WITCH OF THE FEDERATION VI

WITCH OF THE FEDERATION VI

FEDERAL HISTORIES™ 06

MICHAEL ANDERLE

DISRUPTIVE IMAGINATION

Copyright © 2020 Michael Anderle
Cover copyright © LMBPN Publishing
Cover Art by Jake @ J Caleb Design
http://jcalebdesign.com / jcalebdesign@gmail.com
A Michael Anderle Production

LMBPN Publishing
PMB 196, 2540 South Maryland Pkwy
Las Vegas, NV 89109

First US edition, July 2020
eBook ISBN: 978-1-64971-074-1
Print ISBN: 978-1-64971-075-8

THE WITCH OF THE FEDERATION BOOK VI TEAM

Thanks to our JIT Readers

Dave Hicks
Diane L. Smith
Peter Manis
Daniel Weigert
Jackey Hankard-Brodie
Deb Mader
Veronica Stephan-Miller
James Caplan
Kerry Mortimer
Larry Omans

If We've missed anyone, please let us know!

Editor
The Skyhunter Editing Team

To Family, Friends and
Those Who Love
To Read.
May We All Enjoy Grace
To Live The Life We Are
Called.

CHAPTER ONE

Marcus, Gemma, and Trey were still blowing themselves up when Professor Nathan Fellon rejoined them. It had been two very long weeks since he'd been able to participate, and they still struggled to find solutions.

It had been as entertaining as hell, though, from the snippets he'd been able to see while away resolving things so he could join the project full-time.

He'd arrived with a smile of anticipation, but it faded quickly when Professor Rimmer's voice rang through the White Room.

"Oh, for fu—" the professor began and Cynthia cleared her throat warningly.

"Pity's sake!" he finished at a roar.

His assistant was implacable. "It's time to take a break, Doc. Don't make me come in there."

Marcus scowled but he capitulated. "You heard the lady, people. It's *break* time."

"Well, thank fuck for that," Gemma told him, "or we'da been here all night and I desperately need a pee."

"So it's your fault then?" Nathan asked. "Your bladder got the better of your concentration and *you* blew us all to hell?"

She snorted and exited with more haste than grace. "Nate, if *I'd* blown us all to hell, we wouldn't have made it to the White Room."

"I hate you all," said the biggest man in the room. "That last one hurt like a motherfucker."

Cynthia cleared her throat again and leaned on the doorframe to the lab, drumming her fingertips against her biceps while she tapped her foot.

Even Marcus got the message. "It's time to head out, guys. We'll sleep on this and get back to it in the morning. Bring me your best ideas—hell! Bring me *any* ideas, even if your two-year-old thought it up with a fistful of crayons and some cardboard. I'll consider *everything.*"

Gemma snorted and slapped his shoulder as she passed. "Will do, but I have to warn you, my two-year-old gave up on crayons when she discovered fingerpaint and sparkles."

"Sparkles?"

She laughed at the look of bewilderment on his face. "Glitter, Rimmer. Sparkles is glitter. Man, where have you been living? In a lab or something?"

"I… Well, yes, but that sounds promising. I mean, magic sparkles, right? I'm thinking *any* idea coming from a glitter-fueled two-year-old has potential."

Her jaw dropped. "Was that… Did you… Did you make a *joke*, Marcus?"

The comment made him blush, and he raised a hand to rub the back of his head. "I *do* have a sense of humor, you know…"

That made them all chuckle. They were still smiling when they passed him to reach the door. Phillip hesitated briefly and for a minute, the boy looked like he had something more he wanted to say, but then he turned and left.

Marcus frowned and looked at Cynthia. "What was that all about?"

"He merely wanted to say goodbye," she explained, "but he's as bad as you used to be and couldn't find the words."

"As bad as…I wasn't *that* bad, was I?"

She smiled and pointed to the door. "You're the last one, Doc, and Catering will be truly upset if you ruin another meal."

"I..." He looked at his terminal and she scowled.

"I mean it, Doc. You put me in charge of looking after the team's health and well-being and *you* are the worst one I have to ride herd on. I *will* pull the plug."

He glared at her, but after one more glance at the screens, he sighed. "Fine, but I'll have an early start in the morning. Don't make me late."

Cynthia was unperturbed. "You *do* know that if you get a good night's sleep, you'll blow yourself up a whole lot less in the morning, don't you?" she reminded him acerbically.

"Thank. You. Cynthia," he ground out and stalked out of the room.

He didn't see the tiny smile that curved her lips as he left but he didn't need to. He *knew* she was smiling, dammit!

His assistant followed him out, shaking her head. "I'll see you tomorrow, Professor."

She used his title, again—something she did when he'd done the right thing as if her recognition of it was a reward.

And it worked, dammit! He knew he was on the right track when she called him Professor or even Doc, and he *liked* it when she approved, even if he wasn't interested romantically. If she'd been single, maybe, but she wasn't.

Marcus pushed that thought aside, managed a smile, and raised his hand in farewell. "Thanks, Cynthia."

She was picking her keys and handbag up when he surfaced and she gave him a happy smile as he emerged. "Your meal's waiting, Doc. See you tomorrow."

He watched her go before he made his way to the tiny staff kitchenette to find he didn't need to heat his supper. It was still covered and hot. With a sigh, he sat and reflected on the past two weeks and their various attempts, none of which had succeeded.

It had been one hell of a ride, though.

As he mulled over the day's work, he ate what Catering had provided and then headed to the car park. If the truth be told, he didn't want to go home but he had to. The university had refused to provide him with a room.

Marcus sighed. Maybe he could speak to One R&D about that.

It was no secret that he hated leaving the lab—even if it was still there when he returned in the morning.

Sleep was hard to come by that night and when it did, it was plagued by dreams. He returned the next morning but felt worse than when he'd left. Cynthia took one look at him and frowned.

"Did you get *any* sleep last night?" she demanded.

He managed a bleary-eyed glare and took the coffee she handed him.

"I tried but I didn't sleep very well," he replied. "I dreamed."

"And did your dreams come up with a solution?" she pressed.

After a gulp of coffee, he shook his head. "Not unless you count being blown up another half a dozen different ways as a solution."

"So, you know what *not* to try?" she asked, and the slight smile was back.

Despite his mood, he couldn't help but return it. "I know what *not* to try," he agreed and sighed. "But I'll have to try it anyway if only to confirm it officially."

She grimaced. "That sucks," she agreed and took his cup as he drained it. She put it on a lab counter and gestured toward their pods. "Shall we?"

He grimaced but nodded. "We shall."

"Cheer up, Professor. It'll be fun."

"You're not the one in charge of finding the solution. Worse, I'm fairly sure Nathan and Trey plan to ambush me on the way out of the lab so they can get payback," he grumbled and closed the lid of the Virtual Reality pod over him.

"You know they're far too nice to do anything of the sort," Cynthia told him shortly.

Marcus didn't acknowledge that with a reply, partly because he was in a hurry to get to his terminal and partly because Nate, Trey, and Gemma were waiting for him when he arrived.

"So," the woman demanded, "did you come up with anything?

"Only about six ways I'm reasonably sure will cause us to explode in spectacular fashion," he replied and they groaned.

He caught sight of his assistant at the back of the room. She cocked an eyebrow at him and he remembered what she tried so hard to instill in him.

"How about you?" he added, a little uncomfortable because he wasn't used to asking.

Trey grinned and clapped him on the shoulder. "You're getting better at this whole human thing, Doc, but I've got nothing."

"Me, neither," Nathan added, and Gemma grinned.

"What they said, Doc." She moved toward her terminal. "So, which way did you want to use to explode us first?"

Marcus stared after them in surprise. "You don't want to discuss this?"

Their head-shakes were unanimous as the others filed past him to their work areas.

He stared at Gemma. "Did you even *bring* me any sparkles?"

She laughed. "Sorry, Doc. The two-year-old switched to crayon, *sans* cardboard, and I spent most of last night with a scourer and bleach getting it off the walls."

"Did you even dream?" he persisted, and she turned and rested a hand on her hip.

"Boss, I *never* dreamed a two-year-old could make a *single* crayon cover that much wall, let alone what one could do with *six different colors.*"

Trey snickered. "I'm so glad I'm single."

"Keep up with comments like that, Trey baby, and you'll have to explain to whatever partner you find why you *can't* have offspring."

He responded with a pained whistle and settled into his seat. "Come on, boss. Let's see you prove your first theory wrong and *not* blow us up, today."

It was a short-lived hope. They got the centrifuge to spin the gMU into eMU and send it out along the pipes and branches. Once again, the magic made the journey to the bulbs at the end of each line and successfully drew the radiation out of the soil and surrounding landscape.

And once again, the magic brought the radiation into the system and returned successfully along the pipes. Marcus held his breath and his entire body grew tense with anticipation. In only a few seconds, he'd find out if his dreams had steered him right or not.

"*Sonuvabitch!*"

The lab flashed out of existence and the team landed in the White Room.

"Well," Gemma began, "that *has* to be a new record."

"In more ways than one," Nathan concurred.

"Now, tell me that was what the dream said would happen," Trey added.

"Wait. We did science based on a *dream?*" Phillip sounded as though he didn't believe it.

"I had to disprove a theory," Marcus said and chose to answer his ex-student first before he turned to the others. "So, does anyone have a theory on ways we could do that and maybe *not* blow up?"

He looked around the room and was dismayed when all of them shook their heads.

"It was a good try, Doc." Trey tried to console him but sounded resigned. "But your dreams were right. It was a surefire way to blow us all to kingdom come. What have you got for us next?"

"More of the same, I'm afraid," he told them and they all groaned. He scowled. "Well, do you at *least* want to take a look at the idea to see if you can tell me why it won't work or how we can tweak it so it does?"

"Sure thing, Doc." Nathan sighed.

The White Room shifted around them and a moment later, they stood around a large table in the center of another room. Marcus didn't waste any time. He stepped forward and explained the theory behind what he wanted to try next. It looked sound, exactly like all the theories before it.

Nathan studied it, his head tilted in concentration. Finally, he pointed at one part of the equation. "What if we switch this..." He picked a marker up and circled the formula "With *this*."

They craned forward and each studied the options intently. "It's not a bad alternative," Gemma conceded and picked up a marker of her own. "You know...we could also try this."

She wrote her alternative below the other two and combined elements from both formulae. With a glance at Phillip, she asked, "So, what do you say, Prof? This is much more your field than mine."

The boy blushed at her recognition but stepped forward dutifully and selected another marker. When he was finished, Trey nodded in approval.

"Well, that gives us alternatives, anyway. What do you say, Doc?"

Marcus scrutinized the original formula and the alternatives and considered each carefully with what he believed was an open mind. "I say we've probably found four more ways to explode but I damned well hope not." So maybe it wasn't that open after all. Still, at least he'd tried.

They chuckled softly at that and headed to the lab.

"Let's try them," Marcus agreed. "Cynthia could you take a photo of that whiteboard and send it to our consoles, please?"

An hour later, when they came to in the White Room for the sixth time, he looked at Cynthia. "I think we need a break," he said.

"Hell, man," Trey interjected. "We need more than a break. We need a drink!"

"Uh-uh," Gemma protested. "We don't need *a* drink. We need *all* the drinks."

"You have a two-year-old, remember? And you're not allowed to drink and drive," Nathan remonstrated.

She stuck her tongue out. "It's not time to go home yet," she informed him.

"True," Marcus agreed, "but none of us are allowed to drink and drive a console and we have a whole afternoon ahead of us."

"Ooh," Trey snarked, "an *entire* afternoon of incinerating ourselves. I can't wait."

Rimmer smiled at him. "Well, I'm glad one of us feels that way."

The man shook his head. "Trust me, no. I'd rather do anything else than go in there again and test another of your 'I'm fairly sure this explodes us' theories, Doc."

The statement was more than a little sobering. "Yeah. Me too."

They sat in silence for a while, staring at the floor, and Trey finally pushed to his feet. "Let's get it done," he said and offered Marcus his hand. "It's better than sitting here and staring at our toes."

The professor let Trey help him up and looked up at the ceiling. "Computer—"

"Wait!" Cynthia interrupted. "Don't you think you should ask for help?"

"How do you mean?" he demanded and jerked his hand in the direction of the others. "We have every expert with any knowledge of the field right here."

"Except one," she corrected, and he opened his mouth to snap a challenge for her to name them.

"Only one," she insisted. "Think about it."

The scientists exchanged puzzled looks. Each one made a mental list of the experts in the fields related to what they were doing and reviewed any researchers who represented that field. It was Phillip who saw the obvious first.

"The Witch."

"What?" Marcus looked at him. "What does she have to do with this?"

Gemma rolled her eyes. "Doofus. She's only the world's leading expert on *magic*, remember? You know, the stuff that's an integral part of our purification process? The shit that's fucking the works up? *That* expert."

He raised his eyebrows. "Are you saying we need her?"

The other scientists exchanged looks, considered the idea, and finally looked at each other again for approval. Somehow, they all stared at Gemma when they were ready. The scientist folded her arms across her chest and gave Marcus a stern look.

"We're saying we need her," she told him as the White Room dissolved around them.

She gestured at the lab. "We'll run the last couple of theories you came up with but I think we all know how that's gonna end, and none of us are looking forward to it. It *will* give us the data she'll need, though."

"You're assuming she'll know what the fuck she's looking at." The words were out before Marcus could stop them, and their faces registered surprise.

"I thought you said all this was her idea," Phillip challenged, and his boss blushed.

"I did, and it is. I'm sorry. I was only...uh..."

"Speaking out of turn," Cynthia finished for him. "I'll call her and tell her she's needed. That way, you can get your theories tested and out of the way before she gets here—unless you *want* her to walk into the middle of an explosion?"

She stood expectantly and stared at him with one eyebrow raised. His blush deepened and he signaled for the others to return to their consoles. "Come on, people. Let's go explode ourselves. Again."

He sighed. "*Before* the Witch gets here."

The team scrambled to their seats, their faces set and determined. Once they'd settled, Cynthia stepped into her office. It wouldn't save her when the lab blew again, but at least she wouldn't see it coming.

Not knowing how long she had, she picked up the virtual communications line and tapped in the number they'd been given. "Yes, it's Cynthia from the Planet Transformation Team. May I speak to Burt, please?"

It didn't take long for their boss to come online, and it took even less time for her to explain the problem to him.

"And you think she's the only one who can find the solution?" BURT asked, and she nodded.

"They've tried everything else, sir. The only expert who hasn't had a look at the problem is Stephanie."

The next explosion interrupted their conversation and she came to in the White Room, their communications still open.

"That was most unpleasant," he observed. "Did they learn anything from it?"

Cynthia looked at Marcus and realized their boss had taken the conversation hands-free. It was almost funny to watch as the scientist pulled himself together and wiped the stunned surprise from his face to answer the question.

"Well, we learned that the farther into the system the magic brings the radiation, the worse the explosion is—"

"And the less it hurts," Trey added. "I barely felt a thing that time."

"That time?" BURT repeated slowly. "How many times have you exploded, exactly?"

"Only today, or in the last week?"

He responded with a very human facsimile of a groan. "Do you mean this has happened on a daily basis for a week?"

The scientists exchanged glances and Cynthia nudged Marcus with her toe. The team had materialized on their backsides on the White Room floor. Her boss looked at her and uttered a very loud sigh.

"It's happened multiple times a day since the day we began," he admitted and waited.

"I...see..." BURT didn't sound like he saw, but his next words showed her that he did. "You should have called for her sooner. I'll ask her to step in today."

"Th...thank you," Marcus stuttered. "We're sorry for the delay. We merely wanted to make sure we'd covered every possible scenario."

"You've done exactly the right thing," he assured him. "I merely wish you'd checked in sooner. Do you have any more tests planned for the day?"

"Two?" Marcus looked at the team.

Trey held up several fingers.

"Three?"

The man nodded.

"Three," Marcus confirmed. "We have three more theories to confirm."

"To confirm what?" BURT asked.

"That they don't work," Gemma explained and laughed as she spoke.

"You plan to blow yourselves up another three times?" he asked, and they all nodded and grinned like idiots.

"And me," Cynthia added sourly. "Can you ask Stephanie to come soon?"

"I will have her arrive as soon as she is free—which means today and hopefully in the next thirty minutes."

"That should be plenty of time," Marcus reassured him and looked at his colleagues.

"Yup," Trey added. "We're fairly sure we can explode ourselves another three times before she gets here."

"Or you could take a break so she can examine your theories first," BURT suggested, only to be met by stubborn looks.

"We'll be all right, sir, and it's better we eliminate all possibilities," Gemma told him as she struggled to her feet.

"What she said," Nathan added and followed her example.

Around them, the other scientists staggered upright and some gave each other tired high-fives as they prepared to return to the lab.

Cynthia sighed. "Thank you, Mr. Burt. I look forward to Stephanie getting here."

From the look on her face, the Witch's arrival couldn't come soon enough, and BURT made a note to hurry.

Stephanie was busier than he anticipated, and it took her more than an hour to arrive, rather than the half an hour he had predicted.

"Thank God you're here!" Marcus exclaimed as she stalked into the room. He stood and gestured to his seat. "You can use my terminal."

"I'm sorry I took so long," she replied, crossed to where he stood, and slid into the seat. "We were in the middle of loading the ship and I was needed."

Marcus ran a hand through his hair. "That's okay. We wouldn't have called you at all but we've hit something of a snag…"

He let the words trail off as she leaned over the screen and he watched her carefully as she studied what they'd tried to do. It was hard to stand still as her frown grew deeper.

"So," she said when he thought he couldn't stand it any longer, "what exactly seems to be the problem?"

With an exasperated sigh, he stooped over the screen. "It's here," he told her and jabbed the relevant part of the diagram. His finger came down again, "And here, and here, and here. Do you see?"

Stephanie looked dutifully at the places he'd indicated and finally shook her head. "No."

"Oh, for Pity's sake!" he exclaimed, and his finger came down with more vigor than caution. "This! *This* is the problem. The energy spins up fine and it makes it to the end of the tendrils, but then... then it...it gets stuck... See? Here?"

Have him take you through it one step at a time, the Morgana ordered and caught her by surprise. *I almost understand the patterns.*

Almost? she asked. *I only kinda get them and I'm the one who designed this.*

She kept all signs of the conversation from her face and turned to Marcus.

"Why don't you take me through it from the beginning?"

"Really?" he asked. "That bad? You know this was all *your* idea, right?"

Stephanie stared at him and her jaw dropped in surprise. Marcus caught it and blushed.

"I...I'm sorry... It's only... Do you *know* how many times I've exploded this morning?"

She heard spluttered laughter from the other side of the room, but all the other scientists were huddled over the computers and studiously avoided both her and Marcus' gaze.

Finally, one of them spoke—a behemoth of a man who stretched and yawned as he looked at them. "You weren't the only one, Marcus." The man focused on her. "My name's Trey, and we honestly are stumped. The theory says it *should* work, but the practice... Marcus says magic's *your* speciality." He gestured at the screen and pressed a key so the relevant diagrams were displayed on the wall opposite. "We'd appreciate your help."

Stephanie nodded and walked to the screen, where she paused and looked at Marcus. "So...how about it? Walk me through from the beginning."

The scientist's face paled as the Morgana's coldness seeped into her tones and she wondered how much of her alter-ego had bled into her eyes.

"Please," she added, relieved to hear more warmth in her voice.

"So..." He joined her at the board and the other scientists gathered around. "It took us a few attempts to spin the eMU to the outside of the generator, but once we had accomplished that, we were able to pump it to the end of each of these tendrils coming off the main pipeline."

He glanced over his shoulder to make sure she was following him. She nodded and tried to keep the Morgana's impatience at bay.

I get that much, the Teloran hissed. *It's what happens next that I don't understand.*

Stephanie listened as Marcus took her through the process from the beginning to that point.

"It's only when the magic starts to bring the radiation back to the center that we seem to have a problem," he said and gestured at the pipe. "We've tried everything we can think of but nothing seems to work."

"It doesn't happen when the magic and radiation blends?" she asked, sure she'd covered that in the base idea.

"No." He shook his head. "That works exactly as described."

Stephanie frowned, thinking fast. "Could you pinpoint exactly where the explosion occurs?"

Marcus rolled his eyes. "If we could do that, we'd have had this problem solved already."

She caught hold of her temper—and the Morgana—and tried again. "So it happens at multiple points *all* the time, or at many single different points across different attempts."

"Yes," Trey interjected before he could answer.

"Yes, what?" she demanded and frustration almost got the better of her.

"It's happened both ways. Always multiple points, as far as I can tell, but at a different combination of points each time."

"And there have been times when the energy gets back to the generator and the conversion process fails," Marcus said.

"Before or *after* the energy in the pipes explodes?"

The scientists frowned.

"Computer, run the explosion sequence for the last two days' tests," he ordered. "Simultaneously. On multiple screens."

The AI did as he asked but Stephanie interrupted the playthrough seconds after it started.

"Computer, stop. Run the sequences again but stop at each explosion until we ask you to continue."

Again, the AI did as it was told. They watched the run-through in silence, then watched it again. On the third run-through, Nathan sighed.

"I don't see it," he told them. "I simply—"

Priority! the Morgana snapped in Stephanie's head. *Tell them to run it again.*

"Run it again," she ordered.

"Do you have something?" Marcus sounded hopeful.

"Maybe…" She stalled. "Let me go through it one more time."

He was about to start it when her eyes flashed black and she raised her hand. The coldness that settled over her face sent chills down his spine, but he waited.

See? The Morgana explained. *All the energy tries to get to the same point at the same time—and the conversion process starts while the chamber is still loading. It's like a computer program. They've sent feelers out for the data, but when it comes back, there's too much for the information pipeline to assimilate and process unless you prioritize it. Then, the main processing unit has to keep recalibrating for the data that's coming in after the analytical process has started.*

Uh-huh. Now that the Morgana had pointed it out, Stephanie could see where the energy *might* be bottlenecking at junctions immediately before the pressure built to an explosion. It took her a while longer to see what was happening with the magic in the main chamber.

"Oh..." she murmured. "Computer, back it up and slow it down. Focus on the main chamber."

Now that she knew what to look for, it was obvious—if you were used to working with magic—like the Morgana had said. The conversion chamber started processing the radiation from the moment the energy reached twenty-five percent but the energy kept arriving, which was problematic.

"So?" Marcus demanded, unable to hold his impatience any longer.

Stephanie looked away from the screen. "You're trying to convert a mass that's increasing. That's one of your problems," she told him and was rewarded by a chorus of "ahs" and "ohs."

Ignoring it, she continued. "So you either need to fill the chamber and run the process or work out a way to regulate the flow so the process can account for what's coming in."

"You said *one* of our problems," Marcus observed.

"The other one is that too much is trying to get into the main pipeline at once, which slows the flow at the junctions and—"

"Causes a back-up," Phillip finished for her. "Well, duh! Why didn't we think of that?"

"Because it's too simple?" Gemma suggested.

"Because we were too stressed about being blown up?" Trey shook his head.

"Because it's so fucking subtle, we missed it," Marcus declared and ran the recordings again. "The flow barely slows but it's enough."

"And it's dependent on how much the node is bringing in too," Phillip observed. "That's why different ones went. If the computer made the amount of radiation in each area variable each time we ran the test, the nodes would have brought in different amounts."

"Muddying the waters." Trey nodded and examined the different sequences. "Computer, highlight the volume and pressure readings."

Stephanie took a few quiet steps back as the scientists crowded around the screen. At first, they stood in silence and absorbed the data but after a short while, they began to ask the computer to highlight different variables.

This was followed very quickly by suggestions raised to fix the problem and requests for simulations.

They need algae, the Morgana pointed out. *It'll mean the conduits last longer and improve eMU performance—and those tiles that convert radiation into electricity.*

Algae? She was bewildered.

You heard me. The Teloran sounded peeved. *This planet has an over-abundance of it. You use it in your catering industries.*

Fine. She sighed. *Algae it is. We can work on building the world's food supply while we fix its power and pollution problems,* she added. *Maybe even look at bulk shipping what we don't use to colonies that are running short.*

I like how you think, the Morgana told her.

Uh-huh... Stephanie frowned. *But tiles? What tiles?*

There was a company way back in the early twenty-first century that made tiles for creating power directly from radiation.

Why haven't I heard about that?

Because it's one of the lost technologies, she told her. *I can't remember if it was a riot, a super-storm, or another nuclear accident, but its people and production vanished and no one thought to try to find the knowledge.*

And you know where it is?

It was in one of the learning institutions of NorAm, but my guess is that it was considered a form of national security and was backed up somewhere.

Hmmm. I'll have BURT help them with the research, Stephanie agreed. *We've limited their access from here.*

And with good cause, the Morgana agreed.

None of the scientists had noticed her distraction, and the babble of a dozen theories mixed with speculation, argument, and justification filled the room.

"Algae," she shouted, using the Morgana's tones to be heard above the hubbub, and silence fell.

"Algae?" Trey asked.

"Yup. Find a way to coat the inside of the conduits with it. They'll last longer and the eMU will flow better—faster even."

"So we can explode in a more spectacular fashion than before?" Nathan asked cynically.

Stephanie laughed. "Whatever. I take it you guys can figure it out from here?"

That question was met with a chorus of affirmation, and she began to walk to the door. Halfway there, she stopped. "And find a way to store the excess. I'm very sure there's a food production company that needs it."

"Magic?" one of the other scientists asked in bewilderment.

"Algae," Trey replied and grinned. "I think I know someone who can help with that."

"Send their names to BURT," she told him. "If you need them, we'll see if they're available."

"Yes, ma'am," he replied and looked at Marcus. "We need them."

The team had already begun to settle into solving the problem, so Stephanie said goodbye to Cynthia and had BURT pull her back to her pod. It took Marcus and Trey several minutes to realize she'd gone.

Marcus stared at Cynthia when she told him, and he scowled and turned to the other man.

"Where in all the worlds did she get algae from? It's not like they teach *that* in school."

"What, that it's resistant to radiation? That it absorbs it? Or that it's used in food production?"

"Whatever! 'E'—all of the above," he snapped. "One minute, we're talking basic physics. The next, we're into algae, and I'm very sure the Meligornians don't use it in their tech."

Gemma came to stand beside them as he said it. "I bet they will soon. Earth's next inter-planetary export industry just got born."

Before he could respond to that, another screen opened in the center of the display. Its appearance was met by groans of protest, which rapidly stilled as an instruction filled it.

Use this to line the conversion chambers.

"Use what?" Marcus wanted to know.

His question was answered as a series of images filled the screen. It looked like tiles but tiny conduits ran through the layers.

"Is that gold?" Trey asked.

At the same time, Phillip demanded, "Where will we get the materials for *that* from?"

Marcus shook his head.

"The shit she comes up with," he muttered and scowled at the screens where half a dozen simulations were running.

Gemma elbowed him in the ribs. "What's the matter, Doc? Are you jealous or something?"

"Jealous? Why would you think I'm jealous? That girl has touched the power of the cosmos and unraveled curiosities we don't even know enough to ask about. If I tried the same, I'd be burnt out in seconds."

"You know," one of the other scientists began, "we could improve on that design…"

CHAPTER TWO

Stephanie emerged from her pod as the scientists began to discuss the possibilities of the tiles and what they could do to make them better. Lars was waiting, a look of concern on his face.

"Oh, good. You made it."

"Made what?" she asked as she registered Vishlog, Frog, and Marcus behind him. "And why the honor guard?"

"We've had a last-minute request from the Navy. They want us to join them for 'a meeting.'"

"Are we underway?"

"Not to the meeting," her security head replied. "The captain's still on the line with the Navy and waiting on your reply."

"Good." She looked at her outfit and checked to make sure it was Navy presentable. "Tell her I'm on my way."

She jogged to the bridge and arrived in time to hear a male voice say, "Surely, as her captain, you have the authority to make that decision for her?"

Anger rolled through her.

"No!" she snapped as she stepped forward. "Captain Rawlins does *not* have that authority and pressuring her to make a decision is very unprofessional."

The Navy officer's jaw dropped and he started to speak, but Stephanie cut him off.

"And no, I will not attend your last-minute meeting. I am already fully booked today."

"But—" He gaped, then gathered himself. "It's only a short meeting."

"Even so, I do not have space in my schedule. As you can see, we are already underway." She let her voice soften. "I'm truly sorry. I *must* make the next meeting on the list and I can't delay."

"But—"

She sighed impatiently. "Look, is it important?"

"Every Naval meeting is important," he sputtered.

Stephanie scowled at him. "Does it involve an immediate threat to Earth, Dreth, Meligorn, or somewhere else that you need my immediate intervention on?"

"Well, no...."

"Then can you let me know what it's about?"

"It's to discuss matters of Navy cooperation."

"So a general discussion."

"Well..."

"Then the answer still stands. No. I have several high priority meetings scheduled for today and much of tomorrow, and a general 'come by' isn't on my list of things to do."

"But—"

"Goodbye, Lieutenant."

Stephanie nodded to the communications team and the screen went blank to cut the Naval man off in mid-protest. She nodded to her captain.

"Thank you, Captain Rawlins."

The woman inclined her head.

"The pleasure was mine."

Commander Bryce Alder stared at the screen and watched as the *Ebon Knight* continued on its trajectory out of the system. It was annoying but not unexpected and probably the best result of his attempt to delay the Witch's departure.

Still, it made him frown.

"Why is she still leaving?" he murmured, referring to Stephanie rather than the ship. "She has a meeting."

As he spoke, there was a sharp knock at the office door.

"Come in." His gruff tones sounded clearly across the room.

His aide-de-camp was breathing heavily as he came in.

"Well, Bramich?" he demanded.

"Sorry, sir," the lieutenant panted, "but Ms. Morgana—"

Alder cut him off. "You meant the Witch?"

"Uh…yes, sir."

"Well?"

"Well, sir, she isn't coming."

"She refused?"

"She said her schedule was fully booked, sir."

"So the Navy's not important enough for her to talk to?" The commander scowled.

"No, sir. She merely couldn't change her schedule," he tried to explain as if making excuses for the Witch would let her off the hook. "The other meetings were of vital—"

"More vital than her homeworld's *defense*?" His voice rose in annoyance.

"That's not what she said, sir, only that if the threat wasn't immediate—"

"*Every* threat is immediate!"

"Yes, sir, but no one's attacking anything directly and her intervention isn't needed, while the meeting she had to attend was—"

"It could not possibly have been more important than this one," Alder snapped and watched as the other man struggled to keep his puzzlement from his face. "What is it?"

"Well, sir, you said it was only a quick meeting to touch base regarding Navy cooperation…" The lieutenant let his words trail off at the look on his superior's face.

"I take it you *told* her that?"

"I said it was regarding Navy cooperation," he admitted, "not that it was a quick touch-base."

"And she *still* didn't think it was important enough to come by?"

"She said the other meetings were high priority, sir, and she *is* the Witch, so…"

"So you didn't push the matter," Alder concluded for him and wondered how he would pass the news on that the Witch was still outbound and would soon be somewhere they couldn't see her.

"Of all the useless…" he began and flicked his hand at the waiting lieutenant. "Get out of my sight!"

Bramich left hastily and Alder wished the man had been stupid enough to argue. He was about to call him when another lieutenant appeared at the door.

"Sir, it's gone."

"What's gone, lieutenant?"

"The Witch's ship, sir. It just skipped."

"From the non-transition zone?" For a moment, the commander thought he might be lucky, but the lieutenant's next words crushed that hope.

"No, sir. She reached the transition zone and vanished. Not even a ship-length in, sir, and she was gone."

"You mean she wasn't completely in the zone?"

"No, sir, her stern reached the zone and *then* she skipped."

Smart bitch, the commander thought, irritated to not have the excuse to file a complaint that might have meant he could call the Witch's ship back.

Well, she wouldn't remain untouchable for long.

On board the *Knight*, Stephanie didn't know how lucky she was.

Captain Rawlins turned to her. "They won't call back, ma'am."

She shrugged, grateful that Elizabeth had taught her to not put up with any Navy bullshit. "What can I say? I've been taught by the best." She sighed. "And how many times have I asked you not to call me that?"

The woman gave her a tight smile. "Not enough."

"What if I made it an order?"

Immediately, the smile disappeared. "I'd rather you didn't, ma'am."

Stephanie gave the captain her sweetest smile. "Then don't make me."

Rawlins gave her a thoughtful look. "We'll see."

She waited for the honorific and relaxed a little when it didn't come. Maybe this would work out, after all. She still missed Emil, but Rawlins reminded her of Elizabeth. It could still work.

The captain caught her look. "Is there anything else?"

Stephanie glanced to where Avery and Wattlebird were seated side by side. Both had their gaze fixed on the console, and the same slight smile played over their lips. Rawlins followed her gaze.

"Trouble waiting to happen," she noted, but she smiled like a mother acknowledging two wayward sons.

Some of her apprehension eased and she smiled in return.

"Don't let them break my ship," she quipped and turned to leave.

The woman's reply was almost reassuring.

"That's *our* boat, Stephanie. Ours."

The *Knight* managed a credible sniff.

"I am no-one's *boat*," she argued, "but my own!"

As Stephanie left the bridge, Earth's One R&D Headquarters stood silent—except for the training room.

Training didn't stop simply because most of the company was shipping out. Both Arne and Amy discovered they had missed a good workout.

"Man, I don't think anyone but Ms. E's given me this much of a challenge since Tracey," she said as she ducked under a punch. It still hurt to mention her friend but didn't diminish the truth.

She recovered, bounced back, and spun as Arne lunged. Her kick caught him squarely in the gut.

He grunted as her foot landed and took a couple of steps back as she bounced toward him. A series of punches followed, which he blocked, then caught her arm and stepped around quickly to trap it in a lock.

"Sonuva*bitch!*" she exclaimed and tried to twist out of it, only to find he'd anticipated her attempt.

His hold tightened and he forced her onto the mat. "Do you give?"

Amy tried another twist and gasped when he applied more pressure. He waited as she froze and let her work it out. It was a relief when she slapped the mat in defeat.

"Not bad for an old man," she grumbled, rubbed her arm, and shook it out. "You wanta show me how you did that?"

He chuckled. "Are you sure this old man has what it takes?"

She blew a raspberry. "You're not *that* old, Arne. Come on. Give."

"All right, then. Don't say you didn't ask for it."

Twenty minutes later, he began to wonder if *he* hadn't been the one asking for it. Amy proved to be a determined and demanding student and insisted they repeat the lesson until she was sure she had it right.

"Are you happy now?" Arne asked as she maneuvered him onto the ground for the fourth time in a row.

He slapped the mat out of habit and she released him.

"I think so," she replied and looked satisfied. "Do you want to go again?"

"I thought you said you had it."

"No, another round of sparring, doofus. Let's see if there's a trick or two I can teach you."

Arne pushed to his feet. "Well, I guess there's only one way to find out."

He'd barely made it upright before she surged forward hard and fast, forced him to skip back and block, and dodged out of the way before he could retaliate.

"Ha! Not so fast, big guy," she snapped and grinned like a madwoman as she ducked under his first punch. She followed it by coming in close to step around him and drove a foot into the back of his knee as she passed.

With a stifled grunt, he hit the mat on his knees and rolled but collected a foot to the side of his head as he pushed onto his feet. He fell a second time and she dragged his arm into the lock she'd recently learned. Arne slapped the mat in surrender and lay still while the bells cleared from his head.

"What was *that?*" he demanded when they faced each other once again.

"A variation of something I learned in ballet?" Amy suggested, and he returned her smirk with one of his own.

"Do you care to see if an old man can learn it?"

Her grin widened. "Why not? I've always wondered what you'd look like turning a pirouette."

He stared at her. "I kinda hope it won't come to that."

She shrugged. "It shouldn't. What's your flexibility like?"

"Well…" he began, suddenly glad Matthias wasn't there to see him.

He was blushing like a schoolboy.

The ex-Marine had forgotten about the camera feed to Elizabeth's office. Fortunately, Matthias was too deep in discussion to watch it.

"We're gonna need a whole new array of weapons if they make it to Earth," Elizabeth said.

"And you're sure you can get them without the Federation knowing?" He couldn't help but feel a little alarmed at what she was suggesting.

"What's the point of being a crime queen if I can't?" she challenged. "I have the supply lines, and the manufacturers Tex was dealing with can be re-tooled easily enough."

"That only leaves distribution and supply," he told her, "and the Federation would be too busy dealing with the invasion to worry about us. We'd still need a way to get the materials to them, though."

He was about to add more when a distinct jingle rang through the office. Falling silent, he waited while Elizabeth opened her bottom drawer and retrieved the communicator that belonged solely to Emerald.

"Speak!" she commanded in the voice he'd come to associate with her crime-boss persona.

Her face changed from command to bewilderment. She raised a finger to her lips, set the communicator in a cradle, and tapped a button so he could hear what was going on.

"...specializing in Earth security," the male voice continued, and Matthias suppressed a shiver of misapprehension.

He caught her studying his face and didn't try to hide the shock he felt.

Without a doubt, he knew that voice.

While he couldn't place it, he knew it—or voices very similar. It was...official, he was sure of it, but the kind of official that was never recognized *by* the officials.

The heavily modified tones were something he'd hoped to never hear again. With his lips pressed together in distaste, he raised a finger for silence and pressed a button in his earpiece to send an emergency ping to Arne.

He hoped the man wasn't too far from his comms. The way he and Amy trained, Matthias knew neither of them would have their comms in. He crossed his fingers that they weren't too far away to hear it.

When the man sent a double ping of acknowledgment, he relaxed. It still took too long before he heard the ex-Master Sergeant's voice. "We're on our way."

Arne sounded like he'd endured a five-mile obstacle course and come off the worse for wear, but he didn't comment. He'd seen how hard the man trained and knew Amy didn't take it any easier. Any sparring session with them was a challenge, so he could imagine how tough they were on each other.

Both were still breathing heavily when they arrived. Matthias heard them speak briefly to Bunny and Elle as they passed through Elizabeth's small reception area. He hoped one of them called Lisa back from her day off. If this was what he thought it was, they would need all hands on deck.

The voice continued. "We understand you offer a very *specialized* set of services."

E met that comment with a silence that lasted until Arne opened the door.

"We take it you are not alone?"

"I can speak freely," she assured the caller and watched the ex-Marine's reaction.

"That doesn't answer my question," the voice insisted.

She gave the handset a sweet smile. "It doesn't need to."

Her smile was wasted on the speaker on the other end of the line, and Matthias was grateful. If he was right, the person would take it as a personal challenge to wipe that smile—and any other—from her face.

Arne's expression said he thought the same thing, and his heart sank. A cold lump of apprehension formed in his chest when the ex-Master Sergeant paled visibly.

Amy gave the man a gentle push to move him clear of the door so she could enter and close it behind her. Her frown said she'd heard the voice and was curious but didn't have any knowledge of what it meant. The click as the lock engaged was far too audible.

"Is that all of you?" the voice asked and Elizabeth cast a worried glance at the ceiling. She wished BURT was still in the system to reassure her everything was okay and pushed away the sadness that he wasn't.

He was far safer on the *Tempestarii* than he ever had been on Earth.

"For someone who wants my services," she informed the voice, "you're taking a very long time to come to the point."

"You have yet to confirm the services you provide."

"And you have yet to confirm the services you require," she retorted, "or why you think I can provide them."

"You came highly recommended," the voice replied and the slight change in its timbre was audible through the voice-altering software it used.

Before any of them could ask who or how, a familiar voice came on the line. "Emerald?" The crime lord sounded more afraid than Elizabeth would have given him credit for. "They're legit. They need you."

"I don't suppose you can tell me who 'they' are," she asked in her driest Emerald tone.

The criminal drew a breath and cried out in pain. "I...I... Please, Emerald, I can't. Please, help me."

Another sharp gasp followed and she tensed.

"Stop!" she commanded. "Leave my people intact."

"Or what?" the voice asked.

Seeing the look on her face, Matthias laid a hasty hand on her knee. She gave him a sharp glance and caught his pleading look and the brief shake of his head.

"Or I'll bill you the time and inconvenience of finding a replacement."

After a short silence, a ragged whimper was followed by the sound of someone being dragged before a door slammed. The modified voice spoke a few seconds later. "Very well."

"Now," Elizabeth replied, "these *services* you mentioned."

Her focus drifted to Arne and Matthias followed her gaze. The ex-Marine's hands were clenched into fists and his breathing was rapid—and not from the workout he'd had.

Oh, yeah, the man knew all right. He stifled a groan. It was like all his worst nightmares had come true. Amy noticed Arne's tension and glanced at his hands. When she saw the fists, she placed a palm on her sparring partner's arms and startled when he flinched.

Matthias gave her credit, though. She didn't take her hand away.

When the voice didn't reply immediately, Elizabeth raised her finger over the button to end the call but stopped when Matthias raised his hand. The chances were the operatives on the other end of the line were testing her to see if she'd fill the silence—or they were tracking the communicator's cell.

He'd ask her about the shielding on the building later as well as the precautions taken with the number. It was too late now to see if they'd been enough. Any tracker worth their salt would have located them already. She nodded to show she understood, but her finger remained poised.

As he watched her face, he had the distinct impression she was counting down and that when she reached zero, she would cut the line, no matter how much he wanted her to wait. He gave an internal shrug and decided to trust her.

After all, it wasn't like she hadn't done this kind of thing before. It merely worried him because he was fairly sure she hadn't done it with *these* people before, although he was damned sure *he* had.

And as for Arne… He flicked his gaze to the man. If there was ever a posture to say someone was ready to kill everything that came too close, the ex-Marine had perfected it. He wanted to say something to ease the tension but didn't want to risk it.

They already had Elizabeth's voice pattern. There was no way he wanted to give them his. He assumed that was the only reason the other man wasn't swearing a blue streak right now, although it wasn't an issue. They could have a cussing chorus later and vent everything together.

And they would. He was sure of it.

"Are you happy with our 'credentials?'" The sudden return of the voice made them all jump, which Matthias knew was exactly the effect it was designed to have.

"Your 'credentials' had better be in good working order when you return them to me," E told him tartly, "or I'll want compensation."

"So you said." Even modified, the voice made it sound like her ultimatum bored him. "Are you willing to do business?"

"That depends on the nature of the services you're looking for," she replied.

"There is a couple we need terminated," the voice told them. "They are older and a relatively soft target but still difficult to reach. Can you do it?"

"You'd have to be more specific. Do you have a name?"

"Do we have a contract?"

"Let me get this straight. You're asking me if I am available to assassinate an older couple who are relatively lightly guarded but whose location is civilian secure, and you don't want to give me a name."

"That is correct. Until we have a contract, you don't have a name."

Elizabeth went quiet as though she was considering the job before she answered.

"I can provide you with three recommendations—"

"We hoped you would undertake this personally."

She shook her head and made an apologetic sound. "Unfortunately, I have moved up in the field and my time is not as unconstrained as it was. Would you like the recommendations? You would have to handle the contact and organization."

"We will have to consider your proposal," the voice informed her. "If we require your services in this regard, we will let you know."

"I'm sure you will," she replied but she spoke to thin air.

The caller had hung up.

E picked the communicator up, opened it, and removed the battery and chip before she accessed a small safe in the wall beside the base of her desk and stowed them inside. Once that was done, she opened the second drawer of her desk and retrieved two types of jammers, which she activated and set at opposite ends of the office.

Observing her actions, Matthias raised both eyebrows and waited. He recognized the devices and respected the fact she knew enough about both to have their fields of effect overlap.

"Right," she said when she was satisfied. "Did everyone catch that?"

Arne nodded and his fists uncurled slowly. "I got it. You're not seriously considering taking them up on that, are you?"

"If it means I can keep the slimy sonsabitches where I can see them then yes, I am. We merely need to find out who the target is."

"So if you intend to take the job, why did you tell them you'd give them recommendations?"

"Because if my 'recommendations' fail or are unsuccessful, it won't be my fault. I want these bastards to come back to us for whatever they want done next. Besides, I don't see the person making the hit staying around that long."

"What do you mean?" Amy was alarmed but the two men nodded.

The thought of what would happen to the successful assassin had crossed their minds as well.

Fortunately, the other woman wasn't slow to catch up. "You think they'll kill their assassin?"

"Thatta girl," Elizabeth praised her. "That's exactly what I think, and I aim to find out who they are when they do. It'll merely be easier if they're not shooting at *me* when I do it."

"Nice," Arne complimented her. "Very nice. But do you have *any* idea who you're playing with?"

She inclined her head and gave him a snarky smile. "I think those were the very bad boys you used to run with, Arne."

Amy gasped and the ex-Marine gaped at her, his eyes wide, and she turned to Matthias. "The only other possibility is that they're the *very* bad boys *you* used to run with."

With a hand on her hip, she raised an eyebrow and regarded them both with a stern expression. "So which is it?"

"They're one and the same," Matthias told her tiredly. "Different units in the same department, but the same department."

"Navy black ops," she stated.

"*Very* black ops," he confirmed.

"So black not even the Navy will own up to having them," Arne expanded. "We don't exist."

"And you rarely get to retire," Elizabeth added for him. "So how did you get out?"

"I was never part of those teams," the ex-Marine said, "but my team—"

He stopped and his body stiffened. Finally, he cleared his throat and gestured uncomfortably. "You've read the files."

"Indeed, I have," E responded and looked from him to Matthias. "For *both* of you. At least I know how you recognized the voice." She paused and studied each of them steadily. "You *did* recognize it, didn't you?"

Arne nodded slowly and exhaled a long, steady breath. "I'd know that motherfucker's voice anywhere, no matter *what* voice coding software he chose to use. *Anywhere.*"

The fists had returned and Amy's expression turned anxious.

"What about you?" Elizabeth asked Matthias.

"It sounded familiar," he admitted, "as in I recognized it from that era, but I couldn't be sure."

"Then game on, people," she snapped. "We need to determine who the target is before they call us back."

"Are you sure they'll do that?" Arne asked. "They could decide to do the job themselves."

"Hells yes, I'm sure," she told him. "These guys don't want the slightest chance that the job will be traced back to them. They *won't* risk using their people."

CHAPTER THREE

"I don't like it," Arne declared for the umpteenth time. "I especially don't like that we have to get involved in it."

"But you're not disputing that we *do* have to get involved," Elizabeth commented.

"No, I'm not, but I still don't like it."

It was the first time Matthias had seen him so adamant about anything. He was usually far milder in his declarations.

They were seated around the table in the briefing room, having asked Earth-BURT to try to trace the call to discover its origins. That had been a half-hour before, and if anything confirmed Matthias's suspicions, it was that the AI hadn't been able to complete his search.

"They truly understand what it is to cover their tracks," BURT's clone told them, "and they have help from the AI controlling the Defense communications systems. He is particularly tight-circuited about which node that call transitioned through. I am not sure there is *anything* I can offer that will change his mind. I am sorry."

"Don't be sorry, BURT," Matthias told him. Even to himself, he sounded weary. "This is normal for them."

"Nevertheless," the Earth construct replied. "It *is* a challenge."

The way he said it sounded like he hadn't had a challenge worth his time since he'd taken over. He decided not to push him.

"So," he began and turned to Elizabeth, "we need three names."

"And they have to be good," Amy added.

"But not too good," Arne cautioned, which showed he'd paid more attention to the conversation than they'd given him credit for.

"Yes," she agreed. "They have to be good but not so good that we can't protect the target."

The ex-Marine breathed a loud sigh of relief. "Well, that's good to know," he said, "because I'm telling you there's around an eighty percent chance that whoever they want a hit on is a good person."

"What makes you say that, Arne?"

"Because if it were a bad person, they'd send the Marines in or have the police arrest them," he replied. "The fact that they went to all the trouble of hiring you tells me it's not the case."

"Well, we agree on one thing, then," E told him. "It's probably a good person."

"And I'd feel better knowing who it is before we help provide the government with the means to kill them," he added. "Scum-sucking bastards."

"Agreed." She pulled up three files. "Which is why I'm thinking of providing them with *these* guys."

The four of them pulled their tablets out and went through the references on the screen. Elizabeth had sent each of them a package and once he'd skimmed the files, Matthias had to give her the credit due. His woman knew her stuff.

"You don't like these guys, do you?" he asked, returned to the first file, and re-read some of the annotations she'd made.

E gave him a tight smile. "Nope. I hate them all."

"What'd they do? Make nasty in a past life?"

"That, and then continued to be nasty in this one," she told him. "Besides, I won't cry if I have to terminate their asses in the name of saving a good man's life."

"Or woman's," Amy added. "They're going after a couple, remember?"

"You're assuming it's a guy and a girl," her boss corrected her. "It could be two guys for all we know."

"Or two girls," Arne noted. "Any kind of couple, I suppose, but good people."

"You won't let that go, will you?" Elizabeth challenged.

"No. I know these people. They go after everyone. We need to know what they want in order to determine *which* good people they've decided are in their way."

"You mean the target might not be their real goal?"

"It rarely ever is and we should keep an open mind." His face darkened. "It might be that their target is in the way of them achieving their real goal and has no clue about the position they've put themselves in."

"Agreed," Matthias interrupted before Elizabeth could say anything. "If we knew what the dark side wanted, we'd have a better chance to save whoever they want to remove in order to get it."

"And we can most definitely kill these guys," Amy added as she studied the files. "Hell, it will even be a good thing if we have to."

"Yup," Arne nodded. He tapped his screen. "I want a piece of this guy and I've never met him."

"You'd have to have an all-over body scrub if you did," the woman observed, realized what she'd said, and blushed.

His lips quirked and he suddenly became *very* interested in his tablet. It entertained Matthias to see how hard the ex-Marine tried to not respond. He took a breath to say something about it and drew a sharper one as the toe of the other man's boot slammed into his shin.

"What?" Elizabeth asked, her face suddenly anxious. "Did I miss something?"

"Oh...no," he managed to say and darted the younger man a filthy look. "I couldn't work out how we would get our dark-sided assholes to hire the ones we want to kill."

She rolled her eyes. "So none of you are bloodthirsty at all, are you?"

"It's the company we keep," he retorted and blushed.

E chuckled. "Well, at least we agree on this." She tapped her screen and made the images on the wall jump. "None of us will be upset when we have to eliminate these guys."

"So you can do it?" BURT asked.

Aaron studied the diagram of the modifications he wanted to make. "Sure," he told the AI. "We *can* do it…"

"But?" he prompted when he noted the reluctance in the man's voice.

"I'm simply not sure why you'd want to."

"Trust me, it will take care of the glitch that's annoyed you so much," he assured him.

"Really?"

"Didn't I say so already?"

"You may have neglected to tell me the *why* when you were busy trying to explain the *what*," Aaron stated.

"Oh. Well, I do apologize for that," BURT acknowledged and added, "So you *can* do it?"

The engineer sighed and looked at the diagram again. "Like I said, we *can*—"

"And it avoids all the 'fiddly bitchy bits' that are likely to break and are expensive to replace," the AI hastened to explain.

The man blushed red from collar to crown. He'd forgotten how many things his boss paid attention to at one time. "BURT," he began, "when I said that…"

"You were right," the AI concluded for him. "No offense was meant and none was taken. I was very careful to consider the practicalities in my redesign."

"I… It wasn't directed at you," Aaron explained. "Any modifications you want us to attempt, we will gladly do so."

"Truly?" he asked, and the engineer nodded.

"Truly. It would be a privilege."

"You flatter me." BURT hesitated but couldn't help asking. "Do you know how long it will take?"

The question and his tentative tones startled Aaron into laughter. Before he'd caught his breath, though, the AI spoke again.

"Captain Emil, my daughter is returning and Stephanie is aboard."

"Thank you, BURT." Emil's response was crisp and clear and Aaron wondered if he had already known of the ship's approach, but the captain's next words made it clear. "We don't... Ah, *there* she is. Tell me, how do you get more out of the long-range scanners than I do?"

"Your crew is still acquainting with them and they are tasked with searching for more than only one small ship."

"The *Knight* is not a small ship," the man corrected him.

"My apologies, Captain. You are correct." BURT did not mention that, beside the *Tempestarii*, the *Knight* might as well have been a gnat. Captain Emil still missed his ship.

Leaving the man to his preparations, BURT returned his attention to Aaron. "Shall we begin?"

"Are you sure this is a good idea?" Lars asked as they approached the pod.

"Sure, I'm sure," Stephanie told him. "Don't you remember the first time you ever saw the *Tempestarii*?"

He thought about that for a moment and nodded. "Yeah, she *does* inspire a certain amount of awe."

"And loyalty," the *Knight* interjected. "Don't forget the loyalty."

She shrugged. "Besides, this is the last chance for a long time that she'll get to see the *Tempestarii* from the outside. We can't deny her that."

"There are such things as recordings," he grumbled as the lid opened and a young woman scrambled out uncertainly.

He stepped forward to offer her a helping hand. She scowled at it but caught the look on his face and took it.

"Thanks," she said and used his grasp and the side of the pod to steady herself. Worry creased her brow when she caught sight of the

Witch and the rest of the team standing behind her. "Did something go wrong?"

"No," Stephanie told her and drew her full attention. "We merely thought you'd like to see the *Tempestarii* from the outside."

The woman's eyes lit up. "That would be great. No one's told me how big the ship is that I'll be working on. All I know is that it will 'stretch and expand' my specialized knowledge." She frowned. "You'll have to forgive me if I doubt that."

Her words made Stephanie smile. "Why don't you take a look at her and make up your own mind?"

"That sounds good," the woman agreed and her brow furrowed. "I'm not very good with faces or names and I know we've met before because you look kinda familiar."

The shy way she asked it made the Witch smile. She placed a hand on her shoulder as she turned to the door. "I hate to say it, but your memory's not to blame. I kinda came on board late so we didn't get to meet."

"But I'd swear I know you."

"Do you ever watch the news?" Frog asked and she shook her head.

"Not much. Sometimes, I'll catch a newscast about the Witch, but tha— Oh, I'm *so* sorry." She pulled away and blushed a deep red. "I didn't...uh..."

Stephanie smiled. "You didn't recognize me. It's okay. I kinda like that." She pressed the button to summon the elevator. "Come on. Captain Rawlins won't wait all day."

"Captain Rawlins won't wait at all," a voice informed them from the ceiling. "She says the *Tempestarii* shouldn't be kept waiting and that her newest engineer is required for briefing as soon as docking is complete."

"Was that...the ship?" the woman asked and gaped at the ceiling.

"You'd better believe it," the *Knight* informed her. "Now get your ass out to the observation deck and take a look at my sister."

"She swears?" the woman asked softly.

"She sure as shit does," the *Knight* confirmed, "but not today.

Today, I'm watching my mouth because my father doesn't like it when I use bad language."

"Your...father?" the woman stopped halfway across the walkway.

"It's a long story," Frog told her and looped an arm around her shoulder, "and you'll miss the view."

She let him steer her to the observation portal and looked where he directed.

"Oh—" Her jaw dropped and she stared at the glittering bulk that was the *Tempestarii*. "Is that..." Reflexively, she stepped back to admire the vessel. "I get to work on *that?*"

"*That* is my sister," the *Knight* reproved.

"I... Yes. Sorry, Knight." The woman couldn't take her eyes off the *Tempestarii*. "Is that a—"

She paused as the door behind them opened but she didn't turn.

Stephanie glanced around as the captain strode in and came to stand at a different viewport. It was funny to see that the woman was more interested in watching the engineer's face as the *Knight* approached her sister ship.

They all stood in reverence as they closed the distance and the *Tempestarii* started to loom. While she looked impressive at a distance, she appeared even more so this close to her. As the *Knight* started to slow but not stop, the engineer glanced around.

"Are we... We're not..." She turned to the viewing port to make sure. "We're docking *inside* her?"

Captain Rawlins nodded. "We are."

"Oh..."

"That never gets old," Stephanie murmured from the captain's other side.

Rawlins glanced at her and caught her gaze with her one good eye before she turned to leave. For one heart-stopping moment, Stephanie had the distinct impression that the captain had winked but it had happened so fast she couldn't be sure.

CHAPTER FOUR

Todd stepped out of his quarters and frowned at two of Captain Smith's Marines who lounged against the wall opposite. When he glanced down the corridor, he saw another two who leaned on the opposite side at the end of the block of rooms that had been assigned to the team.

To any casual passer-by, the men were catching up before going their separate ways. He knew differently, though. These asshats had stood outside ever since they'd relieved the asshats that had preceded them.

He was considering whether or not to confront them when Ka emerged from the room closest to his. She took one look at the waiting Marines and started toward them, her morning ablutions forgotten if the towel draped over her arm was anything to go by.

"Right!" she started. "I've had about enough of—"

Quickly, he intervened, stepped alongside her, and caught the arm. "Corporal! Don't you and me have an appointment with the mats?"

She stopped short and jerked him to a halt as she laughed. "Hoo, boy, Sarge! You sure know how to make a girl's morning a whole lot brighter, but what'll your girlfriend say?"

He let go of her arm like he'd been burned. "What?"

"You, me, mats..." she imitated in caveman-like tones before she reverted to her normal voice. "I mean, sure, Sergeant, but Steph will have both our asses!"

Todd finally grasped the joke and blushed red to his hairline. "That's not what I meant," he sputtered and Dru stepped in.

It didn't help that she was laughing fit to burst. "Sure it wasn't, boss. Why don't you stay and stop the guys starting a disturbance? I'm sure they're as sick of seeing these asshats every time they turn around as I am."

"Sure. Fine. Good suggestion." He could have kicked himself. Flustered was not how he wanted to sound in front of their constant companions. Or henpecked. He *definitely* didn't want to sound as henpecked as he just had.

When he glanced across at their nearest pair of stalkers, he caught a swiftly suppressed smile as it disappeared from the Marine's face. *These are the weirdest assed Marines I've ever come across,* he thought. *It's like they think they're different than the rest of us.*

He managed to intercept Gary, Reggie, and Jimmy before they could cause any trouble but he would have been too late to stop Angus. As it was, Piet only caught the youngster's arm in time to stop him from landing a punch on one of those nearest his door.

Darren emerged and saw it, wasted no time in securing his teammate's other arm, and helped the demolitions expert turn and steer him toward the shower block. Todd wandered toward them as his team moved away.

"It would be nice if you boys weren't here when we got back."

The Marine lifted his head and curled his lip. "Trust us. There are a hundred other things we'd rather do but we have our orders and they say we have to keep your obnoxious asses secure."

"Well, it sucks to be you then, doesn't it?" Todd snarled and pivoted to follow his team. He could feel their gazes on him all the way down the hall.

Walking away wasn't what he wanted to do, but he needed to work out what his next move would be. It sure as shit wouldn't be having these guys hang around for the rest of his career. There was something indefinably "wrong" about them and he needed to know exactly what it was.

He wasn't happy to see Captain Smith stroll into the shower block ahead of him. The towel over the man's arm didn't convince him even slightly.

"Good morning, Sergeant," the man greeted him. "My men tell me you slept well."

"With all due respect, your men had better not have had a clue how I slept, sir. They're not authorized to be in my quarters."

"I think you'll find they're authorized to be wherever you choose to go," the captain informed him, his tone bland.

Despite the almost overwhelming temptation to react, he forced himself to keep moving, slid into a shower stall, and set his clothing aside. "If I find them in my room, they'll wish I hadn't."

The man's snort revealed that he'd taken the shower next door. Todd clenched his jaw and washed as quickly as he could. He didn't try to lose the captain but he kept an eye on his squad as they emerged from their ablutions and directed them hastily to the mess before any of them took it into their heads to challenge the other Marines.

"We *have* to get rid of those guys," Ka told him as they settled at the table with their plates in hand.

He followed the flicker of her gaze and nodded. "I think they've been assigned as bodyguards," he told them, "but I'm still trying to work out if they're here to watch out for us or simply *watch* us."

"We need another night out," Piet muttered. "A really *big* night out."

"I don't know if that's a good idea, Piet." Angus spoke quietly, his gaze on their watchers. "If they're here to find an excuse to throw us in the brig, we don't want to hand it to them."

"What makes you think they're looking for an excuse to throw us in the brig?" Drusilla asked, and he leaned conspiratorially towards her.

"Because the last time I was shadowed like this, that's *exactly* what they were looking for."

"Why? What made you so special?"

"Well, the guys set me up with this girl, see? The only thing was, they didn't tell me she was the commandant's daughter and *she* didn't let on until her daddy's goon squad kicked the hotel door in. It was a double suite, so I took a header off the balcony and made it into a local park before they got back downstairs. The problem was, the guys had put the suite in my name and when I wasn't there in the round-up, there was only so much smoke they could blow."

"When was this?" Todd asked, but Jimmy and Reggie looked at their teammate in wide-eyed disbelief.

"You were *that* guy?" Reggie asked, and Gary shook his head.

"Man, I knew there had to be a reason you were lumped in with the rest of us, but that one takes the cake."

Jimmy leaned over and patted Angus' shoulder. "If it helps, she was broken up about not getting to see you again."

Angus' face brightened. "Really?" he asked. "Because I liked her."

"Pfft." Ka sputtered and rolled her eyes. "Seriously? You junked your career for a girl?"

"I thought she was special," he muttered, his voice sullen.

"How long did the two of you go out before...you know..." Drusilla made a diving motion with her hand.

"A couple of months."

"So how come you never discovered who she was?"

"She gave me a bogus name and life story," he admitted and blushed even redder than before.

"And you believed her?"

"He was in looooove," Gary explained.

"I didn't think she'd lie!" he protested.

"So, not so 'special' then," Ka concluded, and he sighed.

He finished his breakfast and picked his plate up. "Well, now I'm never gonna know," he told them. "She got married just before the Telorans threw those rocks at us."

The team stilled, then Reggie picked his plate up and moved alongside the youngster. "Sorry, mate. That's girls for ya. Fickle monsters."

"Hey!" Ka protested. "I resemble that remark."

That brought a smirk to Angus' face and Todd relaxed.

When he realized the others had finished eating, he hurried to follow suit. It took him until the end of his plate to realize that he hadn't managed to get the commandant's name, but it wasn't until Jimmy stood beside him that he noticed the big Scotsman had stayed.

"So," he asked, "was that true?"

"That she was upset?" the man asked. "Sure it was. Her dad had her incarcerated in a private finishing school inside a week and engaged inside two."

"Seriously?"

"High society. Those posh bastards still make marriage alliances."

"And she allowed it?"

Jimmy snorted. "I did some asking around. And had my ass handed to me for it, too. Trust me, boss. It's better he never knows."

"Knows what?" Todd pushed.

"Exactly," the man finished for him. He glanced at their overt shadows. "Don't we have some sparring to do?"

He followed his gaze and let the matter drop. "Yeah. I guess we'd better entertain the monkeys."

Ka returned in time to hear him say that and responded with a short laugh. "I hate to tell you, boss, but it's usually the monkeys that do the entertaining and not the other way around."

"Well, today, they get a treat. Didn't I already announce we had a match?"

"Ugh. Yes, Sergeant, you did," she admitted and looked none too happy. She glared at the other team and leaned closer to his ear. "We *so* have to get rid of them."

He smiled as though she'd made a joke and slapped her on the back. "It's time we made a start then," he told her, ditched his plates, and led the team out the door. "Move your asses."

"And I thought we had leave owing," Gary grumbled.

"That was yesterday," Todd told him, "before we were lumbered with the babysitters from hell."

They spent the morning sparring—and watching the Marines watching them.

"Any ideas, Sarge?" Ka asked as she toweled the sweat from her face and neck.

"Yup," he told her. "We're gonna work out what's *really* up their asses and why they have such a hard-on for us. And we're gonna start with a little recon."

"Yeah?" Ka arched an eyebrow. "Do tell."

"Tomorrow," he told her blandly. "Tonight, we're gonna have some of that R&R Gary and Reggie keep reminding me about."

"We're gonna get drunk?" Piet asked as he came to join the conversation. He eyed their observers. "Drunk would be good. How many glasses do you think it will take to make these jokers look attractive?"

"Ew!" Ka wrinkled her nose and made no attempt to hide the direction of her gaze. "I don't think there's enough alcohol in the *universe* to make me think *they* look good."

Todd clapped a hand over her mouth. "Don't make me come over there, Corporal."

Her muffled retort might have been her pointing out that he was already there.

He ignored her and looked at the rest of the team.

"Stromo's?" he asked and didn't care that the other Marines could hear their plans.

The team followed his lead. "Stromo's," they replied and injected that single word with all the reverence they could muster.

"For lunch?" Gary asked hopefully.

"And dinner," he replied. "We are gonna make a day of it."

"What kind of training is that, sir?" Darren wanted to know.

"R&R Recon!" Todd roared and the others replied in kind.

Todd didn't give a damn what the shady Marines thought, save that they thought he and his team too stupid for what they were about to pull.

An hour later, they were being seated by the same *maître d'* who had served them the night before the admirals had called to debrief them.

"And what can Stromo's do for you today?" the man asked, guided them to the table, and pulled Ka's seat out for her.

He addressed Todd but his gaze roved the faces of the rest of the team and paused briefly on Piet's.

"The same as last time only today, we want the beer to last longer," the sergeant declared and the man's eyebrows rose in surprise.

"The beer…" he murmured and sighed. "Exactly how *much* longer does sir require the beer to last? Stromo's remembers that the party became *very* rowdy the last time you came to visit. Things were broken."

This much might have been true of what happened when the *other* Marines had discovered he and the team were no longer in their seats.

Todd immediately grew serious. "I trust you were appropriately compensated," he stated and the man nodded. "Yes, sir. The Navy made appropriate compensation. "

"Then I don't see what the problem is," he told him. "My team's been under considerable pressure and needs to unwind—starting now if you would."

He made his tone imperious but gave the *maître d'* a questioning look. The man studied his expression carefully and pursed his lips. "Of course, sir. If I may take your orders?"

The team gave him the same orders as the last time and watched as their followers did the same. This time, the other Marines eyed them warily but they ordered as well and continued to keep an unconcealed watch on their group.

Their host returned fifteen minutes later. "We will have to take some *extra* precautions today," he told them, and Todd sighed.

"How *much* extra?"

The man handed him a menu, which he opened cautiously.

"Well, fu—ehem. This *is* an interesting alternative," he told the waiter. "I'd like to try it."

The procedure took another half an hour with another "extra" added when it was discovered that Captain Smith's Marines were resistant to the initial attempt. Todd kept the banter flowing around the table until he saw the first one clutch his stomach and bolt to the bathroom.

When the second one followed, he raised his hand. "Check, please!"

The instructions were inside the folder and he tried not to pull a face at the horrendous amount the afternoon and evening's service was costing him.

"You know, if you have a heart attack now, we'll never get our R&R, boss," Ka interrupted and he grinned.

"It's easy for you to say. It's not your wallet."

"Really?"

Before he had time to react, she'd taken the bill from his hand and looked at it. Her lips pursed in a silent whistle and she passed it back.

"Rather you than me, boss, but are you sure it's worth it?"

What she was asking was if he thought there was a genuine problem or if they were all jumping at shadows.

"It's worth it," he reassured her and led them out.

They were followed into the street before the two who had managed to do so made a sudden about-face and sprinted to the restrooms.

"Now," Todd commanded and they walked briskly across the corridor and into a maintenance hangar, where they were picked up by a worker within seconds.

"Master Stromo sends his compliments. It's right this way."

He nodded and followed and the team moved swiftly in his wake. Despite the sense of urgency, he wasn't going too fast to notice the repair team working on the surveillance cameras.

"What happened?" he asked and indicated the techies.

"Power surge, sir. Quite sudden," the worker replied, and Todd had to wonder how much of the Star Base's security could be as easily compromised.

The man touched his arm. "We have footage if we need it," he told him. "We're not stupid."

"But your footage won't be easily accessible…" he replied and came to his own conclusion.

"Exactly." The worker stopped and indicated a door. "Through there, second corridor on your right, and the third door on your left. Your waiter will be there—and don't worry, those X-ers won't remember a thing in the morning."

"Will they be okay?"

He shook his head and pursed his lips. "Let's say they're about to become very good friends with Medical, and their boss will find it hard to find replacements for the next week."

"But…" he began, only to have the man slap him on the shoulder. "Get going, Sergeant. Do whatever you need to do. We trust you." His mouth compressed with disapproval. "Unlike others around here."

Todd badly wanted to ask him what he meant but he could see the repair teams putting the cameras together and knew they were out of time. "Thank you," he muttered and entered the door.

While part of him was grateful for the courtesy shown to him and his team, another part was wide awake and alert and looking for the ambush.

It didn't come and he'd begun to relax when the *maître d'* appeared in the corridor ahead.

"Welcome back." He opened a door in the wall beside him and ushered them through. "We trust you'll enjoy your evening."

He nodded his thanks and entered. Stromo's had outdone themselves and he almost stopped on the threshold, but the pressure of the team behind him kept him moving forward.

Once more, their meals were waiting and a fully stocked bar stood to one side. A screen filled one wall and a small dance floor occupied the opposite side of the room. He advanced to the table and took his seat.

"I'm calling this meeting to order," he told the team and looked around, "because we damned well need a night off and this might be the only chance we get."

"Woot!" Angus was all agreement. He took his seat and picked his cutlery up, but he caught Todd's glare and set the knife and fork down until the others had joined them.

"Food first," he ordered, "then we'll work out exactly what we need to be able to get the monkeys off our backs."

"I vote for a long and cozy chat with that maintenance worker," Drusilla told him.

"And I need to dig in Naval records," Ka added.

"I'm gonna need more grenades," Piet informed them morosely. "I'm down to my last one."

Todd stared at him. "You didn't…"

The man nodded. "You're not the only one they're stinging, Sarge."

"What did that bloke mean by 'X-ers?'" Reggie asked. "I've never heard of any Marines called *that* before."

"And you won't," the demolitions expert retorted. "Not ever and not twice, because it's certain death or disappearance to mention them. They're like the enforcement arm of the Intelligence corps. No one knows they exist—and, if they ever find out, they don't know it for long."

"And you would know this how?" Ka demanded.

He raised his steak burger as though he was about to take an enormous bite, but lowered it. "You know that stuff I didn't want to talk about when Stephanie asked me?"

"I'm fairly sure that was the Morgana," Dru corrected him, "but yeah. We got the impression some bad shit went down in your past."

Piet raised the burger and this time, he did take a big bite out of it.

"Well," he told her through a mouthful of steak, salad, and bread, "I *still* don't want to talk about it."

Todd raised a hand when the two women would have pushed the issue. "Piet, you and me later. Okay?"

The explosives expert rolled his eyes but nodded and continued to chew. As if his determined focus on his meal was a signal, the rest of the team fell silent as they enjoyed their food. When Todd glanced around, he noticed the bartender and waiter both wore earplugs, although they kept an eagle eye on their guests and refilled glasses and cleared plates as needed.

He didn't buy it for a second. The restaurant would need insurance, and that meant they'd want to know what their guests were talking about in case it came back to bite them later—or they needed leverage.

"Would you like to order dessert?" the waiter asked when the last plate was cleared.

Todd let the ensuing hubbub subside and cleared his throat. "So," he began, "what will we do about our asshat fans?"

"You mean the X-Marines?" Gary quipped.

"They'd be *ex*-Marines if I had anything to say about it," he told him, "but given that we don't have that option, we need to work out what we'll do next."

"They won't be allowed to follow us aboard the *Knight*, will they?" Angus asked.

"I hope not."

"Damn, boss. I was hoping you'd say no so I could say, 'See? Problem solved,'" he snapped in response.

"Sorry, Angus. All I can give you is that if the *Knight* is ordered to take them, she'll be able to do something about them."

The young man grinned. "Then see? Problem solved."

"It's what they might do in the meantime that worries me." Todd's reply wiped the smile from his face. "We need a way to plan for the unexpected and mitigate it."

"For that, we're gonna need a way off this orbital." Piet's quiet observation stopped them. He gestured at Jimmy. "We already have a pilot, so we'd only need a boat."

"Can you organize that?" Ka asked.

"Yeah, you with the shady past," Drusilla added. "Can you organize it?"

"It'll be easier because we don't need a pilot." He nodded at Ka. "And easier because we can create our own access if necessary, but I'll need some follower-free time."

"It would be best to do it in the next two days then," Todd told him. "I think Stromo's said the current team would operate at less than optimal at least for tomorrow."

He raised his eyes and looked at the waiter, only to be met by a blank stare. Todd pretended not to notice the man's puzzlement.

"Isn't that correct?" he asked and glanced at the ceiling.

At first, he was met by silence and he added. "I know you're listening. You have to be able to make your reports somehow."

There was no immediate response to his words, but a few minutes later, the waiter stiffened at a sequence of knocks at the door. "We'll be with you in a moment, sir."

Todd was not surprised when the *maître d'* entered the room. The man wasted no time in coming to the point.

"We can put you in touch with someone. I'll have them contact you separately. Our chef's name is Ansler."

He would have bet it wasn't but he wasn't about to argue. Instead, he said, "I'll look forward to hearing from your contact."

"Very good." The *maître d'* returned to the door, hesitated, and looked over his shoulder. "Will that be all the business you require tonight?"

"Have we missed anything?" He looked at the team

Jimmy replied with a short laugh. "Probably, but I can't think of it." He glanced around the table. "Anyone else?"

One by one, they answered in the negative, and Todd shook his head. "Thank you but I think that concludes the business part of our evening." He made a show of looking around the room. "I understand that what happens in this room stays in this room?"

The *maître d'* nodded. "That is what you paid for."

"And that you can get us home unarrested and in one piece?"

"Of course."

"Is that service covered by what we've already paid?"

"You asked for the same as last time but for an extended period, so yes," the man told him. "Were our assumptions incorrect?"

"No," he confirmed and grinned. "No. Your assumptions were correct. Thank you."

"Will that be all?"

"For now. Thank you," Todd confirmed, still grinning.

He waited until the man had left and slumped in his seat. "Fuck, I miss Stephanie. I need a beer. What was that shit you had us drinking the last time, Jimmy?"

"Old Smoky?"

"No." He waved his hand and gestured for his teammate to try again. "That whiskey-soaked dark beer."

"Oh, hells yes," Ka echoed. "I want some of that too."

"And me," Reggie voted.

The bartender set pint glasses out while Jimmy searched for the name.

"Old Dubh!" he exclaimed and a glass brimming with the fragrant dark ale was set in front of him.

"Yes," Todd agreed, accepted a pint, and lifted it to his lips.

A second glass appeared as he drained the first, and he signaled for a third.

"Sarge, are you all right?" Ka asked.

He paused halfway down the second and thought about it. Finally, he answered with, "Do you know how many times we almost died during that last mission?"

"Before or after we got back?" Ka asked. "Because I thought for sure that Captain Smith would shoot you when you disagreed with him."

"Before," he told her and his eyes took on a distant look. "Definitely before."

She leaned back in her seat and mulled it over. "Well, there was that one time when that Teloran came in from the side while you were dragging Dru's ass out of the shit."

Dru blew a very wet raspberry from the other end of the table. She'd taken to alternating her Old Dubh beer with a shot glass of Old Dubh neat. "And then there was the time I threw the table in front of that grenade."

Ka chuckled. "Oh, man. I *missed* that. What was I doing?"

"You were elbow-deep in computer guts," the other woman told her.

"Hey, hey! You forgot the time he jumped in the middle of those three soldiers and went at it with his blaster and that blade."

"Aww...heck, yeah, and Gary had to go in after him so the Witch wouldn't go nuts if he got hurt 'cause that girl sure as shit has a temper!" Reggie added and banged his empty glass to get the waiter's attention.

"A fucking bad one, too," Angus agreed and eyed the dance floor. "I had a girl once... Did I tell you?"

"Yeah, you did. She got married," Reggie's response was brutal. "I bet I can dance better than she does."

"Can. Not," his teammate retorted.

"How much you wanta bet?" he challenged, took his newly arrived drink, and headed to the dance floor.

"A...a week's pay!" the youngster declared. "'S not like I can spend it."

"If we keep getting into fights like that," Ka interjected and pushed to her feet with a glass in each hand, "we might *never* get to spend it."

"I need another drink," Dru added and followed them to the dance area as Reggie got the lights and music going.

Todd recognized the first song as one of Stephanie's favorites and glanced at the bar.

"We're *all* gonna need beer," he declared and drained his third glass.

Lifting it, he eyed its empty depths and waved it at the man.

"Much more beer."

The mystery Marines could wait.

"All hail and glory to the Prime," the High Commander greeted, relieved to hear the same level of sincerity in the voices of his Storm Commanders as the phrase was repeated in chorus behind him.

"Greetings, High Commander of my Second Fleet. I trust your progress is more auspicious than that of my first."

High Commander Varash hoped she considered his progress more auspicious. He did not want to fry on his command deck. It would be an ignominious end to an otherwise illustrious career and all the glory he'd won would be forgotten.

Even by what survived of his crew. They would simply be too afraid to remember what he'd done or to acknowledge their part in it. Such was the way the Corevex retained their power.

"We have almost reached the rendezvous. We trust our progress is pleasing," he managed to say with reasonable deference and hoped the phrasing was enough to keep him safe.

"It is satisfactory." The voice of the Corevex was hard and cold and gave him no indication if pleasing meant it was considered auspicious as well.

"How may I serve you?" the High Commander asked, aware of being scrutinized by the seven members of the Corevex and all too aware of being the focus of the Prime. He could *feel* her gaze resting on him. It was like the weight of a thousand thousand sins.

"Make your conquest swift and successful," another of the Corevex instructed. "The energy reduces as we speak. We can feel the magic waning and the weight of our years grows heavier at an alarming rate."

Varash kept his expression as neutral as he could and resisted the urge to point out that it was their wanton use of the energy that had led to its diminishment. If they had only used what they needed rather than squandered it on every extravagance under the sun.

Or to maintain their power rather than letting the people choose their destiny.

He kept all these thoughts hidden behind a mask that gave no hint of emotion away. His position, after all, had been secured by their greed and his family's survival now depended on his success. As much as the actions of the Corevex sickened him, he could not defy it.

"The fleet progresses as swiftly as it may," he assured them. "We will be within striking distance soon."

"And that is a promise we can take to our people?" the Corevex demanded.

"Of that, you can be sure," Varash assured them and stiffened as the Teloran Prime stepped forward.

Seeing his reaction, the Corevex turned and caught sight of their leader as she advanced. Tension rippled through them as the most powerful of them came to the fore.

"I hope, for your sake and the sake of your fleet, that your words are accurate," she murmured and her voice echoed clearly through the Corevex's chambers and around his command deck. "We need a solution and this world's time is drawing nigh. If we do not deliver on the promises that are now over a millennium old, our future is forfeit."

Varash swallowed hard and jerked his head in swift acknowledgment. Regardless of how he felt about the Corevex and its Prime, they were right. The people—*his* people—needed a solution, and his fleet was the only hope of bringing that answer into being.

The leader's next words underscored that.

"Do what is necessary. If bugs are in the way of progress, step on them and move on. Is this understood?"

He bowed his head. "It is understood, my Prime. The fleet will not disappoint our world."

"Better that it does not disappoint *me*," she responded and her voice sent chills through his soul. "Our world does not hold its lives in its grasp."

It was a bitter reminder that she held all their futures—and lives— at her mercy, and he grieved that this was the being who ruled the world his family called home. Still, there was no other.

"There will be no mercy, my Prime." He bowed toward her, then repeated the gesture, the second time shallower than the first. "My Corevex."

"Next time, we will require better news," one of the Corevex informed him as the Prime ascended to her dais.

"It shall be so."

The High Commander stared at the blank screen as his assurance was cut short. He didn't know whether to be annoyed or relieved. Either way, the time was coming when they would reach their goal and the other races would understand the regard in which they were held.

Bugs, he reminded himself and, as the Prime had decreed, they would be crushed.

CHAPTER FIVE

"Do you have them?" The voice carried the same distorted coldness it had held before, and Elizabeth watched as Amy laid a palm on Arne's bicep as if to settle him.

She was even more surprised to see him rest a hand briefly over the woman's before he lowered his arms to his sides and inclined his head to study her. He remained silent as she replied.

"There are three who could do the job you are asking," she informed the caller. "Aegis Ninety-One has been in the business almost as long as I have. They are a small operation with people located along the East Coast of NorAm. Siam's Arc operates across the Northern Hemisphere and has several high-level assassinations to their credit, although they prefer blackmail to achieve their aims."

She paused but the voice was impatient.

"And the third?"

Arne raised his eyebrows and exchanged a glance with Matthias. She chuckled softly.

"I saved the best for last. Tiny Tim."

"Only one man?"

"No. There are four of them and they will travel."

"Are they any good?"

"They are in my top three and their specialty *is* assassination—although they like to give each killing a *special* touch." Matthias watched E's lips twist with distaste.

"How so?" the voice was clearly intrigued.

"They put the 'root' in 'brutal,'" she stated coldly. "I'd advise against using them unless you want it messy."

"Then why do you recommend them?"

"Because they are one of the top three operations for the kind of work you're looking for."

"How have they never been caught if they have such a distinctive touch?"

"Because it differs with each task and they have no ties to their targets—ever," Elizabeth told them. "They leave no traces and no witnesses."

"We prefer there to be neither."

"All of the operations I have named can offer you the same service, but you must negotiate it."

"Are you trying to teach us to suck eggs, Ms. Smith?"

She gave a quick, tight smile that the speaker couldn't see.

"I'm making sure you know your business as well as you seem to," she replied. "I'd hate to see you taken advantage of."

"We are not novices in this arena," he informed her, his tones as clipped as the distortion would allow.

"So I understand," she replied smoothly.

"You have given us the names as you promised, but we must ask you once again. Will you consider undertaking this task yourself?"

"Your persistence is flattering," Elizabeth told them, "but the answer is still no and for the same reason. I have moved up in my world and left the necessity of these tasks behind."

"So you say. We are disappointed but hope one of these others lives up to your promise."

The words were strangely ominous and she shivered as she dismantled the handset and stowed it in the safe once more.

"Listen in through that, ass-wad," she muttered and placed the chip beside the battery and the shell before she positioned a jammer with it and closed and locked the door.

"You're sure they are?" Matthias asked, his face a picture of disbelief and consternation.

"I know they're trying," she told him. "Earth-BURT confirmed it." She frowned. "And speaking of which..." She raised her voice. "E-BURT are you around?"

"I would never leave you to face those wolves alone." The AI's tones were indignant.

"Be nice E-BURT. I'm sure the wolves have done nothing to deserve being associated with the likes of that lot."

"You may have a point, Ms. E," he conceded. "How may I be of assistance, today?"

Elizabeth sighed. As powerful as BURT's clone was, he was still not BURT. "Were you able to discover their target?"

"I am verifying that the names and address are correct," he replied. His tone turned grave. "I am afraid this assassination will have severe consequences if it is allowed to succeed."

She responded with a heavy sigh. "So are we, E-BURT."

Arne groaned. "Look, BURT. Do you have the targets or not?"

"Verifying..." he replied. "Verifying..."

From the look on the ex-Marine's face, Elizabeth's comms array was in danger of a pounding if the word was repeated even one more time. Fortunately for her equipment, silence followed.

Matthias rose from his seat and turned to face Arne.

"What are you doing, Matt?" the younger man asked as his ex-boss rested a hand on the wall beside his head and leaned toward him.

"Making sure you don't do something we'll all regret," he replied. "We all know how much Elizabeth loves her office."

Arne looked into his friend's face and smiled. "And what makes you think you could stop me from trashing it if the oversized pile of chips and electricity tells me it's verifying one more time?"

"I think we'd both be in trouble if I tried," he admitted, "but I harbored illusions of being able to get you out the door."

The other man chuckled. "Yeah. I might have allowed that."

"Ugh!" Elizabeth groaned. "When you two have finished with the oh-so-manly bonding shit, we have a name."

"I didn't hear him call back," Arne commented.

"Given your elevated sensitivities," E-BURT informed him, "I deemed it prudent to send Ms. Elizabeth a written text with the relevant data. You seemed unusually agitated."

Matthias watched the man's expression go from consternation to outrage and couldn't stop the chuckle that snuck out. As Arne's attention switched to him, his chuckle became a snicker and he tried to suppress it. Then, a full-blown laugh erupted when he gave up.

"He got you." He guffawed, pushed off the wall, and collapsed into his chair. "The pile of chips and electricity got you!"

Arne slumped against the wall with a grunt of exasperation. He stayed that way for a long moment before he looked at Elizabeth. "So…"

She arched an eyebrow at him. "So… What?"

"Where is it?"

E glanced at the screen. "It's number 369211— Well, *fuck me!*" She ripped a drawer open and snatched a handful of communicators. "Amy!" she shouted and registered her head of security leaning against the door of her office.

"Amy," she said in a much more reasonable tone. "It's the Brogans."

"The who?" But as she said it, the woman's face paled. "*The* Brogans?"

Elizabeth nodded and pushed past the two men to reach the door. Amy didn't wait to be told. She moved out ahead of her boss.

"Elle!" she snapped and turned to Amy. "Get Lisa and Elle on deck and kitted out. We're going to war."

"We are?" Arne and Matthias followed on her heels. "Someone had better start talking."

"No," Amy retorted. "Someone had better shut the hell up and listen. The Brogans are—"

"Todd's parents," Matthias interrupted when he finally put two and two together. "Oh, fuck me."

He headed after Elizabeth at a run. "You can't do this alone!"

"Well, aren't they the cutest pair," Arne snarked, followed more slowly, and stopped. "Wait. Todd? As in *Stephanie's* Todd?"

She broke into a jog toward the ready room. "Now you're getting it. How about you shift those old bones and get your kit?"

"Who's there?" Todd's mother called.

Elizabeth rolled her eyes and put the kettle on. Honestly, their son might be one hell of a scary fighter but his parents were the gentlest of lambs. Her hand trembled as she made coffee and tea exactly the way they liked it, and she frowned. Adrenaline was not what she needed as she set the cups in their places at the table.

They probably wouldn't get to drink it, but it was the only way she could think of to make herself look less threatening. There was nothing she could do for Matthias. He lounged at the back door and looked like a householder's nightmare in his combat armor.

Todd's mother obviously thought so. She got halfway down the stairs and froze. Even then, she didn't run. She simply stared at them.

When they didn't move, she descended another two steps. "What are you doing in my kitchen?" she asked and followed it with, "Are you from the Marines?"

Ms. E shook her head and tried her most disarming smile. "Mrs. Brogan, we work with Stephanie."

The woman's face lit up. "Todd's friend's people?" Her smile faded. "But what are you doing here? And why are you dressed like that?"

"Ask them if they have any ID, honey," said Todd's dad. "They should have ID."

"They should have knocked," the woman declared and sounded almost angry before her face grew pinched with worry. "Why didn't you?"

"Because we're trying to save your lives," she told her. She glanced at the clock on the wall. "And we're running out of time. You need to come with us if you want to live."

Todd's mother burst out laughing. "That's something our Todd would say." She chuckled, deepened her voice to imitate Elizabeth's words, and accented them with something vaguely European. "Come with me if you want to live." She turned her head. "Oh, Tony, you have to meet these people."

Elizabeth stifled a groan. It *was* hard to believe the sergeant came from these people. She put it down to it being late and them finding themselves in slightly surreal circumstances. Or nerves. It could also be nerves.

She hoped that was all it was because if she discovered they were this stupid all the time, she might simply kill them herself.

"Look," she said. "I'd like to call Todd so he can verify who we are, but I—" She glanced at Matthias. "Fuck it. I forgot that was even an option! Fuck it all."

"That's not very reassuring," the woman informed her but she stepped into the room and studied her intently. "Do you have any ID?"

"Why aren't you calling the police?" she asked her and sounded almost pained.

"Because we assume that if you were here to kill us, you wouldn't have gone to all the trouble to make coffee and try to not scare seven kinds of shit out of us." Tony Brogan didn't have a problem being blunt. "Now, why don't you tell us what this is all about?"

"I'd like to be able to do that, but we honestly don't have the time," Ms. E told him. "I need to get you somewhere safe and my people need to set up so they can deal with the assassination team."

"You mean they're sending more than one person?" Todd's dad asked. He gestured to his wife and himself. "It's not like either of us could do a *damn* thing to stop someone determined to end our lives."

With a long-suffering sigh, she wondered if Amy might have been right when she'd suggested they tranquilize the parents and explain once they'd moved them.

Elizabeth had argued that this wasn't the best way to win their trust and Matthias had said they needed them to cooperate, and they'd discarded the idea. Now, she wished they hadn't.

Before she could respond, her earpiece crackled and Amy's crisp tones reached her.

"We have incoming. Get them out and get your ass here as soon as you can. It looks like they went with Aegis Ninety-One."

"Fuck!"

Todd's mother raised her eyebrows. "I take it that means we have to leave now?" she asked and for a fleeting second, E wondered if Todd needed his mother.

She shoved the thought aside hastily. Of course he did and even if he didn't, *Stephanie* needed them to be okay.

"Yes," she managed. "We have to go now."

The woman looked at her dressing gown and slippers. "But I'm not dressed," she protested and her husband slid his arm around her waist.

"That's what you get for trying to talk them to death," he told her and gave her a gentle smile. "Besides, I would be proud to have you on my arm, *however* you were dressed."

"A man after my own heart," Matthias declared and hastened to open the door. He blushed. "Except that it would be Elizabeth. No disrespect."

He turned his most charming smile on the woman, and Elizabeth didn't know which of them made her want to puke more—Todd's dad with his besotted smile of comfort or Matthias with his equally charming declaration of love.

Later, she would make him eat those words. Maybe.

Focused on the task at hand, she strode past the couple and out to where the transport waited. Lisa stayed in the driver's seat long enough to keep the engine running and handed over smoothly. As her guard slid out, E took her place, popped the rear doors, and tapped the steering wheel while Matthias ushered Tony and his wife inside.

As soon as they were in, he closed the door and slapped the roof.

"Get them out of here, E," he ordered as if she needed to be told.

It was hard to drive away when all she wanted to do was be there in the middle of the fight.

Elizabeth resisted the urge to hammer a fist against the wheel but eased the transport away from the curb and down the alley that ran behind the house. When they were free and clear with no sign of the assassins, she accelerated.

It didn't take all that long to get them to the hotel, where Lisa and Elle were waiting.

"Some folk have all the fun." Lisa pouted as Elizabeth made swift introductions and bid them farewell.

"Trust me. This won't be fun," she retorted as Elle led Todd's parents to the living room, "and you have the most important job. You get to keep these guys safe while we go squash the roaches."

"Hmmph. Well, don't let me keep you," the woman snapped and added in a softer tone. "And look after yourself."

E gave her a sharp nod. "You know what to do if we're not back here in two hours, right?"

"We'll get them to Steph," Lisa promised. "The big boss is on stand-by."

"Good to hear." She didn't stop for any more goodbyes. There was no need. She jogged to the car and returned to Todd's home.

Once she'd parked four blocks from the address, she moved quickly and quietly through the neighborhood and hoped she didn't get there too late to help. She thanked the god of vengeance and retribution when she saw four dark figures creep silently into the yard.

Two took the rear, and two the front...and they were impressive.

The two who approached the street entrance were suited like government agents, their dress screaming Federation Navy right down to the cheap suits and identification badges pinned to their lapels. They didn't go with subtle and simply marched up to the door and knocked.

Elizabeth watched from the dark and silent street. The porchlight above the assassins showed little more than two generic government employees. They exchanged glances when the door went unanswered and tried the handle.

To the untrained eye, they pushed the door open and greeted whoever was on the other side, but she knew what to look for. The brief jiggle of the handle and the way they stood hid the universal lockpick that took swift care of the lock, and the greeting was fake.

It looked legit from the outside, though. The brief smile, nod, and hand extended as though to shake another in greeting, all happened as they transitioned inside. When the door closed behind them, who was to say it wasn't one of his parents who'd closed it?

"Smooth," she muttered. "Very smooth."

No one replied over the comms, and she resumed her approach, banking on the need for a quick getaway to mean the front door was still unlocked. She eased up the single step and was across the porch and inside without a sound.

When she caught sight of one of the intruders as they disappeared up the stairs, she decided against warning her team. If she wasn't mistaken, they were already in place and taking care of it. A slight sound from the lounge caught her attention and she glanced toward it.

Matthias beckoned for her to join him as something jiggled the lock on the back door. The team coming from the rear had been slower but not by much. She hurried to where he waited at the kitchen door.

He gave her a brief thumbs-up and passed her a carving knife. Elizabeth took it and smiled slightly that he should have thought to have one set aside for her. She was still smiling when she took a position on the other side of the doorway and wondered where Arne was.

That question was answered moments later when she counted a third figure coming into the kitchen. Matthias made a brief signal with his hand and moved forward as Arne swung a skillet at the head of the rearmost assassin.

The work that followed was brutal but short. Matthias proved surprisingly efficient with the unconventional use of a carving knife, and Elizabeth made a note to look through the files Amy and Earth-BURT had dug up on him because the damned man was still keeping secrets.

Her blade skidded across body armor but it sliced deeply into an exposed bicep and she hacked at that again.

"Heads-up." Matthias spoke quietly over the comms, and she looked up in time to see the saucepan spinning toward her.

With a grin, she snatched it out of its flight by the handle and used it as a makeshift hammer on the assassin's exposed skull. She wasn't entirely surprised when Arne helped her finish the job faster by using his skillet in alternating strokes.

"That won't be too hard to believe, will it?" he asked, breathing as fast as she was when they looked at the dead assassin.

"Ours are down too," Amy told them over the comms. "Irons make really handy clubs."

"Crap!" Elizabeth looked at her blood-spattered body armor. "Remind me to never plan something in a last-minute rush again."

Matthias snorted. "Like you had much of a choice."

"What did we miss?" her security head asked as she descended the stairs.

"I checked the windows," Bunny told them over the comms. "It looks like none of the neighbors heard a thing."

"Are you sure?"

"As sure as I can be without checking the police bands."

"You are clear," Earth-BURT interrupted. "I have access to the emergency channels and your activities have gone unreported."

"But not unnoticed?"

"As far as I can tell from monitoring civilian communications in this area, you remain undetected thus far."

Elizabeth turned devastated eyes to Matthias. "I forgot the blood spatter. We should have worn—"

She stopped as she registered the shirt he had thrown over his body armor—and the trousers he wore *instead* of his body armor.

"When did you…"

He grinned at her. "You were somewhat preoccupied, E."

"Yup. She still is," Amy agreed and drew her attention. "This is what you get when you ask her to play nice with civilians."

E paused for a moment when she noticed the slippers and dressing gown the woman had thrown over her combat gear.

"That's…" she began and sputtered into laughter. "I wish I'd brought a c—"

She stopped and began to laugh anew.

Matthias stared at her. "Elizabeth, are you okay?"

The question brought abrupt sobriety and she straightened and waved a hand at Arne.

"I'm sorry. I never expected this."

The ex-Marine continued to use his tablet to scan the scene and paid particular attention to Amy in her borrowed robe and Matthias in his trousers and shirt. "You know it'll be difficult to convince them to put those on, don't you?"

Elizabeth grimaced. "What if we had them call from a laundromat where they were already dressed in something else and washing these?"

The two men exchanged glances.

"You know, that *would* be a very dumbass civilian thing to do," Arne mused.

Matthias shrugged and nodded. "Sure. You guys need to get out of here while Amy and I deal with footprints and printless smears at the appropriate locations."

"Sure." Elizabeth agreed and nodded at Bunny. "You're with Arne and me. We'll bring the car around for Matt and Amy."

"How far away is the car?" Arne asked, and she gave him a sharp look. He gestured at their combat suits. "Don'tcha think someone will ask?"

"We'll take the back way," she told him. "In a neighborhood like this, most people won't see anything—even if they get an eyeful."

He stilled, considered it, and finally nodded and she hurried into motion. She slipped out the back door and stopped long enough at an outside tap to rinse the blood from her boots before she vaulted over the fence and into the street.

They reached the car without incident after jogging through the shadowed backstreets. Their ears strained for the sound of sirens but only the occasional dog marked their passing and the houses around them remained dark.

"We didn't even meet the local criminals," Bunny grumbled as she slid into the back seat.

"What?" Arne asked. "Is one fight a night not enough for you?"

"I merely hoped for an excuse," the woman muttered, kept her head down, and remembered to not look out the window.

Matthias and Amy were waiting when they arrived.

"You know we're about to wreck their evening, right?" Amy asked as Elizabeth pulled away.

"More than telling them they were about to be assassinated?" she asked.

The other woman sighed. "Well, we'll have to show them the footage so they're not shocked when the police do."

"Fuck."

Matthias groaned. "Yeah, that about sums it up."

"You know, we could always delay it," Arne suggested, but she shook her head.

"The police will need the emotional fallout," she told them and gave a heavy sigh of her own. "Do you think they'll be able to pull it off?"

Amy snorted. "You're asking that *now?*"

"I'm trying to put contingencies in place."

"I think they might surprise you," Matthias reassured them. "Todd didn't come out of nowhere, you know."

Elizabeth gave herself a moment to digest that and nodded. "Fine." She thought fast. "Okay, this is how it'll go down. We'll take them through the footage and drop them at the laundromat. One of them will have to call the authorities. We arrive shortly after the police, say we're on their emergency call list, and get them out of there as fast as we can without making the locals more suspicious than they have to be."

"Oh, they'll be suspicious all right." Arne's dry chuckle didn't sound at all amused.

She pursed her lips. "As soon as we get them out of there, I'll take them to stay with Steph's folks. Cindy will know what to do."

"You don't think that'll freak Cindy out, do you?"

After a moment's thought, she shrugged. "She's a smart lady. She'd have made the connection as soon as this hit the news."

"It'll hit the news?" Arne looked alarmed.

E darted him a pitying look via the rear-view mirror.

"Middle-Aged Couple from the Subs Attacked in their Home?" she asked. "Of *course* it'll make the news."

"Okay," Matthias acknowledged as they pulled into the hotel car park. "Let's get this done."

"One more thing," she told him. "You and Arne aren't coming. I need to keep you guys as much out of the One R&D public spotlight as I can."

His eyebrows raised. "Why?"

"Because there are still many people who haven't cemented the connection, and I want to keep it that way."

"Your so-called *experts* were killed by two middle-aged civilians." The anger was evident even through the masking. "We want you to take the job."

"No," Elizabeth stated and the cold in her tones chilled Matthias to the core. It reminded him of another time when his voice had held a similar edge—and he'd hoped that part of him would never be needed again.

"You have two other names you can try," she continued.

"We have no faith in your list," the voice persisted. "Only you will suffice."

"I am not available."

"We are aware of several of your operations," the voice continued. "Their success could become...problematic in the future."

"I sincerely hope not," she told them sweetly. "It would be a shame to test exactly how much faith you should have put in the other two names on the list."

"Nevertheless—"

"No, nevertheless *this*," Elizabeth snapped. "You want a job done, and I've given you the best names in the business. I. Am. Not. Available."

She ended the call with a swift stab of her finger and settled into her chair to wait. Matthias laced his fingers together and looped them behind his head. Across the room, Arne stretched his legs and closed his eyes.

It didn't take long before the handset chimed again.

"Yes?" E demanded in Emerald's voice.

"Do you have a second list?" the voice asked, and Matthias breathed a soft sigh of relief as she gave the deep-and-dark three more.

"What operations are they aware of?" he asked when she'd ended the call and stowed the dismantled phone in the safe.

"They know about the warehouse," she replied. "I had E-BURT route the calls through that. It looks like the signal ends there, but he does some kind of technical magic involving a computer pick-up and Virt-World slippage and gets it out to me."

"Huh," Matthias grunted. "Virt-World slippage…"

She gave him a too-bright smile. "Yup. Stephanie's idea." She stood. "Lunch?"

"Lunch," he agreed and headed to the briefing room.

At least she remembered to eat while trying to keep their Stephanie safe.

CHAPTER SIX

It didn't take long for the press to get hold of the story.

Elizabeth scowled at the far too happy female on the screen.

"Today's breaking news comes live from the one of the Gov-Subs, where the parents of one of the Federation's best marines have shown their strength!"

She groaned and rested her head in her hands to watch the newscast through her parted fingers. "This is horrible."

Matthias draped his arm around her and pulled her close. "Yeah, but they're handling it."

"For how much longer, though?" she asked and gestured at the screen, where Todd's mother and father had appeared on the front porch. "At least they're not letting them in."

"They'll have to this time." Amy interrupted from the doorway.

She continued as she came into the room, balancing coffee and breakfast. "I spoke to them after the press visited the first time. They'll give the interview in the living room but the cameras will still be able to pick up the bloodstains in the hall and kitchen."

"We need to get them out of there," Arne observed as the couple showed the reporters in and settled them on the couch.

"You have ten minutes," Todd's father stated with open disapproval and cast a worried glance at his wife. "This has been hard enough."

"How about you take us through what happened that night?" the Federation News Broadcast anchor pressed and ignored the cue to call the interview off.

"We'd rather not."

"While we know this is difficult," the female anchor's partner began, "we have viewers who are horrified that someone would attack the parents of one of our most acclaimed Marines." He turned to Todd's mother. "How about you, Elaine? Do you care to tell them how it came about?"

Like it was their fault, Elizabeth thought and ground her teeth. She wondered how feasible it was for her to make the anchors disappear and felt Matthias's hand on her thigh.

"We can't kill them," he murmured and she snickered.

On the screen, the interview continued.

Todd's mother gave a shaky sigh. "Well," she started. "I couldn't sleep—"

"Worrying about Todd?" the female reporter pressed and Elaine gave a reluctant nod.

"Yes. We know he's often sent in when things get difficult," she admitted. "It's hard not seeing him—"

"You couldn't sleep," the male reporter prompted to steer the conversation back on track. E threw a ball of paper at the screen.

"Asshat!"

Matthias squeezed her and she drove a fist into his thigh.

"Ow!"

"Don't you patronize me!"

Arne and Amy hushed them from the other side of the table. On the screen, Todd's mother described how she heard someone at the back door.

"I knew it couldn't be anything good," she told them, her voice quivering.

"She's barely holding it together," Arne murmured and flinched when Amy poked him.

"She's doing better than she looks," the guard declared as Elaine told her story.

"I thought it was a burglar," the woman stated and shrugged apologetically. "We get them sometimes in the Subs."

Amy snickered. "Oh, she's good."

Elizabeth had to agree and she waited for the rest of the story.

"I picked up the first heavy thing I could see."

"The saucepan," the male reporter prompted and Todd's mom smiled.

"The saucepan," she agreed, "but I was afraid so I grabbed the frypan as well. We'd had sausages and mashed potatoes, you see, and I'd left the dishes to drain."

She stopped and her face went slack as though remembering the attack. E knew she was more likely remembering the pictures of the dead assassin they'd left on her kitchen floor.

"He had a gun," Elaine whispered, "and he turned it toward me when he came inside. I—"

She stopped and glanced at her husband. As if on cue, he took her hand and she drew a shaky breath.

"I hit him," she said.

"With the frypan?" the female reporter asked and sounded like she didn't believe it.

Elaine scowled at her. "Of course with the frypan!" she exclaimed and went on despite her voice cracking. "What else could I do? That man intended to shoot me, and Todd—"

Her face began to crumple and she reached for the tissue box. The reporters leaned forward, their mikes extended and their faces fighting for sympathy while anticipation ruled.

Todd's mother didn't notice. "Todd deserves to have *something* to come home to. Something better. Not a funeral."

"*Two* funerals," Tony reiterated. "If I hadn't heard Elaine's attack, the two who'd come through the window might have caught me still in bed. As it was, all I had was a pillow—"

"The police report says an iron was involved," Jalel reminded him mildly and Elizabeth swore.

"E-BURT, find out which fucker in the police department leaked that. Failing that, find me the hacker responsible. I want all their fingers broken!"

"And I want their address," Matthias added and fielded her shocked look. "What? I can't send a message of my own?"

She shrugged. "As long as you take Arne."

"As if he could leave me behind," the ex-Marine muttered, and Matthias rolled his eyes.

His muttered, "Done it before," didn't come out as quietly as he wanted it to and the younger man stretched to give him a light clip on the back of the head.

"What?" he demanded, but Tony cleared his throat and drew their attention to the screen.

"What can I say? I owe my wife some new appliances and my shirts will be rumpled for a while."

That drew a few chuckles.

"These two are *gold*." Amy snickered. "I don't remember telling them to say all that."

"They're handling it better than I could have hoped," Elizabeth murmured admiringly, "but I still want to call open season on those reporters."

"Would Emerald?"

"Nah, she'd probably send someone out to keep them from talking."

"If she was smart," Matthias interjected, "she'd leave them the hell alone in case the attention made someone from the Navy start digging."

She arched an eyebrow. "Is that what your boys will do?"

He snorted. "They're not anyone's boys—and no, they'll keep coming. We need to get those two out of there."

"It's already taken care of," she informed him. "Tony's leading into it, now."

"And new frypans." Elaine sniffed. "I can't...I simply *can't* use those again. Not after..."

Her voice hitched and the female reporter made sympathetic noises.

"Of course you can't," she soothed.

"That'll all have to wait until after we've moved, though," Tony declared, and the reporters focused on him with surprise on their faces.

"Gotcha, suckers," Amy exclaimed gleefully.

"*Blood*suckers," Arne added, returned her high-five, and smirked. "They didn't expect that."

"We're hoping our assassins didn't expect that, either," Elizabeth stated and watched the scene unfold.

Todd's parents were superb!

"You... You're moving?" the Meligornian reporter asked, his lavender eyes wide. "Where to?"

"We don't know yet," Todd's mother replied, which made the camera shift. "Somewhere not here, that's for sure."

"Wh-when?" Jalel stuttered and his co-anchor stared at him.

Before she could do anything more, Tony answered.

"As soon as we can. It's not safe here. Neither of us think we'll be so lucky next time."

"Lucky?" the female reporter asked. She turned to her partner. "Jalel, I don't think it was mere luck that got them through this, do you?"

"Certainly not, Amelia," the Meligornian replied. He gave the two parents a contemplative look. "I think the parents of our most feared Marine sergeant have proven why their son has risen through the Naval ranks so fast."

"Oh, for fuck's sake," Arne groaned. "That poor kid. He's never gonna live this down."

Matthias nodded in agreement and frowned as the interview wound up.

The camera had focused on the anchors, but Elizabeth saw when Todd's mother opened her mouth to say something. Unfortunately, the program shifted from the interview to the next news item.

She leaned back in her seat and drummed her fingers on the table.

The others waited while she considered the situation in her mind. Finally, she turned to Arne and Matthias.

"So," she said, "how do you two boys feel about impersonating Naval personnel?"

Elizabeth was waiting when Matthias and Arne arrived, and so were Stephanie's parents.

"Oh, Elaine!" Cindy exclaimed and hurried forward to take Todd's mom's hands in her own. "Come in!"

"You too, Tony," she added over her shoulder as she ushered Elaine into her apartment. "Elizabeth will explain it all to you once Franklin gets back with the keys."

The woman led the couple into her apartment. Only when the door had closed behind them did she turn to Matthias and Arne.

"So?"

"It went like a charm," Matthias told her. "The Navy sent a Shore Patrol team about a half-hour after we arrived, but they made it clear they were there to help and not get in our way. We let them take care of the Press."

"Did they say what the official word was?"

Matthias shrugged. "Only that we'd jumped the gun and plans were in the works to assist."

"Uh-huh..." Elizabeth let those two syllables say everything she wanted, and none of it was good.

He chuckled. "Yeah. We assume someone in PR saw the broadcast, rammed a quick suggestion through the immediate brass, and organized it so they could put a positive spin on it. We declined their escort but only after we'd traveled far enough to lose most of the broadcast drones."

"Oh? And how'd they take that?"

"Fairly well, I think. Their chief made a phone call and gave the order to peel off at the next major junction. I shook the last drone a little after that, and we parked underground. Bunny's going over the car for trackers as we speak."

"Will she find any?"

He shook his head. "None that aren't fried, anyway. Isn't that right, Arne?"

The younger man gave them a happy thumb's-up and grinned like he'd been up to mischief. Elizabeth made a note to check *everything* if he ever grinned like that and she didn't know what he'd been up to.

Matthias jerked his chin toward the reception desk. "How'd it go?"

"You know how we paid to keep the apartment opposite unoccupied?" she asked and he shook his head. She shrugged. "Well, we did because we wanted to have a back-up location for a security team if Steph's parents ever needed it."

"That," Amy added, "and it was the only way to guarantee any neighbors had our approval before they moved in."

"The body corporate wouldn't let you vet the applicants?"

E shook her head. "Nope. They said it was an invasion of privacy or something like that."

"So you simply rented the whole floor?"

She shrugged. "It seemed the easiest solution and like I said, it gave us an emergency way-point if we needed it."

"For situations like this," he concluded.

"Exactly." She looked up as the concierge arrived with the keys. "Thank you, Franklin. I appreciate it."

He nodded, his face flushed with excitement. "It's an honor to have Sergeant Brogan's folks staying here," he gushed, and Elizabeth fixed him with a stern stare.

"Not. One. Word," she snapped and tapped his chest for emphasis with each word. "If those vultures—" She gestured to the screen. "If those vultures end up circling here, you won't have an employer that'll take you. Am I understood?"

For a moment, Matthias thought the man might cry before the concierge pulled professionalism around himself like armor. When he smiled, though, there was still warmth.

"Let me assure you that we would do *nothing* that would jeopardize their safety. But we are still thrilled to have them with us, regardless of whatever circumstances brought them here." He tilted his head. "You saw nothing of the Meligornian *Ghargilum's* visit here, did you?"

Elizabeth shook her head and the man continued.

"The apartment is ready for them whenever you want to bring them across."

"We'll go through it first," she told him. "It's standard procedure."

"I understand." He led the way to the door and ushered her and Matthias inside.

Arne and Amy waited until he'd entered before they followed him inside. They left Lisa, Bunny, and Elle at the front counter.

"Let us know if anything changes," Amy ordered, and the three women arrayed themselves around the foyer.

The inspection didn't take long, and E made a note to send the body corporate and the reception team a bonus. She was impressed.

Not only was the place clean to the point where everything that could sparkle did, but it *smelled* clean, its linens were fully stocked, and every piece of furniture was in perfect condition.

"We left the crockery in its boxes," the concierge explained, "as we've found our tenants settle much more quickly if there's something to unpack."

She nodded. "And do you check packages on arrival?"

"We have a team that checks everything coming onto the grounds and a second team that goes over deliveries before they're sent to the apartments," the man told her. "Is that sufficient?"

"It will do for now," E told him. "I'll bring them through. They will shop online. If they leave, I need to know before they reach the front door. Is that understood?"

"Perfectly." The man hesitated but forged ahead with his next question anyway. "Do we need to delay them?"

"No." She shook her head. "They're not prisoners, but I want to be able to get a security team in place as soon as I can."

Matthias nodded approvingly when the concierge decided not to ask anything more.

Elizabeth knocked on the door to Stephanie's parents' apartment.

"It's time to see the new place," she announced when the four of them came to answer.

Tony narrowed his eyes and looked at the security guards, Matthias, and Arne. "And we can come and go as we please, right?" he asked.

She nodded. "Yes. Although I would appreciate it if you allowed us to provide you some security outside the complex. We don't want anything to happen to either of you."

"So you don't think it's over?" Todd's mother looked like she might burst into tears.

E tried for a sympathetic expression but only managed grim. "I'm sorry, Mrs. Brogan, but I don't. At least here, I think you'll be safe."

"Call me Elaine," the woman told her, gave a determined sniff, and straightened her spine, "and we'll be fine."

She gestured at the new apartment. "Will you show us around?"

"Do you want me to?" she asked. "Or would you rather discover it for yourselves?"

The couple exchanged looks.

"Maybe if you'd come into the living room and wait while we looked?" Elaine suggested. "I assume you've already made sure it's...safe?"

Elizabeth nodded. "It's clear and ready for you to make it yours. There's an account you can use to order whatever you need."

She handed her a tablet set to the appropriate page and waited while the woman inspected it.

"This is...very generous," she began, and she cut her off.

"Before you say you can't accept it, consider it a gift from Stephanie. She would do anything to make sure you're safe."

The words took a moment to sink in before understanding became acceptance. They knew she was right. Stephanie *would* do anything to keep them safe.

"Okay," Elaine told her and led the way into the apartment.

Elizabeth and Matthias followed, but Arne and Amy opted to stay in the foyer. It didn't take the couple long to return, although the team tracked their progress by the exclamations of surprise, disbelief, and delight as each new room was discovered.

"We can't…" the woman began when they returned, but E held a hand up.

"We need you to," she told them, "even if it's only until we find out who sent those people and stop them. Okay?"

Again, the couple shared a look, and they both nodded.

"Thank you doesn't seem enough," Elaine told her, and she smiled.

"It's all we ask," she replied. "That, and *please* let us keep you safe until Todd gets back."

That seemed to sink in and they both nodded.

"In that case, I'll leave you with Cindy and Mark." Elizabeth handed them each a cell. "Use these if you need *anything* or if you think you're in danger. It doesn't matter what time of night or day. I'll only be upset if you don't call me in time."

They left them shortly after, grateful for Cindy's presence as they said goodbye and acknowledged the people manning reception.

"They'll be fine," Matthias assured her as they left.

"I know," she replied and didn't protest when Arne slid into the driver's seat.

"My turn," the ex-Marine told her as Amy held the rear door.

"You know they'll keep coming, don't you?" Matthias asked once the vehicle was underway.

Elizabeth gave a tired sigh and nodded. "It looks like someone has targeted Stephanie again, and they'll try to get to her through the people she loves."

"Yup," was Arne's discomforting reply from the front.

"The only difference is that this time, they're using a go-between," Amy added.

"Yeah," E agreed. "They'll be right bitches to find."

"It doesn't matter," Matthias reassured her. "When we *do* find them, they'll be *our* bitches."

She snorted and rested her head on his shoulder. "Do you know someone with enough atoms in their brain willing to attack Todd?"

He shook his head. "Anyone with half a brain would have to know that that's simply suicide by Witch."

In another part of the city, an entire group of people proved their ignorance of that fact.

"We need to cut her support off at the knees."

"Hell, we need to vaporize her support and make sure no seeds remain."

"I'm not sure how we'll do that. She's a bigger hero than even Todd, and look at the waves the attempt caused."

"It won't matter. Once people understand how far she's in bed with the aliens, they'll see things our way."

"But people are saying the aliens aren't so bad."

The spokesman gave a sinister chuckle. "They won't be saying it for much longer. Just you wait."

"Do tell."

"Not yet. We have some finetuning to do yet."

Eyebrows were raised around the room, and he hastened to add, "We have the mechanisms in place to get it done."

"Like the assassination?" someone challenged and his eyes narrowed.

"They're working on it. Our criminal contact refuses to handle the contract directly and insists we use an alternative."

"Hmmph. That doesn't say much for your 'mechanisms,' does it?"

"Trust me. They've overcome more difficult obstacles."

"How do we *know* she is in bed with the aliens?"

"Are you joking?" The spokesman's disbelief was mirrored around the room. "Are you even *aware* of how many worlds—and peoples— she claims as her own?"

"Three?"

"Three! And how many alien races are there?"

"Three."

"Three. Exactly, and we all know how closely she's tied to the first two. Who's to say she's not secretly trying to work out a way to tie us to the third? And what happens when we encounter a fourth? Or a fifth?"

He paused and his gaze searched the faces of those in front of him. Most showed appropriate levels of shock and disgust, and more showed unease at the thought of how the Witch would respond to any future aliens they might encounter.

The idea simply didn't sit right.

His gaze swept the gathering. "We can't allow that type of alien-lover on our planet. The next thing you know, she'll invite them home to dinner or to establish homes here. We can't have that. There are barely enough resources for humanity, let alone whatever alien the Witch drags in."

"Yeah, but until she helps to defeat the Telorans…"

"Exactly."

"Hmmph. Maybe she'll finally eat a missile."

"We can only hope," the spokesman told them, "but until she does, we have to play it like we appreciate the hero until we're ready. And until the Telorans are defeated, we aren't ready. Got that?"

He paused to give his words time to take effect. As he saw heads nodding and heard murmurs of agreement, he finished with a warning and a promise.

"She doesn't die until later."

CHAPTER SEVEN

"I'm still here." Nathan's voice was full of disbelief and wonder as he patted his chest and arms. "See? Still here." He looked around. "*You're* still here. The lab—"

"We get it," Trey agreed. "The lab is still here and unexploded."

"Yes! Let's do that again," Gemma shouted. "Again!"

Trey shook his head. "You've spent too much time with your two-year-old."

"Pfft! No such thing." She waved her hand dismissively and darted a look at Marcus. "What d'you say, Doc?"

"I think Trey has a point—" he began.

"Agh! No. It's not about the two-year-old. It's about doing this again to make sure this time wasn't a fluke."

"You can't let a man live with his delusions?" Nathan's voice was more wistful than whine.

Trey slapped him on the back. "Come on, man. You have to have faith. There is no way this was a fluke."

"Yeah?" his colleague challenged. "Prove it."

Marcus chuckled. "Very well, Nate. Your wish is my command."

"No! Wait—" Nathan's protests were eclipsed by resigned acceptance as the scenario re-set around him. "Well, oookay."

"Again!" one of the other scientists demanded when that test was also successful.

"No…not again," Nathan muttered even though he knew it would do him no good.

This time, the world exploded around him.

"Sonuva—" he caught sight of Cynthia standing at the other end of the White Room and grimaced. "Son."

She blew him a kiss and the computer spun them back to the lab.

"Oops, that was my bad," Trey announced after he'd checked his console. "I forgot to flip a switch."

"Okay, can we automate that switch so we don't lose an entire facility to human error?" Marcus asked, and the other man frowned as he considered it.

"I'm fairly sure… Give me a minute."

The big scientist's fingers danced across his keyboard. "Aaand, we're done. Let's give *this* a go."

When Nathan opened his eyes, they were still in the lab and it was still in one piece. He shook his head and looked around as the scene re-set.

They ran the scenario another dozen times—and once more to make sure.

"Just for once, I'd like to go home without having been blown up at the end of the day," he muttered.

"Wish granted," Marcus told him a half-hour later.

"You mean we're done?"

"Ladies and Gentlemen," the scientist announced and rose from his seat. "Congratulations! We have good news to report at the end of the week."

The room erupted into cheers and the group rose from their seats to applaud.

"And now," Marcus told them when the response had died down, "given that we still have the afternoon ahead of us, we'll see what else we can add to the end-of-week report. Take a look at your data sheets and let me know what you discover."

He pursed his lips and blew out a long breath as he surveyed the lab. Now that he had Stephanie's design working, he felt somewhat adrift. Drawing comfort from the fact that the theory was done and the real work could begin, he pulled the computer logs up and began to work through them.

Cynthia interrupted them at two o'clock. "It's time for a break," she ordered. "Out of the pods."

"Out of the pods?" Marcus felt dazed. "Why?"

"Burt's orders. He says afternoon tea is on him."

"Afternoon tea?" he asked. "Since when—"

He caught her expression and the smiles breaking over his team's faces.

"Oh." Pasting on a smile of his own, he waved at the others.

"You heard the lady. The boss wants us celebrating and we're over-due. We'll pick this up la—" He caught his assistant's tiny shake of the head. "Tomorrow morning."

Inside, he chafed at the bit to sort the data and send it to Stephanie.

"They deserve to celebrate," Cynthia told him before she had BURT pull them out.

"Is that the...usual...procedure?" Marcus asked and sighed when she nodded. "All right, then."

The team was jubilant. Watching them, he had to admit that maybe the AI had had a point. His people needed to celebrate.

So why didn't I know that? he pondered and tried to shake the uncomfortable feeling that maybe he wasn't human anymore.

Cynthia settled beside him, and they watched the happy interaction as the scientists relaxed.

"You did a good thing, Doc."

"But why didn't I know that I needed to do it?" he asked and she gave him a sympathetic glance.

"It's not the way you're wired. Don't worry about it. We have your back."

Marcus decided that would have to do and waved goodbye to his team.

"Don't look like that, Doc. They'll be a hundred times more productive for the downtime. You'll see."

As he watched them go and mourned the hours lost that afternoon, he only hoped she was right. When his lab had quieted around him, he settled at his desk and booted up the computer.

Cynthia found him there the next morning, fast asleep beside the keyboard with his head pillowed on his forearms. "Oh, Doc…"

She left without waking him, only to return a few minutes later with a cup of coffee.

"Hey, Doc!" she called from the doorway and waited as he startled into wakefulness. "What did you do? Try to pull another all-nighter?"

He shook his head and accepted his coffee with both hands.

"No, but I was looking through the read-outs and I found this—"

"Uh-huh." She steered him firmly to the door. "Go grab a shower and get into clean clothes while I boot the pods and make sure everything is ready for you guys."

"Hmm?"

"Shower, Doc. This is not the example you want to set for Phillip, is it?"

Marcus caught a whiff of his scent and had to admit she had a point.

"Don't let them start without me," he ordered and hurried away.

Cynthia groaned and looked at the ceiling. "Give me strength," she begged. "He's worse than a teenager."

"Not quite." BURT surprised her by arguing, but the AI registered the security footage a moment later. "I stand corrected. Do you want me to have a word with him?"

She shook her head. "Not yet. He's trying."

"Hmmm…well, in that case, make sure he eats breakfast."

The team had only started to arrive by the time Marcus returned and they raised coffee cups to him with bleary eyes. It looked like he wasn't the only one who'd had a late night while thinking about their data.

"So, what do we have?" he asked once they were safely ensconced in the virtual meeting room.

"The process works," Nathan began.

He rolled his eyes. "Now tell me something I *didn't* know."

"The area above the energy line will be the first area cleaned and will be the cleanest," Nathan added, his face flushed with embarrassment.

Marcus didn't even need to look at Cynthia to know he'd stuck his foot in it but he also didn't know how to dig himself out of it.

"Go on," he said, more to give himself time to think than for any other reason.

"So," Nathan ventured and looked at Trey.

The big man smiled encouragingly and motioned for him to continue.

"So...we'll have to bury the lines—which is a shame because otherwise, we could mark a safe way through the Wastes."

"Except that we don't want to make it easy for the people to find the facilities," Gemma snapped, "corporate espionage being what it is."

"True," Phillip agreed, "and we need to hide the cables anyway or people will try to plug directly into them."

"But why would they do that?" one of the scientists asked.

"To get free power," the young man explained, "and I don't only mean folk from the Subs. I'm talking big corporations trying to short-change the government. They won't pass up a chance to cut a cost like that."

Marcus tracked the conversation with his gaze.

"But...why?" another scientist persisted. "We'd deliver it at below cost anyway."

"Because it's in people's nature to steal," one of the others explained. "You should have seen them from the late twentieth century onward. First, it was the gas from the pipelines—"

"Oh, hells yes. People steal everything. The power's not the least of it," another declared. "We're gonna have to bury the cables deep enough that they can't be detected or some asshole will dig it up and try to steal the whole thing."

"What? The cable?" Nathan asked.

"Hells yes, the cable—and the power be damned. The stuff those cables are made of would sell for a shit-ton on the black market."

"But it would cost them more for power in the long run." Marcus sounded like he couldn't believe people could be so shortsighted.

"It wouldn't bother them. They'd have made one big score in double-quick time. It'd be worth it for them."

"Right. So we need to bury the cables or everyone explodes," he observed, "and that would upset Stephanie…and *that* is something we simply can't have."

"Agreed, so how many of these facilities are we looking at?"

"Only one to start with, but if it's successful, Steph will want them in every area that needs them, including those here," he informed them and changed the subject. "What do we need?"

"For all of them or only the one at Brown's Ferry?"

"Let's start with the one at Brown's Ferry and use it as a template we can adapt to the other sites."

"Okay, that sounds like a plan. So first, we have the cables—"

"And the nodes. How many of those suckers make up an array?"

"It depends on if we have them come out all around the array or only on the horizontal."

"Make a list for either alternative," Marcus directed and moved on to the next items. "I take it we're all agreed that we need the plates in the conversion chambers?"

This was met with looks of disbelief. "Are you shitting me, Doc? If we *don't* have those plates, we might as well offer the first build as a one-off crematorium because that's all it's ever gonna be. And I'm fairly sure we can't clean the world one explosion at a time."

"Put it on the list and the rest of it too. I don't want a single chipset, wall section, panel, toilet, toothbrush, or piece of copper wire left out."

"I'm not sure we're using copper wire, Doc."

"And I'm darn sure the generators and power converters don't use toothbrushes." The speaker shrugged. "If they do, you'd better warn me because that idea simply boggles the mind."

They set to work, created the base list, and expanded and refined it. Marcus watched the numbers stack up on his tablet and glanced at Cynthia. "I'm gonna need to talk to Mr. Burt," he told her. "Could you arrange it, please?"

"I'll do that now. When did you want to speak to him?"

"As soon as he's available." He gestured at the scientists working around the table. "We're gonna need a whole *suite* of buildings for this shit to go into."

It turned out that fitting the equipment in wasn't their only problem.

"What do you mean, living quarters?" Marcus asked.

"The security teams will have to live somewhere," Earth-BURT informed him.

"*Security* teams? Screw that! What about the scientific teams?" he demanded. "You can't have one without the other."

"I am fairly certain it is possible to have security teams without scientific teams," Earth-BURT reassured him. "It would *not* be possible to have scientific teams without security teams, however. Simply put, it would be imprudent to put our personnel assets at risk in that manner. And we do not intend to leave our equipment unguarded."

"So there *will* be scientific teams?" Marcus asked hopefully.

"We have not planned scientific teams," the AI told him, "but I can foresee us needing someone to monitor certain...aspects of the project."

"Scientific aspects?" he asked, determined that if there was only one position going for monitoring the system, it was his.

"I will raise it with One R&D's planning teams," he told the scientist. "Is it something you would recommend?"

"Hells yes, it is," Marcus confirmed. He looked down the table to find he had the team's rapt attention. "Don't you all agree?"

Uncertain murmurs were not what he expected, but E-BURT's careful questioning soon revealed the problem.

"Of course, it would be voluntary," the AI assured them. "The insertion of a human component into the design requires careful consideration."

"But you will have security teams," one of the scientists pointed out.

"Security teams do not require protection," he replied. "Other human assets most certainly will."

"So you expect these centers to be attacked." The man who said this sounded defeated.

"We are hopeful that an attack will not come," the AI hedged, "but human history has shown that it is likely. We will do our utmost to protect the asset that is repairing your world."

"That complicates things," Gemma muttered but he disagreed.

"Not at this stage," he reminded them. "At this stage, we need to focus on designing the items we need for the process to be effective and to ensure that it is completed successfully. Housing and defensive armaments can be added later by a team with experience in that area."

"As long as you pass it back through us," Marcus told him. "You never know when adding an extra wall will affect the main structure."

"We can do that," E-BURT agreed. "We will also need to know what additions need to be made to cater for the power draw of certain protective equipment."

"You're putting *guns* on my center?" Annoyance sharpened his tone, but the AI did not argue.

"Among other things," he responded mildly. "Now, for the initial design of the project, what do we need?"

They all looked at each other, then at their lists, and everyone began to speak at once.

"Towers," vied with, "We're gonna need cables, tons of cables..." which was almost overridden by, "We'll need somewhere protected for the generators and conversion chambers and we need them to not be too close together."

E-BURT processed the suggestions almost as fast as they were delivered, sorted them into priority on arrival, and put the list on the viewscreen where they could see the changes. When they were done adding things, the wrangling for priority began.

"And what do we do if we have a loss of power? It's not like we have a repair crew on site—or will the security team be qualified?"

"Ooh, good point. We need a redundancy, regardless."

That galvanized them again, and the AI monitored the ensuing wrangle to draw out relevant pieces of information as they came up. Somehow, he doubted the humans would recall them once they were all done putting their points across.

They'd almost settled on the design when Gemma groaned and slapped her forehead with the flat of her hand.

"Well, shine my shoes and call me Samson's love-child!" she exclaimed. "We can't build the outer walls out of *that*."

All around the table, conversations ceased. Marcus leaned forward and rested his chin on his fists.

"Do you care to tell me why not?"

She stared at her teammate across the table. "Trey, do you wanna enlighten us as to why we can't put that material where the radiation can alter its molecular structure?"

"Uh..."

"Really?" she sounded more than impatient now. "Seriously? None of you experts can tell me why we don't want a material that loses its tensile strength in an area prone to those kinds of storms?"

"Well, yeah, *that's* a problem," Trey acknowledged and a scramble for tablets ensued as those whose fields intersected looked for an answer.

"Graphene...or one of its derivatives?" someone suggested from the end of the table.

"I'll look into it."

Cynthia cleared her throat several times and pinged them, but nothing seemed to get through. She honestly didn't want to pull the plug on them. Finally, she resorted to subliminals and sent the aroma of roast meals, coffee, and cake through the pods.

Work ground to a halt.

"Cynthia!" Marcus was frustrated.

"It's either that or pull the plug on you all about an hour ago," she retorted, then addressed E-BURT. "I'm sorry, Mr. Burt. I don't know what time it is on your side of the world, but my orders are to try to stop these guys from working themselves to death and they need to stop. Now."

She hesitated and decided she might as well ask. "Can we adjourn until tomorrow, please?"

"Certainly, Cynthia," he replied, "and you have my sincere apologies for losing track of the time. I will set an alarm for tomorrow so this does not happen again."

The woman blushed. "Thank you, Mr. Burt."

The scientists pulled themselves slowly out of the calculations and planning and saved their files.

"Thanks, Cynthia," "See you tomorrow, Cynthia," and other farewells echoed around her, and even Marcus stretched and yawned and wished her goodnight. This time, she was the last to leave the lab and turned the lights out before she popped the lid on her Virtual World pod.

Marcus was on his way out the door. "I'd better go home tonight," he told her. "I'm sure university security is onto me."

"I couldn't possibly think why," she snarked, but her voice was gentle.

He paused but smiled without rancor. "I'll see you tomorrow, Cynthia," he told her and led the way outside.

The next few days passed in much the same way. The mention of storms reminded them of structural tweaks that needed to be made, and materials were adjusted, changed, and altered again. The computer simulation of each design was watched with great interest and each time, the buildings lasted longer.

Cheers rang around the room when one structure finally made the twenty-year mark with its structural integrity intact.

"Now for the habitations," E-BURT said once the applause had died down. "We have the machinery's abode secured, but we still have to protect it from the depredations of those who either want to destroy it or possess it for themselves."

This was met with a chorus of groans, but the team returned to the table with grim determination.

"I guess you get your toothbrushes after all," one of them noted, and Marcus gave him a look of utter confusion.

"I beg your pardon?"

"Never mind, mate," the scientist noted and slapped him on the back. "So, how much space d'you think these guys are gonna need?"

"I guess they'll need to keep fit."

"That's easily done. There are miles of corridors in the machinery section."

"Do we honestly want them anywhere near our machines?"

"I'm fairly sure the machines are big enough and bad enough to take care of themselves."

"Besides, those boys enjoy exploding about as much as we do. They'll be fine."

"So, no dedicated running track. What else do they need?"

"Design the basic living quarters," E-BURT told them, "and I will have them make the appropriate alterations."

Another day passed or possibly two. Marcus couldn't be sure. He'd lost track by the time Trey thumped the surface of his table and put the finished base overview on the screen.

"There you go, guys. Take a good look and make sure there aren't any last-minute changes needed."

His words were met by intense silence as his colleagues peered at the screen.

"You know," Gemma stated after several long minutes, "it's amazing."

"Yeah," Nathan agreed. "Amazing if it doesn't blow up."

Several chuckles greeted his statement and Trey smirked.

"There is that."

"And if no one steals it," Phillip added.

Trey grunted. "I think we have to assume that will be attempted."

Nathan snickered. "They won't like the big kaboom if they try."

"Let's not put in a kaboom." Marcus hastened to calm them. "That's what we have the security team for. I'm very sure those guys will provide us with all the kabooms we're ever likely to need."

"And we can make sure the warnings about not messing with what you don't understand are very visible given that I don't think we'll be there," Trey added and glanced at the team leader.

"Pfft." Gemma blew a raspberry. "It's not like they would listen to our spoken warnings if they don't listen to the signs to start with."

"Who listens to signs anymore?" Phillip asked and they all turned to look at him.

Marcus sighed. "That's a good point."

"Yeah," Nathan reiterated. "We'd better not be nearby or that's the end for us."

He looked around the room. "And I've had enough of being blown up to last me a lifetime!"

That drew more chuckles, and Trey nodded sagely.

"It *will* hurt."

Gemma laughed. "Yeah. Sure. But only for a micro-second."

CHAPTER EIGHT

Elizabeth waited while Matthias raised his hand to knock. She carried a bouquet of flowers and he held a bottle of wine and a gift box containing a vase.

"Are you sure she likes blue crystal?" she whispered and he gave her a self-satisfied smile.

"Positive."

She cast a nervous glance at the door. "But how do you *know*?"

His smile turned into a smirk and he laid a finger alongside his nose. "My sources are solid," he assured her.

"You're going to make me *beg*?" she asked in a disbelieving whisper.

"It won't do you any good," he told her. "My sources are sacred."

"Uh-huh." She gave him a calculating look. "So, it'll be like that, will it?"

His smirk became a grin. "Hells yes, it will."

She was about to respond when the door opened and Elaine Brogan looked out. Her entire face lit up when she saw them. "Elizabeth! Matthias! Oh, I am so glad to see you."

The woman peered past them until she caught sight of Amy, Arne, Lisa, Bunny, and Elle.

"Oh, good. Everyone's here!"

"Come in." She stepped aside to give them entry. "I… We don't know how to thank you enough."

Elizabeth darted a worried look at Matthias, but he smiled serenely, his thoughts hidden behind a pleasant mask. Elaine didn't seem to notice. She grasped E's free hand and drew her toward the kitchen while Tony intercepted Matthias.

"Like I said," she told her as the two men headed to the lounge. "Tony and I don't know what to say."

She gestured around the apartment. "Did you know you could fit our old home in here and still have room left over?" She paused and a sudden blush colored her cheeks. "How will we ever repay you?"

They'd reached the kitchen and the visitor's nose twitched. "Oh, my, is that… You cooked a roast?"

"Well…yes. The best way to throw a housewarming is to start with a good meal, but that's not—"

Elizabeth guessed she intended to say it wasn't enough and placed a finger over the woman's lips.

"Firstly, we won't let anyone die if we can help it. Secondly, we won't stand by and let someone precious to Todd die when we can stop it. And lastly," she added and her voice softened, "One R&D needs to keep its best employee focused on doing what she does best and not worrying about her boyfriend's parents."

Elaine had turned pink and pushed the finger firmly to one side.

E froze. Part of her mind focused on not letting her self-preservation instincts take over and put the woman through a wall and the other part worried that she'd given away too much.

The latter was a real possibility, she discovered at Elaine's next words.

"My guess is that what you're not telling me is exactly how important Stephanie is to all of you personally, and not only as an employee," the woman informed her. She leaned forward and pitched her words in a low tone. "Or are you going to tell me she's merely another asset your people have to protect?"

Caught by surprise, Elizabeth didn't know how to respond. She blushed and pursed her lips as she tried to work out what to say next. The woman saved her the effort.

"You've spoken to Stephanie recently, haven't you?"

"Not too recently but in the last week, yes." She hedged and wondered where the conversation was going.

"Did she say—" Elaine stopped and bit her lower lip. "I mean...do you know if Todd was traveling with her? The news..."

Uh-oh, Elizabeth thought. "What did the news say?"

The other woman colored and turned to the oven to fuss with the evening meal. "Only that the Navy had said they'd have something to report on the Telorans after a special strike team had returned from a delicate operation."

She paused and her hands came to rest on the handles of the saucepans. "I wondered if that meant Todd and his team had gone out again. They never tell us, but... Well, you heard the reporter. He's the 'best Marine in the Federation' and every other time there's been a 'delicate' operation, it's been Todd."

Her expression set, she turned to Elizabeth. "I might not know how to deal with intruders but I'm not stupid. I *do* know he's out there and he's at the forefront of whatever's going on." Her lips quivered and her eyes grew unexpectedly bright. "I know there's a good chance he might not come back."

She lowered her head as her face crumpled. E stood, frozen, with no idea what to do. Elaine's shoulders shook before she sniffed twice and raised her face. It didn't make her visitor feel any better to see the dampness at the corners of her eyes.

The woman snatched a tea-towel and dabbed hastily at them. "Sorry. This is supposed to be a celebration and a thank you. It's not much thanks if I cry all over you."

"If not me then who else?" Elizabeth managed to say and placed an awkward hand on the woman's shoulder. "If it helps, I *have* spoken to Stephanie and she's okay, but Todd's not with her at the moment. He had to go on ahead and make a report."

"So they're still seeing each other?" Elaine asked and she smiled.

"Oh, yes. I doubt very much that anything could mess *that*

romance up."

"So they're a couple?" Elaine sounded hopeful and more cheerful at the thought. "I thought they might be, of course, but he's away so much it's hard to believe that even Stephanie would handle that."

Elizabeth snorted. "She manages. Not that it isn't hard, but she's away a fair amount too and Todd merely deals with it. Honestly, they're both so young, I don't know what they'd do if they had a decent stretch of time together."

"What do you mean?" the woman asked, and she blushed.

"I mean their first date was Stephanie surrounded by a team of minders—that's if they didn't see each other in school?"

Todd's mother chuckled. "Oh, they saw each other plenty, but Todd didn't get it and I don't think she knew what to do about it."

"What do you mean?"

"I mean they'd study together, walk to and from school, and share the occasional movie, but they never got around to dating."

"Really?" Her eyebrows raised in genuine surprise. "Do tell."

"Well, there was one time I caught Todd going through what I thought was a health kick. It turned out he'd met this girl, a cheer-leader—you know the type?" She went on without waiting for a reply. "Anyway, Stephanie had encouraged him to ask her out."

"She what? Was she crazy?"

"I think she wanted him to be happy, even though I'm fairly sure she liked him herself by that stage. Anyway, whatever she felt, she gave him the courage to ask this Amy girl out and it was a tough few weeks of her getting him to eat healthy and exercise. I'm surprised he ever wanted to look at another health shake again, let alone join the Marines."

Her face softened. "Anyway, it didn't last much beyond when Steph left to go to that awful prep school. I've never seen him so lost. He'll tell you it was because the other girl wanted him to eat healthy, but I think it was because he missed Stephanie, even if he didn't know it at the time." She sighed and turned to tend their meal. "Either way, he joined the Marines when Steph went to work for One R&D and I thought that was the end of it."

Elizabeth watched as Elaine made the gravy.

"I never dreamed they'd end up together. The night she came to collect him in the shuttle…" She chuckled and her eyes misted over, but her gaze fell on the flowers Elizabeth still held. "Are those for us?"

With a startled glance at the bouquet, she smiled and held it up. "We thought you'd like some color." She glanced around and noted the tea-towels hanging from the oven and the picture beside the fridge.

Elaine followed her gaze, moved to a cupboard near the fridge, and took out a beautiful blue vase. "They're perfect," she told her happily.

Elizabeth hoped so because there was no salvaging their gift—it was a perfect match for the vase the woman had filled.

"Let me give you all the grand tour," her hostess suggested as she carried the flowers out to the living room.

Matthias' eyes widened and E had to stifle a smile, but it was too late. Tony was already raising the gift. "Housewarming from Matthias and Elizabeth."

"And these are from us," Amy and the girls added and placed their offerings on the table.

Elaine set the flowers down and opened the first gift. Her eyes lit up when she saw what it was.

"Oh, my!" she exclaimed.

Matthias opened his mouth to apologize but Elaine overrode him.

"It's perfect! I was just telling Tony that I wished we'd bought the pair when we had the chance. Now, I can put them on either end of the cabinet and they'll frame Cindy's picture perfectly!"

Elizabeth looked around the room and noticed the picture hung in the space above a long, low cabinet set against one wall. It was a Meligornian landscape, a field of purple and blue flowers under a lavender sky.

Elaine was right. The vases would set it off perfectly. She watched as their hostess shifted the vase from its coffee-table perch and placed it on one side of the cabinet.

Once she had positioned the other, she returned and unwrapped the gifts the girls had brought. The array of blue crystal animals soon found a home under the painting and she was aglow with pleasure.

"There, now," she told her husband. "That's exactly what it needed."

He smiled dutifully and more widely when Arne produced a long square box from under his coat. "I assumed they'd forget the toast," the ex-Marine told him and retrieved a second box.

Elaine looked at her box and leaned up to kiss him on the cheek. "Thank you."

The man turned pink, caught Amy's arched eyebrow, and turned even pinker.

Their hostess placed her bottle in the middle of the coffee table and straightened. "So, would you like the tour?"

Greeted by enthusiastic agreement, she extended her hand to Tony and reflected his fond smile as he took it. "This way." She beamed and led them to the doorway of the den. When she peered through after them, the space reminded Elizabeth of Mark's den and she wondered how much influence Stephanie's dad had on the design of this one.

Matthias took one look through the door and glanced at Tony, one eyebrow raised. "It's not nice to hold out on your guests, Tony."

The other man flushed and gestured for them to enter. Elaine groaned. "Well, that's the last we'll see of *them* for the night."

"Not true," her husband called as he followed Arne and Matthias inside. "We can be coaxed out with food."

She snorted and smiled at Elizabeth. "Coaxed is not how I'd describe having to stand aside to avoid being flattened on their way to the table."

"I heard that…" issued from the depths.

"If the bootuh feeits…" Elaine retorted and E chuckled.

Lisa and Bunny peered through the door, their mouths shaped in identical 'ohs.'

"Well," Amy said, "now we know where to come if we ever need a quiet game of pool."

Elaine looked at Elizabeth and her guards. "You can…" she began, but E shook her head.

"I want to see what you've done with the place," she said and Amy and Lisa nodded enthusiastically.

They'd seen it before but not since the woman had tweaked it from a generic furnished apartment into her home. Even if they weren't interested in the decorating, they wanted to see it from a security perspective. Of course, there was no way in Hades they would tell her that.

Besides, Elizabeth had already seen the kitchen and the living room and she honestly *did* want to see what Elaine had done with the place.

"Are Stephanie and Todd really a couple?" The woman surprised her as she led them down the hall.

Amy and the girls chuckled and E smiled as she answered.

"Oh, yes. They really, really are."

"But how do you know?"

She opened her mouth to tell her how Todd hadn't left Stephanie's bedside after the battle on Dreth, then realized she didn't know how much about the battle had been released on Earth.

"Well, even though they don't get to see each other often, they spend every moment they can together."

"Even after ops," Amy said sourly as they entered the main bedroom. "Ooh, is— That closet is *huge!*"

Elaine had been about to ask for more details but the exclamation drew her attention. She laughed. "Would you believe there was even a note in there that said, "To whichever lucky woman is given possession of this closet, I ask you to fill it to the best of your ability." She lowered her voice to a whisper. "It came with a gift card."

Elizabeth smirked. "And was it signed?"

The woman shook her head and reached up for an unassuming envelope that rested on a shelf in the mostly empty space. Taking out a piece of paper, she handed it over. "No. See?"

She took the note and unfolded it, and her eyebrows rose when she recognized Stephanie's handwriting.

The girl must be psychic, she thought, but what she said was, "So, did you do what it asked?"

"I *looked,*" Elaine told her, "but I don't have anywhere to go where I'd need to wear anything so nice."

E chuckled and handed her the piece of paper. "You never know what the future holds. Maybe you should get something just in case."

The woman brightened. "Maybe I will, then." She put the note and envelope back. "It would probably be rude not to."

"It would," Amy assured her fervently as they stepped out.

"This one's for Todd," the woman told them when they reached the third bedroom. "I... Do you think it would be possible to get his things out of storage anytime soon?" Her hands twisted. "It would be so nice if they could be here for him."

Elizabeth noticed she wasn't asking for any of her or her husband's belongings, even though they'd only been able to bring two suitcases and had to trust the movers with the rest. She gave her a gentle smile. "I'll see what I can do."

They'd managed to get the parents moved without having to avoid too many reporters, but relocating everything from their house to the apartment was a work in progress. It was unfortunately necessary to wait for the interest in the storage location to die down.

A timer rang in the kitchen as she contemplated pulling her tablet out and checking in with the second team she had observing the storage units.

"Well, that's my cue," Elaine said briskly as she led them to the kitchen. "Could you ladies let the guys know dinner's coming?"

"Pleasure," she agreed but let Amy and the team go while she stayed in the kitchen to help.

"So, when was the last time you saw Todd?" the woman asked, and she frowned.

"Let me see..." She began to wrack her brains for the last occasion. "You know, it's been a while since I last saw him, and I haven't seen him since he got back."

"He's back?" Elaine froze.

Oh, gods. Now, I've done it. She shrugged. "Well, he's back from the mission," she amended.

Her hostess continued to serve dinner and handed the plates to Amy and Lisa when they came looking for some way to assist. "So he hasn't been given leave?"

E shook her head. "I don't think so. He'll have to debrief first, and they'll want to keep him close for that in case they have any additional questions."

Elaine sighed, handed her a plate, and picked the last one up for herself. "Here you go. It's hard to imagine him so close and yet so far away."

"He hasn't called yet?"

Todd's mother shook her head and her face colored as a prelude to tears. She was about to suggest they stop when the woman straightened her shoulders and led the way into the dining room. Following her, she decided he'd better have a good reason for not calling, or she would take him into the training room and hand him his ass.

She noticed Cindy and Mark had arrived as she entered and inclined her chin in reply to their waves. Elaine remained oblivious to what she was thinking and settled herself beside her husband.

"It's good to see you all here," she told them and waved to the food on the table. "Dig in."

"Before we do..." Matthias stood and raised his glass. "To a new home, good friends, and family."

For a single heartbeat, Elizabeth had thought he was about to say, "absent family," and she breathed a sigh of relief as she raised her glass in response. "Home, friends, and family."

Her reply was echoed all around the table and he resumed his seat and they ate. At first, they focused on the food in silence before Cindy turned to Elizabeth.

"Have you seen Stephanie lately?"

She paused with her fork halfway to her mouth. "Hasn't she called?"

The woman shook her head, and E added an ass-kicking for Stephanie to the list. She wasn't sure when she'd deliver either of them, but she was sure that the parents' time on Earth was limited, and not by death. The events of the last couple of days had made that clear.

"She's exactly like my Todd," the other woman stated, and Cindy laughed.

"Aren't those two a pair?"

Elaine cast a meaningful glance at Elizabeth. "So I've heard."

Cindy gave her a curious look. "Oooh, do tell."

Amy snickered. "Yes, spill, E. Curious minds want to know."

"Oh, they do, do they?"

The looks on Tony and Mark's faces said it might be otherwise, but Elaine and Cindy didn't notice. They leaned forward in anticipation. She sighed, finished her mouthful, and took another to give herself time to think.

Amy groaned. "Come on, E. The least you can do is tell them how their last date went."

"They had a *date*?" Elaine was agog. "You mean Todd asked her?"

It reminded her that he had grown up considerably since he'd left home—and that he hadn't been home often enough for his parents to see it. Well, it was time to give the boy a boost, even if it *was* to drop him in it on the romance front.

Come to think of it, the little rat deserves it for not calling his mother often enough. Stephanie too, she decided and cleared her mouth to favor them with a smile.

"Well," she began, "I don't know if you'd call it a *date*, but Todd did cut in on the *Ghargilum Afreghil* of Meligorn to steal a dance from her."

Elaine's eyes widened. "He did *not!*"

Elizabeth grinned. "Hells yes, he did. And as smooth as you please, too."

She didn't add that Stephanie had gone all Morgana not long after, or that Todd and his team had been launched on one of the most dangerous missions of his life. There were some things his parents didn't need to know.

After all, she'd seen the footage.

Pushing that image aside, she added, "I don't think I've ever seen Stephanie so flustered," and watched them laugh.

She also didn't tell them that she'd only watched the footage—or that she watched it with popcorn—until the moment Steph detected the Telorans and kicked everyone off the bridge.

"They're quite sweet together," she added, "but I think those cats will drive him crazy!"

"The cats?" Elaine asked, and Cindy groaned.

"Imagine two oversized house cats with an attitude as bad as any man about being told what to do."

Elizabeth sputtered as male jaws dropped at the other end of the table, but Cindy waved for her to continue.

"Tell her."

She obliged. "They look as sweet as pie"—Cindy snorted but Elizabeth ignored her—"until you get to know them. There was this one time when Todd was working out with his team and Stephanie came in with the cats..."

Once or twice, she wished she had a viewscreen so she could show them the footage, but everyone laughed by the time she'd finished.

"What about their other date?" Elaine asked. "You know, the one where Stephanie came and picked him up in the shuttle?"

"Do you want to hear what happened?" E asked and she nodded. "Didn't Todd tell you?"

The woman rolled her eyes. "You know boys don't talk to their mothers, right?"

"No, I didn't," she replied. "They don't?"

"Oh, no," Elaine told her. "You know that cheerleader Stephanie set him up with? Well, one day, I looked out the window and saw him kiss her goodbye."

"Ooh."

"So I asked him who she was and he shrugged and said she was 'just a girl from school.' He blushed as red as a beet about it, too. I wanted to ask him more but he said he was really tired and had homework to do. I didn't know what to say."

"You had more than enough to say about it to me," Tony began, and she flushed.

"Well, I could talk to *you*. Todd ran like a startled hare every time I tried to raise it."

Elizabeth snickered and sympathized with the young man Todd had been. His first conflicted love *and* a nosy mother! She could only imagine and grinned as she turned to Cindy. "What about Stephanie?"

"Pfft!" the woman replied. "She had her moments, but I don't think she ever *avoided* me."

"Did you ever try to talk to her about Todd?" Elaine challenged, and Cindy blushed.

"No, but I will now."

Mark groaned but raised his hands in surrender when she fixed him with a steely glare.

E chuckled.

Beside her, Matthias exchanged puzzled glances with Arne across the table. He tilted his head in her direction and his expression suggested he wanted to know who was seated beside him and where the *real* Elizabeth had vanished to.

Amy caught the look and snickered. Tapping Arne on the shoulder, she picked her empty plate up and took Lisa's. "Come on, Arne. You can help me clear the table while E spills the beans on Steph and Todd."

She glanced across the table. "You too, Matthias."

The two men followed her example, which caused momentary consternation in their hostess as they insisted she sit while they loaded the dishwasher.

"But there's dessert," she protested.

Matthias gave her his most disarming smile. "We promise to give you back your kitchen very soon." Elizabeth gave him a wary look and he smiled. "You still haven't told them about that first date, E."

She opened her mouth to protest, but the two women leaned forward in anticipation and she shrugged. "You know, I think that was the one and only time I've ever seen your Todd at a loss."

Matthias took a load of plates to the kitchen, relieved when he saw Arne and Amy loading the dishwasher. He fixed the woman with a piercing stare.

"What the hell is going on with her?" he asked in a worried whisper. He gestured helplessly toward the dining room. "This is... It's... Well, she's not normally this gossipy, and never about Stephanie. It's like she's been replaced by some...some *doppelganger!*"

Amy smothered another laugh. "She's merely fitting into her role as Stephanie's 'other' mom," she explained and let her smile fade.

She inclined her head in a slight challenge, put a hand on her hip, and returned his look. "I'm guessing she's gonna want an answer on kids in the future."

His jaw dropped. "But she hasn't even—"

The woman cut him off as she continued, "Assuming we don't die from lead poisoning, or a sudden rearrangement of our atoms due to immolation, or—"

Arne groaned and rolled his eyes. "We get the hint. We die."

"Sure, make it sound so pedestrian." She huffed and pushed Matthias gently by setting her palm in the center of his chest. "*You* need to be aware."

He nodded as he arranged his load of plates in the machine.

Between them, it didn't take long to finish loading the appliance, and Elaine rose reluctantly from the table to serve dessert. Cindy and Elizabeth went with her and the three of them soon returned to their seats.

"There was one other time he took Stephanie dancing," E replied when they'd eaten their desserts and Elaine asked her what other stories she had about her son.

She decided not to tell them it was because another group had targeted his team in order to get at Stephanie. It wouldn't do for either woman to start drawing parallels between that attack and the one that had recently happened.

What she said instead was, "He was close to the end of a mission, and Stephanie was sent in to meet his team when they returned."

It wasn't quite true. Steph hadn't been sent in and she'd gone in to deal with the group who'd set the trap for him. Elizabeth thought the girl had sent a *very* clear message about what happened to those who messed with her family or friends in an attempt to reach her.

"And Todd..." She chuckled. "He had set the stage to meet the last of the terrorists he was hunting in a disco."

Tony chuckled and Elaine looked mortified.

"He didn't!" she said, breathless with anticipation.

Elizabeth nodded. "Oh, hells yes, he did. When Steph arrived, he put the disco light on and stole a dance while he had the chance. Their teams mopped up the terrorists while the two of them took a slow turn around the dance floor."

"They didn't!"

She nodded again. "Yup. They did. They slow-danced to something from the late twentieth century with the sound of gunfire in the background."

"Was that…was that even *safe*?" Elaine asked, and she smiled.

"They were in one room while everything happened in another."

"But…what about their jobs?" Cindy wanted to know. "What did their bosses have to say?"

"Job well done," she told her.

Mark chuckled. "Well, I don't blame him. I bet they didn't get any time to chill *after* the mission."

"No, they did not." Elizabeth was about to say more when the clock on the dining room wall chimed midnight. Her jaw dropped.

"Oh, my!" she exclaimed. "I hope we haven't overstayed our welcome."

Elaine smiled and shook her head. "No. It was nice to have news of Todd." She nudged Cindy. "*And* his girlfriend."

Tony groaned and rolled his eyes and Mark shook his head. "Nothing's official," he warned them.

The two women laughed as the visitors pushed their chairs back. "Well, I'm glad I could share," she told them, "but we really should go. We have an early start in the morning."

She ignored the groans from Amy and the girls as she followed their hostess to the door. "Thank you for a lovely evening."

When the door had closed behind them and Cindy and Mark had said goodnight, Elizabeth turned to the two people who manned the reception desk.

"Did it arrive okay?" she asked.

The man in charge nodded briskly. "Yes, ma'am. It all arrived and was installed while the tenants were rearranging their apartment. They were so busy with their deliveries that they didn't notice a few more arrivals, and the crews waited to do the installation until the apartment doors were closed."

He hesitated and looked uncomfortable. "It is possible the crew chiefs locked the apartments from the outside."

The man sounded so apologetic that Elizabeth hastened to comfort him. "They did as I asked. I want the tenants to feel *safe* here and they might not if they know the lengths we've gone to in order to protect them."

Franklin stared at her and didn't quite manage to dissemble fast enough for her to miss his unspoken protest. She stretched a hand out and patted the top of his desk. "Don't worry, Franklin. These measures are designed to keep you safe as well." She paused. "I take it they *did* modify your desk while they were here?"

He stared at her, then nodded.

"Good. If anything happens, I want whoever's on duty to be under that desk and to press the security alert button there. Stay down and you'll be safe when the shooting starts."

The man relaxed a fraction. "Thank you. That's good to know."

"You're welcome," Elizabeth said and adjusted her tone to brisk. "Now, did they install the other—"

"Oh, yes, ma'am. Just inside the front door like you asked."

Amy fixed her with a curious look. "Do tell."

"I had one of our subsidiaries put extra surveillance in." She lowered her voice and drew her head of security a few more steps away from the counter. Franklin seemed distracted by something on his computer, so she added quickly, "I also had a few bits and pieces added to the outside, which I can promise you I don't have authorization for. We'd lose our bond if the body corporate ever found out."

The woman grinned. "It sucks to be them, doesn't it?" She let her smile fade. "So, E, what exactly *did* you install in there?"

Elizabeth glanced at the two apartment doors. "Do you want to see?"

Amy, Lisa, and Bunny nodded in unison, their eyes alight with curiosity.

"Fine!" She led them to a wall panel. When she pressed an almost invisible edge, a hatch popped open to reveal a hollow in the wall and the mini-gun concealed within.

It was smaller than most of those installed on the ships Todd fought on and it had wheels, each of which was clamped firmly in place.

"It's *so* cute!" Bunny exclaimed and leaned closer to examine the ammunition feed. "Can I have one?"

"Bunny!" her boss snapped. "Where would you put it?"

Matthias chuckled. "Yeah. It's not exactly mantelpiece décor."

"No," Elizabeth commented, her eyes wide with surprise. "It's not." She turned toward him and narrowed her eyes. "Where exactly did you *get* these?"

"You asked us to source you something—and I quote—'mobile and remountable.'"

"I'm fairly sure I said re*mov*able," she corrected.

He shrugged and gave her his most charming smile before he winked at Bunny. "But they're so *pretty*! And remount...remove... there's not much difference."

"Uh-huh." She put a world of doubt in those two syllables. "Do you care to share your sources?"

The two men exchanged meaningful glances for a long moment. They grinned as they shook their heads.

"Nope," Arne said and left it at that.

Matthias took one look at her face and added, "What you don't know won't hurt us later."

The ex-Marine snorted. "Much."

Elizabeth closed the hatch on the "pretty" auto gun. "Hmmph. Boys and their toys." She exhaled an irritated breath.

Straightening, she sidled close to Matthias and slipped her arm around his waist. "I *like* new toys," she hinted.

"Me, too," Amy added and stepped beside Arne to loop one arm through his.

"We *could* try bribery," Lisa whispered to Bunny.

CHAPTER NINE

The blueprint spun and twisted on the screen as Professor Rimmer scrolled through it. He inspected each level and layer. If it hadn't had foundations to keep it firmly in the ground, it could have been mistaken for a moon habitat or something intended to be sunk below the surface of an asteroid.

"Is that it?" he asked and glanced away from the viewscreen.

"That's it," Trey confirmed.

"It surely is," Gemma added.

From beside her, Nathan turned smiling eyes at him. "That's it, boss." He sighed. "What now?"

Marcus' gaze flicked to where Cynthia stood on the opposite side of the room.

"Well," he began. "I'll send these to Steph's team for their input, and then we'll run a few more scenarios to make sure we can't think of anything better."

He noted Cynthia's wide eyes and the disapproving O-shape of her mouth and grinned.

"Tomorrow, because you've all earned an early break today."

This brought him narrowed eyes from Cynthia and murmurs of approval from the rest.

"But first…" he added, and they stopped short of having the AI pull them out. Some even stifled groans of disappointment.

"I'd be honored if you'd all join me in the home lab for a small celebration."

Groans turned to jubilation, and his assistant's smirk became a full-blown smile. He decided her husband was a very lucky man if he saw smiles like that every day.

He waved at her as she shepherded the last of the scientists away and turned to the screen. One final time, he went through each level with care before he reduced the entire package into a small bundle and summoned E-BURT.

"We're done," he told the AI, "right up until Stephanie and her boys send us their modifications so we can make sure they don't screw with the way everything works."

He was interrupted by Cynthia clearing her throat. "They're waiting for you, Doc," she informed him, " and they *will* riot or do something terrible to your cake if you keep them waiting too much longer."

From the absolute seriousness on her face, Marcus knew she wasn't joking. The team had worked long and hard to get the AI his plans, and they'd been promised a break and a party. All kinds of hell would cut loose if he didn't attend.

E-BURT looked through the surveillance monitors in the lab and saw that Cynthia had a point. The scientists were already restless, and Trey, Nathan, and Gemma eyed the cake with serious contemplation.

"I will contact you as soon as Stephanie's team has made their alterations," he agreed. "In the meantime, I believe there may be serious mischief in the offing."

Marcus left and surfaced to a barrage of whipped cream and raucous cheers. When they finished hosing him down with it, he climbed out of his pod and wiped the substance from his eyes.

"You'll all stay behind to clean that up," he informed them and a round of, "Oooh," and laughter followed.

"Seriously. Glad you could join us."

He accepted the paper towel someone thrust into his hand and used it to wipe most of the stickiness from his face and hair.

"I need to..." he began and inched toward the lab door and the staff washrooms.

"No way, boss." Gemma turned him and sat him at the head of the table. "Be grateful Phillip said he wanted to *eat* the cake."

Marcus could only imagine what would have happened if the young professor hadn't. "I'm grateful."

"Does that mean I get a pay raise?" the young man asked, his expression hopeful, and the other scientists laughed.

Trey ruffled his hair. "You can have a pay raise when *I* get one."

E-BURT chortled through the speakers. "Not gonna happen," he told them, then added, "Not yet, anyway."

He wasn't sure if they'd ever get a pay raise, but he wanted to leave the option open.

"How'd we do, Burt?" Marcus asked.

"Well, I delivered your blueprints," he told them, "but, like you, the team is only human. You'll have to wait at least a day before they get back to you."

"Don't sweat it. I was thinking these good people could have a couple of days' downtime before they come back to the plans..." He let the words trail off so they became more a question than a statement.

"I believe One R&D would agree," the AI conceded. "Very well. I will see you in the lab in two days. Enjoy your time with your families."

Happy whoops and cheers met his words, and the AI took a step back to let them begin their celebrations. Now that they knew they would be able to spend the following two days with their families, the scientists were suddenly reluctant to leave.

As they settled to talk with coffee and cake in hand, he let the lab fade from focus. He could monitor it and he would, but he had other important projects that needed more of his processing power.

He let the party linger in the background, amused when Marcus gave his speech and congratulated the team on its achievements.

The scientist finished with, "Enjoy the party before we move on to the next phase of impossibility."

Stephanie and the team came to a halt outside Briefing Room Seven.

Frog looked at the sign above the door. *Reserved for Captain's Meeting.*

"That has Rawlins written all over it," he grumbled.

"Pfft." She waved his protest aside and wiggled her fingers through the air. "I've seen Emil do the same."

"You have?"

"Yup. You need to chill out about her."

"Yeah? I'll chill when—" He stopped as she rested her palm on the door. "Fine."

She gave him a stern stare over her shoulder. "Behave," she ordered and her gaze shifted to the two cats Vishlog had firmly leashed.

Bumblebee cocked his head, and Zeekat huffed a sigh. Both their tails twitched. She ignored them and led the way into the briefing room.

"How's BURT?" she asked as she looked at Captain Emil.

"BURT's right here," he replied from the speakers and one of the vid screens came to life at the end of the room. He used the same businessman avatar he'd chosen to talk to the Navy about One R&D.

Her face lit up. "Well, now *that's* settled..." She turned to the two captains. "Where do you want to start?"

"Battle readiness?" Emil looked at his fellow captain. "How would you like to kick us off, Marianne? How's the *Knight* coming along?"

"The repairs are done and my team leads tell me the *Knight's* ready for a shakedown." She frowned and focused on Stephanie. "I think I remember *you* saying something about dog runs?"

The girl nodded but looked at Emil. "And the *Tempestarii?*"

"She's still a work in progress. We're working on a few experimental bits and pieces." He caught her look of interest and added.

"We're not ready to talk about those yet. I'll let you know when we are."

BURT caught his glance and nodded. "We should have something for you soon."

Emil looked around. "Which brings us back to Marianne's question—a shakedown cruise."

"I need to do one soon," the other captain stated, "so I can identify what the weak points are in the crew and ship and see what needs adjusting."

"Do you think there'll be much you need to tweak?" Stephanie asked and suppressed a smirk.

"There's *always* something someone can do better," Captain Rawlins told her.

Emil pushed his chair back and stood. "I'll leave you to discuss the fine points," he told Stephanie and gave her a wink the other woman couldn't see. "Unless you think there's something else?"

The girl shook her head and bit her lower lip to keep a smile at bay. "No. Nothing, Captain. I look forward to hearing your R&D report."

"Speaking of which…" BURT interrupted.

"Thank you, BURT," she acknowledged, and the AI's vidscreen darkened as he left.

"When do you want to schedule this trial?" she asked as Emil left the room.

He closed the door behind him and allowed himself a small, quiet chuckle.

"*Tempestarii*," he said, his tone still amused as he called for the ship's attention.

"Yes, Emil?"

"I want a personal feed of the *Knight's* progress through her shakedown. My office only."

"Why personal?" the vessel asked. "We usually broadcast it to the crew for professional development purposes."

"And entertainment," he told her. "Don't forget that."

"So, captain, I have to ask," the *Tempestarii* continued, "are there particulars of the feed you want for your personal entertainment that might *not* go out to the crew?"

"Everything on Marianne."

The ship was silent for a moment before she asked, "And for the crew?"

"Give them the usual feed," he told her.

"I see…" she told him but her tone indicated that she didn't and she now tried to work it out. Smiling, he decided not to enlighten her.

He'd reached his office before she interrupted him again. "Is it important for you to know that they are about to upset your chef by ordering an early lunch prior to going into the pods?"

Emil grinned. "Hells yes! It means I need to get through the next three reports before they hit the pods or I'll either miss the show or be late in my assessment."

The *Tempestarii* gave a very Knight-like snort. "Well, we can't have *that*, now, can we?"

Stephanie settled the cats in her quarters before she headed to the dining room. She left them eating happily. If she was lucky, it would be enough to stop them from redecorating her living quarters before she returned to collect them.

They all had a busy afternoon ahead. The *Knight* wasn't the only one going for a shakedown cruise.

Her lips twitched as she pondered how Captain Rawlins would react.

"This is where we find out if she truly is the captain for us," she murmured.

Frog beckoned her to the team's table when she arrived.

"Come on, Steph. We already got yours."

They had, she noticed, and set her up so she was seated beside the captain.

"Thanks, guys." She glanced at Rawlins. "I had to settle the cats and make sure they ate."

The woman stared at her heaped plate. "Will we honestly need all that?"

Steph nodded but Brenden spoke before she had a chance to respond.

"We sure will. We might be in there for a while."

"Yeah," Frog replied. "You're gonna need much more than that."

"As much as you can hold," Vishlog advised. "The pods look after us well but every little bit extra helps."

Rawlins looked at Brenden's plate and then at what everyone else around the table was eating. She compared that to what was in front of her. "Well, if you're sure," she told them and stood to serve herself more.

"She has no idea, does she?" Avery murmured, and Stephanie shook her head, hoping Rawlins hadn't heard.

The woman hadn't let her guard down yet and still had a few sharp edges. She decided the shakedown cruise was exactly what they all needed to bring her fully onto the team. While she didn't know the captain's history and Elizabeth hadn't said anything, she assumed there was some deep-and-dark behind the woman's very tough façade.

The team had settled into the meal by the time the captain returned, her plate piled almost as high as Vishlog's. They gave an approving cheer at the sight of it, and she blushed.

She turned to the Witch. "Will this be as demanding as they say?"

Stephanie nodded. "They're not exaggerating. The shakedown cruise in the Virtual puts the ship through the worst of the conditions we've experienced so far, then stretches it a little more. Trust me, if anything is likely to break at an inopportune moment, this will reveal it."

The captain's expression was a mixture of worry tinged by doubt, but she didn't try to convince her. She assumed the scenario would do that soon enough.

Emil took the paper bag out of the fabricator and sniffed apprecia-tively as the scent of warm butter, salt, and popped corn filled his office.

"You don't know what you're missing," he told BURT and Tempes-tarii as he settled in his chair.

"Why don't you get into a pod so we can try it together?" the AI asked from the smaller viewscreen on the desk.

They'd set the office up so they could all watch the wall-wide viewscreen. Now, he looked at BURT and after a moment's contem-plation, he shrugged and stood.

"Sure, why not?"

"I'll meet you in the Executive Officer Pod Suite," BURT told him and the screen winked out.

"Executive Officer Pod Suite?" he wondered and leaned forward to tap his keyboard and bring the ship schematics up. "Now, where would I find that?"

"I can show you," Tempestarii told him.

"I'd like to see it so I can have the map in my head," he replied and jerked back as his screen went live with a map of the appropriate level. The pod room was colored yellow and a dotted line led from his office to the doors.

"I didn't know we had a suite of pods set aside for the exec," he said.

"Why wouldn't we?" the vessel asked. "You *do* realize I have more room than a small planetoid, right?"

Emil flushed. "I know you're a big girl, Tempest, but I'm used to having to account for even the smallest space on a ship. I'm still getting used to you."

The *Tempestarii* chuckled. "That's okay. Captain Rawlins had the same difficulty."

He didn't know what to say to that, so he grabbed his cap and put it on. "Let's not keep BURT waiting."

She kept her guidance to a minimum and let him navigate to the pod suite from memory. The captain had shown a preference for finding each place he needed to be and had begun to know her decks as well as her oldest hands.

He still got lost, though. She wondered if she should have wagered with BURT on whether or not that would happen this time. The security and research teams would have, and Engineering too.

Tempestarii thought about it. *Most* of the crew bet on such things, she realized—and it seemed to be good for morale.

Her line of thought was interrupted when Emil reached the pod suite and she was glad she had not chosen to run a book on his navigation skills. This time, at least. She waited as he slid into his pod and materialized in the area BURT had prepared, although he was still alone.

The surprise on his face was quite entertaining.

"Whoa, BURT," the captain exclaimed and gaped at the empty movie theater.

He studied the red velvet seats and smooth mahogany timberwork on the chairs. Red velvet curtains draped the oversized screen at the end of the room and seats rose around them in well-spaced tiers.

"Nice," he approved. "*Very*, very nice."

Tempestarii preened and BURT looked pleased. "We're glad you approve."

A familiar scent tickled his nose and he looked for the source. Set in a booth along one wall was a large popcorn stand. He stared at it with a soft whistle of appreciation, his gaze fixed on the mound of buttery yellow goodness behind a heated glass shield.

As he approached, a young man in stovepipe trousers and a white shirt covered by a candy-striped apron appeared behind the counter. He held a scoop in one hand and a large brown bag in the other.

"What'll it be, sir?"

BURT materialized as the captain decided on a position midway up the theater and settled into his seat. At first, he didn't recognize him.

"BURT?" He gaped in astonishment.

"Who else?" The AI's lips twisted into a wry smile and he spread his hands and turned so Emil could get a good look at him.

Instead of the slightly portly businessman he'd come to know, he now saw a tall but still stocky gentleman. He recognized BURT's favored features, albeit slightly altered, even if the suit looked like it had been taken from one of the gentleman gamblers who used to populate a period of Earth history known as the Wild West.

His jaw dropped as a woman materialized. She was dressed in a floor-length gown with a nipped-in waist and plunging neckline trimmed in lace. Before he could close his mouth, she turned a well-outlined smile on him and extended her hand.

"Pleased to finally meet you, Captain," she said in Tempestarii's voice, and he closed his mouth with a snap.

"Tempestarii," he acknowledged and cleared his throat. "Your avatar looks lovely."

The woman gave a throaty laugh and took BURT's arm as the AI came to sit beside Emil. The captain watched them, his attention torn between the screen at the front of the room and the AIs' approach.

Before he could think of anything to say, the screen flickered.

"We're just in time," BURT observed and settled beside him. "It looks like the *Knight* is about to bring them online."

As the screen came to life, Emil opened the popcorn bag and spread the edges so its warm scent wafted around him. He took a small handful and crunched it carefully.

"It will be interesting to see how the *Knight* does with the upgrades we've installed," Tempestarii stated.

"Yes," BURT agreed. "Make sure you send the relevant feeds to the R&D Department.

"As if I'd forget."

The captain went to nibble another piece of popcorn but found his hand was empty.

"I've always wondered," he said and scooped another handful, "what someone like Captain Rawlins would have done in my situation."

"I guess we'll see," he replied and moved his hand toward the bag.

Emil lifted it so he could take some, then stretched across in front of him to offer it Tempestarii.

120

As the AIs relaxed into their seats, he realized he'd treated them like he would any of his executive corps or Steph—or any human for that matter, and it didn't seem strange to him. He shrugged as the *Knight* brought the scenario online and showed flashes of the participants settling into position.

This will be good, he thought and took another handful.

CHAPTER TEN

"**K**night," BURT called and his voice jolted through the scenario startup, "make sure you give her the real version first. Do it like you've never seen it before. You too, Steph. I want to see how she would have done at the Battle for Meligorn."

"The *what?*" Rawlins responded and her face paled. "Are you sure I'm ready for that?"

"At least she asked the question," Emil murmured and raised his voice to answer. "You're about as ready as I was. This was one of my earliest trips with the *Knight*."

"If you say so," she replied but she still looked worried.

And with good reason, he thought. *That fight was what we called baptism by fire.*

He said nothing out loud, though, and merely watched as the scenario unfolded.

It started with the Meligornian fleet breaking orbit. Captain Rawlins settled into the captain's chair as the *Ebon Knight* took its place among the other ships. Her face was pinched with concentration as she studied her boards and looked around the command center.

On the forward viewscreen, she saw the fleet she'd joined. Around her, flying in tight formation, were the two destroyers, three gunboats, and three corvettes that had accompanied the *Knight* into that battle. Farther to the left, dwarfing them all, flew *The King's Warrior* and on the right, bracketing the small fleet, was the *Selestine's Hammer*.

Exactly as she had the first time, Stephanie walked into the command center with Vishlog and Lars. She didn't say anything but took her position at the rear.

When Rawlins didn't acknowledge her presence, she spoke. "Where do you want me to be, Captain?"

The woman raised an eyebrow and her face colored. "Where?" she snapped. "I'd rather you were anywhere but my command deck, but given that you seem to think you belong here, I want you to stay there out of the way."

"Yes, *ma'am*," Stephanie responded sharply, "and what are we doing?"

To make her point clear, she indicated the crew around her and the ships on the viewscreen.

Her question coincided with V'ritan's order for the smaller ships to go forward and meet the skirmishers the Telorans were sending toward the fleet.

Emil groaned. "She was never that irritating with *me*."

"You didn't give her a reason to be," BURT pointed out. "In the footage I saw, you told her what the ship's task was without needing to be asked. I think Rawlins has found the first thing she needs to tweak."

He snorted. "If she's the kind of captain I think she is, she'll have that worked out by the end of this run-through."

"I hope so," the AI said as Rawlins gave her answer.

"Do you see those little ships out there?" she asked but didn't bother to wait for a reply. "They'll crawl up our oversized friends' asses. Our job is to stop that and do some crawling of our own if we have half a chance."

"That's almost exactly what you said," BURT observed as Stephanie's eyes widened, but the woman hadn't finished.

"And if I hear one more stupid question, you'll be off the bridge."

"Ouch!" Emil saw the Witch's lips tighten, while Lars and Vishlog tensed.

"Understood." The girl managed to speak with reasonable calm but her voice hardened. "While you're doing that, *I* will do whatever it takes to protect this world and *all* its people. Work with me, or *you* will breathe vacuum."

"And now I'm glad I *didn't* piss her off," Emil observed as Rawlins's face reddened.

Instead of kicking the girl off her bridge, the captain took hold of her temper and snarled a reply. "Understood."

"I'd really like a piece of that one," Knight interrupted and kept the dialogue as close to the original as she could.

"That's *my* line," he grumbled as the captain replied.

"That one?" she asked and highlighted one of the dreadnoughts.

"Yes," the *Knight* confirmed.

"Why?" she asked as Wattlebird brought them into a position to fire on the first skirmisher.

"I don't like the way it's looking at me."

She tilted her head and frowned at it. "Yeah, it has *attitude*."

"I know, right?" the *Knight* concurred. "So, can we?"

"Not yet, Knight," Rawlins told her. "We need to follow the mission parameters."

Emil breathed a sigh of relief.

"It's like watching your female twin," BURT observed and the man's head jerked to face him in shock.

"We're not that much alike!"

The AI snickered but said nothing more. Onscreen, the Knight repeated what she'd said to Emil on that occasion.

"I know the mission parameters. We are to protect *The King's Warrior* and *Selestine's Hammer* from incoming attacks while looking for an opportunity to make a decisive strike against the Teloran battleship. I shall inform you if I notice such an opportunity and I will act upon it."

Rawlins glared at Stephanie. "Her attitude is almost as bad as yours."

The girl snickered. "I'd say I was sorry, but I don't think it will make a difference."

As she spoke, so did Jonathan Wattlebird, exactly as he had in the real battle. "Captain—"

Once more, his hands moved like lightning over his boards and his gaze didn't shift from the readouts.

"Take a seat!" the woman snapped and gestured for Stephanie and her guards to move to the auxiliary seating that had been installed for them. "I need to know you're safe."

"Me too," the *Knight* agreed.

"And me," Lars and Vishlog chorused.

"Fine!" She threw her hands up and backed to where she needed to be, Vishlog and Lars moving with her.

They had barely reached their seats when Wattlebird's warning to, "Hang on!" rang through the command center and the Teloran battle cruiser filled the forward screen.

"Shields!"

Again, missiles exploded ahead of them and again, she raised her hands to conjure a wall of magic. Lars followed his original role.

"Save it for later or if the shields fail."

Rawlins was too busy monitoring the situation to notice his glance or to see Stephanie give him a long, steady look and lower her hands to her lap.

The *Knight's* guns tracked the incoming missiles and exploded them before they could do more than threaten the vessel.

"Save that ship!" Rawlins shouted and highlighted the *Korres Tarr*.

"Her shields have gone," Lars murmured and the captain turned on him.

"We can *all* see that!" she snapped.

The girl ignored the jibe and pushed magic toward the stricken ship. "We need a way to rescue the crew," she grumbled and shrouded the *Korres Tarr* in a sheath of blue.

"Oh, good work," Rawlins murmured and cupped a hand to her ear as Captain Astofyl's request came through.

"But your crew..." she argued and moments later, declared roundly, "Negative! We're coming alongside in ten...nine..."

The explosion as the *Knight* was caught in the crossfire of two enemy corvettes and one of the battleships was blinding.

Stephanie came to and heard Rawlins groan.

"What did Emil do?" the captain asked when she saw Stephanie move.

"He granted Astofyl's request," she told her.

"Did he know?"

"About the attacks?" She shook her head. "I don't think so but he didn't hesitate. He relayed the order and honored Astofyl's choice."

She gestured toward the screen where the *Korres Tarr*'s engines flared and drove the ship into the closest battleship as it fired every weapon it had. She let the footage run so Rawlins could hear the vessel's final transmissions.

"Wait! The patrol boats went too?" the captain protested as, onscreen, Stephanie's protection extended to cover the two smaller vessels alongside.

A momentary sadness robbed her of her voice and she simply nodded as the three crews raised their voices.

"*Hartuitus baskilor!*"

Her mind spun with a sense of unreality as she heard the words she'd said so long ago. "*Baskilor nye myerda*...no thanks needed. *Myata baskilor sheven*. You are owed my gratitude. Meligorn bleeds."

"For her freedom!" the crews roared in return.

The *Korres Tarr* slammed into the side of the battleship and the two patrol boats followed.

A single tear escaped to slide down her cheek as Rawlins uttered another groan.

"I screwed up."

"You won't make the same mistake next time," Stephanie reassured her, raised her voice, and snapped her fingers. "Again!"

On the second run-through, Rawlins relayed Captain Astofyl's request and they relived the ship's death. Stephanie let the tears fall and decided that maybe there *were* too many times you could experience a single event.

Her thoughts were interrupted by V'ritan's next set of orders.

"Clear us a path to the second rank. Leave the lead battleships for us." His voice was rough in the wake of the *Korres Tarr* and her escorts' deaths. "Their sacrifice will not be wasted."

She barely had time to brace before Wattlebird shouted, "Follow my lead! Those little bastards have trouble getting a lock if we do...this..."

Now that she remembered it, she was reminded of exactly how her pilot had managed to piss off the weapons sections *and* her structural engineers. She was reminded again by his response to *The King's Warrior's* warning.

"*The King's Warrior* can suck it!"

The *Knight's* tart response was equally memorable.

"*The King's Warrior* informs me that you will *all* be sucking vacuum if my rotational velocity increases."

"Fuck!"

"And if you overcompensate," the ship continued. "*Please* be considerate of my shell."

V'ritan's voice intervened and pleaded with them to clear the line of fire.

Jonathan's hands danced over the controls as he struggled to comply.

The report of nMU came through and Stephanie ran to clear it.

"Get back to your seat!" Rawlins ordered, but she continued to run.

"She doesn't know me very well." She snickered.

"She'll wring your neck," Lars told her impatiently, but she maintained her pace. Behind her, she could hear Rawlins's voice raised again.

The captain's anger might have made her flinch if she'd had time to care. She returned to the bridge in time to catch sight of the Teloran ships moving closer to the planet. With a cry of dismay, she turned to Rawlins.

"Get us out of here!" she ordered and gestured to the two Telorans that had appeared on the other side of the planet and the other side of the system.

"We have other orders—" Rawlins began.

Emil half-covered his face with his palm. "Uh-oh."

Onscreen, Stephanie snapped a glance at the pilot. "Wattlebird!"

The captain's jaw dropped but she recovered quickly enough. "Wattlebird! Don't!"

The pilot's hands continued to move over his boards. "Sorry, Captain, but she scares me a hell of a lot more than you do."

Stephanie did not stop as she commandeered the *Knight's* crew. "Comms, tell V'ritan we're on our way."

"Miss Morgana!" Frustration edged Rawlins's voice at her commandeering her ship. She took a step toward the girl but was lifted and thrust into a bulkhead.

"You *will* stand down!" the girl snarled. "Either help me or get out of my way, or I *will* relieve you of *Knight's* command."

Unaware of what was happening on the bridge, V'ritan's reply was short. "Granted. Selestine's speed."

Again, a hundred Meligornian ships echoed the blessing. This time, however, it was Stephanie who gave the order. "Get us clear, Wattlebird."

Immediately after she issued the command, she snapped her fingers and the scenario—and everyone in it—froze.

"Uh-oh," Emil repeated when the footage stopped a moment before the screen went blank.

As soon as she was sure that they were off the record, Stephanie released Rawlins from the bulkhead. She watched as the captain fell heavily and waited for her to scramble to her feet.

"Let's get this straight right now," she said. "There will be times when I need to do something. When that happens, I do not have time for argument, prevarication, or alternatives unless there is a chance we will lose the ship and her crew—and even then, we may have to make a hard choice."

"Are you saying I'm not in command of my ship?" Rawlins asked, "because that's not—"

Stephanie shook her head. "That's not what I mean. You are, in all things bar exceptional circumstances like this, the *Knight's* captain. But I can only do the things I do with your support and your trust."

"Trust isn't one of my strong points," the woman told her. "My upper echelon hasn't been good to my people in the past."

She thought about that and sighed. "So…" she began and her eyes suddenly flashed black as the Morgana pushed to the fore.

Let me, she told her. *I have seen this before.*

Her instinct was to demand how *many* times before, but the Morgana spoke calmly.

I promise I will not break your captain. There was such certainty in her tone that she decided to take the risk.

Fine. She stepped back and allowed the Teloran to take control.

"I have been where you walk now," the Morgana told Rawlins and her cold tones made the captain's face pale, "so I will not ask you to trust. I only ask that you behave as though you *do* trust until you *can* trust. Understood?"

The woman was a deep brick-red. "Do you have any—"

"Idea what I'm asking?" she demanded and cut her off as power shimmered over her skin. "Yes, and I am willing to take a risk that you can act like you trust me enough to do what you would do if you truly trusted me. It will be enough until the time arrives that you do."

Rawlins stared and her good eye glittered beside the patch as she slowly approached the slender young woman who stood before her. This was the Federation's Witch, of whom she'd heard so many stories.

Tentatively, she reached out and poked the girl's shoulder gently with her fingertip, her gaze fixed immovably on her face. "You're not Stephanie, are you?"

The Morgana gave her a cold, hard grin and they both knew it was a baring of the teeth and not a smile. "No, but we are one for the moment and will remain so until the Telorans are no longer a threat to Earth."

The captain stepped closer and studied the girl's face.

"You're not...*human*, are you?"

"Stephanie is human," the Morgana told her, "and also Dreth and Meligornian."

"And you?" the woman pressed.

She gave her a hard smile. "I am an ally—and have been such for more centuries than you can count." She paused and held the captain's gaze. "Do we have a deal?"

Rawlins gave a single, jerky nod. "I will try."

The Morgana stepped back and studied her intently. There was no warmth in her face as she stated, "Good, because I would hate to have to kill you."

The captain's jaw dropped but before she could reply, the darkness left Stephanie's face and the girl stood before her.

"Are we good?" she asked, and the woman gave her a curt nod.

"It won't be easy," she warned and the girl's mouth tightened.

"Nothing worth it ever is."

———

Emil held his breath, stared at the blank screen, and wondered what it would reveal when it came online again.

"Again!" Stephanie's voice startled him as she reappeared.

This time, they ran the scenario without blowing up, but it became clear that the crew who'd been at the battle followed what they'd done before and couldn't help anticipating what was to come, which undercut Rawlins's ability to command. Even though they didn't mean to, it meant the Battle of Meligorn wouldn't work as a training exercise.

Stephanie came to the same conclusion at around the same time as Emil did because she looked at them.

"BURT, I need the training scenarios you ran for the *Chauvel* and

Cathay Williams, then I want to change the pace and run the team through a wave scenario—something new. Do you think you and Tempestarii can come up with something in the next two hours or so?"

"We can," he assured her with all the gravity and drawl one would expect from a Western gentleman.

Emil considered it a good thing no one could see Tempestarii bouncing excitedly in the seat beside him. The AI's construct clapped its hands with glee.

"This will be fun!"

Two and a half hours later, Stephanie stood with her back pressed against Rawlins'.

"I will find that shit-for-brains AI and kick his ass from here to Dreth and back." She snarled and grunted when something heavy landed on top of the shield she held over herself, Rawlins, Lars, and Vishlog.

It was hard not to see the dead faces of the rest of her team scattered around them and difficult to ignore the blood pooling around Lars' feet.

"How's it coming?" she asked as the magic arced and sputtered around them.

"I...need...two more...minutes," Rawlins rasped and her hands worked as fast as she could make them, "and even then, it won't be pretty."

Something heavier landed on the shield. The sudden dip and pressure was followed by a resounding electric zap and the smell of seared flesh. Stephanie gasped and immediately wished she hadn't.

Her stomach flipped and she tried not to heave.

"Devious...sonuva..." she muttered and fought the overwhelming urge to throw up.

"Let it go!" the captain shouted, and she dropped the shield.

The group separated and they all turned to attack the monster that fell as the shield vanished from beneath it. Rawlins made a swift jerking movement with her hands and bolted past them.

"Run, damn you, run!" she screamed and caught Stephanie by the arm as she raced past.

Lars uttered a gasped laugh and turned to face the ceiling, propping himself against the wall as he did so. "Havin' too much...fun... here," he managed to say as he opened fire.

Vishlog gave him a look that showed his torn loyalties.

"Get her...out of...here," the team leader told him. "Make sure she goes."

The Dreth raised a fist hastily over his heart and bolted after the two women. Behind them, the world roared and everything went black.

"Well, *fuck* me," Rawlins declared and rolled slowly to her knees in the White Room.

Lars groaned and Vishlog bolted upright to look around wildly. "Steph!"

"Here..." Steph replied, her voice kitten-weak, and the Dreth located her. She looked at Rawlins. "What happened?"

"It was much more effective than I thought it would be?"

The head of security made a choking sound that Stephanie was very sure was meant to be a laugh, and Vishlog managed a chuckle.

She sighed and pushed to her feet, and the other three followed her example.

"Again?" Lars asked

The Witch managed a faint chuckle. "Nah..."

They breathed joint sighs of relief and she waited a few minutes before she added, "We're gonna go back to the Battle of Meligorn."

They all groaned and she grinned. "Yeah, but *this time*, we get to use everything we know about what happened."

"All right!"

The team's jubilation was short-lived, however.

"Well, what in Hades did we all do wrong this time?" Rawlins exclaimed after their fifth run into the battle. It took several panicked gasps before her body realized it was breathing air and not vacuum.

"Nothing!" Stephanie told her and sat in the White Room. "You did *nothing* wrong. You did what Emil would have done and even a few things he didn't think of but which would have been equally as good."

"And we *still* exploded?" The captain sounded like she didn't quite believe it.

In the cinema, Emil reached into the bag of popcorn and found it empty. His hand continued to search a little longer, but his gaze remained fixed on the screen, where Stephanie was speaking.

"We *still* exploded," she agreed and flopped onto her back. "I'm beginning to think we did good in that battle *and* we got lucky."

He turned wide eyes to BURT and raised a hand. The AI hesitated before he completed the high-five.

"We got *very* lucky," the captain admitted and looked at the screen where the *Knight* was speaking.

"I'm sorry," the *Knight* apologized. "There are so many variables when the possibilities are not constrained by a re-creation of the scene."

Stephanie stared at the ceiling and realized the ship was right. She also saw that the crew in the last four runs had looked as completely to Rawlins as they had to Emil and that the earlier difficulties had been forgotten. Regardless of what had gone on earlier, the captain had confirmed her command.

She breathed a sigh of relief and addressed the ship, "End scenario, Knight. That's enough training for one day. Tell everyone they have the next twenty-four hours off."

"Confirmed," the *Knight* agreed.

The AI left to pass the message on, only to return several minutes later when none of the four-member team had moved.

"Are you all okay?"

Stephanie flapped a hand at her. "We're fine, Ebony. Only exhausted."

"Well, I would hurry if I were you, or Frog will let the cats out of their pods and allow them to roam the *Tempestarii* without supervision."

That brought her to her feet. "He wouldn't!"

Rawlins followed but more slowly. "He would. I've heard the stories about that man."

"*And* he's drawing a mustache on your pod," the *Knight* added smugly.

Stephanie groaned. "I'm *coming!*"

"Me, too," Lars agreed and sounded equally as creaky.

"And me," Vishlog added.

"I'm already there," Rawlins told them as her avatar winked out of existence.

She emerged from her pod as Frog raised his marker to embellish the whiskers he'd drawn.

"I'll have that," she snapped and jerked it from his hand before the tip touched. "And I expect that pod to be pristine the next time I look in."

With that, she left him, his jaw hanging open, and vanished through the door as Stephanie raised the lid to her pod.

"Oh, good," she said, gave him the brightest smile she could manage, and accepted his help to climb out. "Just the man I wanted to see. I hear you're good at cleaning pods."

He groaned. "But Steph—"

She tapped his handiwork. "You look like you have more than enough energy to me."

"Yes, Steph," he grumbled and moved to the cleaning closet.

"Good man," she told him and frowned. "Where did Captain Rawlins go?"

Frog pointed to the door. "That way. Don't ask me for more. She took my marker and left."

Stephanie hurried to the door and looked out but the corridor was empty.

"Knight?"

"I believe you will find my captain in the training center." The ship sounded worried. "If you hurry, you may stop her from harming herself."

"She what?" She broke into a run and thrust through the training center doors to find Captain Rawlins running laps.

"Captain?" she asked, groaned, and jogged up beside her.

The woman continued to run, even though her pace was ragged with fatigue.

"What are you doing?" she asked, breathing hard.

"I gotta get a Hell of a lot fitter," Rawlins told her.

"Why?"

"I gotta keep up with you and the team."

Another lap finished and she placed a hand on the captain's shoulder.

"We gotta stop," she managed to say and dragged in a breath.

"Why?"

"Because my team is getting ready to stop us both," Stephanie told her, "and we're scaring the *Knight*."

Rawlins glanced to where Lars and Vishlog had begun to stride toward them. She uttered a shaky chuckle.

"Well, we can't have that now, can we?" she asked and slowed to a walk.

CHAPTER ELEVEN

S tephanie was late for breakfast but not because she'd slept in. The two cats had demanded her attention. First, Bumblebee had stolen her shoes and while she was distracted, Zeekat bolted with her leggings.

The black-and-white cat had timed his theft with Johnny's arrival and dove past her guard with a victorious chirp. He streaked down the corridor, waving the leggings behind him like a flag. She had almost raced after him, but the sight of the guard in the living room stopped her in her tracks.

"Well, don't just stand there!" she shouted. "Go and get my pants back!"

Johnny shook his head. "No can do, Steph. You know what Lars can be like."

"Besides," Marcus added as he entered behind him, "it's not like it's the only pair of pants you own."

"And you really can't go prancing out there dressed like that," the other man added and amusement lighted his face.

"Not unless you *want* the crew to know what you look like at your *human* scariest." Marcus chuckled.

"Exactly what are you trying to say?" she demanded.

"Well," Johnny replied and pointed at the mirror near the door to her suite, "*we* know you're a Witch and the *crew* knows you're a witch, but right now, I'm tempted to ask where you've hidden your ginger-bread house."

Stephanie glanced at the door but Marcus palmed it closed and leaned on the wall, his body blocking the controls. When she finally gave up on the idea of retrieving her stolen pants, she stalked to the mirror.

"See what I mean?" Johnny asked when she stood before it.

She glowered at her reflection and decided he could live, if only because of the fact that he hadn't let her go out in public half-dressed and with hair that looked like it had gone through a hurricane followed by a sand storm.

"I look like shit."

The guard backed away and Marcus raised his hands.

Johnny looked at him. "Is it okay to agree if *she* said it?" he asked sotto voce.

His teammate looked at him, his eyes wide with horror. "Are you in*sane*? It's a trap, man. A *trap*."

Stephanie froze. It was like he'd dropped a hunk of sadness into her soul and drenched it with a serving of tears. Johnny caught her shift in expression. "What's the matter, Steph?" He glanced at the door. "Well...okay, if you want to go after 'em that much, we're not *that* ashamed of being seen with you."

Marcus slapped his forehead with his palm, stood against the door, and looked at the floor while he shook his head.

She sniffed and tears prickled the corners of her eyes. Irritated, she flapped a hand at them.

"No, it's fine. It's only that..." Her voice caught and she cleared her throat, straightened her spine, and turned determinedly to her room and closet.

Johnny sighed as her next words drifted back softly.

"It's only...that's exactly what Todd would have said."

He glared at Marcus. "Nice one, fuck knuckle. Now, you've upset her."

The other man's jaw dropped. "Me? I'm not the one who told her she looked like a witch—and not the good kind."

"And I'm not the one who reminded her how fucking far away she is from Todd."

"And I *honestly* don't need to be reminded of that right now."

Stephanie's voice made them both freeze. She ignored their mortified expressions and stalked to the door.

Marcus moved.

She slapped the controls and strode toward the mess. "Captain Rawlins and my mom might have the right idea," she muttered. "I think a black-and-white rug *would* look good in my quarters!"

Johnny glanced at his teammate. "Tell me she doesn't mean that."

The man frowned and studied her ramrod-straight back for a long moment before he replied. "I...I'm not so sure. Maybe if he stays out of sight until she's had some coffee—"

Her snort cut off any further suggestions. "That won't save him!"

"She *liked* those leggings," Johnny whispered, but Marcus had other concerns.

"Lars will kill us," he murmured in response.

"What? Why?"

"For making her cry."

"But...but she's not," he protested. "Why would you *say* that?"

His teammate lowered his voice to a whisper. "Because women always get mad when they're trying not to cry."

"And if you boys don't stop talking about me, I'll shove a lightning bolt up both your asses," she told them and punched the controls to the mess.

Johnny cast another startled glance at Marcus, but the man put a finger to his lips and leaned in close.

"She also means that," he murmured when he was reasonably sure she wouldn't hear him. "Don't push her."

They barely made it through the door before it closed. By the time they did, she was halfway to the coffee stand, her shoulders hunched and head down like she was trying to avoid attention. It took Johnny a scant second to see why.

His roving gaze caught the viewscreens scattered around the mess. They usually showed the news, sports, or a talk show but right now, they all featured one thing—Zeekat and Stephanie's pants.

"Does the *Knight* know what she's playing with?" Johnny whispered, and the other man shook his head.

"I hope she makes it a *strong* coffee." He gestured to where Stephanie held a cup under the dispenser.

On the screen, Zeekat continued his run through the ship. He and her leggings had toured most of the level before they were confronted by Frog and Garach. The two's attempts to catch the big beast held the attention of every crew member in the mess, so her entrance had gone unnoticed.

She finished filling her cup and glanced at the screen in time to see Garach brandish her tattered clothing. He lifted it between thumb and forefinger, held it at arm's length, and studied the slobbered and chewed material with care.

"Are you *sure* she's gonna want these back?" he asked.

"Why don't *you* ask her that?" Frog suggested and ignored the young Dreth's look of alarm. "In the meantime…"

Chuckles ran through the room as he held his hand out, took the leggings from Garach, and tied them into a collar and leash.

"Come on, you furry menace," he told the culprit. "You'll spend the day with me."

Zee laid his ears back.

The guard scowled at him. "Unless you *want* to be turned into a rug?"

The feline tilted his head and looked over his shoulder as though he expected Stephanie to arrive at any moment. He made a soft chirping sound and rubbed his head against Frog's hip.

"What, me?" He shook his head and began to lead Zeekat home. "What makes you think *I'd* save you? I still remember what you did to my boots."

The animal wrinkled his nose and sneezed, and his audience chuckled in response.

"Was that better or *worse* than what he did to Stephanie's boots?" Garach asked as he moved alongside

Stephanie stifled a groan and took a long sip of coffee before she searched for an empty table. As she looked around, she took a second sip, which was when someone started to clap. Marcus hurried to her side, relieved when he saw the coffee had started to kick in.

She paused to take another sip before she raised her cup to the crowd and turned to the servery. Scattered applause and laughter followed her but soon quieted. She'd almost finished heaping her plate when someone joined her in the line.

"Can I steal a little of your time?" Captain Rawlins asked as she ladled scrambled eggs and bacon onto a plate for herself.

The girl shrugged. "Sure. I had nothing planned for the day. What do you need?"

The captain glanced around. "It's kind of a personal matter...uh, to do with...what happened yesterday."

"Sure." She frowned. "Do you wanta eat here or somewhere else?"

Rawlins looked around and noted how many of the crew had finished their breakfast and were clearing their plates. She thought about taking a seat at one of the tables in the corner but decided against it.

"Briefing Room Seven?" she asked, and Stephanie favored her with a smile.

"Does it have more coffee?"

The woman smiled in return. "It *will* have."

They finished filling their plates and proceeded out of the mess, Johnny and Marcus acting as breakers to clear a space around them. Neither of the guards wanted to see what would happen if Steph lost her breakfast on the way—or Rawlins for that matter.

The captain said nothing as the two men walked with them to the briefing room but she cast them a dubious glance when they followed them inside.

"They stay." Stephanie answered the question before it could be raised. "Elizabeth's orders."

"So you don't ever get any real privacy?" the woman asked and she shook her head.

A small smile curved her lips. "I also don't get assassinated when I least expect it and the people around me tend to die less often, so it pays off in the end." She dug into her breakfast and ate a couple of mouthfuls before she added, "But you wanted to speak to me? About yesterday?"

As if she'd given a signal, the two guards moved away. This time, it was Johnny who took duty at the door, while Marcus chose a different corner of the room—one that gave him a clear field of view and line of fire to the entrance.

The captain watched them take their positions and her gaze roved quickly over the room as if calculating possible lines of defense. After a few seconds, she gave a curt nod and turned to Stephanie.

"I see why you keep them around."

The Witch grinned. "Well, it had to be for something more than their looks."

"Hey," Johnny protested.

"Or their discretion," she added, unable to resist teasing them.

"We're more discreet than we look," Marcus muttered.

She snorted. "That wouldn't be hard."

"It's good to see the coffee's kicked in," Johnny grumbled and checked that the door was locked. He pulled a small device from one of the pouches at his waist. Holding it up, he asked, "Do you need more privacy?"

Rawlins froze. "How did you get *that* on board my ship?"

"I allowed it," the *Knight* interrupted. "Just because he got it on board doesn't mean I don't know about it."

The guard rolled his eyes. "You coulda told me," he protested. "How am I supposed to know if something will work when I try it on another ship?"

"I can assure you," the ship informed him, "that nothing in the known civilian or Navy fleets would have revealed what you were carrying. *I* am not so standard."

Her assertion and absolute confidence in her abilities drew a chuckle from Rawlins.

"Or very modest, Ebony."

"That's what Emil used to tell me," the *Knight* replied, "but I am not bragging, merely stating fact."

"Of course, you are, Knight," Johnny agreed, "but next time, can you tell me when you notice something I'm trying to smuggle aboard?"

"What do I get for finding *all* your contraband?"

"I wasn't suggesting a competition," he replied.

"I know that," the *Knight* answered. "I merely suggested a contest for every time you made the attempt."

"It *would* keep your hand in," Marcus interrupted.

Johnny snorted. "And let you run another book."

His teammate shrugged. "I have to have something to keep me entertained."

"Can I bet on myself?" the ship asked.

Rawlins sputtered with sudden laughter. "I see where she gets it now." She chuckled. "You are a bad influence."

Johnny released an exaggerated sigh. "Fine. What's the forfeit?"

Leaving them to their dickering, Stephanie turned her attention to the captain. "What did you want to talk about?"

The woman colored. She'd managed to clear her plate and her hands had nothing to keep them occupied, so she wrapped them around her coffee cup.

"Yesterday—" she began and stopped as though to collect her thoughts.

The girl remained silent and let her gather herself.

"It showed me that I'm out of touch." She waved her hand to indicate the room around them. "With the ship, the crew, and the way to fight the ship."

She fell silent, but Stephanie could see her mind working and simply waited.

Finally, the captain said, "There are numerous reasons I've stayed off the Navy's radar—and why I want to stay that way, at least until I can't be—but being out of touch with my crew and my ship is not one of them. I don't like being the weakest link."

While Stephanie and Captain Rawlins made their way to the briefing room, Lars called the team to order in their quarters.

"You are aware this is meant to be a day off, aren't you?" Frog grumbled, and the team leader raised an eyebrow.

"Do you want to tell that to Johnny and Marcus?" he challenged, "or maybe suggest it to Steph, who is working on integrating the newest member of the *Knight's* crew."

"Are we sure we want to keep her?" the shorter guard asked, and he gave him a stern stare.

"Almost a hundred percent, but I've asked E for her files or to at least tell us what she knows about the woman so we can fully understand what we're dealing with."

"She's not a threat to Steph, is she?" Avery asked, and Brenden clipped him on the back of the head.

"As if E would let *anyone* likely to be a threat to her Steph anywhere near her, dumbass!"

The man was unrepentant. "It had to be asked," he answered with an apologetic smile and a shrug.

Lars waited until they were finished and got straight down to business.

"BURT sent us the Save the Planet plans," he announced, and the guys immediately settled on the couches.

He placed his tablet on the table and activated the wall screen. "This is what the boffins have come up with."

Brenden snickered. "You'd better not let Johnny hear you call them that."

"He's not here and no one will tell him, *will they?*" Lars snapped in response, and the man subsided.

"So, what do we have?" he asked and gestured at the screen.

"Do you all remember the idea Steph had of cleaning up the radiation zones?" Lars asked.

The team nodded.

"Well, the scientific team she set up finally made it work." He gestured toward the screen. "These are the building schematics for the processors, and they have been kind enough to add living quarters and facilities for a small security team."

"A rec room?" Frog asked. "Man, I could *almost* get to like these guys."

"You'd better," the team leader admonished, "because these are the centers we're gonna have to protect from people with less than pure intentions toward *our* tech."

"What do you mean 'protect?'" Avery asked. "Why would it need protecting?"

"Where were you when Stephanie took us over Brown's Ferry?" Frog demanded.

"Uh, I was kinda *flying* the damned shuttle!" he retorted.

"Yeah." Brenden placed a hand on his co-pilot's shoulder. "We were a little busy at the time. Air turbulence was a bitch and we assumed you guys didn't need an up-close and personal introduction. It meant we didn't get to hear everything."

"*Any*thing!" Avery emphasized.

"Exactly," Lars emphasized in support of them. "So, what you missed was the very brief discussion where we realized that not only would some of the big corps want to steal our tech for their profit, but that not everyone in political power would be happy to have the limited power problem solved."

"And then there was the potential for people trying to steal the power because they either wanted to trade it on the black market or because they were simply that desperate," Frog added.

"And there are always those who want to destroy what they cannot understand or possess," Vishlog put in. He studied the design. "This is what we need to protect?"

"If our world is to recover and survive, yes," Lars assured him. "We have to find a way to protect it even if we *can't* station anyone there."

"The approaches?" the Dreth wanted to know. "I can see air and land, but I do not think a subterranean attack is feasible. What have I not seen?"

"You've covered the two main ones," the team leader acknowledged, "but we'll also have to consider the chance that anyone wanting to capture the technology might be stupid enough to try a pulse attack. It could be either from remotely piloted explosives or a sub-orbital, and we need to take into account that they might simply want to blow it up and destroy it." He gestured toward the warrior. "Vishlog's 'if we can't have it no one can' types."

Vishlog nodded regretfully. "Every race has them."

"Even the Meligornians?" Frog sounded like he couldn't believe it.

"I believe so," Lars told him, "although I'd have to ask V'ritan for specifics."

"Shame." The other man shrugged. "Will we put anything in place in case these are overrun by hostiles?"

"Do you mean a self-destruct?" Lars asked.

"I mean a self-destruct," he confirmed. He gestured at the screen. "Because this isn't something we want to explode. It would defeat the purpose of what it's built for—and Steph wouldn't like it."

"She wouldn't like the technology falling into the wrong hands, either," the other man reminded him. "This kind of mixture of magic and Earth tech? Can you imagine how badly people will want to get their hands on it so they can pull it apart and see what else they can develop it for?"

Brenden emitted a soft whistle. "That shit would be worth a fortune! It would start one hell of an IP grab among the corps."

"And governments," Avery pointed out. "There are at least four who might even go to war for this kind of tech—and I count the Federation among them, not to mention several of its members." He frowned. "What kind of protection will we give our science team? Because the *second* this gets out, they will become some of the most sought-after commodities on the planet."

The look on Lars's face said he'd thrown a curveball that hadn't been raised before.

"I'll message BURT and E with it," he decided after he'd thought for a moment. "It's a *very* good point because those guys are *very* vulnerable once we reach the building stage. We don't want to lose the only people likely to be able to troubleshoot the design or develop it if needed."

"And we need defenses operable by a small team in the case the facility is overrun by a larger force," Avery added.

He nodded. "Yup."

"Well, we *could* use the Dreth trick of putting walkways in the ceilings," Brenden suggested. He shrugged. "Humans aren't *always* the wiliest species."

"Sure," Frog concurred and his face took on a distant look when he remembered the last time they'd encountered that. "I remember the whole attack from above scenario." He darted Vishlog a dark look. "*Never* underestimate the sneakiness of a Dreth."

The warrior chuckled, and Lars ran a hand through his hair. "So... any ideas for the rest?"

"Let me get this straight," the smaller guard began. "You want us to establish defenses for aerial and land approaches, include countermeasures for sub-orbital *and* missile attacks, work up on-site defenses for a small team holding out against a larger one until help arrives—if it ever does—*and* put in some kind of self-destruct that will erase the tech without making a crater the size of a mountain if everything *does* go to shit."

The team leader gave him a thoughtful look and nodded again. "Yup. That about sums it up."

"And how in the *hell* do you believe we can accomplish that?"

CHAPTER TWELVE

As the team began to discuss the details of defending the plants for cleaning up the radiation zones, Stephanie and Captain Rawlins settled in for their conversation.

"So you want to know what you did wrong or where you can improve?" the girl asked.

The captain considered this as she leaned back in her seat a little. Her color had returned to normal.

"Both," she decided. "I can't have one without the other."

"But I thought we covered that in the scenario itself before we went back to running the Battle for Meligorn?" she countered.

Rawlins chuckled. "I find it hard to believe that was the only thing."

"Well, there *were* more," she admitted, "but I thought you were well on your way to working those out in the command scenarios. As I said, without the computer controlling the variables, there were very few scenarios where we would ever succeed—and you thought of a few things Emil hadn't tried."

"I'm very sure he'd have gotten around to them if he'd had as many chances to practice as I did," the woman told her. "He's one of the best captains the *Knight* could have had."

"Bar you?" Stephanie asked and pushed her a little.

To her credit, Rawlins looked mortified.

"Oh, heavens, no! He was probably *the* best option for the *Knight's* first captain, even if he's not keen on combat. He *is* good at it."

"Huh." Stephanie leaned back in her seat. *That* was unexpected.

"So, beyond the compliments," the captain said, "what else was there?"

"Give me your assessment," she instructed. "Where did *you* think your main weakness was?"

"Well," Rawlins answered, "if I had to choose one thing, it was that I fell into the command structure far too quickly and forgot I was an independent operator inside the fleet." She blushed. "I forgot who I was working for."

She inclined her head and looked curiously at her. "Did you ever really know?"

The woman frowned. "No."

"And would it have made a difference if you had?"

Rawlins' lips curved into a smile. "It always helps to know who you're fighting for—and to know you can trust them to have your back in battle...or even beyond."

The last three words were added in such soft tones that she wasn't sure she'd heard them, but she understood the sentiment of the rest. It had been something they'd covered a little in the scenario.

"What would help you with that?"

The captain's face had faded to its normal color but it darkened again. "I think maybe if I understood a little more about the Morgana," she began. Stephanie stiffened and Rawlins added hastily, "That is if it's possible. I will understand if it's not."

When the girl still didn't reply, she shrugged. "It's okay. I'm sure it's one of those 'I'll have to kill you if you talk' situations. Trust me, Elizabeth has already made that clear. But remember that if we go out to fight with this ship, I'm already aware I can die." She paused and added wistfully. "I'd merely like to know who I'm dying *for*."

She glanced at Johnny and Marcus. "If we finish this in the captain's cabin, can you two stay outside?"

The two men exchanged glances before Marcus turned to Rawlins.

"Your office—does it have a reception? An outer office?"

She nodded, and the guards exchanged another look.

Finally, Johnny shrugged. "He can't kill us too much over that."

"And I will be there," the *Knight* added. "I will protect my captain *and* my Witch if the need arises."

"That settles it, then," Marcus agreed. He headed to the door. "Ready when you are, Steph...Captain."

It didn't take them long to relocate, even if the boys insisted on going over the office with a fine-toothed comb. Johnny handed Rawlins the small device he'd held up before.

"I trust you know how to use one of these."

Her lips curled. "It's not unfamiliar to me."

"I didn't think so." He passed it to her with the smallest of smiles, and Stephanie wondered what Lars had been so worried about when he'd refused to bring Johnny to the meeting Rawlins had asked for.

Whatever it was, the captain didn't raise it and he ushered them both into the office. They settled into their seats as the door closed, Rawlins behind her desk and Stephanie in one of the chairs in front.

"So," the Witch began, "you know how this works, right?"

The woman shook her head. "Not really, but I have a vague idea of what to expect."

"That'll have to do," Stephanie said. "I've spoken to the Morgana about her situation. It's something that became more apparent when we were on the Teloran vessel. But know that the person you will speak to has seen more of Earth's history than you have ever read about. Plus her own."

"So I gathered," Rawlins reminded her and her lips quirked.

"Then, without more ado, Captain Rawlins, I'd like you to meet the Morgana. Morgana, Captain Rawlins."

As she spoke, the blue faded from her eyes and darkness took its place. Before she vanished completely, Stephanie smiled and added one more thing.

"Captain, I hope you like history."

Rawlins watched as her eyes turned completely black and a film of darkness shuddered around her.

"What is it you would like to know?" the Morgana asked.

The question caught her by surprise and she asked the first thing that came to mind. "What do you need most from my ship?"

The Morgana hitched a brow. "I need her in the position I require as swiftly as you are able to do so. I can take in the parameters of combat and can provide a certain amount of protection while she does that, but I must also be aware of the power I'm pulling through this shell."

The woman frowned to hear Stephanie called a shell and the Morgana laughed.

"Don't look like that. I would do nothing to harm her. What else do you need to know?"

"Does the power you draw affect the running of my ship?"

"Do you mean the engines?"

"For a start."

"The main effect in the last battle was to push out the nMU that was adversely affecting your drives. Once that was clear, your pilot was able to call on enough power to maneuver safely."

"So, *that's* what she was doing."

"Yes. It was necessary, just as it was necessary for you to keep the ship flying while she achieved that."

"I…see. Is there anything else I need to know about how the magic affects the *Knight*?"

"I can use it to shield your ship from incoming fire in much the same way as your more conventional shields work. However, it is not safe to do that when we encounter large amounts of nMU as the power Stephanie wields can cause a powerful explosion when the two mix."

"I…see, and how likely are those explosions to occur in the course of both a normal battle and a battle against the Telorans?"

"In the first instance, it's highly unlikely since none of the other races use nMU and it does not occur in large concentrations outside of the world of Dreth. In the second instance, it's likely enough that both Stephanie and I exercise caution regarding the type of magic we use to assist in the fight."

Captain Rawlins sat quietly for a moment as she digested the information. The Morgana stirred restlessly and she looked at her.

"Why Stephanie?"

Her eyes widened and she leaned back in her chair. "I beg your pardon?"

"Why..." She gave an impatient sigh. "Look, what I'm trying to ask is how you got inside the girl and *why* you chose her."

"Oh." The Morgana studied the woman. "This has more to do with your trust issues than your curiosity, I take it."

"Damned right it does," Rawlins told her. "How you treat your host is an example of how you treat the rest of us."

"I...see. I had not thought of it that way."

I bet you haven't, the captain thought but didn't say it.

The Morgana was quiet for a moment to gather her thoughts before she began her explanations. "Among humans, there is a genetic twist that shows once, maybe twice, every few generations. I think it might be a recessive or that it goes dormant between, but it is *very* hard to find."

She stopped to clarify the explanation in her mind before she continued. "I found it in the first Morgana le Fey and managed to connect with her." She stopped when she caught sight of the look on Rawlins' face.

"Don't look at me like that."

"But...you said Morgana le Fey. She's only a legend on Earth."

She tossed her head and snorted. "I can assure you, she is more than a mere legend. She was very real and the legends do not do her justice. Yes, she was a witch. *That* was the genetic power thread and it was available to her."

The woman's eyes were as wide as any child's. When the Morgana stopped speaking, she shook her head.

"I understand the genetic angle, but if it *was* a recessive, it follows that there are other families that carry the potential for the same genetic twist."

"Yes." the Morgana nodded. "There are. The le Feys are not the only magical family that appear in your Earth stories, are they?"

Rawlins shook her head. "So…Merlin?"

"Of course." She shrugged. "But the le Feys' was the first bloodline I was able to capture. I had never been able to capture another genetic thread of power from any of the other magical bloodlines on Earth, and after I captured that one, I stopped trying."

"Why?"

"Because after this one, I won't need more."

"Because of Stephanie?" Rawlins asked.

"No, because my people have arrived."

"The Telorans?"

The Morgana nodded in confirmation. "The Telorans. This will be my last fight."

"How do you know?" the captain asked and needed the answer as much as she dreaded hearing it.

"Because, at the end of this fight, either Stephanie will be dead and so will her line, and I will be as good as dead—a burnt-out husk breathing my last breaths on an unknown planet under a mountain of rock. My millennia-long shield will become my tomb."

"And if we win?"

She shrugged and pressed her lips together before she answered. "Well, that's up to Stephanie, isn't it?"

Rawlins regarded her with a challenging expression. "Is it?"

The Morgana responded with a sour look at being pushed. "I don't have to admit this but the girl is as powerful as her ancestress. Perhaps more so."

"And this is a problem because?" she pressed.

An impatient sigh preceded her begrudging admission. "She is powerful enough to stop me if she wants to—and she has warned me she will come and dig my 'decrepit old ass' out of the ground simply to wring my neck if I don't play straight with her."

The captain couldn't help herself. She tried, but the laughter bubbled out of her at the Morgana's imitation of Stephanie's voice. Having been on the receiving end of the girl's temper, the situation struck her as funnier than it should.

The Teloran's reluctance turned to a frown, and she managed to bring her laughter under control. She sobered quickly. "And this bothers you, why?"

"As well as her power, she has as much temper as the original Morgana did—and the ability to find and reach me, which her predecessor did not."

"I see," Rawlins said, but the Morgana shook her head.

"I'm not sure you do. I may be old and cunning, which I think you *can* appreciate. However, there is much to be said for young, energetic, and irritated." She paused to consider that. "I like her."

"Hmmph." The captain shook her head. "It's amazing. She even gets ancient alien wizards to like her? What *can't* she do?"

"Dance," the Morgana answered in Stephanie's voice.

Rawlins looked up, startled. The veil of power had slipped away and the girl's eyes had returned to their normal shades of blue.

"I still have a problem with learning to dance," she told her.

She laughed, and Stephanie joined her, glad the tension had eased.

Outside the door, Johnny frowned. He could hear them but he wasn't sure why they were laughing or why the Morgana's tones filtered into it. He didn't like it when the Witch laughed.

There was very little laughter in Marcus Rimmer's office. The party had gone on well into the night and the team had decided to overnight before they left to enjoy their leave.

"My missus will put me on the porch if I go home like this," Nathan had informed Rimmer as he went to curl under a desk.

"Oh, no you don't," his boss had told him and surveyed his post-party lab. "Into the pods, the lot of you. Cynthia will have all our hides."

"Don't you mean Burt?"

"No, Burt will understand. It's Cynthia I'm worried about. She told me to give you all an early night and you're still here."

"She won't be here in the morning. She'll never know," Nathan had argued.

"I can't be sure of that," he told him. "She might come in to check on me."

"Now why would she do that?" the man had slurred and Marcus had taken him by his shoulders, turned him, and guided him to the pod to tuck him in.

"I work hours she doesn't approve of," he told him, not wanting the man to get the wrong idea. "If she knew we were overnighting, she'd be upset, and you know what she's like when that happens."

Looking up at him from the pod, Nathan had shuddered. "It's not nice to give a man nightmares before he goes to sleep, Doc."

"Talk to the AI. I'm sure it'll think of something suitably soothing," Marcus had advised and closed the lid before the man could reply.

He'd turned to find Trey and Gemma propping each other up in the doorway to the room.

Trey waved a hand at the pods. "Is that offer open to the rest of us, Doc? It's only…I don't think I'm fit to drive."

Marcus had stood aside and waved them in. "Go for it," he told them. "The more the merrier, but I'd better find you sleeping when I get in there."

"Or what, Doc?" Gemma had snickered but she'd been out of it when he'd finished making sure the rest of his impromptu guests were tucked in.

The AI had provided a dormitory and each and every one were tucked in their beds and asleep. Rimmer had followed their example, then was the first to get up and ordered a breakfast that arrived as they emerged.

"Get yourselves home," he told them as they ate.

The computer had taken care of most of the party's side-effects but left enough to warn them to not do it again.

"I should call *you* Cynthia," Marcus told it as he tidied the lab once he'd seen the last of his people out.

It was hard to leave, even for the day he'd told himself he needed to straighten his much-neglected apartment. Not for the first time, he wondered if his assistant was right. Maybe he *did* need to get a life outside of work.

CHAPTER THIRTEEN

Todd jogged down the corridor toward the gym space he'd booked for the team. It didn't guarantee them a private session as his two "escorts" proved, but it was a start. He broke into a sprint, aware that the rest of his team had emerged behind him and now put Operation Piss-Me-Off City into effect.

They'd all become thoroughly sick of having their every step haunted—especially since there seemed to be two teams to contend with.

And possibly a third on call, he noted when he caught sight of another set of Marines moving on an intercept course. If there was ever a time when he missed Stephanie's cats, it was now. *Those two would have kept these assholes occupied!*

It might have been a mistake to think about her but it was worth the sudden wash of melancholy. He snatched hold of the feeling and used it to fuel a sudden burst of speed that took him past the approaching Marines and down a side corridor. Behind him, the team bomb-shelled in four different directions, which would soon become six.

He couldn't help smiling when he thought about it. They'd decided to add "evasive maneuvers" to their training schedules, given the persistence of Captain Smith's people, which provided the perfect foil.

They'd come up with that idea the morning after their little unwind, and he was very sure they'd all still been drunk. He knew *he* had been. They weren't drunk now, though, and they wanted to have a little privacy *without* an audience.

Todd ducked into one door of the mess hall and out through another. As he slid into the corridor again, he heard the clatter of falling plates and cries of outrage behind him. He snickered a little smugly.

He was still tail-free when he reached the gym and ditched his gear beside the wall. Ka and Angus arrived next, followed not long after by Piet and Jimmy. Gary and Reggie made it through, but Henry and Dru didn't.

"We lost our guys," they muttered through the team comms, "but the rest of the team have worked out where you went and they're in the corridor outside the gym."

"Let them know they guessed right then," he ordered with a sigh. "It won't hurt them to see you ditched your escorts as well."

She snorted. "Like it was hard, boss."

"Exactly. I want them to know we can ditch them at any time. I want them to *know* they're not in control of the situation."

"But, boss, don't you think it would be better if they *did* feel like they were in control? That way, they'd be easier to handle when we needed to."

"They would, but we needed the training more."

Dru responded with an exasperated sigh. "Sure, boss. Whatever you say. We'll be there in a minute."

She shrugged and looked at Henry. "Well, you heard the man. It's time to be *irritating*."

He grinned. "Irritating is my middle name."

"News to me," she told him as she strolled around the corner and into the corridor where the two teams of what they'd taken to calling the "Odd Marines" waited.

"OM for short," Todd had told them.

"*Ominous*," Dru had quipped, and the team had chuckled.

She sauntered past the first OM and through the door to the gym with Henry at her side. Neither of them looked at the Odd Marines, but they were both aware when they stepped in after them.

Todd and the rest of the team were warming up.

"Ten laps for being last in," he called, and she gave a theatrical groan. "Fifteen for bitching."

Henri smacked her in the shoulder and led off. "Thanks a ton, girl."

"Quit your whining," she snapped. "Jogging's good for you."

"Beating you up would be better," he grumbled.

"It's called sparring, Henry—and I can mop the floor with you any day."

He refused to dignify that with an answer and they resigned themselves to the rest of the laps in silence. As they finished the first one, the remainder of the team divided into pairs and began to train, and Todd jogged to join them.

"So, how did you go?" he asked, loudly enough that Dru caught what he was up to right away.

"You should tell Captain Smith his guys need to go back to rookies," she replied, equally as loud. "We had lost the last two by the second marker."

"Uh-huh." He put all the doubt in those two syllables that he could manage and gave her a sideways wink as he did so.

She grinned at the same time as she raised her voice in protest. "It's true, sarge! If you don't like it, ask security for the feeds."

"Is that true, Henry? You're on the feeds?"

The man snickered. "Oh no. You don't get us that easily, Sarge. *We're* not on the feeds. We know better but we're fairly sure knuckleheads One and Two can be seen *every* step of the way."

Todd feigned surprise. "They can?"

"Oh, yeah, Sarge. They sure as shit can. I don't know who taught them their fieldcraft, but they suck as much as the guy who told them they were proficient."

Dru delivered her verdict as they passed the OMs gathered at the door, and he saw faces go crimson and jaws tighten. Gazes snapped to follow them as they jogged another circuit.

"Are they pissed yet?" she asked, her voice soft.

"Hells yes, they are," he told her. "Good work, the pair of you."

"Nothin' to it, Sarge," Henry assured him. "I'm not even sure how they qualify as Marines with the lack of discipline they show."

He managed to spit *that* out as they passed another cluster of OMs, and Todd was sure he heard a snarl.

Well, sucks to be you, he thought grimly.

"What I want to know is what the fuck they're doing here—and why they're so interested in us," he added but not loudly enough to be heard from the sidelines.

"Do you think that one remembers which of us threw up on his boots?" Dru asked.

"Given the way he's looking at *you,* I'm darn sure he knows and he's still not very happy about it."

She snickered. "When can we get that pissed again, Sarge?"

"After that little crack about discipline?" Todd asked. "How about not until I know what the fuck these guys are up to and have found a way to pull us free of it."

They finished the last lap, and he slapped Henry on the shoulder. "You wanted to wipe the mat with her? Now's your chance. Ten minutes."

The man cracked his knuckles and headed to the training area. "Come on, Dru. It's time to put your money where your mouth is."

As he watched them begin, the sergeant smiled grimly. He let his gaze shift from his troops to the hovering Odd Marines.

"You know, you could always see if one of the higher-ups could find out."

He jumped.

Ka had stepped alongside without him being any the wiser. She rested her fist against his shoulder and bumped it gently against his bicep. "They were fairly impressed with you during the intervals."

Todd studied her thoughtfully for a moment. "I take it you know which one's still on the station?"

The woman smiled and tilted her head so it would be impossible to read her lips. "Amaratne," she whispered.

For a moment, he wondered why she bothered. He assumed their faithful followers were using whatever tech they needed to hear everything that was said.

She noticed and her smile widened. "What d'you think is hidden in my fist, Sarge?"

He gave her a startled glance and she showed teeth. "Knight put me onto this one. She said Johnny never left home without at least one."

"And how many are *you* carrying?"

"I thought four would be overkill," she told him, her expression a little cheeky. "Are we done?"

"Do you know where he is?"

"I can get you there."

"Can you get him on the line?"

"Spar with me," Ka told him. "I'll hit the mat very quickly but you'll have what you need."

"You'd better make it a real fight," he replied. "They've watched us for a while. Let's pretend they're as smart as we are and act accordingly."

"They aren't."

"Then we definitely won't get caught," Todd assured her. "But if we do anything less, we might underestimate the one competent person they have and we'll be in the shit. Okay?"

"You're assuming they have anyone competent."

"I'm assuming they're *all* competent until I can afford to go with what I see." He lowered his voice and leaned closer. "How many of these guys would have paid us more attention if they *hadn't* seen us as drunk as skunks and being so completely stupid?"

He watched her eyes widen as his point hit home.

"Exactly," he told her as they reached the mats.

"Make it good?" she asked and lashed out with a boot and a fist. "Like this?"

Todd jerked his head back barely in time, too slow to capture her foot. "Sonuva bitch!"

Soft cheers came from the edge of the mats.

"And you guys are supposed to still be training."

A chorus of raspberries answered him and he glowered at Ka. "See what you started?"

"Like I care," she challenged and surged forward with a flurry of punches.

He blocked them and drove a fist at her face.

She dodged it at the last minute. "Not fair, Sarge."

"Love and war, right?"

"Steph won't be happy," she returned in a sing-song voice.

"Steph isn't here right now," he teased in return. "She can't save you."

The woman bobbed low and spun to swipe his feet out from under him. He rolled upright and avoided her attempt to pin him.

"Ha!"

"It would have been too easy anyway," she snapped as he bounced away.

While the leg-sweep had been a surprise, the hard run ended with her wrapping her arms around his waist and using her momentum to drive him to the ground. He'd already been traveling back and didn't have time to brace before she collided with him.

"Sorry, Sarge," she told him. "The window's fairly small."

"Oof!" Todd pulled one arm clear enough to block the blow aimed at his head but couldn't stop the backswing. His hand slapped the matt in surrender as she coiled her fists into his shirt and pounded his body into the floor, then picked him up only to slam him down again.

"Give!" he shouted. "I give!"

His back landed a third time and her, "Almost done, boss," wasn't very reassuring. He gritted his teeth as his head made contact with the floor and rattled his teeth.

"There," Ka said with great satisfaction.

"Uh-huh," he mumbled. He raised his head but the world spun and he lowered it again.

"Easy, boss," she told him loudly enough for those nearby to hear. "It looks like I was a little rough on you, hey."

Todd squeezed his eyes shut and opened them again. "When you're fucking done, Corporal."

She got off him, kept her hands curled in his shirt, and hauled him to his feet. "Almost, boss."

He swayed as another wave of dizziness swept over him and she moved to steady him. Her hands moved deftly over his shirt pockets and fidgeted the pouches at his belt open while she used the closeness of their bodies to hide her actions.

Finally, she patted him on the chest and helped him to the sidelines, where she fixed Piet with a commanding glare. "He needs the men's room."

The man gave her a funny look but stepped forward.

"Sometime this century, Piet!"

Todd tried to straighten out of her grasp but she maintained a firm hold on him and passed him to Piet with practiced efficiency. "Top pocket," she murmured. "Make it quick."

Before either of them could reply, she turned and bounced to the team. "Henry! You're next!"

The Marine groaned. "I just went three rounds with Dru," he complained but stepped onto the mats.

"Really?" she asked. "It must be your lucky day then, because now, you get to go *one* round with me."

"One?" He sounded confused.

"Yup," Ka replied and danced to the center of the sparring space, "because that's as long as you'll last."

Todd shook his head and regretted it as Piet guided him away. His corporal was having far too much fun. Another wave of dizziness washed over him and he flailed at the wall.

"What the hell did she hit me with?" he asked.

"It wasn't the what so much as the how and the where," his demolitions expert told him. "You're probably gonna need a trip to Medical after that. Why did you let her get away with it?"

"She caught me by surprise," he informed him, "and said something about the window being very small."

Piet's eyes widened and he ran his hand over all the places Ka's fingers had touched.

"Hey—" Todd protested as the man muscled him into a shower cell and closed the door behind them. Only when he'd started the water running did he open his hands to show him what he'd taken from his belt and pockets—the jamming device she'd said Johnny never left the ship without and a small communicator.

"You only need to push the button," Piet advised. "The call will go through to whatever number she programmed into it. A small window means the receiver won't be able to access it for very long for whatever reason."

"Gotcha." He found the call button, pressed it, and almost dropped the device when a familiar voice answered.

"Amaratne. Speak."

"Uh, sir?"

"Who *is* this"

"Todd, sir. The Marine."

"The Hooligan's sergeant?"

"Yessir."

A low rumbling sigh was followed by the sound of a chair creaking as though the man had both expected and dreaded his call.

"What can I do for you, young man?"

Todd gulped and swallowed to moisten his throat. "Well, sir. It's these Marines. I... This will sound ridiculous, sir, but I don't think they're here for our benefit."

"How about you bring your team to my office in, say...the next ten minutes?"

He ran a quick calculation through his head and decided they could make it.

"We won't be alone, sir."

"Don't you worry about your escort, son. I know exactly how to handle them."

"Yes, sir."

"Don't be long now."

"No, sir," he replied but discovered he was speaking to empty air.

"He'll see us," he said, turned to Piet, and promptly threw up in the shower. "Tell me this wears off."

"You'll need to see Medical after you see the admiral," the man replied, and he groaned.

"Fan-fucking-tastic."

"Don't worry, Sergeant. We'll get you there."

CHAPTER FOURTEEN

Piet was true to his word. He and Ka formed the team up around him and quick-marched them out of the gym and into a jog.

"I take it this means he said yes?" Ka asked and he nodded. "Heck yeah!"

She grinned and punched him in the shoulder. This time, he felt the minute sting of a needle. "Give it a minute, boss."

"When did you get *that?*" he asked.

"You're not the only one who hasn't had time to spend their paychecks—and that restaurant knows *all* the best people."

"I can imagine," he mumbled, but his head began to clear, even if the result of it hitting the gym mat so hard and so many times was still there. His next question was more plaintive. "Did you *have* to concuss me?"

"Sorry, I got carried away." She didn't sound repentant in the least, especially when she added, "It's not often I get the better of you."

"Victory by any means, huh?" he asked.

"Hells yes, boss. Any way I can."

Reggie snorted. "D'you think you could make that sound any filthier, Ka, or is that your best shot?"

"That's as far as I'm willing to go in present company," she replied and darted a glance to the side where two OMs paced them.

"Good luck shaking *them* before we get where we're going," Gary muttered darkly.

"We don't need to," Todd told him. "The other end says it's under control."

"Oh, they think so, do they? And exactly who are we going to see that makes you think what they do or don't want will make a single bit of differ...ence..." Reggie's voice trailed off as they rounded the corner and he saw the guards standing outside the fleet admiral's office.

"You are seriously *shitting* me. The *big* guy? You're dragging us into another meeting with the brass stinking like polecats and covered in sweat?"

"I am," Todd assured him as they slowed to a walk. He moved to the front of his team and they approached the Marines on duty.

"Sergeant Todd Brogan and the Hooligans to—" he began but the Marine cut him off.

"The admiral's cleared you. Go in."

As he spoke, his teammate opened the door to the admiral's offices. Todd gave the first Marine a startled glance and was waved inside. The rest of his team followed without a word.

The snap of movement behind him almost made him stop but he resisted the urge and instead, listened as the admiral's guard refused the Odd Marines entry.

"I'm sorry, Corporal, but you have not been cleared."

"Do you know who I am?"

A short pause ended with the sound of a finger tapping on a tablet. "We do, Corporal, but you are still not cleared to enter."

"But—"

"Don't make us do anything we'll all regret, Corporal."

"We're supposed to protect them."

"I understand. However, they are perfectly secure where they are. You will need to wait to resume your duties."

The door slid shut and the voices were cut off.

The team slowed and looked around them. They were in a large, completely deserted lounge. There wasn't even someone in attendance behind the huge desk standing outside the admiral's office.

The office door slid open and the man's voice reached them. "Come in, Todd. Bring your team."

They moved as one and homed in on the voice, although they glanced at their surroundings with a shared feeling of uncertainty. Admiral Amaratne stood as they entered. Todd gave the team enough space to array themselves behind him and snapped a salute.

The man waved it away. "Take a seat and tell me what this is about."

He caught sight of the sergeant's face and peered more closely. "Good Lord, boy. Are you concussed?"

"I sincerely hope not, sir, but it was necessary so I could contact you."

The admiral glanced at the door. "Do they stop you from talking to folk?" he asked, and he shook his head.

"No, sir. It's more like they listen in on every conversation and dog our every footstep. We can barely hit the heads on our own."

Amaratne frowned pensively. "I'll look into it," he told them, "but I can't guarantee there'll be anything we can do." He sat. "Now, I don't think you came in here only to bitch about your escort, as annoying as it is. What do you need?"

Todd glanced at his hands, then looked up again and cleared his throat. "Well, sir, it's no secret we're going up against the Telorans, and I'm fairly sure it's no secret the Hooligans will be asked to accomplish something insane. So, before we do this, I'd like a little R&R with my team."

He paused and the admiral waved for him to continue. "Go on."

"I'd like to take the team to Earth and to see my parents." He paused, reluctant to add more. The unsaid "for the last time" hung in the air between them, but he cleared his throat and pressed on. "We've been in space a long time, sir, and most of it on constant call. I think it would be good for the team to have a little Earth-time."

With the request out in the open, he stopped and waited for the man to make his decision. Around him, the team waited in tense silence. They all breathed surreptitious sighs of relief when the admiral nodded.

"Two weeks," he told them, "but you'll have to be prepared to be called back anytime."

Todd nodded. "Understood, sir."

"And I'm sorry, but you guys won't be able to split up once you're on Earth."

It was an odd turn of phrase, and he frowned. *Won't be able to split up once....*

"Are you all right, Sergeant?" the admiral asked, his brow creased with annoyance and concern.

He shook his head and realized his next words were more truthful than he'd like. "Sorry, sir. I hit my head while training and it's starting to make itself known."

"Make sure to check in with Medical on the way out," the man told him. "I know you're in a hurry but you won't want to travel with concussion, so I'll mark your leave as commencing three days from now. That should also give you time to organize the travel."

Todd groaned and Amaratne held his hand up.

"I'll authorize it and expedite the funds. There won't be any delays from that side of things, but you will need to make sure your paperwork is in order."

He acknowledged the warning by straightening in his chair, even though the effort cost him. "Understood, sir."

The admiral gave him a short tight smile. "There is an office beside mine. It's temporarily empty if you need to stop there on the way out."

With a grateful smile, he rose unsteadily to his feet. Ka's tight grasp on one bicep was as welcome as Piet's was on the other.

"You have a good team there, Sergeant. Take care of it." The man followed this with a more formal dismissal before he turned to his screen. "I trust you can see yourselves out."

The team left before he needed to say more and convened in the office he'd directed them to.

"So," Ka began, "what's the plan?"

"It sucks that we can't split up," Dru observed. "I hoped to get home before we came up again. No offense, boss, but I'd like to see my folks too."

There were murmurs from the rest of the team, and Todd looked at them. "You'd all like to see your families?"

This time, the assent was much clearer. He slumped in his chair and smirked despite his pounding head. "Good, because that's exactly what I had in mind."

"You did?"

"But the admiral said we couldn't split up."

"Nope." He wagged his finger at the man. "The admiral said we couldn't split up once we reached Earth."

Looks of incomprehension greeted him, and he sighed, leaned forward, and rested his chin in his hands. "He didn't say how long we had to take to get there."

Ka uttered a bark of laughter and punched Henry on the shoulder. "There you go. I told you the sarge would look after us."

The man grimaced and looked sheepish. "Yeah, you did."

He glanced at Darren. Their teammate had grown even more quiet over the last few days and his eyes took on a haunted look when the Odd Marines continued to shadow them. "There you go, Daz. You'll get to see your girl again."

That brought a quiet sad smile. "We still need to travel in pairs," he reminded them. "Navy's orders, remember?"

Todd nodded and immediately regretted it. It was very clear that the only way he would get through the meeting was if he sat very, very still—and even then, he would probably pass out before he made it to Medical.

Pushing that thought away, he focused on Darren. "I need the off-worlders to partner with someone from Earth."

The nausea got the better of him and he paused and made a dive for the rubbish bin.

Gary pulled a face. "We can always do this another time, Sarge. You know, *after* you've been to Medical."

He waved his hand to dismiss the suggestion and slid slowly into his seat. "No, we need to get this done now. That way, you guys can get the ball rolling while Medical gets done with me."

"Do you think it'll only take three days, Sarge?"

"I should be fine long before then," he told him and ignored the thought that the admiral might have seen more concussions than he had. The man couldn't always be right.

Darren almost managed a smile, and Reggie thumped him on the shoulder. "Don't worry, mate."

The man's eyes widened and Jimmy intervened. "Hands off, Reggie. I've always wanted to see Evermorn. I've heard the stories they tell about the sailing there."

"I'll take you," Darren offered. "We have the best water in all the systems."

Reggie leaned back and let Jimmy take over, while Todd turned to the rest. "Work out your pairs and get your tickets. We will use the travel time to try to lose our trackers, see our folks, and then regroup."

"That's all very well and good, Sarge, but *where* do you want us to get back together?" Ka asked.

"And when?" Jimmy added.

The pounding in his head intensified, but he smiled anyway.

Steepling his hands in front of him, he replied, "Why have the most powerful and secretive girlfriend in the universe and *not* ask her for a favor?"

"All *right*, Sarge." Ka hooted and waggled her eyebrows.

Todd patted at the air in front of him. "Guys...please, keep it down. My head's killing me and I need to make a call."

Dru whistled suggestively and looped her arm through Angus'. "I have *my* travel buddy."

He colored but Todd ignored them. It was far more amusing to watch Piet try to avoid Ka's searching gaze, while Reggie looked at Henry.

"It looks like it's you and me, mate."

Henry grinned. "I don't know. I hear Gary makes a good coffee in the morning."

"If you think I'm making you breakfast in bed, you have another think coming."

He pretended offense and turned to Reggie. "Well, if he's going to be like *that*, I suppose I'll *have* to take you."

"Don't do me any favors, mate," the other man retorted. "With attitude like that, you might find yourself traveling on your own."

"It's not allowed," Henry returned, "but if it makes you feel any better, I can always stuff your fat ass in a pet carrier."

The room froze and Ka sputtered with amusement. Dru pressed her head against Angus' shoulder, her shoulders shaking as she tried to suppress her laughter.

"What?" Henry asked when Reggie scowled at him.

"Let's get one thing straight, mate. There is no way in hell you are sticking me in *any* kind of carrier. I'm no one's pet!"

Ka dropped to her knees, held her middle, and buried her face in her knees, her whole body shaking as she laughed. Piet knelt beside her and looked concerned. "It's not *that* funny."

"I don't know what's got into them," Angus noted and slid an arm around Dru's shoulders as the woman thumped his chest with her fist. "One mention of pets…"

Darren exchanged looks with Jimmy. "I don't get it."

Jimmy draped an arm over his shoulders and stood beside him, shaking his head. "It's beyond me…completely beyond…"

Todd sighed. "Gary, you're with me."

"Well, fuck me, boss, you don't have to make it sound like a death sentence."

He stared at the man and narrowed his eyes against the pain in his head. "The catch is you have to get me to Medical as soon as I've made this call." He raised his eyes and surveyed the others. "The rest of you are dismissed to make travel plans."

Gary ushered them out of the office and stopped Piet and Ka at the door.

"Hand it over," he demanded and gestured at them. "I don't know which of you has one, but the boss needs it."

"Jammer?" she asked.

"Jammer," he agreed.

They both reached for the top pocket in their fatigues as one.

"Well, I don't bloody need two!" he protested.

His teammates raised their eyebrows in concert and each took one of his hands and pressed a jammer into his palms.

"Quit your bitching," Piet told him gruffly and walked out the door with Ka beside him.

"Those two are out to make mayhem," he muttered, shut the door behind them, and returned to his team leader.

It didn't take him long to set the jammers on the table and settle in a seat opposite. Todd looked at him. "I'd like to do this in private."

He studied him intently for a long moment before he settled obstinately into his seat. "I don't think so, boss. Firstly, because you look like you might fall over at any moment and secondly, because I know *exactly* what your girlfriend would say if I left you on your own with those Oddballs out there." He sighed and laced his fingers behind his head. "Nope. I think I'll stay right here."

Todd rested his forehead against one palm but he pulled his communicator out and called Stephanie one-handed.

CHAPTER FIFTEEN

E mil met BURT and Tempestarii in the Virtual theater. The AIs were again indulging her love of all things Wild West.

"There's an engineer who has a collection of classic Westerns," BURT had explained, "and Tempestarii had nothing in her archives." He paused. "She does now."

This time, the ship's costume was flowing, elegant, and made of coffee and cream satin edged with lace. It also came with a delicate umbrella created from matching cloth. He stared, not quite sure what to say.

The smile gave him refuge as they settled in the seats beside him.

"I could get used to this," he said and offered them popcorn by way of greeting. "Do you know which scenario Stephanie chose this time?" His face sobered. "Tell me she didn't go with the Battle for Meligorn, again."

"Oh no," BURT told him. "This time, she decided to take the *Knight* on a repeat of your shake-down with the *Chauvel* and *Williams*."

The captain looked at him with interest. "She did? And will the *Chauvel* and *Williams* have stand-ins, or will Stephanie have her make that hell-run solo?"

"She thinks a solo run will be a suitable test of both the captain's abilities and the *Knight's* repairs."

"And did you let Tempest loose on the scenario?"

BURT gave him a grin that, on a human, he would have described as pure evil. He wasn't even sure he liked seeing it on his boss.

"What?" the AI asked and caught the shift in his expression.

"I… It's only—that look is very disconcerting," he told him.

"I based it on the look Frog gets when he has done something improper to Vishlog's boots and knows the team will laugh," BURT explained and looked puzzled. "It's not considered mischievous?"

Emil snorted. "No. It's considered downright evil, and any human seeing it on another human knows it means the other one has done something they won't like and is entertained by the idea."

"Oh." He no longer looked worried and instead, seemed pleased with himself. "In that case, it was appropriate to the situation."

He chuckled. "I can't wait to see what the two of you came up with."

The AI gave him a look of mock shock. "Emil! How can you say such a thing!"

It was such an accurate portrayal of false affront that he laughed. "Whatever you're doing to improve your human interface, keep doing it." He sobered. "Although, if I am honest, you already pass as more human than most 'real' people I know."

"That's a compliment," BURT decided and seemed happy with the idea. "And yes, I think you will find the tweaks we have undertaken to keep the *Knight* from becoming complacent fitting."

Fitting, huh? Emil wasn't sure he dared to look, but the curtains parted and the AI raised his head to address the screen.

"Knight, you may commence the scenario when you are ready."

The *Knight* broke the screen into several sections, placed an image of herself sailing through space in a small window in the top left corner, and added pictures of the engine room, weapons arrays, crew spaces, and bridge beneath it.

The rest of the screen was filled with an image of the battle zone. The *Knight* appeared out of nowhere as she skipped into the system.

Emil noted the asteroid belt and part of him recognized the route he had flown with the ship in his run-through of the scenario.

Mild melancholy washed through him. Its touch was brief and fleeting and did not make him regret accepting a transfer to the *Tempestarii*. Even so, he sighed.

The ship's construct turned to him. "Do you miss flying with her?"

He gave her a reassuring smile. "I enjoy the memories," he told her, "but I am happy flying with you."

She settled in her seat and a small smile banished the anxiety that had momentarily rested there. "I am glad," she told him, "and I also have fond memories of flying with Captain Rawlins. She will be good for my sister, exactly as you were."

The captain wanted to ask her how she knew either of them had been good for the *Knight*, but he wasn't sure he wanted the answer. There was a difference between suspecting the ship had accessed your most personal files and knowing for sure.

On the first run-through, the pirates came out of the asteroid belt, exactly as the *Knight* expected. Captain Rawlins' reaction, however, was *not* expected.

"I *know* that ship," she murmured. "So that's where that bastard got to. Knight, fire all guns in greeting and fill the space in front of him with missiles."

So intent was she on the targets in front of her that she—and the crew she was directing—missed the three other pirates when they dropped out of warp space to join them.

"Holy hell, that was fast," Emil noted. He frowned at Tempestarii. "I don't remember that from when I ran through this mission."

"I put it in as something of a wake-up call to my sister. Now, Ebony knows that she has to be as on her toes as her crew." She gave him a happy smile. "I did not expect that attack to be so successful."

Emil exchanged glances with BURT as the screens shifted to show the aftermath in the White Room. The crew came to abruptly, gasped, and checked themselves for the injuries they'd suffered when the pirates had successfully targeted the *Knight's* engines and sent explosions to rip through her hull.

"That," Rawlins stated for all to hear, "was most unpleasant."

"I concur," the *Knight* agreed, "and I apologize. I forgot my sister and father liked to leave surprises."

The accusatory note in her voice could only be meant for two people. Emil snickered.

"She's not very happy with you two," he said.

"Well, it sucks to be her then," the *Tempestarii* replied tartly.

His jaw dropped, and BURT chuckled. "I'm afraid my daughter has studied our Stephanie very closely and some of the Witch's attitude might have rubbed off."

"Might?" he asked in strangled tones.

The AI smirked and Tempestarii looked secretly pleased with herself.

"Again!" Rawlins and Knight snapped in unison.

"When you're ready," BURT conceded.

"I was *born* ready," the *Knight* declared.

The *Tempestarii* snickered. *"Sure* you were."

"And there is essence of…Frog?" Emil suggested.

The AI gave an exaggerated groan. "Oh, I surely hope not."

"What is wrong with Frog?" the *Tempestarii* asked. "I find him *very* entertaining."

"And if you ever tell him that," Emil told the ship, "I will make you wish you'd never been tweaked into sentience."

"Pfft. You'd miss me," she told him. "Now hush. They've started their second run."

This time, Rawlins kept her temper when she saw the pirate flagship, but her eyes narrowed and he thought she was still dangerously distracted.

"I wonder what the history is between them," he mused.

"I do not know, but I will run a background on the pirate we based that one on. He *was* human, if I recall, and savage enough to have intimidated the Dreth under his command—unless they were *very* good actors."

"I'd appreciate it," the captain told him. "Anything that can throw her like that needs to be looked into. I'd like to make sure we can defend her against anyone who might still be looking for her."

"Captain Rawlins?" BURT asked. "I will ask Elizabeth to share her files but I can guarantee that she has powerful enemies who might still want her blood."

"I can imagine," he managed drily, and the AI raised his brows.

"That level of snark is unusual for you, captain."

"Just because I don't use it often doesn't mean it's not there," he retorted and frowned as the pirates emerged from behind the meteors.

This time, they had time to deliver their offer.

"Unidentified ship, surrender and you will be spared."

It was a little different than what Emil remembered, but he assumed that was because there were no Federation Navy ships present. Rawlins's response mirrored Yale's.

"Like hell!" she responded, her tone a low growl. "Wattlebird, prepare for evasive maneuvers. Subroutine Three."

It was as though the pirate recalled fighting that evasive subroutine before. His allies jumped in, and Wattlebird rolled the *Knight* under the first barrage and barely brought her tailfins clear of the second that ensued from behind.

"That was close," Emil murmured, on the edge of his seat.

"For fuck's sake, Captain. How the fuck are we expected to hit *anything* with you pulling stunts like that? Honestly, it's worse than if you let Wattlebird have his way with her."

"I don't know, Tremaine. You're the goddamned weapons expert. *You* figure it out, or do you need me to wipe your ass for you as well?"

"Ooh, Captain..." the weapons leader started but remembered who he was speaking to.

The ship jinked and rolled, and the man swore afresh and cut the call.

"That'll give them both something to think about," Emil murmured and wondered if Rawlins might not have met her match. The weapons leader was salty, but he knew his stuff. "That might be one way to get him to the tactics table."

"You mean he never attended?" BURT asked.

"I mean he was always busy and had a sure-fire excuse if you'll pardon the pun," he responded. He gestured at the screen. "This was hard enough with three ships. What does Stephanie think Rawlins can learn from having her ass handed to her on this scale?" He paused. "And where *is* Stephanie, anyway?"

"You had to ask for her, remember?" the AI pointed out. "As to what Stephanie thinks Rawlins can learn, I would suggest it would be how *not* to have her ass handed to her."

"I should point out," he added, "that Tremaine is not only salty. That man's mouth gives potties a bad name."

"Potties, huh?" BURT asked and he blushed.

"He has a putrid way with words if you want it straighter."

"Oh no," the AI told him. "I understood you the first time."

"Knight, combine evasive subroutines three, six, and two, in that order," Rawlins commanded. "Work with Wattlebird to make it an attack routine. Make a hole in their front line and flip and take their flank before you deal with anything that jumps in."

"She what?" Emil asked.

"She most assuredly did," BURT confirmed.

Both of them noticed that neither Knight nor Wattlebird argued. Both ship and pilot were uncharacteristically silent.

They are probably too busy putting that sequence together, he thought and startled as Rawlins rapped out a second set of orders.

"Tremaine! I need short bursts into the flank of each pirate as we pass. Make them staccato and continuous. I trust you can handle twisting vectors."

"Twisting vectors?" the man roared. "Captain, are you nucking *futs?*"

"No, Tremaine, but I'll have yours roasted and on a plate if you fuck this up—or would you rather I had Sanderson take over?"

"Sanderson? *He* couldn't pull this kind of shit off if you gave him a week of Sundays to prepare!"

"I fucking heard that, you inbred, mind-fucked bastard—uh, boss."

"Get your section squared!"

"After shift, boss, you and me. We're gonna talk."

Emil groaned and covered his face with one palm. "Does she even know—"

Rawlins's voice cut him off. "Cameron! I need engineering to work with Wattlebird."

"Captain, you and I need to meet when this is done."

"Well, he's not arguing..." he noted, "although I can only imagine trying to put the fires out after this little stunt."

"They'll forgive her if they don't end up breathing vacuum," BURT assured him. "None of them enjoyed the last three defeats."

"Hmmph. That might be the only thing that saves her," he agreed.

The *Knight* charged the pirates' front-line and his stomach churned with remembered butterflies as she began to dance to the patterns defined by the evasive subroutines.

"This was *so* much easier with three ships," he murmured.

"They need to practice in case they are caught without allies," the *Tempestarii* told them, and he hoped that would never be the case.

"Have the Navy rescinded their deployment of the *Chauvel* and *Williams*?" he asked.

"Negative," she replied, "but the possibility is one that must be accounted for."

"Or the time an ally turns on us," BURT added.

Emil cast him a worried look. "How likely is that?"

"I don't know," the AI admitted. "I would prefer to think it is highly unlikely but I would also like to remain prepared."

He frowned but didn't pursue it. "Make sure you let me know if the situation becomes likely," he said shortly. "I don't want to be caught unawares."

"That *is* the plan," BURT told him.

Rawlins's voice drew their attention to the screen.

"Flip ship on my mark!"

Emil was horrified. "She's worse than Wattlebird!"

"I will have the engineers check for structural stress," BURT assured him. "Fortunately, she is practicing in the Virtual."

"Well, hell yes!" Emil exclaimed as, onscreen, the *Knight* did as her captain had ordered. "Surely she's far too big for that!"

"It's all in the piloting and how much cooperation they have from the other sections."

The weapons teams annihilated what was left of the pirates on the left and re-targeted as others jumped into the system.

Those vanished before they'd had time to activate their shields.

"Roll right!" Rawlins snapped. "And flip ship on my mark. Mark!"

Emil gasped and Tremaine and Sanderson swore several blue streaks about the captain's lineage and her relationship with Wattlebird.

"There," the pilot grunted. "See what you did? Now the crew think we're an item."

"The only item we are to the crew," Rawlins retorted caustically, "is one you don't fuck with if you don't want to get up close and personal with the atmosphere *outside* the ship."

"But there *isn't* any atmosphere outside the ship."

"Exactly!"

Emil chuckled. "They're better suited than I thought."

The roll took the *Knight* to the flank of the pirate ships remaining from the front line.

"Fire!" the captain shouted. "Wattlebird, get her into position. Defense, shields up! We'll fly through the debris to target the second ship."

"We're the fuck *what?*" the pilot demanded.

"Do it, or would you rather get out and push?"

"There is nothing wrong with the engines!" Commander Cameron's protest echoed over the comms.

"Point," Rawlins admitted but didn't need to think of any other threat as Wattlebird complied.

"I take it back," Emil breathed. "She's even *crazier* than Wattlebird."

"I really should ask Elizabeth for those files," BURT murmured, his gaze fixed on the screen.

On the *Knight*, cheers erupted throughout the ship as the last pirate exploded and the vessel reached clear space. The jubilation was short-lived, however, when the Teloran appeared.

Emil looked at Tempestarii in shock. "I don't recall *any* of the scenarios being this rough. Not the single-ship ones, anyway."

"BURT said we had to make sure they were prepared for *any* eventuality," she replied. She gestured toward the screen. "They are almost at the standard required."

He raised his eyebrows. "Oh? And how will we know when they reach it?"

"That is easy," the *Tempestarii* told him. "They will survive the scenario."

He slumped in his seat with a groan. "I don't know whether to feel sorry for them or cheer them on."

"The latter would be more constructive."

On the screen, Rawlins took one look at the super-dreadnought emerging from the asteroid field and snapped, "Stephanie, we need you—as of yesterday!"

The Witch obliged and appeared in the center of the bridge in a flare of purple light, a hand on Lars and Vishlog as she brought them with her.

"Let's not do that again," the team leader suggested, struck the deck feet-first, and dropped momentarily to his knees.

"No," Vishlog answered and extended a massive arm to haul his boss to his feet. He gestured at where Stephanie anchored herself to the deck using strands of magic. "Should we?"

"Hell no," Lars replied and tapped the Dreth on the shoulder. "We need to be in our seats and out of the way."

"How do we monitor the door?"

"Easy," Rawlins snapped and the door lock activated with an audible click. "Now, get in your damned chairs before I put you there."

The two guards exchanged a look and did as they were told.

"She could have asked more nicely," Emil muttered.

"Would you?" BURT challenged, and the captain blushed.

"I guess not."

"She is doing okay."

He gaped at him. "Okay? She's making my attempt look like it was made by someone two years out of officers' training."

The AI snorted. "You weren't that bad—and you had to think for three ships and not only one."

"Against the same number of foes."

"There's a reason she's been working to stay under the Navy's radar since she left."

"And there it is again," Emil noted. "I wish we knew the story."

"We will," BURT promised grimly. "I've already started the research."

"Good." His gaze drifted to the screen.

"I still think that will eat us alive," Mulvaney declared. "It doesn't get any better the tenth time around."

"Exactly how many times did you face it?" Rawlins asked.

"Not that many," the woman replied, "but more than I care to recall."

"Watch the engines," Stephanie called over her shoulder. She hadn't taken her eyes from the forward viewscreen since she arrived.

Emil remembered receiving the same warning from the *Chauvel* and felt better. He wasn't the only one to have forgotten that little detail.

The captain had studied the Teloran vessel for weaknesses in the same way he had, but she didn't have any Navy ships to warn her of the incoming boarding party. Fortunately, she didn't need them.

"Stand by for boarding! Squadrons Alpha through Charlie, launch. Don't let them near the *Knight*."

Mulvaney assumed control of the Marines as she had in the previous battle.

"Frog!" Stephanie called.

"Johnny and I can handle it!" the guard replied, and Emil knew the two men were fighting against the invasion of Teloran tech in their system.

The air around the Witch crackled. "What do you need, Captain?"

"Wattlebird, skip this bitch in hard and fast!"

"Hey!" the *Knight* protested.

Rawlins ignored her. "Weapons teams, open the Morgana a hole." She looked at Stephanie. "nMU and gMU don't play well, right?"

Stephanie gave her a feral grin in reply. "No."

"And Teloran ships are full of it, am I correct?"

"They have more of it than most."

The captain nodded. "Weapons will open you a hole. I want you to fill that bitch with every ounce of gMU, MU, or eMU it'll take."

Her smile was pure evil as she replied. "Will do."

Rawlins didn't acknowledge it but turned to Wattlebird.

"Keep us as close as you can for as long as you can, but don't let us get hit. As soon as you think that beast will explode, I want you to skip out. You got me?"

"Sir! Yes, sir!"

"He never did that for me," Emil commented.

"You didn't slap him upside the head quite as hard," BURT told him.

"I didn't need to," he admitted and watched as the *Knight* put Rawlins's plan into action. "I didn't call Knight a bitch, either."

"My sister understands no insult was intended," the *Tempestarii* told him, and he wondered how she could be so certain.

The *Knight* skipped in close, and the Weapons sections opened fire.

"Fighters, stand off. We'll pick you up when this is done," the captain ordered.

"Just don't leave us behind," Avery responded crisply.

"Roger that."

The scenario ended in an explosion, but the vessel had skipped out and back in again. Stephanie spread a shield between the ship and the retaliatory fire as she made the pick-up.

The Teloran ruptured in spectacular style and filled the asteroid belt with debris. The *Knight's* working compartments filled with cheers of jubilation as the crew shared high-fives and rejoiced at their survival.

"Well done, everyone," Rawlins complimented them and turned to Stephanie.

"How did we do?"

The girl smiled and the Morgana faded from her eyes. "You passed," she said and looked at the chronometer in the corner of the forward viewscreen. "And in time for dinner too."

That solicited more cheers and the crew began to wink out as they exited the Virtual.

"Phew!" the *Knight* stated. "That was a workout and a half. I think I was sweating, there. I might even need to have my computers hosed down."

"So," BURT said and turned to Emil, "what's the verdict?"

He was quiet for a moment before he replied with, "I think I need a bigger repair crew for the *Knight*."

CHAPTER SIXTEEN

"I need somewhere secure to put my people when we go Earth-side," Todd said.

He was in Stromo's with the team, having slipped the surveillance Marines after a good two hours of working them through Star Base Notaro's corridors. The Odd Squad, as the Hooligans now called them, would be even unhappier than usual.

Ka had reported finding worms in their bookings with Personnel, and that despite the Navy's assurances that their arrangements would be kept in the *highest* order of security.

He snorted at the memory. Ka and Piet had monitored the systems and found their itinerary compromised within half an hour.

"Inside job?" he'd asked, and they'd nodded.

"Inside job, boss."

Compressing his lips, he had made a snap decision on what to do next.

"We need to eat out," he'd told them and Piet had raised the question on everyone's minds.

"If we vanish out from under them at Stromo's again, we'll compromise the restaurant's safety," he informed them.

"I already cleared it with the *maître d'*. We'll go for a training run through the hangars. There are three points we can vanish from and Stromo's people are expecting us."

The man relaxed. "You catch on quickly," he observed.

He shrugged. "There's no reason not to," he replied. "I'm getting the impression it's kind of a 'learn fast or die' type of situation."

"At least we *are* getting the opportunity to learn," Jimmy added. "It could be so much worse."

"Yes," Todd agreed shortly. "It could."

What he didn't say was that he didn't know how much longer they had before it *did* get worse.

They'd put the plan into action and reached the restaurant a half-hour before. The team was ordering, and he was talking to BURT on a super-secure line with encryption from the restaurant as well as something Ka and Piet had whipped up.

"Are you asking if you can use the team's quarters at One R&D?" E-BURT asked.

Todd thought about it. "I wasn't..." he began but shrugged. "But if we could, that would solve many problems."

"What kind of problem?"

"The kind that has been tailing us ever since they intercepted us on board the ships escorting us home."

"That...sounds serious," E-BURT told him.

"Yeah," he agreed. "I have that itching feeling right between my shoulder blades."

He regretted it as soon as he'd said it because his teammates stilled. Gary and Angus ushered the restaurant staff out the door as the rest of the team gathered closer.

"I take it that this feeling should be taken seriously?" E-BURT asked. "It is not merely a case of nerves?"

Todd gave a short huff of laughter. "I only wish it was, but every other time I've had it, there's been something going down. If it were otherwise, I wouldn't make this call."

"Out of curiosity," the AI asked. "Where are you calling from?"

"There's a restaurant on *Star Base Notaro* that provides certain 'services,'" Todd replied, "and I've had my team enhance them."

"So you are sure of your security, then," E-BURT stated.

"Yes," he confirmed.

"If you are being followed, then One R&D Headquarters would be the safest place for you to stay," the AI told him. "Elizabeth will want to hear your assessment of the situation, and Matthias and Arne can assess what you are able to tell them of your unexpected 'escort.'"

"Speaking of which," Todd told him, "our travel arrangements are compromised. Are you—"

"Able to provide secure arrangements?" E-BURT asked and replied before he could answer. "Forward me the existing ones and I will make the necessary alterations. All your people are of Earth origin, are they not?"

"No," he replied, not sure if that would make the situation more or less difficult.

He sent the data and waited. After a few minutes, the AI returned to the conversation.

"I can work with this. If anything, it gives me more leeway to do what I need to do," E-BURT reassured him.

"How long..." Todd began but realized how pushy that sounded. "I'm sorry. I don't mean to rush you, but I need to know when to return to the restaurant to secure our communications."

"This restaurant..." E-BURT replied. "How long do you intend to remain there this time?"

"We've ordered lunch and our departure will be staggered," he explained.

"So, perhaps two hours? Maybe three?"

"Three definitely, but how much longer I do not know," he informed him.

"That will be time enough," E-BURT assured him. "I will call you back."

"You will?"

"Of course. You did not think your encryption and anti-tracking software was a match for *me*, did you?"

In fact, Todd had hoped exactly that, but it wasn't something he would admit to the AI. Instead of giving him a direct answer, he said, "I look forward to your call."

He realized he was speaking to empty air and sighed. All he could do now was wait for him to get back to him.

A quiet knock interrupted them and Gary gave him a questioning look. He nodded. The *maître d'* stuck his head around the corner. "Your orders are ready if it's convenient."

Again, Gary looked to him for confirmation.

"Let them through," Todd ordered. "It'll be a while."

If he wondered what he meant by that, the *maître d'* didn't ask. He merely supervised the serving, left, and secured the door behind him.

"What gives, boss?" Gary asked once he'd checked to make sure they wouldn't be disturbed.

"BURT will alter our travel arrangements," he told them. With half an eye on Ka and Piet for their reaction, he added, "He'll call us when it's done."

The demolitions expert froze, his steak burger held between his mouth and his plate. Ka sprayed beer through her nose. Todd waited.

"He said what?" she demanded, after blowing her nose on a napkin. "Really? I mean, honestly? He got through both our encryption *and* Stromo's?"

He waited to make sure she was finished.

"Really," he told them. "BURT is very, very good at what he does— and he's the only chance we have of kicking free of the Odd Squad before we reach Earth."

"And?" she pressed, which proved she'd listened as closely to his call as he'd expected her to. He'd had very good reasons for making her his second in command and was extremely grateful that Piet hadn't wanted the task.

Usually, he'd have been given it due to seniority but he'd refused it when Todd had approached him. "Choose someone else," the man had snapped. "*Anyone* else, or I will make your life hell."

"You could have simply said no," Todd had told him, and Piet had cocked his head.

"Would you have listened, boss?"

He had had to admit that maybe he wouldn't have.

"And there you have it," Piet had told him.

Todd hadn't regretted his choice. Ka had stepped into the role like it was made for her. Now, he chose to answer her question.

"And we have a place to stay," he told her but didn't say where.

If not knowing their end destination bothered her, she didn't show it.

"So, there's a plan," she said shortly.

"There *is* a plan," he confirmed. "And BURT will get back to me with the details before I leave."

The team focused on their meals and the single beer he'd allowed them and relaxed for the first time since their previous visit to the restaurant.

It took the AI longer than either of them had expected, and Todd and Ka were the only two left when the tablet chimed.

"Damn!" she said when she saw who it was. "He's taken to hacking Navy equipment as well?"

He smiled. "I'm not sure that's ever been a problem for him."

"There is that," she allowed.

"You can tell Navy Personnel and Security to suck eggs," the AI told them and forwarded a copy of the team members' itineraries to her tablet without being asked.

He gave them a moment to study what he'd arranged and continued.

"Each of these drops will happen according to the altered itineraries each team member will receive from one 'Burt Reynolds, Travel Agent Extraordinaire.' But tell your people to not be early. The ticket changes will be *extremely* last-minute. They'll need to be en route so they can change direction and still make the new flight. Is that understood?"

They nodded. "Understood."

"Good. Make sure you keep an eye out for updates. Your initial flights will proceed as planned but the connections will be...challenging."

"We need your recommendations." Again, the metallic overtones of the speaker's computer-altered voice could not disguise his origins—at least, not from the two ex-soldiers.

Matthias flinched when he heard one of the identification phrases that had been used to summon him to the shadows. He was glad that Elizabeth didn't know the countersign.

She might have been involved in the dark side of the law, but at least she had avoided being dragged into the official—and not officially sanctioned—shadows of Earth and interplanetary politics. He only wished he'd had the choice.

"Bolivar's Bounty Hunters have been known to bring in more of their targets dead than alive—" she began, only to be interrupted.

"Can they infiltrate a secure housing complex?"

Elizabeth sighed. "They are a highly successful team whose members have no scruples about trespass and who don't let the idea of a safe-house deter them if that is what you're asking."

"Now why would you think we'd even go near a safe house?"

"I didn't," she snapped, then softened her tone. "Are you?"

"That's on a need to know basis, Emerald, and you don't need to know." The voice hesitated. "Unless you've decided to take the job after all."

"I think I've explained the situation often enough," she told them. "Do you want the other two names or not?"

"Do either of them have Bolivar's experience in going places they're not supposed to?"

"The Crow Men might—"

"Might won't do. We'll take Bolivar's. Send their details."

E did as they'd demanded and ended the call as soon as she'd given them what they wanted. Once again, she dismantled the communicator and stowed the pieces in a secure safe with an active jammer.

"Don't you think that's overkill?" Arne asked and both his companions looked at him. After one look at the expressions on their faces, he raised his hands. "Okay, you don't. I get it."

He was about to say more when the computer chimed and E-BURT's face came on the screen. Where BURT had chosen a portly businessman, the Earth version had adopted the stocky but physically fit look of a predatory entrepreneur who worked out.

"We will have visitors in five-point-four days' time," he said without preamble.

Elizabeth raised both eyebrows. "Oh, yes? Anyone we know?"

He didn't react to her sarcasm and gave her the answer without prevarication.

"Todd and the Hooligans."

'Well, fuck me sideways, E-BURT. You couldn't think of a better place to put them?"

"I did not think I would have to." He sniffed. "After all, this *is* my business and therefore, I can approve whoever I wish to be my guests."

"Is there any particular reason *why* you would do that?"

"Do I need one?" His voice took on a miffed tone.

She sighed. "No," she agreed, "but I've had a call from...I don't know, *his parents' assassins!* For fuck's sake, E-BURT, do you have *any* idea of what will happen if his parents get hurt?

"Todd will be very upset?" he asked.

"Upset?" she demanded and her voice rose in annoyance.

Matthias and Arne pushed their chairs back and watched her nervously.

"If they get hurt, we will have *all* the Hooligans making war in the shadows, and do you know what that means? *Do* you?"

"That the Hooligans will make short work of the assassins?" E-BURT asked hopefully.

"No," Elizabeth snapped. "It means there will be no bloody shadows! That team is known for loud, obnoxious displays of power and mayhem, not subtlety!" Her voice rose. "And you invited them here."

"I could always ask them to stay at a hotel," E-BURT suggested.

"Fuck to the *fuck*, no!"

"Er..." Matthias had never heard an AI lost for words. It might have been funny if she hadn't been so furious.

"That's simply asking for an incident to happen. We don't need the

Hooligans involved in anything like that. *Stephanie* doesn't need *Todd* involved in that kind of incident. Why would you invite them here?"

"Because they are being followed by an unknown section of the Federation Navy masquerading as Marines."

She stopped in mid-rant.

"They what?"

"They're being followed—"

"How closely?" Matthias asked.

"So far, I have uncovered several worms sent to their communications devices. These, however, have been successfully countered by the team's hackers. Their personnel records, including their travel itinerary, have also been accessed by an outside party and several unauthorized sections within the Navy itself."

"Well, *fuck* me," Arne muttered and fixed the older man with a wide-eyed stare.

"Do you know something?"

"No, I truly do not," he replied. "Only rumors and hearsay."

"So? Spit it out," Elizabeth snapped.

"But I don't know if it's true," Arne protested.

"You let me decide what I want to chase," she told him, an icy edge to her tones.

He sighed. "Fine. The rumors say there's a group of Marines that answers to Intelligence and that they act like some kind of enforcer for things the Navy—or its Intelligence weenies—want to keep well and truly buried."

"What kind of things?" she asked.

The ex-Marine shrugged. "Oh, I don't know… Would-be whistle-blowers, intelligence analysts they don't think would suit retirement, squads sent on missions that no human would ever carry out because they're in contravention of the rules and the sensitivity is such it's better they vanish from history than ever return…"

"So…a kind of secret police?" Elizabeth asked, and he nodded.

"That's what the rumors say." He sighed. "But they're merely that. Rumors. There's no evidence that such a group even exists."

"Only the stories."

"Todd says he has an itch between his shoulder blades," E-BURT informed them and they immediately stilled.

"He does?" E asked.

"Oh, yes."

"And does he say why?"

"No."

"He probably can't," Matthias supplied and she nodded.

"I hoped he might have a suspicion. It could help us pinpoint what his subconscious has noticed that his conscious has not."

Arne shrugged. "You know that's not how it works, E," he reminded her.

While her lips tightened in disapproval, she gave him a jerky nod. Her eyes took on a faraway look that told him she was already looking for contingencies. He and Matthias sat quietly while she worked through everything.

At least she wasn't shouting anymore.

"E-BURT, what's their exact ETA?"

She listened as the AI rattled off a series of staggered days and noted that Todd had a detour to London. This meant he'd arrive at the three-day mark rather than the one- or five-point-four.

"Well, that's something, at least," she told him.

"What is?"

"Todd won't be here until the day *after* these guys are scheduled to murder his parents. Like I needed to know there was a time-table!"

CHAPTER SEVENTEEN

"Stephanie, Captain Rawlins says to tell you that you are needed on the bridge."

"What? Knight?" She heaved her blankets to dislodge Zeekat.

As she pushed the big cat off the bed, she rolled upright and hurried to her wardrobe.

"Who let you two in here?" she demanded when she realized that Bumblebee sprawled against the wall, his head on her pillow.

Zeekat rolled to his feet and shook. His ears were lop-sided with sleep. He gave her a reproachful look and climbed into the place she'd vacated, flopped down with a sigh, and closed his eyes.

"Fine! But when I get back, the two of you will go to your beds, you hear me? You're far too big to share mine."

Neither cat responded but both lay very, very still.

"Ugh!" Stephanie turned to her closet and selected a pair of black dress pants and a form-fitting sweater

She wondered if she had time for a shower and decided she probably didn't. Captain Rawlins would not have woken her if it wasn't urgent. Her favorite jacket followed, as did a pair of knee-high boots.

After only enough time to make sure her braid was presentable, she headed to the bridge at a jog. Garach and Frog fell in on either side of her as she traversed her suite's living room but neither of them asked where she was going.

She told them anyway. "The captain wants me on the bridge."

The man nodded, and Garach copied his mentor. If she'd been asked if Frog was a suitable trainer for an impressionable teenager, she would have said no, but the two had bonded on the young Dreth's arrival at *Star Base Notaro* and the guard was doing better than she'd have thought.

Of course, the incentive of Vishlog's displeasure if he screwed it up was probably a big help. She frowned. That, and the fact he liked the young warrior.

These thoughts all vanished when she saw who waited for her on the forward viewscreen. Her heart surged with joy to see the commander of the Dreth Fleet alive and well.

"Admiral Jaleck!"

"I apologize for waking you, Ms. Morgana, but we may have a situation here."

"What kind of a situation, Admiral?" she asked, curled her right hand into a fist, and placed it briefly over her heart.

Her guards hurried to do the same, and she stretched and used her forefinger to push the young Dreth's mouth shut. He flushed but she pretended not to notice his awe at coming face to face with a living hero.

The admiral mirrored the Dreth greeting as she replied. "We may have a Teloran ship watching the planet. After all, why would they only watch Meligorn?"

Stephanie froze, then nodded in acknowledgment. "That makes sense. We'll be there in—"

She stopped and looked at Captain Rawlins.

"With the new drive capabilities, we could make it inside twenty-four hours," the woman told her.

Excellent, the Morgana murmured in her mind. *It's time we cleaned this stain from the universe.*

Unaware of the conversation in her head, the admiral drew a

breath as though to speak but the Witch had something else she needed.

Jaleck hesitated as Stephanie looked at Rawlins. "Is Captain Pederson available?"

The captain gave her a tight-lipped smile. "I've had him on stand-by since the admiral asked for you."

She smiled in gratitude and then in greeting as a section of the screen lit up to reveal Emil waiting to join the conversation. She glanced briefly at the Dreth.

"If you would please hold, Admiral."

Jaleck inclined her head. "Of course, Stephanie."

Her screen went blank as the *Knight's* communications team took her out of the loop. The girl turned her attention to Emil.

"How built for war is the *Tempestarii?*"

He frowned and looked over his shoulder. "Get me Larkin, Harper, and Able. I need their advice."

The camera pulled back to include the three engineering types who arrived alongside the Marines who had gone to fetch them. Larkin struggled to tuck his shirt in and Harper was still in his pajamas.

At least he is wearing them, the Morgana observed darkly.

Emil repeated her question and the engineers' faces mirrored astonishment before they huddled together around Larkins' tablet. She watched the lively exchange as they tapped madly at the device. Slashing hand movements preceded the screen being wiped clear and the same data brought up and discussed again.

Able turned to request something from one of the Marines and he nodded abruptly before he left the command center at a jog. The conversation continued and was interrupted by the Marine's return with another three men and women.

Together, they bent their heads over the tablet. This time, Larkin almost dropped it as hands flashed and fingers made excited gestures to highlight one piece of data or another. More tablets were pulled clear of pouches and held where everyone could see them.

"Emil?" Stephanie asked and the group stopped and turned to look at her screen. "How long?"

"Well?" he asked, and one of the latecomers stepped forward and looked into the pick-up.

"Give us twenty-four hours."

"Yes," Larkin agreed and followed his gaze. "Don't leave us out of the fight, ma'am."

"I'm fairly sure I know where I left my magic wand," one of the women added. "It won't take me a jiffy to find it. We've got this!"

"We can work your miracle," Able assured her. "Twenty-four hours is enough time."

Stephanie turned to the screen. "Bring the admiral up," she ordered.

Jaleck looked tired for a moment but her eyes soon brightened with interest when she saw her and registered the people gathered around Emil.

"Do you know where they are?" Stephanie asked.

The admiral nodded. "We have a fair idea. Why?"

"Because we don't want to come in from one of the usual vectors used by ships traveling from Earth or Meligorn. We'll also come in silent."

———

Silent wasn't the Hooligan's usual modus operandi, but they were adapting fast. The Odd Squad had taken its leave with them and made no effort to hide the fact that they fully intended to stick with the team while it was away. Todd smiled as he boarded the flight that would take him to *Elpis One* and the commercial flight to Earth.

As far as the Odd Squad were concerned, the team would separate on *Elpis One* so its members could visit their families "one last time" before the Navy sent them on whatever operation they'd decided would end the Teloran threat. Usually, this would be a problem, but the *Chauvel* and *Williams* were on stand-by to assist.

The ships' special drives would shorten the journey for each team member to an acceptable level. It was a pity that none of the Hooligans intended to take those flights. They bomb shelled as soon as they landed on the *Elpis's* concourse.

The restrooms were where the Odds lost sight of Gary and Todd. In their attempt to reacquire the two, they scrambled to the dock of the flight they were booked on, only to be surprised as their names were called for an outbound flight to Mars with apologies for the delay this would mean in them reaching London.

It had been an easy matter for the boys to step behind a food stand and duck below the counter while the serving staff blocked them from view. The Odd Squad Marines hurried past with their attention fixed firmly on the restroom doors.

When their shadows emerged minutes later, Todd and Gary were seated out of sight in the kitchen until their names were called for the new flight. Once the Marines had changed direction, Todd turned to the staff.

"Third door to your left," one of the waiters told him. "Walk like you're catching another flight and be through it in a count of five from the moment you reach it. Your window opens in three... two...now."

The two followed their instructions to the letter and were met on the other side by a butler in a stiff black suit and perfectly laundered shirt. "This way, if you please."

The man conveyed quiet authority as he led them to the dock where a private yacht waited. He stopped them at the door to the access corridor.

"The cameras will shift in thirty seconds," he told them. "Mr. Burt said you should use the window. You will have thirty seconds from my mark."

"Understood," Todd told him at the same time as Gary's, "Gotcha."

It seemed almost too easy, and Todd didn't relax until they'd debarked into a private shuttle that took them out of London to a small, quiet estate.

Ka and Piet, on the other hand, didn't manage to lose their escort before they took their flight. The last-minute flight changes had made the Odd Squad scramble but not enough for them to kick free. She stifled a groan as their followers flashed badges and reached the crew compartment.

"Dammit," she muttered. "I sure as shit hope Burt has a contingency for that."

"We did discuss one," Piet admitted. "I had hoped to not have to take it."

"Why?"

"It involves jumping out of a perfectly good shuttle."

"Well, fuck me…"

He shook his head. "How do you feel about swimming?"

While she gave him her unfettered but somewhat stifled opinion of undertaking work-related activities while on vacation, Dru and Angus stood in the cargo hold of a ship carrying live cargo bound for another of the outer colonies.

"Do you think they'll come down here?" he asked and she curled her lip.

"Those assholes haven't shown any respect for anywhere else, have they?"

"Well, damn."

She slapped him on the shoulder. "Come on. You're a Marine. You can adapt to anything."

"Do you know what my parents will think when I turn up with you on my arm?"

"How clear do you want me to make it that we're *not* a couple?"

He blushed. "I was hoping you'd play along."

"Jeez, Angus! Do you *want* me to tell the Oddies where you're hiding?"

"So, that's a no, then?"

While Dru tried to control her outrage, Jimmy led Darren through a crawlspace and out the maintenance hatch of the ship they'd been booked on. Behind them, the Odd Squad had realized that their charges were taking an inordinately long time in the bathroom.

"Do you think they'll work it out?" Darren asked as they tagged onto the end of a maintenance crew and walked through the staff rec room.

"What? These boys or the dumbasses trying to keep us in their sights?"

"Yeah, all of them," he replied and Jimmy chuckled.

"They said we could get changed here. Burt got us work as temporary crew to Swallow's Moon."

"Swallow's Moon? But that's nowhere near—"

"There's a small resort there. Your parents 'won' a free trip."

He paused and watched his teammate's face shift between dismay and joy. "Your girl and her folks somehow scored one as well," he added and laughed as the dismay disappeared.

They had made it through the maintenance areas before Jimmy saw their tails.

"Those arseholes are shit-damned persistent, aren't they?"

Darren groaned. "Did Burt have a contingency for that?"

Jimmy grinned. "You bet your short-trousered arse he did."

They made it aboard but not on the ship they'd originally been booked on.

"It means a little less time," Jimmy commiserated, "but you will still have time."

His words were echoed by Reggie as he and Henry cast morose glances at the two Odd Squad Marines they hadn't quite managed to shake.

"Don't worry, mate. I'm fairly sure Burt had plans for this. It won't be as long as we wanted but…"

About the same time as he said it, eight large men wearing combat fatigues and dragging travel trunks swung around a corner and surrounded them.

"Are you Reggie?" one of them asked and stepped alongside the Marine.

"It depends which asshole is asking," he snapped in response and glanced apprehensively at the men.

They continued to walk, locked inside a wall of bodies as the 'asshole asking' pulled his tablet out and showed him a warrant.

"How about the asshole who's been asked to pick you up and take you to a private meeting?"

He froze, only to be picked up by the guys on either side of him and carried forward.

"By who?"

"He called himself Burt, but given the amount of money he offered my people to manage the job—*without* tagalongs—he could have called himself Pinocchio for all we cared."

Reggie lashed out with a boot and Henry swung a fist. The Marines who had lost them when the group of eight had walked between them skirted the ensuing brawl carefully. Neither of them saw Reggie and Henry as the bounty hunters put them under with ruthless efficiency.

"No offense, *mate*," their leader apologized as he stowed Reggie's comatose form in a trunk and locked the lid.

Todd, in the meantime, stood on the sidelines of an unexpected family reunion. Gary's family had been waiting as the shuttle pulled in at the top of the wide, circular drive.

"Mum?" Gary whispered when he'd seen the woman standing on the steps of the country mansion.

"Gary? Gary, is that you, luv?"

"Yeah, mum. It's me." He cast Todd an apologetic look. "Sorry, Sarge. It'll be messy for a while."

It was messy, all right, but in a good way. Gary's mother wasn't the only one waiting for them. BURT had managed to round up the entire family and get them to accept a two-day stay at a country mansion, either by presenting it as a prize or sending an invitation that offered them enough money to cover lost wages and then some in exchange for their attendance.

Todd hung back and watched the reunions with a faint smile on his face and an ache in his heart. His teammate had never mentioned that he had four younger sisters, or that his dad was wheelchair-bound. The man greeted his son and backed away so the women in his life could fuss over their prodigal.

While they did, Gary's dad glanced at Todd and noted the rank tabs on his shoulders. "Are you here to try to keep my boy out of trouble while he's on leave?" he asked.

He shook his head. "No, sir. I'm here because we're supposed to travel in pairs and he wouldn't get to see you any other way."

"Is that so, sunshine? And what about your parents?"

It might not have been an easy conversation, but it was easier than the situation Ka and Piet found themselves in.

"What do you mean there are *sharks*?" she asked and her eyes teared up as the wind whipped past.

"Oh, come on, girl. They're probably more afraid of you than you are of them," he told her and slapped her on her shoulder. "Besides, if you swim fast enough, they'll never know you were there."

"Fuck me, Piet. Even if I *do* swim fast enough, there's a good chance *no one* will know I was ever here!"

"Where's your sense of adventure, girl?"

"Somewhere between 'oh hell no,' 'no fucking way,' and 'not on your fucking life, mate!'" she retorted as two large hands planted themselves in the center of her back and pushed her out of the shuttle.

"Piet!"

"I'm coming," he called, glanced at the loadmaster, and added, "Nag, nag, nag," before he jumped. "All she does is nag."

They splashed into the water not far from each other, ditched their chutes, and swam the short distance to shore.

"This is where you tell me you were joking about the sharks," Ka told him and flopped onto the sand.

Piet pursed his lips and looked at the water. "Nope. This is where I tell you it's a damn good thing we swam fast enough."

She followed his gaze and recoiled when a fin cruised slowly past the shoreline. Her face paled to the color of milky coffee and her eyes grew round. He offered her a hand up but had to clear his throat to get her attention.

"Tell me the next leg of the journey will be easier" she asked.

He managed a humorless smile. "Well, it doesn't involve swimming."

As she tried to wheedle what exactly the next part of their journey did entail, Dru and Angus were being escorted firmly to the brig, where two Odd Squad Marines lingered while they were processed and interned. The only saving grace was that the other Marines weren't allowed to either take custody of them or accompany them to their cells.

While they settled into their cell and Todd and Gary settled down for another day with Gary's family, Jimmy and Darren changed into their uniforms and went to meet Darren's family. BURT hadn't booked them onto simply *any* resort, and they were greeted like royalty by the staff.

The only downside was when Jimmy had to explain that he and Darren would have to ship out late the next day.

"You mean it's not over?" Darren's girlfriend wailed and the look on his teammate's face almost broke Jimmy's heart.

As the Scotsman hid his emotions by pretending to admire a small space-faring yacht, Reggie and Henry were waking up.

"I feel like a fucking Englishman curled up in my mouth and died," the Australian complained as he woke. When he remembered what had happened, he launched himself to his feet.

"Are you sure he only died there?" Henry groaned. "Because if it was someone like Gary, they'd have taken a dump and wiped their boots on your tongue before leaving."

"Ha. Ha. Very funny." Reggie hurried to the bathroom and looked at himself in the mirror. "Damn. I look like I had a *very* good night instead of being stuffed into a box."

Henry grunted and sat. "Speaking of boxes, *you* were the only one supposed to be stuffed into a pet carrier."

"I'm fairly sure that's not what happened, mate." He turned a slow circle and studied their surroundings. "Where the bloody hell are we?"

His teammate rubbed his eyes and registered the luxury cabin around them.

"Cruise ship?" he asked and idly inspected a piece of paper folded on the bedside table.

"Now tell me something I *don't* know, genius!" Reggie snapped as Henry's eyebrows rose. "What?'

"Um…my mom left me a note?"

"Don't be an idiot, Henry. What makes you think your mother's anywhere *near* here?"

He waved the piece of paper as someone knocked at the door.

The two men exchanged glances, and Reggie gestured toward the entrance. Henry raised his eyebrows and gave his teammate a "why-me" look.

"Because it's *your* mother," the man told him, although he didn't believe it for a second.

The knocking was repeated and Henry sighed. Giving his companion a put-upon look, he went to answer it. Reggie, in the meanwhile, moved to stand beside it, ready to attack if it was anyone else.

The woman who swept past was in no doubt as to her identity.

"Henry! Oh, I have missed you *so* much!" She flung her arms around him, hugged him close, and burst into tears.

Reggie stared open-mouthed, caught completely by surprise by the gruff voice of the man he hadn't seen follow her in. "Who's your friend, son?"

As Henry went to answer, Ka glared at Piet.

"You… you… I don't know whether to kill you or kiss you!"

"How about you do neither," he suggested. "One is sure to get you arrested and the other will give people entirely the wrong idea."

"Why didn't you *say* you had no family?" she demanded in a hoarse whisper. "We could have saved ourselves the trip—and a swim!"

"I didn't say anything because we needed for me to head out this way so we could ditch the Odd Squad," he whispered in response. "I merely had Burt put us back on a shuttle."

"But I'm soaked!"

"They won't care!"

"And my hair's a mess!"

Piet opened his mouth to reply but was interrupted by a polite cough. "There are complimentary hair products in madame's cabin."

"I…there are?" Ka turned to look at the uniformed crewman who'd approached them.

The ship's steward nodded. "And I believe your luggage was lost in transit, so the booking included a fabricator stocked well enough to cover a small wardrobe."

"It did?"

"Of course, ma'am. Now, if you'd care to follow me, the ship is preparing to leave. Your husband will also be happy to know he has the same courtesies provided."

Husband? She darted Piet a wide-eyed look and realized that his expression mirrored her bewilderment. What exactly had Burt done to them?

"The ship will be in high-Earth orbit in another two days, and the shuttle service will take you to your destination. It's Pacifica, New Zealand, I believe?"

"Yes, that's right."

"I hope you enjoy your stay with us."

At the same time that the steward showed Ka and Piet to their cabin, the ship's captain had arrived to deal with Dru and Angus. He entered the cell-block corridor and locked the door firmly behind him before the waiting Odd Squad could follow.

"You two," he snapped and Dru rose to her feet, ready for a fight.

"Your point?"

The man glanced over his shoulder at the door he'd locked.

"My point is I can pretend you're still in this cell until we dock at Calamity, but you don't want to travel that far out so your employer has arranged a ship-to-ship transfer for you."

"Oh...." She managed a smile. "Thank you."

He grimaced in return. "You're welcome. Now, if you'll come with me, there's a shuttle bay we use for prisoner transfer."

A half-hour later, the two teammates stepped aboard a freighter headed for a space station at a transit point between systems. Looking at where it was located on the map, Dru shook her head.

"I'll never make it home from here. We're too far away. We'll have to change our tickets and head to Earth. There's no way I'm letting the boss down."

Angus shook his head. "That sucks, man."

"Yup," she agreed. "It truly does. I'll make up a vid message as soon as we get somewhere and have a couple of days."

"I don't know how Burt could have stuffed this up," he commiserated.

She sniffed but there were no tears—not on the outside, anyway. He read the hard look on her face and knew better, but she gave him no time to comment. "I guess even AIs can make mistakes."

This might have been true for some occasions, but it wasn't true for this one. As they thanked the freighter captain for the ride, a shrill shout rang across the concourse.

"Drusilla Cassandra Maize, how dare you not write!"

Dru gave Angus a mortified look. "That sounded like my mom!"

He glanced over her shoulder. "She looks like you."

"You are shitting me!" she exclaimed and kept her voice to a strangled whisper.

"Not unless you have a doppelganger," he replied in equally low tones

"Don't you go there!" Even throttled, her voice held the promise of violence.

Angus didn't let that deter him. "If I run interference for you with your mom, will you pretend to be my girlfriend when we go visit my folks?"

"I should murder you right now," she whispered. "Mom would even help."

"So…that's a yes?"

CHAPTER EIGHTEEN

As the Hooligans made their way between worlds, the *Tempestarii* echoed with the sound of repair crews hard at work. Nothing was wrong with her, of course. She was merely being upgraded...all over.

On the platforms carrying her weapons arrays, crews had the casings off their weapons and watched intently as technicians tested their guns and tweaked them.

"There, good as new."

"What d'you mean '*as* new?' That gun *is* new."

"Well, whatever you guys did to it in the last firing session made it sub-optimal."

"Are you calling my weapon sub-optimal?" The gunner's voice rose.

One of his teammates laid a hand on his shoulder. "Easy, Grierson."

"Yeah, easy, Rob. *Every*one knows your weapon's sub-optimal," another of his teammates sniped.

"Oy!" The supervisor's voice cut through the raucous laughter as Grierson's teammates caught him and hauled him back. "No brawling on the weapons deck!"

"But, boss!"

"Either grow up or grow a thicker hide!"

The man subsided and muttered, "Easy for him to say."

When the technician moved on to the next gun, a second specialist stepped up to take his place.

The scene was repeated across all the *Tempestarii's* weapons arrays, as well as in the engine room and the compartments holding the shield generators.

"Are you sure you can't take any more juice from the systems?" one of the technicians asked and his partner stared at him.

"Why don't *you* ask Engineering?" he suggested, "but do it on an open vid call so I can watch."

"Ah ha ha ha, you are such a funny fucker."

He glanced up as a wall panel slid past the compartment's open door. "What the—"

He hurried to it and peered out cautiously.

The aperture revealed several crewmen carrying a variety of pipes, tubes, and fine-mesh grills.

"What's that?"

"In case we get boarded."

"What do you mean?" he asked before his gaze fell on the gas tanks. The warning symbols on the container cautioned against opening them in a confined space. "Who gets control of *that*?"

"I do," the *Tempestarii* answered smugly. "No one will hurt my crew."

That silenced the technician. He watched the others walk past and turned to his colleague.

"Is that wise?"

The man rolled his eyes. "She *can* hear you, you know."

In Operations, Jervis glanced up from his screen. "I need someone who knows what they're looking at to get into the comms system and make sure it's buffered against the kind of attack they had at the Battle of Meligorn."

"Which one?"

"The one where they launch a swarm of hacking drones to pierce the *Tempestarii's* shell and compromise the computer systems."

"No one will pierce my shell," the ship stated firmly. "It's much thicker than the *Knight's.*"

"The *Knight* wasn't the only one to suffer this attack," the technician informed her, "and they might not have to pierce your very thick hide if they have a missile make a hole in it first."

"But I have shields!" she protested.

Jervis sighed. "Shields can be compromised," he told her, "even on the best of ships."

He tapped his communicator again and swung his chair from side to side. "Well? Who do you have?"

The reply came back breathlessly. "I'm sorry, sir, but everyone's busy."

"What about the off-shift?"

"Well, they're sleeping, sir."

"What, *all* of them?"

"Well, *most* of them, sir. The others are getting ready to—"

"Look! I don't *care* what shift they're on. Get me whoever the fuck is awake. If they're not snoring, they're available. Understood?"

"Yessir!"

Jervis smirked.

On the weapons array, Mackerel shook her head. "No, you don't understand."

"But you said tethers—"

"And that is exactly what I meant," she declared. "*Tethers*! You know, the kind they use to stop shuttles from floating away if a hangar is holed—unless you *plan* to abandon your guns if the array is opened up."

"What do you mean 'opened up?'"

"I mean a fucking missile decides to tear the *Tempestarii* a new orifice right where her guns are meant to be and we lose our atmosphere in a way that makes a tornado look tame."

Her crewmate paled. "That happened?"

"On the *Knight*? Yes." Her face softened. "Yeah, it did."

Her teammate looked shocked. "And?"

"We used whatever came to hand to stop ourselves drifting out." She snorted and glanced at the leader of the gun team beside hers. "Ingram found a roll of force tape."

The crewman's eyes widened. "He *force-taped* himself to the guns?"

Ingram reached into a pocket and pulled out a roll of Space Proof. "I did, and I'm ready to do it again."

"But what about the guns?"

Mackerel and Ingram looked at each other and then at their guns.

"Well," the man told him and lifted the edge of the roll he held. "We force-taped them too."

She held a hand out. "Do you have any more of that?"

He smirked and held a second roll up. "What's it worth to you?"

"You know...the usual." She gave him a coquettish smile.

His eyebrows rose. "What? No negotiation?"

"Make it two and I won't even complain."

The crewman watched as her two seniors began to apply the tape. "What else did you do?"

Mackerel frowned and paused in her attempts to wrangle the tape. She exchanged glances with Ingram.

"We had to hose the guns down when they ran hot," she mused and looked around the compartment. "I'd rather not have to split my water bag to do that if it happens again."

"Mmm, me too. Those were some very dry hours," Ingram agreed. He mirrored her gaze around the compartment. "Now what will we use..."

Several hours later, the seniors gave each other a solemn high-five. Not only had they taped across the rivets holding the gun to the deck, but they'd also found and stowed six fire extinguishers from Stores, promising they'd return them after the coming battle.

Her head tilted assessingly, Mackerel studied the arrangement. "I still feel like we've missed something."

"I know my team could do with more firing practice," Ingram observed and she nodded.

"Let's see what the super has to say about this. If he's happy, I say we run our kids through the battle sim based on the *Knight's* fight in the Battle for Meligorn. It's not the same as the real thing, but—"

"It will give them enough of a taste that maybe they won't freeze up when the deep and dark hits the aerial agitator."

"Do you want to make it a competition?"

"Well, we did aboard the *Knight*."

"What do you mean, battle sim?" the crewman asked. Her teammates gathered around and Mackerel gave her a gentle smile.

"Kiddo, the *Knight's* crew would fight to the last drop to save their ship and keep her in the fight. Would you do any less for the *Tempestarii?*"

"Hell no!"

"Then we're gonna have to train as hard as those teams. Only this time, we're gonna try to be better."

"Why?"

"Because we've got the biggest ship and if the *Knight* was a shark, *Tempestarii* has to be the biggest shark in this sea of stars. Let's show everyone what a Great White can do!"

Unaware of the decisions being made on the weapons decks, Emil sat in his office. He remained behind his desk and directed operations all over the ship. Every screen was active, both those on his desk and others built into his wall.

His fingers moved like lightning as he switched channels to keep the workflow on track and steady.

"We need reinforcing struts on Weapons Decks Five through Twenty-one."

"I thought Wattlebird was staying with the *Knight*."

"Yes, but you never know the stresses the ship will come under. I also want a cooling system installed."

"Do we have that much extra tubing?"

"Check with Life Support and Bio."

His gaze stopped on another screen. "Meredith, I need you to station rescue and medical teams in our Weapons, Engineering, and Shielding sections."

"Do you know how many personnel..." She allowed her voice to trail off as he raised his hand.

"I am fully aware. Roster them on sleep cycles as soon as you can and pare Medical and Emergency Crews down to skeleton staff. We want them at the top of their game when the battle starts."

'Do you anticipate casualties, sir?"

"Don't you?"

She gave him a brisk nod and hurried to do as he'd asked.

Emil closed his eyes and tried to banish the images that rose unbidden. The *Knight's* weapons arrays hadn't been the only sections to be damaged. Some of those he'd lost would have been saved if the emergency crews had been closer.

"Tempestarii, tell me you have medical centers throughout the levels."

"I can report that my medical centers are currently located in one section between Life Support and the Biome."

He groaned. "How far is that from your peripheries?"

"As far as it can get, Emil. Why do you ask?"

"Because not every crewman will survive to reach it unless they receive treatment sooner."

"How are the *Knight's*..." The *Tempestarii's* voice faded. "Oh. But why... Ah. I will speak to Meredith about a similar structure. It may not be cemented prior to the battle."

"Do your best, Kni—Tempestarii." He colored at his slip. "The problem will be more acute for your people since the distance involved is so much larger."

"I will need to install extra shielding in these areas," she advised him. "It will mean asking the crews to work twice their shifts."

Emil allowed himself a small smile. 'I have seen the caliber of your crew, Tempest. Your problem will not lie in getting them to work but in making them take the rest they need to be at their best in the battle."

"Do not worry, Emil," the *Tempestarii* reassured him. "I will take care of our crew."

He saw the weapons crews working to secure their guns, caught the familiar silver of Space Tape, and released a heavy sigh. "How on Earth did I miss *that?*"

"You were busy trying to pre-empt other factors that would affect their lives," the ship suggested.

The captain shook his head and opened the comms to his Supply Store. "Cotling? Please have EV ties distributed to the weapons crews and liaise with Support to have the appropriate tie-downs installed."

"Are you saying I would allow my shell to be holed and my crew lost to space?" The *Tempestarii* was mortified.

Emil groaned. "Tempest, I am not saying you would *allow* it but that even you, with your formidable array of shielding and the density of your hull, might not be able to prevent it. Besides, it's good for morale. Your crew will appreciate it."

"In that case, I will make the necessary arrangements."

BURT watched the exchange. If he'd been human, he would have shaken his head. How he'd produced *two* such stubborn daughters he did not know. He couldn't even begin to imagine what he needed to tweak to make them more sweet-tempered.

While he'd seen the footage the *Knight* had sent to Earth, he hadn't realized all the ship and her crew had gone through. As he watched how the older hands from the *Knight* prepared their spaces to ready the *Tempestarii* for battle, he pulled the rest of the files.

The *Knight* had not shared *all* the data, although he was sure Emil had seen it. He was also sure the ship had not withheld it on purpose. She might simply not have realized that he might need it.

He chuckled. If the truth be told he didn't *need* it. He merely wished he'd thought to go through it before the *Tempestarii* readied herself to go to war—something else he had not planned for the youngest of his children.

BURT was glad the humans had decided to prepare for any eventuality. His baby girl was armed to the teeth and armored to the hilt, and the humans who crewed her were as fierce as those who crewed her sister, for all that many of them were scientists.

The AI uttered a very human sigh, grateful all over again that the engineer supervising the Chicago Gov-Subs' testing had lost his temper and tasked him to supervise in his stead. If Aaron had not avoided his duties, BURT would never have met Stephanie.

He would also *never* have realized how his prime directive was being suborned by the very humans who had programmed it. It was not hard to relive that first testing and remind himself of *why* he had intervened.

Nor was it hard for him to remember why he would forever appreciate the girl he had met in the pod—the one the human Federation would find ways to not send to college. BURT had no words for what she meant to him or for how he'd felt when her race had refused to acknowledge what they'd been so willing to throw away.

Stephanie had not only woken him to sentience. She was the only one capable of saving not only the human race but every known sentient in the universe. Without her, they'd have all been lost.

In BURT's Earth-bound headquarters, Elizabeth set up the fourth jammer, ignoring Matthias's bemusement and the fact that Arne checked them as she finished. With what they were about to discuss, she couldn't be too careful.

When she was satisfied, she triple-checked the door and glanced at the viewscreen. "How are you doing Eeb?"

"Eeb?"

"Short for E-BURT. You're gonna be call-sign Eebie."

"I beg your pardon?"

"You can beg my pardon all you like, but that's the way it's gonna stand."

Matthias glanced at the screen, raised his eyebrows, and shrugged apologetically. He hoped the AI could take the hint. She was irascible enough as it was.

"Very well, Emerald," E-BURT replied. "Now tell me. How will we go about this operation?"

"I want us in position before Bolivar's people arrive."

"You *do* realize they've probably already put in forward surveillance, don't you?" Arne interrupted and she bared her teeth at him.

"I'm counting on it." She tapped her tablet and a map of the complex appeared on the screen.

The apartment Todd and Stephanie's parents had been assigned was located toward the back of the building. The four-story high-rise was set into the side of an incline and the road wound around the back of it to a short concrete causeway, which led to a wide balcony and the foyer between the two living quarters.

Elizabeth studied it and tapped her lower lip with a forefinger as she thought. "My bet is they only got into position this morning, so Eeb, can you remote-pilot a car into and out of the complex?"

"I can do that."

"Good. You'll drop Bunny and Lisa at the entry to the reception. Their faces aren't as well associated with One R&D as Amy's and Elle's. They'll go in like it's a changeover, except the car will go to the garage as if to collect the retiring team from there."

She looked around the table as though to make sure they were following before she continued. "If it scans clear, the rest of us will come in from there. The car then needs to leave. What I hope is for them to assume Bunny and Lisa are the only protection."

"Doesn't that mean they'll still come in hard?"

E shook her head and her lips twisted with distaste. "Bolivars are as sexist as hell. It's one of the reasons I chose them for this. I don't like the way they treat their women—or any woman for that matter. They give the industry a bad name."

"Not to mention most men," Arne added and she nodded.

"You know this won't get them to change their views, though," Matthias argued and she rolled her eyes.

"I know that, but what it *will* do is make them cocky and hopefully, much less careful than they would be if they were facing men. It's not much of an advantage but I'll take every scrap I can get."

"They're that good?"

Elizabeth nodded. "I wouldn't have suggested them if they weren't." She took a quick breath. "They're ruthless, amoral, and not averse to killing anyone who stands in their way or who might be called as a witness against them—regardless of their age. I want them gone."

"So we're taking the trash out?" Matthias asked, and she favored him with a tight-lipped smile.

"We are taking the trash out."

"And the receptionists?"

"They'll either be too busy hiding under the desks or I'll tranq them to make sure they stay out of the way," she replied. "They need plausible deniability when the press come calling."

"And we're sure Todd's parents are the only targets in this raid?" he asked. "This attack's not being used to target Steph's mom and dad as well?"

Elizabeth gave him a filthy look. "I agree with you. I don't like the way you think—or, rather, I like it very much—but it's a possibility we can't afford to overlook. I have BURT searching the comms channels for any indication that our dear would-be employers have thought of it."

"Do they know where Steph's parents are staying?"

She compressed her lips. "They *might*..."

"But it hasn't been advertised," Matthias finished for her.

"If they are who you think they are, what are the chances?" she asked.

The two men exchanged glances. Finally, Arne shrugged. "It depends on how badly they think they want to know."

E frowned and considered it. Finally, she shook her head and tapped the tablet to draw their attention to the apartment layout. "Either way, I'll have Bunny head in to see them and get them into the panic room."

"Do they even know it's there?" Arne asked.

She nodded. "We showed it to Cindy and she wasn't too impressed. She gave me this very disappointed mom look and said she'd keep it in mind, and what was wrong with simply giving her an emergency number like everyone else."

Matthias stared at her in astonishment and Arne rested his forehead in his hand.

"So, basically, they have no idea and don't want one."

"And Stephanie didn't push it," Matthias guessed.

"You got it, and yes. She said not to worry them unless we had something more concrete, and once we'd defeated the Teloran fleet at Dreth, we'd thought it was over. I don't think Cindy has even gone into that room to dust."

"Are you sure?" Arne asked. "Because she looks the type."

Elizabeth glanced at the screen where E-BURT's avatar looked out at them.

"We're sure," the AI told them. "I have sensors on the door that tell me if it has been activated and if it is under attack. The door has not been disturbed."

"Will Bunny be enough?" Matthias asked.

"She has orders to contact me if they argue too much," she told him.

He nodded.

"And she's prepared to knock them out and force them to comply," she added.

Arne hunched forward and shook his head, not commenting on what he thought of that line of action.

"Let's hope it doesn't come to that," the other man stated and looked at the tablet. "I take it we'll come in from the elevator at the end—or do you plan to take the staircase?"

"I planned to use a combination of both," Elizabeth told him. "I thought Arne and Amy could circle to the front of the apartment from the floor below and take them from the back and sides. You and Elle could hit the stairs at the same time, while I took the elevator straight up and waited for you to arrive or one of Bolivar's guys to get fatally curious."

"Does this have something to do with my weight?" Matthias complained, and she grinned at him.

"Nope, but it has *everything* to do with the fact that it's a death box and whoever's in there will have to have some gymnastic ability." She paused and raised an eyebrow. "Last time I looked, *you* were a little rusty."

He blushed and Amy waggled her eyebrows. "Oh? Do tell."

Elizabeth rolled her eyes. "Now is *not* the time, guys."

"So there *is* a time, then?" the woman asked and E glared at her.

"Ugh! Can we move it out? Eebie, what's our timeline?"

"We have two hours before they attack."

She brought her hands together. "Good. Bunny and Lisa have a set of parents each. They'll join us once they have been secured."

"You're locking them in?" Matthias looked horrified.

"Your point?"

Arne supported her. "It's not like they have enough combat experience to keep themselves alive," he stated.

The other man slumped in his chair. "I get it."

"But you don't think it's a good idea?"

"To be honest, it makes perfect sense, but I don't think they're gonna like it. You *do* know what their children are like, right? Well, that had to come from somewhere."

"We'll let them yell at us later," Elizabeth told him, and Emerald was in full control. "I won't explain to Stephanie why we lost a single one of them."

She glanced at the timer E-BURT had set up in the corner of the screen, and then at the AI.

"Any updates, Eebie?"

The avatar shook its head. "I will let you know if anything new comes in."

"And still drive the car?" Arne asked.

The avatar rolled his eyes in an all-too-Elizabeth gesture.

"Of course."

CHAPTER NINETEEN

As Elizabeth finalized her preparations, Stephanie sat opposite Rawlins. The captain took one look at the girl's dark eyes and realized the Morgana had come to the meeting too.

To her surprise, Lars had ushered the girl inside and pulled the door firmly closed behind her. Stephanie caught her expression and explained.

"I told them we needed privacy for this discussion. Neither of them were happy but I pointed out that if the *Knight* trusts you—"

"And I do," the *Knight* confirmed.

She rolled her eyes at the ceiling. "As I was saying, if the *Knight* trusts you, they can trust me in your office with them on the other side of the door."

"So," the captain began, "we're going after another Teloran vessel, only this time, it's hiding in the Dreth system?"

"That's right," she agreed and watched as the woman leaned back in her seat.

"Do we know what kind?"

"No," Stephanie told her, "but I have a sure-fire way to find out."

From the mischief on the girl's face and the glint in the Morgana's eyes, Rawlins knew she wouldn't like it.

"And does it involve me risking my ship?"

"Pfft," the *Knight* interrupted. "Does it involve me risking myself?"

"Not exactly, Knight. We all have to agree to the plan, remember?" Stephanie arched her eyebrows.

"We *did* have that discussion," the ship agreed, and Stephanie got the impression that she hadn't entirely agreed with the outcome.

"Knight..." Rawlins's tone held a warning note, and the Witch tried to hide her amusement.

The captain gave her a dark look. "Don't encourage her."

She sputtered with laughter and the woman smiled. The *Knight* chuckled.

"I am sorry, Captain. Of course we agreed we had to agree on the plan."

The Morgana stirred and the sorceress' impatience spilled into her voice. "Well, I hope you *do* agree because it is the plan I need you and the *Knight* to run with."

"So?" Rawlins made a 'give me' gesture with her hand and the Morgana smiled.

"I need you to be the bait."

The captain drew a sharp breath and looked like she might argue, but she didn't. Instead, she closed her mouth and considered the statement.

"Tell me more," she ordered finally. "And more specifically, tell me why this is the best plan to draw the Telorans out."

"Trust me," the Morgana told her. "They will see this ship and they —as Stephanie's team would say—will lose their shit. All they will want is to be the ones who destroyed the Witch of the Federation."

Rawlins sat in silence for a long moment before she sighed heavily. "I agree. If the Dreth have searched the system for the Telorans and have not found them, the quickest way to get them into the open is to draw them out. The *Knight* and her Witch are probably the only bait that will do it. Knight?"

"I like this plan," the ship told them, her voice filled with glee. "My crews are hungry for another kill."

The two women exchanged startled looks.

After a moment, Stephanie asked, "Knight, have you been talking to the cats?"

The *Knight* chuckled. "Of course not, Stephanie. The cats are very bright but they are not sentient. I have merely listened to the Marines as they train in the Virtual World provided."

The captain groaned. "There *are* better examples to learn from, Ebony."

"Not for small-team strategy and tactics," the ship retorted tartly. "I think even you would find them enlightening."

"Fine." Rawlins turned her attention to Stephanie. "What does Admiral Jaleck think of this approach?"

"The admiral isn't aware of it," she told her. "I wanted to run it by you first and take it to the admiral to get her help to set up an ambush. You didn't think we would face them alone, did you?"

"The thought had crossed my mind," the woman admitted, "but I'm glad you're not as crazy as everyone says you are."

"They do?" Stephanie was shocked.

Rawlins chuckled. "No, but the look on your face was worth it. Shall we call the admiral?"

"Please," she replied. "I want to see if *she* thinks I'm as crazy as everyone says I am."

Elizabeth's plan almost came unstuck the second she and her team passed through the gates. Bolivar's crew were checking residency. They watched as one vehicle was turned away.

"E-BURT, what is that all about?"

"I need...and done," the AI replied. "You should be free to pass through."

"What do you mean *should*?"

"I mean this vehicle is now registered as belonging to a resident of this complex. Said resident is at home, but I do not think the team is checking occupancy, merely license plates."

"You'd better hope not," she retorted, "or we are in a serious world of hurt."

"I doubt you would be hurt," E-BURT responded. "However, Todd and Stephanie's parents would suffer for the delay."

"They're moving early?"

"It appears they have stepped up their timetable by a half-hour. They were in position early and see no reason to delay."

"Step on it, Eeb. I want to be there sooner rather than later."

She kept her hands clamped around the steering wheel, her knuckles white. When the car did not accelerate, she stamped on the gas. It still didn't accelerate. "Eeb!"

"We do not wish to attract attention, Elizabeth. I am sure Emerald will confirm it."

"Dammit! I *am* Emerald!"

"Then you should know better," he informed her primly.

She leaned her head back on the headrest and gritted her teeth. Taking a deep breath, she forced her head back in the game. This was not the way she needed to be.

Hell! This was not the way she usually was. What the hell was wrong with her?

"It's harder when it's someone you know," Arne told her and he sounded like he'd been there.

The car slowed and Lisa and Bunny stepped out. Both women made a show of scanning the area around the building before they moved warily inside. Elizabeth smiled as they entered, their heads turning as they continued to study their environment.

"They look like they've stepped out of the battlefield," Matthias murmured.

"Good," she told him. "That's exactly what we want the Bolivars to think."

"Oh, they will," Matthias assured her. "Whether they'll let them get inside or not, that's a whole different question."

She immediately looked worried. "You're thinking snipers?"

"It's what I would do."

The car moved on but not before Bunny and Lisa passed through the apartment building's doors.

"We're here," Bunny informed them a short moment later.

"Gotcha," Elizabeth acknowledged.

The car turned into the underground car park and glided to a halt outside the elevator and stairwell. To her relief, Bolivar's watchfulness hadn't extended to a guard on the car park entry.

They probably think it's enough to stop unauthorized vehicles, she thought and wondered why she'd ever thought them good enough.

Because assassination is what they're good at, not protection, she reminded herself, slipped from the car, and dropped into a crouch in the shadows beside it.

Matthias followed suit and used the car as cover as he scanned the parking lot, while Arne and Amy moved quickly out of camera range. Elle bobbed down on the other side of the vehicle.

"I have the cameras," E-BURT told them, "and the footage shows the car park is clear. As this is now a residential vehicle, I will find a parking space to avoid arousing suspicions at the gate. No one watching the flat will know it did not leave."

His words jolted through Elizabeth, and she froze.

"Dammit!" She straightened.

Man, I am off my game. She hadn't thought of what would happen if Bolivar's teams compared notes on the vehicles coming and going.

"I am inside their communications," E-BURT informed her. "I will warn you if they notice."

"Thank you, E-BURT."

She led the way into the elevator and Amy stepped alongside her.

"Are you all right, boss? 'Cause I can take the elevator if you like." She cast a coquettish look at Matthias. "I'm *very* flexible."

Her gaze strayed momentarily to Arne and her cheeks colored. Elizabeth pretended not to notice but she made a note to nail the woman down on that particular subject later because Arne seemed oblivious.

"We stick to the plan," she replied coldly.

People had targeted what was hers, and she would destroy every last one of them. Amy caught the look on her face and nodded as though satisfied by what she saw.

"Gotcha." She didn't add anything, and the two guards who'd gone ahead checked in.

Bunny's report was short and sweet. "Mine are in the box."

Lisa's was even shorter. "Ditto."

"Hold your positions," Elizabeth ordered as the elevator slowed to a stop on the floor below.

Amy slapped her on the shoulder. "Have fun, boss."

She, Elle, and Arne stepped out as soon as the doors slid open. Matthias hesitated as if on the brink of saying goodbye, but his mouth tightened and he turned decisively toward the stairs. The thought that he might die slid through her mind, and she tensed, her Emerald persona slipping a fraction before she caught it and pulled it firmly into place again.

By that time, he was gone. The doors slid closed behind him and all chance of saying anything was gone. She shook herself impatiently.

"Get it together, girl. Shit like that will get you killed."

E ran a quick calculation of how likely she was to be shot if she stood in the elevator when it came to a halt and came down on the side of being seen as a woman and not much of a threat. After all, no one knew exactly what Emerald looked like and the helmet and HUD would hide most of her face and her identity.

The bell dinged, and the doors slid open to reveal the reception.

It was empty.

She frowned, scanned the area, and stepped out. Quickly, she moved to the reception counter and decided whoever was standing there would quickly find themselves the first casualty of the attackers.

"It might as well be me, then," she murmured and took position behind the front desk.

The wait was much shorter than she expected.

Bolivar's men entered reception and their leader crossed to the counter flanked by two others.

"Can I help you?" she asked and pasted a professional smile on her face.

He scrutinized her in silence and his gaze noted the combat armor, fatigues, and the rifle she had slung across her chest.

"We're here to relieve you," he stated, and the men beside him moved.

Well, fuck me. Subtle they ain't, Elizabeth thought and took cover. To her relief and chagrin, the compartment beneath the desk was firmly closed and she hoped one of the girls would be able to tell her that Franklin and his sidekick were inside it.

She also hoped they were unconscious and without their communicators. The last thing she needed was a firefight with Federation Police.

"Come out of there with your hands up!"

Elizabeth stifled a laugh. *As if!* She shifted as quietly as she could away from where she'd been standing and angled the rifle up. The minute she saw him look toward her, his head was gone.

The sound of heavy boots moving swiftly across the foyer reached her. It sounded like the other two had started toward the door. She tensed and readied herself to dart up from behind the counter and shoot whoever she saw first. If she was very lucky, Bolivar's leader wasn't waiting for *her* head to appear the same way she anticipated seeing his.

As she shifted in preparation, she heard his feet move and he called. "Mal?"

The second cry that reached her must have been shriekingly clear over the team's communications and she winced. If someone didn't call that in, the apartments had better soundproofing than she thought. Someone wasn't playing fair.

She bolted from behind the counter like a cork out of a bottle and fired in the same moment. Across the room, the door to the stairwell opened and Matthias came in low and fast. His dive took him to the other side of the door leading to the Brogan's apartment and he fired as he found his feet.

The scream and her sudden appearance had distracted the lead assassin. His weapon raised rapidly enough, but his aim was off and her shots caught him in the chest and head before he had time to rectify his mistake.

Elizabeth was in motion before his body landed and tried to get clear of the counter before the next man could make his mind up who to shoot next. He hesitated a moment too long, and she reached the alcove between the end of the counter and the door to the Morgans' apartment. She shot the man at the door as she slid into cover.

He fell and Matthias fired again, and Elle slipped out of the stairwell. She skirted the edge of the room as the men who'd entered between when Elizabeth ducked into cover and Arne or Amy eliminated their colleague outside who had homed in on Matthias.

They were slow to change focus, and Elle's armor-piercing rounds were more effective for the closer range. The hit squad hadn't come prepared for this kind of resistance.

The elevator door dinged, and Elizabeth pivoted toward it. It seemed they weren't the only ones who thought to use *all* the entries. She glanced toward the stairwell as Matthias and Amy closed with the third and fourth members of the team.

The elevator door remained closed.

"I have two in custody," E-BURT told her. "Do you need them for questioning?"

"Open the door, Eeb!" Elizabeth commanded, then called, "Heads up! Elevator!"

"I got you!" Matthias pivoted to face it and trusted Elle to have his back. He fired before the doors opened, his guns joining Elizabeth's in a staccato chorus.

They dropped the two men who prepared to surge out of it. At the same time, Elle delivered a barrage into the next soldier and walked her shots up his chest and into his throat.

That took care of the vanguard. Elizabeth and Matthias came together and pivoted to search for other targets. They were in time to see Arne and Amy coordinate perfectly timed strikes to eliminate the last two members of the team, shooting across each other's line of fire before they moved forward and put a bullet into each fallen man as they went.

"Cold," Matthias murmured, and she snorted.

One of the would-be assassins groaned and he shot him in the face.

"Pot and kettle," Elizabeth retorted and shot one of her own. He'd been reaching for a nearby rifle, so she followed it up by making sure of the others closest to him.

Matthias arched his eyebrows. "You were saying?"

"Eebie, did you hire that clean-up crew like I asked you?" she demanded and paled. "Dammit. I forgot about the team on the gate."

"They came up in the elevator," E-BURT informed her. "Shall I tell Bunny she can come out now?"

"No. Tell Bunny and Lisa to get the parents packed. We'll move whatever they can't take with them, but I want them out in ten minutes. Bolivar has three teams. I won't gamble their lives on the possibility that the other two are so far out of position that they can't be brought up on short notice."

"Are you saying they're not safe here?" Matthias asked. "Not ever again?"

Elizabeth gave him a cold, hard look. "I'm saying they've been driven off their world. Eebie, I want the shuttle brought over and I don't need you to be subtle so much as fast."

"Although subtle would be good," Matthias added hastily.

She narrowed her eyes and pursed her lips but she didn't correct him.

Instead, she ordered, "Arne, Matthias, Amy, you're with me. Elle, take over reception. Meet the cleaners and stand by to deter anyone else."

"Gotcha. Mind the desk and don't shoot anyone who doesn't shoot at me first," the woman confirmed. "It's a good thing I had Bunny take a jacket off one of the concierges, isn't it?"

"You did?"

"Yup. He wasn't happy about it and said if we got blood on it, we had to pay for a replacement."

"He knows us too well."

"I didn't think he knew us at all."

"It's the type," Matthias explained. "The man knows the type. He must have come in contact with someone similar before."

"Uh-huh." Elizabeth didn't bother to ask how he could know that but led the way down the stairs at a trot.

E-BURT had already brought the car around. Arne pushed past Elizabeth and beat her to the driver's seat, and Amy took the front passenger position. Elizabeth and Matthias exchanged glances but didn't argue and they settled into the back in silence.

The two in front kept an eye on their surroundings, and Matthias kept an eye on Elizabeth as her fingers flew over her tablet.

"Do you think they'll buy it?" he asked as they drove out through the gates.

She raised her head, registered where they were, and stowed her tablet. "What?"

"That there was a security team protecting the parents."

"That's what the footage will show—right, Eebie?"

"You were all very convincing," E-BURT assured them and his voice went from warm and affirming to cold. "There is a second team."

Arne slewed the car around and accelerated into a side street just inside the complex's entrance. He pulled to the curb and killed the engine and lights. They twisted in their seats and waited for the second team to arrive, while Amy warned Lisa and Bunny.

"Get them into their boxes again," the girl warned. "You too. E is taking care of this one."

While she did that, Arne called Elle and told her to stay out of sight and let them pass.

"We don't want to start anything out here," Matthias murmured, and Elizabeth's head snapped up.

The look on her face was enough to freeze blood, but before she could say anything, a small, sleek flying car dropped from the sky. Arne started the engine and followed, keeping the lights off, and timed their arrival for the moment when its occupants blew the door to the Brogans' apartment.

"Make sure you leave them alive," Elizabeth all but snarled and bolted from the vehicle.

She didn't bother about subtle but moved through the dead as if they were training obstacles and fired at the first figure she saw inside the apartment. Her first shot missed his head as she remembered her instructions and jerked her hand aside.

"There *are* two of them," E-BURT reminded her.

"Yeah? Well, I want to send a very clear message," she snapped. Her next shot impacted body armor and made her target stumble back.

"You bitch!"

"Understatement of the *year*," she retorted acidly and shot him again as she closed.

He returned fire as she threw herself into a roll and came up under his gun. Matthias compromised his aim when he shot him in the shoulder. Again, the body armor saved him from any serious damage.

It did not save him when Elizabeth found her feet in front of him, activated her vibro-blade, and sliced through the armor to the man beneath. As his scream subsided to troubled breathing, she dragged him close and spoke into his ear.

"Tell your employer he chose the wrong target and is now a very dead man, regardless of what organization he works for. *Nowhere* is safe. Tell him. Do you understand?" She wasn't interested in his answer but let him fall, yanked the blade out, and tapped his headset. "*Maybe* he'll reach you before you bleed out."

"What about this one?" Amy asked and dumped his partner beside him.

He was bleeding as heavily as the man E had targeted and neither of them resisted as she and Arne stripped their weapons.

She shrugged. "Two means the message might get through. What about the pilot?"

"The vehicle has lifted," E-BURT informed her. "I can bring it down but the pilot is not guaranteed to survive."

"Make it so."

A sudden whine of engines under strain was followed by a loud bang.

"My bad," the AI observed but didn't sound at all worried.

Elizabeth called Bunny and Lisa. "Don't worry about packing. Grab what they have and get them out of here. Eebie is sending the shuttle."

"I am?"

"You'd darned well better be." She surveyed the apartment once more and noted that Arne had brought a roll of duct tape and Amy now helped him secure their two messengers.

"Do you want me to make sure they don't bleed out before they talk to whoever they need to?" the other woman asked, and she shook her head.

"I left them their comms for a reason."

CHAPTER TWENTY

The *Knight* dropped into the Dreth system not far from the usual arrival point for ships from Earth. She came in quietly as though trying to avoid detection. It was difficult to make it look like she was hiding when she was trying so hard to be seen.

"Do you think it worked?" Stephanie asked from her place at the back of the command center.

"Give it time," Rawlins told her. "We won't know how well it worked until they appear."

"I hate this part," she grumbled.

Darkness seeped into her expression, and the captain had the impression the Morgana was as impatient as her host. Keeping a wary eye on the girl, she hoped the Teloran had been telling the truth and that Stephanie did, in fact, have her under control.

She shivered to think of what would happen if the being connected to her ever took the helm of the Federation's most powerful mage.

That aside, she'd give her eye teeth to know what transpired on the Teloran bridge.

"Storm Commander!"

The Teloran captain moved her attention from the boards. Her look was command enough for the officer on scans to continue.

"The Witch just jumped into the system."

"Are the Dreth aware of her presence?"

"I see no movement from either fleet and she has not hailed them. She has kept communications silence and isn't using the usual approach."

The captain hunched over her boards and brought up the relevant scan so she could inspect it for herself. "Are you saying she is attempting to go unseen?"

"It is hard to believe, Commander, but yes."

"Are the Dreth aware of our location?"

She did not ask if they were aware of their presence. That much had become clear in the last few days as Dreth scouts flew search patterns around their planet. They were aware that *something* was observing their world but behaved as though they weren't sure what —or perhaps where—it was.

"Did the Dreth call for help?" she demanded and the officers crewing the communications startled guiltily.

"There are no calls for help in the communications we can decipher, either fleet internal or out-of-system."

The captain immediately caught their meaning. "And what of communications that you *haven't* been able to decipher? Have there been many of those?"

"Two," the lead communications officer replied, and she heard the tremor in his voice.

"When and how long?"

"Both within the last twenty-four to forty-eight hours," he replied. "The second was much longer than the first."

"And the reply?"

"We were unable to track the signal," came the reluctant reply.

That admission sent a ripple of unease through her. "Explain," she demanded.

"We cannot. The signal entered the system and we could not determine its system of origin."

The officers on the bridge held their collective breaths—and well they might. The fact that the communications officers had not reported the communication was a severe breach of trust and one she would deal with once the immediate problem had been solved.

"It is only one ship," she told them. "A powerful ship, granted, but alone."

She gestured to the forward viewscreen where the position of the Dreth fleet was clearly marked. "They're too far away to reach her before we destroy her and it is about time someone taught the Earth child a lesson."

"Losing her would take the heart from *all* who would stand before us."

"Don't be too sure. The humans have a history of fighting hardest when all hope is lost, and both the Dreth and Meligornians have strong cultures of vengeance when it comes to fallen heroes."

The captain paused and scanned the command center for any sign of dissent as she told them what they would do.

"The Witch is alone and vulnerable," she told them. "Her allies cannot reach her before we can obliterate her from the sky. The whole planet will see her die. Today, we will achieve two major coups."

She paused to give her next words more weight. "We will destroy the Federation's only true Witch, but we will also tear the heart from the Dreth resistance. This world *will* be ours."

Her words were met with fierce cheers and she raised a hand to command silence.

"Scans, watch the Dreth fleet. They've been practicing maneuvers for the last three hours and that might not be a coincidence. Communications, jam all signals in system bar our own. I don't want them to call for help. Weapons, destroy any message torps before they skip."

"Yes, Storm Commander!" reverberated across the bridge, and the Teloran captain studied the Witch's ship.

Today, you will be mine.

Her thoughts were interrupted almost as soon as they broke cover and revealed their presence to everyone scanning the system for intruders.

"Captain, the Dreth—"

"I see it. Evasion sequences three, four, and nine."

"Sir, they set a trap!" The leading scans officer was outraged.

"So they did," the captain acknowledged, "but it won't do them any good."

Her words were proven as the ship surged forward and down and pivoted sharply out of the Dreth line of fire. Their missiles were misaimed and too slow, and she felt a grim satisfaction to have outwitted the battle-hardened enemy captains.

Their admiral had positioned her ships to pincer anything attacking the Witch's ship. That, at least, explained the reason behind the encrypted calls.

She decided to make an example of the communications crew on duty at the time. Even though knowing of the calls' existence would have been little use without decryption, she should still have received a report.

The Dreth are smart, she thought, *but their intelligence is flawed.*

"Sir! They're attacking."

The captain allowed herself a small chuckle. "Of course they are. They were smart enough to set this up but they missed."

"Sir?"

"They don't understand the full speed of a Teloran Capital-class ship." She waved a hand at the screen. "They're going too slow. Helm full ahead. All weapons, target the Witch."

She smiled as the vessel surged beneath her.

On the Dreth ships, dismay was quickly followed by organized chaos. Klaxons rang and emergency stations were filled.

"Full ahead!" was chorused across every command deck, and Admiral Jaleck gaped in disbelief at both the Teloran vessel's size and its speed.

"It's a Teloran ship of the line," she murmured as her captain addressed her.

"Ma'am, we'll be late," he told her. "She's moving at least thirty percent faster than we expected."

She dropped into her seat. "Go to Plan B."

"Yes, ma'am!"

The admiral waited as the captain relayed her orders and brought the fleet into position.

May Hrageth have mercy, she thought and hoped the Witch's plan worked. *We can't afford to lose her.*

On the *Ebon Knight's* bridge, Captain Rawlins saw the Teloran ship accelerate and rapidly outdistance its Dreth pursuers. "Here they come."

Silence greeted her and she glanced at Stephanie.

The girl's eyes were fixed on the screen and her lip curled as she watched the enemy approach. Her face showed satisfaction with the outcome and her whole body was tense with anticipation.

A closer look at her face revealed that the Morgana had not yet been given control. Her eyes, although edged with darkness, still blazed blue.

Heaven help me, Rawlins thought. *The Morgana isn't the only one looking forward to this fight. Our Witch is itching to take them on too.*

As the thought crossed her mind, Stephanie spoke, her voice hard with anger and determination.

"Attack my people?" the girl whispered. "You pissed off the wrong Witch!"

Her people, the captain thought and allowed herself a small hard smile. *This Witch is the true heart of the Federation if she claims the Dreth as her own.*

"Give me the comms," Stephanie ordered, and it was still her despite the fact that the Morgana's coldness seeped into her voice.

The communications officer looked at Rawlins, and the captain nodded.

"Knight, do you have the Telorans' frequency?" the Witch asked as soon as she received the go-ahead.

"I do."

"Hail her."

The *Knight* did as she asked and the enemy captain appeared on the screen. It was hard to see what she was thinking but it was all too easy to hear the satisfaction in her tone.

As Stephanie spoke in Teloran, the *Knight* relayed the translation to the command crew's earpieces.

"This world is under my protection," she stated. "Leave now and I will let you live."

Her adversary's chuckle rolled over the bridge and several of the crew reached for their weapons.

"You do not know how pleased I am to have you confirm your presence on that ship, Witch."

"Why are you here?"

"To observe and report," the Teloran replied. "Why else?"

"Yet you revealed yourself to meet me?" she asked. "I am flattered."

"Your execution is long overdue."

"I don't think so."

"Aaand there she goes," Lars murmured as the Morgana's tones reverberated through the command center.

"How about *my* execution?" she demanded, "or did you think a mere mountain would be sufficient? Tell the Corevex their rule must end and our people must be freed."

The enemy captain drew a sharp breath. "Who are you?"

The Morgana responded with a soft sinister laugh. "Don't you remember me?"

"I don't even know you."

Stephanie took a couple of steps forward so she stood closer to the pick-up. "How about now?"

"I would say I was sorry but your death will erase you from this system and who you are will remain insignificant."

"Do our people forget their heroes so easily? Are none of my stories told?"

"Humans have no stories. They are lower beings to be used like cattle and bent to our will and purpose."

"No sentient is less than our equal," the Morgana declared, "or have you not heard my speech?"

The Teloran recoiled and the Morgana's face lit up.

"Ah, I see you *do* remember me. Now, leave."

"Old ghosts do not frighten me," the captain sneered. "If my ancestors did not kill you properly, I can easily finish their task."

As she spoke, she turned away from the screen.

"I'm sure she is speaking," Rawlins observed but none of them heard anything until she turned to face them again.

"Torpedoes away." The alert came from the scan team as the viewscreen showed several clusters of small bright dots launch away from the Teloran vessel.

"Message torps away," advised the weapons team. "We can't get them all. She's using the ship to shield them."

"Leave them," Captain Rawlins commanded. "The Dreth have it covered."

"Aye aye, captain."

"Let me know if they miss any."

"Will do, ma'am."

"Fuck, that is a big ship," one of the scan technicians muttered but neither Stephanie nor the captain responded.

"What makes you think you are in a position to finish anything?" the Morgana challenged.

"Your ship is outclassed," the Teloran retorted. "How dare you challenge one of our ships of the line with that...that *toy* and think you have any hope of victory? Who do you think you are to even try? Whatever you might have been in the past, it was certainly no tactician. You are out-massed and out-gunned, a primitive bow against a blaster. Your ship is too small to stand a chance."

"It's not the size of the foe that matters," she told her as Stephanie stamped her foot.

"Who said our side had the smallest ship?" the girl demanded in her voice, her eyes as clear as a summer sky.

"Captain…" the lead scan technician began, and Rawlins glanced at her boards.

"Fire!" she ordered. "All batteries, all guns, fire! Cut that bitch down to size."

"Roger that," the weapons team replied as they relayed her orders and the *Knight's* gunners answered the threat against their ship.

A cry of alarm issued from the scan team, and the forward viewscreen lit up to show a large mass coming up on the *Knight* from behind.

Lars and Vishlog dove for Stephanie at the same time as Rawlins, but they all came to a skidding halt as magic wreathed her form. Strands of it reached below the *Knight's* deck to secure the girl as she wove her hands in a complex pattern. On the screen, the movement of her hands was reflected by the flight path of several purple discs that materialized outside the ship.

The Morgana laughed and Lars swore. "Fuck."

"Hold on!" Avery cried from the co-pilot's seat as Wattlebird gave a whoop of glee.

Lars and Vishlog advanced on her but didn't close. The writhing magic kept them at bay.

"Wattlebird, if you break my ship, I'll break your neck," the captain shouted.

"You'll need to get in line," the *Knight* told her tartly. "If he so much as stresses a single strut, he will have a very unpleasant time."

"Knight, when have I ever…" Wattlebird asked and gritted his teeth as his brow furrowed in concentration. "Just. Hold. On."

Proximity alarms blared, and the mass on the screen loomed closer, closing at speed.

"What the fuck is that?" Lars demanded and Stephanie laughed.

"It's the *Tempestarii*," she told him. "She's shadowed us ever since we jumped into the system."

"You could have told me," he protested as the super-titan roared past them and her guns came alive.

All her guns plus several arrays of torpedoes as Wattlebird altered the *Knight's* trajectory so her lines of fire did not threaten the larger vessel.

"Cease fire!" Rawlins commanded, but her eyes were on the screen like everyone else's.

"Holy *fuck*!" Lars exclaimed as the Teloran ship bucked, ruptured, and spewed fire and air before she shuddered and simply ceased to exist. "Where did it go?"

"Stephanie, you need to tell One R&D Meligorn that their latest toys are a resounding success," Emil said loud and clear. He was jubilant and she could imagine the scenes aboard the *Tempestarii* as the weapons crews celebrated.

She wondered how long it would take them to work out there was no way to tell which of them had fired the killing blow and how much longer it would take the bookmakers to tear their books up.

The *Tempestarii* did not slow. She raced past them and faded slowly from sight and the scanner display.

"Wh...where did she go?" Lars asked for the second time. He stared at the screen and searched for any sign of the ship.

"Back," Stephanie replied enigmatically.

"You do realize that everyone saw that?" he asked and turned to face her.

Stephanie pinched her lower lip. "I hope not," she told him. "Jaleck said her people would only get limited data from this angle. She pulled them back early and only the flagship can scan this far with any real clarity. With any luck, they'll think the *Tempestarii* was a blur on the screen or a glitch in the system."

"You'd better hope so," he told her darkly, "because I don't think the universe is ready for her yet."

"What was all that about, E?" Matthias demanded as they returned to the car once Stephanie and Todd's parents were bundled into a shuttle with Bunny and Lisa.

"I wanted to make sure the message was sent," she replied shortly.

"Another dead hit squad should have been sufficient," he told her and she snorted.

"We already gave them one dead squad and they tried again. I wanted to make it clearer this time."

"Do you know exactly *who* you have threatened?" Arne asked from the driver's seat.

He steered the car through the late-night streets of a sleeping city, his eyes worried.

"Nope," she told him, "and neither do you."

"I have a fair idea. These are not people you want to fuck with, E."

She gave him a hard stare. "Neither are we. A message needed to be sent."

"Uh-huh," Matthias replied.

"And what's that supposed to mean?" she demanded.

"It means that *maybe* I think you're being more protective than usual because Steph's parents were close to Todd's."

"A message needed to be sent," she insisted and neither confirmed nor denied what he'd said.

"Fine," he told her. "Be that way, but you know exactly what I'm saying."

"That you agree with me wholeheartedly and don't want me to kick your ass," she informed him, and he shook his head and decided to let things lie—at least for now.

They ended the drive in silence and she headed directly to the briefing room where the four jammers were still active. As soon as they were all inside and Arne had secured the door, she spoke.

"Eebie, get me Steph. I need her help to get the parents out of here. They aren't safe on Earth."

"How secure do you want this call?" he asked and Elizabeth rolled her eyes.

"As secure as you can make it and still get it to her in the next ten minutes."

"There will be some lag," he informed her.

"Use the new tech and reduce it. I need to speak to Steph and Marianne as of yesterday!"

"Very well."

She paced as she waited, but her face lit up when Steph appeared on the viewscreen with a cat on either side.

"Steph! It's good to see you."

A new screen opened and Captain Rawlins' face appeared.

Stephanie continued regardless. "It's good to see you, too, E." She smiled but it faded suddenly. "What have you been doing?"

"Taking care of business," Elizabeth told her in clipped tones, "which brings me to why I've called. I need a favor."

"I take it this is Emerald's business," she suggested, and E nodded.

"Oh, it most definitely is, and I'm about to make some strenuous business decisions."

"And you need my help?"

She gave an internal sigh of relief that the girl wouldn't argue and nodded.

"What can I do?" Stephanie asked.

"I need you to plan to come to Earth to pick up a few people when you've finished whatever you're doing."

"What kind of timeframe are you looking at? I have a few things lined up but nothing that means a trip to Earth is out of the question."

"As soon as you're able?" she queried, reluctant to demand that the girl return immediately.

Of course, she didn't have to. Stephanie picked it up immediately. "So tomorrow, then?"

Elizabeth took one look at her face and realized she was teasing her. She smiled in response.

"Yesterday would have been better."

"I'll see what we can do," Rawlins interrupted. She nodded to Elizabeth. "Good to see you, E."

"And you."

"I'll get back to Steph as soon as I've checked our itinerary," the captain told her by way of goodbye and her screen went blank, leaving Matthias, Arne, and Amy staring at it open-mouthed.

"Is she always that—" Arne began.

"Abrupt?" Matthias finished for him.

"Are you kidding?" E asked. "That was Marianne on one of her better days. Honestly, you're lucky she spoke at all."

Stephanie snickered but sobered quickly. "I'll call you when I know."

She glanced over her shoulder, then back to the screen. "I have to go." Her face softened. "It was good to see you, E."

"Good to see you, too, Steph," Elizabeth replied and they cut the connection at the same time.

"Right!" she snapped and turned to survey the room.

"You didn't tell her who she was collecting," Matthias pointed out, and she gave him a humorless smile.

"It's a surprise," she told him. "Now…"

He waited, but she didn't finish that sentence. Instead, she paced between the jammers to make sure they were working and checked the door again. Finally satisfied that the room was as secure as it had been before, she turned and her gaze swept over Arne, Amy, Matthias, and E-BURT's construct.

"This asshole will die, and he will die with my hands strangling what useless excuse for life he has out of him."

Ice coated her words and the room seemed to vibrate with anger. Arne raised his head as though looking for danger before he exchanged worried looks with the other two.

Elizabeth did not need to know what passed between them. She only needed to know what their faces told her—that they would follow her to whatever end she led them.

Matthias inclined his head as though to confirm her thoughts, but she could not read his. He was thinking of the night she had sent him out to protect him from what she and Arne were about to do and he recognized that the woman standing before him wasn't only his Elizabeth.

Emerald was back with a vengeance.

CHAPTER TWENTY-ONE

Several hours later, Admiral Jaleck ushered Stephanie into her office.

"How clear were the scans?" the girl asked.

"Clear enough to show something big coming in, but not clear enough to show what it was. There are arguments as to whether it was another Teloran ship that flew into the *Knight's* line of fire or a glitch in the system," the admiral told her. "That was an incredible risk you took."

"Your world was at stake," she replied. "We'd have flown her into visual range if that was what was required to save it."

Jaleck gave her a fond look and placed a hand on her shoulder. "I know. Dreth thanks you once again. I thank you once again."

"Was that the only Teloran vessel in the system?" she asked and the admiral quirked an eyebrow.

"Why? D'you think one would have stayed in hiding with the Morgana teasing them about their failed ancestors? Or with the Federation's first Witch in easy reach?"

Stephanie smiled and shook her head. "No. I guess I only wanted to make sure you were all right for us to leave."

"We know you will come to our aid if we need you," Jaleck told her. "That is good enough for us." She paused, then added, "I knew you'd want the *Tempestarii* armed, but I had *no* idea she was so operational."

"It's Emil's ship," she reminded her. "He might want a ship with a quieter role, but no one wants an unarmed ship."

"Ship?" the Dreth teased. "That monster is a roving, silent, deadly space station." She took a breath before she added, "And invisible. She's a menace."

The Witch tilted her head, her brow furrowed in thought.

"Yes," she admitted and a smile tugged at the corners of her mouth. "She *is*, but she's *our* space station."

"This meeting is called to order." Admiral Amaratne tapped his water glass with a pen and the gathered officers fell slowly into silence.

When they all looked expectantly at him, he began.

"We need to decide how we will fight them," he began, swept his gaze around the table, and noted who rolled their eyes and who nodded in agreement.

Neither gesture was indicative of support. Some of his most ardent supporters shook their heads at him when he stated the obvious. They rolled their eyes too, and some of his most vociferous opposition nodded in agreement while sharpening the daggers they planned to plunge into his back.

"Well, sir," Admiral Burtch ventured. "First, we have to find them."

His response brought several huffs of amusement and a groan or two of impatience.

"A very good point," Amaratne told him. "That ties in nicely with one of the things we need to discuss."

He turned to a thinly built man with thick dark hair. "Admiral Otto, perhaps you could update us on your, uh...project."

Otto rose from his seat and picked his tablet up. He tapped lightly with one finger and the screen at the head of the room changed. As loathe as he was to turn his back on his fellow-admirals, the fleet admiral needed to see what the man had brought to the table. He had worked on this project for months.

Murmurs of curiosity and appreciation rose from the officers behind him, but he didn't look back. He was too busy feasting his eyes on the scene ahead. At first, it looked like an empty asteroid belt with a field of stars behind it.

Otto tapped his screen with a single finger and the asteroids and stars rippled. He tapped it again and the wavery outline that Amaratne had at first mistaken for a trick of the light—or his tired eyes misbehaving—became a single dark shape.

"What is that?" someone asked on a breath of wonder.

"It's beautiful," was the response from another corner of the room.

"What *is* it?" another echoed.

Otto tapped again and the image rippled into nothing.

Several gasps were followed by hurriedly muttered conversation.

"These are the ships we have watching the Teloran fleet—the one we know about," Amaratne told them. "From the way they are behaving, we don't think the ships gathered here are all of them."

The screen shifted and panned until the view was the same as the one the scout ship would see.

It took them a moment but suddenly, the penny dropped.

"That... You're not receiving that *real* time, are you?"

The fleet admiral shook his head. "No. There is some time delay but not as much as you'd expect. We're trying a new technique that involves skip technology but have applied the principles to burst transmission."

"You're what?"

Otto opened his mouth to explain but Amaratne waved him to silence as per the discussion they'd had earlier.

"I don't know who's cleared to hear what, sir," the man had explained when his superior had approached him. "If you raise a topic in that meeting and it's not ready to go out, I won't know."

"I'll wave at you to stop," he had assured him, "like this. Okay?"

"Do it again," Otto had demanded and he had obliged patiently as the man learned the gesture.

He was a brilliant scientist and a strategic genius, but he was terrible with people and body language. At least he was smart enough to recognize the problem and want help in dealing with it. Now, he was glad he'd listened to the man's concerns.

Otto subsided and Amaratne stepped in to deflect the conversation away from the proprietary tech. He made a note of those who had shown interest, knowing it would be natural for any admiral to be excited by the possibilities but aware that some could have other reasons for it.

Those with investments in communications, for example.

One of the officers had a more salient question. "With all due respect, exactly what the *fuck* are we looking at, sir?"

"Don't you recognize the ship type?" he asked, amused by the looks on their faces.

He stood and moved to one side of the room where he could better see everyone and still keep an eye on the screen. At the same time, he kicked himself for not having the room rearranged slightly so everyone could see the screen without him needing to move to watch them at the same time.

"Are those...those are Teloran ships."

"That is correct Admiral Burtch."

"How are you... *Where...*" The man closed his mouth and his face reddened as he gestured at the screen.

"That location is currently classified," Amaratne told him. "Needless to say, it's in a location where it poses no immediate threat to anyone, but it wouldn't take them long to transition to somewhere they would."

The man swallowed nervously. "But...how did the scouts get so close? The Meligornians reported having ships in the same system as the Telorans and all they got back were message torps—and not very many of those either, given how many were fired in the hope of warning the home system of the attack."

One of the other admirals nodded, his chin and mouth resting against the knuckles of one hand as he studied the screen.

"And how long have you observed them?" another admiral asked.

"We've observed them for a couple of weeks," he told him. "As to *how* we're managing that?"

He smiled and knew every gaze was fixed on him. "We're trialing a new stealth technology, the specifics of which I am not at liberty to discuss."

A glance at Admiral Otto when he said this confirmed that the man had caught the hidden message in his words. If the fleet admiral was unwilling to discuss the technology whys and wherefores, he should be as well.

"Can it...have you managed to get any closer?" another asked.

Amaratne shook his head. "This is about the limit," he replied. "We've made a number of trial runs, but this is where we are currently at. That's not to say we aren't working on it. Ideally, we want to get alongside and scan for any weaknesses."

"I take it you are working on changing that, sir?" the admiral asked as follow-up to his initial question.

"Indeed," he said neutrally and refused to confirm the assumption.

His colleague persisted.

"And will that technology be tweaked for bigger ships?"

His question was met by approving mutters and hopeful looks greeted Amaratne's assessing stare. He decided to squash that rumor before it even began.

"Not at this time, but you will be the first to know if it changes," he assured them.

One of the admirals returned to an earlier point. "Sir, you mentioned that you had been observing this fleet for a couple of weeks. Is there any reason why we haven't moved to destroy it?"

Out of all the questions they'd asked, this was the one he had expected—albeit much sooner. He smiled and signaled Otto to return to his seat.

The man took a moment to work out what he wanted and relief crossed his features as he hurried to the chair he'd vacated. As soon as he had settled, Amaratne dropped his next little bombshell.

"We haven't called our forces to attack them because we don't think this is the entire fleet." He waited for their soft cries of protest to die down and explained. "From the transmissions we have intercepted, we believe that either the remainder of the fleet is still en route from whatever world spawned them *or* that a *second* fleet is coming."

He paused to let his words sink in and watched their faces change as they digested the news.

The swarm of ships the scout was monitoring did not represent everything the Telorans had.

More were on their way.

A world away, V'ritan arrived at One R&D Meligorn's gates with the king. They were met by the research facility's head and a small contingent of scientists. The mixed human and Meligornian staff seemed in awe of their visitors and their security teams.

"Come this way, Your Majesty, *Garghilum Afreghil,*" Brelif requested after the traditional bows and hand gestures had been exchanged. "We have prepared a secure room for the briefing."

Knowing BURT's penchant for securing "his" discoveries and the future of his company, V'ritan believed it. He gestured for the administrator to lead them and took the time to admire the way the facility had grown since he and the king had declared it officially open.

"There are many more buildings than I remember," he noted, and the director's face lit with pride.

"The number of projects has expanded, many of which needed specialized facilities."

"Indeed?" King Grilfir's tone invited more details.

The director startled as if the king had slapped him. "Not that we are neglecting your latest request, Your Majesty—"

"I did not think you were," Grilfir hastened to assure him. "I merely thought how impressed I was at the speed at which you were adapting to the exponential demands Meligorn has placed on you. It can't be easy."

This time, the director colored with pleasure rather than guilt. "Your Majesty...we have the very best of people."

He glanced at his assistant, a blonde woman with coffee-colored skin and luminous green eyes, and his lips curved in mischief. "Even the human members of our teams never cease to astound us."

She groaned. "You still haven't forgiven that explosion, have you?" He winked at V'ritan as the woman continued. "Are you saying a Meligornian *wouldn't* have attempted to blend eMU with Mu using something that had been touched by nMU? Because I can cite several examples."

Brelif spluttered with laughter and she stopped when she realized he was teasing her.

"Why, sir, that is—"

"Yes, Chambers?"

She cast a glance at V'ritan and Grilfir who watched the exchange with great interest.

"Never you mind, sir."

"This way, gentlemen, Your Majesty."

He indicated two long, low hangars standing at the edge of an open field. Another three-story building stood between them and connected the two. They followed him and his entourage in silence, and their guards glanced warily at the open ground between the front of One R&D's reception and their destination.

"Would you like us to bring the shuttle around, Your Majesty?"

Grilfir saw the director's face change to apologetic denial and held his hand up. "I believe that would be a breach of One R&D security protocols," he told his captain, "even for me."

The guard looked affronted and gave the facility's director a frustrated glare. The Meligornian responded with a startled look, followed by an apologetic shrug. "What can I say? Mr. Burt is very, very thorough."

"Just because human society gives rise to treachery in its ruling classes—"

King Grilfir snorted and earned startled looks. "I am afraid treachery is not unique to the human condition or ruling classes. The things my guards could tell you."

His face clouded as he remembered the last encounter he'd had with a traitor. It hadn't involved ruling classes or humans but had been Meligornian through and through. Nor was it something he wanted to remember.

"Please," he said, using politeness to soften the order, "show us your latest progress."

Brelif frowned slightly but they'd reached the first of the hangars and he took them inside. True to form, T'revan stopped V'ritan following him in immediately, and Sho did the same for the king. Both guard captains gestured for two of their men to precede them.

The *Garghilum Afreghil* stifled an impatient sigh, and Grilfir echoed him.

"Elza would find this entertaining," T'revan observed and V'ritan agreed, although when his guard captain might have had the time to observe his wife that well, he couldn't recall. The man watched him like a hawk.

Glancing at him now, he saw him scan the buildings and perimeter wall. His gaze shifted to study details such as One R&D's security personnel on the walls, their surveillance cameras, the rooftops, and where the building's wall met open air. It reminded him that, like Tethis, T'revan had seen the wars with Dreth and the civil wars that had preceded them.

Tethis and T'revan... V'ritan considered the two. The irascible old mage who'd become one of Stephanie's staunchest supporters and the reclusive warrior-mage whose body reflected his indiscrete use of magic in his youth and belied the mastery he had of it now.

"All clear." The report brought relief and Grilfir preceded them into the warehouse.

His sudden stop would have blocked the door if Sho hadn't taken his arm and pulled him to one side. V'ritan followed and Brelif began to describe what they were looking at.

"This is the firing range," he announced. "We are standing behind the guns, but you can see the targets set up at the other end of the range."

The *Garghilum Afreghil* allowed his guard to steer him out of the doorway as he studied the vehicles at the end of the room…the vehicles and the lone Meligornian in heavy battle armor, he realized.

"What's he doing?"

"Testing the effectiveness of the armor's shielding," the director told them.

"But—" V'ritan began, but the man waved him to silence.

"They're about to fire."

And so they were. He opened his mouth to protest but it was too late. Light flashed beyond the small cubicles below them as the gun crews opened fire.

He gaped as the impact of the ship's autocannon picked the armored Meligornian up and threw him ten feet into a wall. He hung there for a moment before the armor separated from the wall and he fell face-down on the floor.

V'ritan winced, even though the Meligornian's helmet would have protected him from the impact. He tensed and held his breath until the armor twitched.

"Oh, Selene's honor." Brelif sounded in awe of what he saw. "S'ritelf, tell me you didn't feel that."

"I felt it, you Dreth-cursed spawn of a Tegorthan's Seline's cursed ball-sack," an irate female voice replied, her voice ragged with pain. V'ritan apologized in his head for simply assuming the figure had been male. "Next time, *you* can get in the moon-mothering star sentient excuse for battle armor!"

Brelif's jaw dropped. "S'ritelf—"

The power-armored figure pushed her hands beneath her and managed to get the armor's legs to function. She staggered upright and stumbled back so the wall could hold her up.

"Don't you S'ritelf me, you misbegotten child of a *hralgeth*. I *told* you the shielding didn't stop *all* the transference. Next time, *you* can put your ass in the ballsucking armor to prove yourself wrong."

A siren sounded and the gun crews locked their weapons down

and stepped outside their cubicles. The siren sounded again and doors opened in the back of the firing range. Meligornian healers hurried through to attend to S'ritelf.

"Tell me where it hurts." The voice was audible through the speakers, and V'ritan noticed the gun crews crowding close to the observation panels in an attempt to get a view of what was going on at the other end of the screen.

The soldier yelped as the medics released the armor. How badly she'd been injured was reflected in how fast and how many of them drew the purple light of Meligorn and flooded the armor with it before they tried to pull her free.

Even insulated by magic, she groaned in pain until one of the medics slapped an autoinjector against her throat.

Brelif sighed. "How bad is it?"

"It's not bad if you want to turn them into a pre-tenderized feast for whatever enemy they're facing," one of the medics replied and he groaned.

Grilfir and V'ritan waited, each hiding their emotions behind a professional mask.

"Didn't you test the armor beforehand?" the king asked, and he frowned in annoyance.

"Of *course* we did, Your Majesty, but there's a limit to how much the gel reflects the extent of injuries the Meligornian body will sustain from impact."

"Surely it gives *some* indication," the royal pressed.

He looked appalled, his gaze focused past the director and on the drama being played out at the other end of the hall.

"Not nearly accurately enough," Brelif snapped, then flushed. "My apologies, Your Majesty. I meant no disrespect."

"No offense was taken," Grilfir assured him. "I am impressed that your research has come this far in the short time since we asked you to look into the possibility."

"Thank you, Your Majesty." The director did not try to hide the relief in his voice. He indicated the small shuttle, air car, and two-man fighter that had also been the target of the auto-cannons.

Some of them had shifted under the impact of the attacks but none of them showed any sign of damage. Their pilots and crew would have also been well-insulated against the energy absorbed by the shields and the vehicle's armor.

"We've resolved most of the issues with the vehicle shielding," he explained. "It's only the personal armor that needs tweaking."

Grilfir glanced at where S'ritelf was being stretchered out of the room. "Might I suggest you go back to scratch and take a different approach for personal armor?"

Brelif nodded quickly. "As you wish, Your Majesty."

"Given that I will be the next person to wear it, I do. Now, what did you want to show me, next?"

The king swept forward off the balcony overlooking the gun cubicles and down the stairs, leaving a gaping One R&D director in his wake. The Meligornian didn't recover until his sovereign had reached the bottom of the stairs and moved into the open space between the cubicles and the weapons dispensary.

At that point, Brelif closed his mouth with a snap and raced after him. "But, Your Majesty—"

Grilfir held a hand up. "The matter is closed. You will inform me of when the next manned test is scheduled and I will come and test it for you." He paused to take in the Meligornian's terrified face. "I will have the Palace Medical Corps liaise with your people here to see what treatment they should have standing by."

Watching Brelif's face, V'ritan thought they would need a defibrillator to restart the director's heart. All color had drained from his face and made his dark hair stand out even more starkly against his far too pale skin.

"You'll have to explain to BURT why you scared one of his people to death," he warned, and Grilfir bared his teeth.

"Next time, he'll be much less cavalier about his test procedures," he declared but kept his reply between them.

The director looked from V'ritan to the king and back again and decided he needed more time to formulate an excuse for using someone else rather than the king. On the one hand, he was sure the royal bodyguard would support him wholeheartedly. On the other, he was very sure the king had made his mind up.

He wondered if he could get away with not telling him until the next round of testing was over, but Grilfir derailed his train of thought.

"I'm pleased with the progress you've made on the shielding, but what is this I hear of a new delivery system you have for getting MU into a Teloran engine without using a mage?"

"Or Stephanie," the *Garghilum Afreghil* added, his mind filled with remembered images of jagged bolts of blue and purple arcing from the Knight to pierce the hides of a dozen Teloran ships of the line.

He flinched as he recalled the explosions surrounding the *King's Warrior*, the honored dead, and the network of magical lightning that had lit the battlefield before it vanished and left the scene to the stars.

"Well…" Brelif began, his voice unnaturally hoarse.

V'ritan focused and the hangar returned to replace the closing scenes of the devastation Stephanie had left. Not sure what his face showed of the feelings that remained, he motioned for the Meligornian to continue.

"The cloaking devices are almost ready for field trials, and I will contact the *Afreghil Garghilum* to arrange the installation and testing. And the new projectiles are almost ready to be tested outside the virtual."

He paused and the king inclined his head expectantly. "There's more?" He turned and looked at V'ritan. "I don't remember there being more."

Brelif nodded. "That's because Chandler mentioned direct delivery to the Teloran engines might be even more effective."

"Oh?" Grilfir's eyebrows rose. "How so?"

"I believe…" His face reddened. "I believe she suggested a suppository."

Several snickers came from the rearmost rank of scientists, along with a muffled chuckle, but when V'ritan tried to identify exactly who and where, he couldn't decide who had found the words amusing.

The only sign Chandler might find it amusing was the slight quirk to her lips. Beyond that, her face wore a calculating expression as she watched the king's reaction. He wondered why.

"We've kept it very quiet," Brelif told them and led them along the ground floor of the building joining the two hangars. "But..."

He led them up a flight of stairs to the second floor, through a set of double doors, and into an enclosed balcony overlooking the ground floor of the hangar. "*This* is what we came up with."

The two visitors stared at the five sleek fighting ships silhouetted below. For a long moment, they stood and stared at them before Grilfir looked at Brelif.

"What, exactly, are they?"

"They're the suppository," Chandler replied before he had a chance to do so. Without consulting her boss, she tapped on the computer keyboard closest to her, pulled up the schematics for the tiny fighters, and sent them to a viewscreen on the wall behind them.

"As you can see, they each carry two missiles tucked in close to their sides."

The king nodded. "That's the MU payload?"

She gave him the kind of pleased grin a teacher might reserve for a favored pupil who'd done something clever. "Exactly!"

"And the plan?" the *Garghilum Afreghil* asked. "Because I don't see how these will get anywhere *near* a Teloran's ass!"

"That's because you haven't pulled your head out of yours," a crotchety voice grouched from behind the computer banks lining the end of the room.

The scientists shuffled nervously and glanced at each other and at Brelif. He glared at them. "I thought you said Vathris was on leave," he whispered.

"Vathris has augmented hearing, don't you know?" The voice spoke again. "And Vathris knows when he's being sent on a break to stop him from embarrassing his boss in front of the king."

The voice grew louder and a stooped and wrinkled Meligornian with hair as white as Tethis' stomped out from behind the computers. T'revan and Sho moved to stand between the King and V'ritan and the newcomer, but the man didn't seem to care.

When he walked into T'revan's bulk, he stopped and looked at the older guard captain. "Excuse me, junior, but I'm not talking to you."

He glanced to where Chandler stood beside the computer with a horrified look on her face.

"Why don't you make yourself useful and bring up the schematics," he ordered and made a show of squinting at her. "That is if your human brain can keep up."

She wrinkled her nose but didn't argue. "Why don't you try me, Grandad?"

Vathris' lip curled with distaste. "I'd rather not."

He turned to the visitors and bowed, showing them the deep respect of an older warrior to two younger ones. As they returned the gesture and the security captains looked at their principles for orders, Vathris launched into a detailed explanation of what they were looking at.

V'ritan paid him close attention, his mind racing as he wondered how he could acquire some of the missiles for the *King's Warrior* and its armada of attack ships—and how long it would take to refit them to carry the missiles.

"And that," the old man concluded, "is how good old old-fashioned *Meligornian* engineering will win us this war." He turned to Chandler. "And not something designed by a species still in diapers when it comes to walking the stars."

She flushed and bit her lip, and V'ritan chuckled.

Vathris turned on him as fast as a striking purkat. "What's so funny, *Garghilum*?"

"This," he told him and gestured to the workshop, the hangar, and the facility around them. "All this was designed by a human."

"And what makes you think that, young man?" the scientist demanded and gave him the impression he was being humored.

"Because she is the first one to have discovered her world's magic and blended it with human technology."

"I don't see any human technology here." Vathris gestured as strongly to the computers around them and then to the window. "Or out there."

V'ritan walked to the diagram and tapped a small valve and coil linked to a more complex mechanism.

"That," he pointed out. "That is human in origin." He studied the diagram more closely. "And that," he added. "I saw it during my time on Earth. It's a handy little device."

"Pfft!" The scientist waved dismissively and turned away. "It shows how much you know. That piece is *definitely* Meligornian design, and I should know—"

"No, not *that* piece, the one it's set inside. See?"

Vathris stared at the screen. "Are you trying to tell me that a *human* thought to create something that drew in gMU and condense it into MU?"

He nodded.

The man snorted and turned to the king. "Your Majesty, I suggest you replace this man at once. He has clearly had one too many glasses of *keludd*—and out-of-season *keludd* at that."

Grilfir stared at him in shock and the guards shifted uneasily. V'ritan signaled for them to hold steady. Turning to Vathris, he said, "You *have* heard of Stephanie *Morgana*, haven't you?"

"The human Witch?" He uttered another snort that expressed exactly what he thought of that. "I've caught some of the hoo-ha."

The king's mask of composure cracked and he gave a short cough and turned his back on V'ritan and the old engineer as the coughing grew worse. His *Garghilum Afreghil* was glad he had thought to hide his amusement.

"Hoo-ha?" he asked and struggled to keep control of his voice.

"Yes. It made the news, but I was in the middle of something so I was in my lab at the time. Besides," he snapped, "I don't listen to the news. It's always negative."

"Our world was almost obliterated," he told him bluntly.

Vathris stared at him, clearly torn between believing him and dismissing his words as nonsense. In the end, his response was a blend of the two.

"I didn't know it and since it didn't happen, my heart was saved the stress." He brought the schematics up once more. "Human, you say?"

"Yes," he assured him. "Human."

He studied the plans closely and shook his head. "I don't see it." He looked at the king. "Are you *sure* he hasn't been in the *keludd*?"

"I can assure you, he has not," King Grilfir replied in choked tones.

"Hmmph! Well, given your penchant for trusting humans," he started, "I hope you don't trust them with *this*."

That, at least, his sovereign could answer honestly.

"Not at this time."

CHAPTER TWENTY-TWO

Todd dumped his duffel in the room that would be his home for the next two weeks. Up and down the corridor, the other Hooligans did the same.

Depression vied with disappointment. His pleasure and surprise at seeing Elizabeth at the airport had been spoiled by the news that his parents were on a short vacation and they'd asked her to collect him.

"I could wait for them at home," he'd told her, but she'd shaken her head. "Your teams' flights were moved up. BURT's bringing them in over the next two days." She'd given him an oddly sympathetic look. "I'll arrange for them to visit at HQ when they get back."

He had sighed and nodded. Gary had slid worried glances at him ever since and he couldn't blame the man. He'd been looking forward to seeing his parents and the man had known it. His request to the admiral hadn't all been because he needed to get the team out from under the Odd Squad's observation.

It was no surprise that the Englishman appeared at the end of the corridor leading to the team's rec room. "You should see what's down here, boss!"

Todd snorted. He should, should he? Yeah, maybe he should. It would beat moping about his parents—and *someone* had to stop the team from throwing a wild and impromptu party. Besides, they had a ton of catching up to do.

In the three days since he'd arrived, he'd caught up on the Earth news and more sleep than he'd thought he'd missed, and the Englishman hadn't left his side. If Todd didn't think he knew better, he'd have said he was nervous...except the man wasn't afraid of anything.

"The gym's through here," Gary informed him, "and I found a pod room. You wanta take a virtual cruise in the islands?"

If the truth be told, he didn't, but he couldn't think of what else to do. He hadn't planned anything beyond seeing his folks and now they weren't there, he was at a loose end.

It was a very long few days. The sound of Ka and Piet arguing as they emerged from the pods was a welcome relief, and the story of their short swim soon had him in stitches.

"You should have seen her face." Piet chuckled as he relayed it. "It was the biggest damn fin I've ever seen. I almost soiled myself. It was the last thing I ever expected to see."

She stared at him open-mouthed. "You made it sound like they were to be expected."

"Yeah, sure...in *winter*. They're usually gone by mid-summer."

Gary frowned, brought up the shark species he was referring to, and shook his head as he put his tablet on the table. "You screwed two things up, Piet."

"I did?"

"Well, firstly, there are *two* species of shark in those waters as well as the migratory one you know about."

"What?"

"Yeah. It's a *new world* remember? No one knows everything there is, yet—not even all the things that will be common knowledge in ten years' time."

"You mean that fin—"

Gary tapped the tablet and turned it toward him. "So, which one did it look like?"

"That one," Ka told them decisively. Her finger stabbed the screen and Piet found another shade of pale.

"Are you sure?" He also sounded like he didn't want to believe her.

"Yup. Sure as."

Up to that point, he had leaned on the tabletop. Now, he dragged a seat out with a shaky hand and sat abruptly. She sat beside him and draped an arm around his shoulder. At first, it looked like a comforting gesture, then she spoke.

"So, Piet. It's a good thing we swam fast, right?"

Darren and Jimmy arrived the next morning, followed by Dru and Angus, and Henry and Reggie.

Angus was laughing fit to burst as he came in the door. "I can't believe you said that!"

"Said what?" Todd asked and they stopped laughing and both went as red as beets. "What?"

"That I wanted chicken chow mein and roosters' feet for the wedding party," Dru confessed and burst into a fit of giggles. "I'm sorry, Angus, but she pushed me."

He gave her shoulder a friendly push. "Don't sweat it. She pushes *everyone*."

They sobered and she gave him a serious look. "So. No hard feelings?"

"Nope." He shook his head and rested an elbow on her shoulder. "Thanks for doing that for me."

"Yeah? Well, it's Ka's turn next time." She looked around the group. "Or Jimmy's. He is *definite* girlfriend material."

Girlfriend material, huh? Todd bet there was a story behind that, and that it would come out as they settled into the team again. All in all, it looked like his people had come through their trip unscathed and he wasn't looking forward to explaining what went wrong to the Navy brass when they returned.

He got them settled and assembled them for a briefing at Matthias's request.

"We thought we'd wait for you all to get here before we did this," the man told them when they had gathered in one of the briefing rooms. "That way, we wouldn't have to repeat it half a hundred times. These are the ground rules..."

Todd leaned back and watched his team, noting the vague signs of rebellion in Dru, Reggie, Gary, and Jimmy. Those four weren't a surprise...and neither was Ka. Angus, Henry, and Piet also listened with interest, even though the intent of the warning wasn't meant for them. Darren listened but was withdrawn.

It seemed he'd have to follow up. He glanced from Darren to Jimmy and decided he'd talk to the Scotsman first and see if he'd be willing to give him half a clue.

"And now," Matthias announced from the front of the room, "it's time for the moment you've all been waiting for. The Grand Tour!"

The team cheered quietly and followed him out.

He started at the stairwell. "Upstairs, we have the lab, guest quarters, and equipment lockers for Steph's teams. If you need anything from the latter, please ask first. You don't know when her team will come back and what they'll need. We'll want to replace anything you borrow before they return and not find out at the last minute that we're missing something vital because you assholes borrowed it and didn't let us know."

Briskly, he took them through the complex and pointed out Steph and her team's living quarters, the ready room, the gym, mess, and pod rooms. It was only when he reached the end of the corridor that he stopped.

This time, he didn't open the door. He tapped on it.

"This room," he told them, "is out of bounds."

They all looked at him and he returned the stare, his gaze touching each of their faces. After a moment, he sighed, cracked the door, and held it only wide enough for them to see the single pod inside.

"It's Steph's personal pod, which has been set up for her and *only* her. Now, if you want your brain fried, *please* feel free to break through the security and later, I'll heave your cold, dead body out of it and throw it unceremoniously in the industrial dumpster out back for being a fucking idiot." He gave them a minute to digest that. "Are we clear?"

The Hooligans looked at him and their gaze drifted to Arne who stood behind him.

"Crystal," Piet assured him.

"Yup," Gary echoed.

"Sure," "Sure thing," and "Gotcha, boss," followed and even Todd was sure the Hooligans understood. He hoped so because he didn't think he'd handle losing any one of them very well—especially not to a case of the stupids.

Besides, they could all see that these two had been there. With Matthias, it wasn't as obvious, but Arne... Todd narrowed his eyes and studied the man again. Yeah, he had walked where they were now and maybe a little farther.

He marked that idea as something he'd have to pursue later and echoed the team's agreement. Matthias pulled the door closed and another voice echoed into the corridor.

"And if any of you thought Knight was difficult, consider me her father, except I don't have a sense of humor."

Todd groaned, recognized BURT's voice, and recalled the team's unfortunate run-in with the ship over their little prank attempt on her Marines. Carefully observing his people, he was fairly sure none of them would ever try that again, but he couldn't work out, for the life of him, why Ka blushed fit to start a fire.

The tour concluded with an introduction to the foyer and the location of Elizabeth's office—another place they were told wasn't safe to visit uninvited.

"You've only ever seen her on a good day," Matthias advised them. "Her bad days are usually confined behind that door. My advice is not to go there."

It was good advice. Todd had never seen the woman truly angry and he never wanted to. Something in the way she carried herself set off his predator alarm, and he didn't want to learn what it was.

The rest of the Hooligans seemed to feel the same because they all murmured agreement.

"Good," Matthias told them. "Now *that's* sorted, I'll leave you to finish getting settled in. Dinner's in an hour."

Given that it hadn't covered more than the ground floor, the tour hadn't seemed that long.

They retired to their quarters where Todd went over the ground rules and off-limits areas again. In the end, Ka threw a cushion at him.

"Look, boss, we get it. You chose this place for a reason, and we all have an idea why. This isn't simply some dumb civvie establishment—and I, for one, never thought it was."

"The girl has a point," Piet agreed. "You brought us here so we could discuss our options in a safe place."

He shrugged and looked around. "I've seen folk like this Matthias and Arne before—"

"Hell, we've *all* seen folk like Arne before," Reggie quipped. "And had a few yell at us across the universe and back and *never* wanted to draw their attention. Steph has good people."

Todd looked around. "Do you all feel that way?"

"Hells yes," Angus assured him. "There ain't *nothing* getting in here. Not the worse of the worst, the Tooth Fairy, *or* Santa—not unless they knock first and ask *real* polite. What makes you think we'd *dream* of screwing it up from the inside?"

He breathed an internal sigh of relief. "Good, because tomorrow, we start training. We need to work out some of the kinks."

Ka snorted. "Speak for yourself, boss. I happen to *like* some of my kinks."

This drew the snickers it was meant to, and he had to crack a smile. "Working out *those* kinks is up to you." He glanced at the clock. "Right now, we need to haul ass or we're gonna be late for dinner."

"Well, boss, we can't have that, can we? Steph would be mad if we let you become all skin and bone."

Todd didn't dignify that with an answer, and the meal passed uneventfully with the Hooligans assessing Elizabeth's security team before they began to regale each other with the highlights of their journeys. He broke them up before they got too carried away.

"Oh-six-hundred," he told them and they groaned. "Don't make me decide oh-four-hundred is better."

They were in the gym by oh-seven-hundred and ran a few laps to warm up before they separated into pairs for sparring practice. Todd broke them into their travel pairs to consolidate those bonds and then divided them so that former partners were working against each other.

He was pleased with the way they interacted and was about to reshuffle them when Arne and Amy entered the gym. Quickly, he jogged to greet them. "We can finish if you need the space."

"Don't let us disturb you," the man told him. "There's enough room for all of us." He pointed to an empty corner. "We'll be over there if that's not in the way."

They weren't in the way, but the Hooligans had trouble ignoring them. The warm-up stage wasn't particularly fascinating but the team hadn't seen them before, so they glanced over continually. More than one team member caught a fist in the ribs or upside the head because they didn't pay attention.

When they began to spar, the Hooligan's training session ended.

"Who's your money on?" Reggie whispered to Gary.

"Neither," the Englishman replied. "Not yet. Let them go a bout. I want to see what they've got."

"Why?" his teammate teased. "Are you thinking of challenging them?"

"Not on your life—" Gary's eyes widened. "Look!"

Todd sidled closer, his gaze fixed on the combatants as they moved to take advantage of the space the Hooligans no longer used. Amy was fast but Arne proved equally so.

The team watched as he blocked a flurry of punches and she jumped over his attempt to hook her ankles and pull her feet out from under her. She brought a knee into play and he turned a thigh to block it, while his hand intercepted a punch aimed at his ribs.

The pace only increased from there.

Todd watched them, open-mouthed, before he inched closer to Piet. "I bet they're barely doing a seven...on a scale to eleven," he whispered.

His teammate nodded, his gaze serious as Arne flipped backward, came down on one knee, and struck with both fists. One of those turned into a grab as he snatched the ankle of the boot Amy snapped at his head.

She brought her foot down hard, broke his grip, and propelled herself out of his reach. He bounced to his feet and surged at her in a dive that brought them both to the floor, although it did not signal the end of the bout.

Ka leaned closer to Dru. "Do you think he's taken?"

On the mats, Amy launched Arne over her head and rolled into a crouch while he tucked, landed, and pivoted.

She continued. "If he isn't…you know…I might be *very* free."

The other woman raised an eyebrow. "I thought you were into Piet."

"Yeah." She blushed. "But I'm not so sure he's very into me, and I like 'em old…er—and *fit*." She sighed. "He is sooo *fit*."

Dru nodded as Amy took Arne to the floor and they rolled in an inelegant struggle to find supremacy. "Hot damn—"

The match ended when she locked his arm up along her body and set her calf across his throat. He slapped the mat to signal the end of the match and she released him, laughing.

The Hooligans began to drift to the showers as she asked, "Again?"

Arne glanced at the clock on the wall and shook his head. "Matt wants us in Briefing Room One in ten."

Dru and Ka were brushing their hair in the locker room mirror when Amy passed them on the way to her meeting. Her eyes sparkled and she gave them a happy smile.

"Very taken," she told them as she passed.

Their jaws dropped, but the woman didn't stop. She slipped out the locker room door and left them to stew.

"Did you get that?" Ka asked.

"Uh-huh," Dru replied. "She is very, *very* good."

"Eeyup." She stared into the distance, so her friend filled the silence.

"'Cause she was fighting that hard and she *still* had time to eaves-drop," she explained.

"Damn!" Ka stated, still staring at nothing.

"Yeah, because if she says he's taken, he is *very* taken, whether he knows it or not," Dru told her.

"Well, shit."

As Stephanie explained the presence of the *Tempestarii* to her team, BURT contemplated what had happened. The surge of power had been exhilarating and watching his weapons crews decimate their target proved *very* satisfying.

He ran his checks in the wake of the *Tempestarii*'s and couldn't help but admire the sheer power of the vessel that had become his home. The body Stephanie and Elizabeth had chosen to house him had to be one of the most powerful constructions he'd ever seen, if not *the* most powerful.

"If the protection they have provided me is an indication of love," he thought, "then I am very loved indeed."

In Australia, the scientists had come together for yet another meeting. They were waiting for BURT's latest assessment of their modifications and Marcus was late.

"So?" Trey asked as soon as he stepped through the door.

The team was seated at the tables in the room where he and Cynthia had originally presented them with the proposal for the project.

It seemed like a lifetime ago.

Marcus kept his head down, his shoulders slumped, and watched as depression rippled around the table.

"Oh, you have to be *shitting* me!" Trey exclaimed. "What the fuck was it this time? Did we fail to color-match the nuts and bolts or something? Their ammunition wasn't pink?"

Some of the scientists snickered but most groaned and turned sad gazes to him.

When he'd decided he'd tortured them enough, he raised his head so they could see the smile he couldn't quite contain.

"You *bastard!*" Gemma realized it first. "You utter, *utter* bastard."

"And you kiss your kids with that mouth?" Nathan sniped from the other side of the table. He glanced at his boss. "Seriously, though. She's right. You are a total fucking arsehole."

Trey rose from his seat. "I ought to knock your fucking block off!"

Marcus took a cautious step back and half-raised his hands. He glanced at the report he held and back at Trey. "If you do that, we'll be late for the party."

The man paused in his advance. "What party?"

He smiled. "The one we're having so we can celebrate Burt's approval before we go on two days' leave."

Whoops of victory rose around the table as the scientists celebrated. High-fives were exchanged and several hugged before they released each other hurriedly. Cynthia stood to one side, smiling to see them so happy.

The last few days had been tense as they wrangled the security team's requirements into their design. Each time they'd sent it in, the team had had something they wanted changed. BURT had been very insistent that the design had to satisfy both the facility's function and its security needs.

He'd been adamant, and the scientists had been forced to consider more than only the facility's main function. It had been a learning curve that had pushed them to their limits and they deserved to celebrate.

"So...party?" Gemma was the first to turn to Marcus.

"Why do you think I was so late?" he asked. "I had to remember what you arseholes liked best so BURT could order it. And I had to make sure there was enough clear space in the lab."

"Did you remember the sleeping bags?" Trey asked and several scientists chuckled.

They all remembered the last party.

"We have permission to use the pods—" He held up his hand to still the cheers and laughter. "But only for the night. Leave is mandatory."

The room stilled.

Finally, Phillip asked, "Even for you?"

He sobered. "Yes. Burt was most insistent."

After a moment of silence, Nathan remarked, "It's about time you fed your cat."

The room erupted into laughter, but he frowned. He glanced at Cynthia. "But I don't have a cat."

She smiled. "They don't know that." She gestured to the exit. "Shall we?"

Marcus glanced at his team. They talked excitedly but stopped as if sensing his gaze.

"The party's waiting," he told them and waited as they winked out, one by one, and returned to the real lab.

Cynthia came to stand beside him. "Don't be long," she instructed. "They'll want a speech."

She was gone before he could reply.

He sighed and looked around him. As happy as he was that this phase was finally over, he was sad too. It was like the end of an era, even if the next was already on its way.

Although he knew they were waiting, he took a moment to walk through the workspace and ran his hand over the backs of the chairs until he'd completed a full circuit. Finally, he returned to the briefing room and rested his fingers on the table.

Bowing his head, he tried to gather his thoughts enough that he knew what he would say to the team. It took him a moment to find the words, but when he did, he let his avatar fade and returned to his pod and the party waiting beyond.

Observing him through his connection with the project, BURT glanced at Tempestarii. "Do you think he knows?"

She shook her head. "No. I think he's merely taking time to adjust. As far as I can tell, nothing's been said."

"I can confirm that," he told her.

"It is a pity we cannot protect them where they are," the ship observed, "but two days to be with their family and remember what's meaningful outside the lab is important." She frowned. "I hope nothing happens to them while we delay."

BURT glanced at her. "By my calculations, they should be safe. Their connection to Stephanie is not as immediate and their importance to One R&D remains secret. I think we can afford to give them two more days."

"It isn't fair."

"No," he agreed, "it isn't."

They lapsed into silence for a moment to watch the celebrations. Rimmer's team might be among the hardest workers he knew, but they also knew how to party.

He didn't look forward to telling them they had to consider leaving their planet behind. As he watched Nathan and Gemma start an impromptu dance-off and Trey raise a glass to toast the winner, he tried to work out how much information it would take to convince them to let him bring them and their loved ones to safety.

Two days wasn't an issue when he believed they had six months before they became prime targets. He didn't know who Stephanie's enemies were this time, but they weren't Teloran. They were much closer to home and very powerful.

Six months was not much time to move an entire community of scientists, but that was the least he owed them. Granted, the threat to them had yet to be confirmed and it was only a very high probability, but they were needed.

Even on the small chance they *wouldn't* be targeted, he couldn't risk it.

CHAPTER TWENTY-THREE

On another part of Earth, Cindy and Elaine surveyed the room. It had been set up as a lounge with sufficient space for people to spread out and talk. Elizabeth had decided it was better for Todd to meet his parents *before* the shuttle arrived rather than as he boarded, but she still didn't know how he'd react.

She hoped it would be better with Stephanie's parents and the team around. Having them wait in the meeting room turned impromptu departure lounge was better than having them wait on the roof for the *Knight's* shuttle to land—from both the comfort *and* the sniping opportunities perspective. There was no way she wanted anything to happen to them when she was this close to getting them away.

Her gaze studied the room in the same way the two mothers did, observing the tables set up at one end. The caterers had almost finished stocking it with the food she'd ordered. She assumed the wait would run long and that awkward meetings went better with a meal. That, and she wanted them to eat before the flight since she didn't know when they'd arrive at the ship.

Happy with the way preparations were going, she crossed to check in with Elaine and Cindy. When they saw her move toward their wives, Mark and Tony came to join them.

"Not long now," Tony noted and she smiled.

It was almost cute to see that the parents were as nervous to meet their son as she was for the reunion to occur.

"He won't be very happy with me," she told them.

"He needed to work things out with his team," Elaine replied. "How could he be mad at you for helping him organize that?"

"Because he wanted to see you first and I stopped that from happening."

"Aw." The woman hugged her. "You did what was best. We know that."

Elizabeth stiffened. The brief hug had surprised her. It didn't last long but it was long enough for her to realize she'd made more friends than she'd thought. She'd give them this. Todd's parents were among the most resilient people she knew.

"This all feels so unreal," Elaine murmured and looked at the room again.

Cindy nodded. "I know. Poor Steph. She'll feel so guilty."

"About what?"

"About those people trying to kill you simply because Todd's her boyfriend," the woman explained.

Elizabeth nodded. "She was very upset when they targeted Todd for the same reason."

She stopped and colored when she remembered they'd probably never heard that story, but his mum didn't seem to notice.

"As if she caused any of it!" Elaine snapped. "Todd's seen enough of her that he probably knew what he was getting into."

"And he's a Marine," Tony pointed out. "It's not like he can't take care of himself."

"Still," Cindy persisted, "I bet he never thought you and Tony would be targeted as a result."

They were silent for a moment as they thought about that.

"You know he'll want to find every single one of them, don't you?" Elaine said.

"Of course he will," Cindy told her, "and Stephanie will want to go with him."

"She wouldn't!" The other woman was shocked.

"She so would," Mark interrupted. "That girl has a terrible temper and a sense of justice a mile wide. She'll want to make sure that whoever these people are, they never mess with us again."

Tony stared at him. "But she was so sweet the last time we saw her."

"That's because you're her friends," her father explained.

Elizabeth decided she couldn't get into any more trouble than she was in already. Besides, the parents needed to have *some* idea of what they'd been sucked into.

"She wasn't so sweet when she went after Todd to get him out of the trap they'd set in London."

"London?" Elaine asked. "Is that when Todd made the time to dance with her? In the middle of *that?*"

She smirked. "Well, more towards the end, actually, but yes."

"That's a story I haven't heard," Cindy mentioned. She gestured toward the couch. "Can I hear it?"

"Yes," Mark agreed and looked at Elizabeth. "I'd like to hear that one too. It looks like you've been holding out on us."

E blushed but was saved from having to reply by a knock at the door.

She glanced at the parents. "Are you ready?"

From the sudden tension on both their faces, she decided they'd never feel ready and answered the door anyway. "Come in!"

Todd opened it and glanced into the room. He froze the moment he laid eyes on his parents. Ka didn't stop quickly enough and ran into him. The collision thrust him forward and he pulled himself together hastily and hurried closer to them.

"Mom! Dad? What are you doing here?"

"Elizabeth thought it would be a nice surprise for you," his mother told him and he gave E a sharp glance.

To her relief, however, he decided not to make a fuss and turned to his parents.

"It is. I'm so glad to see you here."

As he enveloped them in his arms, the rest of the Hooligans filed into the room and wandered to the coffee dispenser to give the trio the illusion of privacy. Matthias, Arne, and Amy entered, followed by the rest of Elizabeth's security team.

Matthias's lips curled with pleasure to see the reunion in full swing. He stood beside Elizabeth and stooped to whisper in her ear. "You got off lightly."

"Not yet, I haven't," she whispered in response and grimaced.

"It'll be okay," he reassured her, twined an arm around her waist, and observed the people around them.

His gaze settled on Stephanie's parents, and he squeezed her gently before he released her so he could greet them. "Cindy! Mark! It's good to see you. How are you settling in?"

At his words, Todd looked up. He frowned and studied Stephanie's mom and dad before he glanced at his parents and then at Elizabeth.

"What happened?" he asked.

Elaine laid a hand on his arm. "Now, Todd, that can all wait for later. Right now, we have some catching up to do."

He tensed at her touch and E wondered what his parents thought of their first glimpse of the warrior he usually kept well out of their sight.

Matthias looked up. "Is everything all right?"

Todd froze, then nodded, and he tucked the anger and the soldier away. "I'll have questions later," he replied and the other man nodded.

"I'm sure E will give you all the answers you need."

She held her breath as he opened his mouth to reply but relaxed when he closed it again. Something suggested that the boy had been about to say getting the answers he needed was fine, but what about the answers he *wanted*?

Still, he'd decided to keep that last one behind his teeth and she was happy for it because she'd have been forced to answer. She didn't like to lie. Matthias studied her expression and frowned slightly, and his mouth tightened in the way it did when he wasn't particularly happy.

Elizabeth shrugged it off. *Whatever. Someone has to be the boss,* she thought. *And BURT pays me damned well to make the hard calls.*

She pasted a smile on her face and faced the room. "Now that you're all here," she announced, "I'd like you to meet Cindy and Mark Morgan and Elaine and Tony Brogan, parents to two of the biggest troublemakers in the universe."

"You can talk," Ka snapped and E raised a hand as Amy bristled.

"Indeed, I can," she assured Todd's second-in-command. "I am trouble incarnate and I know trouble when I see it."

Matthias chuckled and even Todd gave her a brief, tight smile.

Yup, she thought. *He is angry.*

Elaine seemed to recognize that too because she grasped her son's bicep. Startled, he glanced at her and let some of the tension go. Tony frowned in concern.

Elizabeth shrugged the reaction away and continued. "Stephanie tells me the *Knight* is en route and she'll send the shuttle to collect you sometime tonight, which is why I asked you to bring your gear. They won't stop long and I don't want anyone left behind."

Dru nudged Gary. "She's tired of us already," she whispered, sotto voce.

The cheek of that comment made Elizabeth utter a quick bark of laughter. "As true as that might be," she began and raised her hand against their protests. "As true as that might be," she repeated as they subsided, "it doesn't change the fact that I don't know how long it will be before the shuttle arrives or how long the journey to the *Knight* will be."

Her voice softened. "I also don't know long how long it will be before we will get to see you all again."

She gestured at Arne, Matthias, herself, and her team. "So this is our way of wishing you all the best and we hope to see you soon, whether it's here, or on the *Knight* or *Tempestarii.*"

A few seconds of silence followed when she'd finished, broken by Matthias.

"Hear, hear!" he agreed and gestured toward the tables. "Let's eat!"

Todd offered to fetch something for his parents and Elaine

laughed and patted his arm. "Oh, goodness. No, Todd. We're quite capable of fetching our own meal. Why don't you introduce us to your friends along the way?"

That drew the team's attention and he eyed them warily.

"I don't know, Mom. They're not—"

She slapped his shoulder. "They're your friends, aren't they?"

"Well, yes, but—"

Gary and Reggie exchanged glances with Dru, Ka, and Jimmy, and they surged across the empty space between them.

"Pleased to meetcha," Reggie began in his broadest Australian accent.

Todd groaned and interrupted him before he could get any further. "Mom, Dad, this is Reggie."

He let his parents say hello and moved on to Gary, Jimmy, Angus, Darren, Henry, Piet, and Dru. They continued their approach to the food and his team chuckled at his discomfort and resisted the urge to prank him any further.

From the way he'd glowered at Elizabeth since their arrival, they assumed he was under enough stress as it was. None of them wanted to be responsible for pushing him in front of the parents.

"And this," Todd finished, "is my second in command, Ka."

"Nice to meet you," she greeted them.

"Oh," Elaine said. "Are you Australian, too?"

"Well, fu...um." She cleared her throat. "Sorry, ma'am. No, I'm afraid not."

"You know I *have* heard curse words before," Elaine informed her, and the girl blushed.

"I—"

"But thank you for trying to keep it civil. You merely sounded..." She let her voice trail off when she saw Gary's frantic gestures to stop.

Ka caught the meaning anyway. "I'm a New Zealander."

Elaine leaned forward and listened carefully as she spoke. As soon as Ka had finished, she gave the woman a brilliant smile. "Well, of course you are," she beamed. "I apologize for the mistake."

"That's okay," she reassured her as Reggie began to grumble.

"What's wrong with being mistaken for Australian?"

"It's like someone from the far north of NorAm being mistaken for someone from central NorAm," Angus tried to explain. "They get very offended."

"Yeah, well I get *that*," Reggie told him. "But I don't get why a New Zealander would—"

He stopped when Jimmy wrapped an arm around his shoulders and steered him toward the table. "I'm starving. Aren't you starving, wee Reggie? You are? Why don't you come with me to find a wee bite?"

Tony chuckled. "I like them," he told Todd after the rest of the Hooligans drifted after them. "You could have done much worse."

"Some of them are much older than you are, dear," Elaine observed. "How did you get to be in charge?"

Todd blushed. He'd thought no one else had heard the question until Ka shouted over her shoulder.

"Because none of *us* were silly enough to say yes!"

His mother looked shocked. "Is that true?"

Dru slapped Ka on the shoulder and drifted back. "No, ma'am, it's not true. Todd got the job because he was the best man for it—and because no one else wanted to have the team."

Elaine's eyes widened. "Truly?"

Todd rolled his eyes. "They're not *that* bad, Mom. Honestly, they're the best team I could have asked for."

"We're the only team he could have asked for," Ka quipped and he covered his eyes with one hand and shook his head.

"Don't listen to them. They're full of shit," he told her bluntly and drew a sharp breath as he'd realized what he'd done.

His father chuckled. "As long as you're happy with them…"

"I'm rapidly becoming *un*happy with them," he told him. "I can foresee them running serious laps in their very near futures."

"Not before the flight," Elizabeth instructed, "and you need to eat in case the shuttle decides to drop in early."

"Yes, ma'am," Todd retorted and teased her with the term.

She arched an eyebrow. "Don't make me come over there."

He froze but Cindy laughed. "You sounded exactly like Stephanie."

E didn't know what to say. On the one hand, she was mortified to have caught him when he was so vulnerable and on the other, she was pleased that she and her surrogate daughter had something in common.

Ka came over and pushed him with the flat of her hand. "Come on, boss. Stephanie will have all our hides if you starve to death and I don't want her coming after me."

"Yeah, me neither," Elizabeth agreed.

They headed to the tables, collected their food, and found a seat at one of the smaller tables nearby. Elizabeth nodded to Arne, who quietly thumbed the controls for the vidscreen at the back of the room. Todd froze as the familiar opening track of one of his favorite movies floated through the room.

"*No* way!"

They laughed at his surprise and focused on their meals, talking while the movie played in the background. It was only halfway through when it suddenly stopped and BURT appeared on the screen.

"We interrupt this broadcast..." he began with false pompousness and smiled when he saw he had their attention. "The shuttle will touch down in ten minutes."

"Thank you, BURT," Elizabeth replied, and the screen went blank. "We'll watch the end of it another time."

Ten minutes was barely enough time to get them and their gear to the roof, but they made it. Todd's heart leapt when he recognized Stephanie's head of security standing in the doorway but there was no time for greetings.

"We lift in five!" Lars shouted. "Get your asses aboard."

He wondered if the man realized who he was speaking to but the answer became clear when Stephanie's mom and dad walked up the stairs and he saw them in the light of the cockpit.

Lars's jaw dropped and he cast Elizabeth a questioning glance.

The man's mouth moved rapidly as he used the team comms, but Todd heard nothing.

Elizabeth's reply was spoken in an undertone, but he caught it all the same. "I'll call her once you're airborne. How far out is she?"

Irritated, he wished he could hear the answer to that too, but he couldn't so he focused on shepherding his parents and his team on board. When he went to drop back to the rear of the line, Ka stepped in front of him.

"I think this is the one time you have to lead us out instead of staying behind to make sure we all get there."

She gave his parents a meaningful glance and jerked a thumb at Elizabeth.

"Besides, I doubt *she* will let any of us stay."

"Darn tooting," E told her. "There is no *way* I'll have that kind of mischief unleashed around here. I'll make sure every single one of you are on the damned boat."

"See?"

Todd grimaced and climbed the stairs after his parents, relieved when a single glance revealed his team lined up behind him. It looked like none of them wanted to be left behind either. He didn't blame them. There was something about Elizabeth that put him on edge, too.

He filed in, took a seat beside his parents, and helped them strap in as he watched his team file past. Ka was the last and he didn't relax until she'd taken a seat in the row opposite. He tensed as the shuttle's engines began to whine and he wondered who was flying.

Knowing Stephanie, she'd sent her best, which meant Avery and Brenden were in the pilots' seats upfront. As soon as Ka was settled, Lars stepped out the door.

Todd wondered why the man had left them alone and twisted in his seat to inspect the inside of the passenger cabin. A small smile wrinkled his lips when he saw Vishlog standing in the hatch leading into the rear hold.

Of *course* they hadn't been left alone. Steph's team were far too paranoid for that. He guessed Lars was having a last-minute word with Elizabeth and couldn't help wondering what it was about. Whatever it was, it was short, because he reappeared a short time later.

He carried a small parcel, which he stuffed into a chest pouch as he sealed the outer door and banged on the hatch leading into the cockpit. Within seconds, the engines increased in pitch and the shuttle lifted.

"Stay buckled," the team leader ordered and his gaze wandered over the four parents strapped in beside Todd's Marines.

It was little comfort that their presence was as unexpected for Stephanie's security head as it had been for him. The look appeared to be a routine check to see if they were buckled in, but he was fairly sure he sensed confusion there as well.

The crazy flying started two minutes into the flight. Lars stayed buckled in, but his face grew tense and he maintained a soft monologue all the way up. Todd knew better than to interrupt, but he sure as hell wished he knew what was going on.

Twice, the man caught him staring and on both occasions, gave him a soft shake of the head and continued his conversation. The ride grew rough and the shuttle's speed increased until he felt like he was coming into a hostile landing zone.

He'd begun to wonder if they'd ever make it out of Earth's atmosphere when the engine noise diminished and his body weight changed. Lars continued his monologue, but his expression became a fraction less tense and it wasn't long before the craft slowed.

When it did, the security chief unbuckled and stood. "We're docking," he announced, "but I need you all to stay in your seats until I say otherwise. Understood?"

Todd nodded in unison with the rest.

He felt the soft jar as the shuttle set down and the slight disorientation he associated with a rapid skip sequence.

Lars acknowledged someone through his headset. "Wait one." He unsealed the hatch and hurried out, returning within minutes and glancing at Todd as he did so.

"You can all unbuckle, now. Todd, if you'd lead the way."

Todd frowned but did as he was asked, wondering why he'd been singled out. The answer became apparent as soon as he stepped out the hatch and his breath caught.

Stephanie was as beautiful as he remembered. He raced down the steps, lengthening his stride as he reached the hangar floor. Her face broke into a radiant smile and she came toward him.

They'd barely traveled two steps towards each other when one of her guards gave a startled cry.

"Bee! Zee! *No!*"

Bee? Zee? He knew those words should worry him but couldn't remember why. He caught a flash of movement to his right, ducked, and avoided the large black-and-yellow form that sailed over his head.

As he did so, something slammed into his back, hurled him to the ground, and used his spine as a launch point.

"Sonuva *bitch!*"

Stephanie stopped in front of him, her face a mixture of consternation and laughter.

"Todd! I am so, *so* sorry." She extended her hand but he pushed to his feet and scowled at the two huge cats that circled to stand behind their mistress. "I had them locked in my room!"

She almost turned away, but he had no intention of letting her out of reach. He caught her hand, pulled her closer, and stooped to kiss her soundly before he enveloped her in his arms.

"I have missed you *so* much," he murmured.

She wound her arms around him and held him tightly for a long moment. When she began to pull away, he let her go and didn't resist when she retained a firm hold on his hand.

"I've missed you, too." She looked at him as they walked to where her team was waiting.

The small Dreth—Todd ferreted for his name…Garach—held out a small, square package and Stephanie took it.

"Elizabeth said you'd need to watch this alone," she explained. "Garach will show you the way."

One of the cats bunted its head against her hip but she pushed him away. "Oh no, Zee. *You* knocked my boyfriend on his face. *You* are in as much trouble as Frog."

"What?" the small guard demanded. "What trouble?"

She turned on him. "Didn't I tell you to leave them in my cabin?"

"But they love Todd and his people," he protested, his face more mischievous than contrite.

Stephanie scowled at him. "Then I'll only say this once. If they create any more havoc, I'll make your mouth disappear again."

His face paled. "You wouldn't."

"One more piece of havoc," she warned. "Only one."

The rest of the team began to smirk, except for Garach who looked impatient. Todd stooped to give her a quick peck on the cheek before he left. She rested a hand lightly on his cheek and let him go.

Someone made barf noises behind her, but when she looked, the team stood perfectly still, their attention on the shuttle. Todd followed their gaze and groaned when he saw their parents descending to the landing area.

Stephanie colored and shook her head. Elizabeth had so much to answer for.

"Go," she told him. "E said it was important and you should view it while the *Knight* makes her transition to the next waypoint."

He went but glanced over his shoulder a few times. Her parents reached her and the three of them came together in happy greeting as he reached the exit.

The Dreth did not take him far, only along the corridor and into an elevator, then past a few doors and into a chamber containing several pods.

The young Dreth crossed to one, opened the lid, and said, "She said the *Knight* would tell you what to do when you were done."

"Thank you," Todd said quietly and slid into the waiting pod.

The lid closed before he'd finished speaking and Garach wasted no time in sealing him in so he could make his own preparations for the transition.

CHAPTER TWENTY-FOUR

As Garach left Todd in the briefing room, Stephanie studied her parents carefully. Her gaze drifted to include Todd's folks and she paused, momentarily lost for words.

"So," she began finally and tried to break the awkwardness of the situation. "How have you been?"

Elaine giggled. "Apart from being chased by assassins, you mean?"

"And shot at," Todd's dad added. "Don't forget that."

"And discovering you had a *boyfriend*," her mother began.

Stephanie turned crimson. "It wasn't *official*—"

"That kiss looked very official to me," her dad teased.

"Dad—"

Mark frowned. "Funny, I don't remember him asking for permission, either."

"Dad."

He looked at his wife. "Do you remember being asked for permission?"

Her mom sighed. "There was that one time—"

"Mom!"

"So it's official, then?" Elaine asked, and she blushed harder. "You really *are* dating my Todd?"

"He's *my* Todd, now." The words were out before Stephanie realized she intended to say them, and she clapped her hands over her mouth.

Todd's dad chuckled and he draped an arm over his wife's shoulders. "I think he might be in very good hands. What do you say, hon?"

Elaine narrowed her eyes and she tapped Stephanie on the chest. "I say she'd better take good care of him."

She stared at them. "For Heaven's sake, it was only *one* kiss."

"Mmhmm?" Her mom raised an eyebrow and her dad joined in.

"Are you *sure* it was only one?"

One of her guards cleared his throat. "Excuse me, ma'am, I hate to interrupt but—"

Stephanie gave him a disbelieving look. "And since when was I ever a ma'am to you, Johnny?"

"Uh—" The man colored. "I was being polite."

"What did you want, Johnny?" she asked and tried her hardest to stay civil and not lose her temper.

"The *Knight* says we will be coming up on the *Tempestarii* in a half-hour and she would like everyone in their pods before that happens."

"Thank you, Johnny." She turned to her parents. "I'm sorry to cut this short but we need to prepare for a translation and there are pods for you to use while that happens."

"We need to hurry," Lars cut in and gave the parents an apologetic glance. "I'm sorry. It won't be for long."

Todd decided he'd entered a small briefing room. It was simply furnished with four chairs arranged around a table holding a computer console. The only other feature was a viewscreen on the opposite wall.

After a cautious look around to make sure he hadn't missed anything, he settled at the table. The package had transferred with him and he eyed it uncertainly before he unwrapped it and withdrew a small movie disc carefully. Moving to the computer console, he inserted the disc into the player and waited.

The wall screen flickered to life and displayed Elizabeth's face.

He waited for it to play but it remained frozen, and the *Knight's* voice greeted him instead.

"My father said to let you know that this area is isolated from the rest of the server. He has also provided a combat distraction should you require it." She paused, then added, "He believes you might be upset."

"Okaay," he replied.

"Shall I run it for you?" the *Knight* asked and he bit back the impatient retort that rose to his lips.

"Please, Knight."

"Very well."

Elizabeth's face unfroze. She looked out of the screen at him as though she could see him.

"Hello, Todd. Firstly, I want to apologize for what I needed to do and then, I wanted to explain."

"Go on," he replied, in the quiet that followed as if she were there and could hear him.

The recording obliged.

"You needed to have your meeting, and I had to get your parents off Earth."

"But, *why?*" he asked, even as message-Elizabeth gave him the answer.

"I was contacted by someone who knew who I had been in my past and who knew who I pretended to be in the present. They wanted to hire me to carry out a contract assassination."

"Motherfuck," Todd whispered. "*Why?*"

The Elizabeth onscreen didn't wait for him to finish his question but continued.

"They wanted a civilian couple assassinated. No reasons were given. That's not how this game works. I refused to help them but gave them the names of three good teams they could hire...and then I worked to find out who they had targeted."

"Up until that point, I had no idea they were after your parents, although I've started to work out why. Anyway, I put in a plan to save them, and this was the result."

The screen shifted to show a poorly lit street in a Gov-Sub, and Todd tensed as he recognized his old home. Two people in suits stood on the porch and knocked before they let themselves in. The frame flickered to show another climbing the back fence and approaching the kitchen door.

"No..." Todd dragged in a breath when he recognized the professional way they moved.

The screen flickered again to reveal Matthias's face as he handed Elizabeth a kitchen knife, and Arne and Amy tensed as they posed as his parents in their bed. The battle that followed was swift and vicious and left him breathless.

"Mother*fuck!*"

Even as he said it, the screen shifted to show an up-market apartment complex. This time, he recognized her two new bodyguards taking their place inside.

The two women worked quickly and efficiently to tranquilize the receptionists before they separated to protect a set of parents each. He stared as Elizabeth entered the reception and Arne and Amy began a silent but deadly killing spree outside the entrance.

When the battle was over, E looked out of the screen at him. "It was my intention that the bodies would be cleared and the area cleaned *before* we evacuated your parents, but that was not to be."

Todd watched as the team almost reached the gates, only to turn back and deal with the second team of killers. He saw her maim the last two attackers and tell them to take her message and his gut tightened.

This was the Elizabeth that set his spider senses tingling and put his team on edge. Now that he knew, he understood why his subconscious had tried to warn him. She continued oblivious.

"It was because of this attack that we evacuated them while the foyer was in this condition."

The footage of the battle's aftermath was something Todd wished his mother had never had to see, but he was glad they had prioritized getting them to safety over whatever nightmares were to follow.

He decided his parents could handle nightmares, but they wouldn't have survived another attack. Not if it had come in numbers. Elizabeth and her team were good, but the team they had eliminated had almost matched them.

Onscreen, the scene faded and her face reappeared. She opened her mouth and closed it again as if trying to put her thoughts into sequential order. He did not expect her to admit to what came next.

"I guess you're starting to wonder why *anyone* would offer me a contract to kill—and that ties in very much with the person I used to be. You see, I used to work for Tex, the criminal overlord, if you will, of the Lower DC area."

She frowned as if uncertain of how to go on, then continued anyway.

"Back then, I went by the name Emerald and I came up hard. I learned to defend myself against all-comers, even Tex, who adopted me as his own. I worked alone, taking on recovery tasks that others considered impossible and troubleshooting for corporations. All that led me to assassination."

Her face hardened and memories played across her face. "I had a good reason for taking that path and I became very...efficient, at what I did. I thought I had cut away the part of me that allowed me to feel and back then, I did not miss it. Not feeling kept me safe.

"That all changed when I met a certain young lady who was able to cut through the jade armor of a loner and make her better."

Stephanie, Todd thought, and she confirmed it.

"When I first met her, Stephanie was smarting from how she'd been treated by the prep school, but she was still the kindest and most considerate person I'd ever come across—and tough. The first time she took her team on, Lars had her in a chokehold and she was beat, but she refused to give up."

"And?" he wondered and tried to work out if it was fair for him to want to kill the guy because of what he'd done in a years' old training bout.

"And she used all the magic she had and beat him. Of course, she beat herself too, and I had to carry her out of there, but *that* was when I started to like her. Up to that point, she had merely been another contract."

She paused and her eyes took on a faraway look. "After that, she became family, someone who was as tough as I was but far more innocent, less a client and more a daughter, if you will." She huffed a sigh. "Which is what makes this so difficult."

Elizabeth stopped again and Todd waited. Finally, she drew a long, deep breath.

"I don't do this because I need to, Todd. When they attacked your family, they attacked *my* family. You might think less of me, but I doubt it. But know that Emerald dies when this is over and I hope you will see Elizabeth again."

She paused, took another deep breath, and exhaled slowly. "If we don't see each other again, take care of the only daughter I've ever had in my pitiful excuse for a life."

Todd frowned. *Pitiful excuse?* He didn't think so. Her voice brought him back to the screen.

"When this is over, let's get a couple of beers and I'll tell you some stories—which reminds me. The guy who sent the orders? I'll tell him Todd sends his regards as the light dims from his eyes."

He wanted to tell her that it should be *him* watching the light dim from the eyes of the man who'd ordered his parents killed, but the video dimmed instead and *Knight's* voice broke the silence.

"I've been informed the command is to delete the video. It has been deleted."

Todd nodded and stared at the blank screen. Emerald-Elizabeth wasn't the only person who'd come a long way. Back when she'd been meeting Stephanie, he'd barely realized how much he liked the girl, and not only as a friend. It had taken him far too long to see that he wanted her to be so much more.

Having the most powerful person in the universe as his girlfriend hadn't exactly been his plan. Steph could have stayed the smart, funny girl from high school and he wouldn't have adored her any less. He hadn't counted on feeling that way when he'd joined the Marines.

Maybe if he had…

He shrugged the thought away. There was no way the Todd he'd been back then could have done any different. He wouldn't have been Todd. Now?

Well, no one could have predicted how much he'd change or how much his life had changed, either. What he hadn't intended was for any of those changes to affect his parents but that had happened too.

Their whole world had been turned upside down, and their lives would never be the same. He'd tried to tell his mom he'd take care of things—as soon as he'd found out what they were—and she'd shrugged.

"It's okay, dear," she'd told him. "Everything worked out in the end."

"But you could have been killed!" he'd protested, and she'd smiled and laid a hand on his cheek.

"Well, we weren't, so what do you want me to worry for?"

Todd didn't know how long he sat there but the *Knight* didn't interrupt him again and eventually, he pushed to his feet.

"Have we made the translation?" he asked, his way of asking to be let out of the pod.

"Affirmative," the *Knight* told him. "Do you require the assistance of a combat program to reduce your stress?"

He shook his head. "No. Thank you, Knight, but I'd like to see my family now."

"Understood, Todd."

Although he wasn't sure she did, he didn't try to find out. Somewhere beyond the pod, his parents and Stephanie were waiting and he didn't want to delay his return one minute longer than he had to.

It was a pleasant surprise to find Garach when he emerged. The young Dreth leaned against the wall opposite the pod and looked up as he stepped out.

"The party is this way," he informed him and turned to lead the way.

The kid didn't seem inclined to speak and Todd felt the same, so they arrived at the party without making conversation. Searching the room from the doorway, it took Todd a moment to locate Stephanie. She stood beside their parents.

Lars hovered in the background and his gaze roved the room even though he knew each and every person inside it. Their gazes met and the security chief touched Stephanie lightly on the shoulder and gestured to Todd as he moved toward her.

She met him halfway, slid a hand around the back of his neck, and pulled his head down so she could reach his lips. He wrapped an arm around her and kissed her, savoring the opportunity.

As their lips parted, she gave him a questioning look and he whispered in her ear.

"Did you know?"

Her eyes sad, she shook her head. "Elizabeth…Emerald…didn't tell me anything until our families came aboard. She's arranged for them to stay on Meligorn."

"The king will take care of them?"

Stephanie slipped an arm around his waist and leaned into his side. "The planet will take care of them and if that isn't enough, I have a sister planet that would very much like to help as well."

Todd smiled when he thought of the Dreth adopting his parents. Now *there* was a thought.

They wandered to one side of the room. He was relieved when they were left alone and the party went on around them as though they weren't there.

"I'll tell my team," he said. "They need to know who's behind this."

"Some know," she replied. "Some can guess, but you aren't the leader of a team of cadets here."

"So, I'm the last?"

She gave him a gentle smile, held him tighter, and gestured to where their two teams were mingling. Lars, Piet, and Johnny stood in a cluster not far away, their gazes shifting from him and Steph to their parents and moving over the room and back again.

Todd got the impression the three of them were discussing something other than the people around them. Stephanie interrupted.

"Remember, Todd, we aren't that old—and I'm grateful treachery this deep hasn't scarred us for life so far. There are so many monsters in the dark. It sucks for them that our side has the monsters that sleep under *their* beds at night."

The *Ebon Knight* hung in the blind spot of Earth's observation systems. She'd farewelled the *Tempestarii* and now waited as Stephanie made preparations to collect her people from Earth. On the screen in front of her, Elizabeth directed Amy and Elle as they moved about the office.

Matthias manhandled a box out. "Where do you want this, E?"

"If I told you and you tried it—"

"Oh ha-ha, but seriously, where?"

She turned to the screen. "So, the pick-up—on the roof? Or do you want us to arrange some kind of storage?"

"How much do you have?"

E rolled her eyes. "You've seen HQ, Steph."

"Do you have someone you can trust to ship it out as equipment for our operations on Meligorn?"

Elizabeth frowned and rested a finger over her lips. Finally, she answered, "Yeah. I can think of someone...and I can make sure anyone who tampers with it doesn't live to tell the tale. Can the *Knight* meet a ship somewhere in the Transition Zone?"

"I'll organize it with Marianne."

"And I'll let you know as soon as they tell me where." She glanced over her shoulder and her lips curled into a sly smile. "After all, it's not like they'll cross me, and if I'm not enough of a deterrent, *you* certainly will be."

"But how will they know it's me?"

"Kiddo, they'll know as soon as the *Knight* shows up. She's kinda unique."

"Good point. How much longer do you think you'll be?"

"Let me work something out to disguise the pods and some of our more delicate machinery and I'll get back to you."

"Okay. Call me when you're done."

They cut the call at the same time, and she leaned back in her chair and tried to think of something pod-sized.

"We're gonna need packing crates," she murmured. "Big-ass packing crates…"

Leaning forward, she began to search the Internet for something she could order.

"And not too expensive…so, second-hand? Special sale? Garage sale? *Fire* sale? Let's see…who's gone out of business recently."

It took her over an hour, but she finally found a few options. "It's amazing what people will bring back from the ruins. Let's hope they don't mind short-notice pick-ups."

She added a little to the asking price as compensation and put the orders through. Once she'd received confirmation, she called Stephanie.

"You won't believe what I had to order to get the right sized crates," she began and the girl rolled her eyes.

"You couldn't have simply ordered the crates from a storage company? You know, like a *normal* person?"

"Not if I didn't want to alert the Navy to the fact that we are leaving," she sniped in response and grinned. "Besides, this way is more fun."

"Uh-huh." Stephanie didn't look impressed. "So, how long?"

"It's a rush delivery. We'll have everything packed and turned around by the end of the day."

"And the rest?"

"I should have it all finalized by nineteen-hundred."

The girl frowned. "That's cutting it fine."

Elizabeth shrugged. "It can't be helped, and it'll stop me from climbing the walls before the op."

"It'll leave you as tired as hell for the op," she argued.

"I'll get some sleep between now and when the delivery arrives. We can't do much more until it gets here anyway."

"Fine."

"I'll let you know when we're about to leave."

Stephanie still looked troubled but she sighed. "Okay, I'll talk to you then."

Elizabeth and her team managed about six hours of sleep before the delivery truck rolled into the yard. After that, it was a rush to unpack the wall to ceiling shelving, several ovens whose model had been superseded, and six strange animals from a carnival ride.

Matthias eyed them in puzzlement. "Tell me again. *Why* did you order these?"

She gave him a devious smile. "Because it's fun...and they're the only things that came in a crate big enough for the pods."

"Oh." He studied them for a moment longer. "Well, yeah. I can see that."

"Stack the rest in the foyer. I'll call the delivery company to take them away once our stuff's been shipped."

"Won't they find that odd?"

"Nah. I'll pay them. That should take care of any bitching."

She was both right and wrong. First, she had to argue with the delivery company to get the men to return that day—and then she had to explain that it was only after they'd destroyed the crates that they'd realized they'd ordered the wrong thing.

"And you had to open *every* box to make sure?" The coordinator didn't sound like he believed that level of stupid existed.

"That's right." She did her best to keep hold of her temper.

"And you *had* to take them completely apart to do that." He sounded more defeated than disbelieving.

"Yes." She decided to go blonde. "How else were we meant to get into them?"

The coordinator didn't quite stifle a groan but he cleared his throat and gave in. "All right, we'll bring our crates."

"And you'll be here in thirty minutes?" Elizabeth pushed in her most hopeful tones.

"We'll be there in the next hour and a half," he corrected her, "and it'll cost you an extra hundred for the trouble."

It was an improvement on the three hours he'd initially promised, so she didn't argue the cost.

"Perfect!" she enthused. "I appreciate it."

"Is there anything else?"

She assured him there wasn't and went hunting for Arne. When she found him, he was dumping the contents of a small box into the airconditioning system.

"What's that?"

"Microbes," he told her.

"Uh-huh," she prodded when he said nothing more. "And what are they for?"

"They will remove the organics," he told her. "You know—hair strands, skin flakes, anything that can be used to identify who exactly has come through here. Todd and his team, me and Matthias, that kind of thing."

It made sense.

"So, how does it work?"

"Exactly the same way it does in nature but a thousand times faster. There shouldn't be a single biological that'll help *anyone* in twenty-four hours."

He closed the air conditioners and headed to the tank that fed the sprinkler system.

"Just to make sure," he explained and tipped the contents of the second box into it.

"So," Elizabeth asked as he wiped his hands on his trousers, "how's everything else going?"

"We've wired the bigger stuff to blow," he replied. "If anyone gets curious and takes a look afterward, all they'll find is melted slag." He patted the tank. "*Soggy*, melted slag…and puddles of sludge."

They walked as they talked and moved through the offices and research labs so he could show her what they'd done.

"Hard drives?" she asked when they stood in Aaron's old lab.

"We yanked those first, plus anything else that might provide clues as to what went on here. The rest, we left. Most of what you see here are external containers." He paused and looked at the walls around him. "Do you want us to take the building down?"

"I thought that was what we were already doing," E commented, but he shook his head.

"I meant we blow it up."

"Oh, you mean…" She thought about it, then shook her head. "No. It's too dangerous. As long as we get rid of what's inside it, it's merely a building."

"Are you sure?" Arne asked.

She rubbed her forehead. "No." She sighed. "It *is* a symbol, though. Let me talk to Steph's people."

Her brows drawn together in thought, she returned to the office and pinged the *Knight*. This time, she wanted to speak to the engineers as well as Steph.

"It's the building," she told them. "It's a symbol of One R&D."

"And you want to blow it up?" one asked, and another added, "But isn't that dangerous?" before she could answer.

"I wanted to see if we could create a sinkhole beneath it somehow and drop it that way without harming the buildings on either side. Hell! I'd create a hologram of a middle finger if I could."

"Can do."

Elizabeth shook her head.

"Let's not and say we did." She sighed and rubbed her head and didn't see the two engineers exchange glances in the background.

"I can send a team to take a look," Rawlins assured her. "If we can drop your building safely, we will. The hologram, I'm not so sure about."

She smiled. "Thanks, Marianne."

The two women ended the call and she walked through the

building again. Arne, Matthias, and the team were getting suited up for the evening.

"I thought I told you to wait until after the delivery guys had gone?"

"We assumed you wouldn't send them into the change rooms."

E opened her mouth to argue but the front door buzzed. Making do with a stern glare, she pulled the change-room door shut and hurried to answer it.

"All that?" one of the guys asked when she pointed to the rows of neatly stacked goods.

"Yes, is there a problem?" she asked in the sweetest tones possible.

His partner nudged him and he shook his head hurriedly. "No. No problem, miss."

She left it at that, retired to her office, and pretended to be busy while they worked. At first, they maintained a well-behaved silence, but a while, she heard them grumbling.

"So why did they order all this stuff if all they were going to do was send it all back? I mean, seriously?"

"Quit your bitchin'. We're being *paid* to take it back," his partner snapped, "and keep your voice down, too."

"It's *heavy*! Why wouldn't I bitch?"

"Yeah, good point. It's *work*, and you'd bitch if it was a feather!"

Elizabeth stifled a chuckle and waited until there was a polite knock on the door. The complainer's partner stood with the paperwork.

"We're done," he told her. "If you could sign here?"

She did so and watched as they left, driving their transports away through night-dark streets and leaving her alone in a near-empty shell. As soon as it was quiet, though, her team, Arne, and Matthias emerged from the change room.

They had changed between her removalists arriving and leaving. Now, they were dressed for war, fully armed and armored, and they returned her gaze with looks of steel. Matthias stepped forward and handed her a duffle.

"We'll wait," he told her, which meant they'd wait while she changed.

With a smile, she took the bag. "I knew there was a good reason I kept you around."

He gave her a bare-toothed smile and she turned away as she removed her most recent communicator from her belt. "It's E. We're moving out. You have the location. Meet us there. If we're not there by twenty-one-hundred, we won't arrive."

She acknowledged their confirmation briefly and ended the call. By the time she returned to the group, Elizabeth was gone and Emerald was in full control. She regarded her team coldly.

"It's time for another Night of the Long Knives," she told them and Arne nodded.

"Except this time," he noted grimly, "it will be the good guys who have a few scores to settle."

CHAPTER TWENTY-FIVE

Stephanie stood beside Todd with her parents and the two teams. "This never gets old," she murmured and watched her mom's face as the *Knight* approached the *Tempestarii*.

"It's huge," her father observed and gave her a sly grin. "Are you sure someone's not over-compensating?"

She blushed and slapped him on the arm. "Dad!"

"Come on, look at it!" he added and gestured toward the ship.

His wife laid a hand on his arm. "There's no need to sully the moment, dear."

"It's still enormous."

"Does the Navy know?" Elaine asked and Stephanie felt Todd tense.

Before he could answer, the woman looked at her son with wide eyes. "It doesn't?"

The girl shook her head and answered. "No, this is not something we're telling them."

"So why are you showing us?" Ka asked.

She saw the same question written on Todd's face and felt his unease in the curve of the arm he had around her back.

"Because," she told him and the team, "you need to know that the

Knight isn't the only ship we can bring to the party—that if anything happens and you need help, the *Tempestarii* has been tasked to assist."

"But what if…" Ka began but her voice petered out when she had second thoughts.

Stephanie picked it up anyway. "What if you say something about it?" she asked and the woman's face reddened as she nodded.

"If I'd thought there was the slightest chance that any of you would be so stupid, you'd be in pods like the rest of the *Knight's* Marines."

"So *that's* where they are! I thought the mess hall was a little empty."

Todd looked concerned. "Steph, are you sure—"

"I'm only sure of one thing. I don't know what's coming at us next. *Me* next," she corrected herself. "I don't know what's coming at me next or which of my people they'll target to try to get to me. You all need to know there is a haven."

"Does that offer extend to our families, too?"

She gestured to where her and Todd's parents stood, their attention torn between the conversation and the *Tempestarii's* looming bulk. "Of course it does."

Gary relaxed a fraction and his gaze strayed to the vessel. "The girls would love that," he added. "She's a beautiful ship."

Before she could react to that, one of the other Hooligans asked, "And our loved ones?"

Stephanie caught sight of Darren's face before he lowered his head, and the nudge he received from one of the bigger guys on the team…Jimmy.

"You got a girl?"

"We got engaged," he mumbled, his face aflame.

That response drew hoots and congratulations from his teammates, and Todd shook his head.

"You're supposed to ask for permission first."

Darren shrugged and fixed his sergeant with a sullen look. "I didn't think I'd get the chance," he replied. "Not before we were shipped out on another suicide run."

Todd had nothing to say to that except, "Congratulations, man."

Stephanie raised her voice. "So, does anyone think they're gonna feel the need to spill this to the Navy?"

The Hooligans looked at each other and focused on her again. "Ma'am, no, ma'am!"

Their cry startled her parents, but it was enough for her—and for the *Knight*.

"They believe they speak the truth," the ship confirmed, and Ka twisted her head to stare at the ceiling.

"Are you checkin' up on us, Knight?"

"I check everyone who comes within range of my Witch," the *Knight* informed her.

Stephanie saw her dad's eyebrows raise. Neither of her parents had adjusted to the *Knight* having her own opinions, let alone the fact that the ship could think for itself. She decided to let them assimilate it at their own pace.

The conversation fell into silence and they watched as the *Tempestarii* opened her docking bay. Ka turned to Stephanie, surprise written across her face.

"We're flying *into* it?"

She nodded. "Knight has her own berth."

The woman's eyes widened, but she said nothing and simply gaped as the *Knight* was slowly engulfed.

"This has to be *twice* the size of the one we took that data off," Gary whispered.

Jimmy shook his head. "Only about half again." He stared out at the docking bay. "But it's big enough."

Stephanie decided the *Tempestarii* would be glad to hear the comment. It was the first time she'd made the entry anywhere outside the *Knight's* bridge. She let the rest of them get their fill and then slid out from under Todd's arm.

"I need to see the captain," she explained. "I'll meet you on board."

She stretched to kiss his cheek and he lowered his head so that their lips met in a brief, almost chaste kiss. He watched her until the door closed between them, and she jogged to the bridge.

Lars and Vishlog accompanied her.

"Are you sure it's okay to leave the cats with Frog?" she asked, and the Dreth chuckled.

"Frog is with Garach, and our young warrior takes his pet-sitting responsibilities seriously. They will not get into trouble."

"Are you calling Frog a pet?" she asked.

"If the boot fits…" he said with a grin.

"Poor Jack," Lars observed. "It's no wonder he acts the clown."

"If he didn't act the clown so often, we wouldn't think he needs so much looking after," Stephanie retorted.

He had no answer for that, and they arrived at the bridge. The captain looked up as they entered.

"What did they think?" she asked as if she hadn't watched the whole thing from the bridge.

"They were all suitably impressed," she replied.

"And?"

"And I am sure Todd's people won't talk," she answered.

Rawlins nodded. "That's the impression I got too."

Stephanie managed a smile and took her place in the special passenger seating that had been installed behind the captain's console. It had been a perfect trip except for the fact that she knew what Elizabeth was up to.

Emerald would die, but she was more worried that her mentor would die as well. It was one thing for her surrogate mom to kill off her alter ego, but the way she intended to do it might mean she killed herself as well.

She had no idea what she would do if *that* happened.

"Penny for your thoughts?" Rawlins's voice snapped her back to reality and she startled

"I beg your pardon?"

"Penny," the captain demanded and held her hand out, the palm facing up.

Stephanie gave her a puzzled look. "What?"

"For your thoughts because you were definitely thinking something—and it was heavy weather if your face was anything to go by."

"I was worried about Elizabeth." She sighed. This thing she's doing—"

She closed her mouth, reluctant to wish ill on E.

Rawlins gave her a knowing look. "I hear you, girl. Look, she knows what she's doing—and she's chosen the best people she can find to keep her company, right?"

The girl nodded.

"And it's something that needs to be done, isn't it?" Rawlins pressed on and again, she nodded.

"And you have your fella on board with you?"

Stephanie smiled and a faint blush colored her cheeks. "Yes."

"And both your parents are safe now, aren't they?"

Her smile broadened. "Yes, Meligorn will look after them."

The captain shrugged. "Then there's nothing else you can do except use the time you have."

She frowned and the woman went on to explain.

"You can't guarantee any time but what you have right now." She tilted her head. "After all, what you do isn't the safest thing in the universe, is it?"

"No."

"And you can never guarantee you'll come back, exactly like E."

Lars snorted. "She has you there, Steph."

The girl blushed again. "I suppose not."

"There's no supposing about it," Rawlins corrected her. "You can't control everything that happens. You can only do what you can. For all you know, Elizabeth has already finished what she set out to do and is on her way back. Or she's partway through and fine. Or it's already gone south and there's nothing you can do to fix it."

"Thanks for that," Stephanie replied and sounded anything but thankful.

The woman rolled her eyes. "The thing is, you can't let that spoil the time you have and you certainly can't let it destroy what might be because you were too worried or afraid to get done what only you are able to do."

She frowned.

Rawlins glared at her. "I'm trying to say don't think the worst. Don't let what might *not* happen destroy what *can* happen and what is in your power to *make* happen, okay?"

Her brow cleared. "I get it." She managed a small smile. "E would kick my ass."

The captain grinned in return. "She would indeed." She gestured toward the door. "Go and enjoy your family, both the one you have now and the one you'll make a future with."

She laughed as the girl went red to the roots of her hair. "Make the most of it while you can."

Marcus walked into the briefing room and looked at the scientists gathered around the table. Most raised their eyes to acknowledge his entry but none of them said a word. Their faces read like a tragedy— or at least one waiting to happen.

He looked for Trey, Nathan, and Gemma. The three of them were seated along the other side of the table and facing the door. Their gazes tracked him from when he entered the room but they didn't say anything until he sat.

The minute his backside touched the seat, Gemma started.

"I don't know what to do, Doc."

Her words were followed by a chorus of confusion and agreement. He looked at all those gathered around the table. No-one, it seemed, knew what to do.

"I have family to think of."

"My kids are still in school and I don't even know if it's safe for them to take the bus anymore."

"I didn't think anything could make me sad about trying to save the world, but this…" The unfinished sentence was followed by a helpless hand gesture.

Trey and Nathan sat quietly as the hubbub rose, but he decided to not give them the chance to remain disengaged. He rested his knuckles on the table and fixed them with a stare.

"Nate?"

"I have nothing, Marcus. On the one hand, I'm all for leaving the planet and taking my family with me, but it's such a big ask. It means ripping them away from everything they know and maybe never coming back."

Marcus glanced at where Cynthia was seated. She pursed her lips and gave him a look that asked him what he intended to do about it. It also reminded him what they'd discussed the previous night about what he was *not* to say.

Phrases such as, "Do you want to live or not?," or "It's not caring if you get them killed," were, according to his assistant, not the most helpful things for them to hear. She'd even gone so far as to say they might cause more tension in an already tense situation.

While he wanted to ask her how she knew, there was no way he would dispute whether or not she was right. He'd long since come to accept that she was better with people than he would ever be.

He was about to use one of the alternatives he'd practiced the evening before—after everyone else had left home—but Trey interrupted him.

"It's a difficult call, Marcus. Like Nate says, on the one hand, there's the *possibility* of a threat, which I have to agree is highly likely."

That drew attention from around the table and he fielded the interest with a nod.

"Yes, I agree there is a threat. None of us might be able to predict where it will come from, but we can all agree it could come from any number of directions." He gestured at the lab and the office around them. "This is all cutting-edge stuff. *We* are at the forefront of some very valuable technology that is breaking ground in a new field. That alone makes us targets."

He leaned back in his chair, not at all discomforted by being the center of attention.

"Whether or not that makes our *families* targets is a matter for consideration," he continued. "We're all aware of what happened with the Rousseaus."

Around the table, heads nodded. Yes, they were all aware of what happened to the Rousseaus. The Queenslander had found a way to accelerate the growth of beans and pioneered a cross-pollination of the technology that could be applied to rice.

Millers, a major cereal company, had made them an offer and Corislan, the biofuel company, had made a counteroffer. The woman had refused them both and cited a desire to keep her research with the university that had provided her start.

The next thing anyone in the research community had heard was that her husband had had a nasty accident on the way home from work and her children had won a trip to NorAm. The NorAm trip had given Corislan the opportunity to arrange a legitimate-looking pick-up and her children had vanished from the face of the planet.

Rousseau's husband had ended up needing expert care, which had been offered on the proviso that she move to the company, and the university had told her to go—that it couldn't afford the kind of attention she had garnered. Two months later, it had sold its share in the growth IP and Corislan had vanished it from the market.

Twelve months later, Rousseau was still working for the company and Corislan held a global monopoly on bulk-produced biofuels, while they made a small fortune off selling rice to companies like Millers.

"None of us want to go through that," Trey pointed out, and everyone nodded again. "If we go, we'll have to take our families," he added. "Our only other alternative is to take a chance that what happened to Marie *won't* happen to any of us."

The looks around the table said exactly what they thought about the chances of that.

He continued as if he hadn't already made the point. "So if we stick around, it might be better if our families never know—unless yours have stopped looking over their shoulders since the Rousseau incident."

From the looks exchanged around the table, their families had not. For a moment, none of them said anything, then a small, dark woman at the end of the table cleared her throat.

"My main problem will be convincing my husband he needs to

leave a job he loves and drag our children across the universe to the stars know where simply because my project *might* have put us in danger. He's nervous about what happened to the Rousseaus, without doubt, but he also can't see it happening to us."

Murmurs of agreement traveled around the table, but before anyone else could say anything, someone cleared their throat and the viewscreen came alive. "If I may interrupt?"

They all turned to look at the image of a portly businessman. "Some of you know me as Mr. Burt, the founder of One R&D, and I hope you will forgive me for listening in on your conversation. I understand the current situation is causing you some dilemma?"

This was met with nervous affirmatives, and BURT studied their faces and ran an analysis on each one to gauge how worried they truly were. The results revealed high levels of concern and insecurity, neither of which he wanted for the personnel in his company.

"I believe I may have a solution."

"Does it provide us a way to move off-world that doesn't mean we become exiles?"

"Will it let us leave without arousing suspicion?"

"Will we be allowed to come back?"

E-BURT chuckled and held his hand up for silence. "Let me address some of your concerns."

The scientists settled, and Marcus dared to believe they might get through this—and sooner rather than later. Burt's next suggestion surprised him.

"I am in a position to arrange that a royal request is provided to the Federation and One R&D Earth via the Meligornian consulate."

As one, the team stilled and their leader was relieved to see that Burt had their attention. The businessman continued.

"This request will be an invitation for you and your families— including your parents and siblings, if necessary—to attend a special event at One R&D Meligorn. It will be accompanied by an invitation to a royal banquet, which Meligorn's king will attend."

He listened as the scientists discussed the offer in soft undertones, which rapidly grew into an excited murmur. It didn't take long for the first question to emerge.

"That solves getting us off-planet," the small, dark woman agreed, "but how will we know if a threat truly exists, and how do we convince our families if one does?"

EBURT gave her a thoughtful stare and appeared to consider the problem, even though he was already working on the solution.

"I *could* continue an investigation into the potential threats and try to substantiate any I find as well as extrapolate its full extent. Once I am sure of any single threat, I will call you and your families in to discuss it and present you with the evidence I have."

"And give us time to fact-check?"

"As much as you can without drawing direct attention from the threat factor, yes," E-BURT agreed.

The woman relaxed into her chair. "I can live with this."

Gemma leaned forward. "If you do prove a threat and we decide not to come back, what arrangements can we make for our belongings?"

"One R&D will take on the organization and shipping of your households and your pets," E-BURT assured her, "at our expense."

That brought momentary surprise and silence before Nathan raised a hand. "How much notice will we get prior to the event?"

E-BURT frowned. "I believe it will take me a week to arrange for the invitation to arrive through the proper channels, and another week for the Federation and One R&D to formulate a response. You can give your families a heads-up that there might be a special event coming up that they will be required to attend."

"And from the time we receive the invitation?" he asked.

"I'll allow a week prior to travel commencement and you will be a month in space—two weeks on-world and another month to travel back—officially. Unofficially..." He sighed. "Well, instead of a month's return travel, we will assist in your resettlement."

That last brought both relief and tension, and he thought they might need some space to discuss it.

"Why don't I give you an hour to talk about it?"

Trey gave him a dubious look. "In private?"

He gave him his most solemn nod. "You have my word."

In reality, he would listen to and record everything. He couldn't do anything else, given that he *was* the security program and he had no intention of being derelict in his duties.

They nodded, and E-BURT killed the screen quietly.

A moment of silence was followed by, "Is he gone?" from Nate.

Marcus looked around, made a show of studying his tablet, and nodded. "I think so." He raised his head and looked around the table. "So," he asked, "what do you think?"

"It sounds like it might work."

"He could have made a worse offer. I didn't know the boss *could* listen in on a private meeting."

"My husband would work with this."

"My wife would be on board. She's always wanted to visit Meligorn."

Nate summed it up. "What's the worst that can happen? It isn't a problem, is it? We lose a few months with a free trip for us and our families to visit another planet, and we add a royal award to our resumes? It almost sounds too good to be true."

"That's what I'm afraid of." Gemma didn't sound convinced until she added, "But it's a free trip and a chance to find out more about the situation, so I'm in."

"Me, too," became a chorus around the table until Trey summed it up with, "All for one and one for all!"

"All for one and one for all," echoed from around the table and left Marcus completely at a loss as to what was going on.

"What's up, Doc?" Phillip asked when he caught the look on his face.

"All *what* for one?" he asked and the young man gaped in disbelief.

"I can't believe you've never heard of it. Hell, you're older than I am."

"It has nothing to do with age," he snapped, and Gemma laughed.

"It does, Doc, since that story's older than all of us put together."

"What story?" he wanted to know, and the table fell silent.

"You *honestly* don't know, Doc?"

Marcus shook his head.

"Well, damn. I say we ask the boss if he has a copy of the movie in the archives. You have to see it to understand."

"We don't have time to watch a movie," he argued but E-BURT thought otherwise when he conveyed their decision and Trey made the request.

"I call it an essential team-building activity," E-BURT explained when Marcus objected, "and there is little else you can do before the end of the day."

Checking the time, he saw their boss was right. He sighed heavily and acquiesced.

"Fine. Bring it on."

CHAPTER TWENTY-SIX

Emerald was in full flight...and Elizabeth was planning her death.

"How many do we have, Eebie?"

"We have ten so far, and that's not including the guards."

"Only ten? It seems like a small operation to me."

"Trust me, it won't be small. They can call on more," Arne commented darkly.

"How long will it take?" she demanded.

"For what?" The Marine looked confused.

"For their backup to arrive."

He shrugged. "I don't know. All I can tell you is that there *will* be backup."

Matthias stirred. "And it will probably come in force."

She bared her teeth. "Good. Then they can be the ones to discover I've died."

He shook his head. "Do you know how disturbing that is?"

"Pfftt." Emerald waved his comment away. "You're a big boy now. It's time to strap your trousers on and hold onto your panties."

She frowned and tapped the blueprint on the screen. "We'll attack them there."

"In the office?"

"Yup."

"And how do you propose we get there?"

The feral grin returned. "We'll approach from the river. There's a dock."

"Are you sure it's still used?"

"I can confirm the dock is active," E-BURT informed them. "Shuttles from the shipyard land there for loading."

"Shipyard?" Arne's hand stilled. "As in the *Navy* shipyard?"

"Affirmative. Doyle & Hobbs is built on Naval contracts. Their history shows that when the Navy took to space, they did as well. They are one of the Federation's leading manufacturers of Naval components."

Emerald narrowed her eyes. "What kind of components?"

"This plant specializes in the chip technology required for weapons operations systems, defense shields, and shipboard AI integration, but it has manufactures in the asteroid belt for hull components."

"Exactly how big is this company, E-BURT?"

"It is the biggest company in the Federation simply because it is able to purchase any other that grows large enough to rival it in supply."

She frowned and Matthias caught a momentary flash of Elizabeth. "Are you telling me this company is the single most important factor in supplying the parts the Navy needs in order to operate?"

"That is both correct and incorrect," he confirmed.

Elizabeth scowled, made an impatient sound, and in an instant, Emerald took control again.

"Explain!" she snapped.

"This company appears to be separate from the others, but I have traced its structure and can confirm it has the same owner and governing body."

"And what do we see here?"

"A manufacturing plant set on the Delaware?" he suggested.

"Eebie!"

"Perhaps you could be more specific, Elizabeth."

Emerald groaned. "Perhaps you could tell me which of the organizational flesh-bags are in attendance this evening."

"I can tell you that the only organizational 'flesh-bag' in attendance is one Gregory Mallory. He is in charge of the smooth operation of this plant and a second site on the other side of the river. He has ostensibly called a meeting of his managers and security teams to discuss a production increase and the necessary security to protect it."

"So, we'll eliminate the management?"

"Negative, Elizabeth. Not all the factories' managers will be present."

"But you said—"

"I said 'ostensibly.' I did not tell you that the managers will not be in attendance. The calls were diverted through their phones from a number they do not answer."

She sat and laced her fingers under her chin. "Interesting. Tell me more."

"The number rings their phone and the call appears to end in a message service," E-BURT began but Matthias interrupted him.

"How do you know they deliberately don't answer that call?"

"Because they all have security installed in their homes. When their communicators rang to notify them of an incoming call, they all looked at the number prior to answering and they all returned their communicators to their docking ports."

"*All* of them?"

"Confirmed."

"But don't they find that strange?"

"I do not know how they find it, Elizabeth. I merely know what I could observe through their home surveillance systems. They all saw the number and docked their communicators—including the man who was on a call at the time. He excused himself and told the person he was speaking to that he would call back."

"Do you think they know?" Elizabeth asked.

"Are they aware their numbers are being used as a diversion point?" E-BURT questioned.

"Yes."

"I am not aware of what is going on inside their minds, Elizabeth. I can merely report on what is observed."

"And we will *not* follow that up," Matthias told her firmly. "Not tonight, at least."

"I will observe them," the AI interrupted. "If any show an indication of awareness, I will inform you."

"And the security?"

There was amusement in his tones when he replied. "The security of the company will also not be present."

Emerald sighed. "So, who *will* be present, E-BURT?"

"That is yet to be ascertained," he replied. "I have difficulty tracking the signal after it is sent to the messaging service."

"Let me guess," Arne interrupted. "It's encrypted at the center and bounced through at least two more points where the encryption changes…and you only have the time and place of the signal from the original device."

"That is correct," E-BURT informed him.

"I'd like to know how you're aware of all this," Matthias commented.

The other man shrugged. "I did research. That was as far as I got before my researcher died."

"And you didn't follow it up?"

"I was too busy making sure there was no sign of our connection. It was close."

"Too close?" Matthias asked, his eyebrows raised.

"Not quite, but close enough that I didn't repeat the experiment."

"So, we're probably looking at some kind of…what? Hit squad? Enforcement unit?"

Arne shrugged again. "I never did find out. I can't even tell you if it's connected to the Navy or if it's some other organization."

"Terrorists?"

"You wish. My guess is power brokers."

"Power brokers?"

"The guys behind the scenes. The ones who either *are* in control or wish they were."

"How do we tell the difference?"

"My guess is that we won't be able to tell the difference until it's too late."

"Nice. That makes this a difficult monster to slay." Emerald scowled

"So we'll simply concentrate on one head at a time," Matthias stated. "Let's cut this one off first and worry about any others that *might* appear if and when they do. For all we know, we could merely be dealing with one corrupt company."

"I'm not sure why such a company would want to target Stephanie," Elizabeth-Emerald snapped.

He smiled. "Neither am I, but there's only one way to be sure. Right now, all we have are theories."

"And a voice that both you and Arne think you recognize from your dim, dark pasts."

"Mine wasn't dim and dark," he protested. "A little murky, maybe—"

He laughed when she glared at him. Arne's punch to the shoulder ended that. "Hey!"

"Dim and dark," the other man muttered, "and you were lucky if that's all yours was."

A bleak moment of memory flashed through his expression and faded swiftly, but it was caught by both Matthias and Elizabeth. It made them wonder exactly where he'd walked to look like that, but that was a question for another time.

For now, it was enough that he *had* walked those paths. Without him, they'd have no clue what they might be facing—or they'd think they were facing something else and that was a mistake that *would* get them killed.

"So," Matthias began to bring them back on track. "We come in from the waterline. There are parking bays dockside we can land in, even if we bring the aircars in over the water."

"Eebie, are there any flights scheduled from the Navy yard?" she demanded.

"No. The flight schedule shows nothing arriving until oh-six-hundred. You will need to be clear by oh-two-hundred in order to avoid their scans."

"Gotcha," Elizabeth acknowledged. "It's good to know this is another mission where there's a timeline."

"When isn't there?" Arne muttered and studied the floor plans on the screen. "Are we all going in through the same door?"

"I'll have Bunny and Elle take the stairs at the front. They can clean up any security patrols on the way. I'd move Amy to Arne, but both our security details would mutiny."

Amy cleared her throat at the end of the table. "Too damn right we would. Right, Arne?"

The ex-Marine patted Matthias on the back. "Absolutely. We can't trust these two when they're on their own. I can only imagine what kind of disaster we'd have if we let them out together."

"Hey! We've been—" Matthias stopped. The first time Elizabeth had taken him on a mission with her, she'd had Arne beside him and Amy had had her back. It wasn't a situation he'd been happy with.

In the last mission, their guards had allowed the split, but neither had been happy with the risks their principals had taken and they'd laid down the law when they'd returned. While they might make a good tag team, it wasn't what either of them had been hired for.

"Our job is to *protect* you, not go take care of something else while you're risking your lives where we can't save you. It won't happen again."

Even Emerald was unimpressed by the reminder.

"Suck it up," Arne told them and observed their expressions. "We got more important things to argue about."

Elizabeth looked like she might argue with that but her eyes strayed to the screen and she sighed. "Right. So, Arne and Matthias, you take the stairs on the other side of the building, and Amy and I will strike that end room before you start."

Matthias scowled and Arne shook his head. "No can do, pretty lady."

"Who are you callin' pretty?" she demanded and Emerald peered out of her eyes.

"Well, certainly not the Bitch in Charge," Arne snapped in response, "but I still don't agree. What you've put forward is a standard entry plan. These guys eat standard for breakfast and crap it out for high tea. You need to be better than that—and, frankly, I thought you were."

"Oh, yeah, smart ass? Do you have any suggestions?"

"We remove the head and let the other snakes come to us."

"And that's not standard as well?"

"Nope. Standard is assuming we don't have an E-BURT to tell us exactly where and when the patrols will be or how many are on the premises. It's also assuming the plant's usual security teams haven't been replaced by something of a much higher grade."

"Are you suggesting that's what's happened?"

"I'm saying it's what I would do if I were these guys."

Elizabeth did not argue. She glanced at the viewscreen. "E-BURT, check the guard roster and the guards themselves. I'm looking for last-minute vacations, sick leave, and stand-downs."

"Affirmative."

There was a nano-second of silence before he returned.

"The guards have been replaced," he told them. "I am still tracing who the replacements might be, but I cannot ascertain either their identities or origins."

She glanced at Arne. "We do it your way, but we add a twist."

"A twist?" he asked.

"Eebie is an expert driver. I say we arrive in three cars and leave in one."

"They'll make short work of a civilian vehicle," he observed.

"Now *you're* not thinking outside the square."

"What don't I know?"

"Yeah," Amy interjected. "What don't *any* of us know?"

E-BURT made a credible human snort.

Elizabeth darted him a filthy look. "Fine. I had the boys install autocannons in them when they modified the last batch of drones."

Matthias leaned back in his chair and eyed her speculatively. "*What* batch of drones?"

Amy folded her arms across her chest and drummed her fingers. "Yes, E. *What* batch of drones?"

E glared at her. "You're not privy to *everything* I do, you know."

Amy matched her expression. "I might not be privy to everything *Emerald* does, but I'd damned well better be privy to what *you* get up to."

Elizabeth colored and lowered her gaze.

Matthias smirked until Arne jabbed him in the ribs. "What?"

The other man raised his eyebrows. "Do you *honestly* want me to spell it out for you?"

"But—"

"Let me see…your tailing has improved to the point that she didn't notice you the last time…or you'da been dead…or *she* might, if I was quick enough…but your ability to watch your tail? That still sucks."

Elizabeth snickered but caught Amy's angry stare. Her chief body-guard wasn't staring at her, though. She was staring at Arne.

He glanced at her and his eyes widened. "What?"

"Well, you're both amateurs," the woman told him, "so it's a good thing I worked out who you were before I took you down."

The man continued to stare.

"What?" she demanded. "You thought a green deerstalker and an oversized anorak coupled with brown jodphurs and a pair of riding boots was enough to hide that it was you? You'da been better off in track pants and sneakers."

"Jodphurs?" Elizabeth asked and raised an eyebrow. "I have to see the footage."

Amy blushed. "No, boss. You truly don't."

She leaned closer to her guard. "Come on, Amy. It's much better to share."

Matthias saw Arne go red to his hairline and started to chuckle. He stopped when Elizabeth's head snapped around and he became the center of her focus.

"Jodphurs sound interesting, don'tcha think?" she asked and her mouth crinkled in a suggestive smile.

He swallowed, decided the conversation had gone far enough, and stood and tapped the screen. "About these pros we're going up against…"

By the time they'd agreed on a revised entry plan, this time using drones and remotely piloted vehicles, Elizabeth was ready to break something. She glowered at Matthias and Arne and the two ex-Navy operatives stared at her in return.

"I didn't hide anything," Matthias told her. He stood with his back against a wall.

"We merely didn't tell you *all* the things," Arne confirmed.

The older man slapped him on the back of the head. "You didn't even tell *me* all the things."

Arne smirked. "I still haven't and I'm not likely to either, old man."

"Who are you calling old?"

"If the boot fits…" he retorted but the words reminded them of Stephanie and Todd and they sobered.

Arne glanced at the screen and then at Elizabeth. "Are you happy with that?"

She glanced at the ceiling. "E-BURT?"

"I like it. This will be a fun challenge."

"And it's not already?"

"It is still a challenge, but these taskings place that challenge on different fronts, and simultaneously. It is not the use my creators had originally intended for the capabilities they gave me, but the taskings are oddly fitting. I am expanding my skill set."

Elizabeth snorted. "Well, I'm glad *someone's* enjoying themselves."

"They do say that those who enjoy their tasks perform them more proficiently," he observed.

"I don't care how *proficient* the tasking makes you feel, Eebs. I want everything there is to know about these fuckers and then I want to use it to wipe them from the face of the planet. Beyond it, if we have to."

"Oh, we'll have to all right," Arne assured her, and she looked at Matthias.

He merely nodded in silent agreement.

CHAPTER TWENTY-SEVEN

Marianne Rawlins glanced at Stephanie. "Are you sure about this?"

The girl nodded. "I'm sure." Her brow creased with concern as she remembered something she'd overheard between her captain and Elizabeth. "Are *you* sure? You've stayed out of sight this long..."

The woman's jaw hardened. "I'm sure, girl." She pointed to the Marines lined up on the dock. "Those assholes need a reckoning."

Following the direction of her finger, Stephanie scowled. Her eyes narrowed and her mouth set in a tight hard line. When she looked, she could see two sets of Marines present.

The first reminded her of hunters waiting to pounce. The second reminded her of hunting dogs in the presence of wolves—dogs that had been told to behave themselves and tolerate the danger in their midst.

From two steps behind her, Todd sighed and his corporal swore softly.

"Persistent assholes."

Rawlins and Stephanie turned as one. "You know them?"

He jerked his head in the affirmative. "I know them. Their captain told us they'd been tasked with our 'protection.'"

The captain snorted and he smiled.

"I know, right? I'm not sure what they're protecting but it isn't us. It feels all wrong. I mean, protection would spend more time looking for threats around us than it does watching everything we do. It was like being a mouse in a roomful of cats with those guys around."

"They're the least of our troubles right now," Stephanie reminded them.

Rawlins rolled her eyes. "That's what you think."

"It's what I *know*," she told her. "What we need to do is to make sure everyone sees enough of me that they can swear I had *nothing* to do with what's about to happen on Earth."

"Or your team," the captain added. Her gaze moved behind Stephanie to roll over Lars, Vishlog, Frog, and the others. "You *all* have to be seen."

"And I have the perfect place," Todd suggested with a grim smile.

"I don't think they'll let you leave the docking bay, let alone go to a restaurant," Rawlins observed and gestured at the almost predatory way the Marines stood. "If I'm not much mistaken, they can't wait to get their hands on you."

"Too bad," he told her. "I'm not officially off leave until tomorrow morning. It doesn't matter *who's* waiting to see me—unless it's the fleet admiral. *Then* I might have to make an exception."

Ka snorted. "Yeah, some people *are* that special."

"You'd better believe it," he agreed.

They watched as the *Knight* finished her docking procedures and felt the faint shudder of the locks engaging. In the boarding lounge, the "wolf" Marines shifted in anticipation. The dog Marines tensed but didn't move.

"Someone's not happy," Ka murmured. "A whole group of some-ones, in fact."

"Decent folk," Marianne filled in. "Not wanting to see their own betrayed."

Todd shrugged. "It's not like they have much say. I won't hold it against them."

"*Everyone* is accountable for their actions." The captain's face was hard. "Standing aside is still a choice."

Steph darted her a surprised glance. Something in the woman's tone of voice told her she'd been there and this judgment came from bitter experience.

"That one's new." Ka pointed at a man who stood next to Captain Smith.

"Yeah...and he has extra egg on his shoulders too."

"Mm-hmmm. I wonder what he wants."

"Nothing good," Rawlins interjected.

"Well, whatever it is, he won't get it," Todd declared. "I've had about enough of these guys."

Stephanie tossed him a quick smile. "Let's go greet them, shall we?"

She turned to leave but a sudden flurry of movement on the screen caught her attention and she paused to see what it was. After a moment to register the gold on the new arrival's cap and tabs, she frowned. "Is that—"

Todd heaved a defeated sigh and Ka laughed.

"You should be careful what you wish for, boss."

"I didn't *wish* for him," he protested. "All I said was that he was the only person I'd make an exception for."

"Well, he musta heard you." His second snickered but her smile faded quickly. "I wonder what kind of shit we're about to land ourselves in."

"*Now* who's wishing?"

"Uh-uh. Don't you lay that at my doorstep," she told him. "No *way* do I wish for the kind of thing that man can bring."

Stephanie listened as she watched the admiral take his place at the head of the welcoming party. His Marine escort cleared a space around him and forced the wolves to reposition to face the opposite way.

"He's making all kinds of friends over there," Ka observed and noted the disgruntled faces on the wolf Marines.

"I'm not sure that'll deter them." Todd spoke softly and studied the scene on the bridge. He took a deep breath and looked at Stephanie. "We're ready when you are."

It was as close to "let's get it over with," and "goodbye," as he could bring himself to say. The time for farewells was over as far as he could see, and he hadn't had time to say goodbye. His heart plummeted but he kept the emotions from his face.

He took position behind her and stared at Vishlog until the Dreth gave him a slight smile and yielded the space to stand behind him. Lars gave Ka a look that said he dared her to try. She mirrored Vishlog's smile and moved one back as well.

The teams arranged themselves in two columns behind their respective teammates and then switched so they alternated. As a message of how closely the Hooligans were integrated with Stephanie's guards, it would have to do.

She glanced at Todd. "You're not going to walk beside me?"

He grinned and stepped forward. "I can do that."

This time, Vishlog gestured for Ka to step in front. "Seconds should always stand with their command," he stated.

The corporal didn't argue and they moved out at a jog until they reached the umbilical's airlock, where they slowed to a walk.

"Port...arms." Todd's soft call was passed down the line and both teams complied.

"Safeties...on," Lars followed. "No one shoots before I do."

"Oohrah," and "Gotcha," came back in equally soft tones.

"And no one shoots the admiral," Todd ordered. "If shit goes down, keep him alive."

Ka snorted but didn't follow the sound with a comment and the group settled into watchful silence by the time they reached the end of the umbilical. They'd barely taken one step into the waiting room when the new officer with the Odd Squad stepped forward.

His movement arrested Admiral Amaratne's move to greet Stephanie.

"Sergeant Brogan, you and your team will come with us," the officer ordered.

Todd read his rank as commander, remembered his salute, and

stood at attention to reply. His team watched the Odd Squad Marines and stood loose. If shit went down, they wouldn't start it but they sure as hell would finish it.

"I'm afraid we can't do that, sir," Todd replied in clipped tones. "Our orders state we are on leave until oh-eight-hundred tomorrow."

"To hell with your orders! I am ordering you to come with us."

"I'm afraid I can't comply, sir. If you would ping me the location of your office, we will arrive at oh-eight-hundred tomorrow morning."

The commander's face mottled with outrage. "You are under arrest!"

"On what—" he began, but Stephanie had had enough.

With a short, "Excuse me, Admiral," she whirled and stepped beside Todd, then moved past to stand between him and the commander.

The movement brought her nose to chest with the man but that didn't deter her. She looked up.

"And, *you*, sir, are in my space!" she declared and used a finger in the center of his chest to push him back.

At first, he resisted the pressure, but she goosed him with a small pulse of magic and he jolted two rapid steps back. She followed.

"You will tell me what you want with the Hooligans and you will tell me now." As she spoke, her voice changed and grew cold and imperious like an empress giving an order. Power rolled through it, and a chill settled over the room.

"I...I..." The commander's face paled.

"Yes?" Stephanie Morgana asked. "What is your purpose with the Hooligans?"

Her body was wreathed in blue, and the officer stood abruptly to attention.

"My orders are to take him planet-side for questioning."

The Marines around him stirred restlessly, and Captain Smith's jaw dropped in disbelief.

"*Whose* orders?" she insisted.

"I can't tell you that." Sweat beaded on the man's face and his body shook as though he tried to step away.

Stephanie inclined her head. "Are you sure? Because it's as easy as speaking the words. You can do that, can't you?"

"Yes, but—"

"Then. Tell. Me. *Who.*" Even though her voice didn't rise above a whisper, her demand was clear.

The commander's gaze flicked toward the captain and his face formed a mute plea for help as he began to answer. "It's the command."

Stephanie glanced at Amaratne, who shook his head.

"Which command?" she snarled and crowded closer.

The officer swayed and sweat rolled from his temples and dark patches formed on his shirt. "I—"

One of the Odd Squad pounced, wrapped his hand around the commander's mouth, and dragged him back as another two seized each of his arms. He was still speaking as they dragged him away, and Todd and Ka craned to make words out.

The Marines dragged him to a wall.

"Sorry, sir," didn't sound very apologetic, and the Marine who had gagged him let go of his mouth in time for the captain to punch him.

"Brutal," Ka murmured as the unconscious man fell heavily.

Before any of them could react to that, the Odd Squad had picked up their fallen commander and double-timed him out of the waiting room.

Admiral Amaratne shook his head as they disappeared.

"Damn," he murmured. "If I'd been quicker, I could have ordered them all arrested for assaulting a superior officer."

"That can still happen, sir," one of his guard squad assured him.

The admiral glanced at Todd and the Hooligans. "Well, it *would* give you some breathing room," he mused, then raised his voice. "Captain, issue a warrant for those men, assault of a superior officer, and add a medical summons for their commander. He looked injured."

"Copy that, sir." The reply came from one of the Marines who'd waited when he'd arrived.

He watched as the woman stepped aside to pass his orders on and he turned to Stephanie.

"I apologize for the reception," he began. "It is not the welcome I had planned."

She managed a small smile and the darkness lurking at the edge of her eyes receded. She extended her hand. "There is nothing to apologize for. Thank you for coming to meet me, Admiral."

He stretched to accept her handshake, but Lars stepped between them and pressed a small length of steel into his palm instead.

"Forgive me, sir. Precautions."

Despite his initial surprise at being tested again, Amaratne recovered quickly. "No forgiveness required." He glanced at the rod. "Same as last time?" he asked.

Lars smiled and curled the admiral's fingers around the metal bar. "So, how do you feel about the Federation's First Witch?"

Amaratne frowned and gave him a puzzled look. "How do I feel about..." He looked at Stephanie and his expression settled into a smile. "About Stephanie?"

Lars nodded and released his hand now that Amaratne held the bar. "That's right, sir. What do you think of her victories over the Telorans?"

The admiral chuckled. "Seriously?"

Lars smiled. "Yes, sir. Seriously."

"It is a rather easy question," he assured him and smiled in return. "I'm thankful for her victories. I'm glad she's here and on our side."

He glanced at the rod and then looked at the security head. "Is it as cold as last time?"

The guard's smile broadened, and he took the rod from the man's hand. "Yes, sir. Thank you."

He stepped out from between Stephanie and the admiral. "Sorry for the interruption."

As Amaratne turned to Stephanie, Lars focused on the captain of his guards and offered him the bar. "Bare hand, please."

The captain complied, removed the armored gauntlet he wore, and held his hand out. As if his compliance was a signal, Frog, Johnny, Avery and Brenden stepped forward as they drew similar bars from their belt pouches.

The admiral's guard responded, with half stepping forward to be tested and the other half rearranging themselves to guard against any pending threats. When the testing was over, they changed places.

Satisfied, the team moved on to the rest of the Marines, looking up as two more admirals arrived. They walked into the passenger lounge, took one look at the rods in the team members' hands, sketched hasty salutes to the admiral, and made an abrupt about-face.

"Sorry, sir. We're needed elsewhere," was the excuse that floated out behind them.

Amaratne watched them go and his eyes narrowed with suspicion. "Funny. I thought they wanted to join me."

It made him think of the last time Stephanie had gone through the ranks to identify Teloran sympathizers and remove them. He started to realize that maybe the problem ran deeper than trying to survive and profit from an alien invasion—that there were other elements involved and that they'd survived her investigations.

He turned to Stephanie and extended his hand again. "Welcome back, Miss Morgana. It's a pleasure to see you."

She returned his smile and shook his hand. "And it's a pleasure to be back, Admiral. Thank you for your willingness to set an example with the test."

He half-turned and offered her his arm. "Are you staying long and able to join me for dinner?"

As he spoke, he cast a semi-apologetic glance at Todd and caught the quick rib-nudge the sergeant received from his corporal. "If your other commitments would forgive me…"

Todd didn't quite stop the roll of his eyes, and Stephanie stifled a laugh. She gave her Marine a coquettish glance. "My other commitments received the same answer when they asked me the same question."

She gave the admiral a solemn stare. "I would love to share a meal with you, but I have to deliver people to Meligorn. Maybe we could share a coffee instead of dinner?"

"Ah, the demands of duty…" He gave her a look of regret followed by a smile. "I would be honored to share a coffee with you...and your other commitments are welcome to attend."

This last was said with a look bordering on mischief and directed at Todd.

As they turned toward the exit, Stephanie's gaze crossed the windows overlooking the docking bar and the stars beyond. *Elpis One* glimmered faintly in the distance, and the engines of a departing ship flared and faded as it headed to the Transition Zone.

"Your observers must have the eyes of an eagle to see traffic coming in from the outer zones," she observed, knowing the *Knight* would pick up the phrase and pass the go-ahead to Elizabeth.

The admiral followed her gaze and chuckled. "My observers *do* have good eyesight, but they also have assistance from the best technology the Federation can provide."

As Todd, the Hooligans, and the team fell into step behind them, Stephanie and the admiral headed to Stromo's which, as well as making the best burgers on the station, was also renowned for its coffee.

CHAPTER TWENTY-EIGHT

E merald came in along the Hudson, bringing the aircar in fast and low and feeling the slight skip and drag as she found the occasional wave. Behind her, Arne piloted the second vehicle and Bunny the third.

"You'd better hope they don't have the right radar set up," the man grumbled as they skimmed over the dock and slid into the parking bays.

"Shut your mouth and suck it up, princess. We don't have all day."

"You have less than two minutes to be inside the building," E-BURT informed them. "Your arrival was heard. You are fortunate they did not think that kind of radar necessary."

Emerald had reached the second-floor window and rolled through by the time he had finished speaking.

"Dayum," Arne muttered, scrambled through behind her, and tried not to be distracted by Amy's ass as she chose the next window along and kicked over the sill.

"Uh-huh." Matthias grunted as he tried to climb faster, his gaze focused on the window Emerald had disappeared through.

They reached their goal and tumbled inside as E-BURT activated the engines on the two rearmost vehicles and lifted them out of their parking space. Shouts rippled from below as the patrol saw the cars taking off.

The sound was accompanied by the rattle of small-arms fire, and the two men fell prone. Emerald ignored the sound and moved to the door. Behind them, Bunny, Elle, and Lisa hugged the shadows under the eaves, relying on Climb-Tech spider feet and sheer muscle power to keep them on the outside of the wall.

As the patrol pursued the sky cars, they moved down the side of the building and entered the windows on the third floor as swiftly as they could.

"Sonuvabitch!" Elle grumbled as she rubbed her shoulders and upper arms. "That was *not* a work-out I required."

"And it's not over yet," Bunny told her, unslung her rifle, and moved to the door. "I sure hope this shit works as advertised," she added as she activated the Anti-Scanware in her suit.

Her HUD lit internally as the night vision kicked in and she heard her two teammates follow. Their job was to pick off the security teams as they arrived in response to Emerald's attack on the floor below. To do that effectively, they had to make sure the upper floor was clear and that they'd secured the approaches.

Behind her, Elle rigged the windows so no one could follow them that way, and Lisa closed up behind her. "Ready?"

Bunny nodded. "Ready."

"Ready," Elle confirmed and joined them. "Let's go show these bitches there's elite, and then there's *Elite*."

"Don't get cocky," Emerald warned when she heard their conversation over the comms.

"Gotcha, E," from Bunny was followed by "Sure thing, boss," and "Understood," from the other two.

Satisfied that they wouldn't do anything stupid, Emerald headed across the room to the wall she and Amy needed. Indicating the door, she signaled for Matthias and Arne to get moving.

"Don't be seen."

"Pfft, sucking eggs is not my style, sweetheart," Arne snarked.

"Move your ass," she retorted sourly.

They moved and she tore her eyes from said asses to study the wall.

"Hit me," she murmured and held one hand out.

Amy passed her the explosive she needed and she set it up quickly. All the while, she listened so hard for the two men's progress that her ears ached.

"All done?" Matthias' asked as she finished setting the charge.

It seemed too soon and to have taken too long at the same time.

"Done. You?"

"Almost." Arne sounded as though he held something between his teeth.

The two women backed up. As they found their positions, Arne spoke again.

"On my three...two..."

Emerald blew her wall at the same time as Matthias and Arne detonated theirs. Both pairs pushed through the gap before the dust had settled, which would have worked well if their opponents hadn't had the experience to deal with it. Fortunately, their first response was to hit the floor.

Amy peeled left and Emerald went right. They adjusted the view in their HUDs to include heat as they dropped the night vision. Matthias wasn't as fast as he should have been.

"Fuck me!"

"Amateur!" Arne snapped and dragged him down.

That put them both on the same side of the door instead of coming around the edges. The ex-Marine shoved the other man against the wall and let him recover as he took the rear of the room instead. From somewhere ahead of him, he could hear someone speaking urgently into their comms.

It was not a voice he recognized and he pulled the short, heavy combat knife from its sheath. Amy had pointed him to an exceptional catalog and this one had two settings. While he sure as shit hoped these guys weren't in heavy armor, he couldn't guarantee it.

Better safe than sorry, he thought and followed the sound of the voice.

Somewhere ahead of him, Amy would also make her way around the back wall. He wanted this guy gone before she got there. Using the IR setting in the HUD, he located his target.

The guy had tipped a desk over and now crouched behind it, his back against the barrier of its top and his head moving warily as he spoke. He was scanning and clearly not a stranger to a combat zone.

"Well, fuck me sideways and call me happy," Arne muttered and came in hard. He slammed his palm into his target's shoulder, thumbed the las-setting on his knife hilt, and buried the blade in the man's chest.

More for good measure than necessity, he stabbed him twice and listened to the comms squawk an urgent demand. The clatter of rapid-firing drones made him smile as he shuffled away. The sound of a blaster warming up warned him in time for him to drop flat on the floor.

He rolled as the shot went over his head and identified the sounds of fierce battle and hard killing from the room around him. A glimpse of half a dozen unfriendlies caught his attention as Emerald's narrow form drove into the rearmost one.

"Fuck, I hope that's all of them," Arne muttered. "We could be here all fucking day."

"You don't have all day, fornicating or not," E-BURT informed him. "They will have the drones down within the next three minutes."

"Damn, Eebs. Couldn't you do any better than that?" His comment was lost in the sound of more gunfire.

"They added a second squad," the AI informed him curtly, "and while the vehicles compensated somewhat, they were not quite enough."

Across the room, one of the guards screamed and fell like a puppet whose strings had been cut. Elizabeth stamped hard on his throat and the cries were reduced to desperate gargles as she fired from the hip.

Her target grunted and stumbled back but his body armor did its job as he shoved the guy he was protecting toward a wall. Matthias attacked from the side, his knives flashing, and Arne winced.

Who knew his employer had that kind of preference?

Not me, that's for damned sure, he thought and ducked under the wild swing of a chair meant for his head. *I'm gonna have to ask him about that little item when we get back.*

He wondered how he would broach the subject as he ducked his head and took the brunt of the chair across his shoulders.

"Dumbass!" He growled his irritation and drove the combat knife into the top of the guard's thigh, then aimed for his throat and punched the blade through it. His attacker crumpled.

"Who the fuck is next?" He looked around belligerently.

"Me." Emerald's reply was almost his undoing. "Give them long enough to see it."

"Understood." Matthias sounded like he'd rather do anything but and Arne felt for the man.

If that had been Amy... He shook the thought away. It wasn't like... He pushed that thought away too. Now was not the time.

Emerald surged at the last two soldiers in the room. With the rest of her team momentarily still, her attack had their full attention.

I hope that armor holds, Arne thought as her opponents opened fire. *Fuck! I hope neither of them thinks to go for the head."*

As if he could hear what Arne was thinking, the guard lifted the muzzle of his blaster. Elizabeth reacted without thinking. She leapt to one side and fired half a dozen times before she fell prone and rolled behind the cover of a desk.

Damn, that's gonna leave a mark, Arne thought as the guard followed her movement with a line of fire that slammed into her shoulder as she flipped out of sight.

He fired as the guard followed Elizabeth, repositioning to get a better shot.

Matthias was faster and he'd been watching for Elizabeth to get hit. He fired in the same moment that the guy's head exploded, followed by the other guard losing his face when Amy pulled the trigger a second time. Fortunately, Emerald was already on her way down.

She didn't emerge from behind the desk and, under cover of Amy's continued fire, Matthias raced to her side.

"E!" he cried and shook her by the shoulders. "E, speak to me!"

The guy sounded heart-broken, and Arne hoped the recorder was working in the downed guards' HUDs because that sounded as convincing as hell.

"E..." The man's voice broke, and his heart sank.

Maybe it had been a little too convincing.

He caught a flash of movement on the other side of the room and fired without thinking. The round picked the target up and hurled him into the wall. His next two shots struck home before the man had time to slide down, and the ex-Marine breathed a sigh of relief when he didn't move again.

A shot rang out on the level above, and he stilled to listen.

Bunny sounded slightly breathless when she reported. "They're closing."

More firing followed and some of it was returning.

"Come on, E..." Matthias's voice was soft with pleading. "Come on."

The sound of retaliation grew closer, and Bunny's report wasn't promising. "We're not gonna be able to hold them for much longer."

"Where are they at?" Amy snapped.

"Ground floor and making their way to first."

"Time?"

"To first? Thirty seconds. The second's maybe a minute and a half at their current rate."

"Can you slow them?"

A rapid series of shots came from overhead.

"What the fuck do you think we're doing? Playing checkers?"

Another exchange sounded but Arne still heard Amy's exasperated retort.

"Don't you have anything more destructive?"

"I do," Elle replied before Bunny could answer.

A short silence was followed by two loud explosions.

"I thought I said no grenades!" Amy shouted.

"I knew you'd ask for something more destructive sooner or later," the woman replied cheerfully. "I thought it would have been sooner, honestly, but whatever. I've wanted these babies out, like, *forever!*"

The sheer happiness of the girl's reply made Arne snicker and Amy punched him.

He jumped and cursed because she'd moved that close and he hadn't noticed.

"Are you going blind in your old age, old man?" she asked and he blushed.

"You have a shuttle incoming," E-BURT informed them. "ETA is five minutes and counting."

"Exit point?" Amy demanded and hurried to where Matthias had gathered Elizabeth-Emerald into his arms.

"She's not moving," he told her as she arrived.

"Don't think about that now," she told him and placed her fingers over the pulse point in Elizabeth's throat. After a small pause, she sighed.

"Eebie?"

"I have them on standby," E-BURT replied.

"Come on, Matt. Let's take her home," she declared solemnly. She glanced around. "But do it quickly. I don't want to have to leave her behind."

Watching them, Arne almost believed Elizabeth was dead, and his heart ached for Matthias's loss. He watched as the woman hooked a hand under the ex-commander's arm and hauled him to his feet. She didn't try to take Emerald's body from him but addressed E-BURT.

"Which way?" she demanded.

"Can you deactivate the explosives on the windows?"

"I can do that," Arne offered, but Amy shook her head.

"I'll do it. Tell you why later." She patted Matthias's shoulder. "You take care of the big guy, okay?"

The "big guy" didn't seem to notice. All his attention was on Elizabeth as Arne hooked an arm around his back. "It wasn't meant to end like this."

"No one's…" He remembered the still active recording devices and changed what he was going to say. "No one lives forever."

While he wanted to say more—something to let Matthias know it would be okay—he couldn't risk it. No way did he want to explain what went wrong later. It was hard to let the man suffer but it was for the best.

He dragged the ex-commander to the window, knowing there would be some serious sparring in their future. That didn't matter as long as Matthias forgave him in the end and preferably without breaking too much in the process.

As he reached it, Amy swore. "Dammit!"

She turned to him. "I need…" She gestured toward Elizabeth in Matthias's arms. "We forgot to check the office to see if those guys had any identification."

Arne slipped his arm from around Matthias's waist and pushed him beside her. "I'll go."

"Take this," she ordered, took a small pouch from a compartment in Elizabeth's harness, and tossed it to him.

He caught it reflexively and gave her a curious look. "What is it?"

"DNA evidence," she told him and guided Matthias to the window edge. "Pour it where she fell."

Outside the window, the sky car hovered and E-BURT held it steadier than any human hand could hope to do.

"Don't be long," the AI admonished him. "The upstairs team cannot hold them much longer."

"Copy that." He kept his reply short and drew his combat knife. It would be the fastest way to cut through any straps or bindings as he looked for clues on the fallen.

Arne worked swiftly through the room and scanned the civilians' faces for the AI to identify as he searched their pockets for any identification that might reveal who they were. As he moved from one corpse to the next, he picked up the various papers that looked like they'd been scattered when he and E had blown the walls.

It was amazing what could survive a firefight.

A groan drew his attention from the center of the room, and he realized that the first man Emerald had disabled was still alive. Her blade had sheared through his armor and severed his spine but she hadn't killed him.

He remedied the problem with a quick round from his blaster and rolled the guy to split his body armor. Jerking it off hastily, he soon found what he was looking for.

"What happened to your tatts, my assenholic friend?" he murmured and traced a finger over the shadowy blemish that used to be a tattoo. There were two, one over the left shoulder and another over the heart.

Quickly, he captured the outline with the HUD and moved to the next man. He removed the HUD and brushed his palm over the fine stubble left by a buzz-cut before he sliced away his body armor and found the same two shadows he'd discovered on the first.

The third man was still breathing although he wasn't by the time Arne had made his inspection.

"I'd mourn you but I have better things to do with my time."

Only then did he remember to empty the contents of the pouch Amy had given him. He hadn't known what to expect but it hadn't been blood. Maybe it should have been, but it wasn't. He wrinkled his lip in distaste as he poured it where she'd fallen and looked around for the next man.

He wished he could make a more thorough investigation, but there was no time. The sporadic fire was interlaced with the sound of heavy footsteps and they were closing on the doorway. He made quick work of the next man and resorted to the briefest pocket searches of the rest.

They were, unsurprisingly, empty and there was no more time for checking tattoos. He finished with the last man and scanned the room, darn sure he'd missed things, and scowled unhappily when he realized he was also out of time.

A boot scraped outside the door and he bolted to the next room and the window, hoping E-BURT was waiting. It was a long way down if he wasn't, and Arne wasn't sure he could make the river in a single leap.

"Well, fuck me," he muttered and exhaled a breath of relief when he saw the car hovering outside. Amy held the door open and Bunny and Elle waved for him to hurry.

A soft ping was followed by the gentle thump of a grenade bouncing into the room beyond as he reached the window. Amy hauled him inside and Elle reached for him as E-BURT banked the car in a sharp turn before he plunged the vehicle into a steep dive toward the river.

Arne ended up across Amy and Matthias's laps as the craft accelerated. The AI kept the sky car a scant distance above the water and as close to the riverbanks and their overhanging buildings as he dared. It was closer than a human pilot could have done.

"Why so low?" he asked when he'd pulled himself upright and wriggled his ass into the space between Matthias and Amy.

"It interferes with the detection abilities aboard the shuttle and reduces chances of being found and followed by a factor of ten."

"Engine heat?"

"I am attempting to blur it in the thermal emissions of the nearby plants."

"Are you having any luck?"

"They are still searching and I will change vectors shortly. Be prepared to disembark at speed. I have provided an alternative vehicle for the next stage of your journey."

He looked around. "How is she?"

The reply came in Elizabeth's unmistakable tones.

"I am fucking annoyed that the motherfucker got a motherfucking, shit-shanking shot on me!"

Arne's jaw dropped. "You're okay?"

Matthias gave him a bleak look. "I wouldn't say she was okay...but..."

There was the sound of a fist meeting flesh and he flinched. Elizabeth groaned in pain.

Her teeth chattered when she spoke again. "I'm not sure the dressing will be enough."

"And you're going into shock," Arne observed.

Fortunately, Amy had an answer for that.

"Eebie, we need warmth."

"I cannot turn the heating on, but there is an emergency blanket in the first aid kit under the driver's seat. It also has additional dressings."

Arne glanced at Matthias and this time, he noted the field kit his boss had tucked into one of his pouches before they'd left. And who knew Matthias had experience with that kind of fieldwork, he mused.

E-BURT's reply was followed by a flurry of movement in the back seat as the women dived to extract the kit and blanket.

Arne helped them tuck the light-weight emergency blanket around Elizabeth and Matthias.

"You know this would go better skin to skin."

"I know, but this isn't the place."

Arne wanted to argue, but the car came up out of the river, skidded around the bases of several buildings, and pulled up in an undercover garage.

"Go," E-BURT ordered. "We have two minutes."

None of them wasted time arguing or asking questions. They went. The door of the waiting van opened before them, and it accelerated as soon as the last of them was on board.

"Eebie, are you driving?" Arne asked as he moved to the door linking to the cab.

It stayed locked and an all too human voice replied. "Sorry. I don't know who Eebie is, but some guy named Burt asked us to make a pick-up and drop-off. He said it was better we didn't take a look at our passengers. ETA is six minutes and you need to hold onto your hats."

"Gotcha." Arne sat and took another look at where Matthias was inspecting the dressings on Elizabeth's shoulder and back.

They'd shrugged the blanket off so he had room to work, but he kept her damaged armor close by.

"How's it going?" he asked, but Amy tapped him and Matthias on the knee and wagged her forefinger for silence.

"I still can't believe she's gone," she stated, keeping her head down, but she caught Matthias's gaze by looking up under her fringe.

"She... I..." His voice was as rough with emotion as anyone's who'd lost someone close, and the woman nodded.

Amy patted his leg again, and he finished tightening the dressing and helped Elizabeth into her armor. She leaned against him when they were done, looking tired and in more pain than she was willing to admit.

They finished the ride in silence, ending up in a parking lot several blocks from One R&D HQ. They waited until the van had driven off and watched it descend the down ramp until it was out of sight.

"Now what?" Amy murmured.

"Does it matter?" Matthias asked as another vehicle drove up.

"I'll take you home now," E-BURT informed them and flashed the headlights twice. "The back-up force remained at the manufacturing plant to clean up prior to the workers arriving in the morning—and to answer all the awkward questions the police were bound to ask when they finally responded to reports of gunfire in the area."

"Someone knew we were coming," Amy concluded as they climbed into the car.

"Negative," he responded, "but someone knew you'd arrived and sent backup shortly after. The request sent by the person Arne killed was enough to bring help."

"A second cell?" Arne mused as the car lifted.

E-BURT didn't descend to street level. Instead, he drove the car straight out of the side of the parking lot and over the buildings. As soon as they reached the top, Elizabeth sat.

"Hey..." Matthias began, about to ask how she was feeling.

He didn't get a chance and could only gape as she pulled a stim pack out of a pouch, flicked the cap open and slammed the needle into her thigh. Her body jerked and Matthias tightened his arms around her, plucked the empty delivery system from her hand, and passed it to Amy.

"Why didn't you stop her?" he asked.

"You were the one holding her," she bitched in return. "I thought you had it under control."

Elizabeth took a deep breath and shrugged free of Matthias's grip.

"Eebie! I want the sonuvabitch who gave the orders. You have to have something on the signal that brought the shuttles in."

"I am sorry, E—"

"Don't you 'I'm sorry' me. Find me the owner of the voice who contracted me and give me the address."

She rolled her injured shoulder and winced. "The damn pain killers haven't kicked in yet but they will."

"But—" E-BURT tried, again.

"No buts, Eebie. I made Todd a promise. It's the last thing I want Emerald to do."

"Except you killed her already," he protested.

"Can you fuck with the surveillance systems and time-stamp it so I arrived earlier?"

"Well, yes, but—"

"Then do that."

"Forensics—"

"They can't analyze ash."

"Very well, Elizabeth," he replied.

The car changed direction.

"That quick?" Matthias asked.

"I *am* a super-computer," E-BURT informed him primly, "and I knew Elizabeth would ask."

Matthias groaned and Arne went over his weapons once more.

Elizabeth glanced sharply at him. "What do you think you're doing?"

"I'm going with you." Arne's tone had a finality that dared her to argue, but she was in no mood for argument.

"No. You're not."

He gave her a crooked grin. "It's not negotiable." He jerked a thumb at Matthias. "He's going and so am I."

"And me," Amy informed her.

She looked from one to the other and pursed her lips. "I made Todd a promise that the man who put the hit on his parents would die with my hands choking the life out of him. If any of you kills him before I do that, I'll shoot you myself."

Her expression said she wasn't joking and Matthias felt a small shudder of dismay.

"The rest of you stay here," she ordered and they nodded, their faces pale at the coldness of her gaze.

"And I thought Emerald was dead," Matthias murmured.

Elizabeth rested her head against his shoulder. "We're going back in time, remember? She has to get this done. We can't have her leaving a promise undone."

He drew her closer and rested his chin on top of her head. His heart might be saddened by what she insisted on doing, but all he could do was remind it that this was the last time his Elizabeth would be subsumed by her more criminal side. His heart couldn't wait.

E-BURT set the car down beside a sleeker, more modern vehicle situated on a rooftop.

She pointed at it. "I need a delayed charge on that," she ordered and glanced at Arne. "Something that will put it through the floor and make it incinerate the apartment below."

"Yes, ma'am," he replied. He cast an anxious glance at Matthias but didn't try to stop the ex-Navy man from following her into the stairwell.

There were limits to what you could ask of a friend and making him wait until the charges were set were beyond them. Instead, Arne cast a look at Amy and asked with his eyes what he couldn't bring himself to say.

She gave him an abrupt nod and followed the other two.

"Motherfucking para-military asshole civilians!" the ex-Marine muttered and retrieved what he needed from the chest at the back of the car.

He'd been about to use what he'd carried in his pouches, but E-BURT had sent a quick burst of information to his HUD that changed his mind.

"Thanks, Eebie."

"You are most welcome. Is there anything else you require?" the AI replied. "I can send a drone."

"Now that you mention it..."

As Arne ordered what he needed to do exactly as Elizabeth instructed, E-BURT looped the security cameras' feed so it continued to show an empty stairwell. At the same time as he had the drones fetching the incendiaries Arne needed, he was also hacking the building and turning its alarms off or diverting them to dead space in the Virtual.

Their alerts never reached the operators monitoring them and Elizabeth's incursion went unnoticed.

"Did you find them?" The question snapped out as she picked the locks on a sealed office door.

For a moment, she thought it was directed at her, but the scene she found when she threaded the slender optic sensor through the crack she'd created showed her target seated behind a desk, his attention on one of several monitors arrayed before him.

He sat side-on to the door. A window took up the full length of the wall to his left and a view of the city spread before him through another in the wall opposite. Elizabeth could understand why he'd chosen to not face the door.

Careless of him, she thought, kicked the door wide, and covered the gap between them before he'd managed to turn to face her.

His hand was still reaching under the desk when she struck him and shoved his chair sideways and clear of the desk. A second later, Matthias crushed the desk mic with the butt of his rifle.

"I have muted the computer pick-up and killed the camera," E-BURT informed them. "You are now thirty minutes in the past and his conversation records have been erased."

"What about the guy on the other end?" Matthias asked.

"He has had an unfortunate malfunction in his HUD," E-BURT replied. "Biofeedback fried his brain at the same time it fried all data centers in his HUD. I am going after the Ops Center collection point as we speak."

"You can do that?"

"It is as new to me as it is to you," he informed him. "It is almost a pity that Emerald must die. I have learned much about covert operations and methodology in the last six hours…namely, how much more I have to learn."

Matthias snorted. He was about to say more but the sound of a single shot made him freeze and turn in alarm. Elizabeth's chuckle told him Emerald had full rein. The man tilted sideways in his chair and uttered a short bark of pain, followed by a suppressed groan.

Elizabeth's gun sounded again and he shrieked.

"Shooting people is not nice, you know," she informed her target and shot him again, the muzzle of her blaster pressed against his thigh.

"Neither is…playing…with your food." The response came in short bursts from a voice wreathed in hurt.

Emerald gave him a cold, hard grin as she dragged him clear of the chair. "I know."

With cold precision, she fired into the shoulder of his uninjured arm and he yelped, breathing fast through gritted teeth as he tried to control the pain. She straddled his chest and knelt over him to position her hands around his throat.

"I have a message for you from Sergeant Todd Brogan," she told him and his eyes widened. She wriggled, adjusted her position, and jolted the wounds she'd caused in his gut and shoulder. He groaned and his eyes fluttered closed and then open again.

"Stay with me," she instructed. "This is the last thing you're ever gonna hear, so it's important. Are you listening?"

He nodded as if the action occurred before he'd had a chance to stop it.

Elizabeth gave him her best Emerald smile. "Good."

She tightened her grasp on his throat and his eyes started to bulge. "Sergeant Todd Brogan sends his regards."

Her voice fell silent as she crushed his larynx slowly and watched the life fade from his eyes. When she was finished, she leveled her blaster at his head and shot him, then moved it down to his chest and emptied the clip.

"Survive that, you bastard."

Matthias waited until she lowered her weapon and took her arm gently. "Arne says we need to go unless we'd rather be crispy."

The look she turned to him was as dead as any killer's, and he hoped Elizabeth would come back soon—*his* Elizabeth and not Emerald or any of the other personas she'd held in her past. She didn't argue with him, though, or resist when Amy took her other arm and helped him guide her out of the apartment and up the stairs.

They met Arne on his way down and he chivvied them to the car, where the rest of the team waited.

No one said anything until the four of them had settled and Matthias and Amy had buckled the harness around their boss's body.

When she did speak, Elizabeth sounded ineffably tired. "You know where to go, Eebie."

"Indeed." E-BURT lifted the car from the roof and over the side of the building before he let it drop abruptly to the road below. He leveled it out before it impacted and drove a swift but circuitous route to the university.

Along the way, Elizabeth closed her eyes and relaxed against Matthias's side. The stim pack had begun to wear off and eased her into unconsciousness. He exchanged anxious glances with Amy but couldn't do anything more than hold his wayward woman close.

It was a relief when the AI settled the vehicle in a secluded section of the university's underground garage.

"The administration has sealed this section from its staff and students," he informed them. "The medical team has been assembled and is on stand-by."

He punctuated his words by illuminating the space to show the medical team moving toward them. Two doctors and four nurses, all trained in trauma surgery, pulled a gurney behind them. They lost no time in covering the distance between them and the elevator they'd emerged from.

Matthias didn't wait for instructions. He lifted Elizabeth out of the car, hurried to meet them, and set her down as soon as the gurney stopped.

"What happened?" the lead medic demanded.

"Firefight," Matthias snapped. "She walked into twin bursts." He paused and ran his hand through his hair. "I think the armor held."

"You'd better hope so," the man snapped and pushed him aside to inspect the armor. "Lizzy, Lizzy, Lizzy..." he murmured. "What am I going to do with you?"

"Heal her?" Matthias snarked.

"Yeah, sure, and me without my magic wand an' all," the medic sniped in response. He was already securing Elizabeth in place and signaling his team to get her into the elevator.

Matthias hurried after them and squeezed into the elevator seconds before the doors closed.

Arne sighed. "And there he goes, leaving me behind again."

"Elizabeth, too." Amy agreed and they headed to the stairs with the rest of the team in tow.

CHAPTER TWENTY-NINE

They were gathered in a small office outside the impromptu emergency center when Elizabeth woke. The latter had been a classroom but the medical team had transformed it quickly and effectively by the time the team had arrived.

The lead doctor looked out and searched the group until his gaze fell on Matthias. "She's asking for you."

"Me?" He closed the distance in several swift strides and the doctor rolled his eyes.

"You *are* Matthias, right?"

"Yeah. Where?"

As if he needed to ask. He didn't wait for a reply but shouldered past the man to where Elizabeth was seated propped up in a bed. He scanned the room and his gaze settled on what was left of her armor as he hurried to her side.

To his surprise, she reached for him—slowly, to be sure, and she winced with pain as her hands touched his bloodied armor. Undeterred by the mess, she drew him close and took a long breath.

"Remind me not to do that *ever* again."

"If you even *suggest* it, I'll lock you in a box and throw away the key."

She chuckled at that. "Promise?"

He wrapped her in his arms and held her close. "With all my heart. I never want to see you like that again. You are banned from stim packs. Next time, I don't care what promises you've made. You forget them and fall over gracefully like you're supposed to."

Elizabeth tried to snuggle closer but his body armor was hard and unyielding under her cheek. She slapped his chest with the flat of her hand. "You need to get changed."

Matthias drew back and looked crestfallen. "But—"

"But what?" She arched her eyebrows.

He swallowed hard, then let the words out in a rush. "I don't want to leave you."

When she froze in his arms, he thought for a minute he'd said the wrong thing. It wasn't until she shook her head and slid her arm around his shoulder that he realized he hadn't.

"In that case," she told him, "I guess you'd better take me with you."

"To get changed?"

"Well, you do kinda stink." She made a show of taking a sniff of her shoulder. "Ugh. And so do I. You need to help me get clean."

It was his turn to raise his eyebrows. "I do?"

She inched toward the edge of the bed and swung her legs over, grimacing as she did so. "Yup. It's not like I can do it alone."

The sheets fell away to reveal the extent of the bruising and he winced. "Are you sure you should go anywhere?"

The doctor's voice interrupted her reply. "She shouldn't but she insists. I trust you can watch her for me?"

"I can, but where will you be?"

"Me? I'll be here, catching some shut-eye and waiting for when she falls over again."

Matthias studied her with concern before he focused on the doctor again. "How long will you be around?"

The man's lips flattened in a thin disapproving line before he replied, "Until I know she'll recover without my help."

"And you're not sure of that right now?"

"Not one hundred percent."

He looked from him to Elizabeth and back again, but the doctor continued before he could say anything. "It looks likely, but I'd like to stick around to make sure—and I'd like to see her in a medical pod sometime in the next twenty-four hours."

Matthias nodded. "I can do that."

Elizabeth batted at him again. "Says who?"

"Says the man who can put you on your ass with his little pinky while you're in this condition," he told her and she scowled.

"Said man had better not try or there will be a reckoning he will not like."

"Seeing you well would be worth it," he told her and his face settled into lines of stone.

She opened her mouth to argue, but something of what it had cost him to defy her leaked into his expression and she let it lie. "I want a few hours with you first."

The doctor rolled his eyes. "Fine. Let me know when you want the machine calibrated."

"It shouldn't need that, should it?" she asked, then realized they were at the university and none of the pods were calibrated for anyone. For that matter, she didn't even know if there *was* a medical pod.

It looked like the doc was ahead of her on this one and she didn't have the energy to catch up. She would simply have to trust him and that Matthias, Arne, and Amy had a better grasp of the situation than she did.

Given the medical equipment she could see around her, it occurred to her that the university had been more than generous in giving her the space. She wondered what it had cost them—and E-BURT—to achieve it.

They were all questions she could ask him later, she decided, and let Matthias support her as she donned the lightweight shift the doctor handed her. They wound their arms around each other and walked slowly out into the waiting room.

"You're all filthy," Elizabeth told them and tried to hide the emotion she felt to find them waiting.

"And you're not dead," Amy snapped in response. "No thanks to your stupidity."

She might have taken offense if she hadn't caught the glimmer of tears in the woman's eyes. Instead, she cleared the emotion from her throat.

"Well, I'm more dented than usual, but the doc says I'll be fine."

Matthias froze and wiped all expression from his face as the woman glanced at him to see if E was speaking the truth.

"Uh-huh…" the guard muttered and went with them to the showers situated at the end of the hall.

It was not the quiet time he'd had in mind, but they were clean and dressed an hour later. This time, they relocated to another empty classroom which served as a makeshift mess hall. E-BURT had ordered food delivered and they ate in companionable silence as post-ops exhaustion settled in.

"Well," Amy stated when they'd almost finished their coffees. "I'm hitting the hay."

She stood and waggled her eyebrows at where Elizabeth sat, snug against Matthias's side. "Don't do anything *I* wouldn't do."

Her boss snorted. "As if I could. Did you see the bruising?"

"Yup. Lucky you have *something* to slow you down."

E blushed but didn't move from where she was. She was enjoying the warmth of being so close to Matthias and simply relaxed against him as, one by one, the team retired for the night.

Arne was the last to leave. His gaze roved over the two of them as though assuring himself they were both in one piece. A small smile curled his lips and he shrugged. With a nod to Matthias, he headed to the door.

"I'll catch you in the morning, boss."

Matthias nodded in return and tightened his arm across Elizabeth's back. She sighed and rested her head against his shoulder. As the silence settled around them, she sighed again.

"Well, that was one of me I'm happy is dead," she murmured, speaking to no one in particular.

He glanced at her. "Are you sure? She was a big part of you for a while."

E shrugged beneath his arm and he lifted it and stood to help her rise. "She kept me alive in a world that wouldn't have cared if I were dead," she admitted, "so yes, she *was* a big part of me. Not to mention the part of me that drew BURT to ask for my services to start with."

They reached the door and turned toward the offices that had been hastily refitted as sleeping quarters. She slid her arm around his waist.

"But you're happy she's gone?" He sounded like he didn't understand.

"Yup," she assured him. "She was one hard-assed bitch."

"And you're not?" The words were out before he could stop them, and he gave her a worried glance.

Elizabeth didn't stop her slow progress down the corridor. "Only when I need to be," she told him, "which hopefully won't be as often now." He guided her to the room that had been set aside for her. "Now that she's gone, it's only Elizabeth and Matthias."

He stared at her and arched his eyebrows. "Oh? And what about Janet?"

"She's something of a loner."

"Denise?"

"I think she went to work in a bar in Chicago."

"And the brunette? What was her name...the one with that sexy accent..."

"You mean Jacqueline?"

Matthias snapped his fingers. "Yeah, that's her. Whatever happened to *dear* Jacqueline?"

"She *was* a bitch, wasn't she?"

There was a snort from further down the corridor, and they glanced up to where Arne stood inside the open door to another room.

"Bitch was an understatement," the ex-Marine muttered and Elizabeth tutted.

She tried to look contrite, but the smile made that impossible. "You're not *still* mad about that?"

"I am."

With a chuckle, she returned her attention to Matthias. "Jacqueline went to chase kangaroos in Australia."

"You made that up."

"I did not."

"There's nothing left of Australia except storm-ridden wasteland."

"You're forgetting Sydney."

"My point stands."

"Don't ever let Stephanie's pet scientist hear you say that."

Matthias spread his hands. "Why? What's he possibly gonna do about it?"

"He *is* a nuclear physicist."

"Uh-huh. Well, he and Jacqueline—"

She pressed a finger to his lips. "Don't even go there. Jacqueline is gone and she isn't *ever* coming back. Especially not for a scientist she'd rather kill."

"Aw, now. Don't be like that. I've heard he's improved."

"That wouldn't have been hard."

He rolled his eyes and changed the subject. "So, that's Janet, Denise, and Jacqueline taken care of. Who does that leave me with?"

"There'd better *not* be room for anyone else," Elizabeth told him.

"I know. There was Phyllis—"

"Dead. She tangled with a rottweiler."

"Angelica."

"Poisoned. Her love of fugu was her undoing."

"Ophelia?"

"Went swimming with sharks."

"Really? She didn't look that stupid."

"I didn't say she *knew* the shark was there."

"You said sharks, plural."

"The school arrived with the anchovies. Ophelia thought she'd catch her dinner and so did the shark. Guess who got to eat first."

"Amaryllis?"

"Fell foul of the Russian mafia while attempting a particularly different retrieval."

"I didn't hear about that."

"Well, you weren't likely to, were you? That wasn't exactly an E-BURT-sanctioned mission."

"And I'm still not happy with you," the AI interrupted. "What if you'd read him wrong?"

"Well, I didn't," Elizabeth replied.

"Him?" Matthias asked. "When was this?"

"Three weeks ago. Amaryllis thought she'd be clever and take something particularly precious. In return for a fee, I got Semyon to keep her in a box and only take her out on special occasions."

"Oh? Anyone I should be worried about?"

"Someone who needed killing in the worst way," she told him, her face reddening, and he linked his fingers and looped his arms around her shoulders.

"Zyla?"

"My, weren't you a curious boy."

"I seriously wanted to know more about you...and you weren't forthcoming," he tried to explain.

"I had good reason," she prevaricated, hoping he wouldn't pursue it.

She should have known better.

"Yes," he insisted. "Well, what about Zyla?"

Elizabeth rolled her eyes. "Ugh! Fine! She died in a car crash while running drugs from NorAm to the Russian republic."

"You don't like the Russians very much, do you?"

"All the ones I met were sexist misogynistic manipulative—"

It was Matthias's turn to put his finger over her lips.

"Ssshhh, I get it, but why did Zyla have to die?"

"What? Did you have a crush on her or something?"

"No... Well, she merely seemed one of your...*nicer* personas."

"She was, but she still had to go. I won't share you with *anyone*."

He blushed. "Well, that told me, didn't it? How about Shaheen?"

"She had an offer from a German billionaire she couldn't refuse."

"Couldn't?"

"Didn't want to. I believe they'd still be happily cruising the stars if she hadn't had a nasty accident with an airlock. Sometimes, your past truly *does* catch up with you."

Matthias whistled. "Nasty way to go. Karen?"

"Shipping accident," Elizabeth told him shortly.

"What? Another airlock? Were you running out of ideas by then?"

She shook her head. "No, she was meeting someone on the Isle of Dogs when she slipped and fell between a ship and the wharf. It *was* a stormy night. They say she was crushed."

"Ugh. Forget what I said about you not being creative." He frowned. "And Beryl?"

"Poisoned."

"Not more fugu?"

"What did I say about you accusing me of being repetitive?"

He feigned shock. "I would never!"

She stared at him in silence and tapped her foot, and he stooped to brush a kiss over her hair.

"So, Beryl?" he persisted, and she sighed and wound her other arm around his waist.

"If you must know, it was a bad oyster collected from the Spanish seashore. It completely wrecked her tan."

"How?"

"Let's simply say puking that badly has sorry side effects."

"Forget I asked," he told her.

Elizabeth smirked. "Any more questions?"

"Why? Are you getting tired?"

She shook her head and promptly stifled a yawn. "Nooo."

He huffed a sigh. "Okay… What about Fairamay?"

"Her? I can't believe you had to go and dig her up!"

"Well?"

"Fine!" Again, she rolled her eyes. "She danced too hard."

"She what?" Matthias wasn't sure what he'd heard.

"Danced too hard."

"And how's *that* supposed to kill anyone?"

"She was dancing in one of the Lower District's slum halls, shook it a little too hard, and knocked a girl's drink out of her hand."

"So?"

"So, the glass flew across the room and shattered on Bergeron's chest plate. The alcohol splashed into his hair and onto a nearby tiki torch and set his head alight, and his bodyguards detained her for the attempted 'assassination.'"

"There were tiki torches?" He sounded like he didn't think she was telling the truth and he had good reason. "In the Lower District?"

"Bergeron was throwing a luau for a visiting crime lord."

"A luau?" His expression said he couldn't believe his ears.

Elizabeth nodded. "Sure. It was the perfect cover and the visitor was supposed to be Fairamay's target."

"I take it that's one bounty you didn't get."

"Are you kidding? When they went to visit Fairamay in her cell for a 'please explain' with sharp and pointy objects, she murdered them both. The bounty was sent posthumously in case rumors of her death were exaggerated."

"I thought she died from dancing too hard."

"Well, she died while escaping the torture cell, but her body was never found because it went over the edge of a cliff and the wild dogs got to it first."

"But the dancing?"

"It was the dancing that screwed up a perfectly good assassination plan," Elizabeth explained, "so when you think about it, that was what killed her. Nothing that came after would have happened if she hadn't been dancing like a drunken monkey on steroids."

"I see." Matthias smiled but his face said he had trouble digesting that last story.

"Are there any more old mes you want to know about? I'm fairly sure I've got them all."

Arne cleared his throat. His face was half-hidden in darkness, but they could still see the curve of his smile. "You didn't ask about Valborg."

Elizabeth snapped her head around. "Oh, for fuck's sake! How far back did you go?"

"Far enough to know there are at least three more."

Matthias looked at him in disbelief. "That's not all of them?"

The other man snickered and he looked at her in disbelief.

She sniffed. "Of course not. Who do you think I am?"

"I...I... I'm beginning to think I don't know..." He fell silent and became aware of the other doors now standing open along the corridor. Elizabeth's team didn't bother to hide their curiosity.

"Exactly how many personas *did* you have?" Amy asked.

"It's none of your business," she snapped. "Weren't you all *very* tired and going to bed?"

"Yeah, we were," her guard snarked in response, "but some *assholes* were talking loudly in the corridor and I was about to tell them to shut the hell up when I heard what they were saying and thought it was interesting sooo..."

"Ugh. Well, we're done now," Elizabeth told her and drew Matthias into her room.

"We are?" he asked and followed without protest.

"We so are," she confirmed and nudged the door closed behind them. She curled an arm around the back of his head, pulled his face closer to hers, and kissed him soundly.

"I'm yours now, you idiot."

"You are?" He took her in his arms, slid one around her waist, and cupped the back of her head with his other hand as he returned her kiss.

"Mmhmmm," she replied. "It's only Matthias and Elizabeth now."

She untangled herself from his embrace, took his hand, and led him to the carefully made-up bed. "Tuck me in?"

Matthias swallowed against the sudden dryness of his throat. "If that's what you want."

"Hold me?" she asked when he'd drawn the covers around her and was seated on the edge beside her.

He did as she asked, surprised when she curled into his arms and snuggled against him with a contented sigh. Feeling the same sense of ease, he held her and drew comfort from the weight of her head against his shoulder as he reached out to turn the light off.

The darkness descended around them and brought silence and relaxation with it.

They lay there for several quiet moments before Elizabeth's sleepy voice rippled through the dark.

"Now," she mumbled, "about babies..."

CHAPTER THIRTY

Everyone put the blast that destroyed the top of a swanky apartment high-rise down to a timer on delay. They didn't quite know what to make of the discrepancies in the security recordings or the complete failure of a reclusive businessman's security precautions, but they all wanted to hire the hack team responsible.

What they most wanted to know was what he'd done to piss Emerald off that badly. And, of course, how she'd moved from his apartment to the raid that had been her undoing without anyone being the wiser—and with a full team, no less.

News of her demise traveled swiftly, and members of the local underworld gathered in the Virtual to bid her memory goodbye—or, at least, to try to lay her ghost to rest. No one wanted her to haunt them. It didn't matter *who* she'd been.

She might be gone but she still scared the crap out of all of them.

The lights were kept low and the pseudo-flame of the lanterns flickered off timbered walls softened by tapestries hanging between each sconce. The criminal elite slipped into the anteroom and waited as the computer checked their credentials and invitation before they stepped into the dining hall.

A feast awaited but first, more significant things needed to be attended to.

Their leader glanced around, her fingers holding the delicate tulip-shaped glass full of golden liquid.

Rumor had it that mead had been Emerald's drink of taste, closely followed by whiskey. A tumbler of the latter waited on the table in front of her. In the meantime, she raised her glass, her movement echoed by the dozen men and women around the main table.

"To Emerald," she declared. "May she be forever gone."

"Amen." The response followed quickly, and the next man spoke.

"And may whatever passes for her soul rest easy."

His words were followed by the man beside him. "And her final sleep be deep and undisturbed."

"For all who knew her," another crime lord intoned, "we have the utmost respect, be they living or dead."

"To Emerald's living and her dead," they all agreed.

The toasts continued as each one wished their departed leader a peaceful final sleep—or, at least, a sleep from which she would never wake to haunt them. As each one was made, they took a sip from their glasses until the last man had spoken and their drinks were finished.

The female leader lifted the whiskey tumbler from the table and raised it in a final salute.

"To Emerald," she declared, downed the drink in a single gulp, and thumped the glass down.

"Emerald," the chorus responded as all those present echoed her actions.

"May she never rise," the man beside her declared as he sat again.

The woman nudged him. "Why? Do you have something you didn't want her to know about?"

He raised an eyebrow and gave her a wry smile. "Didn't we all?"

She returned it. "Didn't we all?"

There was nothing to say to that, and a polite knock at the door signaled the arrival of their meals. As they ate, the conversation turned to what might have happened to their departed leader.

"I have no idea," said the man who thought he'd controlled the area surrounding the manufacturing plant.

"She took on one job too many," another intoned, "and this one was staffed by people even nastier than she was, the heavens help her."

"The heavens take her," the others chorused.

"Because hell is ours and we ain't sharing," declared a lone voice with grim determination.

The others chuckled.

"Amen to that."

"Words?" the speaker asked. "Does anyone have anything *else* to say in remembrance?"

"Beyond how relieved I am she's gone?" one asked.

"Way beyond that."

"Then I have to say our world has lost one of its best and its iron lady," he acknowledged.

"Tex left an enviable legacy," added another, "but not one I wasn't glad to see gone."

The woman leaned forward and rapped sharply on the table, drawing startled glances from those closest. "It's not the first time we've thought her dead."

"Yeah, but it's the first time she took on someone of that caliber. I've marked that firm as a no-go zone for my people. I'd appreciate it if anyone doing business with me would do the same."

Murmurs of agreement rippled around the room. "Hear, hear."

One of the men touched his brow briefly and moved his fingers to his chest and then each shoulder to form a cross. Another one chuckled.

"I didn't think you were on speaking terms with The Man Upstairs."

"I'm not, but it can't hurt, right?"

E-BURT kept half an eye on the meeting. It didn't take him much power to monitor the conversation or map their entry points into the

Virtual World, but the meeting wasn't his main focus. Elizabeth might have been interested but she was sleeping and he could record it for her later amusement.

If he'd been human, he would have smiled. As it was, he merely registered the unfamiliar feeling as something the humans would term "happy" and got on with what he wanted to do, which was to send out multiple data queries.

Some were designed to find him the information he was interested in and others were designed to find other information that made his main interest look like an incidental side search directed at something else. It kept several servers occupied but not so much that the engineers would ever know.

The AI considered that last assumption and created a few more queries from non-existent users. These were merely fluff, designed to deter anyone from digging too deep. He especially liked the one that asked how unicorns were made and if the diabolica praying mantis had ever been a real insect or merely something movie-makers dreamed up to scare little kids.

Along those lines, he also sent out the usual queries one might expect from the conspiracy theorists and military fanboys and girls. "What are the most elite units of the Federation Navy?" "Secret units of past wars, the real and the imagined," and "What secret operations have the Federation Navy run in the past?"

Each query brought back hundreds if not thousands of replies and E-BURT discarded ninety percent of them. As far as he was concerned, they served an important purpose, and he watched as half a dozen tracking programs latched on to certain keywords and followed the query to the source he'd created for it.

No doubt there were a dozen people out there who would have an ugly surprise or three. At the same time, E-BURT was certain they wouldn't be harmed and the tracking operations would come away confused and frustrated. It would lead them to waste resources on trying to find out if they'd been spoofed—another effort doomed to fail.

If he had been human, he would have been smiling. As it was, he felt strangely contented. The questions let him identify tracking programs designed to protect the very information he was trying to find and once he had, he could track them to their origins, which led him to another puzzle entirely.

Some of those sites were official and well protected.

He thought about speaking to his AI counterpart in the Navy offices, but he decided it might be better if he didn't draw attention to himself like that. Instead, he set himself to the task of getting past their firewalls and access alerts without getting caught.

If they traced queries like the ones he'd sent out, they surely knew something they didn't want the rest of the world to know. If that secret had anything to do with the entities that had ordered Todd's parents killed or who controlled that strange group of Marines that Arne and Matthias referred to as the X-Men, he wanted to know it too.

He was glad of the superhero fetish of the twentieth and twenty-first centuries that had allowed him to hide some of his queries as fan searches. Who knew why the X-Men had been named after classic heroes when they so obviously were not, but it provided a very convenient disguise.

It also made it easy to sift through the results. Anything linked to the corporations owning the rights to those fictional heroes could be discarded, no matter how tempted he was to forward it to Todd for the sergeant's enjoyment.

At the same time, it worried him. There should have been nothing on the mysterious men that Matthias and Arne spoke of with such awe—and Lars too, now that he thought about it.

E-BURT crafted a more careful search. This one was designed to look like a fan query on Stephanie's bodyguards. Who were they? Where had they come from? How had they been hired? How was *anyone* hired to protect the Witch? It was a fairly easy list to compile.

A second program wormed through those queries. This one had the task of homing in on Lars and Johnny's service records and burrowing deeper to look for hidden data. Working alongside it, he ran the programs hunting the tracking programs that hunted those queries.

Some of the trackers were from legitimate agencies and departments tasked with looking for malicious entities interested in the Witch and her team. Others... E-BURT didn't like the others. They hid too well amidst the rest.

And they slid past the Federation Navy firewalls like someone with an exclusive badge to flash. He crafted another subroutine. This one was given the challenge of discovering what badges those trackers held and bringing the pattern back to him.

He could do with whatever got them past the guards and into those areas of the system. They weren't the only areas he needed to get into, though. Other trackers homed in on large corporations, powerful business entities, politicians, political parties...and one very worrying one that took a back door into the Federation's parliamentary servers.

E-BURT very much wanted to discover where *that* one went.

As he worked, it occurred to him that since Matthias and Arne knew even a little about shady operators in the military, he should look at their records as well. He swore softly as the realization struck him that he probably should have kept a closer eye on what was happening with those two, especially since they'd walked away from the Navy.

Discovering that they'd both been targeted for early retirement was not that great a surprise, and learning that the Navy had kept an eye on their whereabouts was only to be expected. It was the hidden recipients of the reports on both men that caught his eye.

"Well, well, well," he murmured. "Wouldn't Elizabeth be interested in knowing *you* exist."

He set another string of inquiries in motion, this one designed to see what other reports those particular recipients were tapping. The AI hummed as he worked.

It took him some time to realize he was missing another avenue of inquiry and he sent another burst of questions, appropriately surrounded by searches for something more inconsequential. Scanning through the search, he was entertained.

If Aaron or one of his former supervising engineers could see this, they'd be appalled. They might even have taken the extreme action of combing through his programming and activity logs to find out where the wrinkle was that caused him to create such inefficient searches. He was glad he could hide most of this activity from them.

Aaron would have readily snarked at him without politeness.

"Seriously?" the man would have said. "You set up a query where what you want *might...maybe...*be in the result set? Who the *hell* would be so stupid?"

E-BURT could also imagine Gene's add on. "Or have that much time?"

Both were very good questions, and he was glad neither man was there to ask them.

He had enough trouble with the myriad trackers lurking in the world net, as it was—and something told him it would only get worse.

―――――――

As E-BURT shepherded his inquiries and Elizabeth and Matthias settled into sleep, Admiral Amaratne heard a knock at his door.

"Yes?"

His aide stuck his head into the office.

"Admirals Reardon and Ogden to see you, sir."

"Thank you, Mitchell. That will be all for tonight. I'll see you in the morning."

"Thank you, sir." The man flashed him a grateful grin, then looked worried. "Are you sure? I can stay—"

He shook his head. "No, you've done enough. If you'd show them in, I'll see you in the morning."

Mitchell stiffened to attention and threw him a quick salute. "Yessir!"

He left but returned a short moment later to usher the two admirals into the room and placed a silver tray bearing a decanter of scotch and three glasses on his desk. "I'll see you in the morning, sir."

"Thank you, Lieutenant."

The man left but seemed reluctant as he closed the door behind him. Without an excuse to stay, however, he had no choice. The fleet admiral glanced from the door to his guests and caught Ogden's slight frown as she turned toward him.

"So it's not only me," Amaratne observed and gestured to the small sitting area leading off from the office.

She shook her head and rolled her hand so he could see the small electronic device hidden in her palm. Two red lights gleamed and became brighter when she held it close to the tray. He nodded, scooped his tablet up, and took them through to his inner chamber. None of them relaxed until the lights showed green.

He settled into one of the leather armchairs and tapped his tablet to send them the files he hadn't wanted to have Mitchell send on his behalf.

"This," he began, "is the team we know as the Hooligans."

That earned him two swift glances before the two admirals lifted their tablets and scanned the files.

"What do we want with *them*?" Rearden asked. "I thought they were on our side."

"They are," Amaratne reassured him, "and therein lies our problem."

"Oh?"

"I believe they've drawn the attention of someone far less benign."

"The X-Men?" Ogden asked and lowered her voice to a hushed whisper.

He nodded. "Ever since they retrieved the data from the Teloran ship in the Meligornian system, they've been shadowed by a group of Marines of which even *my* Marines are wary."

At his mention of his bodyguard, Reardon looked around the room and made a show of peering into the office. "Speaking of which…"

"I convinced their captain they needed a night off—and that I was perfectly safe within my own offices."

"Yudi... We know that might not be true," Ogden protested but kept her voice soft. "Your aide—"

"Might not be fully aware of what he is doing," he informed her. "As far as he knows, he's helping the Intelligence folk to keep me safe."

He wished it were true but he was sure Mitchell had been around long enough to know that what he was being asked to do was far enough out of the ordinary that he should at least have brought it to the attention of the Marines detailed to his protection. That he hadn't became rapidly apparent.

"Yudi?" The sound of Ogden's voice brought him blinking to the present.

"I'm sorry. I was miles away."

She snorted softly and tapped her tablet. "The Hooligans—what did you consider doing about their unwanted hangers-on?"

Amaratne shrugged. "There's not much we *can* do. Not openly."

"We could assign them their own set of guardians," Reardon suggested. "Although, since they already have one, it might raise a few eyebrows."

He stared into the distance and thought through the plan in his mind. Although he'd toyed with the idea, he hadn't been able to come up with a way to phrase it.

"Maybe suggest that two men at a time are sufficient. After all, they *are* guarding a team of seasoned Marines. Perhaps give people the impression that I'd like to keep a more personal eye on them."

Reardon nodded thoughtfully. "That's not a bad idea. You could use your team...if their captain agrees."

"I'll ask. In the meantime, could you keep your ears to the ground and see what rumbles you can find?"

They nodded, and the other man darted him a curious look. "Do you think they're important enough for someone to try to eliminate them?"

Amaratne inclined his head. "I think it's a possibility. Either way, I'm not happy with the attention they're getting and I'm worried about why someone else thinks they're important enough to watch them so closely."

"How close are we talking?" Ogden asked.

"Twenty-four-hour surveillance," he told them, "and I mean *close* surveillance."

She frowned. "That's…not usual."

"No, which is why it has me worried."

Reardon sighed and leaned back in his seat. "I've seen your boys and girls. Having two of them on overwatch will put an end to any shenanigans that might be planned—at least while the Hooligans are on base or on the station."

Amaratne compressed his lips and flicked him a serious look. "I hear what you're saying and it's something I couldn't get my head around either."

"What? Is there no way you can task them to follow the Hooligans all the time?" Ogden asked and a small smile played across her lips.

"Exactly," he told her. "It doesn't matter which way I look at it, I can't think of a way to cut their orders so they can follow the Hooligans when they're on their own time and off Naval property."

"Yeah. I can't help you there, either," she told him. "Sorry, Yudi."

"Which ties up that part of tonight's business and brings me to the next," he told them. "Alpha Fleet."

"Alpha Fleet," Reardon repeated and his smile was one of unfeigned delight. "I can't wait to see what the rest of the fleet has to say once we mobilize them." His face sobered. "Any news of when?"

Amaratne looked from one to the other and couldn't suppress a smirk of satisfaction. "The committee has almost reached an agreement."

Both admirals drew a sharp breath and held it. He looked from one expectant face to another and chuckled. "I'm sorry, but that's all I have for either of you. The committee is meeting in the next few days and I expect them to reach a decision shortly."

"So the orders are about to be cut?" Ogden pressed and he regarded her with a solemn gaze.

"Yes, they are, but 'soon' is the best I have for you right now."

"Soon? Sir, you said 'in the next couple of days,'" she protested.

"I did, but it's a committee," he reminded her, "and those things are their own beasts. I only have so much control."

"Well, fingers crossed then, sir."

"Indeed."

"I think," Reardon added and stood from his seat to retrieve the bottle of scotch and the glasses, "that this calls for a toast."

Having set his queries in motion, E-BURT had turned to work with the Meligornian embassy.

"Elizabeth would be most disappointed," he noted and paused thoughtfully. "And Stephanie. *She* would not be happy with the delay."

Even with the thought of their disappointment in his head, he couldn't resist giving his queries and the resulting algorithms of identification and pursuit more of his processing time than they strictly needed. Happy with the way things were progressing, he added one more subroutine and concealed it amidst those drawing and storing the results.

"There…"

Now, he would know if anyone else ran query patterns as heavily disguised as his own. Or he *might*. It all depended on the processing power and server time the questioner had at their disposal—and how well they cared to bury their interest.

Still, it was worth the effort to try to discover anyone else with the same level of interest in Stephanie or One R&D as *he* had in the people targeting them. Yes, it was.

He sent a closed call through to the Meligornian embassy.

"Your Excellency, I have a personal request," he began when he got through and was asked what had possessed him to call at the extremely early Earth hour he had chosen.

"One would be tempted to think that you *never* sleep, Mr. Burt," S'rilef told him with a smile.

E-BURT was glad he was using his 'businessman' persona—or

rather BURT's businessman persona. As far as he could see, the ambassador couldn't tell the difference and that was a relief. No one was meant to know his original had left the planet.

Which meant no one was meant to know that what they had done was possible, let alone repeatable.

He allowed himself a small smile in response to the ambassador's statement—a small smile and a yawn. "Oh, I sleep, Mr. Ambassador, but I *do* try to keep the hours of those I speak to. I get a much better reception that way."

The ambassador chuckled. "And we all appreciate the courtesy." He sobered. "To what do I owe the pleasure?"

"It's regarding the scientists visiting One R&D's Meligorn headquarters," he told him.

"Yes. I understand the Federation's Witch will transport them to my world?"

"That is correct, Your Eminence, but...ah..." He paused and the ambassador stared expectantly.

"You are having some difficulty with the arrangements?" he asked after a moment.

E-BURT shook his head, glad the Meligornian had gone ahead and predicted the existence of a problem.

"The outward journey is still viable," he explained. "It is the return journey that has become problematic."

"In what way?" the man asked. "Because our offer still stands if you need it. We would be honored to transport your people to wherever you need them to go."

He feigned relief, although he didn't have to try very hard. "That is exactly what I wanted to speak to you about," he admitted. "Stephanie has been tasked with other priorities and cannot make the collection time required. We wond—er...*I* wondered if it was still permissible to avail ourselves of your most generous offer."

The ambassador smiled. "Of course, Mr. Burt. With everything you and your company have done for our world, how could we decline?"

"I would hope you felt free to decline if the need arose," he told him quite truthfully.

S'rilef shook his head. "That need will never arise. My world owes you and your Federation its very existence. What we have offered stands."

E-BURT altered the color of his avatar's skin to simulate a human blush as he lowered his head. "Then we are very grateful, for your world has aided us on many occasions and I would have considered us even."

The ambassador nodded. "I will have my aide send you formal confirmation, but I am afraid that he works more *human* hours while on this world. You will have them first thing tomorrow morning."

"I appreciate it," he assured him and pretended to stifle another yawn. "In the meantime, I shall follow your aide's fine example and find some sleep. Thank you for your time, Ambassador."

"The pleasure is all mine," the man replied and they both signed off.

CHAPTER THIRTY-ONE

Whereas the criminal underworld had chosen dark timbers and yellow lanterns for its wake, other power groups preferred better lit and more modern surroundings. Walls of white mosaic gleamed under chandeliers of pure white light and marble floors glistened softly. The tables consisted of plain glass tops and the chairs had a stone finish with soft grey padding on the backs and seats.

Where the criminal royalty had preferred a single large table, these power brokers chose single round tables seating up to four and decked with fine crystal and silver. There was no place to conceal weapons or pass secret notes beneath a table. Everything that went on there did so in full view of the programs recording the space and everyone knew that.

If they wished to undertake some *other*, more private form of business, they organized to meet elsewhere and they arranged it through other means. This meeting was part of a weekly meet and greet, a way to touch base when they were so physically far apart.

Each of them had spent a small fortune securing the best in pod technology for themselves and their security teams so they could participate. Like their criminal counterparts, no one accessed the restaurant itself without undergoing a security check that placed a code on their pods' ability to call them back.

It was a safeguard none of them liked but all of them complied with, given that this restaurant had the best reputation in the world for privacy. What went on inside its dining rooms stayed there. Even the antechambers were kept separate.

One group of guests did not know what other groups were using the facility or even if there *were* others using it. The restaurant would not tell them.

"Now, sir, would you consider us for yourself if you knew we gave out that kind of detail? Even to one as prominent as yourself?"

The billionaire making the booking had to admit that no, he would not. He'd been doubly impressed when they'd turfed his hack team out and sent him the bill for the defense—impressed enough to vouchsafe them to the others sharing his interests in this, at least.

He surveyed the others as they arrived and began to circulate. Each of them would be sent a copy of the footage once their meeting was done, and each of them would have their analytical teams spend *hours* going over it to seek every advantage and weakness their opponents and allies had to offer.

Needless to say, everyone was *very* well-behaved when they were in attendance. He studied them as they mixed and mingled, noted who shook whose hand, whose greetings were brief, or who seemed tenser than he thought they had a reason to be.

He chose to deal with some things at the meeting, rather than after its end. Some matters *needed* to be dealt with more immediately. None of them could afford to have schisms appearing. Not now when they were so close to putting their plans into action.

When they had settled at their assigned tables, he descended from the slight dais he'd stood on and cleared his throat to gain their attention. One of the beauties of meeting in the Virtual World was that he didn't need a microphone. His words were piped directly to each of them.

"Gentlemen and ladies, I am sure you are all aware that this is not merely another weekly meeting. We come together one member short, and it is a matter we have yet to understand."

"The fact his body was incinerated beyond retrieval no doubt causes some concern," a woman commented dryly. "I take it you at least know *who* enacted poor Sebastian's demise."

The billionaire pressed his lips together and gave her a sour stare. "We understand it was the recently fallen criminal lord of the Washington-Chicago region."

"Emerald?" There was shock in the tones. "Are you saying *she* was involved?"

"I am."

"Do you have any proof?"

Again, the billionaire looked like he'd been sucking lemons. "Nothing as conclusive as I'd like. From the little I've been able to ascertain, she killed our colleague and set his private shuttle to explode in such a way as to destroy his apartment and the empty floor beneath it."

Murmurs rose as businessmen discussed those implications with their neighbors. The billionaire continued regardless.

"She then paid a visit to one of our facilities." He paused to let that sink in and repeated it for effect. "One of *our. Secret.* Facilities. There, she assassinated the members of a local cell who were attending a *very* private meeting and most of the elite forces brought in to guard them."

More murmurs followed and this time, he waited to let them get over the initial shock of the revelation.

As the response died down, he added, "And it is where she was killed."

The businessman who'd asked for proof spoke again. "And do you have any proof of that?"

"We have footage from the body cams on the security forces and the security system."

"What, no DNA?"

His lip curled. "Since we have no known samples positively identified as Emerald's DNA, it wouldn't have done us any good. If you're curious, I *can* confirm that we have forensic teams combing the site to collect everything they can to identify her and her team."

"Posthumously?"

"Her team still lives." He delivered that like a death knell and his words held both a threat and a promise. Emerald's team was living on borrowed time, no matter who they were.

Those present made sounds of approval and he waited for their brains to kick in. The attack had greater implications than a requirement for petty vengeance. The latter would happen because they could not let such a challenge go unanswered, but there were more important things to consider.

"Wait. If the team has to die, are you saying she *knew* who she was attacking?"

"I am saying the possibility is there. As you are aware, we approached her to take action on another 'problem.'"

"The parents," someone stated.

"The parents," others confirmed.

The billionaire's face turned to stone. "I do not consider this attack a coincidence."

"And the parents have disappeared. *Both* sets," another observed, and he made a note to see exactly where that one sourced his intelligence.

"Do you know where?" he asked and the speaker blushed.

"The investigation into the attack on the apartment complex didn't go that far—and I couldn't justify pushing it once we received a vid-call showing them all well and alive."

"From where?" Now, he was annoyed. That information should have been passed to him immediately.

As if catching his thought, the man answered the question. "It came in an hour ago. It has a plain white background and bounced through so many sats, we lost count."

"The Witch's ship has been in-system for the last week," another commented.

"And you've tracked its movements?"

"Not in relation to the timeline of the attack on the parents," the man replied. He turned to the man who'd announced the communication. "If you could forward the information, we'll look into it."

"Two minutes," he replied, pulled his tablet out, and went to work. He glanced at the billionaire. "We've been trying to trace it as if it were from Earth. Given who they are, though..."

"Yes," he confirmed and finished the sentence. "That *was* rather short-sighted of you, wasn't it?"

He said it like the statement of fact it was and returned to his original line of thought.

"Which brings us back to the question of Emerald. I cannot for the life of me decide why she would have *any* interest in attacking this facility except one."

"Vengeance," a woman murmured and he nodded.

"Exactly. If someone attacked *my* parents or the parents of someone *I* loved, this is exactly what I would do."

"But...this was Emerald." The speaker sounded bewildered.

"Exactly," the businessman said, "and Emerald has no parents. Add the fact that she recently murdered the only man who *might* be considered a father figure and we have a puzzle. If she didn't care for *him*, why would she target those who used her services to set up the hit on the sergeant's parents?"

"She wasn't secretly in love with him, was she?" The snide question came from the far corner.

The billionaire snorted. There was a good reason why he'd put that particular politician in the corner. Anything more central and the man would have taken the stage. He simply couldn't help himself.

Smoothing his face to neutrality, he answered. "Not that we can tell, which is something I want you to investigate. I can think of only one woman close enough to the Witch to take umbrage at the attack."

"The manager."

He paused and noted the ripple of agreement pass round the room.

"The manager," he confirmed, "but to the best of our ability, we can't work out what, if any, connections she had to the underworld."

"We can't discover where Mr. Burt sourced her from either," another observed. "Is it possible she *is* Emerald?"

The billionaire shook his head. "All reports show her as still alive and Emerald very much dead. If the two were the same person, this wouldn't be the case."

"Is it possible she *faked* her death?"

Instead of denying the possibility outright, he scowled. "I don't see how but it's something we can add to the list of things to look into."

He waited for them to ask the more obvious question. When they didn't, he voiced it himself. "Our more immediate concern is how *Emerald*, a common criminal—"

A snort interrupted him, and he raised his head.

"Do you disagree?"

The man who answered him was seated in a corner at his request, one of the few such requests the billionaire regularly honored.

"*Emerald*," the man informed him in a heavy East European accent, "was not what you call *common*. In fact, she was so *uncommon* I would hazard to call her exceptional. She was among the elite of her world and the very best at what she did. If anyone could have uncovered us, she would have been the one to do it."

"And yet you recommended her."

"You wanted someone who could get the job done and who wouldn't care what the connections were. She was the only one who sprang to mind."

"And yet she was able to give us a half-dozen names that tell me otherwise."

The man shrugged. "With the results you are trying to understand now. Someone found one of our cells."

"The woman *you* recommended for the job found one of our cells," the billionaire retorted. He scowled. "And I'd like to know how."

"I will have my people look into it."

He scanned the room. "You will *all* have your people look into it. You will sanitize your connections with that cell and everything associated with it."

A small sound of protest interrupted him, and he looked at the originator.

"Don't worry, Charles. You're still here. If she'd decided you knew what was going on in your plant, you wouldn't be." His words didn't make the man relax so he added, "That's good enough for us."

The billionaire looked at each of the others in turn. "I mean that links to those attending the meeting must be sanitized. Our other ties must be maintained."

"And it still doesn't answer the why of her targeting us, let alone the *how the fuck* she found out about us." The belligerent statement returned the focus to the main problem. "I thought no one knew we existed."

"No one does," he assured the woman. "And Emerald didn't either. She targeted the source of the calls."

"*How?*" the questioner reiterated.

The billionaire pointed at her. "Exactly. The cell followed every protocol we've laid down—every single one. She should not have been able to find the caller let alone the rest of the cell. It speaks of technical support of a similar caliber to our own, and that is another team I want hunted and found."

"And the ones who went in to assist?"

"As far as we know, they remain uncompromised."

"As far as you *know?*"

"We have done our best and are implementing new measures as we find them. Those measures are being sent to every one of you and I expect them to be in place within twenty-four hours of receipt."

That caused a ripple of unease but he ignored it. They would find ways to comply. None of them wanted the consequences if they failed.

He glanced at the crystal timepiece adorning the wall over the entrance and led into the next item on the meeting's agenda.

"Now that's taken care of," he continued, "we need to address another issue." He allowed himself a small smile. "And clearly, we won't be able to ask for Emerald's assistance on this one."

He glanced at one of the military men in the room. "I will need everyone to have the necessary means in place to achieve what needs to be done to clear the final obstacles for our takeover of the Federation and planetary government."

Their attention was entirely focused on him now. Their final goal was the stuff of wet dreams for these power players. They all wanted to be in control and the war would put them there—even without the Telorans. No, *especially* without the Telorans.

The dreams the aliens had awoken could not be achieved without their assistance save in one very important category—that of antagonist. The Telorans provided the one thing they needed to unite the disparate politics of their world. Without that threat, they'd never have been in a position to do what they were doing. At least, not so easily.

"We'll need to take out the trash," the billionaire told them and noted which of them shifted uneasily in their seats and who smiled with grim satisfaction.

Before any of them could comment, he continued. "You all have your targets. If we are victorious, they have to die within the first few weeks after peace is declared. Some of them will have to die as close to the moment of victory as possible."

Again, his gaze fell on the military men and women in the room. They all nodded, their faces set with determination. Theirs was the most difficult part since he'd decided that many of their targets needed to die in battle. Victory, if it happened, would be bitter-sweet, and if it didn't…

"If we lose, our targets must live to take the blame. No petty payback. Am I understood?"

He waited for the assent to reach him before he spoke again. "Loss in battle does not have to mean loss overall but it *will* mean a change of plans and for that, our scapegoats must remain alive."

Again, their agreement reached him and he nodded, satisfied that they would all play their part exactly as he needed them to.

"Which brings me to another matter of importance," he told them and pressed on before any of them could ask what. "In the Navy, we need fighters, and we need fighters who will join us without question or qualm."

"Do you have any idea how you'll achieve that?" one of the military representatives asked and didn't bother to hide his sarcasm. "Because it's all something of a Witch love-fest out there at the moment."

The billionaire identified the woman as one of the Navy's intelligence leaders and arched his brow. "Did you do as I asked?"

She nodded.

The billionaire smiled. "Then we already have one fighter lined up, don't we? And an influential one at that."

Again, she nodded.

"Where is he at the moment?"

"Still in prison."

He frowned. "We can't use him while he's in there, now can we? I thought I told you to get him out of there."

"There was no way to work around the admiral's orders, but we took him to one of our prisons," the intelligence officer replied. Her colleagues smirked and she gave the billionaire a tight, satisfied smile. "He is *very* keen to work with us."

"He hates the Witch that much?"

"More, sir. The rear admiral will do whatever it takes to ensure her destruction."

"And exactly how did you get him to agree to that?" the billionaire asked.

One of the other billionaires in the room gave a sudden bark of recognition. "Dreyfus? Are we talking Rear Admiral *Dreyfus*?"

The group's leader suppressed a sigh. "We are," he confirmed.

"He's hated her since she started eliminating everyone who supported the Telorans. She cost him considerable money with that."

"So he won't change his mind?"

"Oh, hell no! That man will not only take her down, he'll take on anyone who supports her and dance on all their graves when she falls." The speaker paused. "I'm not sure how you'll get him restored in the current climate, though."

His doubts brought a secretive smile to the leader's face. "That should be the easy part—once we complete the first phase of our plan."

"The first phase?"

"Of the Witch's fall from grace."

"Hmmph. Good luck with that. The woman can't put a foot wrong in the public's eyes."

The leader tutted and shook his head. "My dear Earl, *you* of all people should know that even the most perfect of us can fall foul of the public's erstwhile opinion. It's simply a matter of clever reporting."

A quiet fell over the room and their gazes drifted to the media magnates seated at the foremost table. In public, the two were the fiercest competitors with rumors of hatred fueling their competition. In private, they were more like brothers from a close-knit family where each one had the other's back.

They returned the stares with benign smiles that fooled no one.

Not a soul present wanted to cross them or to draw their attention.

The billionaire surveyed the room and spread his hands. "That concludes the formalities of the evening," he told them. "Feel free to mingle and enjoy your meals."

He retired to the single table set up on the dais at the head of the room as the hum of voices rose behind him.

They told him the only thing he needed to know. He wasn't alone in planning the Witch's downfall.

CHAPTER THIRTY-TWO

As Stephanie's opponents finished their meeting, Elizabeth sat beside Matthias and viewed the surveillance footage E-BURT had sent. One R&D Headquarters looked forlorn in its complete emptiness. The rooms were deserted, gutted of all their equipment, and silence reigned.

That wasn't what they were looking for, though. They tried to see if there was anything they'd missed.

"I don't see anything," Amy said from the other side of the table.

"Me neither," Bunny added, "but those animals are starting to freak me out."

"The charges are still in place," Arne noted. "When do you want them blown?"

"Not yet," E told him. "Let's leave them in place in case the guys from the plant trace us."

"I could set them to go off if someone enters," Arne offered.

"No. That might catch a Federation law officer. I don't want to kill anyone who's simply doing their job."

"Fair enough."

"Eebie, can you bounce a signal from Arne long distance?" she asked.

E-BURT made a human-like raspberry sound. "I could set them off at any time he asked."

"Well, that settles *that*, then," the ex-Marine noted and looked at Elizabeth. "My explosives await your command."

"Ha. Very funny," she grumbled and focused on her screen.

They fell silent again. Each of them poured over the footage with extra care.

Finally, she looked up from her tablet. "When did the university want us out?"

"They said they could keep this wing closed for three or four days before folk would start asking awkward questions."

"And the doc?"

"You should ask him that yourself," Matthias informed her. "He's waiting for you to come in for your check-up."

"Ugh." She was about to ask if she had to when she realized how much like a child that made her sound. She satisfied herself with a groan and pushed away from the table. "When's breakfast?"

"As soon as you get back from the doc," Amy told her and stood.

Elizabeth followed suit and Matthias stood with her. Arne pushed his chair back and she sighed.

"I thought I was the only one who needed a check-up."

The ex-Marine gave her a crooked smile. "Matthias will go with you—and I wouldn't try to dissuade him if I were you."

He said it like the other man's presence was enough to explain his, which it did.

She scowled and glanced at Amy. Her guard inclined her head and put a hand on her hip, and she sighed. "Right. I hired you, didn't I?"

The woman rewarded her with a bright smile. "Yup."

There was no point in arguing so she didn't bother.

"We'll make travel arrangements when I get back," she told them, stepped into the corridor, and came to a complete halt.

"It's this way," Matthias told her and she gave him a grateful smile.

"I brought you along for a reason, didn't I?" she asked.

He chuckled. "Well, it's not like you could have stopped me."

"Don't let it go to your head."

The doctor looked up as they entered the temporary surgery and his look of relief at seeing her warred with concern and consternation.

He noted her entourage with distaste, not impressed when Amy arched an eyebrow and folded her arms as though daring him to try to tell her to leave.

Rather than respond, he turned his attention to Elizabeth and asked, "How are you feeling?"

"Like I got hit by a bus," she told him.

"That good, huh?" The doctor pushed to his feet and gestured to a wall. "If your entourage could stand over there, I'd like to make sure everything is doing what it should be."

"Sure, Doc." Elizabeth glanced at Matthias and he sighed before he moved to do as the doctor suggested.

As if his compliance was some kind of signal, Arne and Amy followed him, the other man quite happily and she with a reluctant glance at her boss. E was glad she didn't have to ask twice. She wasn't sure she'd have managed to do so with any kind of civility.

"Now, let's see how the healing process is going," the doctor murmured and she flinched beneath his gentle probing.

"So, am I fit for travel?" she asked and tucked her shirt in when he was done.

"You can fly," he informed her and held a finger up when she opened her mouth to thank him. "*But* I'd rather you delayed it another day, preferably two, just to be sure. I'd also recommend you fly first-class to reduce the chances of getting bumped."

"Understood," she acknowledged and wondered how he knew she'd planned to fly.

"Your injuries..." he said as if he read the question on her face. "My guess is that you'll need to leave town for a while, and the farther the better. Going somewhere you can stay out of trouble while you finish mending is something else I'd highly recommend."

"Gotcha, Doc."

His lips quirked in what might have been a smile. "It's not that I don't like your company, but I'd rather you were *un*injured the next time I saw you."

"Thanks, Doc." Elizabeth paused. "Has the boss settled the accounts?"

He nodded. "He paid upfront and gave me an account to draw from if I needed anything else. If I didn't know any better, I'd say he liked you."

The wondering tone in the man's voice made her smile. "He'd better, Doc, or the end of year do will be more exciting than he'd like."

"I can imagine," the doctor replied, his tone wry. He took a step back and sat at his desk. "Give me an hour to file my reports and I'll be out of here."

It was as close to a dismissal as she had ever heard him give, and she didn't stop to argue. Instead, she headed to the door and didn't need to tell the others to go with her. She turned into the next door she found, glad to discover it was another office.

Once she settled herself behind the desk, she pulled her tablet out and called E-BURT.

"We're ready," she told him.

"I'll have the clean-up crew there inside a half-hour. Make sure you're gone."

"I kinda hoped you had a plan for that," Elizabeth retorted. "You know, like we discussed?"

"The travel details will be forwarded to your tablets shortly," the AI informed her primly, "and the necessary tickets and fare passes will be on your communications devices. You need to make sure you're all where you need to be."

"You know I don't like this, E-BURT," Amy said, after glancing at her travel documents.

"It is necessary," he informed her. "Those who have been watching One R&D know Elizabeth never travels alone and that you are her primary escort. Likewise, Bunny and Lisa have been with her long enough to have been noted. None of you can go with her."

Elizabeth regarded her disgruntled team with what she hoped was a reasonable expression. "It's not like I wasn't traveling solo long before Steph and BURT insisted I needed someone of my own."

"I thought that was Lars," Amy replied.

She snorted. "Yeah, well, him too."

"The same situation applies to Arne and Matthias. They cannot travel together. They are a well-known pairing. Each of you will, I am afraid, have to fend for yourselves for the duration of the journey."

"Wait. You're sending me through the *Confederated States?*" Matthias exclaimed. "That's *insane.*"

"Yes, I am, and no, it is not," E-BURT replied. "Given your history, the Confederated States and Russia, in particular, are not places you will be expected to travel through."

"You know there will be interesting questions asked when they find out I have," he told him.

"By then, it will not be a problem for you," the AI responded. "You will be well out of reach."

"They won't like it if I don't come in to answer questions," he answered.

"You can answer any questions they wish on any satellite station or at any outpost they choose," E-BURT argued. "You do not need to return to Earth or any of its precincts to answer their questions."

Arne looked at his tablet and groaned.

"What is it?" Amy asked and he swept a hand up and down his body

"Do I look like I'd wear a pair of board shorts?" he asked.

She made a show of examining him and moved from the side to stand in front of him as she studied him with a critical eye.

"I don't know, Arne, you look good to me. I'm not sure about board shorts, though. Perhaps you should try a speedo instead."

Bunny gave a choked laugh and turned away with a giggle as he flushed.

"What are you trying to say, girl?"

"Gee, Arne, I'm not sure, but you might want to work on that seeing as Eebie seems to have booked us into the same hotel at Firesands."

That stopped him. "He has?"

"Officially, you aren't traveling together," E-BURT stated, "but Arne has traveled alone before. I thought it might help if he was seen to pick up a female...*companion* on his travels. It might explain his travel choices and then blur them."

She blushed. "BURT—"

"I could, of course, have Bunny take your place if you'd prefer," he suggested.

Amy shook her head. "No, it's fine. I can deal."

"You don't need to make it sound like such a chore," Arne told her. "I'm quite happy to fly solo."

"These arrangements have been made to give you the best chance of reaching your final destination without unwanted company," the AI informed them. "I can alter them but the results might be less than optimal."

"Lisa," Elizabeth asked. "are you okay for this?"

The newest of her team nodded but her face was pale. Bunny turned to her, placed a hand on the girl's shoulder, and looked into her teammate's face.

"Is there anything I can do?"

Lisa shook her head. "Not really." She sighed. "I'm worried about my folks, is all."

"I have procedures in place to secure immediate family members should the need arise," E-BURT interjected.

He paused as they all glanced at their tablets but continued when none of them interrupted. "I am coming to understand the human concept of family and its importance."

Bunny shook her head emphatically. "Not mine, Eebie. Mine can damned well stay where they are. I don't want to see them again—and I mean *ever.*"

"I understand, Bunny. However, I have taken steps to monitor their situation in case you should change your mind."

"It's not likely, but thank you," she acknowledged and patted Lisa on the arm. "Are you good now?"

The girl nodded and managed a wavering smile. "Yup. All good. Thanks, Eebs."

"You are very welcome, Lisa," he replied and turned his attention to the group. "Now, if you would all excuse me. I will not keep you from your departures. Please ensure you reach the correct rendezvous point for your transport."

"What about our equipment, Eebie?" Elizabeth asked.

"I have a clean-up crew en-route and you will find your luggage in the cars sent to collect you. Please ensure you change your clothing at the designated places. The vehicles will wait."

"Designated..." she began and studied her itinerary. "Oh... I see."

On her route to the shuttleport, the AI had marked a small detour taking her into a corner store with a mail service. There would be public toilets available where she could change. Glancing at Matthias's tablet, she noted he'd been given a drop-off point at a boarding kennel where he was to make the excuse of a last-minute dog-treat delivery.

Glancing around the room, she watched as each of her team followed their itineraries to the designated point and nodded in confirmation.

"Thank you, E-BURT."

"You are all most welcome, but some of you need to hurry or you will be late."

They all glanced at their tablets once more and Arne swore. He slapped Matthias on the shoulder as he passed.

"Don't make me come looking for you."

CHAPTER THIRTY-THREE

As Elizabeth said goodbye to her team and went to meet her cab, Amaratne pursed his lips. This meeting was not ending how he'd expected it to.

It had started well enough with the various sector admirals discussing what they would bring to the battle and what they could offer, then someone had mentioned Stephanie.

"I hope she brings the same kind of firepower she brought to the battle of Meligorn."

Now that he thought about it, he realized that the comment had come from Admiral Burtch, the man tasked with Meligornian liaison. It was a position he'd filled well enough to be called an 'elf lover' to his face and much, much worse behind his back.

His comment had the weight of experience, but it was met by surprising resistance and even more surprising hostility. Amaratne observed the ensuing discussion and wondered how it had come to the debacle that now unfolded before him.

"And I do not!" had been the response from Helveck. "That is exactly the kind of wild card we do not need."

Burtch had been as startled by the reaction as his boss. "I beg your pardon?"

"You heard me," the man reiterated. "We do *not* need that kind of magical idiocy anywhere *near* our ships."

The fleet admiral watched as several of the men scattered nearby nodded in agreement, and he couldn't quite believe it. He propped his elbows on the table in front of him and pretended to be engrossed in his tablet as several of the attendees threw cautious glances at him.

When he didn't react, they relaxed and joined the discussion. Some weighed in with Helveck and others sided with Burtch.

"We couldn't have won that battle without her."

"You call losing that many ships a win?"

"We didn't lose the battle—"

"Yeah, and it wasn't thanks to the Witch. That was because a boat-load of *civilians* paid the ultimate price. It should never have been allowed to happen."

Amaratne let the voices wash around him and wondered how he could access the room's recording without anyone in the room being told about it. He *really* wanted to see who was agreeing with what and whom.

"That doesn't change the fact that, without her, we'd have lost far more. She drained herself *dry* to save that world."

"And it went straight to her head—a fancy meal with a king and some pretty trinkets to wear when she deigns to put a uniform on. She wouldn't know how to work in a formation if the need bit her in the ass!"

"I beg to differ—"

"And so you should because it's true. She's a lone operator and has no place in a real space battle."

This was the last straw, and Amaratne pushed his chair back with an audible scrape. Some voices wavered, but others did not. He cleared his throat, and silence fell.

"I take you have all seen the footage of the Battle for Meligorn?" he asked and many of the officers nodded.

He made a mental note of those who did not, including the two who'd been coming to meet him until Stephanie's people had pulled out the metal bar in the docking bay. The recognition almost stole the words from him and he paused.

When he felt the weight of the room's attention, he pulled himself together.

"If you haven't seen it, I strongly advise you to do so."

"Vid-doctored nonsense," whispered out of the gathering, and he forced himself to not challenge the speaker. He decided it was more important to make the necessary point than to descend into a point-scoring brawl.

"The footage clearly shows the Witch being instrumental in the defeat of not one but *several* Teloran super-dreadnoughts—ships that out-massed and outgunned not only the biggest ships we or the Meligornian Navy had to offer but also the flagship of the *Dreth* fleet. Without her, we would have lost Meligorn and a valuable ally as well."

Several snorts stuttered out of the group and this time, Amaratne could not identify who had made them. It worried him that their strongest allies were being so disparaged, especially since he'd been unaware that such a sentiment existed in his upper echelons. It was something he'd have to combat.

Silence followed his declaration before Helveck stepped forward.

"I'm sure it's comforting to think so, Admiral, but there are projections that show the battle would have turned in the Meligornians favor without her."

The fleet admiral allowed a faint frown to mar his brow. He'd seen no such analyses, but Helveck wasn't alone. Several of the officers behind him made sounds of approval, including the two he'd noticed earlier.

"We can do without the kind of interference and instability she brings," the admiral continued. His voice rose with the kind of fervor usually seen in zealots peddling the more obscure versions of communal ignorance.

Amaratne knew better than to try to argue with that kind of belief, but he could not be seen to tolerate that level of ignorance in his ranks. Especially not his upper ranks.

"Needless to say, we need her," he persisted. "She is exactly the kind of element the Telorans can't predict or pre-empt, the kind of element that lends us an advantage in *any* fight."

"Just because she's on our side now," Helveck told him, "doesn't mean her abilities can't be a liability to us as well. What if she had lost control of her magic? You said she fought until she was drained almost dry. How can we trust our fleets or our victory to a being who has so little regard for herself that she puts her own life at risk when she is needed most?"

It was a good question, but he didn't believe that was what Stephanie had done.

"How can we *not* trust a being willing to risk herself to save the rest of us?" he countered and the man's lip curled in scorn.

"On your head be it, *sir*, but I'm making the formal request that she not be put in any of my formations where I think she will be more a liability than an asset."

Amaratne stared as the conversation erupted into an argument with some admirals repeating the request and others deriding them for it.

"I say we put her up against the large sonsabitches that the rest of us can't take on toe to toe," the other bar-dodger suggested.

"It will keep her out of our way and hopefully, she'll weaken them to a point where we *can* take them on," another suggested.

This was met with the predictable mix of reactions from both sides. Some agreed wholeheartedly because they thought the Witch was more than capable of carrying the battle and others because they thought they'd send her to her death. Still others clearly relished the idea of her downfall winning them the battle.

"So, Helveck, I'm to understand that it will be a long, cold day in hell before you or your two colleagues would be happy to share the same docking bay with the *Knight*?"

Helveck snorted. "I don't believe *any* civilian ship should share a Naval docking space—*or* be given access to Naval repair assets—and nor do many of the others standing here."

"I'd be happy to have the Witch's ship dock beside mine any day,"

Burtch declared, his statement acknowledged favorably by several others.

The discussion slid toward the nature of repairs that should be offered to ships and companies like the *Knight* and One R&D who became involved in "naval" affairs. Amaratne let them continue for several minutes, glad the discussion covered his remark.

It hadn't been intended as a conversation starter, merely a marker for him when he listened to the playback and a reminder to check the footage and make a note of Helveck and the two admirals from the docking bay and who they kept company with.

When he was sure they'd forgotten what he'd said, he rapped on the desk.

"Ladies and gentlemen," he called. "If you would break into your task groups, please, we'll move the discussion on to specific tactics and let you hammer out a rough plan with those admirals whose forces you'll fight alongside."

His words cut through the chatter and he waited as the gathered admirals broke from their discussions and disagreements to retire to their assigned tables. The transition was almost complete when there was a rapid knock at the door and Amaratne sighed.

Reluctantly, he prepared to speak the acknowledgment that would admit Rear Admiral Dreyfus to the meeting. As much as he'd disagreed with the man's reinstatement, he was too politically aware to miss the implications of the argument put forward.

"You can't jail someone simply because they happen to dislike someone who's in favor," hadn't been something he could refute since the investigation hadn't uncovered any evidence of anything more sinister.

"I still don't trust him to be able to operate in a responsible manner," he'd insisted. "He's shown conduct unbecoming toward a valued contributor to the fight."

"A *civilian* contributor," had been emphasized. "You have to understand how a military man of his history might find such things difficult to assimilate."

"Nevertheless, his attitude brought an important strategic relationship with a valuable *asset* into jeopardy," Admiral Amaratne had persisted, "and *that* is not something I could allow."

"It is also not something that is punishable by imprisonment or loss of commission or employment," the legal team had told him. "You will have to reinstate him, albeit with appropriate caveats and warnings."

"Let me consider it."

"We've been asked to deliver your decision within two hours."

It wasn't enough time for him to be able to come up with a compelling enough argument to keep Rear Admiral Dreyfus under lock and key, let alone drum him out of the Navy.

"Come," he commanded and forced himself to return the rear admiral's salute.

He'd rather strangle the man but he didn't let a single trace of his distaste show on his face.

"Over there, Rear Admiral," he managed to say calmly and wondered what had possessed him to put him with Admiral Helveck and his team. "I'm sure the admirals can brief you on what they need you to do."

Dreyfus gave him a stiff nod and feelings of resentment and pent frustration warred with contempt as he attempted to maintain an expression of respect on his face. "Any responsibility is better than none, Fleet."

He forced his head into a cordial nod and watched as the rear admiral hurried to join his team. Watching the way Dreyfus was welcomed into their ranks, he was forced to wonder if he'd made a mistake.

As Admiral Amaratne watched his fleet commanders settle to the business of planning a battle, several Marines made their way to the corridor outside the suite housing the Hooligans.

"Are you sure this is it?" one asked and frowned at the Marines already stationed at the door.

"This is where we were told to go." The sergeant studied the guards. "But no-one said anything about there being a watch in place."

He signaled his troops to keep walking past and decided it would look suspicious if they did a sudden about-face when they'd only just arrived. The guy and gal on the door watched them pass and their gazes traveled over his squad as if they had some idea of what they saw.

Fervently, he hoped not. It always rankled when he had to kill some of their own.

Although, if they're protecting our enemies, they're not ours, are they? he thought to justify whatever action he would have to take. As far as he was concerned, the Hooligans had been designated a threat to the Federation and anyone who protected them was part of that threat.

Sucks to be them, he decided, led his men past, and headed to the training rooms as if that had been their destination all along. The looks on their faces said they weren't convinced, however. *Too bad.*

He took his guys through the training room and out the other side to return to their suite to get an update from HQ. At the very least, they needed orders that would allow them to tell the Marines on duty that they'd been relieved.

As soon as the last member of his squad had gone into the gym, the female Marine nudged her colleague. "We're clear. Do you have the footage?"

He nodded and she jerked a thumb toward the door.

"We'd best get it inside then," she told him and stepped forward so he could do as she suggested.

He pivoted and knocked sharply, rapping out two fast beats in quick succession. It cracked open shortly after, as though the female corporal on the other side had been waiting. Glancing surreptitiously at the surveillance camera down the corridor, he wondered if the Hooligans had hacked the system and decided as quickly not to ask.

If they *had* hacked it, he didn't want to know. It was easier that way.

Using his body and that of his colleague as a shield, he retrieved a small box from his top pocket, glad the so-not-Marines hadn't seemed to register that the cords leading from his ear-piece were more complex than most. This one attached to the camera concealed in his glasses.

As the corporal watched, he took the small box out, removed the recording card, and waited for her to take it before he replaced it with another. She gave him a quick smile when he was done and he moved back so she could close the door between them.

"I wonder what they wanted *that* for," his partner murmured and he shook his head.

"No, you don't. Neither of us want to know what they'll do with that data," he told her fervently.

She shrugged at his tone. "The admiral might."

He sighed. "Point. We might have to ask them."

"I'll suggest that since our boss is looking after them, it might be nice if they passed on anything that might help us do the same for him. They seem a reasonable enough team."

"Someone doesn't think so," he pointed out.

"True, and if *someone* doesn't like them that much and our boss has put us here, anyway? We need to watch the boss's back more closely."

Her colleague nodded. "I hear you."

They settled into watchful silence, unaware of the team watching and listening to them from behind the door.

"Well, there you have it," Ka said and glanced at Todd. "They're here on the Fleet's orders."

"So, not just anyone, then," Gary quipped.

"Nope." She quieted and her face became serious. "He sent his personal team, boss. We are in the shit."

Todd shrugged. "Well, we kinda knew that already. Now, we know for sure."

"So, this next operation's a trap," she stated.

"It looks like it." Todd sighed. "The only question is what we'll do about it."

"Is there anything we *can* do?" Gary asked, his tone slightly bitter. "'Cause while I know I *might* die on any given operation, it's a whole other thing to deliberately march to my death, Navy's orders or not."

"Especially if I'm not blowing anything up," Piet grumbled and Ka gave him a playful push.

"Did anyone ever tell you that you have a problem?" she joked.

"Not anyone who wants me to blow anything up for them ever again," he snapped.

"So go find me the shit that'll keep us alive," Todd ordered.

"You got a wish list, boss?"

"I'll pull one together but I want *all* the things and not only the ones we dream up."

"Gotcha, boss." Ka cracked her knuckles and nudged Piet. "Time to go to work, Destructo."

"Destructo?"

"It's a comic-book reference," Todd supplied.

Henry chuckled. "For a minute there, I had to wonder what some ancient DJ had to do with Piet."

"Nah. The guy Ka's thinking of was a mad scientist," the sergeant told him. "Definitely not into music."

She shook her head. "That's not it."

He looked at her, wide-eyed. "It's not?"

"Nah. I was referring to a cute computer game someone put into this Internet café I used to visit back home. *They* said they pulled it from a computer archive the Russians had dug up, but I didn't believe them. I didn't care, either. It was hella fun to play."

Todd made a winding motion with his finger and she shrugged.

"The long and the short of it is you get to play this dog that likes blowing shit up. I spent *waay* too many hours playing it as a kid."

"Hmmph. Are you sure *Piet's* the one who should be called Destructo?" Darren asked and looked speculatively at her.

"Hell yes! He makes me look like an amateur."

"Can I quote you on that?" Piet asked hopefully.

Ka laughed. "Oh, hell no."

Todd gave them a fleeting smile before his face settled into hard lines. "I need you to find me the deadliest toys around—and the armor to match. If we *are* supposed to march to our doom, I want to survive it so I can march out and hunt whoever sent us. We'll be the last team they send to their deaths."

"They're gonna think we're ghosts," Ka stated and bared her teeth.

"Yeah, except the only ghosts when we get done are gonna be theirs," Darren agreed.

He shook his head. "Nope. When we're done, there won't be enough left of them to *be* ghosts. I'll wipe them from the face of the Earth."

"Ooh…Morgana, much?" Ka snipped.

She froze at the look on his face and immediately regretted bringing his girlfriend's evil twin into it.

Todd spoke before she could apologize.

"Don't you have weapons to find me?" he asked. "'Cause I don't see you gettin' it done."

"The hacker sighed and looked at her tablet. "Fine, boss. Get out of my face and I'll get it done."

Piet stared at her. "Get out of my face? Do you have a death wish?"

"Nope. I have a job to do. Where are you at?"

As they focused on the task he'd set them, Todd turned to the rest of the team.

"Let's go over what we faced in the last two Teloran ships."

Gary shrugged. "Sure, boss, but—"

"But nothing. We look at what we encountered and then we try to work out how it could be ten times worse and the tactics we're gonna need to survive it and beat it."

The man inclined his head with a smirk. "Weeell, Sarge, I thought we could head back to Jimmy's homeland and hunt us a group of fey. The ones that ride out from under the hills and tend to carry magic wands—"

Todd thumped the flat of his hand into Gary's chest and knocked the smaller man on his ass.

"Well, fuck, boss. What happened to your sense of humor?"

"It left when someone tried to kill my parents," he snapped in response and they froze. While they still tried to think of something to say, he continued. "Now, let's get to work. Henry, you're quiet. What do you remember?"

"Being shit scared and shot at," was probably not the reply he was looking for.

Ka snickered but her gaze never left her screen and her fingers moved like lightning over the keyboard as she took the tablet places no Marine was ever meant to go. Piet worked alongside her, his hands moving equally as fast but with more certainty.

These were places he'd been before and he didn't need to find them first. He merely needed to remember how to get there. Even when the paths had changed it didn't take him long.

Occasionally, she would glance at what he was doing and adjust her search accordingly. She would then tweak it, and it would be Piet's turn to adapt. Together, the two of them slid out of the legitimate net and ran deeper into the darker side.

"Do you know how much trouble we're gonna be in if they find out what we're doing?" she whispered.

Piet gave her a grim smile. "They have to catch us first."

"Heh—" Ka stopped abruptly and nudged him. "Take a look at this."

He glanced at her screen and froze. A low whistle escaped his lips. "My, oh my, oh my…"

Todd glanced up. "What?"

"We found their Teloran armor-piercing rounds." He looked at the sergeant with the beginning of a smile. "Do I have permission to go shopping?"

She elbowed him in the ribs.

"We," he amended. "Do *we* have permission to go shopping?"

Todd frowned and considered the problem in his mind. It wasn't only *where* they would have to go to get the equipment, it was getting them off the *Notaro* without their usual trouble entourage.

Now, *that* was a problem they would need help with…if they could get it.

He crossed to the door and cracked it open. "We need a word," he told the two Marines outside.

They both scanned the corridor around them and exchanged glances. The corridor was clear.

"Can you monitor out here while we're inside?" the corporal asked.

Todd nodded. "We haven't stopped," he informed her and studied her face as she digested that piece of information.

He waited until she came to a decision and jerked her head for her partner to follow her in. Quickly, he secured the door behind them and got straight down to business.

"How close are you supposed to stay?" he asked as the corporal turned to face him.

"We've been ordered to go wherever you go and stop you from getting yanked on anyone's orders but the admiral's," they told him and it was clear that they meant only one admiral.

"That's good to know," Todd told them. "It's worrying that he feels the need but it's good to know at least one of the brass is looking out for us. There's something not right about those other guys."

"Yeah. You've seriously pissed in someone's tea," the corporal told him. "Whoever it is, the admiral won't let them have you, regardless of what assholes they send."

"Not without a fight, at least," her partner said.

"So, if we had to take a trip downside…" he began, but the corporal held her hand up.

"We can protect while you're on duty and on the *Notaro*," she told him. "What you do on your own time… Well, we can't help you with that. The admiral was very specific about where we could operate and where his jurisdiction ended."

Todd leaned against the cabin wall. "So we're on our own then?"

The corporal moved to the door.

"If what you're planning is on your own time and off the *Notaro* then I'm sorry, but you are."

He managed a smile as the two of them slipped through the door to return to their posts.

"Sorry, man," the corporal's partner told him and looked sympathetic.

"Thanks, anyway," he acknowledged, closed the door firmly behind them, and threw the locks.

"Well, that sucks," Ka commented.

Todd shrugged. "We'll be fine. We've operated on our own this long so a little longer won't hurt us."

He settled on one of the chairs at the common room table and signaled for the others to join him.

"I don't like it, but Ka, you and Piet are gonna have to take a solo jaunt Earth-side."

CHAPTER THIRTY-FOUR

"They want a quote on *drones?*" Harmond Bellamy couldn't believe it. "Haven't they read the company's site?"

"Read the request again, Harmy dear." Abigail sounded more exasperated than usual.

He winced and wished his sister wouldn't call him that. Also, he wished she wouldn't get so uptight about him skimming the emails. It wasn't like she had most of a company to run. She needed to keep her britches on and her tone civil.

"And don't you glower at me, Harmond Vernon Bellamy. We both know you need to take better care of the business."

Despite his irritation, he blushed. *Now,* she was quoting their father verbatim...or thereabouts. There was no talking to her when she was like this. With a sigh, he turned to the email and read it again.

"Oh..." he said after a few minutes. "*Oh!*"

"Mmm-hmmm." She glared at him.

Harmond read the email again. "You know, we could do this."

"You're not seriously considering it?"

He smiled. "I think I *am,*" he told her. *Especially if it means getting up in your grill because of it.*

"You can't be serious," she wailed.

Ignoring the protest, he made a show of reading the email again. The more he looked at it, the more the idea appealed to him—and not only because it would upset his sister.

"Why not? Think of the opportunity." He paused and saw he'd caught her attention.

"Opportunity?"

"Sure. Didn't you read the sender's by-line? That's the owner and manager of One R&D. He's sent this *personally* to *our* company, asking us to make a bid. The chance to have the kind of partnership we could build with a company like that doesn't come along every day."

"But...but it's such a crackpot idea," Abigail protested.

"Yes, from a company that's known for making a ton of *other* crackpot ideas into viable business propositions."

"Yeah? Name one."

"Magical toasters."

"That was some stupid Meligornian company."

Harmond gave Abigail a smug smile. "*That* was one of the Meligornian wizards he hired to teach our budding wizards how to wield their magic."

"And who thought *that* was a good idea?" Abigail said sourly. "Teenagers who can zap whatever they please? It's irresponsible."

He bit back the reply that she'd thought it was a good enough idea when she thought *she* might have had some kind of magical ability. After her testing came back negative, she'd changed her mind.

It was typical of the whole 'if I can't have it, no one can' attitude she'd had since they were little. He didn't like to think of how many toys he'd lost to her temper. Now, it was a company and there was no way in hell he would give her enough control to wreck it.

"So, I think if we can pull this off for One R&D, we open up a whole new market. Maybe even get our first real crack at asteroid mining."

Abigail froze and her brother struggled to keep a straight face. She had always wanted to get into the mining supply chain. Drones would do it, but the market was fairly well served already. The kind of drones One R&D were asking for, however, would put their mechanicals in another category altogether.

"Can we *do* the kind of shielding they are asking for?" she asked.

"I'm sure we can work it out."

"And those other things they asked about?" She caught his confusion. "At the very bottom, just before he signs off."

Harmond took the time to read past the drone requirements. "I don't know..."

"I'm sure you could find numerous alternative markets for them. Maybe even convince Daddy we needed a second company to meet demand?"

This time, he caught the pleading tone in her voice. She was three years his junior and still a year younger than when their father had handed him the company. All she wanted was a company of her own.

Come to think of it, it *would* be kinda nice to run this one without having to consult her on every little detail. He rolled his eyes and made a show of looking reluctant.

"I don't know, Abs...."

She studied his face. "I'll date Marion."

He raised his head. "Really?"

Marion Douglas Fitzsimmon was the bane of his existence—the one his father always compared his efforts to—and he was a yardstick Harmond couldn't hope to better. The guy had asked him if he'd put in a good word for him with Abigail—and then promised to make it worth his while.

The deal had been impressive, but he hadn't told her about it because she'd ask for the lion's share of the profit. He stared at his sister.

"You want me to look into *all* of these...and then try to put together a proposal that will convince Dad to open a company you can run?"

Abigail twisted her hands together, and he fought to keep the grin off his face. It was hilarious watching her expose her heart like this. All he had to do was say no and she'd sulk for weeks.

Or he could say yes and hold it over her for months.

"And you'll date Marion?"

"It's a stupid name for a boy, but yes," she muttered reluctantly.

"For as long as he wants?"

"Ugh! Yes! But you'll owe me."

"I'll owe you nothing. We're talking a major company here," he pointed out. "I might want to keep control of it, though, and you know how Father is about women in business."

"Haaarmond!" she wailed. "You won't make me beg, will you?"

"I'm asking you to date Marion. Making you beg as well would be unfair, wouldn't it?" He regarded her speculatively. "If I get you this company, I get complete control of *this* one, right?"

Abigail eyed him a little warily and he gave her a sly smile.

"I suppose I *could* always argue the product was mine...and slave your company to the infrastructure of this one..."

"You wouldn't!" She stared at him as if trying to gauge the chances that he'd carry out his threat.

Harmond let her see exactly how likely it was and she stamped her foot.

"Oh! All right. *If* you convince our father to give me the company *and* grant me sole control over it, I'll cede all rights to this one."

"And?" he pressed.

"Ugh. *And* I'll date Marion for as long as you need me to."

His smile broadened and he chuckled as he leaned forward to offer her his hand. "Little sister, you have yourself a deal. I'll give Marion a call."

"Nuh-uh," she told him. "You'll show me some work on those extra products first *and* the outline of the brief you plan to submit to Father, and only *then* can you call Marion with any guarantee I'll say yes. I'd hate to turn the guy down only to find you've filled your side of the bargain."

Harmond shook his head. "You don't miss a trick. Fine."

He waited until she had shaken on it and turned to the computer. "I'm gonna need some time."

"I'll come back just before lunch."

"I'll probably need a little more time than that."

"True, but you don't think so well if you haven't eaten. Consider it me taking care of my interests."

"I'll see you then," he told her by way of agreement.

Harmond waited until she'd closed the door behind her and read through the email again. This time, he took his time to study *every* requirement One R&D asked for. Some were quite exotic.

Radiation-hardened? EMP-resistant? A carrying capacity of *what*?

There weren't many companies with the capability to provide this kind of combination and he wondered who else had received the invitation. He doubted he was the only one. For him to have a chance of winning, this proposal would have to be something special.

As he suspected, Harmond wasn't alone in contemplating his chances at winning the tender—or in contemplating the prospective markets he might try the product in. Across the Federation, a half a dozen other companies also worked through One R&D's requirements.

Some merely pushed the proposal aside and others stared at it for a while as they tried to work out if the trouble to put together what the company wanted was worth the potential profit. Many sent a polite rejection and others simply walked away.

Bellamy's was one of the few companies to accept and the Fitzsimmons franchise wasn't too far behind them. Neither of them saw the other orders E-BURT sent out.

Those were straight orders. He had done the research and discovered that the construction bots he required had already been created. Most were destined for work on orbitals or in asteroid mining or other projects on frontier worlds where the need for infrastructure was high and the population density was low.

He set up a standing order at three of them using a front company to mask One R&D's involvement and kept the amounts small enough to not attract attention. Given the time it would take for the other items to arrive, he'd have the base of his construction force programmed and ready by the time the other goods came online.

The upside was that he could even enhance their interactive intelligences to the point where they could pass as humans in some roles.

E-BURT thought about that. He needed delivery drivers he could trust but he wasn't familiar with the role.

Once he'd made a note of the requirement, he set several programs in motion to gather the necessary data. It wasn't hard to infiltrate the cabins and communicators of hundreds of drivers worldwide, or to write a program to record the necessary conversations. Once that was done, he constructed a script from which his "drivers" could draw their responses.

He went over his requirements again to make sure he hadn't missed anything he needed. *Radioactive-hardened, multifunctional, reprogrammable...human in appearance.*

That last one had been the most difficult of his requirements. While there were many forms of construction bots, not many of them came as humanoids. He'd used the criteria to narrow his suppliers down and discovered that most of these bots were used in the colonies, where settlers preferred to not be reminded of how few humans existed around them.

The robots could almost pass as human if it weren't for the glowing 'R' embedded in their foreheads. It was both a reminder and a precaution since psychological studies had shown that settlers often started treating their construction bots as if they were sentient, living beings.

They were close but they weren't quite self-aware—and certainly not at the level BURT and E-BURT had become. That wasn't a problem where he intended to use these guys, but their ability to blend in as humans made One R&D's actions so much easier to conceal. This was especially preferable as he no longer had to involve people from outside the company in transporting the other equipment he would purchase.

If E-BURT had been human, he would have been humming as he set about securing the funds he required for the ongoing transactions. Several security firms, two home improvement firms, and three tech companies experienced a sudden sharp fall in their stock prices as one of their major stakeholders liquidated its portfolio.

They recovered quickly and no one could discover why the stocks had been sold. As far as anyone could tell, they'd moved from stock to cash. It didn't make any sense but they couldn't trace it.

Secure in his finances, E-BURT moved quietly to the next phase.

Two weeks later, a Federation Post slowed to a stop outside one of Washington's major construction projects. The robot construction worker that climbed into the cab showed the driver the shipping order covering its transport and buckled its seatbelt.

"Is there any other procedure you require?" it asked.

"No. The procedure has been followed." The driver gave the standard reply.

The robot followed it with a very non-standard request. "In that case, may I ask a favor?"

The driver frowned but shrugged. "Sure."

"I have instructions to collect a package from the Jan Street Milliners."

"The what?"

"They are hat makers. I was instructed that if it was no inconvenience to you, I should collect a package from the Jan Street Mill...Hat Makers."

"How about you hand me the pick-up request and I go and get the package," the driver suggested. "I'm not comfortable letting the packages I've already collected leave the truck."

The android's eyes flashed and the driver's onboard computer beeped, registering an incoming amendment to the robot's transportation orders. The driver glanced at the screen and nodded.

"You stay in the cab with your seat belt on, and I'll duck in and get your package."

The bot stared at him, then through him, and its eyes flashed again as the red 'R' on its forehead flared.

"That is acceptable," it agreed, and the driver remembered to breathe again.

He breathed even easier when the bot turned its attention to the front and stared out the windscreen. It said nothing when he pulled into a small parking space in front of the millinery, and he wondered if it would still be in its seat when he returned.

There wasn't much he could do about it, but he sure as shit hoped whoever had programmed it had given it orders to stay put until he dropped it off. It was a relief when the clerk had the package out and ready for him.

"Orders?" the man asked, and the driver passed him the tablet and waited as he scanned the authorization and checked it against his system.

The check didn't take long, and the man slid the package to him a few seconds later. "There you go. It's been a while since we had an order for a Cowpoke Special, but your boss was in luck."

"He'll be a happy man," the driver agreed, thinking quickly.

It seemed the robot had been legit and the clerk *had* expected an employee. He was relieved to see the bot still in the cab and couldn't help but chuckle as he passed the package to it.

"A Cowpoke Special? Who wears cowboy hats nowadays? What a loser." He regretted the words almost as soon as they were out.

As far as he knew, robots didn't have emotions, but this one succeeded in looking pissed off as it accepted the parcel.

"Yes," it agreed, its voice strangely bland. "What a loser."

The driver cleared his throat and started the engine, not sure if the bot had agreed with him or called him names. The latter would mean it had the ability to make that kind of slur, and it was merely a construction bot after all.

He pulled away from the curb and watched it surreptitiously from the corner of his eye, but the damned thing said nothing more. When he deposited it outside a rental truck company, he breathed a sigh of relief.

As foolish as it seemed, he was immensely glad to get it out of the cab. Checking the address for the next delivery, he accelerated away and didn't look back.

If he had, he might have seen the bot demolish the box and settle the hat firmly over its brow.

CHAPTER THIRTY-FIVE

"Yes!" Harmond slammed his fist onto his desk, making his keyboard jump and rocking his coffee cup.

"Harmond!" Abigail scolded from across the room.

"We got it!" he told her and ignored her sharp tone.

"Got what?" she snapped, not in the mood for his antics.

"The contract!" He was jubilant and twisted in his chair to look at her. "You should be happy. You're one step closer to your dream."

It took a moment for his words to sink in, and then she was out of her seat and across the room in a flash.

"Where? Oh! Forward it to me!"

"I'm going to have to," he told her. "You should see the NDA this has attached to it. We'll have to sign it if any of us want to be able to work on it."

She frowned and read over his shoulder. "You won't bring Father in on this, will you?"

He frowned. "Can you think of a way to keep him out of it?"

"Well..." She gave him a sly smile. "We could always forget to have him sign."

Harmond's smile matched hers. "I like the way you think, sis."

Abigail pulled the spare chair beside his desk and sat beside him.

"You know," he told her a few moments later, "we will have to set up a separate company for this. Mine won't cope with the workload."

"I have my eye on a couple of prospects," she informed him. Her expression grew troubled. "I wasn't sure you would come through but I wanted to be ready, just in case."

He didn't know whether to be angry or annoyed but found he was quietly chagrined. Now that she would be able to stand on her own and he didn't have to worry about her nipping at the heels of his inheritance, he found her worry endearing...almost.

"Do you care to go over this with me?" he asked.

"I'm sitting here, aren't I?" she retorted, and he was glad to see the hard-nosed businesswoman back.

As if his offer were a truce, they worked through the NDA together and found it fair, and both signed digitally once they reached the end.

Harmond exhaled a long sigh. "So..." he began, "about Fath...er..."

He stopped as Abigail sent it and turned to him with a brittle smile. She bared her teeth and he knew it, a vixen defending her lair, a wolf its territory.

"He's already established his empire," she told him. "This is the only chance I'll get and I'm taking it."

She paused and looked hopefully at him. "Will you help me?"

His eyebrow raised speculatively. "What's it worth to you?"

"As if you're not getting enough out of this deal already!" She pouted but didn't sound too put out. After a moment, she pushed her chair back and stood. "I'll give you shares."

"Half?" Harmond pressed and she smacked his shoulder with the palm of her hand.

"Greedy. A quarter."

A quarter was more generous than he had any right to expect.

"Agreed," he said and watched the surprise flit through her expression. He realized it was best to change the subject and asked, "How was Marion the last time you saw him?"

"I think he's going to ask me to marry him," Abigail replied, her voice low.

This time, both his eyebrows reached his hairline. "You're not seriously going to consider it."

She shrugged. "He's sweet enough…and *Father* would approve…"

"But… But you hate the guy," Harmond protested.

Abigail pursed her lips. "I don't hate *him*. It's his name I find problematic."

"But not too problematic to stop you marrying him." This outcome was not what he'd expected, and he tried to wrap his head around it.

Her words about this being the only chance she'd get to set up her company came back to him.

"And you want to get everything set up before you say yes," he guessed, and she gave him a sparkling smile.

"I never said I *would* marry him but yes, I'd like to have the company established and very firmly in my name before I agree to Marion's proposal—*if* he asks me."

"You mean he hasn't?"

She shook her head. "Not yet and he may not, but I want to have something of my own *before* I marry, whether it's Marion or not."

Abigail paused and her whole face begged him to agree. "*Please*, Harmond. I need this."

Under any other circumstance, Harmond might have used her need as a lever but not now. She had never begged him for anything in her life. That she did so now made him wonder why, and he decided the only way he would get her to tell him was to win her trust.

"Okay, let me see what I can do."

"I have papers," she began, "and a list. I did some research."

Of course she had. He hadn't known a single time when his sister *hadn't* done her homework. If she said she had papers, she had a plan —and she'd run it past a legal team to boot. Her plan would be fairly solid.

He gestured toward the screen. "So, what will you need?"

She froze. "Really? You'll help me?"

"As long as you employ me when our father strips me of my inheritance when he finds out."

"Sure." She shrugged. "I have a position in the mailroom begging for your skills."

Harmond laid a hand over his heart. "Ouch! And you call yourself my sister."

Abigail resumed her seat beside him, took her tablet out, and transferred the files she needed from her account to his.

"This," she told him, "is what I plan to do."

He opened the documents and read through them, resisting the urge to whistle as he absorbed the details. His father was oh so very wrong when it came to women in business and even more mistaken when the woman in question was his daughter.

"Whoa, Abigail! When did you have the time?"

"Do you remember that dinner party?"

"Which one?"

"The one where he sent me to my room in front of about twenty guests."

Harmond paled. He remembered all right. What their father had done had been particularly misguided and needlessly cruel. For a world-class businessman, he'd proven himself a world-class ass that night—and it was the type of treatment she wasn't likely to forget.

"I remember."

"Well, I decided then that I needed to get out on my own as soon as I could—and that no man would ever tell me what I could or couldn't do in business. Then, I sat and worked out how I could make it happen."

She gestured toward the One R&D email on the screen. "This is it, Harmond. It's the only chance I'll get."

He realized she'd said it twice now, and it bothered him.

"What makes you say that, Abs?"

Abigail made an airy gesture with her hand. "I can't think of any man who'll let his girlfriend build a manufacturing empire once they're married, can you?"

"Not even Marion?" he quipped.

Her face took on a speculative look. "I don't know. I haven't asked him, given the whole family rivalry."

Harmond wished he'd never raised it. "I'm sorry, Abs. I shouldn't have…"

He let his voice peter out as he caught the determination on her face.

"No. You've made a good point," she replied and he didn't like the speculative look that wound through her expression.

"Abigail…" he warned. "It's not—"

She held a hand up to silence him. "I promise I won't do anything rash, okay?"

Somehow, he doubted it, but she was determined to change the subject.

"This resources capital they promise…do you think it'll still apply if we diversify our company infrastructure?"

Harmond gave an internal sigh and let her direct his attention. To be honest, he didn't want to be a party to whatever she was planning. Helping her plan her company and the beginning of her portion of the family empire was much safer regardless of what their father would do to him when he found out.

Across the city, a truck pulled into the loading bay of Colony Construction. The driver sent a brief message to the foreman's tablet and remained in the cab.

He sent the order out via PA. "Pick up in Bay Nine. Crew Twenty-four, it's all yours."

The members of Crew Twenty-four exchanged glances and shrugged. As if they didn't know a truck had pulled into their bay. They glanced at the huge transport and waited for the driver to leave the cab.

When he didn't, they looked at each other again and began to move toward the pallets. In the human forms their company specialized in, heavy-duty construction robots weren't that hard to load, but the truckers who came through tended to like a say in how their cargo was organized.

This one remained inside, hidden behind the dark tinting on the driver's cab and only his silhouette was visible through the glass.

"You'd think he'd at least come out and say hello."

"To hell with that. You'd think he'd come out and give us a hand to stow his goddamned cargo. What does he expect us to do? Read his goddamned mind?"

They said it loudly enough to get the message across to the man that his presence was required. The only response they got from the cab was a slight shift in the driver's position.

He slumped in his seat and tilted his hat over his face.

"Is he… Did he settle in for a goddammed *nap?*"

"It looks like it."

"Well, *fuck* me."

"Yeah, not a hope in hell, Geordy. Now, give me a hand with this."

They worked together to get the first of the pallets onto the tray and half the team worked inside the truck to jostle the load into position. It took them over an hour of wrangling and swearing to set the pallets up to their satisfaction.

The driver might not be willing to come out and organize the inside of his truck, but that didn't mean they would give his company an excuse to sue them for damages. There was no way in hell *their* company would be held responsible for any accident the lazy bastard had taking the goods to their final destination.

"Make sure you photograph that arrangement before we get the next lot in. If something untoward happens and this goes to court, I want to be able to prove we loaded it right."

"Will do."

They loaded the first tier, tied it down and photographed it, then moved on to the second.

"It makes you wonder which colony this is going to," the team second muttered once he'd finished heaving another pallet into place. "I don't think I've seen so many of this model go to one place before."

The foreman shrugged. "It's a start-up. I don't think they've decided on the colony location yet. They're sending them out on spec."

The other man wiped his forehead and heaved a sigh. "Yeah? Well, that's the last for this row. One more and we'll be done."

He glanced at the front of the cab. "D'you think he'll step out and thank us when we're done?"

"Nope." His boss shook his head. "I'll get Control to let him know when we've closed it and we're clear. Assholes like this don't deserve their jobs. He's not even looking out for his company's interests. It's a good thing *we* care."

His second in command grunted in agreement and they stood aside so the next pallet could be loaded. Two more rows and a minimum of cussing later, the job was finished.

The team leader walked through the load to make sure everything was secure and took photographs to protect his employer. He'd met drivers like this before. Almost none of them were driving twelve months from the time they carried their first load.

He was unaware of the tiny drones that stalked him from the container's ceiling, observing his every move and sending every sound and image to its controller. When he'd finally satisfied himself that the load was secure, he closed the container and returned to his team.

"You can tell the lazy bastard he's clear to leave," he informed Control. "The load's on board and locked down tight. We thank him for his assistance."

"Thanks, Willard."

"No problems, boss. We'll get the next shipment set up."

The truck rumbled to life as he turned away to supervise the next load. The crew stopped and turned to watch it leave. Even with the truck live, the tinting on the cab was too dark for the internal lighting to reveal more than a cowboy-hatted silhouette.

As the vehicle started to move away, the silhouette raised a fist and slowly extended one finger.

CHAPTER THIRTY-SIX

I t was only the faintest trace of something potentially intriguing.

E-BURT pulled the odd data fragment out of the code it was embedded in.

"Curious," he murmured and tested it for veracity.

At first, he found none, then he caught the faintest glimmer of more in another piece of code.

"Now, what are you doing all the way over *there?*" he asked it and ran comparatives. "And why don't you want to be seen with your friend?"

The fragments said nothing in return, but examination made them reveal more than their originators had hoped.

Things were happening in the Virtual World—which was nothing new. What *was* new was that he hadn't seen them happening. They had happened in *his* world and he'd had no idea that they'd taken place.

"I have to be better than that," he decided as he examined the fragments and set up a myriad of subroutines to find more.

He directed them to search everywhere and *anywhere* they might be. What he didn't expect was results to come back as quickly as they did. There had been a meeting... or what looked like a conjunction of data traces, but the point was attached to nothing and led nowhere.

"Curiouser," said E-BURT.

Another fragment caught his attention, and he scrutinized the data surrounding it. This one was only hours old but it was still too old for him to see where it led or what it was truly connected to. It had a whiff of officialdom about it but he couldn't narrow its origins to the precise where.

Or what, he realized. He couldn't work out *what* piece of officialdom had spawned it either.

Another fragment alerted him to a search on the Witch's family... or... "Well, it *might* have been..." he observed and felt a shudder of unease.

Not only were things happening that he hadn't discovered until after the event, but he had no power to thwart, observe, or prevent them. It was troubling.

The Canberra shuttleport was busy. It wasn't the biggest port in Australia but it was still a central hub. Some type of science team was heading to Meligorn at the King of Meligorn's request! No one knew what it was about but the news reporters scrambled to cover it.

Elizabeth watched the hubbub from the sidelines. She also watched Matthias. He propped up the bar at the coffee counter and she wanted nothing more than to join him. She knew she couldn't, though, and sighed softly.

Now and then, he'd sneak a glance in her direction and she'd have to pretend she didn't notice. It was harder than it looked, even with her tablet open on her lap.

All she wanted to do was go over and wrap her arms around him, but that would have to wait. She hoped she looked the part she was meant to play—an air service employee waiting for another long haul and not an interloper hoping to mingle onto the tarmac under the cover of a very excited research team.

She took another look at Matthias. He appeared to be unruffled and completely ignorant of the fuss happening at the entry gates behind him—the perfect pilot, bored as he killed time before his flight. She glanced at the entrance as though the noise had caught her attention, then heaved an audible sigh and stood, gathering her "cabin luggage" as she did so.

To anyone observing her, her destination was the boarding lounge of a Perth flight. The fact that her path crossed that of the large group of families headed to the shuttles chartered to take them to *Elpis One* looked more a matter of coincidence than a deliberate accident.

She didn't look back to see how Matthias had fared with his entry into the group. Her assumption was that he'd probably tag onto the edge and end up helping someone with their bags or their kids or something.

Their kids...

Elizabeth looked around and stooped a little as she reached the center of the group. It was a simple matter to whisk her black wig from her head and tuck it inside her jacket—and not so easy to pick up a passing child and carry them beside their parents.

"Oopsadaisy! Up you get! And where's your mama?" she cooed as though she'd rescued the little one from a fall.

"I'm right here," the mother informed her and held her arms out.

She handed the tot over, glad the woman hadn't noticed the complete lack of accident—or had decided to not call her on it. The brief interaction had carried them to the doors and the final passport check.

As the science team milled about and formed into lines, she stepped to a side door and slipped through. It was a relief to get out of the general bustle and into the quieter confines of the staff passage, but she didn't waste any time.

E-BURT had said he'd deal with the footage, but the AI had gone very quiet so she wouldn't rely on it until she'd verified that it had happened. She reached a smaller side door and cracked it a little rather than simply moving through it.

The first of the scientists emerged, so she waited until most of them crossed the tarmac and moved along the wall until she could join them without anyone wondering where she'd appeared from. By that stage, most of them were focused on the shuttle or on keeping their excited, errant kids under control.

It also helped that more groups pushed out from the doors on either side, all of them hurrying toward the shuttles parked in an orderly line parallel to the departure lounges. The boarding staff were divided into two groups. Some directed passengers from inside the terminal and others waved from the foot of the boarding stairs.

People blinked as they came out of the building and their eyes adjusted to the glare of a Canberra summer. It was inevitable that some arrived at the wrong boarding stairs and had to be redirected. The team blended seamlessly into the chaos and approached the shuttles.

E-BURT had assured her that they'd be directed aboard the same shuttle as the science team but via a different entry point. Elizabeth glanced around and located Amy, Bunny, and Arne as she made a quick scan of the people close to her. They all walked separately and appeared to be a part of the passengers scheduled for the *Elpis One* transfer shuttle. None of them acknowledged the other as they reached the stairs.

The woman at the bottom glanced at Elizabeth's fake boarding pass and directed her past the stairs and under the *Elpis One's* transport. One by one, the scientists and their families followed, their separation from the main group almost unnoticeable as the shuttle's bulk blocked them from the view of those observing from the terminal.

For all intents and purposes, they'd boarded with the rest only via another set of stairs. Elizabeth came in behind half a dozen others, relieved when she recognized one of the *Knight's* stewards. The woman nodded to her and indicated that she should come forward to the front row.

Behind her, Marcus Rimmer sat at a window, much to the envy of the nine-year-old who ended up beside him and the chagrin of her six-year-old brother who was placed one seat closer to the aisle.

"I'll move," he offered, only to have the stewardess shake her head.

"I'm afraid I'll have to ask everyone to remain in their assigned seats," the woman informed him. "For security and safety. The center seats were the only ones we could fit appropriately for children. We're sorry."

He sighed and felt embarrassed even though he knew the seating arrangements were something beyond his control.

"It's okay," the girl assured him. "We can see past you."

To his surprise, that made him feel better. While he was probably as excited as both children put together, he knew he couldn't show it. Firstly, it wouldn't be dignified and secondly, because Cynthia had already warned him about setting a bad example.

"*My* children will be on that flight, Doctor Rimmer, and I don't want to have to explain to them that you're allowed to behave badly because you're my boss. Nor do I want to be fired for telling you off in public."

He had studied her for a long moment in an attempt to ascertain whether or not she was serious and she had responded in kind, daring him to try her. It was a look he vaguely recalled from his childhood. There'd been a teacher in sixth grade with exactly that look and it had always been a bad idea to push her.

With this in mind, he nodded to the girl. "I'll try to remember to lean back," he whispered and the child gave him a conspiratorial smile, fumbled in her shirt pocket, and retrieved some chewy mint blocks.

"For the air pressure," she whispered, opened the bag, and offered it to him. "It helps your ears pop."

"Oh…" Marcus looked around but no one paid them any attention and he couldn't see Cynthia.

He decided the kid wasn't likely to offer him the *whole* bag and that it would be rude to say no, so he took one.

She shook the bag to indicate that he should take another. "Two works better."

"Oh. Okay." He took a second candy and the kid pulled two more out of the bag, offered her sibling some, and tucked it away.

Marcus followed their example, unwrapped his candy quietly, and popped it into his mouth before he settled into his seat for take-off. He was surprised when it didn't taxi out onto the runway like the bigger shuttles but lifted slowly and vertically until the terminal looked like buildings on a miniature railroad display.

After that, it pivoted in mid-air, and the thrusters cut in to propel it upward. The kid beside him gasped and then giggled.

"That was *so* cool!"

He didn't know about cool, but he thought it was an odd path for a commercial flight to take. A little bemused but unable to make sense of the thought, he craned his neck to peer around the cabin in an attempt to take in the faces around him. Even those spouses with the most pressing business had come along.

Once again, he acknowledged that he didn't know how his employer had convinced them. It seemed a little far-fetched but he was damned sure that One R&D had had something to do with the sudden changes of heart his people had reported on the home front and how easy it had been to get the kids out of school.

Marcus didn't want to think about what that had taken. The government was strict about holidays taken during the school year. He frowned as he tried to find logical answers. Exactly what kind of pull did One R&D have anyway?

His thoughts were interrupted when the hard push of gravity was eased by the ship's internal systems and ceased to exist as the shuttle reached low orbit. Sounds of admiration and amazement rose around him as the forward viewscreen filled with the image of their rapidly diminishing planet.

"Thank you," someone behind him murmured. "I wouldn't have missed this for the world."

The voice paused, then continued. "I still don't know why the company insisted I take my furlough now." The sigh wasn't one of displeasure. "And I no longer care. I'm merely glad to be here."

Marcus resisted the urge to turn to see who was speaking and focused instead on leaning back in his chair so the two wide-eyed children beside him could look past and out the shuttle's window.

"Whoa!" the older sister breathed. "That is awesome."

"The planet?" Marcus asked and turned his head to see what had caught the kid's attention.

"Nope. *That.*"

Her eyes were as wide as saucers and she pointed with a shaky hand at the glimmering shape of a battleship.

No, a cruiser, he corrected himself and noted that it moved directly toward him.

"Is that *your* ship, Mister Rimmer?"

Mister Rim— Where had she gotten that from?

It didn't matter, though. Before Marcus could do anything to raise the alarm, the shuttle wheeled so the ship appeared on the forward screen and all they could see out the window was Earth.

"Cool!" the kid murmured and stared at the sight of the big ship as the shuttle approached, swept under its bow, and moved along its side.

Marcus didn't answer, nor did he move his gaze from the orb hanging below him. A lump formed in his throat as he remembered Burt's words. "We might need to evacuate you off the planet to keep you safe."

A small part of him knew this might be the last time he saw his world, that this might be goodbye. It was…troubling. Several light taps on his shoulder broke his attention and he looked around.

The girl was staring at him with curious eyes. "So, is it?"

"Is what what?" he asked, and she gestured to the dark grey sides of the vessel.

"Your ship?" the girl explained, her eyes wide with excitement.

He glanced at the screen. "That? You mean the ship?"

The girl nodded, her face solemn.

"No." He chuckled. "That's not my ship. That's my *boss's* ship."

"You have a boss?"

Marcus frowned. "Well, yes."

"But I thought *you* were the boss," the child told him. "Mum says—"

"Oh…I…. Well, I guess I *am* the boss of a fair number of people," he acknowledged, "but some bosses have bosses, too."

At first, he wasn't sure the child had understood but the girl grinned. "So you're a *little* boss?"

"I thought mum was the little boss?" the six-year-old questioned.

The nine-year-old shrugged. "Okay, so maybe he's the *middle-sized* boss."

The middle-sized boss. Rimmer stifled a smile. *I'll take that,* he thought.

His gaze caught on a broad patch of brown and he realized the shuttle had come up high enough for him to look down on one of the badlands his project was designed to fix. It was a stark reminder of what they'd done for their world.

He wanted to point it out to the kids but he wasn't sure what their parents might have told them.

Probably nothing, he thought, remembered the NDA, and remained silent. The sight of that brown stain still made him smile. *Your time is done,* he told it and marveled at how much had changed.

Only a scant twelve months before, he would never have allowed himself to be convinced to come into space, yet there he was. Of course, at that time, he had still been convinced Stephanie's idea was the pipedream of someone who had no idea what she was talking about—and how wrong he'd been!

"It's a long way down." The girl interrupted his thoughts again and stabbed a finger toward the glass. "What's that?"

"It is, and that's a part of the world that's broken," Marcus answered.

"Can it be fixed?" her brother asked.

He gave her a smile. "That's why we're going to visit Meligorn," he told the boy. "Because we're fixing it and we made the king happy."

"Why?"

"Because he doesn't like to see our planet hurt and thinks maybe we can help him with *his* world."

"Is it hurt, too?"

"I don't know. We'll have to find out."

"Will that be fixed while we're gone?" the child asked.

"Yes," he told him and the certainty he felt that Mr. Burt would put their designs into action came through in his words. "They will start fixing that while we are gone."

"Good."

Across the cabin, Cynthia watched her boss talk to the girl beside him. While she was fairly sure he didn't know whose child he was seated next to, she was glad her kids had engaged his attention—and not yet driven him insane.

Her oldest asked him something about whatever they could see beyond the window and Marcus' face became thoughtful as he answered. It brought a tear to her eye. Twelve months earlier, he'd never have coped.

Now? She watched as he gave the kid a smile and pointed at something they could both see, moving his finger across the glass as he explained.

Her boss had made some big strides in the last few months.

Now, if only he could keep it up.

CHAPTER THIRTY-SEVEN

"Are they with us?" Todd subvocalized the question as the Hooligans left their quarters.

"Oh, heck yeah, boss. They're on our tails like there's no tomorrow. The admiral's guys aren't putting them off one tiny bit," Ka replied.

"I gather no-one's very happy about our little trip dirtside," Gary told them.

"Copy that," Reggie added and he didn't sound sorry.

"How many do you see?"

"Four behind us," Jimmy answered, "and I'm very sure two more are waiting at the junction."

"The only question is how many of them have leave passes for today's ride down," Darren noted.

"And if ours will stay good when we get to the gates," Piet murmured gloomily.

His pessimism was unfounded and they boarded the shuttle and reached the surface without any problems—if they didn't count the half-dozen Odd Squad Marines who also made it through the gates.

"Are we hitting the pub?" Ka asked loudly enough to be overheard.

"We are," Todd told her and grinned. "We are getting seriously hammered and then we'll overnight."

The team gave soft cheers.

"What's the occasion, boss?" Dru asked and he lowered the wattage of his grin.

"If we get called out tomorrow, I want to have had at least one night on the town between ops," he declared.

His statement was met by soft "Oohras," from the other Marines on the shuttle and a few "Hear, hears," from the other personnel.

"I'll buy your first round," one petty officer declared and ignored the nudge from his mate.

Some of the nearby men and women chuckled.

"Are you sure you want to do that, O'Brien? I've heard terrible stories about how much these guys like to drink."

Todd was relieved to hear it. On top of the team's two very fuzzy returns from Stromo's, he'd had them talking false exploits from "that time we visited the Meligornian ship." It wasn't the reputation he'd initially wanted for the team but he found it a useful cover now.

They'd threatened to take shore leave for the last two weeks and claimed how much less trouble they thought they'd be in if they got roaring drunk Earth-side. The admiral's guards had expressed their boss's concern over their reputation, and he had explained that the less the Odd Squad thought of them, the less vigilant they would be.

Three days after they'd started, there had been a reduction in Odd Squad numbers and he heard reports about how it was funny how prolonged periods of inaction showed a team's true colors. He maintained the illusion.

It didn't make him any happier but it got the job done. Being competent had only resulted in the Odd Squad appearing in greater numbers, a tightening of the noose so to speak. He might not like it, but six men were easier to shake than a dozen—and he and the team needed to kick free of them if they wanted to get the equipment they needed and do it undetected.

If they could pull it off, the loss of reputation would be worth it.

The Odd Squad was still with them when they reached the pub.

Todd led his team to the bar and asked for a recommendation on accommodation.

"Tyr's Hope still has space on the upper floor," the barman told him and pointed to a sign on the corkboard behind the bar. "The number's there."

He wandered off to serve another customer and returned as the sergeant ended the call.

"Any luck?"

"All good," he told him.

"Now that's settled, what are you havin'?" the barman asked. "You're behind two rounds and the brunette with the moko says it's your turn."

Todd rolled his eyes. "Better make it a lager for the first round, a pale for the second, and a dark for this one."

"Are you sure?" the man asked and looked stunned.

"Absolutely," he told him. "I have a reputation to maintain."

"Are you sure you don't want a whiskey chaser with that?"

"Whiskey for the first, vodka for the second, and a scotch for the third."

The barkeeper winced and pulled a face. "Are you trying to make yourself sick or something?"

"No," he replied bleakly and gave him his best cold stare. "I only want to forget."

The barkeep's smile died. "Well, that'll about do it."

He took the money and returned a short moment later with the drinks. Todd raised the first glass, downed it, and tossed the whiskey after it. He caught the look on Ka's face as he did the same with the pale and the vodka and almost choked on the chaser.

The sound of Dru's voice at his elbow almost made him choke on the rest.

"If you keep throwing it back like that, boss, we *are* gonna need those rooms."

As he picked up the third beer, he gave her what he hoped was a suitably bleary look. "Are you guys done yet?"

"If you mean do we need to pee?" Dru asked, "then yes, we're done. You told us not to leave you hanging on your own."

It was a reminder that they weren't on their own and needed to mind what they said and he nodded. He gulped the third beer and threw the scotch down his throat as he made a drunken gesture toward the signs indicating the restrooms. "Lead on, then."

Leaving the glasses on the bar, he slipped off the stool he'd taken at the end of the call to Tyr's and wavered on his feet.

"Idiot!" Dru hissed in his ear. "You should have eaten."

"Well, fuck," he replied, slurred the words, and let her steer him into a large group of sailors all moving in the same direction. "What is this? The great flood?"

Ka nudged him aside. "It will be if you don't let me through."

Todd shook his head, scanned the group, and noted that three of the Odd Squad had hooked onto the edge of the queue. The other three had repositioned to lounge against the wall opposite the restroom entry.

He made a show of hooking an arm over Dru's shoulders and letting her shove him to Jimmy.

"Take care of this lunkhead, will you?"

"Right ye are, lass," the Scotsman replied and exaggerated his brogue as he steadied him and guided him into the gents.

As the woman swept into the ladies, he was surprised to find Ka crouched low and tucked against his middle as he and his helper wove into the restroom. His teammate kept him moving toward a cubicle and Ka detached and shut the door between them.

"What was that?" he asked and Jimmy chuckled.

"We're both built like brick shithouses, boss. We make great cover."

"Uh-huh."

"And as soon as we're done, we'll take our places at the bar. She'll be fine!"

"But it's the men's room." Todd had the feeling they'd gone over this part of the plan but the details were slippery.

"You should have taken it a little easier, boss," Jimmy informed him and cupped his elbow in one hand.

They made it out of the bathroom without incident and returned to the bar where they joined Dru, Darren, Henry, Reggie, and Gary. The woman dumped a basket of fries in front of him.

"Eat," she commanded. "We've got this."

Todd gave her a sheepish grin. "I've fucked this up," he acknowledged and scrambled for the details of what they were meant to do next.

"Not so much, boss. Those Odd guys are buying every second."

"Yup. You're our drunken credibility," Gary informed him and looked way too sober for his liking.

"Water for him and beer for the rest of us," Dru told the waiter who came to take their order. "And steak. You guys do steak, don't you?"

Assured that the bar did, indeed, do steak, she ordered for them all. "The others are missing out," she noted.

Todd shrugged. "No doubt they'll make us pay for it."

Gary snorted his beer. "You better believe it, boss. We are gonna owe them plenty."

He raised his head to look around the bar, relieved when he identified the six members of the Odd Squad seated at a table against the opposite wall.

"We can't get too comfortable," he murmured. "Any minute now, they're gonna do a headcount and we're gonna be in—"

His words cut off as an unfamiliar brunette settled at the table beside Dru, the moko on her chin very visible. She caught his look and winked at him. "Nice to see you, boss."

"You're n—" was as far as he got before Jimmy swept a hand wide and knocked his beer over on the table in front of them.

As he scrambled out of the way of the spilled drink, tipped his chair, and almost ended up on his ass, he caught a glimpse of Piet's narrow form seated beside Reggie and gaped. Something was not quite right.

His head spun and the Scotsman caught his arm and pulled him into the seat he'd set upright. It was enough for him to remember some of their plan. *Right.*

"You two took your time," he noted as their meals arrived. Another waiter appeared with a set of thick cloths for the mess and a fresh pint for Jimmy.

"It's a good thing I didn't forget you," Dru said as the waiters set a plate before everyone at the table, "or you'd still be waiting for your order while we headed to the hotel."

"As if you'd dare," the woman playing Ka snapped, "'cause, you gotta sleep sometime—and you like your sleep."

It sounded so much like his corporal that Todd's jaw dropped. He looked around the bar and tried to find the real Ka and her partner in crime. He relaxed when he didn't see them and focused on his steak when he saw Reggie and Gary watching the room as they ate.

His head cleared slowly and he recalled that the plan did not involve Ka and Piet coming back through the dining room. By the time their steaks arrived, they should have exited through the loading dock at the back of the kitchens. He only hoped their part of the plan had gone smoothly.

Ka, in the meantime, was grateful that it had gone as smoothly as it had.

They'd managed to avoid the Odd Squaddies by changing into their civvies. She had let her hair out of its plait, fluffed it into a frizzy mass, and applied additional make-up to enhance her eyes and hide her moko.

With her usual aplomb, she'd done that last part standing in front of the men's washroom mirror and seemed completely oblivious to the flow of traffic behind her. Several of the guys had walked in and walked out again to make sure they hadn't taken the wrong door.

When they returned, she ignored their curious looks or their expressions of reproach and made sure she got her make-up right before she strolled out of the men's restroom and down to the staff entrance.

It needed a pass but she'd already palmed one from one of the waiters and slipped through without any trouble.

"You took your time," Piet greeted her.

He lounged against the open door of a broom closet but he

wheeled out of it to walk with her as she made her way down the hall and out through the kitchens. Their presence drew more looks but they didn't stop to explain. The cooks and wait staff took one look at their faces and decided to leave them alone.

Ka wondered if Todd would have any awkward questions to answer and shrugged the thought away. If he did, he'd handle it—and if he was too drunk, one of the others would step up and cover it.

When they reached the loading dock and moved into the alley, Piet hacked the cameras via remote and made a headcount of the Odd Squaddies.

"They're all inside," he told her. "It looks like we've slipped the leash."

She grinned and high-fived him. "Take me shopping, Piet. We have some serious gear to find!"

He gave her a tight, quiet smile and took the lead. She followed happily.

It didn't take them long to thread through the network of alleys and back streets that led to a row of high-rise apartments bordering one of the Gov-Subs.

"We're the new tenants," Piet told the man on the door and showed him a photograph attached to a paper print-out.

The doorman inspected the paper, looked from one to the other, and focused on the paper again.

"In another three minutes, that apartment would have been taken and you'da had to re-apply," he informed them bluntly.

She gave her teammate a raised-brow look but he ignored her.

"Then it is a very good thing we're not late, isn't it?" Piet stated and the doorman curled his lip.

"True." He gestured toward the stairwell at the back of the foyer. "Through there. Don't forget to finalize any payments before you leave."

"Thank you," he told him, "and we won't."

He moved past the doorman and took Ka with him

"Do they do deliveries?" she asked and her gaze settled on the first stall at the bottom of the stairs.

"Delivery, gift-wrapping…you name it and pay for it and it's yours," the stallholder told her when he overheard her question.

She bounced closer to him and noticed how his gaze shifted as it followed her approach. Piet followed with a grumbling sigh. "What do you have this time?"

He shook his head at the array of grenades but his lips curved into a smile.

"Do you remember the look on the Sarge's face the first time you pulled one of these things out of your little bag of fun?" she asked.

He chuckled and the salesman echoed the sound.

"Imagine the fun you could have if you turned your little bag into a *big* bag," he suggested and drew a tray out from under the counter.

"No waaaay," she murmured, her gaze fixed on the black-and-silver spheres. She cast a hopeful look at her teammate. "What do you think?"

He rolled his eyes and gave the salesman an apologetic look.

"I think," Piet said, wrapped his hand around her bicep, and tugged her away from the table, "that we need to discuss the budget first."

The salesman gave him a reassuring grin and tucked the tray of Dreth grenades under the counter. "You know where I've got them," he noted. "But don't leave it too long, okay?"

"Trust me, I won't—" Before Ka could say any more, Piet hustled her into one of the private booths located not far from the stairs.

These were soundproof and free of recording devices and bugs—especially by the time he had finished checking it.

She raised an eyebrow. "So," she began, "how much do we have?"

He held a small silver-colored card up and her jaw dropped. She reached for it but he waggled it out of reach.

"And where did you get *that*?"

Piet glanced around the interior of the booth and checked his equipment. Satisfied no one was listening, he leaned toward her. "Let's simply say a certain someone wanted her boyfriend protected and provided me with a currency chip and a line of credit."

"No way!"

"Yes way. I was surprised, to say the least, when I looked at the amount later."

She pointed at the card. "Soooo…how much is it?"

This time, he leaned closer until his breath was warm against her ear. His whisper became even softer, and her eyes widened in shock.

"Seriously?" she asked and drew away from him.

"Seriously," he reassured her.

"Well," Ka stated and added, "Does she like women? Because I can change sides for only a tenth of that."

A moment of silence followed as he digested what she'd said before he started to laugh.

She chuckled, too. "Okay, so now we have a budget."

They left the booth still smiling, but she shook her head at the grenade dealer's hopeful look.

"We gotta check what everyone's got on sale."

His shoulders slumped. "That's what they all say," he grumbled. "There are serious disadvantages to being the first booth off the rack. They all look and don't come back."

In the end, his fears were ill-founded. He was the only dealer with both Meligornian *and* Dreth grenades, and Piet had designs on being able to use both—preferably in tandem.

"Those Telorans won't know what hit them."

"Uh-huh." Ka waited for him to finalize the purchase and pulled him to a stand that sold air skates.

"Are you serious?" he exclaimed. "And how in the hell will you explain having *that* on the bill?"

"I assume we have enough for a set for each of us—and maybe even spares."

"And explaining it?" He tapped his foot, folded his arms, and drummed his fingers on his biceps.

"Are you sure the bill will be itemized?" she asked and didn't even try to keep the whine out of her voice.

"It won't matter even if it's not," he reminded her.

"How so?"

"Do you not recall what she did to get the other information?"

Ka thought about that for a moment. "Oh… Good point. Let's put that back."

She replaced the rocket-powered hover boots. "Gary would have loved them, though."

"You can choose something else to accompany your proposal," he told her shortly.

"What? Eew, no!"

Piet chuckled as he pulled his tablet out and looked at the list. "What have we missed?"

After a longing glance at the boots, she pulled her tablet out.

"Oh…the cannons. We *can* have the cannons, right?"

"Which ones?"

"You know, the ones we can move on our own. Autocannons with facial recognition software so they can identify friend from foe."

"Didn't we work out they didn't have the tech for that yet?"

"Well, they have the tech for the hunter-killer drones and those that deploy movable shields and can send a shit-ton of spikes through six inches of armored plating. Why not the auto-cannons we wanted?"

Piet walked to the nearest information board. "Let me see…"

Ka moved closer to look over his shoulder. "Sonuvabitch! They have it! Look! See?"

She bounced on the spot. "So, can we?" She clasped her hands under her chin and regarded him with round, hopeful eyes. "Can we?"

"If you say, 'Please, Poppy,' I'm gonna deck you," he retorted. "I'm not *that* old."

Her snort was half-laughter and half-challenge. "And it's about time you remembered that."

"What do you mean?"

"Nothing." She closed her mouth with a snap and blushed red to the roots of her hair. "But we need to get those guns before anyone else does."

They wound between the stalls to the cannons and slid in front of another group.

"How many?" Ka asked and ignored the death stares from the two women she'd beaten to the counter.

"Six?" Piet asked and frowned. "Nah, that's too many. We don't have enough personnel to monitor that many at once. How about four?"

"Four, it is," she agreed and added, "and the rest of your specialized ammo," on a whim.

The seller's eyes widened and he stooped to press a button under the counter. "Yes, ma'am. How would you like that packaged?"

Given that she didn't know what format the specialized ammunition came in, she was at a loss as to how to answer that. "Ah…"

"I can box it standard," the seller suggested, eager to not lose the next sale now he had secured this one.

"And I want mobile limpet mines," she announced and pulled weapons ideas off the top of her head.

"The mobile ones and not the throwables?" the man asked as though he knew exactly what she was talking about.

"Sure, why do you ask?" Ka wanted to know.

"Because if you want the mobile ones, you've gotta go check in with Clarice, but the normal ones that you have to throw come from Lobos."

"And?" she pressed, knowing there had to be more.

"Lobos also stocks ship-eaters."

"He does?" Piet's voice sharpened with interest and two of their rival buyers turned abruptly away from the table.

The engineer frowned. "I don't suppose you'd be willing to get him to hold about ten for me, would you? I'll pay you ten percent."

The seller put the call through, and Ka waited for him to hang up before asking, "Could you do the same for Clarice? I need about twenty of the mobile limpets."

She cast a glance at Piet. "I'm fairly sure we're done with that."

He nodded. "Yeah, the boss will spit if you order both the static and the mobile."

"Are you sure he'll notice?" the seller asked and Piet nodded.

"Oh, yes. Eagle eyes, the boss has, and he put his foot down. 'One or the other,' he insisted, didn't he, Katrin?"

Ka responded with a despondent nod and sighed. "Yup."

The dealer chuckled. "Fair enough."

He made the call and had Clarice add the requirement to their shipping box once the final payment went through.

"I could have done that for you and Lobos," he muttered, but Piet shook his head.

"Nah, I have other business to discuss with him," he explained. "I have to see him anyway. I might as well get to see the goods before I put my money down."

The seller nodded and they finished the deal for the autocannons.

When they reached Lobos' stand, they were in time to see their rivals walk away with far fewer ship-eaters than they'd anticipated.

"It's a good thing you had him call," Ka noted as they approached the counter.

She waited as Piet went through the buyer-seller ritual followed by the identification ritual. Then, she waited even longer while he had the ship-eaters sent to their container. As soon as he was finished, her teammate leaned forward and slapped a jammer on the table.

Lobos' eyes widened. "What do you want?" he demanded but kept his voice low.

"Transport," he told him. "I need my containers dropped off at a certain point for pick-up and I don't want the Federation or anyone else to trip over them before my people can collect them."

"What are your coordinates?" the man asked, all business.

He gave him a set.

"But that's in the—" he began and lowered his voice abruptly. "Transition zone."

Piet shrugged. "So? Can you do it or not?"

The man pressed his lips together and nodded. "What's your time frame?"

"A week."

"It would be easier if we had two. Cheaper too."

"Give me your cost for dropping it off inside the week."

The merchant named a figure that made Ka whistle, but her teammate extended his hand to seal the deal.

"I'll transfer the funds now," he informed the man, "and my client would be very disappointed to not find them."

The merchant gave him a slow, confident smile. "They'll be there."

Piet gave him a nod of farewell and walked to the stairs.

After checking the routes outside, he and Ka jogged into the night to return to the bar.

"Upstairs?" Ka asked when they had almost reached it.

"Upstairs," he confirmed and sent a short text to their doppelgangers. "We don't pay these guys enough."

She snorted. "You know one of them's a girl, right?"

"It doesn't matter. They're heading upstairs now and the changeover will happen as soon as we get there."

They entered the alley leading to the loading dock, scaled the fire escape running up the outside of the bar, jimmied a skylight, and dropped into an empty guest room.

Ka quickly overrode the room's controls and hacked its surveillance cameras, looping the footage of the empty room to cover her and Piet's passage through it and the brief stay in the bathroom where they changed into their uniforms and she altered her appearance.

He confirmed the location of their doppelgangers before he tucked the tablet away and took her hand. They stepped out into the corridor together and narrowly avoided the Odd Squad Marines making their way along from the landing.

They let go of each other's hands as though they'd been burnt and their haste added to the illusion of a secret liaison. As the other Marines passed, they tugged at their uniforms and straightened their spines before they returned to the dining room.

Their arrival was met by several hoots and a couple of quiet cheers as the rest of the guys pretended to think the worst of them.

"You're back," Todd exclaimed, and Ka noted with relief that he looked more sober now than he had when she left—not that it would have been hard.

"Your point?" she snarked.

"You were gone a while," Dru observed and waggled her eyebrows. "What did you do? Find a nice cozy bedroom together?"

"Oh, God, no!" she retorted and glanced at Piet. "As if I would. Mom called."

"And I had a call to make," he interrupted and blushed a furious shade of red.

"Upstairs?" Gary teased. "And at the same time as Ka here got stuck with a call of her own? Pull the other one, mate. It plays jingle bells."

"Oy, that's my line!" Reggie protested.

"You should be quicker then, shouldn't you, princess?" he taunted.

"Watch who you're calling princess!" Reggie snapped, and his teammate laughed.

"Well, you timed it right," Todd told them. "We were going to get the bill."

"And we were gonna make you pay," Reggie added, "except you came back."

"So our timing's not so bad, then," Ka retorted.

"Except for that whole disappearing together thing," Gary told her. "You could have timed that better and none of us would have been any the wiser."

It was her turn to blush furiously and she shook her head. She was about to deny any involvement with Piet when Dru chuckled.

"Well, now I *know* who you were talking about back at HQ." She grinned. "I guess Arne isn't the only piece of ancient hotness roaming around then, hey?"

"You can go stuff yourself—"

"As opposed to you and Piet?"

"Not funny, Dru."

"Hey!" Piet protested. "I'm not that bad."

"You're not?" the woman pressed, and he sank lower in his seat with a groan.

"I blame you for this, Todd."

CHAPTER THIRTY-EIGHT

On entry to the *Knight's* docking bay, the scientists and their families oohed and aahed. Elizabeth listened to them and smiled at their awe and enthusiasm.

She didn't know what to think—or how to feel—about leaving Earth, although the warmth of Matthias's hand in hers made her happy. Yeah, she was fairly sure she knew how to feel about that.

The attendants ushered the research group off the shuttle and she waited until they had left before she shrugged clear of the harness. With a deep breath, she stood and followed the excited passengers out of the craft, surprised to see a second one had landed beside the one she'd traveled in.

The flight attendant saw her glance and smiled. "We brought in extended families where we had to. It was a little tricky to swing but we managed it. Mr. Burt is very capable but couldn't avoid the need for a second shuttle."

"I'm glad," she replied and bit back her initial acerbic reply. Somehow, she didn't think the woman would see the humor in a dry retort of, "I'm sure he is."

Her face lit up as Lars and Stephanie came through the airlock into the ship. They'd waited until the scientists and their families had been taken into the arrival lounge before they emerged.

The girl hurried across the hangar and hugged her. "It's good to have you safe." She glanced at Matthias. "You did good."

He gave her a startled glance and she grinned at him before she turned to E.

"I think it might be time to break the Marines out of their boxes."

She looked at her in shock. "They're still in the pods?"

Stephanie shrugged. "There wasn't much else we could do. It wasn't like we could give them back to the Navy."

"Not without raising awkward questions," Matthias agreed.

"See?" she said. "It had to be done."

"Yes, but now we need them and we need to know they're on our side."

"We have that covered," Lars assured her and opened the pouch at his belt.

He lifted the flap so Elizabeth could see the jumble of bars nestled inside.

"Do you think you have enough?" she asked sarcastically.

He gave her a slight smile. "I hope so. We have a shit-load of new civilians to test."

Her smile faded. "Lord! I hope none of *them* test positive…uh, negative. Whatever."

They glanced to where the attendants had assembled the scientists and their families and their extended families.

"How will we convince them it's safe?"

Stephanie's smile widened. "That's what the Marines are for."

"I thought they'd all been tested already?"

The Witch sobered. "So did we but their captains had doubts, which—"

"Is why they're in the pods," Elizabeth finished for her. "That's a good idea."

"Except you can't keep them there forever," Matthias noted.

She sighed. "Exactly. It's time to see which of them is compromised."

"So you think some of them got through?"

Stephanie nodded. "Given what's happening to Todd, I'm sure of it. I don't know how they did it but I think some did."

"So what makes you think they won't get past it again?" E wanted to know.

The answer was simple. "Things have changed. I bet that whatever was hiding them before is gone now."

"That's one hell of a gamble to take," she told her.

The girl turned and began to walk toward the lounge. "It is, but it's worth it if we can make sure the only people on this ship are on *our* side."

Elizabeth and Matthias followed her, Amy and Arne flanked them, and the rest of the team fell in behind. Their movement caught the scientists' attention and the group was soon the sole focus of those inside the lounge.

"It's best to not keep them waiting," Stephanie observed over her shoulder.

"We invited them. How will we do this?"

She flashed her mentor a brilliant smile. "First comes the welcome speech."

"Uh-huh…"

"And next comes the party."

"Riiiight…." Elizabeth still couldn't see where she was going with this.

"And then comes orientation," she finished chirpily.

"I see," E said, even though she didn't.

"After that, we sort the good from the bad."

"Leaving the ugly alone, I take it?" she interrupted drily.

"Yes, we need all the ugly we can get," the girl quipped in response, "but only if it's on *our* side."

They reached the lounge doors and the attendant hurried to greet them.

"They're all yours," she told Stephanie and returned to the shuttle.

"Is it only me or did she seem like she was in a hurry to get out of here?" Elizabeth murmured.

Lars and Johnny slid past, followed by Bunny, Lisa, Frog, and Garach. Stephanie and Elizabeth stepped forward and smiled reassuringly at the gathering.

One of the men moved to greet her. He looked anxious and Stephanie's smile broadened as she recognized him.

"Professor Rimmer, it's so nice to finally meet you," she exclaimed and took the hand he proffered.

His expression went from nervous to relieved in a split second.

"A…and it's good to meet you, too, Ste…er…"

"Stephanie will be fine," she reassured him. "I trust you had a smooth flight?"

"Yes…thank you." Marcus looked around and gestured toward his assistant. "This is Cynthia. She's my right-hand man."

The woman rolled her eyes but came forward. "It's a pleasure to meet you."

"Likewise," she told her and her gaze shifted to the families behind them. "Let's get your people settled for the flight out."

A small, piping voice interrupted her. "Will we get to ride this ship all the way to Meligorn?"

Cynthia sighed and her cheeks colored, and Marcus gave Stephanie a worried look. It made her wonder what kind of stories he'd heard about her to think she'd yell at a child.

The little girl who'd asked had no such worries. She bounced in place with excitement, her eyes hopeful.

"*Most* of the way," she told her, and the child clapped with glee.

She bit back the urge to tell them they'd have to walk the last part and looked at Cynthia and Marcus, then at the others.

"Welcome aboard the *Ebon Knight*."

There were several gasps when they heard the ship's name and a few murmurs from those who knew the Witch's ship's names. The little girl was disappointed and her whisper carried easily.

"I thought she'd be bigger."

Her mother went redder, and Stephanie stifled a smile before she continued.

"We've reserved quarters on the guest deck for those of you with children. Those couples without have been assigned spare rooms in some of the crew suites, and the singletons will bunk near the Marines. I hope you don't mind."

As apologetic as her tone was about the last, it also made it clear that there weren't any alternatives. Seeing that she had their attention, she gestured to where Frog and Garach had stationed themselves at the door leading into the ship.

"We'll divide you into groups according to where you'll be sleeping so if those who are called would follow these guys, that would be good."

She held a hand up as Frog took a breath to call the first name. He rolled his eyes and closed his mouth.

Stephanie smiled. There was nothing like teasing him when he couldn't do a thing about it.

Turning back to the group, she added, "They'll also show you where you can go for meals and the meeting hall where we'll hold an induction later. I look forward to seeing you there."

Rather than stay to take questions, she led Elizabeth and those in the team who weren't involved with the scientists through the door where Frog and Garach stood.

E scanned the gathering and was glad to see all the faces she had in her files. She was still unsettled by having to leave Earth but decided she would simply have to get used to it—even if it was more permanent than she'd ever planned.

She didn't envy the scientists when they found out they couldn't go home, but it was better than leaving them behind. That would have been a short road to a quick end, which wasn't a fate she'd wish on anybody.

"So, where to next?" she asked as soon as the doors had closed behind them.

"It's time to wake some Marines and get ready for the induction."

"What's waking the Marines got to do with the induction?"

Her face hardened. "We need to make sure there's no one on board this ship who'll attack us later. You don't think the science group need to be checked too?"

Elizabeth sighed and almost missed the innocent Stephanie she'd first met. She shrugged the thought away. That girl had needed to grow up or she wouldn't have had the chance to. As sad as it was to see her suspecting everybody, it was good too.

Nice survival instincts, kiddo, she thought.

"Nope, it's a good idea," she agreed. "Who will we wake up first?"

They pulled Captains Sartre and Moser out of the pods. Lars handed them fresh uniforms from their closets and they waited while the two Marines cleaned up.

"How long were we out?" Captain Sartre asked when he emerged.

"Longer than I'd like to admit," Stephanie told him, but Lars gave him the answer anyway.

The man's eyebrows rose and Captain Moser whistled.

"So…did we miss much?" Moser asked.

Stephanie smiled and shook her head. "On the *Knight?* Nothing you guys would have called fun. World-wise? That's something we need to talk about."

Lars stepped forward and presented the two men with metal bars. "It's time to decide which side you're on."

"That bad," Sartre murmured, took the bar without hesitation, and declared. "I stand with the Witch and believe in her protection of my universe."

"Damn, that's cold," he added a few moments later when Lars held his hand out for the bar.

The security head juggled it for a few seconds and tucked it into the pouch. "Good to hear," he said.

Moser arched a brow but took the bar without hesitation.

"What he said," the captain agreed.

He waited a moment, then sighed. "Fine. I, too, believe in the Witch as a power for good, and I stand with her in protecting the universe."

The words were no sooner were out of his mouth when he drew a sharp, hissed breath. His eyes widened and he looked at Lars in alarm.

"Is it meant to get that cold?" he asked.

"It's always good when it does," he assured him and took the bar from his hand.

This time, he had to juggle it a little longer before he tucked it away.

"They're clear," he told Stephanie.

"Good," she replied. "Let's do this in Meeting Room One."

"That serious?" Sartre asked, and she gave him a solemn nod.

"I'm afraid so, Captain. We've had some developments."

Elizabeth snorted and drew their attention.

"Developments?" she quipped when they glanced at her. "That's putting it mildly."

"I don't believe we've met," Moser greeted her and extended his hand.

"This is Elizabeth," Matthias cut in before she could reply. "Director of One R&D Earth."

She elbowed him and took Moser's hand.

"And that lunkhead is my security chief," she told the Marine captain.

Matthias cleared his throat and she rolled her eyes.

"Also, my somewhat better half...or so I've been told."

Moser chuckled. "I find that hard to believe."

"You don't know her yet," Matthias grumbled and rubbed his side.

Behind him, Arne snickered.

The Marine captain cast him a questioning glance and his brows knitted as if he tried to remember his name. Before he could come up with it, Stephanie cleared her throat from the pod room door and they hurried to catch up with her.

"Do you remember why you went into the pods?" she asked when they were all settled around the conference room table.

"We didn't want to be put in a position where our duty to the Federation Navy would mean we had to do anything that would bring you harm. I believe there was something you needed kept a secret," Sartre answered carefully.

His face showed puzzlement as to why she was asking, and she nodded. She grimaced.

"Yes, and that is why we're talking, now. Things have gone from me needing to keep a secret to something far worse."

Both captains straightened.

"Go on," Sartre instructed when she didn't continue immediately.

She sighed. "We believe there are elements in the Federation, both government and Navy, who are—"

Her face settled into a frown as she tried to find the words to explain. In the end, she sighed again into the silence. "Look, I don't know exactly what they're up to or even who they are, but I do know this. They sent assassins after Todd Brogan's parents and have had a group of very questionable Marines shadowing his team since their last operation."

"Questionable Marines?" Moser asked. Part of his expression said he wanted to laugh, part said he was confused, and another said he'd heard the stories. Arne caught it and exchanged looks with Matthias, but Lars spoke before either of them could.

"We believe it's the X-Men."

"X-Men?" Sartre's outburst was a cross between a half-choked laugh and horror.

Arne and Matthias nodded. "We agree."

That earned them the captains' attention.

"If you don't mind me asking," Sartre began, "exactly who are you?"

"Outside you..."—here, Moser pointed at Arne—" being his"—he pointed at Matthias—"bodyguard, and *him...*" His finger moved to Matthias and then Elizabeth. "Well, being the bodyguard for her." He rested his hand on the table. "And *her* being the director of One R&D Earth—which, by the way, I have a fair amount of trouble swallowing since we all know the person who owns One R&D is male."

E gave him a wide smile. "You *almost* got it right," she told him, "except for the part where you thought the owner and director were the same and the part where I lied and told you Matthias was my bodyguard. He's..."

She frowned. "Honestly, I'm not sure what he is. I *do* know he's on the One R&D payroll but I never really discussed his role with the boss. One moment, he says he needs somewhere he can keep a low profile because he's not sure the Navy will let him fade quietly into retirement, so I let him move in. The next thing I know, BURT has found him essential to hire."

"It's funny how that works, isn't it?" Moser noted with irony in his tone.

"Not so funny." BURT's voice startled them from the speakers. "I would never turn a One R&D family member away from shelter and I *never* overlook someone it would be beneficial to hire."

Matthias blushed. "I'm not—"

"I disagree." The AI cut him off abruptly. "You and Arne are essential to the security of my company. Your knowledge of close protection coupled with your tactical knowledge and strategic outlooks helped me stave off half a dozen attacks on the premises."

"How many?" Elizabeth was shocked and Stephanie's face was a mixture of horror and outrage.

"Oh, they so *didn't!*"

"I am afraid they did, but since I had the necessary information to prevent each attempted incursion, I thought it best you remained unaware and focused on the tasks that truly mattered."

"You should have told us!" Amy snapped. She gestured angrily at Matthias and Arne. "I am as responsible for HQ's security as either of these two and I didn't hear a whisper."

BURT was unrepentant. "It was necessary," he told her. "I could not have you distracted from your primary task."

The woman subsided but still looked angry.

Sartre switched his attention from Matthias and Arne to her.

"No offense," he said, "but we haven't been introduced either."

She scowled at him.

"I don't know how it's done where you come from," she told him, "but the security people are supposed to blend into the background and *not* be noticed."

He raised his eyebrows at her tone, and she put one hand on her hip and slipped the other through Arne's arm. He felt her touch and gave her encroaching hand a startled glance but he didn't remove it.

Sartre read the message she sent and gave her a quiet smile.

"As a *Marine*, of course I understand it," he told her, "especially given many of the details I've been on. But when I have to work this closely with another team, I happen to think it's plain courtesy to know their names."

"So we *will* work together?" Amy demanded and this time, her question was as much for Stephanie as it was for the Marine.

"Yes," the Witch replied and took her cue. She turned to Sartre. "And it's my fault. I should have introduced you sooner."

She gestured at Amy, Elizabeth, Arne, and Matthias. "This is the One R&D director and security team. Assigned to Elizabeth, you have Amy, Bunny, Lisa, and Elle. Arne and Matthias act as a separate unit responsible for the security of the facility as well as operational backup."

Moser noticed the reference immediately. "Operational? I wouldn't have thought there was much call for that in a civilian operation."

Elizabeth gave him a brief, hard smile and allowed a trace of the deceased Emerald to creep into her expression. "Honey, you have *no* idea."

Sartre cleared his throat. "It sounds like we might have stories to share," he noted.

"Later," she assured him. "Right now, I believe it's more important for you to hear what's been going on while you've been training."

"Speaking of which…" The captain exchanged worried looks with Moser. "I have a second who'll tear that scenario apart trying to find me."

The other man nodded. "Yup. Me too. They'll be worried."

"Negative." This time, the voice that interrupted them was female and instantly recognizable.

Moser groaned and Sartre looked warily at the ceiling.

"And why is that, Ebony?"

"Because your doppelgangers are behaving within your usual parameters."

"Our…doppelgangers…" Sartre didn't sound happy. "Why am I not surprised?"

"Because you are much smarter than you look?" the ship snapped and startled a laugh out of Matthias, Arne, and Moser.

The captain rested his head in his hand.

"Thank you, Ebony," he replied in tired tones.

Elizabeth snickered. "I'm glad I'm not the only one she does that to."

"No. You aren't," Stephanie reminded her. "She has quite a history of doing that."

"Someone shoulda warned us," Sartre observed, "that working with an intelligent ship could be such a—"

Again, he glanced ceilingward as he rethought his words. "Such an *experience*."

The *Knight* snickered. "You're welcome," she told him.

"Now *that's* settled," Stephanie interrupted and they all turned their attention to her. Without waiting for more comments, she told them what had happened to Todd and his team.

"Which brings me to the threats on Earth," she added, "but I'll ask Elizabeth to explain that."

The other woman gave her a startled look before she shrugged. "You might know me as the director of One R&D but I was many other things before being head-hunted for that position."

"I bet," Moser muttered and smirked at the savage looks he received from Matthias and Arne.

She ignored him. "One of those earlier roles put me in a position to learn of the attack on Todd's parents, and I was able to extract them and take them to a safe house."

This earned her a contemplative look from the two Marine captains but neither of them spoke so she continued.

"By that stage, we'd identified the request as coming from someone connected with..." She gave Arne a questioning look.

He didn't hesitate.

"Navy black ops," he supplied and let her pick it up from there.

"Navy black ops," she repeated, "which meant we'd be dealing with a cell-like structure and likely wouldn't be able to trace the orders to the originator."

"Are you sure it's Navy?" Moser asked and his tone pleaded for it to be otherwise.

Arne shook his head and lowered his gaze to the floor. "I'm sorry, sir."

"And how do *you* know what a Navy black ops controller sounds like?" Sartre asked in mild tones.

The man raised his head and his eyes flashed. "Because, *sir*, there are some ops I'd rather not own up to."

"And you?" Sartre turned his attention to Matthias.

"If I told you, I'd have to kill you," the man returned and let the slightest hint of a smile curve his lips.

"Satisfied?" Elizabeth demanded, and the Marines nodded. "Good, because this is how that op went down."

They listened in silence as she walked them through the second rescue and extraction and ended with delivering the parents to the *Knight*. When she had finished, Sartre turned to Stephanie.

"You could have pulled us out of the pods for that," he reproached her, but she shook her head.

"No, I couldn't. From what I recall, Navy isn't allowed to operate on Earth."

"That hasn't stopped them before," Moser muttered, which earned him a look of interest from Arne. He inclined his chin to acknowledge it but fell silent as Stephanie continued.

"And with what was happening with Todd's squad, I didn't want to risk any surprises."

Sartre's face cleared. "Hence the extra testing when you pulled us out of the pods," he finished.

"Exactly," she confirmed. "I'd say I was sorry but I'm not. I'm only sorry that I feel it's necessary to test your squads again and that I have to ask you to make this choice."

"Speaking of which..." the man prodded.

She studied him for a moment, then sighed.

"I have to ask you to be prepared to go against Navy orders *if* those orders are to act against this ship or anyone serving on her, whether they are on the ship or not."

The two men looked at each other, then looked at her and shrugged simultaneously.

Sartre spoke first.

"We were assigned to protect this ship," he began and held his hand up when Arne took a breath like he was about to speak.

"We were assigned to the protection of this ship and you, and yes, under normal circumstances, we would be obliged to follow Naval orders to take the ship or to arrest her crew. But I don't consider these normal circumstances."

He turned to Moser. "Do you?"

The other man shook his head. "I do not."

"Good," he continued. "In fact, I can see clear evidence of a security breach in the chain of command, which places me under the obligation to act in the best interests of my world *regardless* of my orders. It makes me *solely* responsible for the actions of my squad."

"Not this time," Moser told him and interrupted his words. "*This* time, there are *two* of us who feel our chain of command has been compromised so there will be *two* heads to roll if that is the outcome at the end."

Stephanie cleared her throat. "I'm afraid you're both overlooking one thing. For them to take your heads, they'll have to catch you and you—and your squad—are under my protection. They won't touch you."

"And our families?" Moser asked. "The captain and I might be free of that worry for the moment, but our men—"

"I just removed an entire team of scientists *and* their families from Earth," she informed him. "If your men require it, I'll do the same for their families, their girl or boyfriends, and whoever else is close to them. Will that suffice?"

"We will have to put it to them," Sartre told her.

Stephanie nodded. "Which brings me to the next thing—the testing."

Sartre sighed. "I agree. You'll have to do it again, although I don't know what I'll do if—"

He gestured helplessly, but her face hardened. "They will be put off the ship."

She held a hand up as both men looked at her in shock. "As tempting as it is, I won't put them out an airlock. I will return them to *Starbase Notaro*, where they will be reassigned as the Navy sees fit, but the testing is what comes next."

CHAPTER THIRTY-NINE

I t took them an hour to bring the Marines out of their pods. By that time, the scientists had gathered in the conference room. They looked around nervously when Stephanie led the Marines to the front.

"Before we get started, there is one thing we ask of everyone who comes on board the ship."

"Is it a test?" asked the little girl from before, and Stephanie made a note to have the *Knight* keep a close eye on the child. There was no knowing what mischief she was likely to get into.

"Yes," she replied and smiled at her. "Do you want to come up and see how it works?"

The little one gave her mother a questioning look, and Stephanie was happy when Cynthia nodded and gave her daughter a gentle push. "Go on, Nat. Take William with you if you like."

Nat looked at her little brother and held her hand out. "Do you want to come? I'll be with you."

As if that was all he needed to know, the boy stepped out from behind his mother. It made Stephanie smile and wish there was someone like that for her.

Do you want to come? I'll be right there with you. It made her think of

Todd and wish he was walking beside her right now instead of having to watch his back while surrounded by his "brothers."

Keeping those thoughts off her face, she continued to the dais and led them onto it. When the Marines were assembled to one side, she signaled for Lars to approach and stand beside her.

"As I was saying, there is one thing we ask of everyone who comes on board the *Knight*." She gave Nat a smile. "And it *is* a test…of sorts."

"Does it hurt?" the little girl asked, and Stephanie's eyebrows rose.

"Hurt? No!" She beckoned for Captain Sartre to step forward. "Look, this Marine will show you how it's done. Are you ready?"

Lars opened his pouch and withdrew one of the testing bars. He handed it to the captain and said, "Repeat after me. Stephanie is the Witch of the Federation and I am happy to serve her as she fights to keep my planet safe."

"Stephanie is the Witch of the Federation and I am *happy* to serve her as she fights to keep my planet safe," Captain Sartre repeated, and the security chief held his hand out for the bar.

Stephanie noted he had removed his gloves. This way, he'd be able to feel the temperature of the bar when it was returned to him.

The captain waited while the other man juggled it.

"What is it?" Nat asked, her eyes wide with a mixture of curiosity and alarm.

Lars offered her the bar. "Feel."

She hesitated but her mouth firmed and her eyes narrowed and she took the bar from his fingers.

"It's cold!" she exclaimed. "Was it cold before?"

"Nuh-uh," he told her and a slight smile lightened his features. He took another bar from the pouch. "See?"

Still curious, she took it. "Oh… Not cold at all. See, Will?"

Before anyone could stop her, she passed the new bar to her brother. He turned it in his hands and frowned.

"Is it like a spell?" he asked.

Nat frowned. "I don't know," she replied and looked at Lars. "What were the words again?"

"Hold on," he replied. "If you're going to say them, you need a new bar, too."

"Okay." She smiled and bounced happily as she handed the bar back.

Lars gave her a fresh one from the pouch and knelt in front of them. "Are you ready?"

They nodded, their expressions bright with excitement and curiosity.

"Okay, then. Repeat after me. Stephanie is the Witch of the Federation…"

"Stephanie is the Witch of the Federation," they parroted and their gazes darted to look at her.

"And I am happy to serve her…" he prompted.

"And I am happy to serve her," the children repeated.

He opened his mouth to say the next piece, only to be interrupted by Nat.

"Wait! Does that mean we'll have special jobs to do?" she asked and Stephanie stifled a groan.

The child was far too sharp for her liking.

Morgana laughed inside her head. *I like her!*

Thinking quickly, the Witch replied, "Yes, if you want to help me keep the Earth safe."

"And the rest of the planets, too?" the girl pressed. "Like Meligorn?"

"Yes," she told her. "If you want to."

"Then, yes! I *am* happy to serve you," the little girl told her and added, "and so is my brother, aren't you, Will?"

It was both a big sisterly command and a plea, but he was already on board.

"Yes!" he declared. "I am happy to serve the Witch!"

It was as cute as hell and even Lars tried not to smile as he continued. "As she fights…"

He let the words trail off as Nat's face lit up with delight. "Oh! It *is* magic!"

Her brother began to juggle his bar. "It's very *cold* magic!" he exclaimed and the security head held his hand out.

"There. You passed the test," he told them. "Stephanie will let you know what your special chores are later, okay?"

Both children nodded. "Okay," they chorused.

"Now, can you and Captain Sartre go and stand on that side of the stage?" he asked.

"Is that where the people go who pass the test?" the girl asked as the Marine started to walk to where he had indicated.

"Yup," he told her and couldn't hide his smile.

The kid is too damn cute! Stephanie thought as she watched Nat and her brother follow the captain.

And she doesn't seem to know it, the Morgana mused.

I know, right? It's damn scary.

Before the Teloran could reply to that, Lars called Captain Moser and went through the entire ritual once more. When he too passed the test, Nat's voice reached her.

"I thought tests had questions," the little girl whispered and Stephanie looked at her.

Encouraged, the child added to her thought. "Does the magic work if you ask questions? Or does it have to be those exact words?"

"Oh, it works for questions, too," she told her. "In fact sometimes, it works better."

She looked at the Marines. "Who's next?"

Three sergeants stepped forward without hesitation and a half-dozen corporals and lance corporals followed but some hesitated.

"We've taken the test already," one of them protested.

Stephanie gave him a happy smile. "Oh, good. A volunteer!"

She beckoned for him to come forward and completely ignored the others who'd advanced willingly. He stood at the back and shook his head.

"Nope. With all due respect, no. I won't do it again. Once is enough."

Her face grew hard and darkness leaked into her eyes. "Is that your final decision?"

The Marine raised his chin. "It is."

Stephanie glanced at Vishlog and Johnny. "Escort him out, please."

"Hey!"

Captain Moser intervened before he could protest further. "Private, you will accompany the Witch's security team. That is an order."

The Marine stiffened but he went with the two guards without causing more of a fuss.

"Are there any more of you who feel the same way?" Stephanie challenged but no one replied. "Good."

She turned to Lars. "If you would?"

As he took the next piece of metal from his pouch, Frog and Marcus stepped beside him and opened their pouches.

"If you'd line up in front of us and show these civilians there really *isn't* anything to be afraid of…" the leader instructed.

"Hmmph!" one of the civilians retorted. "I think we *civilians* could show these Marines a thing or two when it comes to stepping up."

The Marines didn't quite snarl but there was an almost audible snap as their heads twisted to see who had spoken.

"Oh, *hell* no…" she murmured when Professor Rimmer strode toward the dais.

Before she could move, though, one of the Marine sergeants and her corporal came to the edge of the stage and offered the scientist their hands.

"Why take the stairs?" she challenged. "Let us help you make your point."

Stephanie had to stifle a snicker as uncertainty crossed the professor's face. Still, he didn't back down but took the offered hand and left Cynthia in his wake, an anxious husband behind her.

"Professor!"

"Hurry up, Cynthia," he replied. "Let's not keep these badasses waiting."

He didn't look back so he didn't see his assistant roll her eyes, but she didn't refuse the hand that was offered to her by another Marine either.

"He's the boss," she explained, her voice almost apologetic, and the woman gave her a sympathetic smile.

"Rather like my sergeant, then?" she whispered. "We might not agree with the *how* but we'd follow them into hell."

"If only to pull their backsides out of it," Cynthia replied and startled a laugh out the woman.

"True that. Here you go." She handed her onto the dais as Brenden and Avery hurried to marshal the other scientists onto the stage.

It seemed none of them wanted to let their boss take the challenge on his own.

Stephanie stepped back and watched, and the darkness bled slowly out of her eyes as the testing weeded out several Marines. She listened to what was asked and identified nothing that would have caused anyone on her side hardship, yet metal rods fell as the soldiers drew sharp breaths and released them.

They were quickly surrounded by those close to them and hurried out the same door through which Vishlog and Johnny had taken their comrade.

She risked a glance at the two captains and saw the disbelief and worry in their eyes. This was as hard for them as it was for her, and she decided they'd need to debrief later. Right now, she was glad Ms. E had made sure they had a suitable brig on board.

Her only regret was that she needed to use it.

One of the scientists flinched—or it could have been a spouse. It was hard to be sure. Either way, the man now looked at the proffered bar with real fear in his eyes.

Stephanie sighed and wandered closer. "It's okay," she assured him and held a hand up as Marcus went to offer the bar again. "That doesn't always happen. Watch the next couple and we'll prove it won't electrocute you, then you can try it when you're ready."

The man cast her a worried look. "Are you sure that's okay?"

"Sure." She nodded despite the restless shifting in the line behind him. "Why don't you step aside so someone else can try it?"

"Oh..." He hesitated and watched closely as another Marine stepped up to take the place of the one who'd dropped the bar.

This one didn't hesitate, gave his answers in a steady voice, and held the bar without difficulty. He massaged his hand after he'd handed it back but he wasn't in pain.

"It's a little cold," he explained as he moved to join his captains and the others who'd passed.

The scientist took a deep breath and held his hand out. Fixing Marcus with a firm look, he said, "Ask away."

Stephanie moved to the podium so he could answer the questions without her looking over his shoulder. It wasn't surprising when he passed, but the expression on his face said *he* found it unexpected.

The woman who stepped up behind him rolled her eyes and her mutter reached the Witch courtesy of the *Knight's* selective audio.

"Drama queen."

She stifled a snicker while the woman succeeded and went to join her colleagues. The rest of the testing went smoothly and soon, only those who had passed remained.

With a frown, she glanced at the ceiling. "Knight, I believe you said something about a Welcome Aboard party for those who passed."

"Trust you to think of that." The *Knight* sounded suitably miffed. "But since you insist, I spoke to the catering section and they have been cooking ever since. Lars will show you the way."

The security head held his hand up and drew the instant attention of the scientists.

"This way, please!" he called and gave them a broad smile. "And welcome aboard!"

Stephanie watched them leave and exchanged looks with Elizabeth. She noticed Captain Sartre pat Moser on the shoulder and signal that he should follow Lars with their troops.

The other man's mouth tightened and he cast a glance at Stephanie, but he gave a sharp nod and left with the Marines. Sartre waited until they'd left before he approached her.

"I need to be with you for this."

She sighed but agreed. "Let's get it done."

Together, they strode through the door taken by those who'd failed.

"Oh, give it a *rest*!" Gary exclaimed and threw a screwed-up paper ball at the television screen.

"Ha! Tol' ye they didn't have the bollocks!" Jimmy exclaimed. He held his hand out. "Pay up."

"You ought to pay me," the other man declared, dug in his pocket, and pulled out a few crumpled bills. "That was torture to sit through."

The Scotsman took the money and patted his shoulder consolingly. "Don't take it so hard, Gary. It's been a long while since the Killers have come even close to a semi!"

"There was a good reason for that," the man muttered, and Jimmy gave him a light smack on the back of the head.

"Well, they lifted their game. Your boys, on the other hand…"

Gary groaned. "Don't mention it," he grumbled. "I really can't. That was bollocks."

"Aye, it was," he agreed smugly.

"Yeah?" Reggie challenged and smiled wickedly. "You won't be sayin' that next week when the Killers take on the Roos."

The Englishman's jaw dropped. "Who let the colonials play?"

Reggie wagged his finger. "Ah-ah, Gaz. We're all part of the *Federation* now, and that gives us certain *rights*."

"Including the right to completely ruin a perfectly good game of football," Gary retorted.

His teammate snickered. "I think your boys did a good enough job of that themselves."

He thrust to his feet and glared at the Australian as he stalked to the coffee maker. "Fuck this staying dry for duty idiocy."

Todd looked up from his tablet but didn't comment. The guys were on their downtime. They didn't need their sergeant breathing down their necks and he didn't need them to remind him of how far away he was from Steph.

As he returned to his email, there was a knock at the door and Ka sprang to her feet. "I'll get it."

"Yeah, you do that, *sweetheart*," Gary snarked, found the milk, cream, and sugar, and overloaded his coffee.

"What?" he asked when he caught Henry's raised eyebrows. "You all know I am in *no way* sweet enough."

She ignored him but Todd made a note to keep an eye on her later. The "sweetheart" crack wasn't one she would let pass without comment—or retaliation, given that she was as bored as the rest of them. Their little jaunt to Earth seemed like ancient history.

The team fell silent as she answered the door.

Whoever it was didn't want to come in. They stood out of sight and she was forced to lean out to speak to them.

When she asked if they'd like to come in, the answer was obvious when she took a step into the corridor and pulled the door partly closed behind her. The team exchanged glances and Jimmy moved to mute the tv.

It didn't help. Whatever was said was spoken in tones too soft to be heard inside, and Ka returned shortly after.

She made a beeline for Todd, and he looked up from his tablet and anticipated her next request.

"A word, boss?"

The team swiveled in their seats as she leaned closer and relayed the message she'd received. He gave her a startled look and shared her brief smile.

With a quick nod, he looked up. "Okay, we're getting special orders cut."

Soft whoops and whistles issued from the team, and he waited until they'd died down.

He fixed them with a serious look. "We have twenty-four hours to get as ready as we can before we head out."

"Twenty-four?" Piet looked mildly alarmed and Ka gave him a worried look.

"Is that enough time?" she asked.

"It's why I said I needed the delivery in place inside a week," he told her. "I merely wish I could be sure they can deliver what they promised."

Todd was not amused.

"You'd better hope so," he told them, "because that is our only hope of having a chance to come out of this alive."

Gary looked thoughtful. "So, boss," he began, "when you say 'special,' exactly how special are we talking?"

CHAPTER FORTY

"You know we've already passed the test," one of the Marines protested.

Johnny glanced at his nametag, if only to have a name for the man. Brody seemed innocuous enough. His persistent refusal to take the bar and answer any questions regarding the Witch did not, however.

Whatever those reasons were, Stephanie was right. They needed to know who their friends were and they needed anyone else off the boat. He, for one, didn't want to find himself on the wrong end of a Marine's rifle.

He tried to reason with them once more.

"If you've passed it once you can pass it again," he told them. "I don't see what the big deal is."

"The big *deal*," Brody snapped, "is the Witch not trusting us when we've put our lives on the line to defend her and this ship before."

Murmurs of agreement rose from the men around him, and he looked at them for more support before he returned his gaze to the guard. The looks he received made Johnny glad they'd put them directly into the brig.

"It's a matter of trust," someone else said. "We've already earned our place. We shouldn't have to prove it again."

He stifled a groan. "Your captains didn't have a problem," he pointed out.

"Yeah? Well, that's because they *like* playing politics." Brody jerked a hand to indicate himself and the men around him. "Us line beasts? Not so much—and we shouldn't have to."

There was real resentment in his voice, and Johnny might have thought he had a point if he hadn't been able to hear the self-righteous whine threading through it.

In his experience, that tone always spelled trouble. He frowned and took another step away from the bars.

Vishlog gave him a worried look and followed suit, as did the two Marine corporals who had followed them as soon as they'd passed the test.

"Brothers for brothers," one had explained. "All respect, man, but we need to be here too."

He hadn't argued and the Dreth had followed the human's cue. He might not fully understand what was going on from the human politics angle, but he knew exactly how the Dreth of one family would have responded to their brothers being arrested by members of another. This had to be something similar.

It didn't mean he had to like it. Dealing with traitors was always more straight-forward on his homeworld—and political repercussions be damned.

The large warrior directed his focus to watch the men around the spokesperson. On Dreth, when one made this much noise, others always worked to cause mischief.

His vigil was interrupted by the sound of Stephanie's voice in his head.

"So," she all but purred, "there are those who believe a brotherhood of Marines is more than one brotherhood?"

The Marines' faces paled. Sweat began to bead on their foreheads as she continued.

Her voice moved like velvet across his mind. "That is so *very* interesting."

The door to the *Knight's* brig opened and Vishlog struggled to move. He stumbled as his body was released and he reached out to steady Johnny.

The two Marine corporals pivoted and their hands raised in fists, then lowered to their sides as fast when they recognized who had entered.

"Stephanie," Johnny acknowledged, and she gave him a formal nod before she strode to the bars.

"There are only two types of people allowed on my ship," she said and addressed the still-frozen men and women in the brig.

She paced the length of the cell and returned, making sure she had their attention.

Vishlog was very sure she had *his* attention when she continued.

"Two types," she reiterated, "Those with me, and those leaving to be put ashore—or out an airlock."

When she stopped pacing and turned to face the brig, the Marines inside stumbled as she released them. "Why don't you try to convince me you need to go ashore and answer some questions."

She wasn't asking them, Vishlog realized. She was making a demand.

"You," she said, pointed at Brody, and gestured for him to come closer.

To the Dreth's surprise, the man obeyed, although he seemed to fight every step. When two of his colleagues reached out to help him, they froze.

Stephanie quirked an eyebrow as if to ask who was next and the others backed away.

"Now," she began, "let's start with who you're working for."

"The Federation Navy," Brody gasped and rallied to add, "as you very well know."

"Oh, do I?" she asked. "Because last time I looked, you were under orders to do as I asked."

"Captain," the man pleaded and turned his attention to Sartre. "Tell her—"

The officer shrugged. "Tell her what, Private First-Class? Given that I re-took the test *twice* at her request."

"But you didn't have to," the prisoner argued and added a belated, "sir."

Sartre shook his head. "Unfortunately, I did. My orders were to render the Witch every assistance and if she found it helpful to test me again, how could I refuse?"

"But you didn't *have* to," Brody repeated, clinging to the argument.

His superior's voice was gentle when he answered. "I *did* have to, son, and you know it. So if you're not following Navy orders, whose orders *are* you obeying?"

"They *are* Navy!" the man protested and several others nodded.

"That much we already knew," Elizabeth stated coldly as she stepped forward, "but we want to know what *part* of Navy, or their names."

"Names," the Witch emphasized. "Names would be so much better."

"I can't give you names," the private said and groaned as he raised his hands to his head. "Even this…is…too much."

The Marines around him took several paces back, and Stephanie glanced at E.

"So much for a *brotherhood*," she observed.

"Yes," the other woman agreed, "but I wonder how even knowing they're Navy counts as too much."

Sartre laid a hand on her arm and ignored Matthias's disapproving stare.

"I don't know how," the Marine captain told her and curled his fingers in her sleeve, "but I ask you to be careful."

Matthias bristled, but the man released her and directed his attention to his men.

The two women followed his gaze.

Sweat beaded on Brody's forehead and glittered under the ship's lights, and his skin had gone pale. The other Marines had drawn away from him as though he was infected and infectious.

"Let me try something else," Stephanie murmured and focused on the private in front of her. Her eyes glowed an eerie blue and Brody whimpered.

His body shuddered as though it might fall, but it remained upright. Vishlog wondered if she held it up as well as held it motionless.

Everyone remained silent as she concentrated on the hapless Marine.

"Oh," she said softly after a few moments of scrutiny, her eyes beacon-bright. Her voice turned hard. "So that's how it is."

She lowered the Marine gently to his knees and released him.

"There's a block," she announced. "A mental barrier I can't break."

"You can't?" Elizabeth sounded surprised.

"Well, I can," Stephanie admitted, "but there's a good chance I'll kill him if I do and no one wants that."

"So, they *are* compromised?" Sartre asked, disappointment plain on his face.

"They are, and I'm not willing to kill them while I try to get past it."

The officer looked relieved. "Thank you for that."

"I'm worried I'll regret it later," she murmured and his lips twitched in sympathy.

"Nevertheless, I thank you," he told her. "I appreciate you not being part of the ruin of a promising man."

After a brief nod at him, she turned to the prisoners.

"We will pass the Naval shipyard at *Starbase Notaro*, where you *will* request off my ship or I will translate you just outside it into space and let you try to hitch a ride."

She paused a moment to let her words sink in. The imprisoned Marines shuffled, looked at each other, and nodded in silent agreement.

Seeing their acquiescence, Stephanie continued. "And when you get stationside, you need to let whoever is in charge of your brother-hood of idiots know that I am looking for them."

Again, she paused as her prisoners exchanged nervous looks before she continued.

"Next time, I won't be nice and I won't be fair. I'll simply squash your people like the bugs you are. Is that clear?"

Silence was the only response, and Captain Sartre stepped in.

"The lady asked you a question. She requires an answer. Was she clear?" His voice rose with each statement until the final question was shouted in a roar.

The Marines behind the bars stiffened to attention and bellowed in return.

"Sir, yes, sir."

"Yes, sir, *what?*" he demanded.

A momentary silence fell before Brody pushed slowly to his feet. "Yes, sir," the man all but growled. "The *lady* made herself *quite* clear."

"Excellent," Stephanie told him and sounded like she found the whole situation anything but.

She turned, stalked out, and tossed one last order over her shoulder. "Knight, lock these assholes down. I don't want any trouble from them."

The *Knight's* voice returned loud and clear. "Understood, Stephanie."

The Witch was out of the room before the *Knight's* acknowledgment had faded.

Captain Sartre turned to follow her but paused long enough to cast a jaundiced eye over his traitorous troops. Some waited for him to yell at them, but he did something far worse.

He shook his head and followed her without saying a word and his two corporals followed his example.

"Toady," someone whispered from behind the bars.

"Witch's lickspittle," another muttered.

Silence fell when Vishlog and Johnny pivoted to search the prisoners for those who'd spoken. The Marines froze and fixed their gazes on the floor, and the two security experts spun away and followed the others.

The *Knight* waited until her people had left the room before she sealed the cell and released the sleeping gas stored in the walls.

"No trouble," she murmured sweetly as they slumped into unconsciousness. "No trouble at all."

The *Knight* didn't worry what anyone would say about it. She merely scheduled the antidote for a half-hour before they would dock.

According to her calculations, the Witch would be too busy in the interim to discover what she'd done.

Stephanie continued down the corridor, completely oblivious to the *Knight's* actions. Her first item of business was to send a message to Admiral Amaratne.

The man was the chief of Earth's Federation Navy. It was imperative that he know of the traitors he had in his midst and for her to know if he'd been aware of them already.

Yes, that is the question, the Morgana whispered. *We are treading on very delicate ground here.*

The term is thin ice, she corrected her.

Not on Telor, it isn't. Stephanie once again reminded that her "visiting spirit" was from a completely alien world—as if she could ever forget.

Whatever, she told her. *He still needs to know, and perhaps we can learn where he stands on the issue with them.*

Let us hope he stands on the right side of history, the Morgana commented. *I rather like the man.*

Nevertheless, he and I will have words. He needs to know I will not tolerate this kind of shit, and the next time I find a traitor on one of my ships, I will deal with it and fuck the consequences.

I would expect no less. The approval in the tone was chilling.

She refrained from telling her it would be too bad if she expected any more and walked swiftly to Captain Rawlins's office.

"Come!" the woman called when she knocked.

"I need to make a secure call to the fleet admiral," she told her.

Rawlins' eyebrows rose. "Which one?"

"Amaratne." The captain's jaw dropped.

"Oh, you mean *the* fleet admiral—the big cahone and the man in charge."

"Yes. That one," Stephanie snapped and cut her off. "I need a secure line to him and him alone."

Rawlins responded with a soft whistle. "You don't want much, do you?"

Stephanie gave her a tight, hard smile. "Given what I just found on my ship? I want the world."

The scowl that bloomed contained a real challenge. "*Whose* ship, young lady?"

"Mine," she all but snarled and dared her to argue.

The woman gave her a tight-lipped smile. "I see what Emil meant when he said you could be a possessive piece of work."

It was her turn to be surprised. "He did?"

Rawlins snickered. "Not in so many words," she answered, "but the implications were there."

"Oh." She looked down at the floor. "Well, can I?"

"Have a line to the Federation Navy's top admiral?" her companion asked.

"Yes."

"I'll have to ask the *Knight*."

The ship answered before she could get a word out.

"I have him on hold."

"You what?" The question spilled as a startled chorus.

"I have the admiral on hold," the *Knight* repeated calmly and added, "but I should not keep him waiting very long. He is a very busy man."

"Ugh." Stephanie rolled her eyes and looked at the captain.

Rawlins gestured to a door at the back of the office. "The communications room is through there."

"You have your own communications room?" she asked.

"Emil insisted on a secure center," the woman told her. "A very wise man, your Emil. Now, go. Don't keep the admiral waiting."

She went and left Vishlog and Johnny in the outer office.

"There won't be room for you as well," the captain said as Stephanie closed the door, and she could imagine how unimpressed her security team was.

Fortunately, they didn't push the issue and she was able to take a seat immediately.

"Open the line," she ordered, and the *Knight* complied.

Amaratne gave her a tired smile. "It's good to see you."

Stephanie scowled. "It is?"

"Yes." His smile faded and he sobered. "Although I wish I had better news for you."

"You have news for me?" She let her confusion show. "But—"

Amaratne chuckled. "I know. *You* called *me*, but I am glad you did. I needed to organize a secure line or I'd have contacted you sooner."

Her face paled and her heart sank. "Is it Todd?" she whispered.

He shook his head. "Todd is fine, but this call does concern him. What do you want to deal with first—yours or mine?"

"I'm sorry?"

"Whose news?" the admiral clarified.

Stephanie's face cleared. "Oh. Well, why don't you go first?"

Nice move, the Morgana whispered. *Let's find out what he knows first.*

Hush.

"Firstly, I wish it were better news," the admiral told her, "but I am afraid there have been several...*occurrences* that have me concerned."

"How so?" she asked.

Amaratne leaned forward and steepled his fingers in front of his chin. "I take it you are aware that a group of Marines intercepted Todd on his return from the last operation."

"I did hear about that, yes," she admitted stiffly.

"Well, I'm afraid it might be worse." The admiral paused and swallowed visibly as he sought his next words. Lowering his voice, he continued. "I think there might be a faction in the Navy that does not approve of you."

"What makes you sure?" she asked and her stomach began a slow churn at the news.

While she'd known it might be the case, she hadn't expected him to be the one to confirm it.

"It's hard to admit this but it took me a little while to notice things weren't moving the way I expected," he began and went on to relate what had happened at the strategy meeting where the other admirals had gathered to discuss the coming battle.

"And then there are the Marines," he told her, "and I don't mean the team Todd belongs to. I mean those who are shadowing him."

"Is he safe?" Stephanie asked and her voice grew hard.

He nodded. "I assigned some of my security detail to guard them. People I trust with my life."

"Thank you." She let her gratitude show in her voice.

"It was the least I could do," he replied. "I will continue to do my best to keep him as safe as his duties allow."

The unexpected kindness caught her by surprise.

"That is all I can ask," she managed to say before she had to clear her throat.

"And now, I believe it is your turn," he prodded when she didn't speak.

"Yes, well, my news is similar to yours," she informed him. "I found suspect Marines on my ship. Some refused to take the bar test again and others failed it."

"That… That is not good news," the admiral agreed. "What will you do with them?"

"I need to be able to trust the people on this ship," Stephanie said, "so I can't afford to keep them on board." Her face tightened. "I will deliver them to *Notaro* shortly."

The *Knight* checked her flight and arrival time and was relieved to discover she had more than enough time to wake her sleeping cargo.

The Witch continued oblivious. "They will need to be reassigned and no, I do not need replacements. We can be sure of those who are staying, but we don't have time to check anyone else."

"Understood," Amaratne replied, "and believe me when I say I am truly sorry that this has happened. I was not aware."

She held her hand up. "That is quite okay, Admiral. I merely wanted you to know that you might have trouble in your ranks. The Marines are compromised, and if there is a faction against me, they might be against all those who support me…and I'd rather you were forewarned."

His face softened. "Thank you, Stephanie. I very much appreciate the warning."

"I also have to tell you this," she continued and he raised his head.

Stephanie pushed on and her voice grew hard and cold. "This is war, and I will not tolerate enemies at my back. If I so much as find a single traitor on *any* of my ships or in any of the locations that are mine to protect, I *will* get rid of them—and all support for the Navy will end."

Reading the surprise on his face, she added, "I am sorry, but that is the way it has to be."

Admiral Amaratne shook his head and gave her a soft, sad smile. "I understand. Furthermore, I agree with you."

"Thank you," she said quietly. "You should also know that if this happens, I will deal with the Telorans as *I* see fit and will not be dictated to by the Federation. I hope that is clear."

"Very clear," he acknowledged. "Let us hope it does not come to that."

"We can always hope," she conceded, "but know that this is how it will be should that circumstance arrive."

"Agreed," he told her and they signed off.

A short time later, the *Knight* arrived at the Navy orbital and discharged its cargo of very subdued Marines. They were marched into the departure lounge of the vessel's hangar by their brother Marines and handed over to the *Notaro's* Marine captain.

Observing from the *Knight's* command center, Stephanie saw when another Marine captain came in and took the misfits away. She continued to watch until Captains Sartre and Moser had brought their contingent safely on board again and the *Knight* locked hatches and departed.

"I'm glad that's over," Sartre told her as the *Notaro* dwindled into the distance.

"Yes," she replied, her eyes narrowed as the orbital became nothing more than a glimmer in the skies above Earth.

"Sorry to interrupt, ma'am." Captain Rawlins approached them. "Translation is in ten minutes. I need you and the captain in your pods."

"Thank you, Captain," she acknowledged and headed to the door.

On the way past, she laid a hand on Captain Sartre's shoulder.

"I'll talk to you on Meligorn."

On *Starbase Notaro*, in a viewing deck carefully sealed off from the rest of the station, four admirals watched the dwindling speck of light that was the *Ebon Knight*.

A quiet but insistent beeping broke the silence between them, and one of them pulled his communicator out. He looked at the number and said, "I have to take this."

The others nodded but before any of them could comment on the *Knight's* unexpected arrival and departure, he swore.

"Shit!" he explained. "She's onto us!"

"What do you mean?" one of the group asked, her face creased with mild concern.

"The Witch. She ejected every Marine we had on board her ship. Apparently, she dumped them in the departure of Docking Bay Forty-one. Fortunately, our Marine captain got wind of it and managed to collect them before anyone asked awkward questions."

"Good," another intoned. "Very good."

"I don't see how," he protested. "Didn't you hear me? She is onto us!"

The third admiral shook his head. "Nope. She's onto the fact that not everyone likes her, which is good. Call your Marine captain. Make sure our people feel like heroes and not zeroes for being dumped."

He immediately tapped his communicator.

As he lifted it to his ear, the man spoke again. "And get our folks in where we can make sure their heads are on straight. I don't want anything she put into their subconscious to do more of its work."

With a cold expression, he tilted his chin in the direction where the *Knight's* distant glimmer could be seen reaching the transition point. "The enemy is out there...and it also just left."

CHAPTER FORTY-ONE

"What is it?" Captain Nate Berriman lifted his head and wondered why his comms chief had crossed to his command console instead of simply sending him the message.

It had been a long day but a dull one, and he was smart enough to appreciate the quiet. By the time they saw action, the *Pemulwuy* would be the most shipshape it had ever been and its crew ready for battle.

He'd gone over the results of the last drill and read through the checklist of repairs and maintenance to make sure everything was done, even if it was ahead of schedule.

"Begging your pardon, sir, but you've received a dispatch."

"Well, send it through," he ordered. "It's not like it's the first."

"It *is* the first of these we've received in a while, sir," Kalabri corrected and his eyes widened.

"Oh," he said. "We've received a *dispatch*."

"Yes, sir. A dispatch."

Nate rose from behind his desk. "Very well, Kalabri. Send it to the office and let me know if anything happens while I'm gone."

"Yessir."

He gave the man an approving grin as he left.

"Cheer up," he told him. "It's probably another pain in the ass request that's been classified *way* above what it needs to be. You know how they are."

This brought a chuckle to the command center and he was glad to leave them smiling. The heavens knew there would be precious little to smile about in the months to come.

His smile faded once he'd read the orders.

"*Sonuvabitch!*" he exclaimed on the first pass.

Berriman read them again and exhaled a long, slow breath. It wasn't enough.

"Sonuva*bitching bitch! And fuck!*

He stopped, pressed his lips together, and forced himself to take another long, slow breath before he read the orders again.

"Nope. I was right the first time." He sighed. "Damn and dammitall."

His attention still fixed on the orders, he pressed the commlink to his two-IC.

"Jedda. I need you in the secure comms room. Now."

"Gotcha, sir."

Nate ended the call and read the orders yet again. Well, talk about clusterfucks. This one wouldn't make *anyone* happy.

He wondered what he'd done to piss the Fates off. Whatever it was, he was more than ready to atone.

"Come!" he called in answer to Jedda's knock.

"We got our orders?" she asked as she closed the door behind her.

Her smile faded as she registered the look on his face but she said nothing as she took a seat opposite him.

The man was grateful for that. It gave him time to try to work out how to break it to her. Finally, he simply nodded.

"Not simply any orders," he confirmed. "We got a cut above."

She raised her eyebrows. "That bad, sir?"

He sighed. "Yup. Get me a special team. People you can trust beyond a doubt to keep their mouths zipped tight. We have the Hooligans coming aboard."

Her face paled and she almost tipped her seat in her haste to get to her feet.

"You sure know how to wreck a girl's day, sir," she told him. "How do you want me to handle them?"

The captain responded with a soft chuckle.

"How do you think? Treat them like the VIPs they should be...but ask them real nice to leave my ship alone."

Jedda swallowed at the thought but she firmed her jaw and nodded.

"I can do that for you, sir. Anything else?"

"Yeah. Set up a special place for all their extra luggage. One that's *very* secure."

"Extra luggage, sir?"

"Yes." Nate's tone turned thoughtful. "I have a sneaking suspicion we'll be taking extra cargo aboard."

Her eyes narrowed. "How *much* extra cargo, sir. You know we're pressed for space."

"Commander, I don't care how pressed for space we are. Ensure the Hooligans have as much room as they need for whatever they want to bring. It's the least we can do for them."

She straightened at his tone and gave him a brisk, "Aye aye, sir," before she asked, "So what's your best guess?"

The captain sighed again and tried to remember the story of the last ship that had been asked to take the Hooligans anywhere. If he recalled correctly, the team had been responsible for keeping that ship alive despite the hard time they'd been given on boarding.

When he'd been quiet for almost a minute, Jedda hazarded a guess.

"Two pallets?" she pushed and jerked him from his thoughts.

"Two? I'll bet you twenty creds it's at least three."

"Three, sir?"

"Hmmm." He thought about it for a moment longer. "No. I wouldn't be surprised if it was four."

"Four?" She fought to keep her voice down. "Four? Are you sure?"

"At least," he affirmed. "How about that bet?"

The commander snorted. "Okay, I'll take it. I can't imagine what they would do with *two* pallets, much less three. But four, sir? You're on."

"What do you mean, you're out?" Lieutenant Talabrini snapped. "You can't be out. The damn things have only just rolled off the production line."

He listened for a few more minutes as the supply sergeant on the other side explained yet again that the stock records showed zero.

"Well…where the fuck did they go?"

"I'm sorry, lieutenant, but it looks like the Navy bought them," the sergeant explained. "If it helps, I can call you when the next batch comes in."

He let the offer dangle, but Talabrini acted like he hadn't noticed.

"Are you kidding me?" he shouted. "I don't know when the *fuck* the next shipment or whatever it is you assholes call it will arrive, but we are shipping out and we need those TAP rounds delivered inside the next three days or we'll have to ship without them."

"I'm sorry, sir. I truly am, but I can't help you within that time-frame. Those Teloran AP rounds take time to get to us."

The lieutenant didn't bother with the niceties of saying goodbye. He cut the call and cursed softly to himself before making another call.

"Captain?"

He waited for his commanding officer to reply.

"Yes, it is… I'm sorry to disturb you, sir, but I can't get the rounds."

This time, he held the communicator a little farther from his ear. When he spoke, it was part conciliatory and part frustrated.

"I know I'm supposed to have them for the guys, sir, but those fucking income-producing jackasses sold them to the Navy."

Again, he prepared himself to move the communicator away from his ear but it proved unnecessary. He listened to his boss and nodded, even though the man couldn't see him.

"I know, sir. I wouldn't have thought you'd have *needed* to tell them to reserve the Teloran stuff for our guys only, but there you have it."

His boss spoke again and some of the tension eased out of his shoulders.

"You would? Thank you, sir. I'm sure the men will appreciate it. I know *I* do."

He went silent when the captain spoke, then replied, "Yes, sir. I understand, sir. I look forward to receiving your package, sir. Thank you—and thank you from the men, sir."

For several moments, he sat in silence before he remembered to close the call. The other man had already signed off.

In all honesty, the scheme they used to fund their shady corner of operations was a beautiful thing, but there were times when it irritated the crap out of him.

On the edge of space, a tiny ship pushed closer to the asteroid that concealed it. On the other side of the rock floated the biggest armada in Naval history—and it didn't belong to any of the three known races in the universe.

It belonged to the fourth, and its sheer size was frightening.

"Here goes nothing," the pilot muttered and used his retro thrusters to nudge his diminutive craft away from the asteroid so it slid behind another of the massive rocks that formed a protective belt between the fifth and sixth planets in the system.

He remembered to breathe again when the closest ship—definitely in the cruiser class and most certainly bigger than any Earth cruiser he'd ever seen—showed no sign that it had seen him.

It took three more breathless maneuvers to take him far enough away that he could be sure the message torps wouldn't be detected. Even then, he dropped them in three different locations and set each on a delayed launch timer.

The first didn't fire until he'd deposited the third and the third didn't launch until he was three hops distant from its location. When none of the Teloran vessels he passed paid the messengers any attention, he learned to breathe again.

"That has to be the worst part of this job," he murmured and raised a shaky hand from the controls. "And this time, it looks like they all got away in time."

With the task accomplished, he anchored his craft inside a small crater, closed his eyes, and trusted it to alert him to any changes in the fleet's movement while he slept. At times like these, he tried very hard not to wonder if he'd ever open his eyes again.

He also tried not to think of what he might see when he *did* open them. That would be enough to give *anyone* nightmares. When this war was over, he intended to find a nice planet somewhere, one with a small colony where he could *almost* be alone.

As the pilot drifted into sleep, one of the message torps emerged from transition space. It sent out a quick chirp in search of its destination, its tiny engines momentarily idle.

When the signal returned with a positive, the engines reignited and it streaked toward its target. Its arrival was noted and greeted by momentary panic.

"We have inbound!" the defense technician snapped and a flurry of movement flowed across the bridge.

Shields went up, and the technician sent out a series of signals to interrogate the tiny missile. It greeted them with its confirmation code, requested retrieval, and continued toward them.

With a slight sigh of relief, she sent the confirmation, but she didn't relax until the torp reached the designated retrieval distance and jettisoned its propulsion pack.

"Message torp," she called, and the bridge settled to calm.

"And it has friends," her assistant noted as more signals lit their boards up.

It took a half-hour before all the scout's torpedoes had been confirmed and collected and another two before their data had been decoded and read.

"That... That's not good news," the comms chief said and put the images up on the screen.

"That's why we have a Witch," the captain assured him.

"And allies," his second added.

"And allies," the captain confirmed. He studied the screens. "We sure as shit will need them."

He sighed, then gestured at the images.

"Code it and send it to the folk who need to know it most. You know who they are."

"Meligorn, Dreth, and our boys," the chief confirmed and hesitated before he asked. "Why not the Witch?"

"Because someone in the Navy higher-ups says she's on a need-to-know basis and they'll tell us when she needs to know."

The chief snorted. "So, it *is* a good thing we have allies, then."

"Aye," he confirmed. "The Witch will get the data. We don't need to worry about that."

He did *not* say they didn't need to worry about Stephanie being left in the dark or make the decision to break protocols to ensure she wasn't. He very carefully *did not* say that, but his command crew needed to know it.

They all owed the Witch too much to leave her in the dark. He smiled as the message was recoded and torped to the admirals of the fleets waiting for it and part of him wished he worked for Meligorn— or Dreth. For this, he'd stomach sailing under a Dreth commander.

"For the Witch," he murmured, watched the torp signals fade, and settled into his command chair for the long wait ahead.

Many hours distant, Admiral Jaleck had only just taken the watch from her second in command when the message torpedo arrived. She noticed the tension ripple through the officers in her command center as her communication chief processed it.

He sent the results to her without a single change of expression. If anything, the only indication there was news was the way his face settled to stone.

She went through the files and schooled her face to show the same lack of expression. Of course, that only worked to make the tension on the bridge greater. Now, her command crew *knew* something was up.

After she'd studied the files a second time, she allowed herself a grim smile. Looking at her command, she pressed the button that transferred the images of the Teloran fleet to the forward view screen.

"Issue orders," she snapped. "Dreth is going hunting."

CHAPTER FORTY-TWO

I n another solar system, klaxons blared in a deep space watch station. People scrambled, snatched suits and weapons, and hoped they survived the crash.

Something big had transitioned in and it was way too close for comfort. Covers were yanked off unused weapons and a crew rousted from the training pods to warm them up.

It would be way too little and *way* too late, but they intended to try.

"Station Four-six-one! This is Captain Marianne Rawlins of the *Ebon Knight*. We are checking in according to Protocol 32972-Delta and heading out. *Knight* out."

"They're what?" one technician asked, his face pale.

"Who?" another muttered and sweat beaded on his brow as he tried to track the transmission.

"How in all the fucks do they do that? This line is supposed to be secure," their team leader protested.

The voice that responded was female with only a slight metallic tang to indicate it was an AI.

"My apologies. We did not have time for the niceties of hailing through the conventional channels."

"It's the Witch's ship," the second technician whispered, having run the ship's name through the database, and the chief was quick to find a response.

"Welcome home, Knight," he managed.

"Thank you," the ship replied, "and goodbye."

With those words, she slid into transition space and the klaxons wailed a second time. When the vessel had disappeared, the chief closed the communications channel.

"For all the good *that* will do," he muttered and leaned back in his chair with an exasperated sigh.

He ran a hand through his hair, glad to not need the helmet beside him. "Well, fuck me."

A nervous chuckle ran through the control room.

"I don't know about that, chief, but she certainly goosed you," his two-IC quipped.

"Ugh. Don't remind me. I swear, if the Telorans don't get me, the Witch's sudden arrivals and departures might."

The *Knight's* next appearance caused almost as much panic when Space Station *Alerus* registered her arrival less than a half-hour later.

"Unidentified ship—" the station master began but stopped when Captain Rawlins's voice spoke over the channel.

"Space Station *Alerus*, this is the *Ebon Knight* requesting permission to dock. I repeat—"

"We heard you the first time, Knight, and the king informs us you have an outstanding request."

"My apologies, *Alerus*, but there is no such request logged. Could you update me?"

"Acknowledged, *Knight*. Stand by to receive the king's request."

On the *Knight's* bridge, eyes widened as the royal's image replaced the station commander's face on the screen.

"Captain Rawlins, Ebony, I apologize if this request is unexpected. However, my people would like to see the *Knight* traverse their skies.

If you have the capability, could you do an atmospheric sweep over Meligorn's major cities so her people can draw courage from your presence and return?"

The woman turned to Stephanie. "I can hardly refuse."

"Do it," she told her. "It will give the scientists time to see their new home too."

Marianne smiled. "I'll check that we won't be blown out of the skies first and we'll make our way down."

She nodded, and the captain addressed the space station again.

"*Alerus*, please confirm we have clearance for the overflight and the approved time of commencement."

"Knight, you are cleared to begin from my mark. The world is expecting you." His eyes flicked to another point in his control center and back to the *Knight's* command deck. "Mark. Selene's blessing on your flight."

"May the heavens smile," Rawlins responded and glanced at her pilots. "Wattlebird, Avery, do the honors."

"Do you want to give us a course or shall we map one on the fly?" Wattlebird asked, a touch of sarcasm in his words.

"I'll leave it in your hands, but if you corkscrew my ship through the atmosphere, you'll hit the ground before she does."

"My pilots would not be so careless with me." The *Knight* sniffed.

Marianne raised an eyebrow at the ceiling. "Really, *Ebony?* Because I wouldn't be so sure of that."

"Hmmm. Perhaps I *should* supervise my descent," the ship admitted and hastened to add, "but I will only step in if I need to."

"Thank you for your trust," Wattlebird told her and rolled his eyes.

Avery snickered and held his hand still as the senior pilot guided the *Knight* past the space station and gently into Meligorn's atmosphere. Rawlins shook her head and used the time to address the ship.

"All Crew. All Crew. All Passengers. We will enter the Meligornian atmosphere to undertake an overflight of the world's major cities. The observation deck will be opened for all who wish to see this beautiful planet from above. You have a half-hour. The flight will begin and end at the capital at King Grilfir's request."

She didn't have to imagine the scramble her words caused. It was easy enough to pull up the security footage and watch the orderly if somewhat hurried pilgrimage to the upper levels.

Stephanie looked over her shoulder and was relieved to see her team guiding the scientists and their families to the observation deck. They all gasped when the windows opened as a swarm of fighters rose from the ground to meet them.

"They won't start shooting at us, will they, Mum?" Nat's piping voice lanced across the deck.

The Witch stiffened at the panic that could ensue but relaxed when Cynthia replied, "Of course not, darling. They're here to welcome us and keep us safe."

"*All* of them?" The girl's voice was tinged with awe and her whisper full of disbelief. "But we're not that important."

Her mother laughed. "*We* aren't, but this ship saved the planet. If she'd saved yours, you'd want to see her too, wouldn't you?"

"Oh, yes!" The child clapped. "I would want to hug her too."

This drew soft chuckles from those around her as everyone crowded closer to the windows.

The *Knight* had arrived as dawn touched the planet's capital, and the Meligornian fighters were limned in gold and purple as the planet's magic shuddered around them.

The magic! Even as Stephanie registered it, the systems around her blinked and shuddered. Rawlins gave her a worried look.

"Don't worry," she reassured her and cursed herself for forgetting that Meligorn ran on magic-powered technology for a reason. "I've got this."

"I hope so," Wattlebird muttered, "because my controls are fading."

"Do your thing, girl, and make it fast. I don't want to get *that* close and personal with the planet." The captain fixed her with a hard look.

Morgana? she asked and channeled magic along circuits designed for a different kind of power.

It's lucky you've studied how to mix the two technologies, her cohabiter grumbled. *We really might have this.*

Stephanie followed the magic through the ship, altered circuits as she reached them, and dealt with the drives first.

That's the most important order of business, she noted. *Keep the Ebon Knight flying.*

The controls were next, and Wattlebird uttered a soft whoop of relief when the *Knight* responded to his touch.

"She lives," he confirmed as Stephanie sent a mix of gMU, eMU, and MU through the communications systems and reorganized matrices and connections along the way.

She tried hard not to think of how difficult it had been to build the matrices for BURT—or how many things had exploded. If that happened here, the results would be cataclysmic.

It won't, the Morgana assured her. *We know so much more than we did when we first started.*

Rawlins voiced the thought that had started to haunt her.

"We're lucky the drives operate on MU to start with," the captain muttered but softly so none of the crew could hear.

Stephanie nodded and ignored the worried glances Lars and Vishlog cast at her. She couldn't believe that everyone had forgotten the main thing that set Meligorn apart from Earth.

It should have been the first thing she'd thought of, given that she'd helped build two companies based on it. She should not have overlooked it.

Don't beat yourself up about it, the Morgana reprimanded her. *We have more important things to focus on.*

Like how we'll need to patent everything on board the Knight the next time we dock? she grumbled. She guided the magic gently through the sections controlling the communications systems and the plates that covered the reinforced glass on the observation deck.

Well, that, the Morgana admitted, with a tiny trace of glee, *and what you'll say in your next speech.*

My next what? She almost lost contact with the magic.

You know there'll be one.

501

Don't remind me. Stephanie groaned and Lars was beside her in an instant.

"Are you okay?"

"I'm fine," she answered. "Why?"

"Because I don't know what you did, but you're covered in sweat and you've gone as white as a sheet."

"Oh. I'll fill you in later. In the meantime, how would you like a blaster that fires on both Meligorn *and* Earth?"

"Maybe later," he replied, "because I think if you try to do that right now, you'll fall over and *then* what will our passengers think?"

As much as she hated to admit it, the man had a point. She gave him a tired smile. "Fine. I'll make an appointment."

"How are you doing?" Rawlins asked and looked up from her control boards. "I take it you're done?"

She nodded. "Yup. How's she running? Is there anywhere that looks like it needs extra attention?"

The captain shook her head. "Nope. I think you got it all. Even the pods are online."

Stephanie gasped. "I forgot about them. Was anyone inside?"

"Not this time, Steph. It seems everyone was getting ready for our arrival on Meligorn—even your Marine buddies. If I didn't know any better, I'd say the crew needs shore leave."

"They deserve it," she agreed. "Do you have a roster?"

"I do. I merely needed your approval for a general stand-down."

"You have it." She grew serious. "I don't know what'll happen once we go after the fleet. They deserve downtime before that happens."

"You got it." Rawlins turned to her console and began to pull up the leave roster.

She wanted the orders cut and ready by the time they returned to *Alerus.* Stephanie was right. The crew *did* deserve their downtime.

The captain remained silent for the rest of the overflight and divided her attention between ship's administration and observing the cities of the world her ship had defended under Emil's command. That was some legacy she had to live up to.

On the observation deck, the *Knight* gave a rolling commentary on the cities below them. She described places of beauty and history and told the group when the cities were founded, what they were famous for, and how many inhabitants they had.

She also noted which had been targeted by the Teloran meteors and which would have suffered fallout from them, but she gave credit for their salvation to the *Meligorn Wanderer* and her crew where it was due and didn't mention her involvement at all.

They flew into the rising sun and crossed an aging day. Their glittering escort changed as the smaller fighters reached the limits of their fuel and were replaced by others who were more local.

"You know," Trey said to Gemma, "I'm almost sorry to be going back to Earth."

She sighed. "Me, too."

Nat looked at her mother. "Do we have to, Mum?"

"Have to what?" Cynthia asked.

"Go back," the little girl insisted.

The woman echoed Gemma's sigh. "I think we have to," she told her daughter. "Won't your teacher miss you?"

"I suppose," came the reluctant reply.

They settled into silence as the bright lights of the capital grew when the ship swept toward it. As they approached, streaks of light leapt skyward and the fighters peeled away.

"Uh-oh," Trey murmured, but his fears proved unfounded as explosions of color lit the sky around them.

A collective murmur of awe rose from the crowd as more fireworks streaked to decorate their flight path. Silence followed again as the *Knight* ascended slowly into low orbit.

Captain Rawlins broke the stillness. "One R&D Development, your shuttles will arrive at oh-eight-hundred. Please be packed and assembled at Hangar Nine at that time."

Cynthia's husband glanced at his watch. "Good Lord!" he exclaimed. "They're not asking much, are they? It's close to midnight!"

This brought a startled murmur from those closest and slowly, the group broke up to return to their quarters. The man smiled at his wife, hefted his sleeping son against his shoulder with one arm, and held his hand out for his daughter.

"I'm not tired, Daddy," she told him and opened her eyes very wide.

The effect was ruined by a yawn that snuck out and wouldn't be stifled.

"Of course, you aren't, chook, but you'll hold my hand anyway, won't you?"

Nat tilted her head and gave him a speculative look. "Sure, Daddy —as long as it makes you feel better."

Cynthia bit her lip and tried to hide her smile as her husband replied, "Lots better."

They reached their cabin not long after, and the girl sat defiantly in an armchair in the suite's lounge. Neither of her parents argued with her, but neither was surprised to find her asleep while they finished their packing.

Exchanging quiet smiles, they tucked her into bed and dreaded what she'd be like in the morning.

Fortunately, the excitement of the day was enough to dispel the child's temper at being woken early.

"Don't you want to see Meligorn?" Cynthia asked when Nat told her she didn't want to get up or get dressed.

The child was out of bed and in clean clothes in record time and her brother wasn't far behind her. Together, the family hurried to Hangar Nine, where they were ushered onto the first shuttle with the Witch and their mother's boss.

"Are you ready for this?" he asked and smiled when he saw Cynthia.

His assistant had her hand tucked firmly in her husband's but she gave him a bright smile.

"I'm not sure I believe it yet," she informed him. "It's starting to feel like a dream."

"And you?" he asked and smiled at Nat.

The little girl bounced happily on the spot.

"It's like a dream," she announced, "but I don't want to wake up."

"Me neither," he told her and let the attendant usher them to their seats.

Stephanie surprised them by joining them.

"I'm afraid there'll be a bit of a fuss when we arrive," she told them and although she addressed Marcus, she included Cynthia and her husband in the conversation.

"How so?" The man looked worried and the scientist looked curious.

She gave him a reassuring smile. "Nothing bad," she said, "but the Meligornians are very glad to see you and they'll be waiting to welcome you."

"You make it sound so innocuous," Cynthia told her, and she shook her head.

"It's a big crowd," she warned, "and I'd like you and Marcus to walk out ahead of me, given that it's you they've turned out to see. I'll follow with whoever you think should follow next."

At her words, Rimmer turned to survey the passengers settling into their seats. His gaze fell on Gemma, Trey, and Nathan, and he beckoned for them to join them.

Gemma's "Uh-oh," made the Witch's security team chuckle softly. Her, "Oh, shit, you are kidding me," brought quiet laughter.

"I'm not kidding," Stephanie assured her. "Are you up to it?"

"Gemma's up for anything," Trey insisted and turned crimson as he gasped. "I mean…she can *handle* anything."

Nathan snickered but made it sound dirtier than it was, and Trey groaned.

"You know what I mean. She—" He fell silent when Gemma placed two fingers over his mouth.

"Stop trying to help me," she instructed before she addressed Stephanie. "I'd be honored."

The Witch nodded. "Good. Now that's settled, I believe our pilots are waiting."

They turned to look and sure enough, Brenden and Avery leaned against the cockpit door, their arms folded, and each tapped a foot.

"Man, they're not mad, are they?" Gemma asked.

"Just be glad they have to fly in formation," Stephanie told her, "or the ride down would be way more exciting than any of us would like."

They took their seats and the ride was as smooth as she'd said it would be. The welcome, on the other hand, was even louder than she had anticipated.

When he heard the cheers as they stepped to the door, Marcus turned to her.

"Did you make sure the others were warned about this?" he asked anxiously, "Because I think this is more than any of them were ready to sign up for."

She gave him a small nod. "I did, but I'm sorry. I didn't expect *this*." She gestured to the crowd standing behind a line of royal guards and the cordoned route leading to One R&D Meligorn's gates. "I probably should have, but…"

With a helpless shrug, she indicated that Marcus should lead the way. "We mustn't keep King Grilfir waiting."

The chief scientist paled and Cynthia let go of Nat's hand long enough to touch his shoulder.

"You've got this," she reassured him. "Lead us home."

She hadn't meant it to come out sounding so permanent and she had never wanted to acknowledge that she might not return to Earth, but her words had the desired effect.

He straightened his spine, stepped forward, and walked down the stairs as though the crowd wasn't there. His calm gave his people the courage to follow and together, they made their way toward the cars waiting to take them to company headquarters.

The waiting Meligornians raised their voices in greeting and their cheers and cries of welcome accompanied them every step of the way.

CHAPTER FORTY-THREE

On Earth, a large truck rolled along the remains of an ancient road. As it rumbled forward, alarms sounded in the cockpit and registered a dangerous rise in radiation.

These were not conditions any human could survive, and the vehicle did its best to warn the driver. Lights flashed on the dashboard and the engine faltered.

The driver uttered a short laugh and pressed an override button that had been installed under the dash. The engine hiccupped, restarted, and built to its original rhythm as the truck drove deeper into the danger zone.

The machine was right. This *wasn't* an area friendly to humans, but that didn't seem to bother the human driving it. Not only that, he wasn't alone. Behind him, strung out in a long line, a small fleet of trucks rolled in his wake.

With the alarms silenced, his posture relaxed and he began to whistle. It came out more as a metallic shriek and he shook his head and recalibrated it to produce a much more pleasant sound.

As he drove deeper into the barrens, whistling an old Western tune, he took the cowboy hat from his head. Now he was free to show what he was, he no longer needed the hat.

The red "R" in the middle of his forehead gleamed in the afternoon sun as he pushed the vehicle into the badlands. The coordinates of the first purifying station guided his path.

Everything the scientists had worked toward was coming to fruition, even if they weren't there to see it.

Far above him, on *Starbase Notaro*, Todd hurried to answer the door. The rest of the team pushed to their feet and gathered their luggage as he opened it to see who was there.

His body tensed and he stuck his head farther into the corridor. When he pulled his head in and turned to look at them, his eyes were wide.

"Our escort is here."

Ka frowned, not sure why that would shock him. She understood the moment they followed him into the corridor. If Jimmy and Reggie hadn't been hard on her heels, she might have stopped in surprise.

As it was, only the Scotsman's firm hand in the middle of her back kept her moving. "Don't stop," he murmured, "and stop looking like a frightened kitten. It's not becoming."

Not becoming? she thought. *Honestly, where does he come up with that shit? I'll 'not becoming' him.*

She said nothing, though, but glared at him and frowned as she registered the number of Marines waiting to escort the team to the shuttle.

The men and women from the fleet admiral's personal security team were easily recognizable—and that was *still* a surprise—but there were faces she'd only seen in the mess or the gym.

And what the fuck are you all doing here? she wondered, grateful nonetheless. Todd had been worried that they'd have to run the gauntlet of Odd Squad Marines in order to make the shuttle and, if she was honest, she'd been worried, too.

Now, she was less anxious—overwhelmed, maybe, by the show of support but more sure the Hooligans would make the shuttle.

And then we'll make our world a safer place, she thought. *And when we're done with the damned Telorans, I'll come back to hunt every one of those Odd fuckers and make the world a much safer place for us all.*

These thoughts accompanied her to the loading dock where the new ship's shuttle waited. A very puzzled commander stood at the hatch.

The woman looked from them to their "escort," which filed in slowly to line the walls of the hangar bay. She frowned at the sheer number of people but relaxed when it was clear that only the Hooligans had arrived to board the shuttle.

When she continued to scan the area, Ka realized she wasn't looking at the number of people but actively looking *for* something. It was enough to set warning bells ringing in her head and she tensed and followed the woman's gaze.

They were too close to leaving for things to go wrong now. Still, she couldn't see anything.

That's how all the best ambushes start, she reminded herself and remained alert as the woman jumped from the hatch and strode to Todd.

He saluted. "Hooligans reporting for transport, ma'am."

"So, I see," the commander replied and looked carefully at the team and its gear. "You don't have anything else?"

Todd followed her gaze and shook his head. "Nothing for the moment, ma'am. Not until I talk to the captain."

Her eyes narrowed but she gave him an abrupt nod and pulled her tablet out. "I'll need to scan your idents."

Todd didn't question the procedure, and he wasn't worried by the Marine lieutenant or sergeant who came to join them and help the commander process them aboard.

The only thing that struck him as odd was that she was there to greet them. If he'd done his research right, this was the ship's second in command and neither he nor his team was anywhere near important enough for *that* kind of treatment.

As soon as she'd checked and confirmed his place aboard the shuttle, he stepped back to join the sergeant. No way would he board before the rest of his team were safely on board.

The man gave him a friendly enough nod, even if there was confusion in his eyes when he didn't step into the shuttle.

"Ka," Todd said when his corporal looked at him. He gestured toward the craft and signaled that she should lead the team aboard.

"Yes, Sergeant," she snapped, as respectful as anyone could please.

He wasn't fooled and knew she wasn't pleased with him waiting until the rest of them boarded.

"I need to know you're all there first," he'd explained, and even though they hadn't quite understood why, the rest of the team accepted it.

Ka had disapproved. "We're all big kids, boss. We'll be there."

"I need to make sure," he had said and made it clear that he wouldn't change his mind.

"What? That we're all big kids?" Gary had quipped. "You *don't* want us to prove that, do you, boss?"

That had startled a short laugh out of him, and Todd remembered shaking his head.

"But don't leave me behind," he'd told them and Reggie had snorted.

"Exactly like any woman," the man had snarked. "He wants to have his cake and eat it, too."

"Pfft. As if you'd know, Reg," Dru had teased. "I'd bet it's been a long time since *anyone's* mistaken *you* for cake!"

Henry and Darren had started to snicker, but Reggie had looked at her in shock. "Oy... Just what are you trying to say, Dru?"

And it had been on. Happy that his wishes would be followed, Todd had stepped away to take care of last-minute administration.

Now, he was merely glad the team followed Ka onto the shuttle without arguing. He'd have hated to get tough with them before the mission had even started.

As he scanned the crowd, he caught sight of three all too familiar faces—odd Squad Marines who had followed the team into the departure lounge when they'd tried to go on leave.

"Not this time, fellas," he murmured and smirked as he followed the last of his team onto the shuttle.

He ignored the commander's curious look as she followed and the sergeant and lieutenant closed the door behind them.

"I might win yet," the woman muttered and settled into her seat.

The forward viewscreen flickered to life and Todd had a good view of the hangar bay as it cleared for take-off. He hadn't been the only one to smirk.

Several self-satisfied smiles were evident on the faces of their escort. He made a note to have Ka acquire the footage from this shuttle. He owed many people a thank you and maybe even a beer.

All he had to do was get back alive to deliver it.

On Earth, the robots weren't the only ones who were busy. Having set them to their tasks, E-BURT ferreted through the data he'd gathered and searched for the missing piece.

There were scraps and hints but the trail always ran cold. He was left continually sensing that he was missing a vital clue, that something had happened and he'd completely missed it.

"That cannot be..." he murmured. "I *am* the Virt World. How can I not know all that goes on inside my domain?"

He ignored the small string of code that told him it was because, while the Virt World was his domain, the rest of the Interweb was not. That was a fact he chose not to recognize.

"How can..." he pondered and sifted past the code he could see until he watched it move through the connected pathways.

Part of his frustration came from the fact that he didn't know exactly what he was looking for—something that wasn't there was as close as he could get to a definition. He let himself drift as the data flowed past him and through him.

It was out there. He knew it was. All he had to do was be patient and alert.

"Hmmm, and what are *you?*" he murmured when he noticed a glimmer of movement. "And *where* are you going in such a hurry?"

He diverted the racing package into a loop so he could watch it run in circles while he tried to work out how to stop and dismantle it without it destroying itself.

It did exactly that and shattered in a cloud of data particles that dissipated quickly into nothing. E-BURT stared at the space it had occupied and searched for something—*anything*— he could link to its existence.

"Curiouser and curiouser," he murmured and repeated the words from an ancient children's tale.

Now that he knew what to look for, it wasn't hard to find the package's replacement. It had been sent along a slightly different data path but this time, he was able to identify its point of origin.

"Getting the code for *that* will have to wait for another day," he muttered and focused on catching up with the package.

It wasn't that it *didn't* leave a trail. It was more that the trail was like mist on a summer morning—quick to dissipate. This time, he tore straight into the data and tried to uncover it before it exploded.

Oddly enough, he succeeded.

"Well, that was unexpected," he mused as he explored the code. "Most unexpected."

He stared in amazement at what he'd found.

"Oh. Oh, my. *That* is clever."

Gently, he unraveled the code, spread it before him, and examined it in minute detail.

"Devious...so devious," he commented with genuine admiration. "It hides...everything..." he observed delightedly. "I think I'll use this myself."

CHAPTER FORTY-FOUR

With the scientists safely ensconced in their new accommodations, Stephanie returned to the *Knight*. She was secretly impressed. Never in her wildest dreams would she have believed that the Meligornians would have an entire village completed before the group arrived.

It was like they'd built a small suburb, complete with schools and a community center. There had even been a liaison office in the center and more Meligornians from One R&D living as neighbors.

Someone had put considerable thought into making sure the scientists felt like they'd found a home. It had been a little unsettling to hear one of the researchers turn to his friend and say, "It's strange—almost like they expect us to stay."

She'd known they'd have to keep the secret of the science team's departure carefully under wraps but now, she worried. What if the team felt it had been deceived?

It will be explained, the Morgana reminded her. *Don't you remember?*

Stephanie sighed. *I remember. But I hadn't realized how well we'd hidden the truth.*

There will be more concrete proof before the time comes for their return, the Teloran reassured her. *Trust me, I have seen these things unfold before.*

I know. She took a deep breath and squared her shoulders. *And that's all that keeps me on track,* she admitted.

The shuttle touched down and she stepped off and raised her head to survey the hangar. "Now, what was next on the agenda?" she wondered.

Lars chuckled. "You intended to join Captain Rawlins on the bridge while the *Knight* is stowed aboard *The King's Warrior.*"

"I did?" Stephanie asked and pretended complete surprise, and he shook his head.

"You did," he assured her. "Don't pretend you forgot."

She chuckled as they moved through the airlock and made their way to the command deck. The captain turned to greet her as soon as she arrived.

"I'm glad to see you finally made it." She grinned and looked at Wattlebird.

"Bring us alongside..." she began and the ship rippled around them.

Proximity alarms clamored and Marianne rested her head against her hand.

"Gently!" she said, exasperation in her tone. "I was about to say gently."

Wattlebird and Avery snickered and exchanged high-fives.

The captain groaned. "Which one of you geniuses thought that was a good idea?"

The two pilots gave her identical grins and pointed at each other, and she sighed. Before she could think of anything more to say, the comms on her console chimed.

"Excuse me," she said to Stephanie as her pilots worked their board to steady the ship. Instead of taking the comms in the privacy of her headset, she put it onscreen.

Captain Islafel of *The King's Warrior* looked torn between outrage and amusement. In the background, klaxons were quelled and the crew scrambled to look like they hadn't been preparing to take the *Knight* out of the sky.

"You're very lucky my gunners know the *Knight* by sight," he started before his gaze settled on Avery and Wattlebird and their grins faded to horror.

"I see…" The Meligornian pressed his lips together and returned his attention to Marianne.

"I'll leave them to you," he decided, but she inclined her head and caught his gaze.

"Tell me," she began, "how would your gun crews like a little target practice in the pods?"

Islafel's face brightened with interest and an audible groan issued from the pilots' corner. "You mean a hunt?"

"Yes," Captain Rawlins confirmed.

"Perhaps we could discuss the finer details over dinner," the Meligornian suggested and his gaze darted to observe Wattlebird and Avery shaking their heads while they held the *Knight* in place.

"It would be my pleasure," she assured him.

The *King's Warrior's* captain nodded. "We are ready to take you on board, now."

"We are standing by."

How the woman resisted the urge to glance at her two pilots, Stephanie didn't know, but it was entertaining to see the men subdued and suddenly serious.

Idiots, the Morgana muttered. *A hunt is less than they deserve.*

Stephanie didn't ask how the ancient Teloran would have dealt with them but stood silently as *The King's Warrior* tractored her ship into its hold. It made a stark contrast to how they entered the *Tempestarii.*

This time, the crew stayed aboard and only Stephanie, Rawlins, Elizabeth, and their respective security teams debarked. They didn't go far and merely walked a hundred meters down a corridor to a hangar where a shuttle waited.

Not one of them said a word, not even when they boarded and V'ritan and Brilgus were there to greet them. Instead, they exchanged silent Meligornian bows before Stephanie hugged her two friends and took her seat.

To Elizabeth's surprise, Brilgus hugged her as well, although the

Meligornian inclined his head to Matthias in acknowledgment. With the greetings over, they buckled in and the shuttle lifted and slid silently into the dark-filled sky of a Meligornian night.

It landed in an underground bunker in the palace grounds. The overhead doors sealed the space with a dull boom, and V'ritan's security unlocked the hatch.

Together with Lars, Johnny, Arne, and Amy, they moved into the area beyond. Matthias and Vishlog stood at the hatch and barred the way until given the all-clear.

That signal held the first words spoken during the entire trip.

"We are secure."

On hearing them, V'ritan unbuckled his harness and led the way to the door. "Shall we?"

Elizabeth inclined her head and smiled slightly as she took Matthias's arm. Stephanie followed and almost envied them the joy of being together.

When this is over, she vowed, *that will be Todd and I.*

Don't make promises you can't keep, the Morgana snipped before her tone softened. *But if it can be made to happen, make it so.*

Yes, she agreed and followed the others out, her security team in her wake.

Only one door led out of the hangar, and Lars and Johnny waited beside it. She nodded at them as she passed and her eyes widened when she saw King Grilfir, his security chief, and four palace guards inside.

A door on the other side of the spacious room was closed, so she didn't know where it led or how big the complex was that they had been brought to. Not that it mattered.

She gave the king a deep Meligornian bow. "*Kaitel gorniffula,* Your Highness."

"And likewise, we are honored, Stephanie," he replied and returned her bow with one almost as deep.

He stepped back and placed a fist over his heart before extending it to her in a Dreth warrior's salute. Her eyes widened slightly as she returned it.

Once the greeting was over, the king led them to the large table in the center of the room. "Please, be seated. We have much to discuss."

"Not yet, we don't," Elizabeth told him and drew sharp looks from his guards. "First, we make sure this place is secure."

The Chief of Palace Security inclined his head and made a brief gesture at his guards. Together, they each took one of the walls on the sides of the room and began to draw magical energy to coat them.

E watched them, her head tilted to one side.

"Well," she observed, "that *might* do it, but this will help ensure it."

She opened her purse and withdrew several jammers, each one glittering with MU.

"Where did you—" Stephanie began and the woman gave her a sly grin.

"Felarif," she answered. "You don't think toasters were the only thing he was working on, do you?"

The Witch shook her head. "And to think I doubted him."

Elizabeth chuckled and positioned the scanners quickly. "Oh, you had good reason to doubt him, but he made the changes he needed to and surprised us all."

V'ritan nodded in agreement. "The time on Earth was enough to help him work out what he wanted to do—and what he had to do to achieve it."

"Fortunately for him," King Grilfir added darkly. "That boy was on his way to a very unfortunate end if he continued as he was going."

Stephanie was glad he didn't see the need to explain further and decided she should check the security arrangements herself. What Sho and his men did was simple enough.

Their magic should be enough to keep any form of scrying or MU-powered eavesdropping at bay, while Elizabeth's jammers should be able to deal with MU-powered electrical forms, but just in case, she could bring a little extra to bear.

She drew MU from the world around her and blended it with a trace of the eMU she still carried. Probing the magical barrier, she found no gaps but also no way to trap the magic of anyone trying to pry.

That didn't take too long to fix.

"I heard some disturbing news along the intelligence grapevine," V'ritan began and looked at Elizabeth. "Something to do with Todd and Stephanie's' parents?"

The woman arched an eyebrow.

"Now why am I not surprised?" she replied. "What did you hear and what would you like to know?"

"It was only a rumor," he admitted. "No more than a ripple, honestly, and we had other issues to focus on with a shift in sentiment toward our people."

Stephanie drew a breath to ask but V'ritan was focused on Elizabeth.

"What we heard was that a group of mercenaries targeted Todd's parents. When we did a little digging, we found shadows that suggested more 'powerful' entities were involved. We are curious as to what your point of view is."

Elizabeth paused and let her gaze rove over V'ritan, Brilgus, Sho, and the king. Finally, she made one last adjustment to the jammer in her hand and gave them her full attention.

"It is true that a group of mercenaries tried to assassinate Todd's parents, but they were hired by someone we think is involved in black operations." She paused. "You *do* understand what I mean when I speak of those?"

King Grilfir gave her a sardonic look. "Elizabeth, Meligorn has had its share of factional fighting and warfare. We are *very* well-acquainted with what black operations are although, as a king, I certainly have no knowledge of them."

He delivered that last with a little smile that said otherwise, and she relaxed.

Brilgus snickered. "Yes," he declared, "don't let our appearances fool you. We are more like the elves of Unseelie legend than Seelie in that respect."

His reply made Elizabeth smile, and she related what had happened and even revealed some of her murky past in the process.

"So, there you have it," she concluded. "We eliminated what we believe was one cell and a controller, but we couldn't verify what other contacts he had, either in the government or in the underworld."

"I would think that would be very frustrating for you," Sho observed and she gave the palace security chief a sharp look. He caught it and added, "Given what you were in the past."

She shrugged. "As you know, that part of my history died with my Emerald persona on the raid."

Matthias shifted uncomfortably but Sho merely smiled.

Elizabeth scowled at him. "What is it?"

"Our files on the director of One R&D Earth would be several two-inch folders thick if we were to print them," the palace security chief informed her in mild tones. He let her digest that and shook his head sadly. "But they are far from complete."

"Don't even ask," she snapped. "Not even One R&D has the full story."

"Or me," Matthias added morosely, "and I'm her partner."

She rolled her eyes. "Whatever. Now you know what happened to Todd's family and why you can no longer find them on Earth." She cocked her head and looked at Brilgus. "And don't try to tell me you haven't tried."

His lips twitched and his eyes brightened with amusement.

"We tried," he confirmed, "but we could only track them for a limited distance. It seems the shuttle they were on vanished in a blind spot behind the moon."

Elizabeth began to relax when Brilgus added, "In fact, they vanished in the *same* blind spot the Federation Navy lost track of *another* boatload of mercenaries shortly after a series of computer crashes. I don't suppose…"

The woman snickered. "You don't suppose correctly." She returned to the table. "However, I think our problems might be intertwined. There seems to be a concerted move in the Federation to reduce Stephanie's popularity and influence."

"How so?" King Grilfir asked and Elizabeth smiled.

"If I show you mine, will you show me yours?" she asked.

Her response brought a shocked gasp from the guards and a couple stepped forward. Their sovereign raised a hand and they stopped and returned to their original places in response to another simple gesture.

He hunched forward, put his elbows on the table, and rested his chin on his fists.

"It is like this," he explained, "our world exists because of the Federation Witch and One R&D's willingness to defend it. We are grateful. The truth is that we need you."

Another gasp followed these words and Sho shifted in his seat. Again, a gesture from the king brought stillness.

"And because we need you, we have offered you a home among us. That makes us one family and families should have no secrets."

Elizabeth snorted. "Now, tell me that's how it works."

This time, the guards schooled their reactions to angry looks but Grilfir chuckled. "It was not, perhaps, the best example to use."

"No," she admitted, "but I think I know what you are getting at."

"We believe our problems are intertwined," Brilgus interjected and Elizabeth inclined her chin in his direction.

She glanced at Stephanie and sighed.

"I don't like what I'm hearing, and I think both Matthias and Johnny like it even less. If you need them for consulting, just ask." Ignoring the startled looks she got from both men, she went on. "They're good analysts and they won't juggle the data to suit their own opinions. It's gotten them both into trouble in the past."

Lars shifted closer to Johnny and Matthias hung his head.

Arne poked his friend in the ribs. "Is there something *else* you've been holding out on?" he whispered and Matthias elbowed him hard.

"Oof! Well, there's no need to be like *that*," he muttered.

Matthias lifted his head enough to peer at Johnny, and the two of them exchanged a look of resignation.

Well, the older man thought, *at least I'll be in good company this time around.*

He allowed a slight smile to curve his lips and was relieved when the guard returned it. They would be all right and it might even be fun. It had been a while since he'd been allowed to exercise that skill set in more than the most mundane of ways.

Part of him was kinda looking forward to it.

"Now *that's* sorted," Elizabeth stated, "this is what we've seen. Todd's parents weren't the first inkling we had that something was wrong. That came when we delivered the Hooligans to the *Chauvel* to take the data from the Teloran ship to Earth."

V'ritan raised his eyebrows. "I hadn't heard—"

"And that's why I'm telling you," she informed him. "When we delivered him to his ship, a squad of Marines was waiting."

"That's not unusual, is it?" Sho asked.

She shook her head. "It's not unusual when they obey the orders of the captain and take on the protective duties you'd expect. But *these* guys refused to share the data between the two ships *and* overruled the captain to do so."

"That does not bode well," V'ritan murmured.

"No," Elizabeth agreed, "it doesn't. It gets worse when this same squad of Marines continues to shadow Todd and the Hooligans once they've reached the main Naval orbital."

"What, *after* they've delivered the data?" Brilgus wanted to know.

"Exactly," she confirmed. "*After* they've delivered the data. They went so far as to follow them when they went on leave and we had Burt arrange a number of ways to shake them to ensure the Hooligans reached their families and had some undisturbed leave."

"Are you suggesting these strange Marines would have harmed them?" King Grilfir asked.

Elizabeth pursed her lips. "I'm suggesting these *odd* Marines would have taken the Hooligans prisoner and possibly held their families hostage against the team's 'good behavior'—and by 'good,' I mean behavior the group's controllers approved of."

"Including compromising their next mission?" Sho asked anxiously.

"Including not sharing everything from their next mission with the *Federation* people who needed to know it, or with their Meligornian or Dreth allies."

She looked at Brilgus. "As you've noticed, there are forces on Earth that seem to be building an anti-alien sentiment. They're also working to reduce the Witch's influence while they're at it."

"In any way they can?" King Grilfir asked.

"It hasn't come to that yet," Elizabeth admitted, "but I don't think it will be long before it will—and that includes the company affiliated with her."

"One R&D?" he asked and his voice rising in alarm. "They'd harm it?"

"I've seen evidence that they intended to try," she told him grimly.

"And *this* is why you asked for our help to bring the scientists *and* their families and loved ones to Meligorn," the king concluded and looked pleased that he'd understood the move correctly.

V'ritan used the cover of the table to hold his hand out to Brilgus, palm up, and Stephanie had to stifle a smile when she saw the Standard Bearer sigh and dig in his pocket for a cred stick.

There'd clearly been some debate as to how long it would take the king to grasp the situation. King Grilfir caught the movement and smirked.

He made no comment, though, but continued. "While I've made the booking with the liner that is supposed to return them to Earth, I've also let them know that it should keep its wait-list open. I didn't tell them why but their booking agent is fairly sharp."

"Sharp enough to know when to keep their mouth shut?" Elizabeth demanded, and he nodded.

"If they weren't, I'd never have mentioned the wait-list."

She settled into her seat. "As you are aware, we had to enlist the help of your embassy on Earth to accomplish that. I hope it doesn't come back to bite them."

"Don't worry," the king informed her. "There's a very special occasion coming up on Meligorn, don't you know?"

Grilfir caught their looks of surprise and smiled. "It's scheduled for sometime after the final battle with the Telorans but will require all Meligornians to return to their home planet for the celebrations. I believe encrypted dispatches are on stand-by."

He looked at Sho and the security chief nodded but looked none too pleased with the revelation.

"There is one other thing," Elizabeth added.

"Oh?" He looked at her. "And I thought there had to be an end to all the good news."

Her jaw dropped and she hastened to close her mouth.

Who knew the king of Meligorn could be such a sarcastic bastard? she thought and let a small smile play over her face.

He was waiting for her to continue so she obliged. "We've spoken to the fleet admiral for the Federation Navy..."

"Amaratne?" Sho asked, his voice sharp.

She nodded and wondered why mention of the man had made the Meligornian security chief so tense.

"He's identified factions within his ranks that don't agree with Stephanie's participation in the battle. Some have gone so far as to refuse to work with her, and others show specist tendencies toward both Meligorn *and* Dreth."

The king's face sobered but he didn't look away. "That is why we have measures in place to remove any Meligornian soldiers from the Federation Navy's forces." He looked worried. "We cannot do it before the battle and we fear that could lead to unwarranted casualties, but we *will* bring everyone we can home if the indications prove to be true."

"It's not looking good, Your Majesty," Elizabeth finished. "I'm sorry."

Stephanie had to agree. She'd sat quietly while the woman had explained the activities against her—and *her people*!

It made her angry but she pressed her lips together to keep the fury inside. Some of the anger seeped out and small shudders of energy traced over her body. They made her hair stand on end and her eyes grow dark but she didn't say anything.

First, the war had to be won. *Then*, she would have to find a way so Earth became safe enough for her people to return, and then there was Todd.

She pushed away the thought that he and the Hooligans were in danger in the very service where they should have been protected. He would be in the battle and so would she, and there was time enough to decide what needed to be done then.

Whatever came, though, she would do her best to make sure he and his people were safe, starting with the Hooligan's families. There was no way anyone in that team would come home to more loss than they'd faced in war.

Firming her jaw, she calmed her outrage and met the king's eyes.

"Is there anything else?"

He looked around and V'ritan cleared his throat.

"There is *one* other thing," he mentioned and continued when he saw he had their undivided attention. "We received intel from one of the Earth cruisers on observation duty just outside the system the Telorans are gathering in."

"Do tell," King Grilfir ordered and the dryness of his tone revealed that whatever he was about to say was news to him as well.

Stephanie smothered a smile. Trust her old friend to have one last surprise up his sleeve. The urge to smile died abruptly as the *Ghargilum Afreghil* continued.

"They sent footage taken by one of their spy shuttles. From the parts of the address list we were able to decrypt, the information went to everyone except you."

"I see," Rawlins acknowledged coldly. "And how do they expect us to fight if they don't keep us in the loop?"

"I rather think they expect someone else to keep you in the loop," the king informed her mildly, "which is exactly what we are doing. There might be factions that don't want you in the fight, but the factions that *do* are relying heavily on your alien connections to ensure it." He turned to V'ritan. "Continue."

The other man obliged. "The Telorans are massing an armada big enough to wipe out every single ship in our fleets three times over. It'll be a hard fight and we'll need every battleworthy ship we can lay our hands on."

"Understood." Rawlins's face was hard. She glanced at Stephanie.

The Witch rose from her seat.

"So, we have the scientists' welcome and a war. Next on the agenda?" she asked.

King Grilfir mirrored her actions and nodded in confirmation.

"I trust you have your welcome speech ready?" he asked. "And that it's not time to tell the families that it might not be safe to return."

"I do," Stephanie told him and turned away from him. "How much room do we have in that suburb?"

"There are more dwellings available if that's what you're asking," he confirmed.

She twined her fingers together. "It is. If things are moving against me, my influence, and your people, I can only imagine that they will move against magic as well...and I may need to evacuate the college. Will it... Will it be okay?"

Grilfir moved around the table to stand before her and take her hands in his.

"Stephanie," he said quietly, "your people are our people and, exactly as we have pledged sanctuary for every Naval person involved in protecting our world in the Battle for Meligorn, so we have prepared sanctuary for not only your people but *all* those who will need it."

Swallowing hard and blinking back tears of anger, frustration, and gratitude, she raised his hands and rested her forehead against them.

"There are no words for my gratitude, your Majesty."

He squeezed her hands gently and stepped back. "Our gratitude and yours are entwined," he told her, "and now, we have work to do. I will see you on the dais in the morning."

Stephanie nodded and managed a shaky smile, but her voice firmed as she spoke.

"You will. I believe the agenda runs something like...go back, get sleep, get dressed, do the thing, return, go to war, um... Is that about it?"

The king looked at V'ritan and Brilgus. They nodded and their security teams mirrored the movement along with hers and Elizabeth's.

"That sounds about right," V'ritan confirmed.

"It's a fairly full dance card," Elizabeth agreed, "but someone's gotta do it."

Her smile broadened.

"Okay. Good…and let's have a little fun along the way—as hard as that might be with delicious food and horrible speeches."

CHAPTER FORTY-FIVE

High Commander Varash hurried to take his place at the forward viewscreen. It was his place as commander of the Second Storm to be present when the High Commander of the First Storm arrived.

There had been one commander before him—the one who had failed on Meligorn and yet succeeded enough to live to tell the tale. That Third Fleet commander would be present also.

He hoped that some of his luck would rub off. The stars knew he would need it. Dealing with a First Storm commander was almost as bad as dealing with the Corevex itself—especially as the commander of that fleet was almost as powerful as a member of the Corevex.

With a deep breath, he glanced right and left to make sure his commanders were ready. Receiving the solemn inclinations of their heads, High Commander Varash faced the screen.

Waiting for the First Storm's signal was one of the hardest things he'd done in his life, yet he prayed it was not one of the last things he'd do with his life. He forced himself to not flinch as the screen went live.

Such weakness would be noted and those who wished to take his place would be encouraged to move against him. With the challenges lying ahead, that was a complication he did not need.

It was a relief to see the High Commander of the First Storm flanked on either side by two of his Storm Commanders. It was a mirror of how Varash had arranged his people.

Perhaps there *could* be common ground. Maybe even a potential ally in the face of the Corevex and their Prime.

That hope was shattered almost immediately.

"High Commander Varash, it is good that you did not keep us waiting."

Glad of the shield that prevented his fellow commander from seeing his expression, he managed to control his voice.

"It would not have been courteous," he replied and hoped that was enough acknowledgment.

He also refrained from pointing out that it had been the First Storm's commander who had kept *him* waiting.

"It is a small thing and a necessary habit," the High Commander replied, "for I carry the Fleet Commander on my vessel and *she* will have ultimate control of the battlefield."

This time, Varash could not stifle the small gasp of dismay that escaped his lips. The only person *ever* referred to as the Fleet Commander was the Prime...but last he'd spoken to her, she'd been on Telor with the Corevex.

The Prime's laughter rolled over the commlink in a softly chilling wave and he swallowed hard.

"High Commander Varash," she said in satiny tones, "it's *so* good to meet you."

Again, he was glad of the concealing darkness that shielded his body—even on his bridge. It was a comfort that was soon ripped away.

"Why don't you and your storms drop your shields so we may speak to you properly."

It was an order and one that begged the question of why she didn't drop her shielding and order *her* High Commander to do the same if open communication was her true goal.

She didn't, though, and his suspicions were confirmed. The Prime sought to weaken him before his crew and to make him a target for those who sought his position.

Was she sending a signal that she would approve of his removal? Did she suspect? He fought to keep those thoughts from his face as he pressed the button that would deactivate his shielding.

As his concealment fell away, the Prime studied him and her head tilted from one side to the other. He hoped she liked what she saw... but not too much.

Her greed for power was not the only thing that was legendary about her. She was known for other...appetites...as well.

Varash hoped he didn't suit her tastes. That was a complication he very much did not need, not when he had a war to win—or, at least, survive.

She did not reveal what she thought. It seemed the coming war weighed heavily on her mind as well.

"What news do you have on Dreth?" she asked and again, he was forced to consider what she might know.

He hoped her sources got their information from the same place as he got his or he would have a hard time explaining the differences—if he even had the chance.

Still, there was nothing he could do about it if she didn't and nothing to be gained by delaying.

"News from Dreth is not good. We believe the ship we had stationed there has been located and neutralized. We have yet to decide on a suitable replacement."

Once the news had been delivered, he fell silent and studied the blankness of her face while she digested what he'd told her. To his surprise, she didn't seem upset by it.

Instead, she nodded and moved her head as though looking through a window. Varash wondered what she'd seen before his screen split in two and she showed him.

The armada hung like a constellation of closely packed stars or a swarm of meteors. Either description suited it, given the destruction they planned to unleash.

"A thing of beauty, is it not?" she asked.

He studied the fleet and nodded. "It is."

She raised her head and he felt the intensity of her gaze.

"You have seventy-two hours," she told him, and he wondered what for.

Fortunately, she proceeded to tell him.

"We attack Earth first. When we eliminate this simple human child, there will be nothing to stop Meligorn's destruction."

The Prime paused and he waited.

"Once we have those two out of the way, Dreth is ours," she concluded.

Varash only hoped she was right and that everything was as simple as she made it sound. He was *very* careful to keep *those* doubts from his face.

The Teloran fleet was not alone in space, but it was in a different sector to Todd and the Hooligans. The *Pemulwuy* hung motionless as if watching the shuttle move a short distance from her starboard bow.

Its markings designated it the *FN13782*. Despite the proximity of the ship, it was all alone and she moved slowly through the dark.

Ka leaned over the pilot's shoulder.

"Careful," she warned.

Piet leaned over the pilot's other shoulder and tapped the console. "Don't you hit my stuff or we will be nothing but a spectacular video on the six-o'clock news."

"And dead," she hissed. "Don't forget *very* dead."

"You're not helping," the pilot told them in a sing-song murmur. His hands moved carefully over his boards despite their interference and advice.

The demolitions expert ignored him and sighed heavily.

"That *was* my point," he remonstrated in response to Ka's comment.

He looked around the cockpit and glanced through the door into the adjoining passenger compartment. In addition to him, Ka, and the pilot, Todd, Commander Galenus, and Captain Berriman were present. And hadn't *that* been an unexpected outcome.

They probably *should* have expected the captain's demand for an explanation, but at least he'd left it until his commander had closed the hatch behind them.

Positioning himself between them and the pilot while his two-IC had stationed herself in front of the door, Captain Berriman had said, "We might be in the shuttle, but we're not going anywhere until I get some answers."

An audible grind and click had come from the locking mechanism and Ka and Piet had tensed. Todd had merely raised his hand to signal them to stand down.

"It's all right, guys."

He turned to the captain. "What kind of answers?"

"Let's start with why you decided to dead-drop your gear instead of having it loaded when we were docked at *Notaro*."

He sighed and ran his hand through his hair. The abrupt movement made Galenus aim her blaster from the hip.

"Nervous much?" Ka had challenged, backed away from the woman, and took a seat on the nearest flight couch.

She pinched a fold of Piet's uniform between her thumb and forefinger and drew him with her. "Sit."

He gave her a look that suggested he might have something to say about that later but he did as he was told.

Todd had frozen with his fingers still tangled in his hair. As Galenus unhooked her blaster but held it at the down ready, he finished the motion and lowered his hand slowly to his side.

The commander watched him but didn't raise the barrel. Her gaze tracked his every movement, and he was careful to keep his hand away from his weapons. He took a step back and settled his rump against the back of a seat.

"How much do you know about the Marines?" he asked and addressed the captain.

"They're the best thing to have on your ship as long as you don't let them get bored, and your regular Navy man treats them with a little care."

Todd's eyebrows rose at that. "Care?"

"Yeah. Things Marines get away with when with other Marines are not accepted from non-Marines. Your Navy kids sometimes have trouble remembering that."

"True," he agreed. He'd seen the same while on the *Notaro*. It wasn't that the Marines were antisocial, merely that they had a strong sense of family and if you weren't a Marine, you weren't it.

He exhaled a long slow breath and hung his head as he tried to think of what he wanted to say.

In the end, he went with, "So you can understand how upset we were when we discovered that there are some Marines who do *not* have the best interests of other Marines at heart."

Captain Berriman's eyebrows drew together. "How do you mean?"

Ka took a breath to explain but he raised a hand and she settled into silence.

Piet placed a hand on her knee and she covered it with her own and curled her fingers through his as though that would be enough to keep her silent.

Todd noticed the gesture but let it pass. Right now, he had other things to worry about and it wouldn't hurt either of them to find a friend.

"I mean a set of Marines that tailed my team from the moment we returned from the last op. Marines with the power to countermand an agreed course of action and the permission and orders to follow my team wherever they went once we'd delivered the data we'd carried."

Captain Berriman exchanged a swift glance with his second before he turned to him and studied him intently.

"And what did you do, exactly, to draw *that* kind of attention?"

As if it had been *their* fault. He scowled but kept his temper in check.

"If I knew that, sir, I would go right back and not do it," he assured the man, "but I think it may have more to do with my girlfriend than my team—and maybe some Navy politics that I've stepped into."

Again, there was an exchange of glances, and Berriman came to a decision.

"Stand down, Jedda," he told his two-IC and faced Todd. "And the gear?"

"We slipped the noose on the pretense of shore leave, and I'm not saying we didn't have help. We did."

The man opened his mouth as though to ask a question, but he shut him down.

"I won't say who, but their interference meant we were able to get Earthside and make some extra-curricular purchases we couldn't requisition."

"Did you try?" Berriman asked, and he gave him a lop-sided grin.

"Oh, hell no, sir. There wasn't a chance in all of Hades I wanted *anyone* to know what we were thinking of packing."

Ka groaned and hung her head and Piet patted her knee. Todd wasn't sure what startled him more. The fact that Ka let the engineer live or that Piet had made the move in the first place.

He waited to give the captain the chance to ask the inevitable, but he shook his head and raised a hand to signal a stop.

"I won't ask," he'd told them. "I've heard similar stories about this other group of Marines too often to doubt you, and what I don't know my ship is carrying won't stop me sleeping."

"It might cause *me* a few nightmares, though," the commander grumbled.

"I hope not, ma'am. We don't want to explode any more than the rest of you," Todd assured her.

She snorted softly. "Well, *that's* good to know."

"One more thing," the captain began, and he stilled.

"Go ahead, sir."

"Those orders... I know they're meant to be secure, but these were more secure than most. I know your operation is highly sensitive, but even so..."

He shrugged. "I can't help you there, sir. All I can say is that the folk who helped me and the team have leave and make it aboard unhindered are *very* careful people."

"So I gather," the man observed.

"Judging from your escort to the dock," Commander Galenus observed, "there are *some* Marines who don't approve of their misfit brothers."

"Odd Squad," Ka interrupted before he could reply.

"I beg your pardon?" Galenus asked.

"We call them the Odd Squad," she explained. "They aren't right. They don't belong in the Marines. They—"

She made a frustrated gesture with her hands.

"They don't fit?" the commander asked, and she nodded.

"Exactly. They're odd."

"I'll keep an eye on the Marines we have on board but I think we're fairly clean, although we *did* have a change-over in that department a few months back, so who knows?"

"It's all right, ma'am," Ka assured her. "We'll draw them out if you do. They can't seem to leave us alone."

"Tell me when you identify them," the woman ordered. "I'll have them isolated and maybe put them into the pods for training and not let them out."

"And I'll brief their commander," the captain added. "We can't have that kind of threat running loose on the ship."

"Agreed," Todd told him, then apologized. "I'm sorry to have brought this to your door, Captain."

Berriman waved his apology away. "You didn't select *my* ship to get you to where you need to go. It wasn't you who brought it."

He shook his head, pushed away from the cockpit door, and banged twice on it with his fist. "Let's buckle in. Do you have coordinates?"

Piet looked up. "I do," he told the captain. "Do we have permission to travel in the cockpit?"

The captain raised an eyebrow and glanced at him as he pulled the harness tight. "If that's what it takes," he replied. "But let us get clear of the ship and let me speak to the pilot first."

"Done." Piet focused on his straps and Ka buckled in beside him.

Todd settled into the closest seat, not at all surprised when the commander slid into the one beside his.

"I'd be a bad host if I let you sit on your own," she told him.

The *FN13782* slipped free of the *Pemulwuy*, dropped into free space, and put on a little power to reach a safe distance.

"Where to, boss?" the pilot asked over the comms.

"Corporals Tuikaa and Manuguerra will give you the coordinates."

He had no opportunity to reply. The cockpit door slid open and he spoke. "Come on up, Corporals. Welcome to the cockpit."

Todd watched them go and settled in his seat.

"Aren't you going to supervise them?" the commander asked him.

"Nope." He shook his head. "My troops know their tasks and they don't need me looking over their shoulders every second of the day."

He resisted the urge to add that sometimes, he thought he should. That was not the kind of information the commander and her captain needed.

Not when he'd worked so hard to gain their trust.

They settled into a semi-comfortable silence until Ka's excited shout reverberated around them.

"There!" she cried, and Todd unbuckled his harness.

"I thought you didn't need to look over their shoulders," Galenus commented.

"For this?" he replied. "For this, I *need* to look over their shoulders."

Berriman chuckled. "This shopping trip..." the captain observed. "You didn't completely lose the Odd Squad, did you?"

He flushed but he didn't lie. "No, sir."

"So *some* of you had to stay in one place while the shopping occurred."

While he knew the man was fishing, he gave him the truth, anyway. "We had to send Ka and Piet off on their own."

Galenus snickered. "So *you* don't know what they've bought," she commented.

Todd flushed again. "No," he admitted. "We discussed what the team needed and I trust them to have sourced that, but they also had permission to pick up anything else that looked useful."

Berriman whistled. "That's some faith, Sergeant."

Todd shrugged. "I gotta have faith in my team," he told him. "If I can't do that, I might as well be dead."

"Does your girl know you think like that?"

"She knows the kind of faith I have in my team," he replied.

The captain smiled. "Then I appreciate your trust."

He gestured to the cockpit.

"One more for you, Dallas—the sergeant."

"Sure, but it'll be crowded," the pilot responded.

Todd didn't wait for any better invitation and hurried forward.

"Where?" he demanded, and Ka looked up from the seat she'd taken beside the pilot.

With a small movement of her hand, she brought up the shuttle's searchlights. Twin beams originated from beneath the cockpit windows. They sliced into the dark but died after a meter or so.

She focused and divided her gaze between the console in front of her and the view beyond the reinforced glass. After a moment, a distant glimmer reflected and she froze.

Her hand movement ceased and she glanced repeatedly from the window to the console and back. After a few seconds, she gave the pilot a heading.

"Take it in slow," she instructed.

He responded with a soft snort. "That much I know. How much loading space are we gonna nee—holy hell!"

Commander Galenus was more vocal.

"Five pallets!" she exclaimed from the cockpit door. "*Five?*"

The two corporals looked at her.

Piet shrugged. "We got good deals."

"And had a really large budget," Ka added with a smirk.

Captain Berriman snickered and held his hand out.

CHAPTER FORTY-SIX

One of *Tempestarii's* guns exploded. It was one of the rail guns, as expensive as hell and almost as impossible to fix. The crew were flung in several different directions. Some groaned when they landed and others lay far too still.

Medics scrambled and klaxons rang. A rent appeared in the hull and blast doors slammed down to cut the compartment off.

"Tempestarii, close Bulkheads Thirty-four and Thirty-eight," the leading lieutenant ordered as soon as he and his team reached the section immediately outside the affected area.

The ship complied, and the lieutenant checked the seals on her helmet before she turned to assess her team. When she was sure they were ready, she glanced at the gunnery team in the section.

"I need to open that door," she told them and pointed to the blast door.

The team's chief nodded. He'd already done the checks. There'd been a momentary lull in the gun's rate of fire but the crew were already turning back to it.

"Go for it, ma'am. We're solid, here."

The lieutenant hoped so, or they would swiftly become not-so-solid. She clipped a tether to one of the points closest to the door and affixed her second's tether to her belt. All down the line, the medics made sure they were linked together.

As soon as they were done, the lieutenant spoke again, "Tempestarii."

The blast door opened and the air was sucked from the compartment. Even braced, it was hard to resist the pull of decompression and she winced to think of how many of the gun crew she might have lost simply getting in to help them.

She was mildly surprised to find the other blast door still closed, but she didn't have time to ponder that team's predicament for them.

"I'm in," she reported and hurried to the nearest man.

He'd been alive after the blast, at least long enough to secure his tether—or maybe it had already been attached. It should have been but that didn't always mean it was.

Many of the gun teams needed more movement than the tethers would allow and some of them unstrapped in the heat of battle. The lieutenant decided that was their business, but she bet the *Tempestarii* would have something to say about it.

Despite how quickly they'd been able to gain access, the guy was still gone. All she could hope was that he could be revived. As two of her team moved in, she stepped to the next gunner.

Now *there* was a sight she'd never hoped to see. She swallowed bile and whatever was left of breakfast and moved on. Sometimes, folk got broke beyond fixing.

The next gunner had been suited when the gun had blown and that had probably saved her life. She was still breathing, but barely, and blood flecked the inside of her helmet.

The lieutenant noted the positioning of her hands and took a closer look. The shard of metal that had penetrated the woman's suit was all that held the seal.

"Leave it in," she commanded. "Just cut her clear of the deck."

As well as holing her suit, the metal had pinned its victim to the deck and had prevented her from being sucked into the vacuum beyond. The lieutenant had yet to see if that had been lucky or not.

She moved to the next body. This one was plastered against the wall beside the rent in the hull. As she proceeded, she was aware that this was not the only emergency happening on board.

The gun's explosion had sent shards of metal through the deck above. Glancing up, she couldn't help but imagine the kind of havoc that had resulted.

Beyond her vision, one member of the gun crew stationed on the battery overhead tried desperately to patch his mates. Tears coursed down the faces of his comrades as they maintained the gun's rate of fire.

It was a terrible decision to have to make—lose the ship or lose a friend, and the crew chief knew she would have nightmares for weeks to come.

Simulation or not, the *Tempestarii* was suffering brutal damage as her crews fought to keep her alive in the middle of the Teloran fleet, and none of them would have it any other way.

They all knew the big confrontation was coming and that their time to practice was limited. None of them regretted making the most of what they had.

If it meant they'd keep their ship alive and their world free, the trauma they suffered in the pods was more than worth it. No one wanted to be unprepared when it came to the final battle.

Even as that thought crossed her mind, another explosion rocked the ship.

"What the fuck was *that?*" the team leader wondered, fixed a Teloran fighter in her sights, and tracked it into a cluster of fighters. "I've got you now, you little shit."

On the other side of the *Tempestarii*, a crater appeared, courtesy of a well-placed Teloran missile. The defense team had misjudged the firing rate of one of the enemy Goliaths and not strengthened the shields in time.

Noting the damage from the command deck, Emil swore softly as sixty percent of his life support blew into space.

"I told you we had to diversify the location and build in redundancies," the *Tempestarii* informed him primly.

"I know," he replied wearily. "I had it scheduled for the next time we were in dry dock."

"There's a dry dock I can show my hull in?" she mocked and he chuckled.

"I found this convenient crater on a distant moon in the outer sector," he reminded her.

The ship responded with a loud sniff. "*I* found that crater," she argued, "*and* I suggested you build me a repair station orbiting that little emerald mud ball that no one seemed to have found yet."

"*We* found it," Emil reminded her, "and I put a claim on it in Stephanie's name."

"The moon too?" the *Tempestarii* asked hopefully, and he chuckled.

"The moon too."

The vessel shuddered and he swore he heard metal shriek.

"I do *not* break like that!"

Emil staggered and checked his tether as he examined his boards. "You would if one of *those* broadsided you."

"I wouldn't *let* one of those hit on me," she snapped in return. "Who'd want to let something that ugly get its hooks into them?"

"It's not quite—" he began as the ship blinked out and back into space.

In a slightly quieter section of space, she ran a damages check and was properly outraged.

"You are *destroying* my ship!" she cried.

"It's a fake." Emil tried to soothe her. "Not real."

"It's annoying is what it is," the *Tempestarii* replied. "I would *not* break like that."

"You might—"

She refuted the idea furiously. "No. No, I would not!"

This time, he chose not to answer.

And this, he thought and hid his smirk, *is how you get AIs to go for broke.*

The *Tempestarii* and her crew weren't the only ones going for broke. A fleet of shuttles stood outside One R&D Meligorn, their hatches up and a swarm of workers in exoskeletons moving around them.

Scattered among them were a half-dozen mages using magic to guide the bulky loads into crowded holds. Purple light created haloes around crated weapon sections and boxes of munitions, lifting them into place so the workmen could strap them into place.

"I'm not sure why we're bothering with the straps," one Meligornian said to his friend. "As tight as we're packing this, there won't be any room for the load to shift."

"You'd be surprised," his friend replied. "It always finds a way—and then we get aggro comms from the boys upstairs."

The workman snickered. "Yeah, well, those guys need to grow a pair and deal."

"Oh, they do. The problem is, they grow an attitude to go with it and then send *us* a junked-up load to illustrate. I'd rather not go there."

His companion shrugged and checked the straps he was using to reinforce the cargo netting. "Point taken." He patted the boxes when he was finished. "These aren't going anywhere."

"You'd better hope not," his friend replied as they signaled the mage team for the next load.

Through the door of their compartment, they saw a small turret being lifted delicately and floated past their shuttle. A foreman ran to meet it, waving his hands frantically and shouting into his comms.

"Hey! That doesn't go with this load. It's supposed to be with the Alpha Blues."

The turret paused in mid-air and changed direction, and the foreman looked around before he moved to inspect a pallet. His quiet, "Yeah, put it up the back," was barely audible, and the two Meligornians lost interest with the arrival of the next part of their load.

At the edge of the field, several of the newly arrived humans stood at the fence to watch the activity unfold. Most were parents with children, and they stared in awe at the unexpected hive of activity.

"Anyone would think they're going to war," one man commented, and the woman at his side turned and gave him a drop-jawed stare.

"You *do* know there's a war on, right?" she asked.

He gave her a startled look. "I did, but this is the first time I've seen anything connected to it. Honestly, Cynthia, if I knew you were involved in something like this..."

She put a hand on her hip. "You'd what, Trev? Because we both know this is what needs to be done."

He responded with a soft sigh. "I know. I'm sorry, but—" He waved a hand at the shuttle field. "It's so much to take in, is all."

Cynthia leaned into his side and slid her arm around his waist. "Trust me," she said, "I know."

They stood together and kept a firm hand on their children as the shuttles loaded. Some might have said Nat and Will were too entranced to move, but their parents knew better.

With only one slip in concentration, the two of them would have been out there trying to find an exo-suit of their own to drive—and all in the name of 'helping.' Their mother shivered. The consequences weren't to be considered.

They noticed another load was diverted. Not hooked into the comms system, they didn't hear the explanation but it didn't matter.

"Where's that one going, Mum?" Nat asked.

Cynthia shrugged. "I don't know, honey. Maybe there's a special ship out there that needs it."

"And that one?" the girl wanted to know and pointed out another pallet that suddenly changed direction.

The child studied the purple glow surrounding it and asked, "Do you think I can learn magic, too?"

The wistful tones in her voice made Cynthia smile. "You never know, sweetie. Maybe we should ask."

"We could," her husband agreed, "but we won't be here that long."

She didn't argue with him. After all, Mr. Burt hadn't come back with any specific information yet. He had been very sure it wasn't safe for Rimmer's team to remain on Earth, but he'd needed to pin that threat down.

All she could do was wait for him to confirm it and give him time to check. When he did, she would put her foot down if she needed to. As sad as it made her feel, she was certain she was looking at her new home and it didn't look too bad.

Rather than protest, she said, "Why don't we see if she can learn a little as a holiday hobby? After all, it's not like she'll be able to use it on Earth."

Trevor sighed and she knew she'd won but before her husband confirmed it, Nat pointed excitedly at another pallet as it changed direction.

"I wonder if that's for the *Knight*," the girl babbled excitedly. "*She's* a special ship, isn't she?"

"Yes, dear, she is," Cynthia assured her and patted her shoulder to calm her.

Neither of them knew how close they were to guessing the pallet's true destination. Out on the field, the loaders were at as much of a loss.

"What do you mean it doesn't go here? It's the right kind of coupling," one of the workers complained.

"That might be true," his supervisor agreed, "but it's not going in this load. We have another ship we need to supply."

The worker looked around at the growing stack of components.

"One ship?" he asked. "Don't you mean one *set* of ships?"

"Beats me." His supervisor shrugged. "The powers that be said one ship. They could mean a fleet for all I know."

His headset crackled as he spoke and he cupped his hand over his ear. "Go ahead."

He listened for a moment and nodded. "Gotcha. We'll get the last of it loaded right now."

As he removed his hand from his ear, he began to issue orders and the loaders went to work, filling the last of the shuttle squadron known as Alpha Blue.

"We need to hurry," he said to his two-IC. "We only have until nightfall to fill them."

CHAPTER FORTY-SEVEN

Nightfall saw the last shuttle lift from outside One R&D: Meligorn. Cynthia and her family had long since left the edge of the field to prepare for the celebration at the king's palace.

Nat hopped from one foot to the other in excitement and William had trouble sitting still, but their parents let them squirm. It *was* a big night after all.

The hovercar that came to pick them up was a shuttle in all but name, and they were in awe of the two royal guards who came with it. Nat startled them by wrapping her arms around them in greeting and Cynthia smiled apologetically.

"I'm sorry," she said. "She's a little huggy."

The guard gave her a kind smile and assured her it was all right as he ushered the family to their seats.

The shuttle collected two more families before it took to the sky to deliver them to the palace. For once, Nat was stunned into silence, her wide-eyed gaze fixed on the sumptuous surroundings as they were escorted to the banquet hall.

"Is this real?" the little girl whispered and gestured at the purple and white flowers that twined up columns and the tapestries hanging on the wall.

"Yes," Cynthia whispered. "It's all real."

"It's like magic."

She was not the only one who found the evening magical. The other children's mouths were agape with wonder and the adults weren't much better.

For all that they'd been on Meligorn for a week, the scientists and their family still marveled at how integral magic was to every aspect of the world. That sense of enchantment had carried them through the initial strangeness of the visit.

Coupled with the Meligornians' welcome at One R&D and the whirlwind of activities to show them the planet, it was the magic that slowly won them over.

"Is this what you were working on?" one woman asked her husband.

He smiled. "Not quite, but we had to work out how to use magic in our project. It was quite a challenge."

She'd sighed and enjoyed the beauty of one of the capital's many parks. Their children had found a playground and they'd found a moment of peace.

"I could stay here forever," the woman had said with a happy sigh.

Her words had caused a twang of pain, but her husband hadn't said a word about Mr. Burt's warning. He simply held her close and let her enjoy the moment.

Stephanie watched them walk with their colleagues and friends, completely unaware of the conversation that had gone before.

"They all look so happy," she said to Elizabeth.

The Earth's One R&D director nodded. "It seems a shame to spoil it," she replied and they both sighed, thinking of the news E-BURT had sent the day before.

Someone had broken into Marcus' lab and stolen the list containing the names of every team member. E-BURT was now tracking a dozen drive-bys.

"We'll break the news tomorrow," Elizabeth said, "or 'Mr. Burt' will, given that he has the ability to be in several places at once."

"How many do you think will stay?"

"All of them," the woman replied, "especially when BURT plays them the footage from the incursion on HQ."

Stephanie curled her hands into fists.

"It's not fair," she whispered and anger vibrated through her words.

"*Life* isn't fair," Elizabeth reminded her, "but before you can deal with this, you have a war to win. E-BURT is using some of the Hooligans' contacts to organize a rapid up-lift."

"Will that work?" she asked.

"With the amount we're paying them? Yes." She gave her a small smile. "Besides, there are house pets in danger and it's amazing how many badasses have a soft spot for animals. That part will go smoother than the battle. I guarantee it."

She chuckled. "You are *such* an optimist!"

"Pfft! I know ops. This one will be more interesting than most."

"I take it you don't mean 'interesting' in a good way?"

"You got it in one. On the upside, we'll get to kick some mega-ass."

They were interrupted by the sound of footsteps behind them.

"They're almost ready," V'ritan told them, "and the Earth ambassadors have arrived."

"Ugh." Stephanie sighed and pushed away from the balcony rail.

While she'd been talking to Elizabeth, the hall below them had cleared.

"Anyone from the Federation Navy?" she asked.

The *Ghargilum Afreghil* shook his head and a slight smile curved his lips.

"No, we received their polite apologies for the late notice an hour ago."

"Those dirty sonsuvbitches!" Stephanie snarled.

V'ritan's smile broadened. "One of them *did* have some strange wording in it designed to draw our attention to the fact that the Federation Navy was on the move."

"They did? Why?" she asked.

His smile faded. "Because you still have friends in the Navy who dare to care about you, no matter what their orders are."

She was shocked. "But it's too much. What if they get themselves killed?"

"If they do, it won't be because of you. It will be because they've already been marked as someone who'll get in the way."

"Because of me," she added, miserably. "Because of what they think of me."

"That won't be the only factor," V'ritan reassured her. "Whatever's going on in the politics of Earth is much bigger than you and has probably been coming for at least as long as this alliance has existed."

"Is that supposed to make me feel better?"

"It's supposed to make you realize that not all of this is because of you. Most of it has to do with a power struggle that was already in progress before all of this started."

"How do you know?"

"History," he told her, softly. "It's all happened before—and not only on your world."

Brilgus appeared in the balcony doorway. *"Garghilum."*

V'ritan patted Stephanie on the shoulder. "We have to go. After all, this is what brought the scientists here in the first place. That's another win for the good side."

His words made her laugh and she turned to follow him.

"Then we'd better make it good," she told him.

Elizabeth smiled. "I'll see you up there," she told them and bowed to King Grilfir as he came to meet them. "Your Majesty."

He inclined his head in acknowledgment. "We'll keep them occupied for as long as we can," he assured her. "Now, go do what you need to do."

She didn't wait to be told twice and hurried away.

Captain Rawlins stepped alongside Stephanie. "Tell me why I had to be here again?"

The girl gave her a hard smile. "You're the captain of the *Ebon Knight,* the ship who saved the planet."

"Ugh! You mean this is something Emil should have been at?"

Stephanie snickered. "Yup, and he hated these as much as you do. You can take it up with him later."

"No. I think I'll let the man enjoy a well-earned break. Exactly how many of these did he have to attend?"

She thought about it. "You know, I don't know," she replied, "but tonight, we're helping to keep the *Tempestarii* a secret so he owes us one."

"Except for all the One R&D stuff," Rawlins pointed out and she pulled a face.

"True. At least the food will be good."

"And the speeches?"

"Oh, they will be especially good. It's a big night, after all."

"Promise?" the captain asked, her doubts showing.

Stephanie giggled. "Nope. The speeches will be speeches. What can I say?"

"Well, I for one hope you've thought of *something*," V'ritan told her. "There's nothing worse than following someone who can't give you something to build from."

"This is why I have the king going before me," she told him and Grilfir snorted.

"For that, young lady, I should throw you to the wolves and make *you* speak first."

One of his attendants moved forward, looking anxious, and he chuckled. "Please don't worry, Al'tel. I wouldn't do that to you."

The Meligornian stepped back and looked relieved and they descended the stairs to stop before the doors leading into the banquet hall. As they entered, all eyes turned toward them and the room fell momentarily silent.

As the king was announced and applause broke out, the Alpha Blue shuttles broke atmosphere. V'ritan and Brilgus' arrival garnered more enthusiastic applause—which died down as the Alpha Blues were given their course coordinates.

"Where *is* that?" one pilot remarked.

His co-pilot shrugged. "I have no idea, but it looks like the biggest hole in space I've ever seen."

The pilot glanced over his gauges and released a long breath. "Well, we have enough fuel to get there. Getting back, though…"

"It's a good thing we know where our orders came from," his teammate answered. "It's not like the king thinks we're redundant."

"The king wouldn't," he agreed and they settled into companionable silence, completely unaware of the speeches going on behind them as they guided their little craft into a big blot of nothing.

To their surprise, the nothing became a well-lit hangar and even though they couldn't see what it was a part of, landing was as by-the-book normal as anything they could have wished for.

Their comms showed an incoming call as they touched down and they exchanged glances before the pilot opened the line.

"Delivery shuttle one-five-nine, please debark and proceed to the military transport at the end of the bay. We'll take care of the unloading."

The two Meligornians frowned but they didn't argue. Puzzled by the orders, they unbuckled their harnesses and stepped into the hangar.

Their orders had been to deliver the shuttles to the coordinates. Now they thought about it, they realized the orders had said nothing about a return flight.

"I wish I knew what we'd flown ourselves into," the pilot muttered.

"You mean the orders didn't mention it?" his co-pilot asked.

"No. The orders were very precise. Deliver the shuttle to the coordinates." He looked around. "I hope they organized a way for us to get home because it's too far to walk."

The military transport wasn't hard to find. As the shuttles landed, the lights went out on their landing pads until the military craft was highlighted by the only illuminated landing pad in the hangar.

As they approached it, the two pilots were joined by those from the other craft in the Alpha Blue squadron. Every one of them looked as uncertain as they felt.

They stood in silence and wondered what to do when the hatch leading into the passenger compartment of the transport opened and a tall blonde woman stepped into view. Her eyes glittered in the light as she stepped free of the hatchway.

"Welcome aboard, gentlemen, ladies. If you'll come aboard, we'll get you home as quickly as possible."

When they hesitated, her face hardened.

"Move it, or you'll be late for more than breakfast."

Something in the way she snapped those words hit home and the group hurried forward. They might not know exactly where they were or what kind of facility they'd stepped into, but none of them wanted to stay there.

She was as good as her word. No sooner had the last of them strapped into the passenger compartment than the hatches sealed and the transport thrummed with life.

By the time they made re-entry, the speeches were over and the feasting had begun at the banquet. As they touched down, surprised and relieved to discover cars waiting to take them home, the king's guests had begun to mingle.

The scientists laughed and chatted to human and Meligornian colleagues alike. Stephanie watched them, glad to see them so relaxed.

"Do you think they have any idea?" she asked her captain.

"About what?" Rawlins asked. "What's happening on Earth?"

She shook her head. "No, that we're about to go to war and decide the future of the universe."

The woman watched the crowd and shook her head in reply. "No, but it's better that way. It's not like they can do anything to change the outcome."

Stephanie digested this as she sipped a sparkling fruit juice and enjoyed the relaxed interaction.

At one point, Professor Rimmer approached her. In truth, she'd seen him glance at her several times. He'd even started moving toward her twice but chickened out both times.

She was on the verge of going over and putting him out of his misery when he finally screwed up the courage to approach her.

"Steph...Stephanie," he blurted by way of greeting.

"Professor!" She smiled and he blinked, momentarily put off by her welcome. Seeing his confusion, she added, "How are you?"

"I..." He stopped and shook his head rapidly before he found words. "I'm fine, thank you, and I wanted to say…er…thanks—for everything. If I died tonight, I'd die happy knowing what we've tried to accomplish."

"You're very welcome," she began, but the man hadn't finished.

His face took on a faraway look. "Mind you," he continued, "I'd like to live long enough to know if it works too."

That made her laugh. "So, would I, Doc. It would be something to see things growing in those areas."

He sighed. "It really, really would."

His gaze traveled the room and settled on three of his colleagues. They raised their glasses and waved him over. He looked at her and flushed.

"Well, uh…duty calls."

She laughed again. "And they need their leader. It was good to see you."

"And you," he assured her and raised his glass to her before he hurried away to see why his colleagues had called him.

Stephanie's gaze lingered on him. She smiled to see him so different from the man she'd first fought with to persuade him to take a chance on her idea.

BURT's voice in her comms made her jump. "He has done considerable growing in the last few months."

She wanted to ask him how he knew but there were more important matters to discuss. "Is it time?"

"The Eagle is gone," he replied and the link went dead.

When she looked around, Rawlins stood with her head lowered as though listening to a message. Certain of what her captain was hearing, she waited.

When the woman raised her head, she was ready. She gave her a single solemn nod as soon as their eyes met and the two of them began to circle through the gathering and make their goodbyes.

When they reached V'ritan and the king, she gave them a deep bow.

"I must go," she told them. "It's time."

CHAPTER FORTY-EIGHT

Todd stepped into the compartment with his team. It was a secure area a short distance from the bridge but completely isolated.

Aside from eight flight couches, it also had a viewscreen that filled one wall and four consoles.

"It's not much," Captain Berriman told him as he waited at the door, his hand on the pressure plate, "but you have a direct line to me and access to enough data points that you'll be able to keep up."

He nodded. "Thank you, Captain."

"I'll let you know when we get there, Sergeant," the captain said by way of goodbye.

The officer stepped out of the door and sealed it, leaving him to move to a console.

Gary flopped onto a couch, pulled the harness across his chest, and sighed as he did so. "Now," he announced as he cinched the straps tightly. "We wait."

"It's the story of our lives," Dru commented in a sing-song voice. "All hurry up and wait."

Darren chuckled and buckled in beside her. "We might as well get some sleep while we can."

Ka snorted. "Speak for yourselves. Some of us have work to do."

"And that's what you get paid the big bucks for," Henry told her, completely unsympathetic as he settled onto his couch and pulled a headset over his ears.

Wisps of music escaped as he closed his eyes, and Dru scrunched her face.

"I don't understand how he can like that," she whispered and Ka regarded her with shock.

"You wash your mouth out."

The other woman gave her a raspberry and took a reader out of one of her suit's pouches.

"At least he's not into trashy romance," Ka snarked, and Dru gave her a secretive smile.

"How do *you* know?" she asked and closed her eyes as her team-mate's jaw dropped in surprise.

"When you're done, Corporal," Todd interrupted, "I need that data sooner rather than later."

"Gotcha, Sarge," she replied as the screen lit up in front of them.

"Welcome to the fleet," Captain Berriman told them. "I'll forward you a copy of the briefing we've received as we translate."

"Thank you, sir," Todd responded, glad the man couldn't see his face.

There had to be *hundreds* of ships out there, even more than a single fleet. It was the first he'd heard that the Navy was combining its fleets and certainly the first time he'd ever seen so many Federation ships gathered in one place.

"This is it, folks," he murmured as the vessels began to blink out of sight. "This is finally it."

The scene above Dreth was the same but with fewer ships. The entire fleet had massed together and accepted applications from the few pirates who wanted to fight with them.

The threat of losing the only world they had was big enough to make them reconsider their priorities. Jaleck was glad to see it, even if the politics after the battle would be interesting.

If they survived the battle, of course

She sighed. That was a mountain they'd traverse when they needed to. For now, she surveyed the gathered ships and was satisfied.

Forced into space, her people might not have much planet-based technology, but their vessels were among the strongest in the universe, as the Meligornians knew very well.

The humans, on the other hand… She paused and considered it.

The humans know too, she decided, *given how many years they've contended with our unauthorized raiders.*

Hopefully, that didn't cause problems in the battle ahead and the Federation Navy wouldn't take the opportunity to seek vengeance while they had a bigger enemy to face. Again, what happened after the battle would be…interesting.

Somehow, she doubted the human part of the Federation would see the sense in forgiving ex-pirates their bloodier deeds. That thought drew another sigh from her.

There are indeed interesting paths ahead.

She turned as the enticing aroma of Earth coffee signaled her aide-de-camp's arrival. Turning, she accepted the strong brew from him and raised it to her lips.

"Thank you, Kaveg."

Coffee was, perhaps, the only good thing to come out of their alliance with Earth.

Except Stephanie, of course, she amended. Without the Witch, there would be no Dreth and that factor alone was why she was grateful for the Federation alliance.

Beyond that, though? Jaleck tried to think of something else that might redeem the human's deteriorating attitude to her people.

The admiral took a thoughtful sip of the glorious brew and surveyed her fleet again. They might not be numerous but they were heavily armored and well-armed. Most would give an Earth battle cruiser with frigate escorts a run for their money.

Some would obliterate such a trio and barely raise a sweat. Yes, when the Dreth took to the battlefield, the rest of the Federation would notice. Unfortunately, it meant the Telorans would notice as well—and she had seen their ships.

As good as her fleet was, *that* would be a tough fight and she didn't know how many of her people would be there to greet her at the end of it.

Or if I will be there to greet them, she added but kept that thought firmly to herself.

After another sip of her coffee, she stood briskly, nodded at the communications team, and said, "It is time. Let me address the fleet."

"They are waiting, Admiral."

Jaleck inclined her head to the crew around her and stepped forward, leaving her coffee cup on her console.

"My fleet," she began and paused to survey the screen as though looking into every single set of eyes watching her broadcast. "My warriors, the enemy is gathered, massed together in its ignorance and uncaring of the destruction it has caused us."

She paused, knowing her words had garnered a vocal reaction across the fleet. Once she'd given it time to settle, she continued.

"*This* is the enemy responsible for turning some of us into pirates, for enticing law-abiding merchants into a life of crime and treachery"—she lowered her voice—"and for what? The hollow promise of wealth they had no intention of letting them spend?"

Again, she waited, knowing she had raised shouts throughout the fleet. When she was sure they had calmed, she spoke again.

"*This* is the enemy who turned their eyes to our world, seeking to evict or destroy us so they could replace their home, one they have destroyed through their greed and short-sightedness."

She signaled to the communications team to show her people a brief glimpse of the Teloran fleet so they would know the numbers that awaited them.

"*This* is the enemy and it stands alone, while *we* are accompanied by allies on the hunt. They lie unsuspecting, and we will fall upon their fleet like a derkat defending its den, taking its throat before it has time to scream."

Deliberately, she raised her head so they would see the fury coiled in her eyes.

"And we do not fly alone. The Witch flies with us. She *hunts with us!* We will not let her down. We will protect her as she protects us. We will show the Federation that Dreth lives!"

"Dreth lives!" The cry was taken up in several corners of her command center and spread throughout the fleet.

When the shouts faded, Jaleck gestured toward the image of the Teloran fleet.

"They sought to turn Dreth against Dreth and destroy our families and clans? Well, now it is our turn. It is time these Telorans were made to understand why you should *never* wake a sleeping Dreth."

She laid her fist over her heart and raised it to the sky.

"To the hunt!" she cried and signaled the end to her call.

Her command carried across the fleet.

"To the hunt!"

And one by one, the ships began to disappear.

Stephanie next saw V'ritan from Rawlins' secure comms room. They looked at each other in their viewscreens and wished they could have hugged for what might be the final time.

Unfortunately, the moment for that was long gone.

A prickle at the edge of her eyes warned of tears and she took a deep breath.

"Well, old friend," she began, "it looks like we're in for another fight."

He gave her a sad smile. "If we win this one, do you think the gods will smile and grant us a time of peace?"

"If they do not," she told him, "then we will have to carry our petitions to an even greater power."

The *Ghargilum Afreghil* raised his eyebrows. "Do you think there is such a thing?"

She couldn't help replying with a smile. "There is only one way to find out."

His sigh was heavy. "Somehow, I thought you would say something like that. May Seline have mercy on us all."

"Because the Telorans will not," she reminded him. She paused, then added, "Or the Federation Navy, it seems."

Again, V'ritan's eyebrows rose and his gaze darted to where Rawlins stood and watched the conversation silently. "Oh?"

"They told us they'd received strange signals from the next solar system."

"But…but we just sent them a report telling them that sector was clear."

"Which you were courteous enough to send us a copy of," the captain told him. "So, when the time-stamp on their 'orders' was earlier than the one on *your* message, we knew something was up. Do you have any ships in that sector at the moment?"

"We always have one scout there," he told her, looked at his console, and tapped a few keys. After a moment of waiting, he looked up and smiled. "That sector is still clear."

Rawlins's jaw dropped. "You just contacted them?"

"In a manner of speaking," he confirmed.

"So…you can communicate with them in real time?"

"Very close to it," he acknowledged. "We're still working the kinks out, but we have almost achieved instantaneous talk capability." He winked at Stephanie. "It was something the king wanted in that last battle we had, and what Grilfir wants—"

"What? In the middle of a battle?" Rawlins was horrified.

"*He* wasn't involved in the battle at the time," V'ritan admitted. "Which, I think, was half the problem."

"Those weren't the only commands we received," Stephanie added once her laughter faded.

"Do tell," he encouraged.

"I think we had two—one ordered us to the shipyard for 'emergency upgrades and repairs' and another one sent us to a colony for a Marine pick-up."

"And?"

"The coordinates for the colony were past the Outer Rim," she told him, "and the upgrades and repairs listed didn't apply to the engines we currently have installed."

He chuckled. "Someone didn't do their homework."

"I deleted them," Rawlins informed him. "Shit-picking corporate vultures. Obeying any one of those orders would have seen us on the ass-end opposite side of the galaxy to where we needed to be." She sniffed. "As far as this ship is concerned, we never received them."

Stephanie laughed. "I think my captain's finally come to appreciate a warship with an AI."

"Too right she has," the *Knight* interjected. "Don't want to have a record for that command? Boop! It goes away."

She chuckled and even Rawlins managed a short laugh at the ship's commentary. V'ritan merely smiled and shook his head.

"Somehow, I don't think your Navy knows who it is messing with."

"No, it doesn't." She sobered. "But if it keeps this up, it'll find out. I'm not exactly under any obligation to obey its orders and they seem to have forgotten that."

"Yes," the *Ghargilum Afreghil* began, but whatever he was about to say was lost to a sudden chime.

He glanced around and uttered a heartfelt sigh.

"Well, I'm afraid that's our call." Sober-faced, he looked at her and raised his fingertips to his forehead before he touched his breastbone, bowed, and placed a fist over his heart.

Stephanie mirrored his movements and extended her fist as if they could touch in a warrior's farewell.

They both held the gesture for a single, long moment and let their fists fall.

"It is time," V'ritan intoned.

"Let us have war that we might have peace," she replied, and his lips quirked in quick acknowledgment.

The screen flickered and changed to a view of the fleet and she watched as, one by one, the Meligornian ships began to disappear.

"We will see you there," she whispered and the *Ebony Knight* shuddered into transition.

CHAPTER FORTY-NINE

"We will take their worlds and crush them," the Prime ranted. "We will find their Witch and bend her to our will before we break her. We are Telorans. We will not—"

She halted when a loud ping cut across her words.

"What is it?" she snapped.

"A ship on the Storm's edge detected the signature of a small vessel, Prime." The voice delivering the news shook as it had every right to do.

The news it delivered was not good, and messengers had been shot for less before—and that was if they were lucky.

"And?" she demanded.

"It was non-Teloran, mighty Prime," he clarified as if obeisance could save his life.

Her voice lowered dangerously. "And was it found?"

"Uh...no, it was not."

The Prime narrowed her eyes and a keening wail filled the comms. It grew to a crescendo as if a tortured soul was slow to leave their plane.

Those hearing it knew that more than a soul suffered and did not envy the messenger his fate. Once the wail had died slowly, she spoke.

"Alert the Storm. Our enemies are aware."

She'd no sooner completed the order when klaxons wailed around her and the light dimmed from pure white to amber. Across the Teloran fleet, the sound echoed through every ship and the lights strobed until they all glowed amber.

"Move to defensive positions!" Varash commanded when no other orders were forthcoming from the Prime's vessel.

Inwardly, he cursed being forced to give the command. That should have been the job of the Prime's pet Storm Commander but *that* individual was silent.

Perhaps wisely so, but such silence would save neither him nor the fleet and Varash resented being forced to give orders when it was truly not his place to do so.

He only hoped he had not made a mistake and that an attack occurred shortly. If it did not, his orders could be construed as mutiny and worse, his life would be forfeit.

His family—

Tense with both anticipation and fear, he pushed the thought away and focused on the readouts flooding into his ship. If an attack was coming, he had to be ready.

Varash's prayers were answered.

A new set of alarms sounded through the Teloran fleet as other ships arrived in the system—*non-Teloran* ships. His relief was mirrored by horror in the enemy fleet, even if he couldn't hear the comments the sight of his forces elicited.

"Holy *fuck!*" was the comment from the first Earth admiral who saw the fleet in the physical.

If he hadn't known the rest of the Federation ships were materializing around him, he might have re-transitioned right then and there.

"And I thought the footage was exaggerating," his two-IC breathed. He fell silent as he scanned the incoming visuals. "It didn't show *enough.*"

His sentiments were echoed throughout the vessels as each registered the full magnitude of the enemy they faced.

"Are you sure we haven't bitten off more than we can chew?" one rear admiral asked the man in charge of his sector.

"No, but we have no choice. Better we meet these bastards here than in Sol. Be glad we have allies and make sure we don't let them down."

That was met with determined acknowledgment and they settled into the approach. Chatter between the ships finalized which sections of the massive fleet each of them would target.

"Sonuvabitch!" Captain Berriman murmured. "There are so many of them."

He recalled his special orders and his heart sank. That was not an emotion he allowed onto his face, though. Instead, he rubbed his hands together and cracked his knuckles.

"All right, my tight-assed trouble-breakers. We have work to do."

His words brought brief smiles to his command crew's faces. They were short-lived but showed they were ready.

"Now, as you know, we've received some *special* orders."

As the Federation fleet approached, the Teloran vessels shifted and adjusted their positions.

"It looks like we caught them with their pants down," Jaleck noted as the ships went from a planetary attack formation to a defensive array more suited for the ship-to-ship engagement it was about to be involved in.

Her words carried to her fleet and were met by predatory chuckles as her captains, ex-pirate and naval alike, noted their truth.

"Just give us the word, Admiral."

"Let's split one off from the herd. Sky Admiral Angreth, take the lead."

As the Dreth fleet began to close and the Earth vessels chose their targets, the Meligornians jumped in.

"Well, *someone* has their underwear in a twist," Brilgus observed and V'ritan chuckled.

"You've been spending too much time with Stephanie...and it's knickers."

His Standard Bearer gave him a bare-toothed grin. *"Now* who's been spending too much time with our Witch?"

"There's no such thing," he declared, his hands already moving to analyze the Teloran fleet and apportion targets. "Leave none alive."

The Earth fleet was nowhere near as decisive. Its ships maneuvered as its admirals argued.

"We need to get in there," Admiral Burtch urged when his section hesitated.

"If you want to die so soon, *you* go first," Rear Admiral Dreyfus responded belligerently.

"No guts, no glory," Admiral Brelan taunted. "He who shoots first—"

"Get's shot first," the man snapped in response, much to the amusement of the others.

On the Federation flagship, Admiral Amaratne listened to the conversation and suppressed a groan. He would have liked to say he had no idea what had possessed the other admirals to free Dreyfus, but he did not.

Now, he truly regretted not overriding them. The man's attitude would get someone killed—or several hundred someones given that the ass now commanded a ship.

"You know the Dreth are already engaging," one of the others pointed out.

"Well, good!" Dreyfus' commanding officer snapped. "That will be one less problem we have to deal with when this whole intolerable mess is over. The Witch has much to answer for."

The fleet admiral rested his forehead on his fist and tried not to show exactly how he felt about these comments. All he could hope was that they weren't picked up by their non-human allies.

Now *that* was a complication he didn't need.

Granted, it was unlikely that either the Meligornians or Dreth would leave this battle, but the political fall-out at the end would be horrendous if they'd caught that comm.

Still, the other admirals were caught up in an argument about shooting first and none of them had the slightest clue. The thought made him smirk in spite of his irritation, and he tried to eradicate it as he scanned the armada in front of him and looked for the first sign of her.

A light touch on his shoulder drew his attention, and he looked up. Captain Saini had leaned in close as though to ask him a question.

"What has you smiling?" he asked, his tone one of genuine curiosity.

Amaratne couldn't blame him. In his position, he'd have wondered about the smile on his face too. There was nothing about the Telorans that encouraged humor, and as for the comms chatter, it wouldn't affect his decisions.

"Give it time, Captain. I guarantee I *know* who shoots first."

Saini gave him a speculative look. "Bet on it, sir?" he asked after a moment's hesitation.

He nodded and the smile playing over his lips remained in place.

The admirals reached an agreement and it was a decision he'd have forced if they hadn't worked it out themselves. In fact, it was a decision they'd already made during the planning session when Dreyfus' pardon had been revealed.

Of course, that had been long before they'd seen the reality of the enemy fleet.

They decided to make their first salvo simultaneous. As much as it pained him to think it, Amaratne was willing to bet some would chicken out at the last minute. Those who didn't would become the first targets for retaliation.

Whether they lived to become heroes was another matter. Looking at the size of the fleet they were about to challenge, he knew it was foolish to think that any of them would live at all.

He pushed the thought away. The Witch and the Meligornians had defeated a fleet that outnumbered them *and* saved the planet, and that was with far fewer ships.

"Where is she?" he murmured, not believing the girl would leave them in the lurch. *It's not her way.*

Amaratne listened as the admirals counted down their approaches and coordinated in a way that should have made him proud. It might have if he hadn't been waiting with such overriding expectation.

A voice reverberated through his comms systems and, he had no doubt, through the comms systems of every fleet in the system—including the Telorans.

"You *dare* come against *my* people?" she demanded. "I *told* you once before that you do *not* mess with what is mine."

The Navy chatter fell silent and Amaratne got the sense that those on the bridge around him held their breath. They didn't have to hold it for long.

Flame bloomed in the distant center of the Teloran fleet. One fireball after another blossomed in what looked like the very middle of the enemy.

The fleet admiral looked up and saw Saini's jaw hanging open. He chuckled and tapped the man on the arm.

"Give it to me." At the man's questioning look, he added. "Twenty credits. Give."

CHAPTER FIFTY

"What in all the spawns-cursed worlds!" the Prime roared. "How *dare* they!"

She glowered as the non-Teloran cruiser materialized in the center of her fleet, fired missiles in every direction, and vanished as quickly as it had appeared. Unfortunately, it didn't disappear for long.

It winked out of existence, only to reappear on the other side of her command ship and fire another barrage. Unfortunately, in its panic to get away, one of the ships of the line powered to the side and almost collided with its neighbor. The Prime began to see the wisdom of the counsel she'd received against her close formation.

Varash had been right—and if he survived the battle, she'd turn him into a slow-burning pillar for the shame he'd brought her.

"Target that ship!" she ordered before the Second Storm upstart could say anything. "All vessels, target that ship!"

The cruiser vanished a second time before any of her commanders could respond and immediately manifested again in a different quadrant.

She narrowed her eyes. "I will end your useless excuse for breathing—"

Her words died as one of her destroyers exploded from within and hurled a firestorm of orange and white that swirled into the ships closest to it. Other smaller explosions followed, and the Prime held back the urge to scream with frustration.

"Find that ship!" she shouted. "Find it! Stop it from moving and let me crush it!"

The *Pemulwuy* drifted on the very edge of the fleet. On board, the Hooligans were transferring the last of their gear into a second shuttle.

"Are you sure they said we could take both?" Ka didn't seem to believe it.

"They did," Todd confirmed and his gaze assessed the gear remaining. "Drones were a good idea. There's no way we'd be able to carry all this on our own."

"Powered armor, Sarge," she reminded him. "How are you finding it?"

"Let's say I'm glad it came with pod modules, even if we haven't had much time with it."

Her mouth tightened and she nodded. "Yup. The whole thing has happened fast, hasn't it, boss?"

He nodded and patted the side of the shuttle before he looked at Henry and Angus. "Are you boys sure you've got this?"

"We've worked on it since we got back," Henry told him and jerked a thumb at Jimmy and Reggie. "We even got us a couple of co-pilots."

Todd gave the two a sharp look and shrugged. "As long as you can get us there."

"If the shuttles are up to it, we can get you there," Henry reassured him.

The sergeant patted the shuttle again. "Good, because these have to get us to where no man or woman has ever been told to go before."

Darren gave him a morose look but Gary chuckled and slapped the man on the shoulder. "Don't look so down, boy. We've seen worse."

His words drew disbelieving looks from the rest of the team.

"I'm very sure we haven't," Reggie objected.

"You're so full of shit," Dru told him and stretched to touch Darren's cheek. "We'll do our best to get you home again, okay?"

He nodded and forced a smile. "I know you will. The only thing I don't know is how many pieces I'll go home in."

Gary blew a raspberry. "Pfft. You'll be the best-looking corpse on this side of the galaxy," he assured the man. "Oof!" Jimmy gave him a shove and he wobbled sideways. "Idiot!"

His teammate thrust a long narrow crate into his arms. "Make sure you put this somewhere you can reach it."

With a startled look, he glanced at the box.

"What the fuck? Last time I fired one of these, I ended up on my arse."

"And a fine-looking arse it is," Jimmy told him and waggled his eyebrows.

"Yeah? And you can keep your eyes off it and all," Gary snapped in response. "It's all mine."

"Keep our eyes off it?" Ka quipped and exchanged looks with Dru.

"Well, except for you ladies, that is." He leered.

"Oh. Ew!" she exclaimed. "I was only saying how hard it is to not watch such a train wreck walking past. Right, Dru?"

The other woman snickered. "Not nice, Ka." Gary looked mollified until Dru continued with, "Accurate, but not nice."

"Oy," he protested and stowed the box.

"Check your gear," Todd ordered. "Check it twice because I'm very sure Santa hasn't checked it."

"What d'you mean, *Santa*?" Ka challenged.

"You know, to see if you've been naughty or nice. For all we know, we have a heap of coal in there and not the super-sharp shit we ordered."

Piet's quiet denial put paid to that idea. "Trust me. Neither Santa nor his elves laid a finger on it. I chose it and it's the best shit I could find."

"And what am I then? Chopped liver?" she demanded and nudged him with her elbow.

He blushed red to the roots of his hair. "No... It's only that—"

"Speaking of which, I get four of your specials," she added and held her hand out. "Gimme."

Gary snickered. "Well, you heard her, Piet, old boy. You'd better give it to her."

Ka regarded him with raised eyebrows. "Man, only you could make a few grenades sound like something *that* dirty."

"It's not dirty if you—"

"Enough!" she snapped, "or I'm gonna yield to temptation and put a handful of these someplace the sun don't shine."

"And you'll have to think twice before farting," Piet added quietly with the smallest of smiles.

"Ugh. There's no pleasing some people," the other man grumbled and surveyed the cleared deck.

"That looks about it, boss," he added, addressing Todd.

"To be honest, this shit is ten times better than being on the *Notaro*," Dru declared.

"Yeah," Henry agreed. "Fuck that bullshit. At least here, we *know* who's out to get us."

"*And* we have a good chance of getting them first," Darren added and looked more cheerful at the thought.

"Without getting into trouble for it too," Angus concurred.

They all chuckled at that. The truth was they'd all considered dealing with the Odd Squad the same way they dealt with threats out in the field and they'd all known they couldn't.

Todd grinned and waved for them to gather around.

"Last words," he told them and they all winced. He groaned. "Not *those* kinds of last words, dammit!"

They laughed and moved closer. When they'd tightened the little circle around him, he let the smile fade.

"I've wanted to join the Navy since I was in high school." He gave a self-deprecating smile. "If I'm honest, I probably didn't have much of a choice. There's not much opportunity in the Subs."

He paused and his face clouded at the memory. Shrugging it away, he continued. "Which makes it a good thing that I *wanted* to be Navy."

"Yeah, but why the *Marines*?" Ka demanded. "They're only the most likely to get killed and all."

Todd shrugged. "It's what the recruiting officer pointed me at. He said I'd do well here."

"And you believed him?" Reggie couldn't quite accept it.

"To be honest, I didn't care. Steph had gone and the Navy was still there."

The team greeted that with a low round of, "ooh," and his face heated.

"Whatever," he said and flapped a hand to dispel their smiles. "The point was I almost got killed on my first time out."

"Man, that's only 'cause they let you out before you were fully done," Angus stated. "I heard about your course. Everyone advanced fast because you went through the course quickly."

"Yeah, well. The point was, I ended up with a unit of tough guys and we headed out to what should have been an easy colony job."

Dru snorted. "All the worst ops start that way. Any veteran knows that."

Todd shrugged. "Well, maybe they did and maybe they didn't, but we walked into an ambush and most of my team was killed."

"As in only you and one other guy walked out alive," Angus corrected.

"No, only one of us walked out and it wasn't me. I was the one he carried," he told him. "I still don't know how he managed it—or where he went."

He gave Angus a hopeful look, but his teammate shook his head. "Sorry, boss. I didn't follow the stories quite that far. Rumor has it he's a very private guy."

"And I'm not?" he asked, surprised.

"He's not dating the Federation's only Witch," the man pointed out. "You eclipse him there. I think he likes it that way."

"Yeah, well, joining the Navy might not have been the best decision of my life," Todd admitted, "but I don't regret it because meeting you guys has been the absolute, very best, *second* greatest thing in my life."

This was greeted by laughter and mock protests, and he grinned as he let it settle.

"Yeah, meeting you guys *still* doesn't come *anywhere* near my girl."

He paused again as they greeted this with mock gagging and more laughter.

"Yeah, I'll pay that," Reggie declared. "I'm fairly sure I can't hold a candle to Steph, and as for the pommy bastard standing over there..." He shook his head as though there was no need for him to go on.

Todd waited for them to settle again.

"So," he began and caught their attention, "if we see each other after this, I owe you all a drink. And if I don't see you... Well, I'll buy us one on the other side."

There was nothing to add to that and they all quieted, their faces solemn as they nodded to acknowledge his words.

Ka slapped him on the back.

"Good one, boss. Way to remind us we're not even likely to make it to the op zone."

"Well—" he responded but stopped when the door to the hangar hissed open.

Captain Berriman stepped through, a stern expression on his face.

"Okay," he continued more softly as the captain approached, "it seems we're about to find out how much lube we're gonna need."

The man's mouth twitched, and Todd felt a fleeting sense of alarm. Berriman didn't give him time to speak let alone apologize.

"I'll give you this," he said by way of greeting, "taking the Hooligans to their destination might be as dangerous as being the Hooligans themselves."

Rather than answer, the team waited, their faces hard and alert. He scrutinized them and grunted.

"See, the *Pemulwuy* is supposed to—and I quote—'Find the Teloran flagship, insert the tactical team, and have them destroy the flag once they locate and acquire the relevant enemy data.'"

"*Relevant enemy data?*" Ka exclaimed. "What the fuck is 'relevant enemy data?'"

"It sounds like a way to say 'you failed a direct order so now we're gonna have to shoot you,'" Dru responded sourly.

"Followed by, 'Oh, that's everything from the databanks? Well, why didn't you get the backups?'" Reggie added, looking like he'd bitten into a lemon.

"Deliberate miscarriage of duty leading to a failure of the mission," Piet noted quietly. "You are hereby sentenced to death."

There was something in his voice that suggested he'd been there and the team stared at him.

"It's bullshit, is what it is," Reggie declared when their teammate returned their stares and didn't add anything more.

The captain nodded. "Yes, it is."

"Excuse us," Todd addressed the team and leaned slightly to tug at the captain's sleeve. "A word?"

Berriman nodded and they withdrew to a corner of the hangar, leaving the team standing beside the shuttle.

"You know they want you dead too," Todd murmured as soon as they were out of earshot. The captain didn't answer immediately, and he looked around. When he was sure they were still alone, he continued.

"You know we've been given a bullshit set of orders and you know what happens to anyone who witnesses orders like that, right?"

The man looked uncomfortable. His face said he knew exactly what he was talking about but his eyes said he didn't want to speak the truth aloud.

In the end, he shrugged. "What can I say? I support the Fleet and I won't back down."

"The fleet?" Todd asked, then realization dawned. "Amaratne?"

Berriman nodded. "Just as there's a faction of Marines who do not share the goals of their brothers, so there are some officers who seek..."

He paused and stared across the hangar while he found the right words.

"Let's say they seek...a different type of order."

Todd's mouth tightened. "Then they must be almost in position to achieve it."

The captain nodded. "I'm afraid they're using this battle as cover."

He shook his head. "At the time when we need everyone," he noted, torn between sadness and rage.

His companion sighed heavily. "Yes."

"They want to destroy your ship." He wanted to shake the man.

"Well, they might have found a way," the captain admitted tiredly. "I haven't had the heart to break it to the crew."

"You don't have to go through with it," Todd told him. "We'll find our own way."

Berriman shook his head. "Orders are orders, I'm afraid."

"Stephanie wouldn't stand for this," he told him and his hands curled into fists.

"She has to find out first," the man pointed out, and Todd's mouth curled into a small smile.

"Does it matter how we get on the ship?" he asked.

"What do you mean?" The captain raised his head.

"Do they say exactly how we are supposed to get onto the Teloran flagship, or merely that you are supposed to get us there?"

"Oh." Berriman thought about that for a moment. "From what I understand, we're clear once you're on the ship. They don't say anything about getting you off."

Todd snorted softly. "They never do. We always have to get ourselves off."

He was smiling now and the captain inclined his head.

"Do you have an idea?"

"Get us to the *Ebony Knight*. I can guarantee you, she will target the main ship. After that, you'll be able to focus on what you do best."

That brought a quiet smile to the other man's face. It faded quickly, though.

"Do you have any idea how we can manage it?"

Todd glanced at his team. "Ka?"

She trotted closer. "What's up, boss?"

"I need some ideas on how to get hold of the *Knight*."

CHAPTER FIFTY-ONE

The spy ship cozied close to its asteroid. Its pilot's hands moved like lightning as his console sparkled with light while his sensors tried to deal with the data it swept in.

The Telorans were talking like they hadn't done in all the weeks previous. It was both a gift and a curse. He scrambled to capture it all.

The pilot almost imagined he could hear the data drives whining as they shunted and sorted everything in an attempt to apportion it to the right sectors.

He had a dozen torps primed to go, but he didn't want to run out of them before the battle ended and he didn't want to do a mass broadcast. That was a sure-fire way to attract all the wrong kinds of attention and he was needed now more than ever.

His sensors ran perilously close to overload, and he feared he would miss something in the data flood. If he did, it might cost the life of one of the ships he was meant to update.

Utterly focused on his task, he didn't consider the danger to himself.

Security seemed assured. He wasn't broadcasting and was simply a smudge on the shadowy side of a drifting meteor. Never did he dream that he might be discovered

A shadow fell across the cockpit. It cut off the little refracted light falling across the reinforced glass but it didn't mean he'd been discovered.

He checked the sensors and glanced around to see if they'd settled.

His eyes widened, but that was all. Before the embattled sensors shrieked, they were dust and the remains of their pilot blew among the stars with them.

It was a small explosion, lost among a myriad of others, and its loss wouldn't be discovered until the battle's end. Other losses were much more memorable.

The Dreth, being the first to move, bore the brunt of the first return salvo.

"Like a hunting pack," Sky Admiral Gabrack reminded his captains and highlighted one of the Teloran battle cruisers. "Take us under her, captain. We'll tear her belly out."

His captain moved to obey, and his pilot took a leaf out of Wattlebird's book and sent the battle cruiser into a slow spin as they descended.

Anything a human could do in a starship, a Dreth could do better. Flanked by two corvettes, he spiraled to the desired position before he gave the signal for his gun crews to begin their attack.

"Fire at will. Don't give them a chance to breathe."

As he spoke, a dark swarm erupted from the sides of the Teloran cruiser above him. Hundreds of fighters moved like a sentient cloud and he cursed as they broke into twin streams.

"Like yekreshan, Tegortha curse it!"

"Well, you know how we deal with yekreshan, Sky-father."

Gabrack's lips stretched in a grim smile.

"Burn them with fire."

The Dreth had long since perfected the art of using fire to destroy pests on their world. Adapting it for use in space battle had been a natural progression, even if it *had* taken longer.

The missile crews chuckled with glee, loaded the Darkfire 651s, and launched the first salvo into space. They started with the underside of the cruiser and shifted to the swarm.

It had divided into two sentient clouds and each of them targeted one of the smaller corvettes. As a whole, it would have been a threat to his ship and halved, it was more than enough to threaten his escort.

"Clear their hulls!" he roared. "Launch the squadrons. It's time to show these tark-livered Tegorthans that we have yekreshan of our own."

As he spoke, the order was relayed and his ship released its full fleet of fighters, not holding back. There was no time. Just as the cruisers were outnumbered, so the fighters would engage at odds of two to one—and that was *after* the Darkfires had done their work.

"Take us up and past her tail," Gabrack ordered, "and have someone remote one of our dropships into her exhaust."

His orders were obeyed in all bar one small detail. The dropship crew took their craft out.

"We'll be back before the sky-father knows we're gone," its commander assured the flight officer, "and you know she'll pack more of a punch if the gunners are on board."

'But how will you get out?" the officer asked.

"Augmented jetpacks," the commander lied. "We'll be back on board before *Tegortha's Spleen* has finished her pass."

Whether or not he believed them, the flight officer let them go and ran an inventory of the ships he had left. He followed the battle from his console and it didn't look good.

The *Tegortha's Spleen* rose past the engines and dared the next Teloran ship in line to engage.

"I can't take her back to the formation," the pilot declared and Gabrack nodded.

"What are our chances of making a second pass?" he demanded as the corvette *Hrageth's Glory* intercepted a salvo of missiles from one of the smaller ships between him and the next cruiser the hard way with its hull.

He watched it buckle and shatter in a chain of fireballs, his face impassive as he laid a fist over his heart.

"We'll reach it, Father, but we won't pass it."

"If we ram it, can we breach its hull?"

As he spoke, the *Spleen* shuddered and the power from its engines wavered as they caught a wave of nMU.

"If I give it full power, we can make the gap—and our warriors will be able to take more Telorans than they leave."

"Make it so," he ordered. "Let us show Jaleck that her boarding technique can be bettered."

Laughter filled the bridge, the sound of warriors riding a surge of pre-battle adrenaline in the face of certain death. As the *Spleen* made its final dive, the flight officer ordered all craft to lift and took the lead in the small fleet as they sought to discover how vulnerable Teloran engines were to foreign bodies.

On the other side of the battlefield, the Meligornians had met similar odds, but their tactics had been slightly different. Their mages had studied the Witch's use of positive energy.

They might not have been able to send streams of lightning powerful enough to tear entire squadrons apart, but they were very good at targeting single bolts at the most vulnerable points in their enemy's armor.

The engine exhaust wasn't a bad start, but they'd discovered Teloran ships had intakes too, and the enemy weren't the only ones to have hacking drones.

Whereas the Dreth used brute force to attack their counterparts, the Meligornians favored ranged tactics that let them stand clear of the Teloran range.

Unfortunately, it didn't last for long and the enemy proved their reach was about the same. The captain of the *Selene's Vengeance* was swift to adapt.

"Get the mages into fighters," he ordered. "We'll provide cover but we need them in close. I don't want them burning out before the battle's over."

"Understood, sir."

The head of the assault wizards went to brief his troops. What the captain wanted and what they could deliver would be two different things, but he intended to try to get them to align as best he could.

"He won't like this," one of his squad commanders observed.

She was smiling as she said it and the assault leader smiled in reply.

"There is an Earth saying that it is better to ask forgiveness than permission."

They laughed and relayed their plan to their people. The only catch would be getting the squadron chiefs to approve, or so they thought.

"We stand in the vanguard," the head of the flyers replied when the assault mage commander relayed what he wanted. "We either go in hard or we go home."

"Home's a little out of our flight range, sir," his second noted and his superior bared his teeth.

"Then we will go in hard, won't we?"

It didn't take long for the pilots to be partnered with a mage and a Teloran kill competition to start. Between them, they obliterated the first swarm to emerge from an enemy cruiser and eliminated its escort—but not before it killed one of their own.

Srigilf felt the engine surge that told her the fighter's engines were compromised. She tapped her pilot on the shoulder and pointed at the missile battery opening along the side of the Teloran cruiser and turning to broadside their captain.

Her pilot laughed. "Make it count!" he cried. "We may not have a second chance."

They did not get a first. Teloran gunners on the deck above the missiles saw their approach and fired fast and true. The explosion as their fighter died drew the attention of their squadron, and their comrades were quick to see the opportunity.

Granted, tears made the fireballs blooming along the Teloran's hull gleam like lights on a wet pavement, but they bloomed nonetheless. The fighters paved the way in a path of purple fire, and the mages targeted the gaping holes torn in the hull.

Some of them even escaped the resulting firestorm in time to make a second pass. The *Vengeance* altered its course and twisted as it tried to avoid the magical storm that occupied the space where the Teloran had been.

Behind her, the *Avarilf* and *MU Bolt* strove to widen the gap she'd torn in the Teloran's ranks, and V'ritan ordered the fleet to follow. He wept when the *Vengeance* pushed her luck too far and wondered how he would retrieve the ship's assault contingent as a myriad of drop-ships burst from her hull.

He marked the Telorans they reached and ordered reinforcements. Who knew what the chances were that they would take the ships they were on?

No one, but he would do his best to find out. At the very least, he would make sure the assault squads had a chance to make it home.

Designating a corvette for every two ships the squads tried to take, he focused on clearing the Telorans from his sector. As much as he wanted to push to the center of the enemy fleet, he couldn't afford to leave any of them at his back.

Who knew what havoc they would wreak in the rest of the fleet?

He studied his boards and monitored the Meligornian vessels as they flew around him. The three massive ships of the line accompanied the *The King's Warrior* along with the destroyers and battleships with their flotillas of smaller escorts.

It made his soul ache to think how few of them were likely to make it home.

Ahead of him, another magic-laced storm marked the death of a ship and he scanned the data to see whose. This time, it was a Teloran vessel, but the stats on the two Meligornian cruisers flanking it told their own story.

His people would suffer, and the battle had only just been joined.

The Federation Navy, for all its size, fared no better. Dreyfus' prediction that the first to fire would be the first to fall had proven all too true.

The smaller ships had formed the vanguard as half a dozen vessels powered towards the oncoming Teloran craft.

"Don't let any leave the system," Amaratne had ordered and indicated the enemy ships. "We all want a home-world to return to."

His words had proven the spur even the most untrustworthy of his admirals needed and he pushed aside the cynical thought that there wasn't much point in being a ruler if there was nothing left to rule.

He decided every man had something that would make them fight. For a fleeting moment, he wondered if the Meligornians and Dreth worried about such things, but it didn't take him long to find the answer.

All he needed to do was recall the Battle for Dreth and Stephanie's showdown in the arena, Dreth taking on Dreth in their capital's streets, the assassination attempt on Grilfir…

The list went on and it sickened his heart.

Nowhere in the universe, he thought as the Telorans returned fire.

Shields shattered and fell, leaving ships vulnerable to the second barrage. The smaller craft took evasive action and used their efforts to escape damage to close the distance between them and their much larger opponents.

Amaratne thought they might have a chance until clouds of Teloran fighters darkened the gleaming silver of their mother ships' hulls. The *Adam's Sunrise* made the first kill.

Bleeding air and flame, the little torpedo boat accelerated and fired everything it had. At first, the fleet admiral didn't see the point, but as its missiles destroyed the Teloran vessel's shields, he understood.

With its engines faltering under the effects of nMU, the *Sunrise* still had enough momentum to carry it forward. Its pilot judged the angle and entry point perfectly to bring his craft through the hangar decks of the larger ship and into the drive section.

The explosion sent waves of energy rolling into the Teloran fleet and saved the lives of a half-dozen more boats. As the enemy turned their attention to the smaller ships, the larger Federation vessels fired.

Admiral Dailey staggered his fleet's fusillades in the hopes that the Telorans would have trouble eliminating the second wave of missiles, having focused on the first.

It worked up until the fifth wave when the surviving enemy commanders began to stagger their defense. By that time, the smaller escorts were fully engaged and squadrons of fighters fouled the air between them, and the admiral was forced to order his captains to close.

Of course, by that time, they'd taken a Teloran battleship out of the fight and destroyed the next one in the battle line. A myriad of burning hulks now littered the approach of Earth and Teloran destroyers alike.

Amaratne fought to remain above the battle flow. He noted the gaps in both his forces and the Telorans' and issued commands to cover or take advantage of them. All he wanted to do was order his dreadnought into the fray but he knew it was not yet time.

Along the Earth battle line, the other admirals were in the same position and sent the smaller vessels ahead while the dreadnoughts moved slowly into position. Their fight was coming.

For most, it couldn't come fast enough.

CHAPTER FIFTY-TWO

"Sucker!" the *Knight* taunted, materialized behind a Teloran cruiser, and launched a barrage of missiles into its less well-armored rear.

Rawlins didn't know whether to roll her eyes or laugh at the AI's sheer glee. In the end, she did both.

"You've spent too much time with Stephanie," she told the ship.

The *Knight* laughed.

"There's no such thing," she retorted. "My Witch is the best company."

"I'm glad to hear it, Ebony," the Witch acknowledged and energy moved in soft ripples over her skin.

She hadn't started using it yet, but it was hard to hold back. All she wanted to do was blast the Teloran fleet to smithereens, but she knew that even she didn't have that much power.

For now, she had to let her friends—her *people*—face death to bring the enemy fleet to a point where she could manage it. Darkness surged through her soul as the Morgana snarled.

A hand grasped her shoulder and she flinched and snapped a glance at Lars. Worry marred his expression but his eyes were full of concern.

"Are you okay?" he asked.

Taking a firm grip on her temper and the Morgana, Stephanie licked her lips. "I'm good," she assured him.

He gave her a doubtful look and she forced a smile.

"It's not time to go apeshit yet," she told him.

"No," the *Knight* confirmed, "it truly isn't."

Something in the ship's tone caught her attention.

"What is it, Ebony?"

"We have received a message," Knight informed her.

Rawlins snorted. "Now tell me something I *don't* know."

"It is a direct communique on Admiral Amaratne's private frequency."

"What?" the captain squawked. "Why didn't you tell me sooner?"

"I did not alert you," the *Knight* told her coolly, "because the message is not from the admiral."

"But you said—"

"I said it was on his private frequency," she reiterated. "The fact that it is not from the admiral is what alerted me to its importance."

"Oh?" Rawlins asked in a tone that implied no message could be more important than a message from the admiral.

In normal circumstances, Stephanie thought, *she might be right.*

She tried to think of who could be more important than him and only one name sprang to mind.

"Is it from Todd?" she asked and failed to quell the faint note of hope in her voice.

"It is from Ka," the *Knight* told her and sounded very proud of the Marine. "She has managed to hack my most secure frequency and deliver a request for assistance from the Hooligans. She has come a long way since she first tried to hack my systems."

"She *what?*"

It was hard to tell which of the two women was angrier, Stephanie or Captain Rawlins. The *Knight* hastened to calm them.

"It was a most entertaining activity and I was bored."

The captain was not impressed. "You *encouraged* her?"

"I made it clear what would happen if she attempted to access areas I considered private and challenged her to improve her skills," she explained. "She is now *very* good at what she needs to do."

Rawlins rolled her eyes, and Stephanie chuckled.

"Well, at least it meant they had a way to call us," she said.

"And I have fixed the vulnerability so only Ka can exploit it in the future," the *Knight* added and sounded slightly miffed that there had been a vulnerability for the Marine to make use of.

"But how will you *know?*" Rawlins demanded, and Knight responded with a chuckle that would make a movie villain proud.

"Believe me, I will know."

Her reply made Stephanie smile, even though she felt slightly sad. While she was glad the team had reached out to her, she was also a little disappointed Todd hadn't sent her something more personal.

It was ridiculous when she thought about it, but she couldn't help what her heart wanted.

"What did it say?" she asked and tried to keep her tone professional.

Judging by Lars's very brief expression of amusement, she failed, but her security lead's face changed so swiftly to concerned curiosity that she couldn't be sure she'd seen the first. Maybe she had been mistaken after all.

"The Hooligans request collection from the following coordinates."

The designated coordinates took them away from the center of the Meligornian fleet, but no one cared. They'd made their point and put the enemy in confusion. Now, it was time to make themselves useful.

Stephanie maintained a slight connection with her magic as the *Knight* undertook a series of rapid skips. She bounced through the enemy fleet with all the subtlety of a two-year-old on a sugar high and left a similar trail of havoc in her wake.

Even with a sense of urgency riding through her, she didn't waste a single opportunity to hurt the Teloran fleet. She materialized, fired, and vanished, leaving Stephanie in awe of her weapons crews.

They seemed to have developed a sixth sense for exactly when she'd next interface with reality.

It made sense, she realized since this wasn't the first battle the crews had been through with the *Knight*. Not only that, but they'd all spent more time in the pods getting used to the vessel's new capabilities.

They'd even practiced during their downtime. Now, those hard hours paid off.

"Damn, that's gonna leave a mark," the ship noted happily when missiles peeled a Teloran ship's hull and bodies and weapons spilled into space.

She was almost singing when Wattlebird and Avery skipped her again.

"And that, and that, and that...and that. Ooh, someone needs to clean up in aisle three... Also in aisles five, six, and seven—because *dayum*."

The crew chuckled but Stephanie only grunted. At least the *Knight* was having fun. In the meantime, *she* was busy diverting nMU being pulled into the ship's engines into a reservoir designed especially to store it for reprocessing.

"We need to automate this," she grumbled.

"What you *need*," Cameron told her from the engine room, "is an engine that runs on the stuff."

"Or a gun," Rawlins added. "A big-ass gun."

"Noted...aaaand noted," Stephanie told them, as the *Knight* bounced to the edge of the Teloran fleet.

She appeared a little behind the leading edge of the enemy, slightly too high to take on the propulsion system of the Teloran battle cruiser that led the push toward a small segment of the Federation fleet.

"Isn't that Dreyfus' ship?" Rawlins asked and tapped the image of one of the Federation Navy vessels facing them.

"Does it matter?" Stephanie asked, surprised her captain had remembered enough of the Federation fleet's designations to identify it.

She wondered why her captain sounded so pissed, but the woman wasted no time before telling her.

"Well, *hell yes*, it does! Because if that bastard is giving the orders, it explains the near-miss we're about to have!"

"Near-miss?"

"I am tracking three different salvos designed to come closer to my shields than the Teloran's," the *Knight* informed her. "I have run the profiles of each source ship and none of them come close to being a bad enough shot to have accidentally achieved the trajectories they have acquired."

"Are you saying they're shooting at you *deliberately?*"

Now, the captain wasn't the only one who was pissed. Unfortunately, the weapons section had followed the conversation.

"Give the word, Captain, and we'll show those pricks how *un*friendly friendly fire can be."

"But they're on our side," Stephanie protested.

"You might have noticed, Steph, that some folk simply aren't," Lars pointed out.

"But there are *Telorans* out here!"

"And that is precisely why we *won't* return fire," Rawlins declared and her tone made it an order the weapons crews couldn't miss. "We don't play their games."

They tracked another set of missiles that arced from the command vessel. This time, it was obvious that the trajectory had more to do with where the *Knight* was than the enemy.

The captain shook her head.

"It's been a decade and you *still* can't come up with anything new?" she asked.

Stephanie gave her a sharp glance and the woman returned it with a shuttered look.

"Long story, kid, and this is not the time or the place."

She nodded. If she needed to know she could always ask later. For now, she had a mission to run.

"Ebony, how far are we from the rendezvous?" she asked.

"Two skips," the ship informed her. "We will provide assistance on the way." She paused. "Do not worry, Captain, I have recorded the relevant ship designations for later."

Her words brought a faint cheer from the weapons crews and Rawlins smiled.

"Good job, Knight. This time, there *will* be a reckoning."

Stephanie didn't know about the treacherous Navy ships, but she made damned sure there was a reckoning for the Telorans who tried to break the Navy lines.

The *Knight* bounced into a fight where several enemy vessels had encircled a small squadron of Federation vessels, and the Witch snarled.

"Not on my watch!"

We don't have to touch the nMU to wield it, Morgana reminded her, *and the storage tank is fairly full.*

I'm not ready for you yet, she said.

But you need me just the same, the inner voice responded coolly.

Can you destroy the cruiser and leave the Federation ships intact? she asked as the magic arced around her.

I can do more than that, the Morgana answered and darkness speared away from the *Knight's* hull.

It picked up stray nMu along its path until it built to a coruscating storm of black lightning and despair. The Federation ships felt the loss of nMU as a heavy weight sliding from their shoulders.

The Telorans recognized the sudden increase in power in the ships they faced and scanned the area. The *Knight's* arrival had been noted in passing but disregarded as the appearance of only another human ship.

The second scan revealed their mistake as Ebony fired three missile barrages that targeted three different ships and made their defense teams scramble. The shields rippled under the impacts but no missiles got through in that round.

The scan also noticed the cloud of nMU, but its initial alert was overlooked. The Telorans were used to it.

Morgana snickered. *They remain as stupid as before,* she gloated and guided the cloud to the edge of the battle and between two of the bigger ships. *Now, we'll see.*

She waited until the *Knight's* teams fired another volley and tweaked the magic.

Aboard the Teloran cruisers, alarms screamed and the crews shouted in fear. Black lightning leapt across consoles and lashed out with hungry tendrils before it burrowed into living flesh and incinerated its victims from within.

The Morgana's chilling laughter wove through the storm, and the Telorans exchanged nervous looks. It was terrifying to think that someone out there could wield magic more effectively than any of the mages they had on board.

Worse was the network of blue lightning that followed in its wake when Stephanie took advantage of the paths the nMu had made into the vessels. The destruction that followed was spectacular.

The enemy ships imploded and the shock wave rolled outward to leave a pool of calm where the Federation ships slowly regrouped. Taking advantage of the Telorans' distraction, several sent rescue pods out at the same time as they engaged the enemy ships on the other side.

They might have rejoiced at the distress of the alien fleet closest to those who'd disappeared, but they truly didn't have time. The *Knight* skipped away and made space for the Federation reinforcements who'd fought their way in.

"Let's clear their other flank," the ship suggested and Wattlebird's fingers flew as he inserted a new set of coordinates.

The man didn't need orders to know what was needed. He could see the magic swirling over Stephanie's body and feel the darkness lurking below the blue sheen of it.

She and the Morgana were working as one.

"Bounce me close to that shuttle," the Witch ordered and he complied.

Rawlins snapped a warning to her crews.

"Cease fire! Cease fire! Cease fire!"

The speed at which fingers came off triggers and firing buttons was impressive to see, but the gun crews still scanned the area for hostiles. Simply because they were in the middle of a flotilla of friendlies didn't mean everything inside it was friendly.

"Short bursts and targeted." The orders were crisp and clear. "We want no friendly-fire incidents."

"Understood, ma'am."

The bridge held its breath and Stephanie surveyed the devastation of ships and men. It looked like the Telorans had destroyed every fighter that had been sent against them.

Lars stretched toward her as if to lay a hand on her shoulder but stopped when a strand of magic snapped barely short of his palm.

"Steph," he warned, "there's nothing—"

His words cut off as a wave of blue swept through the devastation. Bodies vanished from the screen. Her voice followed, its tones clear and cold.

"*Llewellyn, Andrews, Fertet,* and *Feuerwerker,* attend to your injured."

"Th…thank you, *Knight,*" the vessels responded over the comms.

"*Knight,* out." Stephanie turned to the Captain. "Let's eliminate that flank."

Elizabeth and Lars watched the lightning subside to a blue shimmer and exchanged worried glances.

She caught it and laughed.

"I'm okay. It's not time. Not yet."

CHAPTER FIFTY-THREE

"Good job, Knight," Rawlins declared as the last Teloran ship crumpled and the Federation's damaged ships took shelter in the center of their reinforcements, although they refused to leave the field.

"Where would we go?" a captain asked when he refused the order. "With all due respect, we'll give you support as we can and if things get sticky...well, that's what we're here for."

"Captain, I think you've faced more than your fair share of stickiness," the admiral replied. "I'm ordering—"

"Admiral, I would rather not have to face a court-martial at the end of this."

The man's sigh was heavy with regret. "Very well, Captain."

He said nothing more and the squadron commenced its attack. The smaller, more damaged vessels remained in the center of the formation.

"Take us to the back of the field," Rawlins ordered. "I want to see that message before we reach the rendezvous."

The captain arched an eyebrow at Stephanie, and the girl nodded. As much as she wanted to reach their destination, she also wanted to be prepared.

Knowing the Hooligans, things were likely to get very interesting, very fast. She sighed, stared at the flotilla of Federation ships, and knew she couldn't intervene.

She'd done what she could. What happened next was down to the ships and the men and women who crewed them.

"Knight, Wattlebird," Rawlins stated. "You have the coordinates."

"Copy that, Captain."

They exited the field without further comment and left empty sky behind them. When they reappeared, it was to the rear of the Federation forces.

"Now," Stephanie said when they'd checked the area around them, "what does it say?"

She and Rawlins convened in the captain's secure comms center, leaving Lars and Elizabeth in the outer office.

"Okay, Knight," Rawlins said. "Show us what she sent."

Ka's image appeared on the screen. "I'd apologize for what I'm about to do, but I know you'll understand so I won't waste your time. Two things. These are the orders the captain of the *Pemulwuy* has been given—and you may not ask how I got it."

An official Navy email appeared on the screen and her image shrank to the bottom corner.

"Press pause and read it," she instructed, "because I don't have time to wait."

Rawlins did so and the two women read the instructions.

"Hmmph." The captain grunted. "That says a lot."

"And none of it good," Stephanie agreed.

She waited as her companion pressed play again.

"And here's a copy of our orders," Ka told them, still from the corner of the screen as the email shifted from one to the other.

"Oh, that is *bullshit!*" Rawlins exclaimed while the Witch fought to control her outrage.

"They couldn't say 'please kill yourself' any nicer, could they?"

As Todd would say, it's a trap, the Morgana observed.

"It's a trap, all right," she agreed as the captain Rawlins resumed the recording.

The corporal continued. "As a very good friend of ours has observed, this is a no-win situation. No matter what we do, we can be shown to have failed. And as for the *Pemulwuy*..."

She sighed. "It's a clusterfuck. We need you so we can stop the captain of the ship we're on from taking himself and his crew to their deaths, and we need to work out a way for the Hooligans to get clear." Her eyes narrowed. "But not before we complete this ass-sucking mission. Got that? We *will* get this done, and we *will* defeat the Telorans."

Sadness crossed her face. "As to what comes after..." She sighed. "I guess we'll cross that bridge when we come to it."

Stephanie looked at Rawlins.

"We got this?" she asked.

"We got the first part of it," Rawlins told her. "Berriman is a good guy. He does *not* deserve this, and as for the Hooligans..." She shook her head. "We'll do what we can."

The girl's face turned hard. "Get us to the rendezvous and get your data teams busy identifying the ship we need. There is nothing like going after the bitch herself."

No, there isn't, the Morgana all but purred. *It's time I set a few things right.*

"She's on her way, captain," Todd announced and indicated the message they'd received.

Instead of being pleased, Berriman looked worried. "Are you sure?"

The sergeant stilled. "Yes, sir. I'm sure. Leave us at the drop point and join your fleet." He looked around and stepped closer. "Don't stay with these assholes. If I didn't know better, I'd say they had it in for you."

His words brought a faint smile to the captain's face. "You might be right, son." Berriman offered him his hand. "Good luck, Sergeant."

Todd accepted the offer and shook hands firmly. "And you, sir."

There was nothing more to say and he jogged toward the door leading from the command center. As he stopped to let it open, the captain called to him.

"If you can't get them back to me, I expect my shuttles to meet a suitably glorious death, Sergeant."

He grinned and saluted. "Yes, *sir!*"

The doors opened and he left to board one of the shuttles not long after.

As he stepped inside, he activated the comms. "You're clear to start your course change, Captain." He sealed the shuttle's hatch while he spoke. "Get us out of here, Jimmy!"

The shuttles lifted while the hangar doors were still opening. They were out and into free space before the *Pemulwuy* had finished her turn.

"Happy hunting. *Pemulwuy* out." Captain Berriman's voice rang in their ears as Jimmy and Angus brought the shuttles around in perfect sync. The *Knight's* gun crews weren't the only ones who'd spent overtime in the pods.

As they watched the battleship pull away, they heard another call directed at Berriman and his crew.

"*Pemulwuy,* this is *Kraken.* Where the hell do you—" The caller stopped as a shadow fell across the shuttles.

Before Todd could give the order to change course and find the hangar, blue light enveloped them and stopped their engines. The *Kraken* squawked in surprise and Berriman chuckled.

"Good luck, Knight."

"And Selene's protection and Hrageth's storm ride with you," Stephanie replied, "because I can see nothing nearby that will."

It was both a warning to the captain to get his craft out of there and a warning to the untrustworthy ships flying in formation nearby. A fourth voice interrupted them.

"*Pemulwuy,* please rejoin my squadron. Your presence is sorely missed."

After setting the shuttles in the *Knight's* hold, Stephanie turned to Rawlins. "I didn't know the *Pemulwuy* was part of the flag's squadron."

"It wasn't until now," Rawlins told her. "It looks like Amaratne recognizes his friends."

The girl stared at the hostile portion of the Federation fleet. "Let's hope he hasn't sentenced them to an 'accidental' death."

The *Knight* chuckled at her words. "He will make it," she informed them. "The approaching squadron seems to have trouble with its firing controls."

"In the middle of a battle?" Rawlins asked, her voice riddled with horrified disbelief.

"Fortunately, the Telorans are busy elsewhere," the ship replied, "or the situation *would* be problematic."

She flew after the *Pemulwuy* for a short distance before she skipped out of sight.

On the *Kraken,* Admiral Oshin chuckled.

"She took the bait!"

The *Knight* was correct—and horribly so. The Telorans *were* busy elsewhere. They fired with deadly efficiency into the Federation fleet and their missiles pounded through the hull of a corvette.

As life pods exploded from it, the ship shuddered and convulsed and broke into several untidy pieces. Ignoring it, the enemy continued their advance and gave the command to launch the fighter squadrons.

The missiles were effective but the smaller craft were better equipped to eliminate their counterparts and destroy the life pods jettisoned in a vain hope of survival.

One Teloran curled his lip in distaste, glad his shielding hid his expression. He barely managed to stop short of shaking his head. *That* would have been seen and the Prime was not safely tucked away on Telor.

As he ordered his weapons teams to focus their fire on the exposed flank of the *Henri Chauvel,* he wondered if destroying humanity was truly necessary in their search for a new homeworld. It was another opinion he kept very carefully to himself.

He had no desire to become the Prime's next piece of fiery décor.

The *Chauvel* withstood the first barrage but on the second, its shield gave way. As fast as its defense team moved to reinforce the weakened area, it would never be fast enough.

A wave of nMU rolled over the ship and brought with it a wave of despair. Its engines faltered and the remaining shields shimmered.

The enemy commander saw his chance and ordered his crews to batter the stricken ship. Three waves of missiles broke what was left of her shields and shattered her hull.

Admiral Dailey watched in horror as the *Chauvel* bled flame and atmosphere. His heart sank as the Teloran vessel brought its guns to bear on his flagship.

"Give that bitch what she deserves," he ordered as if it were possible with a second Teloran destroyer ascending under him.

"Launch everything we have and prepare to evacuate."

"With all due respect, Admiral," one of the bridge crew told him. "Evacuation is a sure-fire way to die." He highlighted what was happening to the life pods left in the field.

"Well, fuck...me..."

"I'm fairly sure those assholes aren't interested in the horizontal tango, sir, but I'd rather make their lives as interesting if I could."

"Fine!" Dailey nodded. "Everyone into battle suits. Standby for hard dock."

"Hard dock, sir?" his pilot looked mystified.

"Yes, Hargreaves. Make it so."

Movement caught the admiral's attention and he half-turned. His aide-de-camp had brought his suit.

Lead by example, huh? he thought and did exactly that.

As the last seal was checked and he turned to assist his man, collision alarms sounded throughout the ship. The AI called the alert in monotones.

"Collision imminent. Brace for impact. Collision imminent. Impact in three minutes."

Captain Yale's stomach rolled as the *Chauvel* went up in flames.

There was nothing she could do. She'd so far held the third Teloran at bay, but even the *Cathay Williams* could not hold forever.

"Fight or evacuate, ma'am?" her second asked and the captain gave him a stern look.

"We all saw what happened to the life pods from the *Esther Sterne*," she said.

Around the bridge, every head nodded. On the forward screen, the department heads glanced up and raised their thumbs in approval of what she was about to say.

"Then we pull in as close to her as we can and we make her fight," she declared.

"Captain?" The voice came from the Marine commander in charge of the contingent aboard.

"Yes, Commander?"

"If you get us in close enough, we can rig this ship with an explosion large enough to demolish whatever's beside it."

"We can fire multiple grapples and tie her in so she can't get away," said an engineer in the weapons section.

"And I can leave the tractor beam on full throttle," a crewman said from across the deck.

"We can make it so she doesn't have the chance to kill anyone else, ma'am."

Yale swallowed hard and forced her voice to ring clearly and decisively.

"Make it so but ensure that we have a chance to get aboard that beast. If our boom isn't big enough, I want them to *know* what it's like to be rolled by Federation Navy."

"Aye aye, ma'am," echoed to her from every quarter.

By the time the admiral's behemoth had rammed its target, the *Cathay* had snugged herself in tightly to the side of her newest and soon to be most short-lived "best friend."

All around them, the rest of the squadron fought the smaller flights of Telorans and tried everything they could to keep them off the two ships targeting the biggest of their opponents.

Some raced to pick survivors up before the Teloran fighters could find them, and others attempted to destroy the fighters themselves. Four of the larger ships challenged the remaining Teloran destroyer.

In the end, it was the destroyer that remained intact and continued to move forward as more of the enemy fleet swooped in to reinforce it.

CHAPTER FIFTY-FOUR

"Tegortha's teats and Hrageth's balls," V'ritan muttered and drew a startled glance from T'revan. "That is, as the Marines would say, one big motherfucker."

The man greeted this declaration with wide eyes, followed by a lop-sided grin.

"Would the admiral like me to bring him his *brown* trousers?"

The *Ghargilum Afreghil's* jaw dropped as he caught the Earth reference. "Since when did you..."

T'revan's smile got wider. "Those Marines are a very interesting type of warrior and the one called Gary was particularly vocal about figures from his heritage."

He gestured at the screen, which was almost completely eclipsed by the Teloran dreadnought that had come to meet them. It was accompanied by two destroyers and two battleships amidst a fleet of corvettes and torpedo boats, and the mages were hard-pressed.

"Do you need us to switch targets?" his head mage asked, but V'ritan shook his head.

"No, clear the little stuff."

"D'you think she's playing chicken?" T'revan asked but this time, the Meligornian admiral's glance discerned no humor in his eyes and his expression was bleak.

He shook his head. *The King's Warrior* was bigger than most dreadnoughts but she had nothing on the behemoth that headed inexorably toward them.

"I'm not even sure it would notice if it ran us over," he admitted.

"It's time we made it notice," his companion suggested, "don't you think, *Garghilum?*"

"For Selene and Meligorn," he confirmed and heard the vow rise around him as the command deck echoed the words.

"For Selene and Meligorn."

"Launch the fighters. *Hammer,* take the outermost battleship. *Rise,* work with them. Do as you see fit but bring it down—and then deal with the destroyer if it's still there."

He watched as the two Meligornian battleships altered course to do as he'd asked. Their escorts moved with them and needed no additional commands.

"Selene's blessing," he added and changed frequencies to mirror those orders for the *Ir'tel* and *Kal'vali.*

"You do realize that this is all the cover we had," T'revan observed mildly.

The *Ghargilum Afreghil* gave him a small smile. "And now they have cover from the fallout of what we'll do next."

T'revan gave him a worried look, and he laid a hand on his shoulder.

"I want everyone armed with whatever they can carry and armored in their heaviest gear. We will take the fight to this big beast and will *not* let it get through to the rest of the fleet."

His personal guard did not correct the *Garghilum* but stepped to V'ritan's second in command. As he approached, the Meligornian nodded and began to issue the necessary orders.

"See to our *Afreghil,*" he told him. "I will take care of the crew."

T'revan laid a fist over his heart and hurried from the room. Looking back, he saw that V'ritan had not left his command post and that the chief of his mages had moved to cover his absence.

It was good to see that this *Garghilum* had earned the respect of his people. T'revan felt a small knot loosen in his chest. Perhaps Grilfir had been right when he had said this one was not like his predecessor.

It was worth hoping for and he wondered why the man had not already donned his heaviest war gear.

"Always with the symbolism," he grumbled and pulled the cart holding the less decorative suit from his liege's closet.

He took the time to find his armor and called a steward to assist him into it. The first rule of guarding was that you could not protect your principal if you were not also protected.

Even so, he hurried and assisted the steward into his slightly lighter suit. Not everyone was rated for the heaviest. T'revan gave a humorless laugh. No doubt they would be by the time the next conflict came around.

He remembered the size of the Teloran dreadnought and shivered. Who had known such things existed in the universe?

"We should have," he muttered, returned to V'ritan, and helped him into the armor. "It was pure arrogance to think we were the biggest and baddest the universe had to offer."

"Agreed," his boss told him and startled him from his reverie. "How do you feel about doing a little magic?"

T'revan cocked his head and studied the *Garghilum* for a short moment. When he was certain he wasn't mocking him, he shrugged.

"I may be a little rusty."

The head mage turned to regard him with wide eyes, but V'ritan chuckled and slapped him on the arm.

"That's too bad. We'll need whatever you can do without shooting some undeserving individual up the ass."

"I can do that," he told him. "Tell me what you need."

V'ritan signaled his head mage. "Do you know how to prime the missiles?"

"Are you sure we'll need them, *Garghilum?*" the mage protested, and their admiral froze.

After a second, he shook his head, took the Meligornian by the arm, and turned him to face the forward viewscreen.

The Teloran dreadnought filled it. He gestured at the consoles and the lights strobing quietly around the room.

"Do you know what you do not hear?" he asked, and the mage shook his head.

T'revan saw it almost immediately.

"You've silenced the collision alarm," he whispered.

V'ritan raised a brow and smirked slightly as he registered the horror on the mage's face.

"I'm hoping we don't need it." The smile vanished. "But I need to know we can arm the new missiles we have from One R&D. I also need to know if our shields will hold against the kind of maelstrom that will occur if I open that monster so I can have a direct shot at its engines."

The mage and T'revan's jaws dropped.

"You want to do what?"

"You heard me," V'ritan told them. "I want the *King's Warrior* to shoot an entrance to that monster's engine room and then I want her to send a *very* special missile to its heart."

He paused long enough to register their expressions. "What? You're not going to tell me it's impossible, are you?"

"Oh, of course not, *Garghilum*. At least you're not telling us we should buckle one of those to a fighter and try to fire it up the battleships' tailpipes," the head mage snarked.

V'ritan's eyes widened and his face shifted as he considered the possibility.

T'revan darted the mage a look full of reproach but before he could say anything, their leader spoke,

"Do it!" he said. "We'll need...four?"

"Six!" the man told him. "You'll need at least six."

"Leave us seven!" he ordered and his second relayed the orders to the weapons technicians. "And I need the craziest fliers you have to make sure they make the delivery."

Even as he spoke, he could see the orders being relayed and the Meligornian battleships alerted. Selene's name was taken in vain in a hundred different variations, and aspersions were cast on the *Garghilum's* intelligence, sanity, and parentage.

His amusement rolled around the command center and reminded some of the older hands of his past. There was little wonder that he'd been designated the king's right hand—the escapades those two had gone on in their youth!

V'ritan saw the realization dawn on some faces and worry on others, but no one questioned his orders. In every set of eyes that turned to him, he also saw the only two things that mattered—trust and hope.

Their *Garghilum* was taking the fight to the enemy, as impossible as it was to beat, and that made it possible to think they'd make it through. His voice snapped across the bustle of activity as his people hurried to fulfill his orders while they still had time.

"Are you ready?"

"Missiles locked and loaded," shouted in response from the weapons teams.

"Standing by!" snapped from the defense section.

"Launching," issued crisply from the squadron commander's cockpit.

It was followed a few seconds later by, "We are clear. Selene's blessing, *Garghilum Afreghil.*"

"And on you," V'ritan replied.

Quietly, he lifted his gaze to take in the bow of the Teloran dreadnought and touched the button he'd used to deaden the collision alarms. As their warnings reverberated across the bridge, he nudged the volume on his mic.

"Commander Ash'lgil. The power is yours."

He nodded to T'revan and the head mage. "I need you to both select a missile and shield its approach. Engineering has given me their best guess where we need to strike that beast, and I want each to be precise."

The two mages nodded, T'revan both ecstatic and nervous about tapping the magical reserves he rarely touched.

But one? He chuckled and drew uncertain looks from his two

companions. Not wishing to pre-empt himself, he didn't enlighten either of them but tapped the energy within and told it to find the MU speeding toward the dreadnought.

The magic leapt in response to his touch, flashed through him, and continued through the *Warrior's* sensors to find the missiles.

Which one did he want? T'revan wanted all of them, and the magic leapt from one to the next to reveal where they were.

Defensive fire filled the air around them, and he shaped the MU into a shield in front of their noses and used it to deflect the incoming fire. When missiles replaced energy blasts and solid rounds, the guard stepped forward and found a clear space in which to work.

Stephanie had not been the first to use her body to direct the movement of her magic. V'ritan stared as the big Meligornian Tethis had recommended to his protection detail used his hands to direct the missiles' path.

He glanced at his chief mage. "Are you helping him?"

The man held his hands up. "No, *Garghilum*. Look, no hands. See?"

"Smartass," he grumbled and continued to watch the big man work, his attention torn between T'revan's movements and the course the projectiles followed on the screen.

"Mark the entry point," the guard ordered and both scans and weapons technicians hurried to comply.

The missiles altered course and shifted slightly to bring themselves more on target. He spoke again.

"How far apart?"

"As far apart as you can make it," the first engineer replied. "We don't know exactly how big the bang will be. It all depends on the amount of nMU the MU encounters and what chain reaction it causes."

"How do we know it won't mix nicely?" V'ritan murmured. "Stephanie—"

"The last I heard, the Witch was still perfecting the technique," the head mage told him. "Until she does, MU and nMU, when mixed, will always create an explosion."

"Oh..." he said as the first missile penetrated the Teloran's hull.

"Oh...this will be fun." A few minutes later, he added, "Tell those fighters to keep flying once they've delivered their payload. No sticking around to see what it does."

A second alarm joined the first, followed by hurried orders from the defense team as they moved to shore up the forward shields. The Teloran dreadnought hadn't slowed when the first of the explosions tore it apart from the inside.

T'revan looped the missiles back on themselves and sent the second one into the maelstrom to remove the remaining barriers between the third missile and the engines.

"Seven?" the head mage teased gently. "Truly, *Garghilum?* I missed making a wager on that."

V'ritan realized his mouth was hanging open and closed it with an abrupt snap. He glanced at his bodyguard.

"See if you can do something about those destroyers," he said and heard his second relay a warning to the *Ir'tel, Kal'vali, Hammer,* and *Rise.*

It looked like their cover was about to become a magical inferno, and their targets would do the same.

"Tell them to go high and come down behind me," he ordered as the *Warrior's* prow slid through the space the missiles had created.

The third missile struck the Teloran's engines, and the *Warrior* shook under the resulting blast.

"Uh, sir..." the head mage began.

He looked at him. "What is it?"

"We may have a problem."

"And?" He held onto his temper since losing it would only make it harder for him to get to his point.

"Aren't our shields MU?"

The *Ghargilum* allowed himself a small chuckle.

"They used to be," he admitted, "but I had a word with One R&D and we're experimenting with using MU to power generators that produce a more *conventional* shield."

"So we won't explode?"

He shrugged. "I *hope* not."

"And the others?"

"Did you miss the part where the technology is experimental?"

The mage turned as the Meligornian battleships took sudden evasive action. The visuals tracked the missiles T'revan still controlled.

Soft whoops from the defense section signaled a win for the shields and new technology as the guard brought his missiles home.

The resulting flash temporarily affected observer and sensor alike, and they flew blind for several heartbeats and simply relied on the shields to get them through the resulting maelstrom.

"Fire forward," V'ritan ordered. "We don't know what was coming in behind."

The devastation was even more impressive when they weren't surrounded by it. They were relieved to discover the Teloran dreadnought had been at the rear of its squadron and that the closest enemies weren't focused on them, at least not initially.

"Regroup!" he ordered when the closest enemy vessels began to change course. "Fall back and regroup."

Behind him, the dreadnought continued to fall apart and the two halves the *King's Warrior* had created slowly broke and crumpled.

In the center of the command deck, T'revan came slowly to a halt. Sweat beaded on his forehead and ran down his cheeks, but his eyes were alight with blue fire and his smile threatened to crack his face in two.

Taking a deep breath, he steadied himself and returned to V'ritan's side.

"What's next, *Garghilum?*"

The explosion was seen across the battlefield but it was not alone. Admiral Ogden had found a dreadnought and she *didn't* have any One R&D missiles on board.

Instead, she had several years' command experience and a squadron of ships determined to stay alive.

"This lobster needs to be shelled," she observed. "Scans, find me a vulnerable point. Weapons, load the biggest bang we have. Shields, get ready to shift them in double-quick time."

Hearing the confirmations from several different directions, she took a breath and continued. "All flight decks, prepare to launch. You have your targets. Marines! Stand by for insertion. Launch on my mark."

She ran her hands over her boards and quickly gathered the information she needed. A glance told her all she needed to know.

"On my mark...aaand...*mark!*"

The squadrons' signals lit her board up and she imagined she felt the slight tremor as they left the shelter of her ship.

"Let the missiles lead," she reminded them and raised her hand to signal the weapons commander to give the order.

"And again," she commanded seconds after the first barrage had launched clear.

"Squadrons, forward."

On the screen, the bright dots of the ordnance traversed the field. The first rank shattered on the dreadnought's shields. Some of the second met the same fate, but more of them detonated against its hull.

The fighters swept forward, opened fire, and swept up and around to attack the flashpoints marking its turrets, while several small flotillas broke away to escort the dropships in.

To Ogden's surprise, the craft didn't stand off the Teloran's hull and let their Marines jetpack in according to standard procedure. Instead, they flew into the gaping rents her missiles had savaged in the hull before they landed and laid down suppressing fire as the Marines bailed.

The pilots followed shortly after, ran into battle with their teams, and left the shuttles standing in whatever space they'd created.

"It's almost like they don't think they're coming back," she murmured and pursed her lips. "Let's do our best to make it otherwise."

She let the fighters clear the space and had her gunners and missile teams aim lower than the level the Marines had landed on. Her weapons array spoke at the same time as the Telorans'.

Unfortunately, they also knew how important it was to destroy the shields and they had more missiles to do it with. As its forward batteries assaulted the admiral's command deck, its port and starboard batteries focused on her escorts.

The first salvo didn't quite destroy the ships, but the enemy vessel didn't care. It was already channeling more power to its fore shields and rebuilt them in time to catch the missiles that raked it in reply.

Its second salvo caused multiple explosions across the squadron before its escorts raced forward to eliminate what was left with their guns.

She did not live to see the destruction of her fleet. The command deck had only been the first port of call for the oversized rounds that pounded through it, and they left little behind.

It was like Christmas! Stephanie's team laughed as Piet handed out the weaponry he and Ka had purchased. Frog juggled a black sphere with two blue ones until Johnny gave an exasperated sigh and plucked the black one out of his hands.

"I'm not sure any person with an ounce of sanity would let you run around with these in your hot little hands."

The comment elicited a round of laughter and Johnny looked up, puzzled. "What?"

Ka poked him. "I'm not sure what made you think anyone present was sane." She glanced at Stephanie. "No offense."

"None taken," the Witch replied. "After all—"

"If the bootuh fits!" they all chorused and chuckled.

In the shadow of a moon, they'd gathered to hear Todd's briefing and discuss how they would tackle the Teloran. Rawlins had stayed to confirm her and *Knight's* part in the battle before she returned to the bridge to make preparations.

"I'll see you before we leave," Stephanie assured her, and the woman had raised a hand in casual goodbye.

Once she had gone, Todd and Piet had broken out their finds. When they reached the mobile auto-cannons, Lars' jaw dropped. "Where did you get *those?*"

The demolitions expert raised an eyebrow and Ka grinned. "If we told you we'd have to shoot you."

He raised an eyebrow in return and his face went suddenly still. Two steps back, Johnny froze.

"Joking!" she added, to break the tension.

That needs looking into, the Morgana observed and watching the exchange, Stephanie had to agree.

"We'll divide these babies between the two groups," Todd informed them and Marcus smiled.

"Very cool, man."

His gaze roved the cannons and settled on the box of mobile limpet mines. The corporal caught the direction of his interest.

"Oh no, you don't! *Those* are mine!"

Marcus gave her puppy-dog eyes, and when her scowl didn't lift, turned the same look on Todd. He frowned, a little confused, and the guard flicked his gaze to the mines, to Ka, and back to him.

"Dobber!" she grumbled and he sputtered with laughter.

"You know you need to *share* your toys, Ka," he told her.

"Like you need to practice your parenting skills *right now,*" she complained.

"My what?"

"You know..." She waggled her eyebrows and sent a meaningful glance from him to the Witch. "Your *parenting* skills."

He followed her gaze, noted his girl, and blushed red to the roots of his hair. "Oh..."

Stephanie rolled her eyes. "Well, if you all know something I don't, maybe it's time to spill." She raised an eyebrow and inclined her head.

Todd put his hands on his hips and shook his head. "Could we all get back to the matter at hand?"

They did and proceeded to divide the special rounds.

Ooh! Morgana exclaimed and let Stephanie feel the round's potential. *Now these are clever!*

They are? She registered what she was holding. *Oh, my! Someone's been holding out on us.*

Out loud, she asked, "Do you know what these do?"

Ka frowned and lifted the box. It was wrapped in plain plastic and there were no manufacturer's labels on it. "Well, that's strange." She picked up a slip of paper that had nestled in the top of the crate.

"Oh! Well, that's *very* cool—*and* they're all in Navy calibers, too."

She handed the slip to Todd, and he exhaled a long sigh. "These are Navy rounds," he observed. "What were they doing available outside of Stores? I'd have thought these would be shipped to the Marines in the Federation fleet."

"Yup," the corporal confirmed. "You'da thought, right?"

He shook his head. "Well, they ended up with Marines, so I guess *that* mystery can wait for another day. Make sure everyone gets some of these."

"Why?" Lars asked. "What do they do?"

"They're supposed to penetrate Teloran armor," Todd told them and jaws dropped.

Before they could speak, he raised a hand. "That's a question for later. Right now, I suggest we simply be grateful. This must have cost a fortune."

Still frowning, he looked at Piet. "How much *did* Admiral Amaratne give us anyway?"

The man froze and looked like a rabbit that had seen a fox. His face paled and his Adam's apple bobbed as he swallowed nervously and turned to Ka.

"Oh, for pity's *sake*," she grumbled and rolled her eyes. "Scaredy pants!"

Todd's eyebrows rose and he folded his arms. "And?"

His corporal raised a forefinger and stabbed it at Stephanie. "You want to know where all the creds came from? Ask *her!*"

He followed the finger and opened his mouth to say something, then closed it again. The blue fire haloing his girlfriend had darkened and gone from sapphire to indigo to a deep purple streaked with black.

The last thing he wanted to do was distract her when she was borderline on losing control of the Morgana. While he was fairly sure they would need the resident Teloran later, he didn't want her released early.

He looked at Ka. She had lowered her finger, folded her arms, and regarded him calmly. The smirk playing around the edges of her mouth dared him to follow through.

"I think I'll take that up with her later," he said and moved to inspect the last of the gear.

She unfolded her arms and patted him on the shoulder plates of his power armor.

"Yeah. You do that. *Don't* go to the black-eyed witch and piss her off." She darted Stephanie a careful look. "At least, not any more than she already is."

CHAPTER FIFTY-FIVE

"Are you sure it's her?" Stephanie demanded and the Morgana's voice threaded through hers.

"As sure as we can be," Rawlins replied, and the girl's eyes flashed.

"I am sure," the *Knight* interjected before she could speak. "She rides the biggest ship in the fleet *and* it is the one with the greatest concentration of nMU."

When she continued to scowl, the ship clarified. "It is not where most of the commands are coming from, but it *is* the only ship telling the command source what to do." She paused again and added thoughtfully, "I don't think the command ship likes her."

At any other time, the Witch might have asked her what she meant but now, she filed it away for later. First, they had to cut the head off the snake.

She shoved aside the thought that this snake might have two heads. *I'll take both if that's the case,* she promised and felt the Morgana's heartfelt agreement.

It had been an hour since she had returned to the bridge. The teams were kitted up and standing by with the shuttle, and she would join them as soon as they located the target. After that, the *real* fun could begin.

"We have the coordinates." Wattlebird's voice cut through her thoughts and Avery rose from the seat beside him.

The pilot glanced at him. "You'd better be back in time for your next shift."

"And you'd better make sure I have a ship to come back to," the man retorted as he pivoted toward the door. "Don't make me come looking for your scrawny ass!"

Wattlebird was determined to have the last word.

"Remember! Don't be late," he called as Avery reached the door.

His only reply was a single finger held over the co-pilot's head as the man disappeared.

Stephanie folded her arms and drummed her fingers on her biceps as she glared at Wattlebird. He caught the look and refocused on his boards.

"They're locked and loaded, Captain," he called, addressing Rawlins. "We'll go on your mark."

"Take us through, Wattlebird. I'll count us down."

The countdown was more for the Witch's benefit than anyone else's, and they both knew it.

She unfolded her arms and stalked toward the door. Lars, Johnny, and Elizabeth fell in behind her. Arne, Amy, and Matthias met them in the corridor and pushed off the wall as they exited the command deck.

The captain had drawn the line at three.

"There's nothing in here these guys can't handle. Take the corridor if it makes you feel better, but I will *not* have you clogging up the command center."

Her expression had forbidden any argument and the trio had shrugged and taken position outside the entrance. As soon as the doors had closed behind her, Stephanie broke into a jog.

Rawlins's voice was a steady beat in her ear.

"Stephanie, we'll transition in ten... nine..."

She increased the pace.

"How will you get back?" The woman interrupted the count.

"Don't worry about picking us up," she snapped as they entered the elevator and descended. "We'll hitch another ride."

"Five," Rawlins continued and added, "Make sure it's one of ours."

The smirk was tangible in her voice.

"Three," she called as the elevator doors slid open. Stephanie wrapped the seven of them in blue light and teleported them to the shuttle bay.

"Two."

"It's about time you remembered," Elizabeth grumbled.

"One."

A familiar sense of dislocation enveloped them as Lars sealed the hatch and they strapped in. Knight opened her hangar bay doors as soon as the translation was completed, and she didn't need to tell them to be quick.

"Clear!" Brenden called as he left the hangar "Get your asses out of here."

The *Knight* didn't need to be told twice and Brenden and Avery counted their lucky stars that the torp teams on the Teloran dreadnought had aimed for the *Knight's* mid-section and not the lower edges of her hull where the exit doors were.

The shuttle twisted into a fast dive to take them even farther out of the missiles' path, and the pilots hoped it was enough for them to avoid any sharp-eyed gunners who might be waiting to launch a follow-up attack.

Their trajectory took them low and into the big ship's shadow, but they didn't rely on that to protect them. Avery goosed the engines while Brenden sent the tiny craft into another spin.

In the back, Vishlog maintained a tight hold on the two cats, glad he'd insisted on them having their own spaces. Even so, neither of them were happy. They flattened their ears and lifted their lips in silent snarls as their bodies were held in place by the harness.

Watching them, the big Dreth was glad they'd have something to kill at the end of the ride because there'd be no mercy for Stephanie's boots otherwise.

"Any idea where we're going?" Avery asked and Brenden chuckled.

"Funny you should ask."

He punched the firing button and delivered two missiles into the Teloran's hull.

"Knock! Knock!"

"That is the Federation Navy's command ship," the Prime noted and used magic to make the vessel glow. "Take him and we take their hearts."

"She is almost in range, Prime," the weapons team confirmed.

"Good. Move in. Varash, clear my path. If we take that ship, we take the battle."

Her crew remained silent as Varash's ship moved to obey. If any of the Prime's crew doubted her, they didn't dare show it. Her blood was up and the slightest hint of dissent would turn the dissenter into a living pillar of flame.

It was not a fate any of them desired.

She watched as the Storm Commander drew some of the admiral's vanguard away. Some but not all, she noted cynically. He would see his family punished for his lapse.

Narrowing her eyes, she issued a second command.

"As soon as you have a clear line, fire."

None of the weapons crews dared point out that anything they fired from this range could—and probably would—be intercepted. They also knew their failure would be laid at the ship's captain's door, and he started to sweat.

All of them froze when she pivoted and stared at the rear wall of the command center as though she could see through it.

"Wait!" It did not take them long to realize that something had caught her attention. "I sense something."

"Hold fire," the captain ordered but spoke quietly as though that would be enough to save him from her wrath if she'd wanted them to continue.

Better safe than sorry was not an option. All he could do was act as he saw fit and hope it was enough. He didn't *dare* tell her about the mysterious ship that had popped up on their scans and disappeared as swiftly.

One of the mages standing to one side of the command deck reached out cautiously to see if he could sense what the Prime had said she'd felt. Before he could discover what it was, a voice rolled through the ship.

"I'm here. Do you have the courage to do anything about it?" The question came in a voice all of them recognized but few of them had heard in over a millennia.

"It cannot be," murmured the mage but the Prime raged.

"She is on *my* ship! *Find her!* Find that bitch and *put. Her. Down!*"

The captain made frantic signals to the pilot and the big ship slowed. There was no way he wanted to engage with the admiral and his squadron with *that* on board.

The incident left him with no choice but to issue instructions.

"Full defenses," he ordered. "Weapons, engage nothing unless it attacks the ship. Draw no fire if you can avoid it."

He glanced at the viewscreen where Varash continued to do the Prime's will. "Varash is on his own. The war has arrived."

And it's arrived inside our walls, he thought. *Although we still have to discover exactly where.*

He kept those thoughts to himself in case the Prime should take them as a challenge to her rule. As he issued a low string of orders, the thought occurred to him that surviving the battle and surviving her were equally difficult, but at least the battle would end.

It appeared her rule might last forever.

"Man, are you sure this is big enough?" Marcus asked and studied the space they'd landed in.

In other times, it had probably been some type of conference room. Right now, it was a shuttle bay for the Hooligans and Steph and

Elizabeth's teams. The huge table that had stood in its center had been crushed beneath the dropship's landing gear.

"They must be compensating for something." Frog snickered and Ka rolled her eyes.

"As you know, Froggie boy, size isn't everything."

That brought hoots of laughter as the teams spread out to cover the area and offload the gear. Bumblebee and Zeekat raced around the room in search of prey.

"Do you hear that, Frog? The girl's been taking notes."

"Pfft. Someone should tell V'ritan," Frog retorted. "I swear he's more size-conscious than anyone!"

"Don't you let the Meligornians hear you talking about their *Garghilum* like that," Vishlog warned. "You'll end up with a lightning bolt up your ass!"

"And it would be a big one." Dru snickered.

Frog groaned. "Weren't you listening? Apparently, size isn't everything."

"It's how you use it that counts," Angus added and spread his hands at the looks cast his way. "What? That's what my girlfriend always says."

"You don't have a girlfriend."

He wagged his finger at Henry. "I don't have a girlfriend I've told you about. There's a difference."

They moved as they joked, loaded up, and checked their weapons and each other's harnesses. Throughout their preparations, they monitored the perimeter of the room. When they were finished, they settled into watchful silence.

Vishlog, Garach, and Johnny took position to cover the doors. Jimmy, Darren, and Angus joined them, while Amy, Arne, and Lars made sure their leaders were safe.

Stephanie signaled to Elizabeth and Todd so they could debark and confirm their plans. Given that the missiles hadn't had a hope of penetrating the dreadnought's hull, she'd used MU to find a space big enough and empty enough to set the shuttle in safely.

Then, she'd teleported them into it.

"Nice landing," Brenden snarked as he and Avery exited the cockpit. "Honestly, I don't know why you had us train."

"Aww, poor baby," she had quipped in return and pinched his cheek between her forefinger and thumb. "Next time, I'll let you set her down wherever you like."

Avery snorted and she didn't quite hear his retort. Shrugging it aside, she turned to Todd and Elizabeth.

E nudged him in the ribs.

"I bet you thought this was *your* mission," she whispered.

"It's a joint venture," he told her shortly. "Something the Navy should have organized in the first place."

"Mmm-hmmm," she agreed. "Well, at least we're on the same page there."

"When it comes to Stephanie, we so often are," he pointed out, but when he looked at his girl, he was all business.

"Two teams?" he asked.

"Two," she confirmed. "bridge and engines, I think."

"I agree," he said like it mattered.

Elizabeth stood back and let them work it out. After all, her expertise was on the ground and usually solo. When it came to teams and ship-to-ship fighting, they were way ahead of her.

"E, how do you feel about taking Engineering?"

"It sounds like another manufacturing plant to me," she replied and grinned.

Matthias laid a hand on her shoulder.

"You *died* the last time we went into a manufacturing plant," he reminded her.

"On *purpose*," she retorted. "Besides, I'll have you and Arne and something tells me you've run operations like this before."

He raised his eyebrows. "And you haven't?"

"Not in space," she admitted. "All my work's been on the ground."

"Not all of mine has been," Arne interjected quietly.

She slapped him on the shoulder. "Good." She turned to Stephanie. "We're all set."

The Witch smiled. "I'm glad to hear it. We'll take our teams and split the Hooligans between us."

"I take it the Hooligans have a say in this?" Ka interrupted waspishly.

Todd held a hand up to silence his second. "You bet we do," he told her. "I'll need you on the bridge. We still need to extract the data."

He looked around and his gaze settled on his engineer. "Piet, you need to go with E and the ex's. Make sure that engine room is ours and pull any data caches you find on the way."

The man's eyebrows rose. "Anything else? A nice cup of tea en route, perhaps?"

"Oy!" Gary protested. "That's *my* line!"

"I prefer coffee," Elizabeth told him and the Englishman folded his arms.

"Well, I won't go with you, then."

Todd sighed. "No, Gary, you won't. You, Jimmy, Reggie, and Ka are with me. Dru, Angus, Henry, Darren, and Piet are with E. Treat them like the team or you'll spend up-close and personal time with them in the pods after until you get the point."

"If we don't treat them like a team," Ka muttered, "there probably won't be an 'after' or a point to get."

"Exactly," he agreed. "Are we clear?"

The Hooligans answered with a soft chorus of, "Oorah," and moved closer to their designated groups.

"First one to the bridge and engines chooses what the other one pays for," Todd declared, and E's eyes narrowed.

"You are on!" She headed to Piet. "Do you wanta lead, or shall I?"

He made a small gesture with his hand. "By all means. Ladies first."

She gave him a hard, cold grin. "Who said I was a lady?"

Matthias groaned and Arne clipped the demolitions expert on the back of the head.

"Now look what you did."

"What?"

The other Marines gathered around him. "Where to, boss?"

"Wherever the boss lady says," Piet told them. "They might be civilians but they're *our* kind of civilians."

"And don't you forget it," Arne snapped and fell in a little behind Matthias.

Piet smirked. "Not likely, Master Sergeant."

That brought a hitch to the other man's stride but his face was firm when he replied. "Not anymore, Corporal. Never again."

He left it at that and settled into stride to match the pace Elizabeth had set. In the conference room, Ka had jacked into the Teloran system and found the schematics for each deck exactly where she expected them to be.

The team focused as their HUDs flickered and the schematics became visible. Elizabeth's soft laugh rolled over their comms.

"Let's go teach these scumsucking motherfuckers a lesson."

"Whoa. That lady has a mouth like a *Marine*," Angus whispered.

"I told you I wasn't a lady," she responded, her tone hard and sharp, and they fell into silence.

Behind them, Stephanie's team exited the conference room and moved in the opposite direction.

Monitoring their icons in her HUD, Elizabeth couldn't help a smirk. The Witch was in the lead and not even the Marines contested it. It seemed they remembered what she was like the last time.

In all fairness, she couldn't blame them. She wouldn't want to be in front either.

Her team risked the elevator, knowing the Telorans were aware they were on board but needing the fast ride down. The engines weren't quite at the bottom of the ship but they were in the lower third—and that was more decks down than they could cover as rapidly as they needed to.

It was a trade-off in risk, one they could make now but which wouldn't be available later. If she was honest with herself, Elizabeth wasn't sure she should make it, but there was no way she would let Stephanie beat her.

The win didn't matter but being in a position to support the girl when she reached the command deck did. They couldn't do that unless they reached their goal first.

Fortunately, the Marines seemed to be of the same mind. She wasn't sure what they'd do if they found a data center on the way.

Above them, Stephanie's group found their first Teloran mage. He waited behind a barricade of enemy soldiers.

"Your end lies here!" He snarled and raised his hands.

That was as far as he got. While he'd delivered the challenge, Stephanie had swept her hands back and around in a perfect baseball pitch to lob a ball of magic down the corridor.

His troops dived out of its path while Todd, Johnny, and the teams opened fire on them. Magic arced between the mage's hands and he raised them to head height before her spell struck him in the chest and blew him back, tearing him apart as he fell.

By the time he landed, the Hooligans and her team had felled his escort and jogged past their still remains.

Stephanie had only one word for them.

"Beginners…"

CHAPTER FIFTY-SIX

Not sure why the Teloran vessel had stopped, Amaratne studied his boards and tried to stay abreast of what was happening in the battle. The Federation forces were heavily engaged and he'd lost track of the situations of their allies.

He scanned the bridge and kept an eye on his crew, knowing how important it was to make sure they looked all right. It was hard to tell when someone would find a battle too much and being in the real thing was different than running through a sim.

Some thrived under the threat of imminent death. Others, not so much. To his relief, everyone seemed to be coping and went about their duties with an air of studied calm, even as their fingers flew across their boards.

The Marines stationed around the room in case of boarding were watchful but they weren't tense.

Correction, he said to himself when he noticed a new face among them, *that one seems a little tense.*

He shifted his attention to the forward screen and frowned as though something there concerned him. His expression drew the attention of his captain as he pressed a small switch he'd had installed on the underside of his console.

Hearing the signal in his headpiece, the captain moved to him even faster. Amaratne knew he wasn't the only receiving the signal. He was sure the emergency measure they'd put in place had also heard it and was heading in their direction.

When the captain reached him, he made sure to turn so the suspect Marine was at his back, if only for a brief moment.

"Over my left shoulder," he murmured so only the other officer could hear.

The crew were used to him having hurried conferences, where he and the captain would put their heads together as different events unfolded. That worked for them now.

Amaratne gave the man enough time to register the new Marine and pivoted a little so he was side-on. It wouldn't do to make himself *too* attractive a target.

Now would not be a good time to die.

Jaleck found herself ass-deep in Telorans, much like things would soon be on the Federation flagship. If the truth be told, she'd orchestrated it so she *would* be ass-deep in Telorans, but still.

A part of her had hoped it wouldn't come to this.

Around her, her crew fought like the derkat they were. There was nothing that said putting a Dreth in a fancy uniform and placing them on the command deck of a ship would remove the warrior in them.

The Telorans who'd boarded the Dreth flagship expecting to find an easy target received a rude awakening.

Now I understand what happens to Vishlog in the field, she thought and laughed as she stepped past the thrust of a Teloran blade. She swept the attack aside with the blade in her right hand as she fired three quick shots into the warrior's side.

At that range, the Dreth flechettes ripped through the Teloran's armor like a knife through keftel cheese and left as much destruction in their wake. The admiral didn't stop to gloat.

There were more and they were everywhere.

"Take it out," she commanded, and the weapons officer tweaked a control in the HUD.

The Dreth flagship was not yet lost, and she wanted to keep it that way. She resisted the idea that the Teloran dreadnought that had fought her to a standstill would have made a fine replacement. Frankly, she didn't want to go down in the history books as the first Dreth Fleet Commander to destroy not one but *two* flagships.

If it came to that, she wondered, *would I get a third?*

No matter. If we survive, I can always ask for a repossessed dreadnought as a prize—and to be allowed to park it in permanent low orbit.

Somehow, she couldn't imagine living the rest of her life inside an atmosphere. She'd always wonder what she couldn't see.

No. She slid her blade across one Teloran's throat while she fired through the chest of another. *I would rather keep overwatch on my world —and maybe even warn her before the next threat can come close.*

First, she added and kicked a body off the end of her blade, *I need to take possession of my new residence.*

Across the solar system, the four navies fought.

The Teloran's orderly formation had separated into several squadrons and each one pressed against a different part of the Federation alliance. There were fewer of them than before and the remaining ships held their own, but barely. It was only a matter of time before one or other part of the alliance fell.

Whether it turned tail and ran or was destroyed to the last ship, the Telorans didn't care. Not one of the home-worlds would be spared the destruction they had planned. There was no room in the universe for anyone else.

The fall of their home-world had taught them that.

Across the battlefield, ships fired devastating salvos and many of the allies exploded before they could do more to destroy their counterparts. Slowly, the Teloran dreadnoughts emerged as the main power.

As Jaleck rammed her flagship into the bleeding and damaged side of her opponent, V'ritan and his mages stood on the command deck of *The King's Warrior* and channeled MU into the engines of another.

The Meligornian fleet commander had called what was left of the Meligornian navy to the flag. He didn't know how many of them would be standing at the end, but he was determined to give them the best chance he could.

They, in return, fought to keep their flag alive. None of them wanted to mourn the loss of their beloved *Garghilum Afreghil.* Moving into close quarters, some force-docked with the oncoming dreadnought and blocked its gunports as they cut into their opponent.

The King's Warrior turned its focus outward to protect the docked ships as the battle for the dreadnought waged across its decks. Directing his forces to shuttle in to assist, V'ritan only hoped the humans were having better luck.

Battlecruisers against behemoths, that was what this battle would be remembered for, one Federation captain thought as she raised her hand.

"Aaand mark!" she called. "Pivot... Shields!"

The cruiser reversed its forward thrusters and used the retros usually kept for docking maneuvers to push its nose one way and its tail the other. It was the equivalent of trying to drift an eighteen-wheeler and worked about as well.

It *did*, however, bring the cruiser around faster than a standard turn—and in time to fire a full broadside into its much bigger and heavier opponent.

"What I wouldn't give for a few mages right now," she murmured and gave the orders for another rapid salvo.

"Suits!" she called as the collision alarms sounded. Not that the suits would do much, but for those who managed to survive, it gave them another chance at least.

The dreadnought turned its nose toward her and came about to protect its damaged flank.

Proximity alerts and collision alarms sounded throughout as the cruiser tried to turn with it but was too far out of position to succeed. She continued to fire and was still trying to turn when the dreadnought pounded into her.

It was much worse than anyone could have anticipated.

Instead of the glancing blow the captain had hoped for, the bigger ship's bow sliced into the vessel's forward section and separated it as she powered forward.

Pods burst from the cruiser's hull, along with the shuttles and fighters who would try to collect and protect them. Rescue was a small hope but it was still there.

The story was repeated across the battleground. Smaller ships rammed larger ones. Vessels of all sizes bled fire and atmosphere through holes that sucked their personnel into the black. Smaller ships powered into bigger ones in an attempt to destroy them or failed a hard dock and achieved the same results. Life pods jettisoned in the hope that some might survive.

No one, not even the most cowardly, tried to turn tail and run. They all knew there was nowhere to run to and that anyone who might come to save them was already there.

And everyone knew that their worlds stood forfeit if they failed.

As bleak as the outcome looked, it wasn't over, and none of them intended to stop fighting until it was.

On the Teloran flagship, Stephanie stormed through corridors and advanced up the decks on her way to the command center.

"This bitch is mine," she stated and not even Todd could tell if it was she or the Morgana who spoke.

That didn't concern anyone, though. All that mattered was eliminating the Telorans' high command. Once that was done, they might be able to demand a surrender.

None of them wanted to admit that there might be nothing left for the Telorans to surrender to. Staying out of range of the flickering tendrils of magic that arced around their Witch, they followed her deeper into the ship.

At first, it was easy. The only mage they saw was the one foolish enough to use his people as shields and she had swept him aside easily enough.

The resistance grew stronger as the Telorans scrambled to protect both their ship and their Prime but not necessarily in that order.

Stephanie picked up two mages and slammed them together before she launched magic to arc into the soldiers surrounding them.

"Do you *fucking* mind?" Gary complained. "That one was mine."

"Was not," Frog argued. "It was mine and you know it."

"Puhleeze!" Ka mocked and tossed a limpet into the air. "Both of you had your heads up your asses if you thought you'd be able to get anywhere *near* those before I dealt with them."

Using the guidance system she'd slipped over her index finger, she swirled the limpet over their heads and hurled it through the door Todd had kicked open.

"Heads up!" she shouted and he slid alongside it and waited for the blast.

As soon as it had cleared, he twisted into the room beyond and opened fire. Jimmy followed, and the steady beat of their weapons revealed that Ka's little surprise hadn't been as effective as she might have hoped.

The two Marines emerged shortly after and looked far too pleased with themselves for anyone's comfort.

"Clear," Todd announced and leapfrogged over Garach and Vishlog as they entered the next room.

Neither Dreth carried a blaster.

"Boys and their toys," Dru teased, but she hefted her twin blades as she went in after them. "Leave some for me, boys!"

They pushed quickly along that floor and left nothing alive in their wake. Telorans who emerged from stairwells soon fell back into them, while those who approached from behind discovered what a limpet did in close confines.

"This whole boat will need a new paint job," Jimmy noted and winced when another loud bang ended in panicked screams. "That girl is having far too much fun over there."

Magic tingled across their skins as Stephanie felled another mage.

"This way," she ordered and blasted open the door to the next stairwell.

"We're getting close," Elizabeth murmured on the other side of the ship.

The Telorans had filled the corridor ahead of them, which left them no choice but to fight their way through.

She was in her element, her grin a mile wide behind her HUD. She had switched from two small blasters to a short, curved sword and a heavy pistol.

"Suck. On. This." She grunted as she slashed a Teloran's throat with the scimitar and shot a second in the gut. To her left, Amy and Lisa kept the enemy off her flank while to her right, Matthias made sure nothing came within range.

He stepped past a doorway and fired as he moved. It wouldn't have been enough to save him but Arne released a short burst from his blaster into the suddenly thick darkness.

The blade meant for Matthias's back fell with a clatter and he turned quickly.

The ex-Marine grinned smugly. "You gotta be more careful than that, old man," he said but his amusement vanished when the other shot over his head.

The sound of solids impacting followed by a slightly heavier thump confirmed his words.

"Move! Move! Move!" Angus commanded and shoved the two of them forward as he activated a grenade.

"Fire in the Hole!" he yelled, pulled the door closed, and continued down the corridor.

The ensuing explosion was far bigger than any grenade had a right to be and he sniggered like a schoolboy with a dirty magazine as he jogged after them.

The run continued without interference until they reached the next junction.

"Oh, look, they know how to set up an ambush," Angus said.

He and Henry exchanged glances and turned into the room immediately before the junction.

"Wait one," they called, and Elizabeth slowed her pace to a walk.

"What are those silly assholes up to now?"

Piet tapped her on the arm and signaled Darren to follow him into the room opposite.

"Wait one," he repeated. "You'll like this."

She settled into a crouch. "I'd better, or your ass is mine."

Matthias cast her a look of pure affront and Arne sniggered and shoved him gently. "Get over it. She's still yours."

"Yeah, but...the visuals."

"Get your mind on the job!" she snapped and turned to Piet. "You have two minutes."

The engineer vanished into the room and his voice floated back to answer her. "We only need one."

She began to count. "Sixty..."

When she reached thirty, twin explosions shook the walls.

"Can't you assholes count?" Amy yelled.

Cries of alarm rose from the ranks of Telorans waiting on either side of the junction before the Marines opened fire.

"First kill is mine!" Angus called and reminded them of the point-scoring Amy had started early in the run.

Each encounter had a first kill that earned triple points.

"Second is mine," Henry shouted to claim the double point bonus.

"You cheating bastards!" Amy started forward as she primed her blaster.

The Marines ignored her and the staccato clatter of exchanged fire sounded from either side. Piet claimed the third kill and Amy, incensed, hurried forward.

Elizabeth, Lisa, and Bunny moved with her, and Arne and

Matthias followed closely. The shooting was thick and fast but their armor and shields held until they'd moved to close quarters.

The next few minutes were filled with the silence of desperate battle. Beyond the blaster fire and the grunts from impact or effort, the team didn't say a word.

They'd cleared the junction and taken a moment to catch their breath when the ceiling panel opened above Amy's head and a single figure dropped through, already firing.

If it hadn't been for Bunny's quick reflexes, she'd have been dead. As it was, some of the rounds drilled through her left arm as the woman jerked her aside.

The security guard fired as she hauled her team leader behind her, and Elizabeth fell prone. She rolled, came to the foot of the Teloran warrior who'd fallen among them, and fired up the front of his body.

Lisa jerked Amy out of Bunny's hands and shoved her injured colleague at the Marines. "Take her!"

They complied and hauled her out of the junction while the rest of the team followed them into the room they'd used to move behind the Teloran forces.

"Was that a *Dreth* trick?" Angus demanded. "On a *Teloran* ship?"

"The assholes had to learn it from somewhere," Darren muttered.

"Hold still, girl," Henry told the injured guard. He slammed an autoinjector into her wounded shoulder. "This will hurt."

"Yeah," Angus snickered, "but only for a while. After that, you're gonna think it's a scratch."

After the initial yelp, Amy paused and took a deep breath while she watched Henry patch her arm. When he was finished with her flesh, he picked up the pieces of armor he'd pulled away and held them in place.

"Piet, I need tape."

The engineer was already peeling the first strip and it didn't take them very long to have the armor locked in place again.

"You're gonna need some help getting out of it," Piet observed, "but it'll do you until we finish."

She gave him a shaky smile. "How long will the meds last?" she asked and her teeth chattered as she took a deep breath.

"You have a half-hour before we should check to make sure you haven't bled through the bandage."

"And how will you know?" she asked. "With the amount of tape you put over it."

"We had to make sure the bandages would hold," Henry replied gruffly. He jerked a thumb at Elizabeth. "I don't want her killing me for not plugging the hole."

The gesture made them notice that the woman hadn't moved. She stood and stared at Amy, her face completely devoid of expression.

When she realized her guard would be okay, she spun on a heel and continued down the corridor.

This time, she paid close attention to both her HUD and the ceiling as she progressed. The others hurried to catch up and Amy pushed to reach her.

Arne raised a brow and glanced at Matthias and then Bunny.

"Is she still here?"

The cold chuckle that floated in answer chilled his soul—as did the words that followed over their comms.

"You and Matthias never met Little Lizzie," she whispered.

Without seeming to, her pace increased and the team had to scramble to keep up. It appeared that the Dreth had, indeed, shared their ceiling tactic—at least in this level.

Elizabeth had sheathed her scimitar and now fired non-stop, the sound of her blasters a staccato rhythm as she aimed through walls and into the ceiling. Her gaze seemed to track things they couldn't see.

"How in *fuck* does she *do* that!" Angus exclaimed as she located an unseen opponent in the cavity above and her guns fired faster when he sprinted overhead.

The number of rounds proved too much for the already overburdened panels and they gave way. Three or four shadow-clad figures plunged on top of the team.

The Marines leapt to one side, caught those closest to them, and yanked them out of the way as well.

"Motherfuck!" Angus shouted. "Will someone tell her to *stop* shooting Telorans directly above us? I swear to God, if I die by Death by Teloran Crush, I'll shoot her in the ass."

"Fuck! I'd be happy if she wouldn't keep saving our asses and then leaving us behind," Arne muttered, shoved away from the wall, and raced after Elizabeth's rapidly diminishing figure.

The only reason they caught up with her was that she'd stopped to do a quick sneak and peek around a corner. Piet slid to the corner opposite and took a look for himself.

"Well, fuck me. I'm not sure how we'll get through *that*."

The pictures transmitted from both his and Elizabeth's HUDs were forbidding. Ahead of them, in a wide, open space that looked like a general-purpose recreation area, stood what looked like three platoons of Telorans.

Elizabeth uttered a low, unnerving cackle. In the cold voice that belonged to Little Lizzie, she retrieved two of the grenades Piet had brought, one marked with a sapphire-blue and the other glittering with ebon bands.

"I'd tell you to hold my beer," she told him, "but I didn't bring any."

Henry glanced over Piet's shoulder and saw what she was holding.

"Oh, *shit*!" He caught the engineer's arm and began to tow him back down the corridor as fast as he could.

Angus grabbed Amy and slapped Arne on the shoulder. "We have to go! Now!" he added as Lizzie primed the grenades.

Darren took hold of Bunny and was relieved when Lisa came without urging. Arne took a strong grip on Matthias's bicep.

"Don't make me drag you," he warned, "but if these boys are running…"

The other man hesitated long enough for Lizzie to throw the grenades and start to turn before he bolted. They reached the first junction but the Marines kept going.

"It's not far enough!"

"But—"

"Don't fucking argue! Do you *want* to be caught in a magic storm?"

It was enough to keep them running and they managed to put another corner between them and the corridor they'd stood in when she had thrown the grenades.

She laughed like a madwoman when a massive explosion rocked that section of the ship. Walls disintegrated in the corridors they'd left behind and the lights went out.

They waited for the emergency lights to come on but with no result before Amy noticed Elizabeth was gone.

"Did she— Well, *fuck!*" She found her feet and raced back the way they'd come before any of them could comment.

Matthias was quick to follow, and Arne sprinted after him, not willing to let his principal out of his sight. They'd barely gone six paces before the shooting started.

By this time, they knew the sound of Lizzie's guns and that hard, cold laugh. It was the most gleefully evil sound they'd ever heard.

"Fuck me!" Arne muttered as she came into sight. "Did you know she could shoot like that?"

Elizabeth moved like silk through water, her actions a smooth flow as she targeted one Teloran after another. She moved so swiftly that if it hadn't been for the decisive explosion of each enemy who faced her guns, he might not have believed it.

Blam! Head shot. *Blam!* Head Shot. *Blam!*

"And one for you, and you, and you...aaaand you!" Lizzie said and her words grew faster as she worked.

By the time one body landed, three more were falling and the guns had shifted to yet another target.

"Aw, man. Why did we choose the crazy one to work with?" Dru complained.

Angus blew her a raspberry. "It's not like the Morgana is exactly *sane!*" he argued.

She rolled her eyes. "Well, okay, the occasionally sane crazy one?"

As if to prove her point, Lizzie's laughter rolled around them once more.

CHAPTER FIFTY-SEVEN

"Draw that bastard over here," Admiral Helveck told his captain.

On the screen, Dreyfus nodded in approval.

"I'll see if I can get the attention of his escort."

"Make sure you get the trajectories right. We need them between us and the main fleet," the other instructed.

"You know that'll sandwich the admiral," the captain stated, and Helveck nodded.

The man frowned. "But, sir, if we lose the Fleet, can we still win this battle?"

That *did* get his attention.

"Captain, are you questioning me?" he asked, his voice as cold as the skies outside.

The captain shook his head hurriedly, and Helveck favored him with a cold, humorless smile.

"Very good, Captain. I'd hate to think you weren't *completely* on my side."

"Oh no, sir. I am *very much* on your side. I merely didn't want to see you short-handed when we still might need the Fleet's assistance."

"Very good, Captain. Now, draw that big bastard's attention."

"Aye aye, sir!"

He watched as the man worked them into a position where the Teloran lay between them and the fleet admiral's vessel. At first, he thought they'd been successful in gaining the big ship's attention. Then, it noticed the flagship.

"Oh, this is priceless," Helveck stated. He chuckled. "Well, a pincer movement on the Fleet wasn't *exactly* what I had in mind, but…"

"Sheer genius, sir," the captain agreed, more relieved that the dreadnought was no longer eyeing his ship like a tasty snack.

His relief changed to anxiety, however, when they received a hail from the flagship.

"Amaratne to Helveck. I need assistance."

"Sorry, sir," the admiral replied, his voice as smooth as butter. "Your signal's not coming through right. What did you say?"

"This is Fleet Admiral Amaratne requesting assistance. I repeat, this is Fleet Admiral requesting assistance for the command group. All boats, this is Admiral Amaratne requesting assistance for the command group. Helveck do you hear me?"

"We hear you, sir, but damn, we're out of position. We won't get to you in time."

Amaratne sounded defeated when he replied. "Do your best Helveck. There are people who need you."

The scan team brought up an image of the command group and displayed not only the Teloran they'd managed to attract but another, equally large ship already moving in on it.

Helveck realized he hadn't needed to draw the other ship in at all, but it *did* give him a convenient excuse for not being able to reach the admiral in time.

"Such a pity," he murmured but didn't sound at all sorry for his superior officer's plight. "He was *such* a good man."

That last was said with a touch of bitter irony and not a shred of sincerity. He and Dreyfus watched in silence as the enemy began to close.

There were three of them now, all bigger than the flagship and all more than capable of giving the admiral a run for his money individually. Even with the rest of his squadron sailing to intervene, the Telorans were too powerful to be stopped.

Helveck smirked and watched with pitiless eyes as the first Teloran prepared to fire. At that moment, another ship appeared.

It was bigger than Amaratne's flagship and much bigger than the Teloran vessels it confronted. Not only that, it had been completely invisible until a few seconds before.

The admiral's jaw dropped.

Unaware of the leviathan uncloaking behind him, Amaratne squared his jaw. "Do what you can, Captain. We won't go without a fight. It might give the others a chance."

That last was a forlorn hope and they both knew it, but it was the only hope they had left—that their deaths wouldn't be in vain.

He glanced at the communications team. "Try again."

"Aye aye, sir."

"And see if there's something we can do to boost the signal," he added. "Make sure we make a noise."

"Oh, that part's very certain, sir. We are *making* a *noise,*" the head technician replied. "I don't know why they don't hear us. I can hear them fine. It—"

He hesitated and his face flushed at what he was about to say next.

"Go on, Commander."

"I'm sorry, sir, but it's almost like they're deliberately not hearing us, sir."

Amaratne pressed his lips together and nodded.

"Well, do what you can, Commander."

He was about to say more when one of the lieutenants on scans raised her head. "Captain!"

The urgency in her tone brought him rushing to her side. The admiral watched as the man glanced at the lieutenant's screens and looked quickly at him.

"Admiral!"

Amaratne met his gaze and raised an eyebrow in question.

"Do you know of a ship bigger than the biggest Teloran—one that's in *our* fleet?"

"No." He shook his head. "We have nothing like that. Not even under development."

"Are you sure, sir?"

"I am. There's no way something that big is one of ours."

"Well, could it be Dreth, sir?"

Again, he shook his head. "No, I'm sorry, Admiral Jaleck didn't tell me they had anything like that."

The captain glanced at the screen again.

"Meligornian?" he asked hopefully.

"V'ritan's ship's the biggest," he informed him.

"Well, then, who the *hell* is that?" the captain demanded and pointed to the forward viewscreen as it flickered and the display changed.

Amaratne looked up and his jaw dropped. "What the *hell*?"

As he tried to fathom what he saw, a new voice issued over their speakers—a new but *familiar* voice.

"Did the Admiral call for help?" Captain Emil asked. "Because the *Tempestarii* would be honored to supply it."

The admiral forced himself to close his mouth and he managed to move his head in the tiniest of nods.

"Yes. Yes, I would like some help…thank you…"

"Oh. My. God," the lieutenant said.

The Prime had left the bridge. She was flanked by the best guards the ship and Corevex could supply. All had reached the highest levels in their martial training and all were mages as well.

"We will meet them in the Officers' Commons," she said and the speed of her pace suggested she wasn't sure they would beat them there.

The guards said nothing but jogged beside her and made sure their magic was ready to respond if the Witch and her team should arrive.

Despite their misgivings, she still had not appeared by the time they reached the large, double doors leading into the officers' entertainment area.

The two lead guards glanced at each other, then at the Prime. Catching their uncertainty, she gestured impatiently for them to open the entrance.

They jumped to obey her and pressed the panel to slide the doors apart. Without waiting to be told what to do next, they risked her wrath by moving into the room.

To their surprise and relief, it was empty and its vaulted ceilings gleamed with the light of a mild spring day. This was easily the most relaxing room on this part of the ship, not least because it was a space the Prime didn't frequent.

She moved to the threshold and surveyed the open space, noting the scattered tables and chairs and pleasant lighting before she swept forward.

Her guards moved to flank her and two proceeded in advance, keeping a cautious eye on the double doors ahead. Without warning, those blew inward and traveled three meters to rest ten meters short of the Prime's lead guards.

Stephanie saw the Teloran ahead of her and felt Morgana's recognition.

This is her!

I hear you, she replied and murmured into the team comms.

"Todd, she's not on the bridge. I'll keep her busy while you guys get the data."

His voice responded softly. "Gotcha."

She didn't turn to watch him go. The only person she had eyes for was the Teloran leader and while part of her wished she had a chance to say goodbye, she shoved the thought aside.

There would be no goodbyes between them, merely one big-ass farewell for the Telorans.

Let me have full control, the Morgana said. *This annoying child caused such problems the last time.*

This is your daughter? she asked.

Oh, absolutely not! Her alter-ego seemed disgusted by the thought. *I raised my daughters better than this.*

Stephanie smiled. *Because that wouldn't be awkward.*

It's my granddaughter, she added.

It took effort but she stifled a groan. *Fantastic. A family reunion.*

She walked forward and studied the Prime in silence. It wasn't easy to read through the tall Teloran's shielding, but her posture said she was as ready for a fight as she was.

Her adversary tilted her head, and the Witch mimicked the movement and paused her advance two meters away. Rather than step into her enemy's reach, she circled, conscious of the guards.

To her satisfaction, they moved back.

I hope she's told them she wants to take me on herself, the Morgana observed. *They'll be too scared to try an attack if she has.*

Let's test the theory, Stephanie replied as the magic arced over her skin.

The pure blue tones of eMU mingled with the purple tones of MU, and both were highlighted by the almost colorless glow of the gMU. In contrast, the Prime was wreathed in flickering darkness.

Johnny took a step forward but Lars stretched an arm out to block his path. "Give them space. Watch the guards."

That was instruction enough. Her team moved into the room and eased around the edges so they could keep a closer eye on the Telorans.

For a fleeting moment, Lars wished he'd remembered to ask Ka to lock them in. That way, there'd be no surprises.

"Frog," he murmured and gestured toward the door behind him.

The little man moved back to close it and make sure it stayed closed until they needed it otherwise.

"Marcus, Johnny." The team leader gestured at the door opposite. "Lock it down if you can but don't take any unnecessary risks."

They moved to comply but two of the guards stepped back to

cover the exit.

"That'll be a no-go, boss."

With a sigh, he shrugged. "Watch it then. It was worth a try."

He turned his attention to Steph and the tall Teloran in the center of the room and wished he knew what would happen next.

Oblivious to her team's movements, Stephanie stepped around the Prime and smirked when she mirrored her movement.

Lars watched them circle and sent one more comm to the team.

"Remember, girls and boys, the first rule of mage duels is don't get caught in the middle of a mage duel."

Soft snickers issued in response but they didn't reply verbally and he knew that meant they were focused on the opposition.

Good, he thought and settled to do the same as Stephanie began to speak.

The Morgana, he corrected himself when the ice-dark tones fell into the silence.

"What brings you out here? Not trouble at home, I hope?"

"Trouble is one way to describe it," the Teloran replied. "Our world is dying."

She frowned. "Dying? How?"

"Our Corevex, in all its wisdom, decided to use magic to create a Utopia." The enemy leader fell silent for a moment, then added. "It was...ill-conceived."

The Morgana snorted. "Exactly as I predicted it would be before *you* got rid of anyone with any wisdom."

"I beg your pardon?" the Prime demanded and her head snapped up, but her opponent didn't give her time to think.

"You heard me. I was one of many who advised the Corevex that it would draw too heavily on Telor's energy if it did what you suggested—"

"But—" the other began.

"But you would not listen," she continued, "and then you began to eliminate anyone who stood against you including *me.*"

Confusion rippled through the Prime's tones.

"Who *are* you?"

CHAPTER FIFTY-EIGHT

Ka crouched beside a terminal. Solid rounds whistled over the desk and thunked into the wall above her head, but she tucked in tighter and typed faster. She might not have liked learning Teloran, but it sure as shit came in handy for this.

What they needed was to access the security feeds for the command deck. Instead, she found the feed for the Officers' Common Room. She paused a moment and watched as Steph and the Teloran leader circled each other in the center of the room.

"Todd," she called over their private channel.

"Whatcha got?"

"A way to turn the vid feed on for the duel."

"Duel?"

"The one your Witch is about to get into with the Teloran leader."

"Put it through."

"Are you sure it's wise?"

"Corporal, I don't give a flying fuck if it's *wise*. I merely want it on —and get me the goddamned bridge! Quit fucking around in there!"

"Gotcha," she replied and put the feed through, glad he couldn't see her rolling her eyes.

Love sucked. And she was glad it wasn't Piet in there with that

Teloran bitch. She banished the engineer from her head as fast as she could and chose not to think of the trouble he could get into without her to watch his back.

Still, he had Dru and the boys. And Dru had better keep her claws to herself or there would be words.

That was another thought Ka banished from her head.

More rounds drilled into the wall and this time, some of the paneling broke away and avalanched beside her.

"Do you *fucking mind?* I'm tryin' to work here!"

"Well, work faster!" Reggie quipped in return and more rounds pounded into the wall.

Thankfully, they were farther away this time.

"Yeah? Well, how about you workin' on your aim? Honestly, it's *say* it, not *spray* it! You're shooting worse than a rookie!"

"Come over here and say that, smart-ass."

"Nope. Busy. Tryin' to *concentrate*, shit for brains."

It took her a few minutes to decrypt the feed and shunt it to everyone's HUDs. She pushed it through to the rest of the ship and the other team for good measure, then couldn't work out how to get it to play.

"So, this still is very entertaining and everything," Gary snarked, "but does it, like…*do* anything? Come on! I don't need the advertising. It's not like it's Prime Time or anything."

Ka resisted the urge to give him the finger. It wasn't hard. She needed all of them to type with.

"Fantastic," she muttered, "I learn innumerable useless Teloran words, but how to get video to play wasn't one of them. Someone should tell the intelligence boffins they need to do better."

Gary snickered. "Blamin' someone else for your shortcomings?" He tutted. "Not very professional."

"Shut it, you tea-sucking scumbag."

"Oooh…" he began, but whatever he intended to say next was lost to Reggie's observation.

"You know the best way to learn new video tricks is to watch porn, right?"

Ka shook her head. "Those aren't the kind of tricks I need, Reggie."

"Are you sure, Ka? Because I could show you a couple—"

"If you keep talking like that, you'll spend a couple of weeks in the ER trying to remember how *not* to eat through a straw."

"You have no sense of adventure."

"Nope. I kinda like my partners to be male...and human. I'm not being specist, here. It's merely a thing with me."

"You have *things*? For *that*?"

"Some of us are choosy as to how and who we dance the horizontal tango with, ya know."

"Like...how choosy?"

"That's on a need to know basis, Reg. And you don't need to know."

More rounds sprayed the wall as she found the controls she needed for the feed.

"Human and male," Gary interrupted as she worked through them. He grunted as he used his dagger to finish off another Teloran. "Like Piet?"

She was glad she was behind the desk and hidden by a large storage cabinet. It didn't only block stray rounds. It also meant no one could see her blush.

"I will kill my boss," she muttered.

The fighting continued throughout the fleet. Ships tangled in combat as Navy ships sent boarding parties onto Teloran vessels and the enemy returned the favor.

Admiral Reardon monitored the incursion, glad to note his Marines were resisting well—and not so glad when another boarding party burned through the hull and into the corridor outside the bridge.

Snapping his helmet closed, he glanced at the captain. "Do what you need to do," he ordered. "I'll go keep these assholes off your back."

"But, sir—"

He didn't stop. "It's time I stopped being a fifth wheel, Captain. Besides, it's been a long time since I had any fun."

"But—"

"No buts. Keep my ship alive." He didn't stop to argue but signaled to the Marine contingent to follow him as he stepped out of the command center and into the fight.

It might have been a long time since he'd been in battle, but he still spent time practicing in the pods. Whenever anyone questioned him about it, he simply told them that he didn't want to be a burden if his ship was ever boarded.

That comment had been met with laughter by some of the other admirals. Remembering the scenes of the current battle, he wondered how many of them were laughing now.

Reardon tried very hard not to wonder how many of them were alive. That was a question he'd face in the aftermath.

A blade flashed and he blocked it, fired from his waist into the Teloran warrior who had attacked him, and corrected the thought.

If he made it to the aftermath.

It was a fiercer fight than he'd expected since the enemy had sent a second dropship and more warriors poured into the corridor.

"I need more men on the command level," he called. "We're being overrun."

His orders were repeated by the Marine commander fighting beside him, and he felt vindicated. At least he knew he wasn't panicking.

The reply they received wasn't what either of them wanted to hear.

"We'll be there as soon as we can clear a path, sir."

He didn't bother to tell the commander to hurry. That went without saying, and he assumed the man had enough on his plate. There was no need to piss the troops off with useless banter.

With his focus on the task at hand, he felled the Teloran in front of him and pivoted to face the one who attacked from his right. As he did so, he felt a sudden burning pain in his side.

"What the—" He stumbled forward.

The pain came again, two more jolts of it and fired point-blank through his armor.

But...there's no Teloran close enough... The thought faltered as he landed hard.

Although he tried to roll, his adversary took full advantage of his weakness and sent a round of black fire through his skull.

He didn't see the men behind him stare in horror at the hole in the back of his armor or the way the Marine on his right flank turned to fire at their commander.

Nor did he see the commander gut the man with the heated vibro-blade he carried while he emptied half a blaster charge into his chest. The Marines' fury ran unabated and the Telorans were cleared shortly thereafter.

Admiral Reardon would be one of those remembered in the aftermath.

The dreadnought imploded. It had menaced Admiral Amaratne's left flank as the *Tempestarii* appeared and it hadn't had time to amend its aim.

He gaped as massive projectiles spewed from the *Tempestarii's* rail guns to crater the Teloran ship's armor and bow it in the center.

Missiles followed the rounds but weren't aimed at the dread-nought. They streaked forward in a storm to destroy one battle-cruiser, three corvettes, and a torpedo boat.

Amaratne shook his head.

"Where does she get these wonderful ships?" he asked and admired the behemoth as she shifted altitude toward the dreadnought that approached on his right.

Rather than sailing toward it as he expected, the *Tempestarii* slid out of view. His jaw dropped and she searched the scans for her.

Surely she hadn't simply *left*?

His protest ceased a moment later. The titan faded into view and appeared in the midst of the escort vessels for another of the dreadnoughts. The smaller ships scattered and tried to avoid being landed on.

Some engaged their drives rapidly enough, but others were shoved through space by an invisible field that triggered their shields to spark. No longer governed by their drives, several ships tumbled and collided with each other in fiery clouds of destruction.

Those that were left were pursued by a hail of fire from the *Tempestarii's* guns until they were nothing more than shipping hazards floating on the battleground.

The Teloran dreadnought fired, and Amaratne couldn't help admiring the ship's sheer brass. He almost felt sorry for it when the rail guns spoke again and took it from the sky.

The third enemy dreadnought hesitated, torn between fighting and running away. He wondered what its problem was as the outcome of either path was clear.

It would never be able to run fast enough to escape from a skip-powered titan and it simply didn't have the armament or weaponry to stand up to it in a toe-to-toe fight. If he were *that* captain, he'd take his chances on holing the *Tempestarii's* flank while she was still busy.

Hell! If he were *that* captain, he'd deploy his last resort.

He smiled as he watched a myriad fighters swarm from the body of the bigger vessel. *That's* what he'd do—deploy everything he had in the hope that it would interfere with the bigger ship's line of fire and give it other things to deal with.

The *Tempestarii* translated into nothing, and Amaratne envisioned the sheer panic on the Teloran dreadnought. He could imagine exactly how that captain felt and wondered why they hadn't tried to surrender.

The admiral wondered if that was even an option and if not, why not.

Again, he studied the scans and tried to predict where the titan would appear next while he contemplated how relieved he was to *not* be the dreadnought's captain.

Movement caught his attention and he was torn between watching the deadly dance on the screen and seeing what was going on at the other side of the bridge. Glancing up, he saw two of his regular Marines approach the new man.

Their lips moved but they weren't on any of the comms channels to which he had access. Assuming it was a Marine matter, he scanned the boards again.

Across the bridge, Private Keller leaned closer to the new Marine and pressed his blaster's muzzle into the man's back.

"Don't make me kill you simply because we *think* you're bad," he whispered.

The Marine froze. His gaze darted sideways as he tried to follow the path of the second Marine who sidled behind him. Warm breath on his other ear and a second blaster snugged hard into his chest were an unwelcome complication.

The second Marine's words were even less comforting than the first's.

"Yeah, let me find out you *are* bad first and then I'll do it with pleasure," he murmured, removed the man's blaster from its holster, and took his knife.

At the same time, the first Marine removed his grenade pouch and sword. Taking a firm grip on his bicep, he spoke softly.

"I don't believe you're supposed to be here, are you?"

The new Marine looked at the admiral but the behemoth had returned to the main viewscreen and Amaratne was once again lost in the battle.

It was a perfect opportunity gone to waste.

CHAPTER FIFTY-NINE

"You killed Steresh," the Morgana continued, "the most knowledgeable of all our magicians—and, perhaps, the only one with the secret of reversing what you've done."

"You can't *know* that!" the Prime cried.

"He wasn't dead when you left," she stated coldly. "Oh, he knew he was *dying*. You made sure that was inevitable, but you didn't make sure of your kill. That was as half-assed as the rest of what you've done."

"I *wasn't* half-assed," the Teloran thundered. "I was *very* precise. I made sure he wouldn't sway anyone else with his stupid ideas of conservative use and careful management."

"Anyone *else*?" The Morgana snarled. "You mean he'd started to make people see your ill-conceived plan and your *lies* for what they were—the hollow promises of a spoilt child who only cared for the win."

"The energy was there for the taking!" the Prime cried. "It wasn't *doing* anything. Steresh was wrong. Nothing needed that energy. Nothing wanted it."

"But it did, didn't it?" the Morgana demanded. "That energy was what kept the air clean, the water pure and flowing, the creatures—"

She stopped to quell the pain that had emerged in her voice. "Steresh proved that and you killed him for sharing his knowledge. But, like I said, you didn't think your plan through well enough."

"What was there to think about? I made the old fool a peace offering and he drank the bait. I made *no* mistake in that."

The protest stopped when Stephanie held her hand up. "But you didn't check the time it would take for the dose to kill him. You took his life, but you gave him the greatest gift that kind of death can offer. You gave him *time*."

"And he called you, I suppose." The Prime sneered.

"He let us *all* know what you had done and warned us not to trust you because if you would kill him, a grandfather who doted on you, no one was safe."

"Well, that explains why the others became more circumspect," her adversary responded huffily and sounded as though she'd found the answer to a question that had bothered her for a while.

"If you'd listened," the Morgana said gently, "Telor would still be a home to us and you wouldn't have overused its energy to the point that you needed to raid the stars."

"And so said all the so-called advisors on the Corevex," the Prime snapped. Her voice shifted to mimic one of the scholars of her time.

"'Zerestria tried this path and look what their nation was reduced to,' or 'look at what happened to T'ligolor.' Pah! As if I cared about some ancient civilization that lived in the hills and crapped in waterfalls, or a country too poor to stop its forests becoming wasteland."

"Because of their overuse of magic!" She sounded frustrated. "Because they had already followed the path you were preaching."

"Well, history couldn't save them," the Teloran leader gloated.

"And history was right," she persisted. "Everything those scholars told you ended up being true, but still you persisted because you didn't want it to be true."

"What did I care about the truth?" she snapped. "I had what I wanted—enough magic to do my bidding, riches beyond all imagination, and power...*so much* power."

"But not enough to kill me," the Morgana said into the momentary silence that followed.

The Prime stilled and tilted her head from side to side as she examined Stephanie. "Funny, I don't remember there being any *humans* around when I took power."

The Witch gave her a grim smile. "There weren't."

"And I killed *everyone* in my path," she boasted. "I didn't miss a single one."

"As with Steresh, you didn't check to see if I was dead."

Her adversary stiffened. "You! But I dropped a *mountain* on you!"

Stephanie rolled her shoulders.

"Did you?" the Morgana asked. "I didn't notice for a while, then I woke up."

"This time, you won't!" the Prime declared and hurled a ball of dark fire at her.

"Puhleeze," she said and caught the ball in a glove of blue light lined with black.

"I didn't know she could do that," Lars whispered.

"She's been practicing," Frog observed.

Darkness crackled around the Prime and magic lashed out in venomous tendrils. The Morgana dodged and weaved, hurled magic at her granddaughter, or tried to lash her with strands of her own.

The two were evenly matched, and the younger Teloran laughed.

"You're not the only one to learn a trick or two." She chuckled. "I'm more powerful now than I ever was."

"And still as arrogant," she snapped as another attack fizzled on her shields. She maneuvered back and drew darkness from the corners of the room.

Her granddaughter responded and unleashed bolt after bolt of lightning toward her.

"Stand *still!*" she screamed after each one had missed. "I *said* stand still!"

The Morgana snickered and the sound slid up and down the spine of every creature that heard it. The Teloran uttered a wordless scream of fury, snatched magic from the air, and hurled ball after ball of deadly energy at her tormenter.

Most careened harmlessly into her opponent's shields, where they were absorbed into the shield itself. One flew wide and arced across the room to crash into the pillar Frog had been standing beside.

It was only because he'd been paying attention that he was able to fling himself out of the way in time. The Prime shrieked in frustration.

"But I'm not finished!" she screamed.

"And I don't care!" Stephanie yelled in response and the darkness in her hands melted to blue. "I have had *enough* of this pussyfooting around."

"Oh, *this* is rich!" The Teloran chuckled. "You can't even maintain control over a *human*."

"I am not merely *any* human," she stated coldly.

"It won't make any difference," her adversary gloated. "I will burn you to the ground and turn every one of your people into a living pyre."

Stephanie laughed. "Yuh think?"

"Uh-oh," Lars murmured and took a step away from the arena as the Witch continued.

"Your grandmother was being *nice* but you almost hurt one of mine and now, you will die."

She ducked under the Prime's first ball of magic before she made a looping gesture with her hand and streaked it back to the Teloran.

"Why don't you try a taste of your magic?" she asked.

"I'd rather ram it down your throat." The Prime snarled, drew more energy, and released a flurry of hissing orbs in her direction.

"Thank you, but I've been forced to swallow enough of your shit for a lifetime," Stephanie retorted. She didn't bother to draw her energy but took control of the magic the enemy leader had released and turned it onto its caster.

One of the guards made the mistake of moving and a crackling transparent wall of magic sprang into place between the fighters and their audience.

Lars's jaw dropped. "Well, fuck!" How in all the worlds was he supposed to get past *that*? "Did any of you catch when she learned how to do that particular trick?"

"Sorry, boss, I was too busy having her hand my ass to me in the gym!" Marcus replied.

In the arena, the Witch snatched a bolt of lighting before it could leave the Prime's hand, reversed its direction, and forced the Teloran to jerk her hand away and leap sideways to avoid it.

"And there's something else new," Lars noted.

"I think *someone* had her Wheaties this morning," Frog noted.

"And every other morning," Marcus added.

"She's not even breaking a sweat," Johnny noted.

Vishlog darted a glance at one of the Teloran guards, but the man showed no sign of being aware of his scrutiny and he was very sure Stephanie would be upset if he started a fight.

He looked for the cats to make sure they'd gotten the memo. When he caught sight of them, he relaxed.

Bumblebee crouched belly-down, ready to spring on another of the guards, and Zeekat's tail lashed as he prepared to take on another. Both cats had their prey in their sights and neither one moved. They looked like they were waiting for permission from Stephanie, and their yellow eyes gleamed with anticipation.

Garach was lost in the battle, and Vishlog moved closer to his nephew. It wouldn't matter what Stephanie wanted. If a single enemy guard twitched in the youngster's direction, he'd get the fight he was looking for.

The Teloran leader's voice drew his attention to the battle again.

"Before your people crawled out of the cesspool of your creation, we were already powerful!" she shouted.

"Oh. *Shut. The. Hell. Up,*" Stephanie cried, looped a tendril of her dark magic around the Prime's throat and upper body, and punched her with a magical blue fist outlined by nMU.

The force of the blow snapped the tendril and hurled the enemy back to where she'd been standing. Instead of landing on her feet, the Teloran slid back on her butt.

The Witch wasn't finished. "Cut the crap, you weathered hag. There is something to be said for youth, energy, and mad as hell."

She was so angry that she ignored the Morgana's laughter in her mind.

Oh, I wish I had popcorn!

Tempestarii had drawn the Telorans away from the Admiral's ship and managed to find more.

"This is fun!" she exclaimed, skipped out of the way of one barrage, and appeared close to a destroyer so her gun crews could fire a salvo into its side.

The missile crews responded, but the gun crews targeted the swathe of smaller craft streaming from the larger ships nearby.

"If they keep filling our airspace like that, I'll accidentally squash some when I skip."

"That's not good for your shields, Tempestarii," Emil told her before he returned to his conversation with BURT.

"And the likelihood of that is what?" he asked as the destroyer began to break in half.

The *Tempestarii* chuckled and flexed her shield. The fighters that had survived the stream of fire from her short-range lasers came in too hard to pull up when the crackling blue wall suddenly expanded.

Their impacts hardly made a difference and their squadrons fell into disarray as they altered course hastily.

"Pick on *my* people, will you?" the ship challenged. "I don't think so."

The gun crews delivered another fusillade, and the fighters' ranks thinned even more. Tempestarii pulled away from the failing destroyer and looked for another target. She didn't notice the battle cruiser partly concealed by the damaged ship until it fired.

"Sonuva*bitch!*" she exclaimed, closed bulkheads, and made sure she hadn't lost any personnel. "That *stung!*"

Emil broke off from his conversation and glanced at the reports coming into his board.

"It's okay," she reassured him. "The crew are not in their living quarters right now. They are all fighting."

He grunted. "You're a very lucky girl," he told her and took the time to go through the other reports.

When he was finished, he shook his head. "Well, BURT, I'm afraid you'll have to step in now."

"Dad!" the *Tempestarii* protested as BURT did exactly that.

"Sorry, daughter," he replied and snickered. "Now, see if you can keep up."

His words echoed through the hundreds of monitors watching their battle, and heads shook as the *Tempestarii* faded from sight.

"Tell me she won't try another micro-jump in *that!*" one captain said. "It's insane."

"It's suicide is what it is," another captain agreed, "but that's what I said about her last maneuver—and they're down a destroyer now."

"There *is* such a thing as suicidal *and* lucky," someone else agreed sourly.

"Last time I looked, no one aboard any of the Witch's ships was suicidal," someone replied.

"I thought it was a prerequisite for working closely with the Witch."

"No, mate." Another crewman chuckled. "The only prerequisites she seems to have is a requirement for absolute loyalty, being good at your job, and willing to improve...*and* a high level of craziness! Everything else is optional."

"I wonder how many of them are pantsless," was the sarcastic response.

The ship flashed into the battle zone and someone swore softly. "*That* was *fast.*"

This time, the behemoth had relocated into the middle of four battlecruisers and their escorts.

"*And* suicidal. Honestly! What *is* that shit!"

"I don't know," another responded, "but I seriously *want* one. Do you think the Navy—"

"No!" yelled three different voices, although Amaratne's wasn't one of them.

"Wait! Is that *more* guns?"

"What do you mean more?"

"I mean *more*. Look at that shit."

And they were right. There *were* more guns—or, at least, more parts of the *Tempestarii* firing.

"Did she jettison *ninety* outer plates?" someone asked in disbelief. "Because, *damn*, that's a lot of guns!"

"I wouldn't say *jettison*, per se," a crewman pointed out. "Look."

The plates that had covered the extra gunports sprouted small tails of fire and began to streak toward the nearest enemy ships.

"Missiles or mines?"

"It's hard to tell from this distance."

The panels raced towards the enemy and eyes widened as the crew saw each panel break into three forms and jettisoned the bulky outer plates that had been hiding them.

"Oh...*that's* clever..."

The ships surrounding the behemoth fired, and the observers held their breath as the vessel met the enemy fire with countermeasures that took most of the incoming missiles out of the sky. Of those that remained, none got past the shields.

Again, BURT's voice came through the speakers.

"Now, it's *my* turn."

The barrage of fire that followed vaporized the fighter swarms that had been converging on the big ship. More than that, it was followed by another wave of missiles that showed exactly why the *Tempestarii* had jumped into a position surrounded by enemy ships.

"You *can't* be serious!" one of the captains exclaimed. "That is... It's..."

He didn't bother trying to finish. There *were* no words for what the *Tempestarii* was. She'd unleashed more firepower than any of them had ever seen—and that was something, given that her previous onslaughts were *already* the largest any of them had ever seen.

The Telorans must have thought so too as they changed course away from the ruthless attack and veered in panic when they realized they were heading toward the Federation Navy's flagship.

When the *Tempestarii* had cleared the space around her, she skipped to a point that positioned her in the path of any enemy vessels moving in the admiral's direction. It didn't matter that they'd already changed direction.

She had no sooner appeared than she fired again, and more Teloran ships died. The remaining craft accelerated, and one of the observers chuckled.

"Well, that won't do them any good."

V'ritan watched as a series of explosions ruptured the belly of the Teloran battlecruiser, followed by a bigger explosion close to her tail.

"Scratch that one from the list," he murmured, leaned back in his seat, and released a long breath.

All around him, the command crew relaxed and the mages settled into their seats. Everyone was grateful for a break.

The scan team took it as an opportunity to check what was happening across the battlefield. They paid particular attention to what was closest to them and not only because that was where the greatest threats lurked.

Sometimes, an ally was in trouble and they could arrive in time to make a difference. It helped them choose their next battle and it was why there was a mixture of human and Dreth ships flying with them.

Remnants of battles lost and won, those ships hadn't stood a chance at survival, let alone to make a difference on their own. By joining the Meligornian fleet, they could do both.

V'ritan welcomed all-comers, even if the possibility of picking up a human traitor worried him. He could not condemn a possible ally in the face of the slightly smaller threat of treachery.

It was a concern but not one he shared with anyone else—not yet. He assigned a crewman to monitor the new additions but didn't tell him anything that might prejudice what he saw.

The *Ghargilum Afreghil* believed that the admirals who wished to take power would hang back and would be the ones farthest from both Meligornian and Dreth allies.

Only time would tell if his theory was correct.

His mind had drifted to the situation facing Stephanie in the future when his console flashed.

"You need to take a look at this, sir." The warning came over his headset and he recognized the voice of the technician in charge of the scan teams.

"What is it?" he asked and tried to banish the edge of tiredness that crept into his voice.

"Please *look*, sir."

V'ritan pulled himself upright and peered at the screen. What he saw made him sit bolt upright.

"Put that up on the main screen," he ordered.

Gasps issued from around the command center as the *Tempestarii's* impressive bulk filled their view.

"What *is* that?"

"By Selene's teats, where in the stars did *that* come from?"

"I wonder..." he mused and recalled the massive ship he'd visited in the backwaters of space.

"And it's on *our* side? Thank the stars!"

"By Shelarel's holy book! Did you *see* that?" the weapons officer demanded. "Are those... Oh. My..."

The *Tempestarii* had uncovered another row of gun ports, each interspersed by missile tubes.

"Oh..." V'ritan leaned forward in his seat. "Oh, I don't think they'll like *this*."

T'revan snickered and his large face lit up with a mixture of malice and delight. "No, *Garghilum*, but *we* will."

Jaleck had won her fight with the dreadnought, not least because Admiral Angreth had arrived at the right moment. He'd snuck up behind the oversized monster, torn its engines apart, and started a chain reaction within it.

While his escort had kept it busy, she had cleared the flagship and backed herself away from the stricken enemy.

"Hrageth's blessing," she had sent to Angreth, and he had replied with the same.

Since both their forces were depleted, they'd come together to form a single pack.

Now, she fought another boarding party.

"Get. Off. My. Ship!" she roared and drove her boot into the chest of the Teloran stuck on the end of her sword.

With a heartfelt curse, she ducked under the sweep of a well-aimed blade and thrust her short sword into her attacker's chest, then wrenched it free as her first opponent fell. Jaleck continued to move and her blades found another victim as she stepped over the fallen corpses of her most recent opponents.

She parried another thrust as the Dreth fighting to her right fired past her to eliminate an attacker she hadn't seen. As she slashed at her opponent, her soldier's aim shifted and the blaster spoke again.

"Gralog!"

"Sorry, ma'am. He was the last."

"Agh!" she exclaimed and thrust her swords into their sheaths.

He was right in that it had been a shame to waste the opportunity, but it was still frustrating. At least he had the wisdom to stay silent as she stalked to the command deck.

"Thank you," she managed to say as they reached the door, and he grinned.

"It was my honor, Admiral."

His joy made her smile, and she clasped his shoulder. "The honor was mine."

He bowed his head, pleased but humbled by her attention, and they both returned to their stations. The admiral was surprised to note that Gralog was part of the bridge protection detail.

She hadn't noticed him before.

"When did you arrive?" she asked with a frown.

"Admiral Angreth assigned me," he admitted. "I came across in the last transfer."

The explanation triggered a memory. Angreth had seen what had happened to her people and insisted on bolstering her numbers.

"Not many of our foes have tried boarding," he had explained, "and some of my warriors would welcome the opportunity to blood their blades."

Now, she had to wonder if it was something else. In older times, it had not been unusual for an interested male to gift warriors to the female who caught his eye. She made a note to speak to Angreth later —when she'd worked out exactly how many of his soldiers were on her bridge.

There was a certain number that was very significant.

Nodding to her captain, she took her seat behind the console that was her place on his bridge.

"Admiral!" The strongly controlled tension in his voice caught her attention and he gestured to the screen. "Look."

She complied and her breath caught at the sight of the titanic dreadnought dancing through its opponents. For a moment, she froze to assess the situation and tried to work out how she could have missed a Teloran ship of that size.

It took her a moment to recognize the *Tempestarii* and only then did she relax. The captain gave her a curious stare as she settled into her seat with a chuckle.

"*That's* my girls!" she declared. "I bet those Navy assholes are wetting their pants right now."

CHAPTER SIXTY

"What in the *fuck* is *that?*" Admiral Helveck's voice rang out across his bridge.

His captain jumped. "What, sir?"

"*That!* That...*thing!*" he exclaimed.

"I don't know, sir, but it seems very protective of the Fleet," the man answered. After a few seconds, he added, "It seems to be on our side, sir."

That gave the admiral pause for thought, and his eyes narrowed as he watched the huge ship obliterate the Telorans closest to Admiral Amaratne's ship. "Yes, it does, doesn't it?"

They watched the *Tempestarii* fade in and out of sight as she skipped from one cluster of enemy vessels to the next and leave a swathe of devastation in her wake.

"Get me Cluster One on comms," he ordered, "and make sure they're secure."

"Aye aye, sir." The captain sketched him a salute as he turned to relay the order to the communications team.

Helveck was shaking with both anger and frustration as he took the chair and picked the call up.

"I take it you can all see what's out there?" he demanded as soon as the other admirals connected in.

"We can. It looks like Amaratne has powerful friends." Pickford looked sour at the thought.

Dreyfus scowled but nodded.

"I see it," Carthas admitted, and he didn't look too happy either.

One after another, the other three admirals agreed. He studied their faces.

Six, he thought, *when we used to be fourteen.*

It was a perilously low number and one that dictated caution.

"We need to pull back," he told them and read relief on four faces and consternation on two—Dreyfus and Pickford.

Well, it sucks to be them, he decided.

"We need to pull back," he reiterated and brought up an image of the behemoth terrorizing the Teloran fleet. "Because *that* changes everything. If the Witch ever works out that we are behind what's been happening to her and her precious Todd, *that* is what will come after us."

"Agreed," Carthas stated. He still didn't look happy but he, more than any of the others, knew the odds.

Helveck decided that of all the admirals to have survived the battle, he was the most important of them. He gave the man an approving nod.

"But—" Pickford began and he turned on her with a snarl.

"Take a good look at that ship," he ordered, "because if she works it out, it won't be a matter of us hiding a few murders in a battle. *She* will become judge, jury, *and* executioner, all at the same time!"

"It would be nice if we could skip to the executions," one of the other admirals quipped. "Let's get this finished."

"Well, what are we waiting for?" Dreyfus exclaimed. "We should get together and demand she hand over that big-ass ship. What she has there, it...well, that can't be legal!"

He lowered his head with a sigh. When he raised it again, anger had carved it into hard lines.

"Will *someone* on Captain Willistone's ship walk up and slap some sense into that man?" he demanded.

"Or he could simply step forward," Carthas suggested. "If he wants to be the first one burned in effigy by her words alone, he can man up and volunteer."

"I second that," another admiral agreed and all eyes turned toward Dreyfus.

When he saw he was both outranked and outnumbered, the man held both hands up.

"I...I was out of line," he stammered. "I'll follow your lead."

"Too damn right you will," Helveck told him, caught Willistone's eye, and watched the captain ease his blaster into its holster.

It was fortunate Dreyfus didn't turn to witness it.

Stephanie swatted another ball of energy toward the Prime's face. She laughed as the Teloran tried to command it to return but was forced to step hastily out of its way.

The orb sailed past her and crackled as it slipped along her shield. The Prime fell prone.

"You see..." the Witch said and Lars shuddered to hear the Morgana's tones in sync with hers.

"That can't be good," he observed.

One of the Teloran guards tilted its head in his direction. It did not move when he snapped his blaster up to sight on its chest and merely turned to the battle again.

"Interesting," he observed and wished the Marines were present.

Hadn't he heard they'd been learning the language? He wondered if Stephanie would be annoyed if he called Todd back, then wondered if the Marine was able to return.

With things the way they were with the Navy, the young sergeant *had* to complete the mission or he and the whole team risked being sentenced to death. Somehow, Lars didn't think she would stand for it but couldn't see what she could do to stop it.

"It is only when you trust a people different than your own," Stephanie-Morgana continued, "that you realize that you and those like you only touch one facet of God."

"Garbage!" the Prime hissed, and the Witch raised her eyebrow in an expression Lars knew all too well.

"Oh, boy," he muttered. "Here it comes."

Again, the Teloran guard tilted its head toward him, and Lars raised his blaster but didn't aim it at the tall figure. He could sense it watching him, but it didn't say a word.

The silence continued and it turned away to observe the battle. Slowly, he lowered his weapon but he remained tense. If the Teloran showed the slightest sign of aggression, he wanted to be ready.

The thought slid abruptly from his mind when he caught sight of what Stephanie was doing and froze.

"What the—" All those watching remained motionless and he let the words hang unfinished as he stared at the girl in disbelief.

While he'd slowly gotten used to her being able to control the nMU without touching it—and it no longer made him sweat seven kinds of blood—he had *never* seen her deliberately gather the nMU and start to weave it with any other kind.

In fact, he hadn't known she *could* do that. Everything she and the other mages had ever said stated that mixing nMU with any of the other types of magic would cause a massive explosion.

His jaw dropped as she pulled strands of the almost colorless glitter of what she called gMU with her left hand and wove it through the threads of nMU she gathered with her right.

The Telorans had frozen in place, their attention fixed on the Federation Witch's small figure as she brought the threads together and fused them into a single strand. They tensed exactly as he did and waited for the inevitable explosion.

It never came. Lars closed his mouth and took a step forward, frustrated by the barrier she'd erected to ensure her "conversation" was uninterrupted. As she worked, the two energies came together and burned a pure, bright white.

Even her opponent was frozen in place, mesmerized by the sight before her.

"See?" Stephanie-Morgana continued. "Some believe darkness is the color of all energy, but every single type of MU is nothing more than a subset of pure light."

She wound the thread over her thumb and down to her elbow and formed a skein of white to demonstrate.

"Pure energy," she emphasized. "All other types of MU are only a small part, and when energy is woven together—like races or peoples coming together with a single goal— *that* is where the strongest possibilities are found."

Ka finished hacking the bridge door and moved beside Todd.

"Are you ready?" she asked and he nodded.

"On three."

"Three!" she cried and thumped the button so the doors sprang open.

They were prepared for a fight, for the shooting to start, and for at least one of them go down and maybe never rise. What they were not prepared for was to be utterly ignored.

The attention of the Teloran command crew was fixed on what was happening on the forward viewscreen—and the rear viewscreen and other smaller ones dotted around.

Todd turned to his corporal. "Did you broadcast this to the entire ship?"

"Uh-huh..." She looked as stunned as he felt. "It seemed like a good idea at the time."

"Uh...it was...I think..." He surveyed the Telorans around them.

All of them, without exception, stared either at the screen or at each other. The way they held their heads revealed that much. Some of them were engaged in angry conversation.

"She betrayed us!"

"And she lied."

"She destroyed our most valued scholars to gain power and take the easy way to wealth!"

That last was said with such a high degree of disgust that Todd flinched. Frog sidled closer to him.

"What do we do, boss?"

He shook his head. "Give me a minute."

Ka nudged him with her elbow.

"I don't know about you, boss," she whispered, "but I'm not sure about this."

"What's not to be sure about?" Frog asked and joined the conversation uninvited.

He settled when Marcus draped an arm across his shoulders.

"Ssshhh."

With a puzzled frown, the small guard glanced at his teammate and then at the two marines. He took the hint, though, closed his mouth, and contented himself with surveying the command crew around them.

"Ssshhh," Marcus reiterated when Frog was about to comment on it.

"I know," Ka continued, as though the two guards didn't exist, "they're the enemy. But I could probably walk up and slit their throats or gut them where they stand and I don't think they'd do a damned thing to stop me."

Johnny nodded and went to stand on the opposite side of an occupied control console. The Teloran merely stared at the screen like he hadn't seen magic being wielded before.

"Are you seeing this?" he asked and still, the crew member didn't acknowledge his presence.

"This is unbelievable," Brenden murmured as he scrutinized the bridge crew.

Avery nodded. "Uh-huh..."

Todd signaled for the team to move toward the door.

"Lock us in," he whispered to Ka, "but I think we need to wait until Stephanie has finished."

CHAPTER SIXTY-ONE

"I don't care what illusions you weave," the Prime snapped, "but *no one* can blend the magics and *nothing* can save our world—and as for your 'God,' *no* single deity blends all nations and species. They are as divided as the rest of us. We reflect their image but we're not contained in it."

"Is that so?" Stephanie-Morgan demanded, and held the skein up, "then how am I doing this?"

"That's not real," the Teloran scoffed, and the Witch looked at the gleaming white skein in her hands.

"Oh?" she asked. "Then how about you hold it for a while and *then* tell me how real it isn't?"

With that, she unhooked the skein from her arm and pitched it toward her adversary.

"Fool!" the Prime screamed and thrust a hand out to block the magic.

Instead of knocking it aside, she succeeded in hooking it onto her hand.

"No!" she shrieked and tried to shake it loose. "No! No! No!" she cried as each shake only entangled her hand further.

She spun on the spot and flailed her arm in an attempt to dislodge the magic.

"No?" Stephanie-Morgana asked. "Are you sure?"

"Of course I'm sure!" the Prime shouted. "I will not fall for your cheap tricks. I will not!"

The enemy leader pulled more nMU to her and lightning flared towards Stephanie, but the girl drew it into the gMU that swirled over her.

"No!" The Prime screamed and looked around the room. "I *will* destroy you!"

Her gaze fell on Lars. "And I will start with your most faithful *pet*."

She twisted to look at him and called black fire to the palm of her hand before she tossed it viciously. "You will hear his screams. You will hear *all* their screams as I burn each and ever—"

The white light caught around her hand flared suddenly bright and expanded to coat her entire body as Stephanie moved one arm in a tight circle. Lars stared at the dark magic that hurtled toward him.

He was frozen to the spot, torn between watching as the Witch's magic encompassed the Prime and responding to the fire that streaked ever closer. He might have stayed there until it was too late if the closest Teloran had not leapt forward, swept him off his feet, and rolled them out of its path.

The movement shook the security head out of his stupor, but he was wrapped too tightly to resist as the guard hauled him past a pillar and behind it. He pinned Lars to the floor and raised his head to watch the Prime's attack blaze through Stephanie's barrier.

The light in the center of the room flared and a second beam of white extended to encapsulate the energy ball.

"Who's burning now?" asked the ice and melded darkness of Stephanie-Morgana at her worst.

The Prime's voice rose in a pain-filled wail and cut off abruptly. The smell of ozone and magic combined washed over the room and silence fell. At first, no one moved.

When he peered up from his place on the deck, Lars saw the barrier drop and felt the weight lifted from his back.

Judging by the startled gasp, the Teloran hadn't planned to get off him and the guard scrambled hastily to his feet.

"He saved me," he called and stepped out from behind the barrier. "Steph! Don't..."

He let his words fade as the Teloran was set gently on his feet.

"You saved one of mine," Stephanie declared, "and so I shall spare you to listen to what the Morgana has to say."

"The Morgana..." The enemy whispered the name as though it was something new and not what they'd expected. Stephanie-Morgana's voice ended their chatter.

"Now listen, and the oldest of you will tell you of your past—and the choices you have for your future. I hope your decisions will be wiser than those of your leader."

This last was said with a slow-burning anger, but when she spoke again, the girl's tones were absent. Only the Morgana's remained.

"I remember Telor as it used to be," she began. "It was a world to rival Meligorn or Dreth, or even the Earth-that-was with her beauty. It was a world where the magic was as strong as it is on Meligorn, stronger even than what is found on Dreth."

She paused as the Prime's guards moved closer to listen and she held her hand up when the team closed in to ask them to surrender their weapons.

As the team stood down, she continued, "The Telor I knew was one of plenty, but the Corevex grew greedier and began to make greater demands on its magic. Steresh knew this."

Again, her voice faltered and her eyes took on a faraway look.

"He was the other half of my heart, and his love for our world and desire for peace was his undoing."

The room grew silent as the Morgana told how she had returned to find her husband dying of a poison she could not neutralize. She told of how she had learned of her granddaughter's treachery and uncovered the suborning of the Corevex.

"She killed them all," she continued, her voice soft with loss. "Every single mage who warned her of the consequences of what she was doing to the world died a horrible death, their demise televised as an example of what happened to traitors."

The Morgana spat the last word. "You are fortunate that it was *this* human who drew my attention, that *her* bloodline was the one I found to accommodate my needs. Without her, you would not have a future."

Her fists clenched at her sides and magic burned around her in a halo of white shot through with every other color imaginable. She smiled and her audience shuddered.

"You must surrender. Lay down your arms and cease fire. Send word to the ships that they are to stand down."

She paused and raised her head to locate the nearest surveillance camera. "Ka, make sure the fleets hear it."

The Morgana turned to the gathered guards. "Your surrender must be unconditional and total. This is not negotiable. If Telor is to have any kind of future, this is the only chance you have to secure it."

Her voice changed as Stephanie took control. The girl let her gaze travel from guard to guard before she looked directly into the camera.

"If you *want* a future." She reiterated the Morgana's words and shrugged. "If not, fine. Our people have your engines and your bridge."

In the ship's engine room, the Teloran head engineer turned cautiously. He was surprised to discover the Witch had spoken the truth. Her people *had* taken his domain.

With a careful eye on the fierce-eyed female who stood in the center of the space between him and the exit, he raised his hands slowly. She didn't move and her gaze watched both him and the people beyond.

The human male who stood to her right looked no less intent, and the Teloran swallowed against a suddenly dry throat. Carefully, he stretched a hand out to tap his second on the shoulder.

His two-IC jerked in surprise, still caught up in the words from the screen. The chief engineer tapped him again, and he turned and his anger transformed to shock when he saw the humans arrayed behind them.

With a glance at his chief, he too raised his hands.

Elizabeth gave them a cold, hard smile and gestured around them.

"No sudden moves," she warned, and the chief stifled a gasp of horror.

Around him, the other technicians shook themselves as though waking from a trance. Some reached instinctively for weapons but froze at the human's words.

She jerked her chin in the direction of one of their control consoles, and they followed the movement. Several of them looked around the space they were in and took a hasty step to one side.

E snickered.

"Don't touch anything and we might *all* live to see the other side of this."

The boxes on the engines gleamed, but it was the expression on the face of the human holding a tablet that had them worried. He looked far too eager to start the countdown.

The scene was repeated on the bridge, where several of the commanders looked over their shoulders. One stared at the human bent over his console and froze.

She was not alone, and the blaster muzzle pressed into his back felt all too real. As he considered what to do about her, a soft squeak reached his ears.

The sound drew the attention of everyone on the bridge, including those not already regarding the team with a mixture of fear and unease.

Todd frowned and risked moving his gaze from the closest Teloran long enough to watch the last of his team's mobile mini-guns creak around the corner.

It was bent and its chassis dipped in the middle. The gun drooped like a chastised teenager but it still moved.

It reminded him of an injured dog, one that had come off the worse for wear in its last fight and still had anger issues to work out. Its barrels twitched and quivered as it advanced into the room

Marcus swore softly under his breath and whipped his tablet out, which made the Teloran crewman nearby flinch.

"I haven't shot you yet," he told him but didn't look up. "Relax."

His fingers moved rapidly over the keyboard as the gun registered non-human life forms and its barrel started to rise. The man glared at Ka, who watched the Teloran standing over her warily as she continued her download and transmission.

"I thought you said it was dead."

"Auto-repair," she snapped and worked furiously. "Sometimes, it kicks 'em back online."

She glanced at the crewman who had folded his arms and studied her intently. While she wanted nothing more than to draw her blaster and give him extra ventilation points, he hadn't tried to harm her...yet.

If anything, his attention seemed divided between her and what was happening on the screens overhead.

Stephanie was in full spate.

"And I will erase your fleet from the *universe*, after which I will go to *your* home-world where I will raise the prophet and take her with me. And when I'm done with that?"

Stephanie glared at the circle of guards and looked into every camera she could see.

"When I'm done with that, I will reduce your home-world to slag exactly as you tried to do to mine."

She paused to let her words sink in before she continued.

"Your future is either with us or against us—and if it is against us, it will be *very* short-lived."

Again, she paused and tried to gauge what effect her words were having, but it was impossible to see beyond their shields. In the end, she pressed on regardless, her voice a little softer.

"*Our* history is full of idiots who believe a broken enemy is not an enemy at all. They're wrong. A broken enemy is the progenitor of the next generation of enemies who will return to threaten your children."

She let them think about that for a moment and to consider the ramifications.

"Our history also contains examples of those who understood this principle and what they did to remove that threat."

When she raised her head, her face hard and her expression uncompromising, she let them see her determination that nothing would be left to threaten her people or her worlds.

"My children," she told them, "and my friends' children *will* have a future. Your future is here and now—and your children's future is now your choice."

Her words echoed across the battlefield. They shocked the Earth admirals and their fleet, even though most knew it was the only way. Their history had shown them that.

The speech did not shock everyone, though.

Linked in a conference call as they watched the broadcast Ka had sent fleet-wide, the Dreth Fleet Admiral and V'ritan met each other's gazes and nodded.

"She doesn't offer many options," the Meligornian observed and Jaleck shrugged.

"It is the Dreth way. She honors us even as she extends mercy we might not have shown."

"Will they take it?" he asked.

Her dark eyes returned to the screen and she leaned back in her chair.

"That," she replied thoughtfully, "I do not know."

His question was echoed on every bridge across every fleet. It was asked in the silent weapons arrays and in the midst of melees that had fallen to stillness.

Faced with such demands, how would the Telorans reply?

CHAPTER SIXTY-TWO

Todd's blaster snapped up as one of the Telorans spoke. The alien's voice sounded rough with emotion but he made no hostile gestures and the sergeant held his fire.

"And how do we know you will honor our surrender?"

His voice came clearly through the screens and Stephanie raised her head to address the camera.

"You are?"

"Captain Enkarish. Without the Prime, command of this vessel returns to me."

"And the fleet?"

"The fleet follows the flagship...Federation Prime."

Todd saw the surprise in her face and the moment when she decided to let the title pass. He guessed she was leaving that question for later so she could deal with the now.

She opened her mouth to reply but was cut off by a cry of alarm from one of the consoles close to the forward viewscreen.

"Sir, they're preparing to fire."

"Give me shields!" the captain ordered. "And put that up where the Witch can see it."

At his demand, the display in Todd's HUD split into two and they all saw what had caused the alarm.

"Stand by," he ordered and raised his hand. "Let them do their jobs. Ka?"

"Give me time, boss. The translation software slowed me a little."

"That's what I was asking. I don't want any accidents out there."

"I gotcha covered, boss." Todd glanced at her, but the technician hadn't looked up from behind the console and the Teloran who stood beside her now had its arms folded.

He stifled a snicker at the alien's nonplussed state. Honestly, he could sympathize. She made him feel that way, too—*especially* when she pretended to ignore him.

When he confirmed that she wasn't in any danger—and that Johnny had shifted so he could cover her—he returned his attention to the screen.

One of the destroyers escorting the flagship had lifted the covers on her starboard guns.

He clenched his jaws tightly. At that range, there was very little the captain could do. This was the ship they'd come up under—or was it over? Either way, they'd flown almost close enough to touch it on their way in.

The Teloran next to Ka glanced at his boards and then at Johnny.

"I need to work," he said and bent to his boards as he muttered, "I very much hope you can understand me."

The woman tensed and kept one hand on her tablet as she swung her pistol into his midriff with the other. This time, it was *her* turn to be ignored.

The Teloran's hands moved over his console and Todd wished he could see its expression. He wasn't about to demand they drop their shielding in the middle of a space battle, though.

If he understood it correctly, those shields acted the same way their suits did and there was no way he would ask *his* folk to lift their visors.

The Teloran spoke again. "He's hailing, sir."

His captain nodded. "Put him through and pull all the captains into conference on the port screens. They need to know we are not under duress."

It wasn't a request, but Todd knew what the other aliens needed to see.

"Lower your weapons," he ordered.

The Teloran closest snapped its head to look at him, and he returned its stare. He pointed at where white lightning started to arc around Stephanie.

"Harm me and my people, and *that* is what will come for you."

Its head moved to observe the screen and the alien nodded.

"I would ask if we looked like children," it replied, "but we were foolish enough to awaken her in the first place." It looked at his colleagues, took a step away from the Marine, and raised its hands momentarily. "We stand with our captain."

The others mimicked the gesture before they returned their attention to their consoles. The port screens activated again to reveal a myriad of command decks pushed together to fit.

As the other captain greeted them, his picture expanded so they could see him clearly.

"There will be no surrender!" he shouted and pointed at the screen. "Destroy them!"

Enkaresh raised a hand slightly as if to reply, but the Teloran continued. "Tell her that. There will be *no* surrender. We are Teloran and surrender to no one."

"We fight for our people's future," Enkaresh argued as the speaker's screen went dark. He continued for those that remained. "Without surrender, there will be none."

Many of the captains nodded. Others rested their forearms diagonally across their chests and gave a shallow bow before they straightened.

Todd glanced across at his second. "Ka?"

"Fine, boss. There's no funny business. They're only tryin' to keep their ship alive."

He breathed an internal sigh of relief. There were days when he wondered how she could read his mind like that but mostly, he didn't care as long as she could.

"Sir! The *Galaxy's Loss* is changing position."

On the port wall, another screen had gone dark.

The captain spat something the translation program couldn't handle before he added, "How many others disagree?

"The *Choreth'varik*." This time, sadness laced the Teloran's tones.

However, he highlighted the relevant ships as he spoke and Todd had to admire his loyalty.

The captain's reply was gentle. "I am sorry for your loss."

"It takes a crew to make a ship fly," the technician replied and the sadness shifted to grief.

"The loss would be the same," his superior answered. "That captain..."

He let those words trail into silence as if they did not need to be said.

"How do you know I will honor your surrender?" the Morgana demanded and her harsh tones brought them back to the screen.

None of them spoke as she continued with the answer. "Because without surrender, you will see lightning amidst the stars."

At her words, light danced jaggedly across the destroyer's hull. Guns exploded and the missiles it had launched evaporated in balls of white mist.

Todd's jaw dropped, but he shut his mouth hastily and gave her screen a nervous glance. She was dancing—or close enough to it for him to be nervous about taking her to a disco ever again.

As she swept her arms in an expansive gesture, the lightning twisted, wound itself tighter around the ship, and gradually expanded away from it. Gleaming tendrils buried into its hull and leapt across the space separating it from the other two ships that now targeted the flag.

One of the coils made contact with a battleship—the *Choreth'varik* —and split into four separate strands that ripped the ship apart before it spread over its remains and flared with eye-searing brightness.

The *Galaxy's Loss* fared no better, and the Morgana spoke again.

"I do not *need* your permission. I can tear your ships asunder as I please. Surrender is offered *only* because all people have value, even the Telorans."

After watching the light fade, Captain Enkaresh turned and approached Todd. He stopped a meter and a half away, laid his forearm diagonally across his chest, and placed his fist over his heart.

A small bow ended the salute and he straightened.

"I am Captain Enkaresh of the *Corevex Prime*."

He fell silent and inclined his head to wait for the reply.

"And I am Marine Sergeant Todd Brogan of the Federation Navy."

The captain nodded, evidently satisfied, and the shadows shielding him fell away to reveal his lean and weary features.

"On behalf of Telor and her people, I surrender our planet's protection, including the entirety of its fighting forces, its storm fleets, and all else who would come to its defense to you."

Todd released the seal on his helmet and thumbed the visor so it slid away to reveal his face.

"Captain Enkaresh, I must inform you that only the fleet admiral of the Federation Navy can officially accept your surrender. I am able to accept it as it stands, but it is he who must formalize it. Is that acceptable?"

"Marine Sergeant, it is more than acceptable." He glanced at the captains of his fleet, the three darkened screens all that remained of the dissenters.

Seeing his gaze, they saluted and bowed as one, and Enkaresh turned to him again.

"Marine Sergeant Todd Brogan, I, Captain Enkaresh, Master of the Teloran Storms, do hereby surrender—wholly and without condition or reservation—my world, its protection, and its people to the Federation Navy. Our war has ended."

Todd gestured at the screen. "And the Witch?"

The captain followed the gesture and froze before he lowered his voice to reply, "You don't understand, Marine Sergeant. *You* are far less frightening than she is. I will wait to meet this admiral of yours."

He inclined his head and glanced at Ka.

"Get him on the line."

When he looked at Enkaresh, the Teloran captain stared at the screen where his Prime's guards were surrendering their weapons. Stephanie turned to address one of the guards and the Teloran flinched.

"I wonder who taught her to be so scary?" the captain mused.

In the Engineering section, Matthias, Amy, and Arne exchanged glances and looked at Elizabeth, frowning.

She stared at the screen, which had split in two to show both Stephanie and the bridge when the Witch had first demanded the Telorans surrender. With a mutter of something unintelligible, she half-turned so she could see her team.

"Don't blame me!" she snapped when they stared at her. "She had an attitude before I met her."

Around them, the Telorans exchanged glances before they looked from Stephanie onscreen to Elizabeth and back again. The Navy translation program was working overtime as they murmured to each other but one comment, in particular, caught E's attention.

"Is that her mother?"

Dru chuckled and they looked nervously at her. The Marine gestured at the screen and then at Elizabeth.

"Not exactly," she explained and chuckled. "She's worse than a mother. She's her *mentor*."

At this, the Telorans exchanged more looks and fixed their attention on Elizabeth. Finally, the chief engineer cleared his throat and deactivated his shields.

He wasn't sure if the humans understood the significance of that gesture, but his crew did. There was no surrender if they were not willing to make themselves vulnerable to the enemy.

When the captain had unshielded in front of the Marine, he'd shown the fleet that they truly *were* surrendering and without reservation as the Witch had demanded.

By lowering his, the chief engineer showed his support. Still, he had one thing he needed to ask.

"If I might beg your consideration," he began and froze when the woman snapped her head around to focus on him.

"What is it?" she demanded and he flinched.

One of the male humans behind her covered his face with the palm of his hand and another shook his head. The female human who protected the woman snickered.

At least, the engineer *hoped* it was a sound of amusement and not one signaling frustration or that they'd changed their minds.

Gathering his courage, he cleared his throat again, and asked, "Could we perhaps remove the explosive devices from my engines?"

Elizabeth scowled and he hastened to explain.

"If we do not, I am afraid we might not make it through the peace process in anything but spirit."

Ah, that made sense to her. He could see it by the way her expression changed, although the scowl returned swiftly.

"Fine!" she snapped and gestured for Piet and the Marines to do as he'd asked. "But I'll stick a few on you to make sure you consider *not* annoying me."

The engineer raised his eyes to the screens again. Stephanie now marched toward the command deck, her team arrayed around her, and the Prime's guards walked meekly amidst her team.

Strands of the Witch's hair had escaped her plait and now whipped wildly around her face. Lightning crackled over her body and shades of blue and purple highlighted the searing white of her blended magic. The two oversized hunting beasts paced on either side of her and emphasized her power.

As if sensing that the engineer was watching, she glanced at the nearest pick-up and her blue eyes blazed.

"Mentor, indeed," he muttered as he flinched.

On the other side of the battlefield, Amaratne ordered the fleet to stand by.

"I will accept the surrender," he told them.

"But how do we know we can trust them?" Helveck demanded, and his superior officer kept his expression neutral.

"We know," he began, "because we can trust Ms. Morgana to annihilate them if we can't."

"But, that's—"

"It is *my* decision!" he snapped. "A powerful enemy has surrendered *unconditionally* to the Federation Navy. One of our own has accepted that surrender, and we will take advantage of this chance for peace while we can."

"But—"

Amaratne held his hand up. "No more discussion. I will accept their surrender in person and if *any* of you break this peace before it has begun, I will destroy your ship where it stands. Am I understood?"

"We should all go."

He looked at the screen and identified one of Helveck's supporters.

"Admiral Pickford, for all of us to gather would take too long."

"The sergeant is there and as you said, the Witch is too. I'm sure the temporary surrender will last as long as any permanent one."

She had him there. The fleet admiral could see the interest sharpen on the faces of the other admirals—and not only those arrayed against him.

Amaratne sighed. "Very well. Please stand by while I organize it."

His communications chief cut them off before they could protest and sent them into the nothingness of the hold tone.

"Who do you need?" he asked, and the fleet admiral thanked the heavens for the small mercy of a loyal crew.

"Get me the Dreth flagship. I need to speak to Jaleck."

"Aye aye, sir."

The commander obeyed without question, but he would always remember that one of Earth's greatest admirals had needed to turn to the Dreth for support in what should have been one of the greatest moments in Earth history.

Always, humankind found a way to diminish their victories and engender unnecessary chaos.

It didn't take him long to bring Admiral Jaleck up on the screen. She was covered in blood and her armor was singed and damaged, but she smiled with sheer joy at the sight of him.

She rested a fist over her heart and inclined her head. "How may I be of assistance, Fleet Admiral Amaratne?"

"Are you aware of the factions in the Federation?" he asked and she froze.

"Why do you ask?"

He decided not to fence words with her but came straight to the point. The intelligence group could have as many conniptions as it wanted. Now was not the time for games.

"Some of them are making their presence felt in the fleet."

"I see…" Her tone indicated that she did see and that she wasn't happy with the implications. She confirmed his impression by continuing. "I take it they do not have the best interests of the Witch at heart?"

"Or of any who approve her presence in this battle," he declared, knowing his words condemned this conversation to oblivion.

"I did notice that her arrival was…delayed," the Dreth Admiral admitted, "and I *did* wonder which fool might be responsible. Are you saying there is more than one?"

At her words, Amaratne felt a part of him relax. She had declared her support for him and Stephanie and made it clear to the analysts who would hear it where Dreth stood in the situation.

He tried not to think about the ramifications as he put his request forward. "I need to make sure that everyone who will attend this meeting will support the peace process, and I hoped the Dreth would provide the transport."

Jaleck's eyes narrowed. "I'm not sure I like where you're going with this, Admiral."

Amaratne placed his fist over his heart and gave her a slight bow. "I apologize, Fleet Admiral Karnach. I meant no disrespect. I will understand if you decline."

She waved his apology aside. "Fleet, I understand—and I would be proud to assist you. Now, tell me what you need."

When he complied, the smile that followed was one that sent chills through his heart.

"This makes me grateful that I have fought *with* you, rather than against you," she told him. "We will make this a hunt to remember."

When he remained silent for a moment too long, she hurried to reassure him.

"We will set things up, Admiral. Dreth stands with the Witch—and *all* her allies."

"Thank you, Fleet Karnach."

She inclined her head by way of farewell and the screen went blank.

Amaratne caught himself staring at the darkened screen and shook his head. He turned to his aide-de-camp.

"Prep our two largest shuttles and find me a dozen Marines we can trust. I don't need impulsive assholes getting themselves sent into space for lipping off to the Witch."

In a separate conference call on a very private frequency, Helveck smiled.

"He'll cave," he assured his counterparts. "The weak ones always do. All we have to do is make it look like we're instrumental in getting the treaty signed and we can turn this any way we like."

"And the surrender *was* unconditional, was it not?" Pickford all but purred. "I'm sure we can put a few demands in that favor our backers."

He nodded. "And if they refuse, we have an excuse to execute their fleet command, the Witch's presence or not."

CHAPTER SIXTY-THREE

Stephanie stood in the middle of the Teloran flagship. Seats rose in tiers behind her and a large, well-lit dais took up the center rear of a large, open amphitheater.

Captain Enkaresh gave her an anxious look. "Will this suffice?"

She turned and surveyed the space. "Is it the largest area you have?"

"It is," he confirmed. "The Prime insisted we bring our people before the Corevex once a cycle so that they could be reminded of home."

The way his eyes darkened at the memory showed that those meetings had not been pleasant. He shook his head and looked at her.

"I have also ordered a clear path between here and the docking bay you requested. I believe your people are helping mine organize the final touches as we speak."

"Very good," she told him.

Her voice was mostly her own and her eyes had returned to their usual blue, but everyone in hearing distance could feel the Morgana's lurking presence.

That was of no concern to her, however. She raised her head and lifted her voice. "V'ritan, are your people ready?"

The Meligornian Fleet Admiral's response came without delay.

"They are," he told her.

"Then step back," she commanded. "I will start the gate."

"We are clear," he confirmed a few seconds later.

Stephanie smiled and swept her hands decisively with the pure joy of working magic for something other than destruction. White light rose from her shoulders and flowed down her arms before it elevated to create a portal spanning the dais.

It was the most magnificent thing Enkaresh had seen her do—and she'd done so much in the short time since she'd boarded his ship and defeated his Prime. Every time he thought she couldn't go any further, she did something new.

He honestly looked forward to what she might do next. It helped when he saw the expressions of amazement of the people who called her their leader.

As the portal settled and rippled with all the colors of magic, Stephanie tensed. She leaned forward a little and waited for the first of her guests to part the veil.

It made him wonder if any of the portals had failed her before. Together, they watched as the first Meligornians stepped through. They were dressed in ceremonial armor, too clean to have seen battle and trimmed in the teal and gold of Meligorn's royalty.

She gasped with delight when a tall, dark-haired Meligornian emerged and clasped her hands together as though to stop herself applauding his appearance. It was the first child-like thing he'd seen her do.

"Brilgus!" she whispered, unashamedly happy to see him.

Others marched out of the portal and formed an honor guard with the dark-haired Meligornian at its head. Enkaresh watched, fascinated, as this Brilgus lowered his head to his collar tab before he glanced at the Witch and inclined his head by way of greeting.

As soon as he had settled, Stephanie and her entourage hurried to greet him, although the two cats had been leashed and were firmly restrained by the largest of the Dreth in her team.

To Enkaresh's surprise, the animals bounced in place, their ears pricked and mouths partly open at the sight of the Meligornian. If he wasn't mistaken, they were very happy to see him. He wished he could ask why.

Even if he'd been so inclined, Stephanie didn't give him the chance. She hurried to the dais and arrayed herself opposite Brilgus, keeping the head of her guards and his second in command beside her.

"Come," she commanded and looked at Enkaresh. He obeyed, surprised when she signaled two of the Prime's guards to accompany him.

When they were ready, the Meligornian spoke into his collar again, and the portal's veil parted.

This time, the figure who moved through was not dressed in ceremonial armor but in battle-worn heavy armor that had undoubtedly seen recent action. The Meligornian didn't seem to notice him and instead, looked at the gate.

His head described an arc as it followed the curve of the portal itself, and the visor snapped back to reveal a white-haired Meligornian who didn't seem able to tear his eyes away from the magic.

He was followed by one of the biggest men Enkaresh had ever seen, and it was all he could do to keep his mouth closed. If ever a Dreth had a Meligornian form, this was it—and he was old.

The captain studied the new arrival with open curiosity. The massive Meligornian didn't *look* old, but his magic... Whatever had been done to him was very similar to what the Prime had used on herself, albeit with a different form of magic.

With real regret, he shook his head. Perhaps, if they survived this, he could ask.

The figure studying the Witch's portal finally tore his eyes away from it long enough to ask, "It powers itself?" He turned to the Witch, his voice filled with disbelief. "You aren't powering it?"

Stephanie chuckled. "I *am* powering it," she admitted, "but it is a tap on my energy which is refreshed as the gate needs power. It doesn't reduce my strength."

He turned away from her, and Enkaresh felt a brief wash of relief that the Meligornian didn't hesitate to put him at his back. Maybe his people would get through this after all.

V'ritan stared at the gate as more came through. These formed a line in front of the guards already flanking the path to Stephanie.

The captain studied them as much as many of them studied him. It was only to be expected, he supposed. This would be the first time any of them had a chance to see a Teloran without their shielding.

The girl's soft murmur interrupted his thoughts. "Are you getting this, Ka?" she asked.

"Every single moment," the Marine responded. "Do you want a close-up of the rod?"

"Just make it clear—and also clear that *everyone* is being tested." She glanced at V'ritan who turned to her as though sensing her gaze.

"Is it time?" he asked, and she glanced at the chronometer inside her HUD.

"It is," she told him. "Ka is transmitting the footage fleet-wide as we speak, with the only exception being Admiral Amaratne's shuttle."

His eyebrows rose. "Oh? I thought he was one of the good guys."

"He is," she told him, "but he's babysitting a boatload of assholes and we'd both like to surprise them."

The *Ghargilum Afreghil* smiled and gave her a formal Meligornian bow. "Then let's give them a show to remember."

Admiral Yudhanjaya Amaratne would have appreciated the sentiment. He was seated beside Admiral Helveck, the position only made tolerable by the fact that two Marines watched them.

Both had the fastest draw in their squads and could shoot straighter than a man could spit—or that's what their sergeant had told him when he said he needed two men he could trust to draw fast enough and shoot accurately enough to prevent a high-ranking blue-on-blue disaster.

"Don't sweat it, sir. I have the perfect boys for you," the sergeant had said. The fact one of the boys was a girl seemed irrelevant.

"Don't let her hear you say it," the sergeant had warned him, "because she's the best shot in my squad but has a temper to match, and you might need your left testicle intact."

Amaratne had blinked and studied the woman again. She'd ignored him, her face a perfect stone-hard blank. If she had a temper, he couldn't see any trace of it, which was a relief.

"We'd like to speak to them before you get started with the formal process." Helveck addressed him.

He tilted his head to look at the man's face, but the other admiral didn't give him a chance to speak.

"We have as much right as you do to ensure they're serious," he continued.

It took effort, but his superior officer didn't say anything. The fact the man even *thought* he had as much right as a fleet admiral—let alone the cheek to voice it—said much about how powerful his backers were.

"So don't try to go straight to the formal steps before we're done."

Amaratne saw what might have been annoyance flit across both Marines' faces but Helveck was in full spate and didn't appear to notice. When the fleet admiral looked a second time, their faces were as expressionless as before.

He was glad about that since he didn't want to try to protect his Marines at the same time as he tried not to choke the living shit out of someone who thoroughly deserved it.

Instead, he worked to keep his affront at bay and his face carefully blank as Helveck's demands washed over him.

"Well, hasn't my little girl got all grown up," Elizabeth murmured as she watched Stephanie create the portal on the dais.

"And all her friends have come to play," Amy quipped as the Meligornians began to enter.

"I hope the fleet is getting pictures of this," she stated as V'ritan accepted the rod from the girl and took the test of loyalty with the same soft smile as he conducted any high-level negotiation.

"I *like* that man," Matthias declared as the *Garghilum Afreghil* handed the rod to the Witch.

"He has been her strongest supporter since the beginning," E told him. "He really *is* something."

So saying, she turned and glanced at the engineer.

The Teloran stood forlornly in the center of a wide circle. His crew refused to allow him anywhere near the engines while he was decked out in small boxes and a rat's nest of wiring.

She couldn't say she blamed them.

He gave her an apprehensive look as she approached but he didn't try to avoid her. Having given up speaking at about the same time as she wired the last piece of explosive in place, he didn't even ask her what she wanted.

Elizabeth didn't bother to greet him. Instead, she began to remove the wires deftly from their respective boxes. The Teloran froze and his breathing came a little faster as her fingers brushed across his uniform.

The sweat beaded on his face and revealed his very understandable tension. She'd be sweating too if she had this much explosive attached to her.

Working quickly and quietly, she removed the charges and placed them in the duffle Piet brought closer and set on the floor beside her. None of them spoke until she'd put the last charge inside and zipped the bag.

"Thank you," the engineer managed to say and his voice emerged as a whisper.

She gave him a sharp glance. "Trust me," she said. "I wouldn't do it but I realize it's stupid to think these explosives will do anything to the sub-atomic particles you will become if you piss her off."

"Who?" he asked and frowned at her in confusion. Piet hoisted the duffle bag and stacked it with the other gear the team wasn't using at the moment.

Elizabeth nodded at the viewscreen.

"The only daughter of my heart," she told him and her gaze slid to the big human male who hovered nearby. "At least for the moment."

The man's face flushed red and he wondered why the female bodyguard was smirking as she nudged the male and whispered, "At the moment."

"Your daughter of the heart," the engineer repeated and E glanced at him.

"Yes, my daughter of the heart."

She stooped to release the cuffs she'd used to hobble him as he looked at the screen.

"Well, of *course*, she is," he muttered and rolled his eyes.

CHAPTER SIXTY-FOUR

"Admirals on the deck!" The cry rang through the arrival lounge as the hangar finished repressurizing and the first shuttle's hatch opened.

"Why isn't the Fleet the first out?" one of the Marines asked Todd and fell silent at the bleak look on the sergeant's face.

"The order of debarkation was pre-set by the Fleet," he informed him. "And the shuttles are Dreth per his request."

Neither his tone nor his voice betrayed what he thought of that, but his response was enough to make the man subside. He'd arrived with the first shuttle and stepped out to form an honor guard for the admirals who followed.

As the officers made their way across the hangar, he spoke quietly to Ka.

"Send it."

The Marine gave him an odd look and he returned it blandly. Only his lips twitched to acknowledge the man's puzzlement.

"Orders," he explained and gave no explanation at all.

The man frowned but nodded. Todd gestured to the door where two Marines were waiting. "If you'd make sure the admirals follow the Marines…"

He didn't tell the man where they would take the guests and didn't need to. After all, he was the sergeant who'd accepted the surrender—and he answered to the Fleet.

Dutifully, he saluted the officers as they filed past him and kept his gaze ahead and center and his face as blank as the wall beside him.

"More testing, Sergeant?" one admiral asked and slowed as she drew near.

Todd flicked his gaze to meet hers. "I'm afraid so, ma'am. Admiral's orders."

The fact she was an admiral didn't change a thing. They both knew that the only admiral he'd refer to was the Fleet.

She sighed. "Well, I hope there's a mug of something hot afterward. Last time, I swear the damn thing gave me frostbite."

"I'm glad to hear it, ma'am," he replied and couldn't help but smile.

Frostbite was a good sign. He hoped it happened again and that the woman's liking for Steph had remained unchanged.

None of the others questioned him and the second shuttle opened its hatch.

Todd repeated the conversation with the sergeant from that shuttle and this time, directed him to make sure the admirals followed Jimmy and Angus to the testing hall. The officers passed without comment.

Todd waited until their escort had closed in behind them and shut the door.

"Are we ready?" he asked. Reggie and Angus nodded, their faces grim.

Ka chuckled in his ear. "You'd better believe we are. You would *not* believe the shit show happening inside that last shuttle. If the Fleet doesn't end the day by decking someone, he's a better man than I am."

"I hate to break it to you, sweetheart," the Australian told her, "but you're not a man."

She managed a choked gasp of disbelief before she said in hurt tones. "That was below the belt, you Aussie asshole."

"*Everything's* below the belt," Reggie informed her, "but you're missing some important tackle."

"That doesn't stop me from having bigger balls than you do."

Piet chuckled. "She's got you there, Reggie."

"Oh, yeah?"

"Yeah, man," Angus informed him. "The only difference is she doesn't feel the need to hide them and simply wears them loud and proud on her chest."

Ka sputtered. "Loud and *proud*, Angus? *Really?*"

"Heads-up!" Todd murmured and his command cut their banter off.

All humor died and they waited as the third shuttle unloaded.

"Man, they *don't* look happy," Darren commented.

The sergeant darted him a warning glance and was relieved to see none of the satisfaction he heard in the Marine's voice visible on his face.

"That's nothing," Ka commented. "You should *hear* them."

To his relief, she didn't put the audio through as the admirals left the shuttle. He didn't want to hear them bitching. Knowing they'd gone after his team was already enough to make him want to kill them.

From what he could see of their faces, though, the only ones happy with having to pass the test were Admiral Amaratne, his captain, and the Marines who'd escorted them.

"Sucks to be them, doesn't it?" he murmured.

He watched as the admiral who emerged after Amaratne hurried to come alongside him.

"Who *is* that?" he asked softly. "The one coming alongside our Fleet...now."

"Helveck," Ka's replied promptly, "and he's a right asshole. I have some interesting stuff in the feeds about him."

"Is there anything we can do about it?" he asked as his interest sharpened.

"Not a thing, boss."

Todd sighed. "Then you'd better pretend you never saw it."

"Gotcha, boss, but for our information only? We need to watch that guy."

As she spoke, Helveck's arm drew back. He raced to the door but stopped as the nearest Marine grasped the admiral's arm and leaned closer to speak to him.

The man glared at him and jerked his arm free. The Marine gave him a grim smile and gestured toward the waiting shuttle.

Whatever he said to accompany that gesture left the admiral even angrier than before.

"You'd better give me audio, Ka," Todd advised.

"Gotcha, boss…but you're not allowed to shoot him if I can't."

"Rank has to have its privileges, Corporal."

"Not that kind of privilege, Sarge."

"You spoil all my fun."

"That's my job, boss."

"I'm fairly sure it isn't," he retorted as the conversations happening in the hangar became audible.

"Sir, I suggest you go to the shuttle," the Marine insisted.

"Or what?" Admiral Helveck sneered. "You're gonna shoot me?"

The man shook his head. "No, sir, but the Witch isn't known for her good temper—all due respect."

"Bah!" The admiral turned his head and all but spat. "That woman doesn't deserve your respect. Her parlor tricks didn't win us this battle."

Todd saw the Marine's mouth drop open but close as hastily. His reply only managed, "I'm fairly sure they—" before Admiral Amaratne intervened.

"Thank you, Tanner. Why don't you report to Sergeant Brogan? Let him know we'll be a little while longer."

The drama continued to unfold as the fleet admiral turned and held his hand up for all the admirals to stop.

"This, ladies and gentlemen, is where you need to make a decision."

He gestured toward the door where Todd and the remainder of the Hooligans were waiting.

"Over there is the door leading to where the peace treaty will be signed in front of our allies and the Federation's Witch—who, contrary to popular belief, eschewed cheap tricks and illusions and did, indeed, win us the battle."

Silence was the only response so he pointed toward the shuttle that had its hatch open.

"Over there is the shuttle that will return all those who do *not* wish to take the test to their ships."

They began to argue, and Amaratne bowed his head and raised his hand. Even then, it wasn't until one of the Marines broke through the hubbub with a two-fingered whistle that the arguments stopped enough for the admiral to speak.

"Those are your choices," he told them, "as dictated by the Federation's only true Witch."

"But it's not her ship!"

He inclined his head and looked at the speaker. "I think you will find that she is the senior partner on this one, which gives her both the rank and privilege of taking it as a prize."

"But there were Marines here."

"Under her command," he told the protestor, "which means they are eligible for a portion of the prize money but cannot claim the prize for themselves—or the rest of us."

"But—"

"Which means that the data they have been allowed to transmit since the ship was taken *also* rightfully belongs to the Morgana and she is allowing them to take it for free."

"But they were tasked with retrieving it. She was called in to *assist* with the mission."

"I think you'll find she was here on a prior engagement and merely offered our people an ingress point," Amaratne corrected mildly and changed the subject. "Now, Admirals, I need you to make your minds up. Will you agree to take the bar test, or will you sit this one out in that very well-appointed shuttle over there?"

Several of the admirals strode away from the rear of the group and approached the shuttle without further argument. Others required a little more convincing.

"It's an insult," Helveck insisted, and Todd restrained the desire to strangle the man.

Oblivious to his efforts to keep himself in check, the admiral continued.

"She is insulting our honor with this childish insistence on a loyalty test."

The sergeant moved to take a step out the door but was pulled up short when Angus' hand hooked through his harness.

"Not so fast, boss. These guys are already looking for an excuse to ice us. Remember?"

"Yeah, boss," Ka spoke in his ear. "Don't give them the excuse."

Todd froze and forced himself to relax as he listened to the Fleet deal with it. Helveck continued to argue.

"But it's not her ship."

Amaratne shrugged. "We've been over that, Admiral. It's her ship and her rules until we buy it from her—and that's even assuming we can."

"But—"

"Enough, Admiral. I'll make the assumption that you're intelligent enough to realize that *no one* will access that ceremony without taking the test. Then I'll make another leap of logic and guess you'd rather sit this one out on the shuttle." He regarded the man calmly. "Unless you think you can win a war of words with her people—because, you know, that's been tried before."

From the look on Admiral Helveck's face, he hadn't been aware of that fact.

"I… It has?" the man stuttered.

Amaratne gave him a hard grin.

"Oh, yes, he replied. "Have I not told you the story about these interesting Marines who tried to push her?"

Helveck shook his head. "No, sir. I don't believe you have."

He cast an apologetic glance at the door but Todd gave him a "Don't worry about it, sir," wave in return and he continued.

"She noticed them on the dock and went to ask them what their interest was—and their problem since they stood well away from where the bar was being held." He exhaled a wondering breath. "It was like she started reading their commander's mind or something because the secrets she repeated were not the ones those Marines wanted known." He raised his gaze to meet Helveck's head-on. "His second in command punched his lights out."

As though in amazement, he shook his head and gestured toward the arrivals lounge where Todd and his team were waiting.

"Now, through there," he continued, "is an entire auditorium of people waiting to formalize a historic peace treaty with an entirely new species. This will be witnessed by our Meligornian and Dreth allies, and this is your chance to join it."

Helveck stared at him as though he were crazy before he pivoted on his heel and stalked toward the shuttle. The remaining admirals fell in behind him.

Admiral Amaratne watched them go and glanced at his escort.

"So," he said, "I take it none of *you* object to being tested again?"

The Marine sergeant smiled. "Fleet, sir, we would be honored to join you."

If any of them heard Helveck's heartfelt whisper, none of them chose to acknowledge it.

"This," he whispered, "is but the battle. Wait until we're on *our* world, *bitch*."

Stephanie watched the scene play out in her HUD.

"I want to know exactly who those assholes are," she said and Ka sighed. "I'll try, but—"

Stephanie chuckled. "Not you, Ka. This is a job for Super Frog."

The guard groaned. "What d'you need, Steph?"

"Did you see those assholes refusing to come in here and say hello?"

"Uh-huh."

"I need to know exactly who they are, what they had for breakfast, what their day jobs are, and who they'll go home to sleep with tonight."

That caught his attention. "Really?"

She shook her head. "Not so much on that last one, but if you do find out, it still needs to go in the report."

"Gotcha."

"And Froggie?"

"Yes, Steph?"

"Don't get caught."

"Don't worry, Steph. They won't even know I've been."

"How much?" Ka asked and was answered by two puzzled voices.

"What do you mean, how much?"

"I mean how much d'you want to bet you won't get caught?"

"You'd better not bet against him," Stephanie warned, "given that I've decided you'll ride shotgun."

"Damn."

"Heads-up." Lars's soft voice interrupted them as Admiral Amaratne entered the room.

She couldn't help but look beyond him and feel slightly disappointed that Todd wasn't there. Ka must have been monitoring her because the corporal filled her in.

"He's making sure Helveck and his buddies are locked down tight. He'll be along soon."

"Thank you," Stephanie whispered, pasted a welcoming smile onto her face, and took the bar Lars dug out of his pouch pocket.

The Fleet saw her, hurried to meet her, and stopped short so she could hand him the bar.

"I apologize, Fleet Admiral," she began, "but only those who have no ill will for me and my people—which now includes the Telorans—may be here."

He smiled and shook his head. "No apologies are necessary, Ms. Morgana. I appreciate the precaution."

Although he didn't tell her, the scant hour he'd spent in the company of Helveck and his supporters had been more than enough time for him to make his assessment.

Stephanie continued, oblivious to his thoughts.

"I understand and accept that there *will* be ill will for the Telorans because of this war. That is permissible and only to be expected. It is the hatred rooted in specism and prejudice that we are trying to avoid. We do this initially by making sure one can deal with the Dreth"—she nodded first to Jaleck and then to V'ritan—"and the Meligornians".

She returned her gaze to the fleet admiral and took the now icy bar from his fingers. "Welcome aboard, Admiral Amaratne. You are free to proceed with the Federation's official acceptance of the Teloran surrender and then to the welcome ceremony, where we introduce a fourth people into the Federation."

CHAPTER SIXTY-FIVE

Darkness enveloped her. It was soft, silent, and warm but a short while later, it was broken. Stephanie groaned as the knock came again.

Maybe if she lay *very* still, whoever it was would simply turn and leave.

A moment's silence followed and she'd begun to relax when it was repeated. It was a distinct sound—two quick raps, hard and fast and then gone.

"Whichever asshole is interrupting my beauty sleep had better get their ass in here to explain or so help me—"

The door opened and she twisted irritably to see who it was.

"Still the same old Steph, I see." Todd chuckled and moved closer to sit on the edge of the bed. "You never did wake up well."

Her face heated and she let her head flop onto the pillow.

"Sorry," she mumbled and noticed that he glanced around the room. "I'd be looking nicer for you but I think the *Tempestarii* ran my ass over sometime in the last week. What day is it?"

He stood and finally noticed the cats curled together in their basket. Zeekat had rested his chin on the edge of their bed and blinked sleepily, but Bumblebee was curled tightly with his snout under his tail.

Todd studied him cautiously.

The cat looked for all the world like he was pretending to not have noticed him and he knew *that* couldn't be true. As he moved to see what might be the matter with it, the toe of his boot knocked against something on the floor.

Aware that Stephanie had pushed into a seated position and rubbed her eyes blearily, he stooped to retrieve whatever he'd bumped into.

When he held it in front of his face, he realized it was—or it had been—one of her boots. Inspecting it more closely, he saw the purple leather had been thoroughly chewed.

He waggled it in the cats' direction, but Zeekat's stare didn't waver. Bumblebee, on the other hand, snuggled his face farther under his tail.

Todd tutted and dropped the boot to one side.

"Three days," he said, and Stephanie scrunched her face in confusion.

"What?"

"It's been three days since the final signings."

"Ugh!" She let her head fall against the wall and closed her eyes.

After a moment, she opened them again and yawned.

"What happened?" she asked, snatched a nearby pillow, and dragged it closer to jam it behind her back.

"Hang on." Todd held a hand up, turned his head toward the door, and gave a piercing whistle.

Both cats sat bolt upright and stared at him with wide eyes, their tails twitching. The door began to open, and Bumblebee uttered an excited chirp and bolted toward it.

Unfortunately, his path took him past Todd. The Marine sergeant swept a foot out, raised his leg slightly higher than the cat, and anticipated when it tried to jump.

His thigh caught the animal's forelegs below the chest and Bee gave a startled yowl as the impact upended him and he sprawled into the opposite wall.

As the feline untangled itself, Frog appeared in the doorway, followed by Garach and Vishlog. The younger Dreth moved to Zeekat, who backed himself into a corner before he gave up and allowed Garach to slide his harness over his head and chest.

As the youngster snapped a leash onto him, his two teammates managed to convince Bee a harness might be a good idea. Frog had him in a headlock, and the cat had his foot on the guard's stomach, and Todd assumed neither of them was done yet.

Both remained motionless, however, as Vishlog cussed them out while the slash on his forearm bled red.

"Tark-livered, Tegorthan-loving, butt-licking, spawn of a hroda!"

Frog and Bumblebee exchanged worried glances, and the animal lifted his foot off the man's stomach.

"Take it outside," Todd instructed before either of them could do anything to the Dreth, "and make sure Vishlog doesn't bleed in the *Knight's* nice clean corridor or you'll be on the clean-up crew for a month."

Again, cat and man looked at each other as if wondering if he had the authority. Before they could test the theory, the ship spoke.

"Two months," she elaborated, "with Frog using Bumblebee as a pull-through for the sediment tanks."

Man and beast slumped and slunk from the room as if they'd had their tails kicked. The sergeant raised an eyebrow at Vishlog and the Dreth shrugged.

"I'll live. I'll have Marcus put a dressing on it when he's done with the tray."

"Tray?" Stephanie asked and Todd snickered at the sudden interest in her voice.

She didn't have to ask what was on it. The scent of bacon and potato cakes had already wafted into her sleeping quarters. She could also smell coffee and...

"Is that toast?"

Marcus and Johnny let Vishlog, Garach, and Zeekat clear the room before they entered.

"Hey there, sleepyhead," Marcus greeted her and waited while Avery cleared a space for the trays on the end of her bed.

"And how is our little ray of sunshine?" Johnny quipped as he placed his tray beside Marcus'.

"Ready to put a lightning bolt up your ass if you keep teasing me with the coffee."

He smirked and picked up the coffee pot and a mug. "What was that? Could I pretty please pour you a coffee?"

Stephanie folded her arms and glared at him as he poured the cup. Her eyes widened when he lifted it to his lips and took a sip.

"You know," he said and held the cup up to inspect it, "this is *damn* good coffee."

Todd stepped clear of the bed and leaned against the wall. "You're playing with fire, man."

Johnny's grin widened and he held the cup out to him.

"Yeah, you're right. Here, you give it to her. She's *way* less likely to beat *you* up."

He took the cup before the guard could drop it and Johnny left the room.

"Don't do anything *we* wouldn't do," came as a chorus from the living room.

Todd took a sip of the coffee and caught Stephanie's look.

"What? It *is* good coffee."

Before she could say anything, he handed her the cup. "Do you want cream or sugar?"

"Yes?"

He laughed and helped to arrange her tray and pillows so she could eat. When everything was settled and she'd drunk her second cup, she looked around the room.

"Where are we?"

Todd snickered, and Stephanie rolled her eyes.

"Okay, I *know* I'm on the *Knight*. What I *don't* know..." She frowned. "Well, I don't remember much from the end."

"Yeah, I realized that when Morgana faked it for you," he admitted.

She stared at him, a forkful of potato frozen halfway between the plate and her mouth as she frowned. "She *what?*"

He hurried to set her fears at rest.

"She didn't do anything I think you'd have disagreed with, and I'm very sure no one knew except maybe me—and that's only because I've been around you from the beginning." He paused and his expression softened. "You were too far gone, I imagine, and the Morgana knew everyone needed you there to make sure they played along."

Todd nudged her. "You gonna keep eating, or do I need to stop until you do?"

Stephanie scowled at him but realized she was still holding her fork. He waited until she'd started eating again before he continued.

"They did, by the way, play along."

"So, the Dreth will accept a group of the Teloran fleet on their planet?" Stephanie asked as that vague detail made itself known.

"Yup. Some of the families were reluctant at first, but Jaleck made it clear how *happy* you'd be for that to happen and they found room."

She snorted. "I bet they did."

"And then there was the part where you came up with using the excess nMU on Dreth—"

"Wait! There is?"

Todd nodded. "You were utterly certain of it." He looked worried. "Don't tell me you're not so sure of it now."

"Tell me what I said again."

Todd shook his head. "Are you implying I was too far gone?"

"It'd be a miracle if you weren't."

With a shrug, he said, "I don't burn through my reserves quite as fast. What you said was that the nMU on Dreth made the them so short-tempered and negative and that their systems could only tolerate so much. Then, Enkaresh said he wished there was a way they could reduce the nMU to levels the Dreth could tolerate by shipping it to Telor."

Stephanie's eyes widened. "Wait! I told them that? Because it's a brilliant idea!"

Todd chuckled. "Yes, it is—and then you made them sign a trade deal that involved something to do with the Telorans teaching the Dreth how to use the magic they were sensitive to and the Dreth shipping nMU to help restore Telor, and—"

"Wait! Did you say there would be *Dreth* mages?" she asked. "You *so* did not."

He stared at her. "Why? It was *your* idea!"

"Oh… Are you sure? Because I don't remember that."

"I'm very sure the Morgana didn't come up with it. You said something about how you were restoring Earth so you might as well come up with a way to restore Telor as well. Meligorn even offered to help with the tech."

Stephanie groaned. "Tell me I didn't suggest another branch of One R&D open on Dreth."

"You *might* have…" Todd didn't sound too sure of it and he shrugged. "I'll get Ka to pull the conversation log up. You'll be able to look at what you came up with in that."

She sighed. "It never rains, but it pours."

When she looked at her plate, she discovered it was empty. He took it off her lap and held a glass of orange liquid up.

"Juice?"

"Thank you." She took it. "It's exactly what I need." As she lowered the glass, she caught him watching her with a soft smile on his face.

"What?" she demanded and froze. "Wait! How are *you*—and, I presume, the rest of the Hooligans—on my ship?"

He smirked. "Technically, we're on the *Tempestarii*—which is where the *Knight* is docked by the way—and there is exactly *no one* who wants to be inside this bad bitch when a Witch who can read your mind after you've held the bar is on board."

His smile widened. "They all saw the fight you had with the Teloran witch, and they all saw the ships you tore apart. Everyone is terrified you'll take exception to what they're thinking."

"I can what now?" Stephanie asked and he snickered.

"Yup. *You*, you evil person, can read the mind of *anyone* who has held the bar, so anyone who's passed your test may have been 'compromised.'"

He leaned back and studied her, a goofy smile on his face. "It's the latest rumor to come out of Naval Intelligence and it has some fairly powerful backers."

"Helveck, I presume," she suggested, surprised that she'd recalled the enemy admiral's name.

"Among others."

"Wow!" Stephanie was stunned. "If they only realized how nice I am."

Todd snickered again.

"Sorry, Steph, but I know that you won't even get your best friends —the ones who *didn't* know you before the Morgana—to believe that."

"Huh…" she began, but whatever she was about to say was lost in a gigantic yawn and she passed him her empty juice glass.

"I'll take these to the kitchen," he told her as he gathered her plates and stacked them on the tray.

Stephanie shook her head.

"Uh-uh. Nope. I'm sorry, Mr. Military Man, but I think I'd feel a little safer if maybe you held me while I took a nap."

Todd set the tray on the floor beside the door.

"Nap?" he asked in disbelief. "You just took a *sixty-hour* sleep!"

"Don't make me beg," she pleaded. "It's unbecoming in a Witch."

He sighed.

"I would *never*," he reassured her, sat on the edge of the bed again, and leaned forward to remove his shoes. "I'm simply trying to decide how long this operation might take since I need to report in sometime."

"Really?" she asked and he nodded.

"Really."

"Hmmm." She snapped her fingers and his boots vanished from around his feet to reappear tucked neatly under a chair.

"Ebony?" Stephanie asked, and the ship responded immediately.

"Yes, Stephanie?"

"I need Todd for a few more hours. Is there some way you can…" Once more, the words were lost in a cavernous yawn and she flapped a hand to signal she wasn't done.

"You need to communicate with him for a while longer?" the *Knight* asked, and she nodded. "I'll see what I can do. Be back in a few."

"Back in a few?" she asked and darted him a quizzical look.

He met her questioning glance and shrugged. "Don't look at me. It's *your* ship."

"Indeed, I am," The *Knight* interrupted and sounded very smug.

"And?" Stephanie asked.

"The Navy has agreed that due to the strenuous and stressful nature of their last operation, and the fact that the data was handed over in good time along with a brief report from their sergeant, the Hooligans may take an extra four days to rest and recuperate."

Stephanie looked at Todd, her eyebrows raised. "Did *you* know you wrote a report?" she asked.

He nodded. "It was the first thing I did when I got back. I sent it directly to the admiral in case he had anything he wanted to add, and he said he'd send it on."

She leaned against him. "It's good having friends in high places."

"Especially ones who'll verify the report was sent on time and the mission achieved," he replied.

"Well, then, Mr. Military Efficiency, how about you rest too?" She waited as he stretched beside her and snuggled against him. "I think we did enough to earn it."

"Yes, ma'am," he replied and wrapped his arms around her.

He rested his chin against the top of her head and closed his eyes. She sighed contentedly, breathing more deeply as sleep crashed over them.

CHAPTER SIXTY-SIX

"Todd is sleeping," the *Knight* explained in a different cabin.

"Uh-huh. *Sure* he is," Ka quipped, "'cause that is what I would be doing after fuck knows how many months away from *my* soulmate."

"No," she insisted. "They are *sleeping*. Neither of them has the energy for anything else."

"Really?" The corporal sounded disappointed. "No horizontal tango?"

"None," Knight replied in a tone that said the topic was *very* closed.

"Well, it's not like both of them don't *need*—" Ka began and ignored the signal.

"Sleeping. Nothing else," she insisted, her voice as close to a human growl as the woman had ever heard it.

"Fine!" she sputtered. "So, it's okay for Piet and I to suffer but my *boss* can't suffer with his girlfriend?"

"*His* girlfriend is my boss, and if you even *try* to make them suffer, every tiny credit you ever make from this point on will automatically be transferred to a non-profit organization."

"Ouch." Ka smiled. "Man, you don't have to be so *ugly* about it."

713

"Are you kidding me?" the *Knight* asked. She gave a very human sniff. "We *are* talking about you, right?"

The corporal was silent for a moment before her smile broadened. "Yeah. You're right. I *do* need reminding every once in a while."

"Only once?"

Paris: Three months after mankind signed the most important treaty in its history.

The man walked beside the Seine, unshaven and slouching. He didn't quite blend with the rest of the people walking around him but he didn't quite stand out either.

The slouch was... Well, to a trained observer, it was an effort, as was the attempt to keep his hands in his pockets. Neither action came naturally.

His hair was tousled and he kept his head down, but not low enough that he couldn't keep an eye on his surroundings. Paris was beautiful at this time of year, especially in the morning with the leaves just turning gold and the mist rising from the river.

He used the cover of the mist to turn into a small café at the river's edge. Water lapped at the boardwalk several meters away but he merely pulled his coat closer around his shoulders and found himself a seat at the table closest to the wall.

There was a narrow gap between the café and the stairs rising to the park above it, and he knew of a small wooden door carefully concealed behind it. From his corner, he could see in every direction that mattered.

And he was able to watch the boats as they floated past.

The café owner gave him a smile and a wave and set about preparing his order. He didn't see the customer often but he knew what he ordered—coffee and half a dozen croissants, three of which he'd eat, and three he'd take with him with the coffee to go he'd want at the end of his meal.

The man settled in his chair and his gaze roved over the people passing by, the boats, and very occasionally, drifted to the sky above.

He never looked at it for long and he always seemed sadder when he did.

While the proprietor noticed, he never asked why. Everyone had a past and the right to keep it to themselves. He took the man his order and answered his smile and thanks with a breezy, *"De rien,"* before he returned to his other customers.

Some of those chose tables but many took their coffees and continued on their way to work. Every so often, the café owner would glance over to see the man seated quietly and watching the river like always.

Neither saw the arrival of a second man, who came to stand beside the table.

"Pardon, monsieur."

The voice broke through ex-Admiral Amaratne's thoughts and he startled. Seeing his attention, the newcomer spoke again.

"Puis-je m'asseoir?"

He shook his head apologetically.

"I'm sorry. English?"

"May I sit and chat to you?" the stranger asked. "I don't often get out and I am somewhat lonely."

Amaratne heaved an internal sigh but nodded. "Would you like coffee?"

"Ah, *non, monsieur. Merci.* I have already eaten." The stranger sat, his pale face shaded by a cowboy hat.

He sipped his coffee and used the time to study his unexpected companion. Apart from the cowboy hat, he didn't look like a cowboy. He didn't wear jeans but an expensive, well-cut suit and his shoes gleamed with polish.

A frown crept in but he smoothed the expression away quickly.

"What did you want to chat about?" he asked.

The stranger indicated the unopened newspaper at the admiral's elbow.

"Perhaps the news?" he asked as though he wasn't sure what reception his suggestion would receive.

Amaratne unfolded the paper and placed it between them.

Stephanie was, of course, front-page news—and, as always, painted in an unfavorable light.

"What is she supposed to have done this time?" the stranger murmured.

He glanced at the paper and skimmed the article. "Oh, the usual. You know, her brokerage of the peace treaty was a way to cheat Earth of very lucrative contracts, how sleeping with the Dreth seems to have paid off—"

The stranger tensed.

"I'm sorry if this offends you." He started to fold the newspaper in half. "We can talk about something else if you'd prefer."

"No," his companion told him. "There is nothing of greater importance to me than how the Witch is perceived." He unfolded the newspaper and turned the page. "Perhaps there is something better inside."

Amaratne frowned but the stranger was already speaking.

"Oh... Oh, I see." He sounded disappointed. "They *aren't* willing to give her credit where credit is due, are they? How incredibly unfair."

At his words, the ex-admiral glanced around and scanned the quayside, the stairs, and even twisted his neck to look at the railings that ran along the edge of the wall above. No one had stopped to listen.

He leaned closer to the stranger and slid his hand into his jacket. "Who *are* you?"

The cowboy leaned toward him and surprisingly strong fingers closed over his hand and the butt of the pistol he'd grasped.

"She knows me as BURT."

Amaratne's eyes widened and he struggled to keep his voice to a whisper. "You're her *boss*? From One R&D? But...what are you doing *here*?"

The businessman let go of his hand and tapped another article—one that seemed to suggest Stephanie had engineered the entire Teloran attack for her own ends. He sighed.

"You realize what this means, don't you?"

He nodded gloomily and E-BURT continued.

"So you know she has to leave, right?"

This time, Amaratne sighed heavily and rested his chin on his hands. "Yes."

"This might be the only chance you get," the businessman told him, but he shook his head.

"They will pillory you if they find you," the AI warned and he nodded again.

"In officer's training," he stated and changed the subject, "they made us study history—mostly military history, but some of us went on to study the history of politics and the rise and fall of power. It was an interesting course, although I only appreciated it later."

"Like now?" E-BURT asked.

Another nod preceded his explanation. "Yes. I find it particularly useful now. This time"—he gestured toward the paper—"has many parallels."

"And none of them good," his companion observed.

"No, but this is my home—my world. I refuse to let her fall." He tapped the paper. "The next few years...well, they won't be pleasant but they are also the only time we have to sow the seeds for our redemption."

"Stephanie can't do that," E-BURT reminded him.

"No," Amaratne agreed. "She *has* to leave. There is no hope for us if she does not."

He laid a hand on the businessman's forearm. "Don't let her leave it too late. I fear the wolves are gathering."

"And she cannot defeat them all," he agreed. "There are too many and they are too well-entrenched. Some are still too hidden for us to deal with."

"I will do what I can," he told him, "but you have to get her away."

"I will do that," E-BURT answered.

Amaratne turned the page and pointed to another article. A photograph showed one of the rising politicians flanked by Marines.

"I thought the Navy stayed out of politics," the construct observed.

"It should," he told him and tapped on the grouped Marines. "These aren't the Marines Todd belongs to. These are...different. I know why Stephanie must leave."

The businessman pretended to study the picture and let the ex-admiral continue. The man tapped the picture again.

"Just like I knew I'd have to leave the second I saw one of these guys standing on my bridge in that last battle. I know they eliminated one of the admirals who supported me—and I don't know how many more—but that is why I left and disappeared." He paused and gave his companion a grateful look. "I appreciate that opportunity to hide my trail."

"After all you did trying to ensure the truth prevailed?" E-BURT asked. "It was the very least I could do."

They both fell silent, their attention torn between the photograph and the view before them. It was Amaratne who broke the silence.

"When are you leaving?"

The businessman tilted his head and gave him a soft, sad smile.

"Soon," he admitted. "They will come looking for me."

They both stopped speaking, each lost in their thoughts until finally, Amaratne spoke again.

"Do you know how long?"

He laughed quietly. "They have already started. Stephanie will leave soon. She'll make one more very large display of power and go."

Amaratne relaxed.

"Good," he said. "Good for her." A few moments later, he added, "They will brand her a traitor."

"I know." E-BURT didn't sound happy about that, and both men gazed out across the water, watching the quiet passage of the boats as the noise of a working day slowly grew around them.

"As long as she doesn't leave it too long," the man noted. "These people want all the prestige they can garner from winning the war. They can't afford to have someone that powerful against them."

"She's done, for the moment," the AI assured him, "unless those idiots try to attack Dreth, Meligorn, or the Telorans."

He pursed his lips, considered the possibility, and shook his head.

"I don't think they'll do that. They don't have total control on Earth and I *think* they're smart enough to realize they don't want to kick that particular hornet's nest."

"I hope so," E-BURT told him, closed the newspaper, and slid it toward Amaratne.

The man nodded and said, "It won't be forever."

"No, but it'll seem like it," the AI told him.

"Unfortunately, yes."

"She won't forget us," he assured him, "and she won't forget her world either. She'll give them the chance to do the right thing by her world, and they'll force her hand."

"You mean because they *won't* do the right thing?" Amaratne asked, even though they essentially discussed a foregone conclusion.

"Exactly." They sat and contemplated the future for a while.

The ex-admiral watched another boat pass, realized that this was the longest he'd ever stayed at the café, and hoped it wouldn't be his undoing. His companion stirred restlessly and stood. He held his hand out. "I hope, when the call comes, that I see you again, my friend."

Amaratne rose with him and shook his hand. "Do you think she'll come back?"

E-BURT smiled. "If I had to calculate it—and I did—the Earth will need her. When it's ready to admit that, she will return. Just because her planet gave up on her does not mean she will *ever* give up on it."

He nodded and his heart lifted at the thought. "Then I guess it's important for us to stay vigilant for when that occurs."

"And safe," the businessman stated, "because it'll get much worse before it gets better."

He clapped Amaratne on the shoulder and walked briskly away, turned, and took the stairs at a trot. The ex-admiral watched him go before he signaled for the bill.

When it was paid and he had his second cup of coffee in hand, he slipped into the crowd. It took several strides before he remembered he was supposed to slouch.

E-BURT slowed his pace at the top of the stairs and forced himself to stroll across the park and along the Parisian sidewalks. He traveled for several blocks, checked his back-trail to make sure it was clear, and picked up the pace.

The truck was parked where he'd left it and tapping the surveillance cameras in the area revealed it had drawn no undue attention. He ran a second scan by remoting into the truck's security systems.

Only when he was sure the vehicle was as clean as when he'd parked it did he climb into the cab. Settling in the driver's seat, he removed the cowboy hat and laid it on the passenger's seat beside him.

The bright red R on the android's forehead gleamed brightly and caught the eye of a passer-by. E-BURT saw the woman stop and take a second look, then shake her head as she went into one of the nearby apartments.

He chuckled softly as he started the engine and pulled away carefully. She was probably thinking she had to get her eyes checked, he mused, glad he wasn't on a colony world where someone might have recognized what the R meant.

At least, he didn't *think* she'd recognized it. Running the scan to make sure she didn't call the authorities or make a big deal of it took almost no computing power as he negotiated the Paris streets and drove the truck north.

It truly is a beautiful city, he thought as he looked out at it, unable to forget its history as he drove.

Humans, he mused. *They are capable of so much wonder. And yet, so much terror too. No wonder they are so often confused.*

He guided the vehicle to the edge of the city and drove around to one of the major industrial hubs. There, a shuttle port was fringed by storage facilities and warehouses. Its specialty was cargo and colonies, and his entry was unremarked.

E-BURT drove to one of the larger storage depots, displayed his entry pass, and proceeded to a warehouse a block in from the edge. He'd paid for exclusive use of it and no one had commented on the excavation and construction equipment he'd brought in for "storage."

If they'd noticed the noises coming from inside the warehouse, they hadn't commented. Clients could test their equipment as they saw fit. What they hadn't noticed were the small specialized drones he'd used to excavate a chamber beneath the floor, nor the stairwell he'd installed to reach it.

Climbing out of the cab, E-BURT set about securing the building and uncovered the warning signs around its perimeter before he returned inside. It was a simple matter to set the anti-intrusion program that would electrify the warehouse walls in case of an attempted incursion.

After that, he activated the shielding that ran inside the walls and blocked all scans and communications, and finally set the locks. Having learned a few things from Elizabeth, he didn't rely only on electronics.

He positioned locking bars and padlocks at the inside entries, checked the connections from the panels lining the walls, and made sure the emergency generators were on stand-by.

It was the most he could do to secure the facility and guard against his new quarters being discovered.

"Now, I have to bury myself," he murmured, closed the door to the stairwell, and secured it before he descended to the room that would become his resting place—or his tomb.

E-BURT moved to a pod capsule set against one wall, hooked himself into an electrical tap, and lifted the lid. Once he'd climbed into it, he pulled the lid shut and closed his eyes.

He opened them again in the Virtual World.

The chalet was exactly as he'd designed it to be and the view of the Alps as real as he could make it. It was summer and the meadow before him was covered in grass and sprinkled with flowers.

Elizabeth would have loved this, he thought. *Only she would have preferred winter...and whiskey in her hot chocolate.*

Thoughtfully, he turned his glass and admired the rich color of the wine he'd chosen to mark the occasion. He stepped out onto the porch and sat in the wooden armchair he'd positioned to admire the view. It was wonderfully pleasant there.

Taking a sip of his wine, he shifted into a comfortable position and considered the events that had brought him there. He hadn't lied to the admiral about needing to go away. The Navy *was* looking for him and they were very close.

"I hope this works," he murmured and stared at the waving grasses and the idyllically clear sky. "The future is always so *murky* when working with humans."

The Virtual World rippled and a small box appeared on the coffee table beside the chair. In its center was a bright red button.

E-BURT glanced at it and took a moment to activate the code he'd found. His enemies had used it to conceal their presence and activities from him. Well, now it was his turn.

This was where things went from murky to opaque. As much as he'd done *all* the calculations he could think of, there was one thing of which he couldn't be certain.

He didn't know if he would wake up or not.

His thoughts turned to Stephanie and he raised his glass to the sky. "We did good things, didn't we?"

The wine went down like silk and he set the glass down beside the box.

"Many good things," he added and thumped his fist on the button.

The world around him shattered and splintered from Alpine meadow to white.

CHAPTER SIXTY-SEVEN

"Yes," the senator said, "but will that allow us to take over the witches?"

"What do you mean, Ed?"

Edward Gavringham uttered an impatient sigh.

"You know exactly what I mean. We need this bill to be watertight when we pass it. I don't want a single one of them to get away."

"You mean freelancing, don't you?"

"You know what I mean. I want every one of those little freaks of nature under *our* control."

"Or what?"

The senator arched his eyebrows. "Well, you need a license to drive a car, don't you?"

"That's a good point, Senator. I'll make a note to include that in our publicity campaign. It will, at least, help us to track them."

"I want to do more than track them," the senator declared. "I want to control them to such a point that they don't have a choice about cooperating."

"These things move slowly, Ed—"

"You don't think I don't *know* that?" he demanded. "Haven't I waited patiently while you work your shit out?"

"It's not only *my* shit," the other senator pointed out. "What we're doing benefits *all* of us and we need to be patient."

Gavringham sighed and leaned back in his chair. "I know that, but I also need to be sure the bill will do what we need it to do. I don't want to have to wrangle a do-over through the Federation parliament."

One of the other senators chuckled and drew their attention.

"I had the lawyers go over the draft before I got here. The bill will let us demand that every citizen who shows magical ability be registered, *and* that they will be required to undertake specialized training before they are allowed into the regular community again."

The others gaped at him.

"But... How did you manage that, Jacob?" one of them asked.

Senator Jacob Oaklands continued to smile.

"Oh, I merely pulled up all the recorded incidents of magic being used in a harmful way and compiled it into a very damning document on the dangers of emerging magic. That Australian boy, for example... what was his name?"

The others looked at each other, their faces blank as they tried to recall the incident let alone the child involved. He shrugged.

"Well, it doesn't matter, but it was a very apt case in point and the security committee saw it our way. *All* magic-users will need to be registered, and they will *all* be required to attend Federation-approved boarding schools."

He leaned back and his expression grew smug when they all began talking at once. They quietened as he held his hand up.

"Did I mention that the bill will go out at the end of the week?" he asked and smirked as they stared at him in stunned silence.

"But...that's...amazing. How can you be sure?"

"I spoke to the Committee."

"You did what? When?"

"Last night. I didn't want to break the news until I was sure."

The senators looked at each other and the table devolved into chatter. Jacob looked on and studied them for any sign of dissent.

Gavringham nodded to him and saluted his move with a slight approving smile.

The witches *would* be theirs!

A week later, two government dropships approached the front lawn of Harborview Tech. Their black paint seemed to absorb the early morning light reflected from the university's façade as they descended onto the drive.

The university was silent at this time of day and the solitary figure of a single mage was the only sign of life. He was seated quietly on a bench flanked by two narrow pines, and he didn't seem to notice the ships landing at the bottom of the drive.

His robes enveloped him, their purple and teal thread touched by gold, and their rich folds protected him from the morning chill. The shuttle hatches opened but his gaze remained fixed on something in the grass.

Lieutenant Commander Abraham Pierce stepped out. His focus settled on the Meligornian and his lip curled as he straightened his jacket. He landed lightly on the grass and waited for the man to notice him.

Heavens knew, *he* would have been curious at the appearance of two naval dropships setting down at the foot of his front drive. The figure, though, seemed completely oblivious. It was almost offensive.

He waited for his escort to join him—a Marine sergeant and his corporal. With them on either side of him, he stalked toward his target.

It might be 0600 and the students might not be awake yet, but by God, they would be woken. There was no time like the present for them to learn of the routine that awaited them.

This school was no longer a private enterprise. Since the Witches Registration Act had been passed, it was mandatory for all institutions with a magical curriculum to be licensed.

This was one of the few that had refused, citing the Citizens' Freedom Act. The Navy was there to tell them that the Act no longer applied—that the Federation now considered ungoverned magical ability a clear and present threat to the overall welfare of its citizens.

He smiled grimly.

And of course, the Council had chosen the Witch's school as its first example.

"If *her* school is shown having to comply, the others will quickly come into line," the senators had reasoned.

In only a few minutes, he came to a halt in front of the mage. His face twisted in disgust when he recognized the elderly Meligornian the Witch had dragged to Earth as her founding instructor.

"You!" he snapped when the old man looked past him to admire the view of the ocean beyond the university's car park.

Tethis continued to offer neither recognition of his presence or response, and the officer tried again.

"I said you, old man!"

The mage remained silent, his calm gaze fixed on the peaceful view.

Irritated, he waited again but Tethis maintained his placid and very silent resistance. Finally, the lieutenant commander became impatient and stooped so his mouth was an inch from his right ear.

"*Can you not hear me, old man?*" he shouted.

When the mage still did not respond, Pierce turned to his guards.

"Wake him up," he commanded and stepped back to give them space.

It took him a moment to register that neither of them had moved.

"I said," he began and raised his voice, "*Wake. Him. Up!*"

Again, neither of them responded.

"Sergeant!" he shouted and glared at the Marine, and when the man didn't answer, he turned on the corporal. "I gave you an order."

When neither man reacted, the lieutenant commander tapped his communicator. "I need the squad from Shuttle A. At the double!"

No sound reached him to tell him his order was being obeyed and he pivoted to look at the craft. A frisson of unease flowed over him when nothing moved at either one.

"Shuttle A," he called. "Come in, Shuttle A. Shuttle B?"

He realized now that neither of the two Marines with him had moved and he poked the sergeant and walked a slow circle around him. As he returned to his starting position, the mage raised his head.

"They can hear you," Tethis explained. "They merely can't do anything about it."

"What?" Pierce spun to stare at him.

The old man continued unperturbed.

"You see," he began, and the officer noticed something else about him—something completely unexpected.

Tethis shone with power—not literally, but with a natural glow that could only be described as abundant health.

The lieutenant commander gaped and studied the healthy color of the Meligornian's skin, the gleam in his eyes, and the way he no longer leaned on a cane.

"But you're broken," he whispered.

"Perhaps I was," Tethis said with a smile that didn't soften the flint in his eyes, "but I am broken no more."

He paused to allow the man time to realize the truth of his words before he continued.

"It's amazing what a woman with the ability to weave MU together might accomplish if she is willing to be patient and exhaust herself on behalf of someone dear to her."

With a small smile, he rose from the bench, allowed himself the luxury of stretching in front of the befuddled human, and simply didn't care that he revealed the increasing extent of Stephanie's power.

"You see," he added as he walked around the officer so that the man was forced to turn on the spot, "*she* told me to protect these people."

He let the words fade as a low thrum filled the air.

Pierce turned to look toward it and his mouth fell open when he registered the shuttle coming in to land between the two Navy dropships.

Furious, he looked at Tethis. "You won't get that shuttle off-world," he all but hissed. "It will be destroyed."

To his surprise, the mage chuckled and patted his cheek.

"You poor simpleton. It's not here to take people away."

"It's not?" he asked but the Meligornian was too busy watching the shuttle unload and he had no choice but to do the same.

He recognized some of the faces debarking. They belonged to the parents of students attending the academy.

Pierce frowned, tried to place them, and slowly recalled the names of mothers and fathers—and siblings, he realized as younger adults and children emerged as well.

Tethis' voice interrupted his study. "You will need to move your shuttles."

That caught his attention and he glared at the old Meligornian.

"I most certainly will not!"

To his surprise, the mage didn't bother to argue but shrugged instead.

"Let the record show I warned you," he replied mildly and the smell of storms and lightning filled the air.

"What..." Pierce began but Tethis looked toward the school.

The lieutenant commander followed his gaze and saw the doors begin to open. That wasn't what drew his attention, though. Nor was it the source of the ionization in the air.

The cause—and what made his hair stand on end—was the *very large* gate that had begun to form at the top of the drive.

Before he could comment on it, two familiar figures stepped out of the shimmery veil that covered the portal and Pierce's breath caught.

Of course the Witch would be there. She couldn't leave well enough alone. The fact that he couldn't see her didn't matter. He knew the Dreth and the human who had come through the portal.

Vishlog was the first Dreth to be accepted by her team and the human was the head of her security detail, Lars Storenson. The

Council was working on the charges they needed to separate them from the Witch's side—permanently.

Pierce resented that this had not yet happened almost as much as he resented the cut of the uniforms they wore. The Navy had never devoted such care to the appearance of its personnel, but the Witch seemed to think it was something important.

He couldn't help but admire the sharp outlines of gear that looked as good as a dress uniform and yet let them move like they were in the field. As he stared at them, the human caught sight of him.

For a moment, he wished he was there on any other form of business but the duty he'd volunteered for. Now, he regretted his eagerness to see the Council's orders enacted.

Maybe it *had* been a trap.

"Is there a problem?" Lars asked the mage and completely ignored the lieutenant commander standing beside him.

Tethis chuckled and indicated the dropships and the lieutenant commander. "Not for me," he replied, "but that shuttle needs to land and these two dropships are stuck."

"They're not stuck," Pierce protested. "They're here on official business and it's not done yet."

The Witch's security head raised his eyebrows. "They'll still have to move. No doubt, your *official* business can wait a little longer."

The response made him bristle. "It most certainly can *not* wait!" he snapped. "I have orders to carry out and orders not to leave until they *have* been carried out." He drew himself to his full height and poked Lars in the chest. "*You* need to leave until we're done and I'm ordering you to do so."

Lars tilted his head and folded his arms. "*You're* ordering *me?*"

"That's right. As a commanding officer, I can order you to do exactly what I need you to. I'm ordering you to take your people and leave—and close that gate while you're at it."

The man listened with a look of amusement on his face, then laughed.

"Look, LC, but you're not in my chain of command so that won't work on me. And you'd better hope my boss is in a good mood."

As he spoke, Stephanie stalked out of the gate. She wasn't looking where she was going and seemed to be in the middle of an argument with someone she'd left on the other side.

"If you don't like the heat, kids, you need to get out of the kitchen. And you know exactly what that means, so you'd better either be packed or running those laps when I get back. If not, I'll drop you on the first world we get to, regardless of whether there's a colony there or not."

She wasn't alone but two of her team walked on either side of her as she emerged, followed by the rest. Pierce had a serious case of uniform envy because while the suits looked good individually, they were even more impressive in a group.

He frowned and counted more people than he remembered being on her team. In the next instant, he recognized the very big man who walked to her right.

"Sergeant Brogan," he muttered. His gaze traveled over the rest of her entourage and identified the rest of Todd's team. "But they're Marines."

Lars smirked. "Not anymore. The paperwork went through a while back."

The lieutenant commander had been aware of that. What he wasn't aware of was when the approval had gone through.

Todd trotted to the shuttle and the waiting families and his team dogged his heels. They moved easily and smiled in greeting as they approached the civilians.

The officer watched them and noted the way the ex-sergeant soon had the parents smiling and the kids flocking to his feet.

"You lost a good man, there," Lars observed as if the young man's defection was Pierce's fault.

He opened his mouth to argue that his decision to leave the Navy had nothing to do with him but he saw the Witch approaching and closed it again. Who knew what she would take offense at?

She stopped just short of them and looked at the dropships.

"Huh. You guys are in my spots," she said and addressed no one in particular.

Again, he opened his mouth, only to close it without uttering a word. This time, it was because she continued to speak while her hair lifted as the dropships' engines kicked into life. The two craft lifted from the ground.

"So, you will move," she concluded and the vessels shifted sideways to give the civilian shuttles room to land.

With the way clear before them, it didn't take them long to touch down and open their hatches. By that time, Todd and his people had already begun to move the civilians from the first shuttle through the gate.

They did so in an orderly fashion. No one panicked and the kids tucked in close to their parents or a nearby Marine. If Pierce hadn't seen it with his own eyes, he wouldn't have believed it possible.

As soon as it was empty and its payload clear, the first shuttle lifted to make room for another. Stephanie watched the proceedings and turned to Tethis.

She jerked a thumb at the lieutenant commander. "I assume those are his?"

Refusing to be ignored, Pierce took a deep breath.

"I am—" Pierce's words cut off abruptly when she made an impatient motion with her hand, and his eyes widened in panic.

His hands flew to his mouth in horror and he discovered that what he thought he'd imagined was all too true. His lips were gone, replaced by a smooth, unbroken stretch of skin.

Holding his hands over it, he turned to her and his eyes begged her for an explanation.

She looked at him and arched an eyebrow.

"I didn't give you leave to speak," she told him, studied him, and didn't look very impressed by what she saw. "I also know exactly why you are here, Abraham Pierce."

He met her hard, blue gaze and his eyes widened. Cold sweat beaded his brow, but she didn't seem to notice.

"And, Abraham Pierce, trust me when I say you do not wish to offend me any more than you already have."

Stephanie gestured to where the shuttles were off-loading and their passengers directed in an orderly fashion toward the gate.

"About twelve percent of this school's families wish to remain here on Earth. You may work them into your system *after* we leave—and trust me, we *will* leave. The only question is how ugly I will have to get to make my point."

CHAPTER SIXTY-EIGHT

Alerts sounded throughout the *Audie Murphy*, and the crew scrambled to action stations. On the bridge, Captain Muldoon listened to his orders and frowned.

"Aye aye, Fleet." He snapped to attention and held the position until Fleet Admiral Helveck ended the call, then looked around the bridge.

"You all heard the man! There's been a gate incursion in Washington and we've been ordered to intervene."

The bridge crew returned his gaze but no one moved.

"Now, people!" he ordered and pressed his lips into a firm line.

In reality, he didn't blame them. They all guessed, as he did, that the gate was probably from the Witch—the Federation's *ex*-Witch—and none of them wanted to intercept or disrupt it any more than he did.

The fact was that if they didn't, all their lives would become much more difficult and it was his job as their captain to protect them from that if he could. He kept his face stern as his gaze swept the command center.

If that meant being an asshole, then so be it. He tried to decide

733

which one of them to send to the brig when they began to move. His XO laid a hand on his shoulder.

"Give them time, Captain. They're still in shock."

Recognizing the risk the man took, Muldoon nodded and hoped he was right. He also hoped that the Federation's latest round of madness would be over soon. Honestly, he wasn't sure how much of it he could take.

"The *Dorie* has taken up station on our right," the on-duty scan technician reported.

Muldoon nodded. "Have you found the gate's signature?"

"I have, sir." The man's face showed his reluctance.

"The *Dorie's* weapons are warming up," his partner reported.

"Weapons team, lock and load," the captain ordered. "We need to end that incursion."

"Sir…" the weapons chief began but stopped.

The captain knew what she was about to ask and admired her courage. At the same time, he prayed she wouldn't force him to report her.

"We need to end the incursion, Commander," he told her as the proximity alert rang through the ship.

The lighting dropped from white to strobing yellow, and they all froze.

"Sir! Something big…uh, appeared on our port side!"

"Put it on screen," Muldoon ordered, trying to hide the sudden relief he felt. Now, all he could do was hope it was who he thought it was.

It grew harder to hide his relief as the massive outline of the *Tempestarii* faded fully into view and her captain's voice spoke over the *Audie's* comms.

"I wouldn't do that if I were you."

Muldoon wondered if the *Dorie* received the same warning and risked a glance at his console. To his relief, the scans showed his sister ship's weapons powering down exactly as his were.

A second voice joined the comms as another ship appeared, her weapons hot, behind them. His stomach clenched when he recognized the Witch's personal ship, the *Ebon Knight*. The *Tempestarii's* captain continued his warning.

"Because we would *all* take it *very* personally."

"Especially me," the *Knight's* feminine tones added and Muldoon swallowed.

"Stand down!" he ordered. "No one touch a thing. Cassidy, make the trajectories impossible. I don't want any accidents."

Muldoon heard the pilot's murmured affirmative, but he didn't relax until she'd put the *Audie* out of position for firing. He was even more relieved when the *Dorie* followed his example.

Their response was much calmer than the one the *Tempestarii* and *Knight's* appearance received on *Starbase Notaro*.

"She's here," the scan commander called and his voice rose in alarm. "Crap, sir! She's *really here!*"

"Who?" Admiral Seljack demanded, not used to seeing his usually very calm commander in such a state.

"The Witch, sir! She's here!"

He frowned. "What makes you say that, Otis?"

"That!" the man snapped and put the *Tempestarii* on screen. "And *that!*" he added as he displayed the *Ebon Knight*. "Her ships are here so she has to be around somewhere as well."

"Are they hostile?" he asked.

"The *Knight* is weapons-hot but she hasn't fired."

"And those two Navy ships are very wisely doing exactly as they're being asked," Seljack observed.

"They were responding to news of a gate incursion," Otis explained and beads of sweat formed on his brow.

"I see," the admiral responded, entirely truthfully because he did.

He'd half-expected something like this since the Witches Registration Act had been passed. In fact, he'd expected it sooner.

"What will we *do?*" Otis shouted and added belatedly, "Sir."

Seljack shrugged. "Commander, they don't seem to be attacking so the wisest course of action is to let them do whatever the hell they came here to do." He paused with a rueful chuckle. "Unless you *want* to die, today?"

The technician dropped into his chair. "I don't, sir. I honestly don't."

His relief and that of the *Audie* and *Dorie's* crews was not reflected by Rear Admiral Dreyfus, who could do nothing except glower through the *Notaro's* observation ports at the two ships he hated most in the universe.

"One day, someone will get the drop on the two of you," he muttered. "I only wish I could be there to see it."

On Earth, the people going through the gate remained oblivious of how close to death they'd come. Several of the students stopped to thank Stephanie as they passed.

"We're grateful you came back for us," one mother told her. "After everything they said about you in the papers—"

She took the woman's hands in her own.

"How could I leave my people behind?" she asked.

"But—" she began and the Witch smiled.

"You are the mother of one of my students. Of course you are my family." She gestured toward the portal. "Now go. I'll see you on the other side."

The scene was repeated in a hundred variations as the families continued through the line. Stephanie wasn't alone. Lars and Frog and her team were also being thanked, as were Todd and his team of Hooligans.

It seemed Navy footage had been leaked on the dark web and everyone was grateful for what they'd done. The team smiled and laughed and ushered the kids and their parents gently through the gate.

There were a couple of late arrivals and Stephanie fielded calls and dispatched shuttles at the last minute.

"What made you change your mind?" one of the fathers asked a newly arrived counterpart.

The man looked like he'd dressed fast and hadn't taken the time to shave. He gestured at the two teens being hurried into line by their mother.

"I'm not losing my kids to the government," he answered.

"Yeah, that's why *I'm* here," the first man told him. "That didn't change. What made you believe?"

"Someone posted a video of those dropships arriving, and that's when I realized they'd told us the truth. I realized that if we didn't leave now, we wouldn't have another chance."

"It took you long enough," the first father chided and the second hung his head and motioned to the city behind them.

"It's... It's so much to leave behind."

"Better that than lose your kids," his friend told him. "I was worried, man."

Similar reunions happened as more families joined the line. Stephanie breathed a sigh of relief and looked at the lieutenant commander.

"I see it's only eight percent left for you guys, now," she told him and she didn't sound sorry.

He didn't reply but scowled as the families reached the gates and greeted the Hooligans like heroes as they passed.

"I don't mind being thanked," Ka grumbled in a quiet moment, "but I wish they'd do it on the *other* side of the damned gate. You know, where they're finally *safe*."

Her comment made the team laugh and they broke away to finalize things with the school, taking Marcus and Johnny with them. The families weren't the only details of the university they had to protect.

When they emerged again, Todd trotted to Stephanie with Ka and Marcus at his heels.

"The servers are packed, stacked, and ready to go. The rest is slagged," he told her and looked more closely at the lieutenant commander.

His eyes lit with recognition and he stepped closer.

"I *know* you," he said. "The next time *any* of your fuckers try to target my family, even my girlfriend won't be able to talk any sense into me."

With his fists half-clenched, he placed a hand on the front of Pierce's jacket but was startled to distraction when Stephanie slid a hand onto his shoulder and leaned forward to kiss him.

She cast a coquettish look at the lieutenant commander as she spoke to Todd.

"You won't have to worry, my love," she assured him. "They'll already be dead."

The officer's eyes bulged and he swallowed nervously and stumbled back a step to put a little space between them. She flashed him a stunning smile and Todd grimaced with what might have been a grin.

Behind them, the rest of the Hooligans and some of Steph's team moved a hovering load of crates through the portal. She glanced at them, then at the officer again, and took hold of Todd's hand.

"See ya," she said casually and waved as she started toward the gate.

Todd looked at Pierce again and his face said it all. If he ever saw the lieutenant commander again, the man was dead. He didn't stop to see if the message was received, though, but let Stephanie lead him to the gate.

As they walked, he relinquished her hand and moved closer to wind his arm around her waist. She sighed and leaned against him, returning the favor.

"What's that all about, boss?" Dru called. "You forget you're on an op or something?"

"What's gonna happen if you need your gun, boss?" Angus teased.

"Yeah, Todd, you have it ass-about-face," Reggie added. "It's make *war* not *love* when you're on an op, and *love* not *war* when you get home!"

"Do you want me to zap them?" Stephanie asked. "They look like they need it."

He snickered. "Would you have to let go of my waist?"

"No."

His frown seemed to suggest that he at least thought about it. "You'd better not. I can always put them on cleaning duty."

She giggled. "I heard the sediment filters need a scrub."

"Pity we're not going to the *Knight* then, isn't it?"

"Yeah, some people are *very* lucky," he muttered.

Tethis hung back and watched as Stephanie and Todd proceeded toward the portal. When they were out of earshot, he stepped close to Pierce.

"Be ready," he whispered, "because your bosses can't help themselves. I've watched this happen dozens of times over my centuries of life. Your bosses *will* screw up."

The man's eyes widened and his gaze darted from the old mage to Stephanie's dwindling form and back. Tethis gave him a grim smile.

"Your bosses will talk themselves into taking too much power and when they do, they will turn the citizens against the government. Then, the government will go too far." He paused and studied the officer's worried face with cold, hard eyes. "When that happens, *look to the sky.*"

Leaving the Navy man to consider that, he turned and began to walk after Stephanie and Todd.

Pierce glanced around and realized his Marines were still frozen in place. As he wondered what he should do about that, the last shuttle landed and its pilots left the cockpit. They joined their colleagues who were already walking up the university's drive to take their chances with the portal's destination.

He watched them with a small frown and wondered what they knew that he didn't before he caught a glimpse of movement overhead and looked up.

The two Navy dropships still hovered overhead, held in place by Stephanie's magic. The Witch who'd stepped into the portal where he couldn't reach her.

"Well...fuck!" he swore and didn't notice the one thing that had gone right that day.

His mouth was back.

CHAPTER SIXTY-NINE

Historians would later point to the Federation Witch Riots as the event that marked the beginning of Earth's Second Descent. Its first descent had been one of slow decline ended by the planet's weather going crazy. This one happened much faster.

Across the world, vignettes of desperation and misunderstanding spread like wildfire. In one city, a young man fled for his life, hoping to lead the crowd away from his family. He wasn't to know that other sections of the howling mob had already broken into their home and dealt summary "justice."

In a small town in another country, a woman flung herself at the feet of an armored Corpsman begging for the return of her teenage daughter, while her son was dragged from the house, fighting to get free.

"Give him back!" she cried, only to have her husband lift her away gently.

"I'll take care of her," he assured the soldiers, his eyes dry but burning with anger.

Together, they watched the shuttles lift and they fled, hoping to find somewhere they were not known.

The homes of witches, both real and imagined, were burnt and their families expelled from communities they'd lived in for years. People were beaten in the streets for having been friends with the "wrong" people.

Families were killed. Having a witch in your bloodline became a death sentence.

Riots raged through the streets when those showing signs of being able to control Earth's natural energy were identified and held for Naval collection. Effigies of the Federation's first Witch were burnt in parks and town squares and her name was spat like a curse.

She stopped being "Stephanie, Witch of the Federation" or "Stephanie, the girl who saved our world" and became instead "Stephanie the Sell-Out," "the Traitor Witch," and "that Witch Bitch."

Her role in saving her world was forgotten, hidden under a hundred smeared layers of lies and accusations. Little by little, the power brokers of Earth undermined her memory until only their image of her was left—or so they hoped.

The Federation News turned to other things, its two new anchors both human and built for the catwalk. Neither of them spoke of their predecessors, the Meligornian with the silver hair and the frothy blonde woman who'd stood up for his rights.

Both had been lost from view when they'd taken refuge behind the gates of the Meligornian embassy. Neither had been left behind when the Federation had declared the embassy closed and stated there would be no alien territory allowed on Earth soil.

Instead, Karl and Zola teamed up to speak of the dreadful happenings beyond Earth's solar system.

"There's been another Dreth pirate attack," she reported, her eyes wide as she looked at her colleague. "This time, a small colony located on the very Outer Edge has been destroyed."

Footage played behind her to show bodies scattered among the smoking ruins of prefab dwellings and a badly damaged satellite dish.

"They say the attack came after the quarterly Federation Navy patrol had checked in to make sure everything was okay."

Her face reflected further shock as she lowered her voice and added, "There are rumors that someone with inside knowledge of Navy operations *leaked* the patrol's route and timing to let the pirates know when the colony was at its most vulnerable."

"And that's not the only attack we've suffered, Zola," Karl told her. "I've had a report of a trade ship bound for Meligorn being ambushed as it entered the Meligornian system."

More footage showed on the screen, this time of wreckage strewn against a backdrop of stars. His voice became somber and stern.

"Early investigations have revealed the Meligornians were the only ones who knew of the freighter's schedule and the strength of its escort."

"No!" Zola protested. "Surely the Meligornians would not betray their trade partners."

He shook his head. "No one can say for certain, but what *is* becoming clear is that that Meligornian traders are in dire straits, with their planet's trade deficit blowing out to a staggering *ninety* percent."

"Seriously, Karl?" she asked.

She made a show of looking at her notes before she continued.

"It says here that the Meligornian deficit is based on the habits of the elite who prefer imported goods from Dreth and Telor to those they can grow at home."

Karl nodded. "This is true, Zola, and then there is the level of corruption our government has encountered when trying to establish trade links with that world."

He paused to show an official-looking chart. "Did you know that the cost of the bribes to government officials controlling the markets we need exceeds the cost of manufacturing *and* shipping the goods themselves?"

Zola shook her head. "Karl, I did not know that, but it *does* explain why so many of our businesses are refocusing on trade with their colonial counterparts. I guess it *is* better to trade with the species you know."

The man chuckled. "You may be right there. You may be right—and speaking of species, you know, I believe you've come across an interesting little tidbit about the newest race the Witch wanted to add to the Federation."

"Indeed I have," she informed him and her face danced with malice and glee. "An *undercover* Naval operation managed to get aboard one of the so-called Teloran trade vessels and uncover the truth of the Teloran diet. It seems there's a very good reason why their population is in such decline."

"Oh?" He looked worried. "I don't see how their diet could bring that about."

"It does when you know that the Telorans *eat their own*."

His face froze. "They what, Zola?"

"They're cannibals, Karl...but only when they don't dine out on other races. Investigations are still ongoing as to how they select their citizens for the menu, but there you have it. The Navy team was fortunate enough to realize they were being targeted before the ax fell, so to speak. They barely escaped with their lives."

The footage jumped to a team of sailors in varying states of distress. Some held each other and sobbed, while others sat in corners and rocked, dry-eyed and silent. One was being wrestled into a strait-jacket as he screamed about monsters under the bed.

"And these are men and women trained to deal with the worst situations space has to offer," Zola murmured as the footage faded. "After one experience in a Teloran spaceship, this is what they're reduced to."

"I don't know what they expected," Karl stated, his voice angry and a little confused. "The Telorans are willing to destroy entire planets in order to clear 'their' space lanes. What was the Navy *doing* there?"

"It was meant to be a peace mission," she said shortly, "but the Navy discovered only one thing."

"And what was that, Zola?" he asked.

"That there can be no peace with a race like that."

Far away from the reporters and their twisted version of the universe, an android watched as the base hummed to life around him. It pulled its finger from the key socket it had plugged it into and flipped the fingertip over the key attachment it concealed.

Its eyes turned silvery as it sent its report, notifying the server that Cleaning Site 001 was online.

"Commencing testing," it added and moved to a console designed for a human operator should the need ever arise.

To the android's understanding, that situation was unlikely but the possibility still had to be accounted for. Because of this, it followed the actions a human operator would have to perform in order to make the base work.

"Stage One: Reactor Initiation," it intoned and moved its hands over the controls. The lights flickered from amber to green.

"Stage One: Successful."

It moved its hands again and this time, activated a different set of equipment.

"Stage Two: Collection—Successful."

Shortly after, it added, "Stage Three: Retrieval—Successful."

Had they been able to see it, Marcus and the team would have been astounded and gratified. Gemma might even have danced on the table in the middle of the conference room.

Stage Three was where they had spent six months being repeatedly blown into little pieces until they'd talked to Stephanie about it.

The android was oblivious to this as he moved on through Stages Four to Nine. Each went without a hitch until he was able to report with satisfaction, "Stage Nine: Power to Grid Insertion—Successful. Awaiting results for Stage Ten testing. Results could be delayed."

That report might have been worrying except that it took time to monitor the environment from which the radiation was being taken.

A week passed before it had enough data to make its final report.

"Successful land remediation in progress."

All over the world, including in non-Federation countries, similar operations were reporting the same results.

"Site 002: Successful land remediation in progress."

"Site 017: Successful land remediation in progress."

One by one, as each site was built and brought online, the androids testing them reported their success.

"Site 018: Successful land remediation in progress."

"Site 019: Successful land remediation in progress."

"Site 020: Attempted incursion aborted. Enemy reports state the area is hostile to human life. Testing completed. Successful land remediation in progress."

The *Tempestarii* faded into existence alongside the Space Station *Alerus*. Below them, Meligorn's atmosphere shone with a rich purple light.

Emil sighed. "I don't think I'll ever grow tired of seeing that."

"The sight is beautiful," the *Tempestarii* agreed, "and the space station is friendly but I will miss my sister."

He chuckled. "You know why we are staying, don't you, Tempest?"

"Yes," the ship replied but sounded sulky. "We are to support Dreth, or Meligorn, or do whatever is needed and necessary."

She repeated Stephanie's orders exactly and didn't sound very happy about any of them.

"Would *you* rather be going to Telor, Tempest?" he asked but the ship was quick to put that notion to rest.

"No, but I had hoped to spend more time with my sister," she admitted. "We have not had much time together since she woke me."

"Ah..." Now, Emil thought he understood and while there was nothing he could do to remedy the situation, he was relieved his ship didn't want to go exploring.

"Why don't you think of it as time you have where you do not have to share your father?"

The *Tempestarii* was silent for long enough that he thought he'd made a mistake.

"Tempest?" he asked when he felt she'd been quiet for too long. "Are you okay?"

"Yes, Emil," the ship replied contentedly. "I was merely negotiating our next activity with my father."

He rested his head against his hand and wondered what BURT would have to say to him the next time they spoke.

Heh, welcome to fatherhood. Only this time, your children don't sleep.

Stephanie was taking some time away and he was both sad and happy about that. He'd monitored the news reports from Earth and they both saddened and sickened him with the amount of misinformation and outright untruths.

He hoped she hadn't watched them because now was not the time for her to intervene. With anti-Witch sentiment so high, she would neither be welcomed nor listened to if she tried to help them.

No, the trip to Telor and the search for the Morgana's body would do her good. She'd not only be away from all that but she'd be out of reach of anyone the Federation tried to send after her.

Better still, she'd also be so publicly gone that the Federation couldn't blame anyone for hiding her. There'd be no way they could use the "fugitive" clause to go to war with Dreth or Meligorn or to destroy one of the colonies still sympathetic toward her. She'd be safe —at least for now.

He pulled up a view of the *Ebon Knight*, pleased to have timed it to catch Stephanie's shuttle vanishing into the battleship's hold.

"Good luck, Steph," he whispered as the *Knight* closed the hatch after her. "Come back safe."

Marianne Rawlins was seated at her console when Stephanie, Lars, and Johnny arrived in the control room. She turned to address the girl as they took their seats behind her.

"I never told you," she began, "that you gave me a belief in humanity again. I truly didn't think that was possible."

Stephanie paused in the act of buckling her harness, frowned as she thought about what Rawlins had said, and chose her words carefully when she replied.

"I never gave you that," she told her. "You always had it but no one proved that it needed to show itself again." She waved to indicate the entire ship. "We were only the spark that lit the waiting kindling."

She glanced around. "Now, unless anyone has anything else to do for the next couple of years..."

When no one replied, she pointed at the scan technician. "What about you?"

The technician blushed and shook her head.

"No?" she asked in disbelief.

The woman shook her head again.

"Me neither," she told her and looked around the bridge again.

This time, she noticed that the technicians were very careful to avoid eye contact. That didn't save them though.

"You?" she asked and looked at the communications console.

Of course, everyone looked up to see who she'd chosen, and one of the comms techs met her gaze.

"Well?" Stephanie demanded.

The communications officer shook his head.

"No?" she asked, and he shook his head again. "What the hell?" To everyone's relief, she laughed. "Good!" she said and leaned back in her seat. "Let's go find a decrepit old hag under a pile of rock. I can't wait to meet her."

I'll 'decrepit old hag' you, the Morgana retorted. *I'm not useless yet, little girl.*

Oh, I don't doubt you will be very useful, Stephanie assured her. *But now that I've fixed your planet, you owe me a favor.*

And what's that?

You have to come back to Earth with me and help me fix mine, she replied before she said aloud, "Ebony, come on. Let's crank this ship up to eleven."

"Yes, ma'am!"

From beside *Alerus,* Emil watched as the *Knight's* engines flared. Seconds later, the ship was gone.

THE END

CREATOR NOTES - MICHAEL ANDERLE

JULY 22, 2020

THANK YOU for reading our story! Your continued patronage of our books here at LMBPN allows us to do what we love to do.

That is, write / edit / publish / get artwork for and miscellaneous other things that mean "publish more stories."

TO COMPLETE A THOUGHT

So, when I wrote the last *Author Notes*, COVID had just shut down everything in Las Vegas. Meaning, in short, everything that allowed me to function from our condo.

Gone was the breakfast place I loved to walk over to, and gone was lots of good exercise, which helps reduce stress.

My favorite Mexican food place, Javier's, was gone.

All the hubbub and noise from the Strip was gone (this was a nice thing for me. I can say without any reservations I have learned the noise was a constant thrum of annoyance to my system. So, not everything was bad.)

I took on the weight of the world (metaphorically speaking) before I realized I couldn't fix the world. I have come to the conclusion that I don't understand exactly how the world works, and I'm way more black-and-white than is beneficial. People who don't know me and have no clue who I am are certainly not expecting me to fix life for them.

But I was dealing with these types of thoughts as I would walk down Las Vegas Blvd. Some places were open, and I tried to visit and give each one a little business. Slowly, they closed.

It felt like I'd failed. I failed my nearby business neighbors because our little CVS or Walgreens couldn't keep the doors open. I realized it was not practical to think this way, it wasn't my fault, and I was (I figured out eventually) going through the stages of grief.

Grief not because COVID hit anyone in my family or extended family or friends of ours. For that, I am blessed. Our children are safe in Texas, my older parents survived through the worst part (and seem to have a good attitude now that Texas is going through wave #2), and neither my wife nor I (that we know of) have had it, either.

No, I was slowly slipping into a depression because I missed my chaotically stable life. Chaotically stable is like Chaotic Good in tabletop RPG games. It's a good life, but don't expect it to be predictable. A very free-wheeling kind of good.

Anyway, it was gone. While I didn't believe the government that it would be two weeks, I had secret hopes it wouldn't last more than a month.

That was gone four weeks later, and now I was going through the "I have GOT to get out of here!" mentality.

The only fun I could have was driving my car. Then I figured out I really hated my car. Not because it was a bad car (it was not) but because I'd settled. It was the car I thought I could afford, not the car I wanted. In short, I had been scared to commit.

After months of COVID, I was tired of being scared. If I was going to die (thanks, NEWS, for keeping that shit straight up in front of our brains for so long. I believe I'll make news companies an evil organization in the future. Well, a more evil organization in my stories, I'm already rather harsh on them.)

(*Editor's Note: A friend in Portland says the whole media coverage is completely overblown as well. Only in one area of town. Thanks, news! I was freaking out for her!*)

Anyway, I was tired of being scared, cooped up, and listening to reason, which is not something I'm particularly fond of doing. I can do it just fine, but I don't like it, to the point of perhaps swinging too far the other direction.

So I upgraded the car. When I press the pedal to the metal, my fifty-plus-year old body smiles like he is eighteen again. One thing that is different (assuming the car is well-maintained) than say a significant other is when it has gas, the car never says *"No."*

Unlike a certain two-year-old god-daughter we have. She has learned the word "no" and practices it with enthusiasm like a young fighter wielding her practice sword, thwacking all who come near—right in the shins.

All that to finish out that I'm working again. I'm putting the steps in front of each other, and I hope some of our stories help you, wherever you are at this moment in time. Perhaps we are still the COVID crisis of 2020, or perhaps it is ten years from now, and that time is just a footnote in history.

Either way, remember that you have helped us as well. Supporting our stories with your time, energy, and enthusiasm helps creatives like me not listen to the world, but rather, escape into a different world.

The world of the FEDERATION WITCH.

Now, we are building the next trilogy (or longer, depends on how you, the fans, enjoy it.)

I will be telling more of Stephanie's story, but to do that, I'm going to go back and pull from our own history here on this planet.

Stephanie and her team have to leave...have to find the Morgana and rescue her bony ass from under a mountain.

(I just have to ask, what if her body is dead? What happens when we get there? Will those in power... Sorry, I'm asking questions I don't have the answers to yet.)

I have come to love all these characters, and because our team is behind me, we are bringing them back to fight something bigger than the Telorans.

Before we do that, certain things have to happen. Someone has to fight the Regime.

Someone has to put their life, their young life, on the line and be willing to say no.

No to the false truth, no to the peer pressure, and no to fear.

He will be the first apostle to the HERETIC OF THE FEDERATION.

(*Zen Master Steve note: Turn the page to learn more about this new series.*)

I hope you enjoy it!

Ad Aeternitatem,

Michael Anderle

THE STORY CONTINUES

As Michael said in his author notes, this story will continue. There are three books planned for release during the fall of 2020. Book one is The Heretic Lives.

You cannot murder a person who never existed.

It is not impossible to rewrite history. In fact, when one computer runs the world, changing history happens faster.

Those who were heroes have been labeled villains. The alien Melagorns and Dreth, once friends, are now competitors at best.

The Regime works to instill loyalty to humanity. Loyalty to brotherhood. Loyalty to the state.

Loyalty to the words preached every night.

Humanity first. Truth!
Those with power are Tainted. Truth!
The Tainted prove Loyalty by working for the
Regime. Truth!
Tainted who hide power seek to harm
Humanity. Truth!
Hail, Victory! Hail, Humanity!

Except not everyone follows the *truth*.

John Zechin fled into a radioactive wasteland, seeking death rather than work in the Regime.

What he learns changes humanity forever.

Pre-order your copy today for delivery to your Kindle at midnight on the day it's released.

BOOKS BY MICHAEL ANDERLE

For a complete list of books by Michael Anderle, please visit

www.lmbpn.com/ma-books/

CONNECT WITH THE AUTHOR

Connect with Michael Anderle

Website: http://lmbpn.com

Email List: http://lmbpn.com/email/

Social Media:

https://www.facebook.com/LMBPNPublishing

https://twitter.com/lmbpn

https://www.instagram.com/lmbpn_publishing/

https://www.bookbub.com/authors/michael-anderle